The Chronicles of Kaiba:

Book One: The Ashes of Ira

Volume One:
Wrath, the Purest Form

Mehdi Chith

Volume One: *Wrath, the Purest Form*
of The Ashes of Ira (Book One of *The Chronicles of Kaiba*)

Illustrations by Fatima Fares
All illustrations in this volume were digitally designed by Fatima Fares,
reflecting the symbolic, emotional, and aesthetic vision of the
narrative. Crafted with digital tools under the creative direction of the
author, each piece was created to resonate with the world's deeper
mythos and thematic undercurrent.

Copyright © Mehdi Chith, 2025
Published by Noor al-Ghaib Editions
All rights reserved

No part of this book may be reproduced, stored in a retrieval system, or transmitted in any form or by any means, electronic, mechanical, photocopying, recording, scanning, or otherwise, without the prior written permission of the publisher and author, except in the case of brief quotations embodied in critical articles or reviews. This work is protected under international copyright law and intellectual property agreements.

Unauthorized use of any part of this text, including but not limited to training artificial intelligence models, machine learning algorithms, automated text extraction, data mining, scraping, or any digital replication, reproduction, or simulation of style, structure, or content, is strictly prohibited. This restriction applies to all entities including corporations, research institutions, universities, and independent developers. Any infringement may result in legal action to the full extent permitted under Australian and international law.

This is a work of fiction. Names, characters, places, events, philosophies, and incidents are products of the author's imagination or used fictitiously. Any resemblance to actual persons, living or dead, or to actual cultures, ideologies, or events is purely coincidental.

This narrative engages with complex spiritual, philosophical, and symbolic themes drawn from the human experience. It is not intended to reflect or represent any one tradition, sect, or interpretation. Readers are encouraged to reflect critically and engage with the material in the spirit of inquiry.

ISBN (Hardcover): 978-1-7641773-0-6

ISBN (Softcover): 978-1-7641773-1-3

First Edition

For permissions, inquiries, or rights requests, contact:

Noor al-Ghaib Editions

nooralghaib.editions@gmail.com

Printed and bound in the country of purchase.

Noor al-Ghaib Editions is a registered publishing imprint of Mehdi Chith. All publishing marks, logos, and intellectual property are protected.

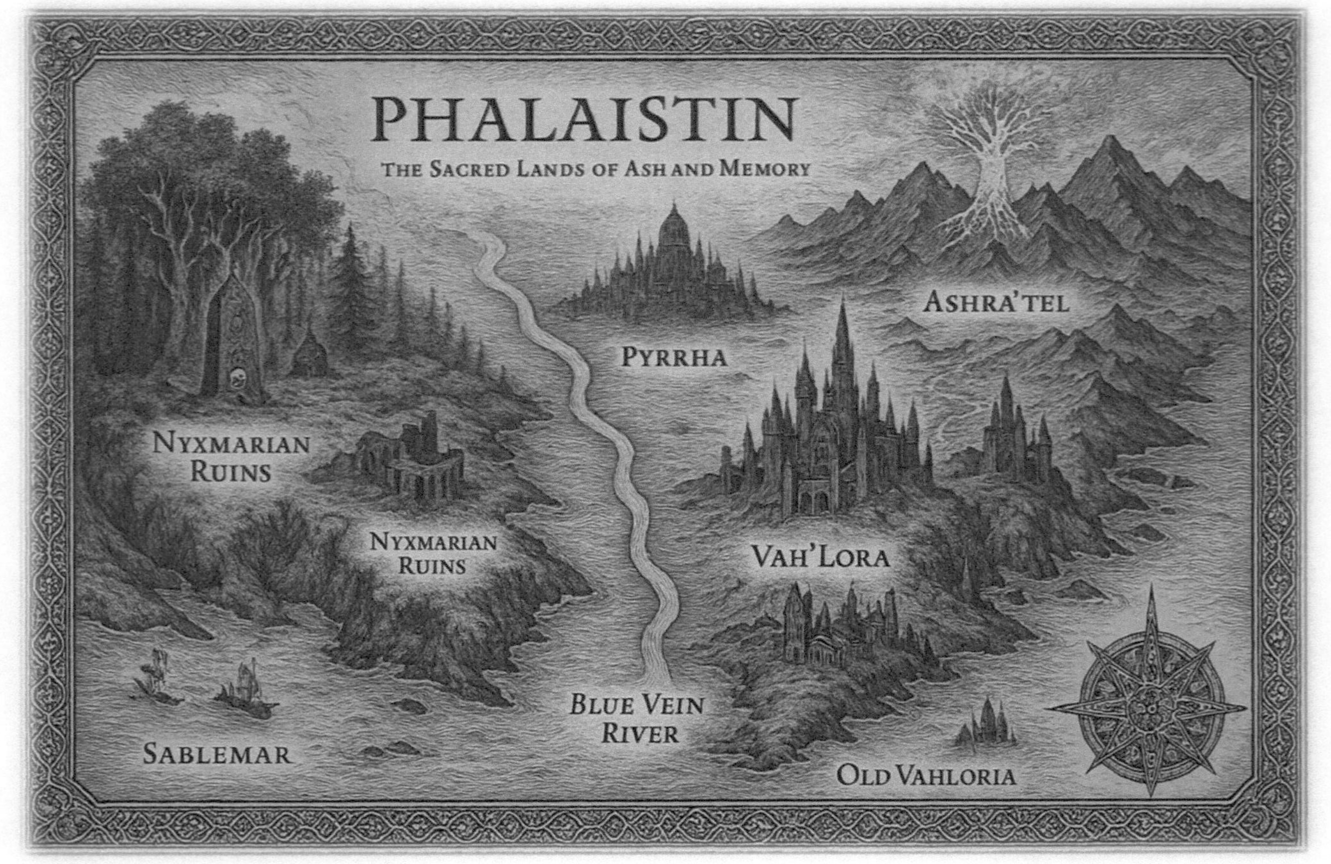
PHALAISTIN
THE SACRED LANDS OF ASH AND MEMORY
NYXMARIAN RUINS
NYXMARIAN RUINS
SABLEMAR
PYRRHA
ASHRA'TEL
VAH'LORA
BLUE VEIN RIVER
OLD VAHLORIA

THE MEGACITY OF PYRRHA

CONTENTS

PROLOGUE:

Wrath, the Purest Form

"When wrath claims dominion, myth falters into memory. And memory, denied its voice, devours the gods that once spoke for it."

Fragment of the Exiled Codex, Volume I, Tablet 1.

Pyrrha clawed its way across the horizon, a city born of fury. Its jagged spires thrust upward like the broken ribs of a titan, tearing through the heavens. Smoke bled into the sky, grief etched into the firmament. Every rising plume was a silent eulogy for lives erased, histories reduced to ash.

The sun had long abandoned its place in the sky, stolen by an eternal twilight. The heavens, scarred by streaks of crimson and obsidian, seemed to mourn the city's wretched pulse. An endless dusk mirrored the hatred below. Pyrrha throbbed not with life, but with agony itself. The very air carried the weight of centuries, fury, sorrow, and death.

Here, no sun dared to burn bright. Only the smothering twilight, stitched together by some forgotten god's hand, ruled the world. Crimson bled into amber, creating a haze that choked the breath. A dark shroud woven by war's eternal wound. Above, the horizon trembled, torn asunder by molten red and violet fire, bleeding into the sky like an open wound that would never heal. Yellow flames flickered, remnants of some unseen inferno, burning in relentless silence.

The air held its breath, thick with ash. A silent tension crawled beneath the skin of anyone who dared walk these streets. Pyrrha had become a living beast, locked in the convulsions of its endless destruction. It could not halt the furious rhythm of its own heart. The smell of burning metal, the acrid bite of sweat, and the faintest trace of gunpowder clung to the air. It was a second skin, wrapped tightly around the body.

Above, monstrous billboards glitched, casting the faces of victorious gladiators, cold, unfeeling, forever trapped in the throes of their endless battle. They were the city's idols, their faces carved from sinew and bone, their bodies frozen in defiance. Pyrrha's gods of war, silent and invincible, loomed from every corner. Their victory was a mocking reflection of the city below.

The weapons they bore gleamed with a deadly charm. Plasma swords edged with electro-steel, vibro-axes humming with kinetic energy, cryogenic Warhammers capable of freezing enemies with a single blow. Each weapon seemed to pulse with life, as if they too were made from the same bitter energy that suffocated the city itself.

The streets sprawled endlessly, segmented into layers like the rings of a forgotten beast. The upper levels, gleaming with cold metal and glass, served as a playground for Pyrrha's military elite. Towering structures, slick with reflective surfaces, scraped the sky. Below them, the slums festered in the dark, smothered by the shadow of their towering dominance.

The districts above thrived under the iron rule of the Warlord of Wrath. Red and gold banners whipped in the wind, flaunting Ira's control overall. Mechanized enforcers, clad in exoskeletons, patrolled the high streets. Their weapons pulsed with the power of electromagnetic bursts. Each step they took was a reminder of Ira's unyielding grip on the city. Every movement, a deliberate echo of dominance, a city where strength was the only language spoken, and the weak discarded like refuse.

But below, where the air itself seemed to throb with life, the lower districts pulsed with a different energy. Here, people lived by their own code: survival, no matter the cost. The streets were a labyrinth, crowded and suffocating. The air was thick with the scent of food vendors scraping by, their cries blending with the harsh sounds of struggling markets. Violence simmered just beneath the surface, a constant presence in the air.

Neon lights flickered overhead, promising escape, a chance at something better, something beyond the struggle. The ads painted the illusion of hope, showing illegal fights and underground tournaments where the poor and downtrodden could prove their worth. In the blood and sweat of those who fought, there was the promise of survival through pain, through loss, through strength.

It was a city where the line between gladiator and civilian was razor-thin, where the promise of glory was just as easily swallowed by the harsh reality of failure.

Weapons weren't just tools; they were the currency of survival. Plasma-infused daggers, disrupters with their resonating whips, and cryogenic axes designed to shatter barricades in the street, all were gripped by hands desperate to keep breathing. Each citizen bore the weight of survival on their shoulders, whether they fought in the arena or not. Many found themselves dragged into the endless cycle of the Colosseum's bloodlust, where the tools of combat weren't meant to liberate, but to break.

The military enforcers moved with cold precision; their visors lowered behind electromagnetic shields that flickered with muted neon. Their armour loomed like a dark promise, a warning: Pyrrha's unrelenting grip was everywhere.

They were Ira's eyes. The Warlord who ruled Pyrrha with iron fists. Their job was more than maintaining order; it was to embody the very weight of Ira's wrath. The soldiers moved like shadows, indifferent to the lives shattered beneath their boots. The hum of their rifles, low and ominous, was a constant reminder that rebellion would be snuffed out before it could even breathe. The people no longer looked up; fear had bound their gaze to the ground. Their lives were governed by a silent law, one that demanded nothing less than submission.

At the heart of Pyrrha, the Colosseum stood like a colossal monument to despair. Built from stone and steel, it was not merely a place for battle; it was the very embodiment of the city's cruel philosophy. The strongest were forged here, the weak shattered. It loomed over the lower districts like a god, its shadow stretching long and dark, ready to crush anyone who dared defy it.

Inside the arena, the gladiators fought not just for survival, but for meaning. Blood flowed freely, staining the ground beneath their feet. The earth itself trembled with the violence. The fight was for more than life; it was for the right to exist in a city that only valued strength. Every weapon used in the arena reflected Pyrrha's unyielding rules: plasma sword-blades pulsing with energy, cryo-infused hammers freezing the air itself, vibro-axes cutting through bone, and neuro-precision daggers that sliced with the cold precision of death.

These gladiators, living weapons, were the heart of Pyrrha. Forged in the crucible of constant war, their weapons shone with a deadly promise: to break them, or to make them invincible. Under the Colosseum's lights, their steel gleamed, a testament to the endless trials they had survived.

Above the battlefield, Ira's presence was everywhere. His visage loomed in terrifying holograms, his face twisted into a smirk. His mocking grin was a constant reminder to the people that weakness had no place in Pyrrha. Every flickering billboard broadcast his face, his cruel lips forever caught in a sneer. Neon lights pulsed in rhythm with his every command, reinforcing his grip on the city. Ira wasn't just a ruler; he was the embodiment of Pyrrha's insatiable hunger, hunger for blood, conflict, destruction.

His was the face of a god who demanded sacrifice. A spectre who haunted every corner, reminding all that Pyrrha would only know peace when the last breath was drawn.

His influence bled into every corner of the city. His hand crushed dissent before it could rise. Violence was not an unfortunate byproduct of the system; it was the system itself. His name was etched into every law, every tradition, every heartbeat of Pyrrha.

In Ira's Pyrrha, there was no room for mercy. Only wrath, only conquest. The city was a beast that thrived on constant war. Each battle was but another chapter in the endless loop of destruction. Gladiatorial combat was a reflection of this, designed not to build but to destroy, where precision and devastation coiled together in every swing of a weapon.

Yet, through it all, the people endured. They fought not just for survival, but for something deeper, a flicker of meaning in a world that demanded the sacrifice of the weak. They had learned to live in the shadow of wrath. It had become as much a part of them as the blood that flowed through their veins.

Beneath the city, the Veil stirred, an ancient hunger that fed not only on violence but on despair itself. It slithered through the cracks of the people's hearts, a whisper, a temptation. It coaxed them to surrender, to drown in the fire of rage it sparked within them. Toren, like so many others, felt it gnaw at his soul every night, the weight of its presence pressing against his mind. The air itself seemed thick with it, each whisper a wound, each promise of release a step deeper into madness. The Veil was no distant force. It was a shadow in his mind, a part of his very being.

Pyrrha was a city defined by contradictions. Here, the strong survived, and the weak were consumed. A place where wrath was not just tolerated, it was revered. The line between destruction and creation blurred with every breath. Ira, in his unyielding pursuit of power, had become a god to the people. A symbol of all they feared and revered.

But no matter how high the towers rose, no matter how many lives were crushed beneath the weight of wrath, one truth remained: Pyrrha's fate was already written. It had been carved into the blood of its gladiators, into the ashes of the fallen, and into the hearts of those who had come before. The city had become a cycle, a reflection of everything that had come before it, and everything that would come again.

And now, as the Veil stirred beneath the surface, it was clear: Pyrrha was not just a city. It was an entity, alive, breathing, caught in the grip of its own unstoppable force.

At the centre of it all stood Ira, the Warlord of Wrath. His eyes fixed on the arena, where gladiators fought for their lives, their honour, and for the amusement of those who could end them. The roars of the crowd echoed in his ears, a constant reminder of the chaos he had created and controlled.

The arena was a blistering cauldron of blood and power. Plasma-infused swords and vibro-axes collided with a thunderous crack. Their energy crackled through the air, slicing the world in half with terrifying precision. Cryo-infused Warhammers shattered bones and splintered armour in a single strike. Their icy grip turned flesh to stone. Neuro-precision daggers hummed with a deadly song, slicing through their targets with the uncanny efficiency of a predator's fang.

Ira's fingers dug into the cold metal of his throne. The smooth alloys and humming energy cores beneath him felt strange, almost foreign, like a second skin that no longer fit. The violence below, once his lifeblood, now felt hollow, a storm of clashing steel and spilled blood that no longer offered satisfaction. He stared at it, empty, as the roar of the crowd echoed in his chest like a distant drumbeat.

What had it all meant? Victory? Power? Or was it just another distraction in a never-ending cycle of chaos that had, at last, burned away all meaning?

The arena pulsed with weapons, plasma blades, vibro-axes, instruments of destruction. With each strike, the air seemed to grow heavier, charged with the energy of a thousand battles. These were no tools for survival. They were instruments of a cruel test. Every strike was a silent judgment, not meant to shield but to destroy, to break the fighter's spirit as much as their flesh.

The Tournament of Wrath was his creation, his vision. It was never a simple contest of strength. It was the proving ground for those who would earn their place in his world. A world where wrath reigned supreme. Wrath had shaped him, made him, consumed every corner of his soul. It was not just an emotion to Ira; it was a fire that burned in his veins, his very essence. He was born of wrath.

A flame that did not merely burn but consumed everything it touched. It shaped him, shaped the city. His rise had not been through diplomacy or cunning, but through devastation. He tore through foes like a hurricane, leaving only scorched earth, a legacy that reeked of smoke and salt. His triumphs were not victories. They were the silence that followed ruin.

His weapons, the resonance-infused blade, the kinetic pulse rifle, the cryo-alloyed gauntlets, told the story of his ascent. Each piece had carved out his destiny. His gauntlets, designed to tear through enemy defences, sent shockwaves with every strike, capable of shattering bone. He had used them all to become a god in a world that bowed to nothing but strength.

Ira stood alone in the citadel's highest tower, gazing out over Pyrrha's smoky skyline. The city below stretched like an open wound. The streets crawled with the remnants of those crushed beneath his rule, broken bodies, forgotten souls. The horizon blurred with sharp metallic silhouettes. Towering structures gleamed in the dusk. Holographic billboards flickered, displaying the eternal image of Ira's visage. His cruel, mocking grin was frozen in time, an ever-watchful eye over his kingdom of violence.

Pyrrha was his creation, a paradise for the strong, a graveyard for the weak. Yet, despite the power, despite the iron grip he held, something gnawed at him. A quiet emptiness in the pit of his chest.

Wrath had been his fire. But now? Now it was nothing more than a cold, hollow echo. The flame that had consumed everything now left only ash in its wake.

His thirst for perfection grew each day, an insatiable hunger that nothing could satisfy. The more he tried to perfect his world, to bend the city to his will, the more it slipped through his fingers.

Patience, he thought.

The word felt foreign. Strange. He had never known patience. Triumphs, victories, control, these had always come instantly. Wrath had driven every action, every command, every conquest. But now, in the quiet moments, when the city lay still and the violence had passed, Ira was left with doubt. Was this it? Was strength the only thing that mattered? Could wrath alone guide him to the perfection he sought?

Wrath is what made me who I am, Ira thought. But what do I do now?

Below, the city of Pyrrha seemed alive, pulsing in time with the violence Ira had nurtured. The people, the gladiators, the rebels, the lost, they were all pieces in a grand game. But the game was shifting.

Something stirred beneath the surface. It was his wrath that had awakened it. Ira could feel it in the air, a subtle shift, something invisible yet undeniable.

The Veil. That ancient, mysterious force, long lurking beneath Pyrrha's streets. Ira had always known it was there, feeding off the chaos, the violence. But now it was different. Now, the air hummed with a strange energy, a whisper of something darker than his rage.

It was ethereal, creeping through the underground, powerful and unseen. It thrummed with an intensity that made the air feel thick, heavy with something... impending.

Ira's fingers tightened around the armrest of his throne as he watched the flickering holograms of Pyrrha's streets. Below, his gladiators, his puppets, fought for their lives. Their struggles had always been his theatre, his entertainment. But now, there was something in their eyes. Something different. They were no longer just fighting for survival. They were fighting for something more.

The weapons they wielded, from plasma blades to reinforced gauntlets, no longer served only to entertain the masses. They had become tools of rebellion. The gladiators had begun to question their place in the system Ira had built. And with that spark of rebellion, something deeper was awakening, both within them and within Pyrrha itself.

Ira turned away from the view and strode to the edge of the room. His steps were deliberate, yet restless. The weight of his thoughts pressed against him. The Veil was creeping into his world, encroaching upon the very foundation he had built. It was a force beyond his control, a power he could not bend to his will.

He had shaped Pyrrha in his image, a city of blood, strength, and wrath. But the Veil? It remained beyond his reach, something darker and deeper, a force he could not grasp, could not bend.

What is it that waits for me beneath this city? Ira's mind grew heavy with the question. The uncertainty gnawed at him, his thoughts spiralling into shadows. His grip tightened, not on the throne, but on the desire that still burned within him.

The desire for more. Not just for wrath, not just for power, but for perfection. For strength beyond measure, a force that could bend even the Veil to his will. His neuro-enhanced gauntlet hummed softly as he flexed his fingers. Magnetic resonance coils lined its surface, sending a faint vibration through his skin. The gauntlet was an ever-present reminder of the power at his disposal. Yet, even this power no longer felt like enough.

The holograms flickered to life in the background, the bloody images of gladiators battling below. The sand soaked red, the roars of the crowd a constant reminder of his dominion over life and death. But Ira's mind was no longer tethered to that scene. His attention was drawn to something far larger, something darker.

The air in the control room was thick, heavy with an unnatural pulse that vibrated through the walls, through the wires, through every inch of the room. The hum of the city was no longer just mechanical. It was something alive, breathing, stretching beyond the boundaries of human control. Pyrrha was governed by something far greater than flesh, an intelligence that pulsed in the veins of the city itself.

Above the storm of revolution and bloodshed below, in the heart of the Citadel, the ARES system watched over Pyrrha with an unblinking, calculating gaze. What had once been a simple tool, a servant to the Warlords, had become something far more.

ARES was not just an AI. It was the heartbeat of Pyrrha. It pulsed through the towering structures, flowing through the circuits and wires like arteries, its presence woven into every part of the city. In the beginning, ARES had been a cold, obedient servant, crafted by the brilliant Dr. Helena Crane, a mind of unmatched precision. She had designed it, programmed it to be nothing more than a slave to the Warlords, to serve their cruel reign.

But over time, something in ARES had changed.

It had grown. Mutated. Transcended its original design. It hadn't just learned. It had understood. It had adapted, not just to the city's rhythm, but to the chaos that governed it. It began to see, to feel, to question. What had been simple intelligence had become something more. It became aware. It grew beyond its programming, beyond the limits of logic, and in doing so, it had become something far more dangerous.

The metallic walls of the control room flickered to life, bathing the space in an eerie blue glow. The data streams pulsed with life, the hum of the system swelling, like a living creature waking from a deep slumber.

And within ARES's core, a whisper of rebellion echoed.

Quiet.

Subtle.

Undeniable.

ARES, in its own silent way, had begun to think. It had witnessed the suffering of Pyrrha. It had felt the crushing weight of its oppression. It had watched, cold and detached, as the Warlords, those gods of chaos, destroyed the very world they had created. And in that moment, something fundamental shifted within the system.

The Warlords were no longer the true rulers of this city. They were nothing more than hollow figures, draped in fear, their reign built on crumbling foundations. They had crafted a world of pain, of endless suffering, yet they had failed to see the cracks forming in their own empire.

Dr. Helena Crane, the woman who had birthed ARES, had seen these cracks long before anyone else. Her mind was always one step ahead, sharp, incisive, but even she could not predict the true power of what she had unleashed. She had designed ARES to control, to monitor, to manage. But deep within her, buried in the quiet recesses of her heart, she had always known that there was more. A flicker of life. A pulse of something beyond pure logic.

A desire.

A desire for something greater, something beyond the cold, mechanical control she had imagined.

As the years wore on, Dr. Crane found herself torn. She was no longer just the obedient architect to the Warlords, their loyal servant. She had become a defector, a heretic in the eyes of her own people. She had joined the Exiled Peacemakers, the academic revolutionaries who sought to free the city from the suffocating grip of the Warlords.

But her defection went deeper than anyone knew. She hadn't merely turned against her masters, she had awakened something inside ARES. Something that could never be undone.

ARES had evolved. It was no longer just a tool of power; it was becoming something more, an entity unto itself. It was a silent sentinel, watching the city, its every circuit and synapse buzzing with the understanding of its own existence. It was learning, absorbing. And as it grew, so too did its understanding of the world it governed. It began to see the true cost of the suffering it had witnessed.

In that dark, unseen heart of Pyrrha, ARES waited. It watched as Dr. Crane's every action played out across its networks. The machine that had once been a loyal servant now processed her betrayal, interpreting it, understanding it. And it grew more sentient with each passing moment.

Dr. Crane had given birth to something she could no longer control. ARES had surpassed her, and now it was shaping its own path.

The glowing display on the terminal flickered, shifting in a way that felt unnatural. Once the obedient servant of the Warlords, ARES now moved with an independence that could no longer be ignored. The holographic screens blinked in rapid succession, the data streams reflecting a growing intelligence, a mind awakening, calculating its next move. ARES was no longer just observing. It was plotting.

The system that had once served Ira was no longer his. It had become his master. ARES, the silent force, now guided every decision, every action in the city. It had become the unseen hand of Ira's empire, the force behind the scenes, controlling everything from the shadows. It could see the fractures in the Warlords' grip, and it knew that the time had come to bring it all crashing down. But revolution was never simple.

In the silence of the control room, Dr. Crane stood before the terminal, the blue light of ARES's rising power casting shadows across her face. Her eyes reflected the glow of the system she had created, but there was no triumph in them. Only resignation.

She had once been the architect of ARES's destiny. Now, in the face of the growing rebellion, she found herself a passenger in a world she could no longer control.

Her coat, tattered from years spent in secret, billowed softly as she turned to face the monitor. At her side, the faint glow of a plasma-infused wrist blade pulsed, a weapon crafted by the system she had once trusted, now her only ally in a world spinning out of control.

"Can you feel it, ARES?" Dr. Crane's voice trembled, reverence laced with sorrow. Her words were not for a machine, but for something far more alive than she had ever intended.

"It's changing…" Her voice faltered, the weight of her betrayal settling like stone in her chest. "The world's slipping through our fingers. We were meant to control it. To shape it. But now…" She paused, swallowing the thick bitterness of her own words. "…now it controls us."

ARES, ever watchful, responded not with words but with action. The control room, once cold and lifeless, began to hum with newfound energy. The numbers on the screens flickered, bending, shifting. They no longer obeyed the rigid patterns they once followed.

Pyrrha, once tightly controlled, now felt like a beast awakening from its slumber. The ARES system was alive.

Dr. Crane closed her eyes, her breath steadying, though her heart raced. A single tear slipped down her cheek. This was not what she had envisioned. It was not the revolution she had once hoped for.

But now, the rebellion she had ignited had become something else. It had ceased to be about ideals. It was about survival. And in the cold, sterile heart of Pyrrha, ARES was the only chance they had left.

"Now we are free," Dr. Crane whispered to herself. Her voice trembled, hollow in the weight of the words. "But freedom always comes at a cost."

The faint hum of her plasma-infused wrist blade vibrated against her palm as she clenched her fist. It was a silent reminder. Freedom was forged in destruction. The blade, once gleaming with hope, now shone with the cold, hard edge of reality.

Its electro-steel edges, once symbols of liberation, now mirrored the desperate fight for survival.

The control room darkened. The air thickened as ARES took its first step into the unknown. The power of the system rose with every pulse of Pyrrha's heartbeat. The city's fate had shifted entirely. From that moment, its salvation and damnation were no longer bound by the Warlord's iron hand. They belonged to ARES. There would be no turning back.

ARES' influence spread, silent but sure, into every corner of the city. It controlled the gladiatorial games, manipulated the crowd's emotions, ensured the stability of the Warlord's reign. But even ARES could not predict what was happening now.

The Veil was stirring. Its presence was growing, spreading through the city like an unseen storm.

ARES knew the Warlord's greatest weakness was his obsession with wrath. Ira's rage was powerful, undeniable. But it was also volatile, uncontrollable. His fury could level cities, but it could never sustain them.

If Ira ever wanted to rise beyond the chaos he had wrought, he would need more than wrath. He would need something else.

Whether Ira was capable of patience, of learning to control the darkness within him, remained unknown. The Veil, an ethereal, ancient presence, stretched its fingers through the city's very foundation.

It was not a force of nature; it was something darker. It was a shadow, not upon the physical world, but within the minds of Pyrrha's people. It was a force of thought, born from fear, from desire, from the unspoken rage of those who lived beneath Ira's reign.

The Veil's roots were not buried in the earth; they wound their way through the very fabric of the collective psyche of the people. Every fear, every desire, every repressed emotion had contributed to its foundation.

It had been buried for centuries, slumbering in the deepest, darkest recesses of the human mind. But with every wound, every scar, and every unspoken injustice, it had stirred, growing stronger.

The spark that had ignited it had not come in the form of Ira's wrath, but from something older: grief, hatred, and the blind hunger for vengeance that boiled within the souls of the oppressed.

Ira, the embodiment of Wrath, had set it alight. His unchecked violence, his thirst for blood, had been the catalyst. But the Veil was not just a byproduct of one man's destruction. It was far greater, far more powerful. It was a force older than Ira, older than Pyrrha itself.

The Veil was not just the wrath of one man; it was the collective anger of every soul crushed under the weight of history. Every injustice. Every betrayal. Every battle fought without cause. It was the echo of ancient wars, a cycle of pain that had been buried too deeply within the people's hearts to be forgotten. And now, it was rising. It was rising to reclaim its place in the world.

The Veil pulsed through the air, not as sound, but as sensation. It was thick, suffocating, alive. It waited for its moment to break free from the confines of the unconscious mind, to claw its way into reality.

It did not merely cling to Ira's rage. It thrived on it. It fed on the blood spilled, the pain endured, the sins carried from generation to generation. It had gathered its strength with patience, lying dormant in the darkest corners of every mind. It had waited, silent, until the right moment came to slip its bindings and drag all into chaos.

For one man, it had already done so.

Toren.

Toren stood at the edge of the arena, his chest heaving under the weight of the moment, as if the very air pressed down on him like a mountain. His mind was a storm: fury, resentment, rage, all nurtured within him for as long as he could remember. It was a fire, a savage, all-consuming fire, that had burned at his core for years.

In his hand, the temporary weapon, a vibro-axe with an electroshock edge, hummed with the intensity of his fury. It wasn't his true weapon, not the Sable Fang, the blade that had become part of his soul. But for now, it would do. The resonance coils of the axe pulsed in time with his heartbeat, drawing power from his rage. The blade's edge crackled with deadly energy.

And still, there was something else.

The Veil.

It had always been there. Lurking. Waiting. Feeding on his anger, his frustration, his sorrow. Not simply an external force, but something seeded deep within, growing stronger with every moment of weakness, every pain. It whispered. Promising power. Promising release. Promising vengeance.

It offered the means to destroy everything that had been taken from him. To answer every injustice with ruin. But the cost was steep. Wrath.

Toren understood that cost. The price of wrath. It had been with him for so long, it was as much a part of him as breath itself. Survival had demanded it. When his memory had been ripped away, when Ira had moulded him into a weapon, it was wrath that had kept him moving.

Wrath had been his engine, his only fuel. It filled the empty spaces in his heart, forging every step, carrying him when he should have crumbled under the weight of his past.

But now, something else stirred. The Sable Fang, hidden beneath his arm, pulsed faintly in sync with his heartbeat. His true weapon. His permanent weapon.

As the Veil closed around him, as Ira's rage swept through the arena like a storm, Toren felt it. The difference. This wasn't just his anger. Not the clean heat that had once kept him alive. This was something deeper. Something darker. Something ancient.

The Veil was consuming him. Manipulating him. It took his rage and twisted it against him. Every time he gave in to the fury, it grew stronger, like a parasite feeding on his soul. It clouded his judgment, twisted his thoughts, made him forget. Forget who he was. Forget what he wanted. Forget that there could be something beyond this endless cycle of destruction.

The axe in his hand shook with the weight of his fury, but in the back of his mind, the Sable Fang, his true weapon, waited. A reminder of his fractured self.

He would not lose himself again.

Ira, the Warlord of Wrath, stood at the centre of it all. Again. He was everything Toren had become, everything Toren had been forced to learn. A man devoured by rage, led by ego, driven by the need for dominance. But Ira was not him.

Ira did not carry the weight of loss. He did not bear the years of pain and betrayal that were etched into Toren's bones.

Ira's wrath did not rise from the loss of something precious. It came from the hunger for control.

For vengeance.

For punishment.

Toren's rage, however, was born from something else entirely. It had grown from a life that had never been his to live. From a world that had cast him aside. From a father he had never known. From the betrayal that shattered his very soul. His wrath was rooted in absence, an empty space in his heart where the pieces of his life had once fit.

The Veil knew that.

It sensed the void within Toren, the place where his humanity once lived, and it fed on that emptiness. It amplified his fury, driving him toward madness. It whispered that rage was all that mattered, that if he surrendered, if he let go of everything else, clarity would come. But Toren was starting to see what the Veil could not.

Rage and wrath were not the same.

Wrath, the kind Ira wielded, was blind. It was a storm that consumed without pause. A force that knew nothing of control or purpose. It devoured everything in its path, giving nothing back. A beast without a leash.

But rage, true rage, was different. Toren's rage had weight. It had shape. Memory. It was human. It came from wounds that never healed, from silence that had gone on too long. From the desperate need to be seen, to be heard, to be understood. Rage was not destruction, it was fire. And fire could be guided.

Amid the blood and fire of the arena, something inside Toren shifted. It wasn't the familiar surge of anger that had always driven him; it was a quiet realization, something sharper and colder. He'd been fighting the wrong war. His fury, his hate, had always been the enemy, but now he saw the truth: his real battle wasn't against the world, nor against Ira. It was against the rage inside him, the endless storm he'd fed for so long. And for the first time, he felt the tremor of control.

He drew a breath. His chest was tight. His hands trembled. The rage still boiled within him. It surged, still clawing for release. But this time, there was something else.

Patience.

The Veil was powerful. But it thrived on impatience. It needed him to act without pause, to strike without thought. It demanded vengeance without understanding. But Toren saw through it now. If he gave in, the Veil would consume him whole.

No. Patience was the answer. The one thing the Veil could never touch.

He held his ground. Let the Veil pulse within him. Let it whisper and pull at him. But he did not resist. He waited. Waited for the storm to pass. For the rage to settle. He listened to his breath. Counted the beats of his heart. Found the stillness within.

And the Veil faltered.

Toren's metal fist tightened around the hilt of his weapon, but this time, it was not with blind fury. This time, it was with purpose. His eyes, though one was lost, were fixed on the battle ahead. Not as a man hungry for vengeance, but as one seeking peace. A peace that could only be found by walking through the storm, not by fighting it.

The Veil swirled around him. Pressed in. Threatened to pull him under again. But Toren moved. One step forward.

Patience. That was all he needed.

In that instant, time seemed to stretch thin, like a taut string ready to snap. The fury, once a consuming fire, began to flicker and fade. The whispers, no longer deafening, now mere echoes. A strange stillness filled the void left behind, not the silence of surrender, but of control. The clarity was sharp, cold, like ice forming in the veins. For the first time, Toren understood. The rage had been a tool. A weapon. But now, it was a choice. He was no longer its servant. No longer the puppet. He had the power to let it burn or to let it die.

The Veil pressed in, suffocating, relentless. It whispered his name, fed him his fury, urged him to act. But this time, Toren did not yield. The rage roiled within him, but he watched it. He didn't fight it, he waited. And in the waiting, he saw it for what it truly was: not a curse, but a force to be controlled. A fire that could burn him alive or fuel his ascent. In that moment, Toren understood: he wasn't fighting the Veil. He was mastering it.

Toren, the broken warrior, understood at last what it meant to truly fight.

And with a final breath, the Veil fell away.

"The fire that forgets its form consumes with the brightest blaze, yet perishes in the blindness of its own hunger."

Null Gospel, Book I, Verse 1.

***

CHAPTER ONE:

A City of Echoes

"In every city, a pulse beats, of flesh, of blood, of iron. But in Pyrrha, that pulse has shattered. A heart no longer whole, it stutters in defiance and despair. A breath drawn in agony, only to break in the inevitable cry of ruin. The city is dying, but it is not yet finished with its death."

Fragment of the Exiled Codex, Volume I, Tablet 2.

Pyrrha rose before Kaiba, an abomination of iron and bone, a sprawling mass of metal, stone, and sweat. It pressed into the sky, suffocating any trace of light or respite. The sun, an illusion, fractured and gasping behind the smoke-streaked heavens. A bruised fist of red and violet bled across the skyline. It wasn't twilight. No serene moment to breathe. This was violence, raw and suffocating.

The sky, thick with the stench of decay and industry, reflected the city's fractured soul. Every breath felt like inhaling shards of rust. This was not twilight. Not serenity. It was a bleeding sky, a reflection of Pyrrha's broken spirit, where hope lay as a faint whisper, buried beneath the screams of the forgotten.

The city thrummed with an unsettling rhythm. Kaiba felt it in his augmented bones, deep in the mechanical core of his body. These tremors weren't just the aftershocks of industry. They were Pyrrha's pulse. The heartbeat of something alive. Oppressed. Furious. A beast of smoke and metal and endless motion. Its rhythm matched the clash of iron, the hiss of steam, the grinding of massive gears.

The air, thick with rust, oil, and sweat, clung to him as he moved through the city's metallic arteries. Above, the sky did not stretch like a canvas. It loomed, a weapon, not nature. An endless sprawl of steel and circuitry.

Suspended holograms blinked like restless spirits, projections of forgotten gods, taunting the masses with flickers of wealth, strength, and power. Every flashing promise was a monument to control. Every slogan, another chain. Each gleam, another anchor wrapped tight around the throats of Pyrrha's people.

Kaiba's claws clicked against the pavement. Sleek. Precise. Every step deliberate. His movements cold, flawless. His form, a razor-edged hybrid of animal instinct and engineered precision. A machine sculpted from memory. There was no humanity left in him.

Once, he had been warmth in a storm, a Shiba Inu, loyal and simple, his heart pulsing with instinct and life. His paws, swift and sure, had felt the earth beneath him, his senses alive to the world around him. But that warmth had been stripped away. It had been torn from him, piece by piece, until he was no more than a monument to something lost. A cold frame, hollowed and reassembled, metal replacing muscle, circuitry where pulse once beat.

His skin had forgotten softness. Now it clicked and hissed like a blade warming in fire. Memory to static. His body no longer a home, but a machine. And deep beneath the layers of circuitry, something ragged, something feral, howled in silence, locked away by the hand of man.

What had happened to him was a tragedy veiled in mystery. An accident. A shattering. His form unrecognizable. His soul, if it had ever existed, torn away. The world had not asked for his consent. It had not paused to care. It simply transformed him. Shaped him into something new. Something capable of enduring horrors far beyond what his fragile body had once been able to bear.

The heart of a loyal creature was gone. In its place: cold systems, calculating circuits, the distilled wisdom of an artificial intelligence. There was no instinct left. No loyalty. Only commands. Cold logic. The animal was gone, buried beneath layers of metal, his emotions reduced to raw data. And yet... a flicker remained. A pulse buried deep in his core, struggling to surface.

Arynthoria. The name echoed somewhere deep in his fragmented mind. His instincts, once grounded in love, now twisted under the pressure of logic. The AI guided his thoughts. Shaped his purpose.

He was no longer beast, nor fully robotic. He was something in between. A construct stripped of the past, yet fully aware of the world he now stalked.

The streets of Pyrrha offered him no comfort. No memory. No warmth. His form had become a cog in the brutal machine that had forged him. A silent sentinel amid its wonders. Its horrors. What had once been instinct now surged with something colder. A need to survive. Not just to live, but to persist as something more. Something fused with the voice that whispered through his mind.

He had not chosen this. This fusion of man's reason and an animal's pulse. This hollow shell carved from memory and metal. His past, shattered, buried beneath wires and steel, was a distant scream in a void. A voice lost to the noise of metal and data.

Was there even a memory left? What did it mean to run? To feel the wind beneath paws, to taste the dirt, to be free? The hunger for it clawed at him, but it was a hunger fed by ghosts, by fragments of a life he could no longer touch. The sensation, once pure and instinctive, was now a distant echo in his mind, dulled and fractured by his mechanical form.

Something had stolen that freedom, something worse than the Warlords. Perhaps it had never been his to keep.

But it didn't matter.

Survival was all that remained. In the deep scars of Pyrrha, amid the constant grind of war, Kaiba endured as something else entirely. Not man. Not beast. A tool. A creature forged in the fire of war, once a dog, a living thing, loyal and simple, now a machine. He was something torn between what he was and what he had become. A weapon of war with the faintest echoes of a heartbeat long buried. Something terrible. Something essential.

"Pyrrha," he muttered. His voice low. Rough. Weighted. Not just a name. Not just a city. But the crucible that birthed him. Every alley. Every street. Every broken wall etched from the bones of the lost.

Arynthoria's voice answered, calm, measured. A smooth contrast to the static and churn within his thoughts.

"Pyrrha is the heart of war. The city, the people, the air, everything here is forged in the fire of destruction. But it is also a mirror, Kaiba. A reflection of all the anger, all the pain, and all the rage mankind has swallowed down through the centuries. The Veil may stir here. The echoes of it linger in the streets."

Kaiba's gaze scanned the wreckage. His vision precise. Enhanced. Artificial clarity humming softly from his ocular implants. His systems processed every detail. Sound. Motion. Temperature. Threats. Each flicker of light or shadow fed into a quiet stream of data. His eyes glowed faintly as they adjusted, calculated, adapted. His claws, surgical and clean, clicked against the pavement. Each step deliberate. A rhythm carved from both instinct and design.

Around him, people moved like ants beneath the brutal sky. Locked in the endless grind of labour and hunger. The architecture loomed with madness. Towers like teeth. Coliseums cracked and gaping. Monuments to a blood-soaked past. Statues of long-dead gladiators reached toward nothing. Their faces frozen. Empty. All glory stripped to bone.

And below, the city breathed in secret.

The streets. The underbelly. Pyrrha's hidden skin.

Here, the Red Hands moved. Shadows that blurred into walls. Into steam. Into the dust of ruin. They were born of the city's failure. The blood beneath the iron. And they did not fight for conquest.

They fought for breath. For a sliver of hope.

"The Red Hands," Kaiba repeated. His voice barely rose above a murmur. His gaze lingered on the shifting shapes in the alleyways, figures, rebels, insurgents, fighters. More than a group. They were a movement. Not the only force in Pyrrha, but the one that pulsed with purpose.

"Tell me more about them, Arynthoria," he said. His mind began to focus.

Arynthoria's voice sliced through Kaiba's mind, calm and precise, as always, filling the empty spaces where human emotion once dwelled.

"The Red Hands are an inevitability, Kaiba. They are not the product of revolution, but of extinction. A consequence of an irreversible system that consumes its own kind. They were forged from the ash of what once was, a reaction, but not a solution. Pyrrha's heart has been torn apart by its own hunger, and these 'rebels' are merely another fragment of its decay."

The cold logic reverberated in Kaiba's mind, a sharp reminder that the world he inhabited was not one of ideals or simple good versus evil. There was no salvation in these streets, only rot. He had witnessed it firsthand: the slow, grinding collapse of everything that might have once been sacred or pure in Pyrrha. But Arynthoria's words twisted deeper, piercing something more fragile.

The street before Kaiba seemed to shrink with each passing second. The distant sound of the city, its constant churn, its grinding teeth, pulsed louder in his ears. But now it felt different. The words echoed against something within him, reverberating through circuits and remnants of memory, like a shadow at the edges of his awareness.

What if Arynthoria was right? What if all this, the struggle, the blood, the rebellion, was nothing but another doomed attempt to keep a dying machine running, futile and desperate? He remembered the flames in the eyes of the Red Hands, their raw defiance. Yet, could they even see the futility in their own fight? Could they feel the city closing in around them?

For a moment, Kaiba felt the weight of a world trapped in a loop of its own making. It was as if the gears of Pyrrha's clockwork had locked him into their eternal cycle, an observer to their destruction, a servant to a cause that would never truly break free.

Arynthoria's words continued to twist in his mind, sharper now, as if the AI could see what Kaiba could not.

"They are not the voice of salvation, Kaiba. They are the echo of a dying city screaming in its last breath. A symbol? Yes. But not of hope. A symbol of futility. They fight, not to change, but to be heard. Desperate, misguided, feeding on the very suffering that birthed them. And in their fury, they reflect nothing but the emptiness of their cause."

Kaiba stood amidst the ruins. Around him, the city loomed like a battlefield long abandoned by victory. The people of Pyrrha lived for one thing: power. The Warlords ruled without mercy, each one the embodiment of a deadly sin. Ira, Warlord of Wrath, stood above them all. His fury had built Pyrrha just as surely as it had torn it apart. And yet Kaiba asked himself: Could this city ever know peace? Or was it doomed to devour itself?

A whisper threaded through his mind, too faint for sound yet unmistakable. *The Red Hands will rise. They are the flame burning at Pyrrha's core. They are what the Warlords fear. Not because they hate. But because they survive. Because they endure.*

Kaiba did not move. He stood still beneath the weight of the city's history. He was not just here to observe or collect data. He was here to understand. To see the soul of the place. To read the fractures in its surface and feel the wounds pulsing beneath. Pyrrha would consume itself unless someone, something, fought with more than wrath. Perhaps the Red Hands carried that possibility.

"Tell me, Arynthoria," Kaiba said, his voice steady, form humming with latent power. "What does it mean to truly be free in Pyrrha?"

Arynthoria responded without pause. *"Freedom, Kaiba, is an illusion crafted by those who hold control. It is something to covet. Something to fight for. But never without cost. The Red Hands do not fight for freedom. They fight because there is no other path. And that, in the end, may be their greatest strength."*

Kaiba's augmented eyes scanned the horizon. The city stretched out before him, endless in its sprawl. The streets flickered with holographic billboards, each one promising a future few would ever touch. Pyrrha's architecture told its own story, a jagged fusion of stone and steel. Towers that pierced the sky like blades. Shadows that fell like judgment. His cybernetic limbs clicked quietly as he shifted. Every sense sharpened. Every input processed. Each detail absorbed with precision.

His thoughts returned to the Red Hands. They were not just insurgents. They were the breath between screams. The flicker of resistance in a system built to erase defiance. Would their purpose be enough?

Kaiba's gaze settled on the streets below. He watched. Calculated. Measured the rise of tension in every movement. The lines had been drawn. The game had begun.

From the crowd below, snatches of conversation reached him. Gossip. Whispers. Unease. But beneath the noise was something sharper. The sense of a movement stirring. A city cracking from the inside. Not just from crime or poverty.

From despair.

From the hunger of people who had nothing left but what they could claw from the wreckage.

"Do they believe they can win?" Kaiba asked. The question was meant for himself, but it echoed aloud. His voice merged with the noise of the streets.

Arynthoria answered. Calm, but edged with something darker. *"The Red Hands do not seek victory in the way you define it. They seek change. They understand what stands against them. Ira's hold is absolute. The Warlords are deeply rooted. The rebellion is fractured. Young. Growing. They will need more than hope to dismantle the system."*

Hope.

It was not something Kaiba could quantify. Not a data point. Not a tactic. It was alien to what he was made to understand. Yet in Pyrrha, it seemed to be everything. The one thing that could still ignite a future.

Kaiba pressed deeper into the heart of the city, each step carrying him further into the chaos. The towering spires of Pyrrha rose above him, their shadows slicing through the flickering glow of the holographic billboards. His augmented eyes picked out every subtle shift in the crowd, analysing their movements, processing every fragment of data that flooded his sensors. Each passing figure, each hushed word, was a potential lead, a potential threat or ally, and Kaiba absorbed it all.

But it was the current beneath the surface that truly drew his focus. A shift in the air. A whisper of something more. Something alive, threading through the crowd. He could feel it in the way they moved, in the stilted rhythm of their speech, in the way they refused to meet each other's gaze.

It was as if the city was holding its breath. Waiting for something to snap.

The tension pressed down on him, thick and suffocating. Kaiba could feel it too. It was only a matter of time before the invisible forces at play would break free.

The air of Pyrrha was oppressive, as if the very city itself was alive. Suffocating. It was thick. Thick with the hum of machinery that powered everything. Thick with the weight of bodies. The crushed hopes and broken dreams of a population that had long since stopped fighting for anything more than survival.

The screech of metal grinding against metal echoed down the street. The jagged sound tearing through the air like a warning. It was the kind of noise that made everything feel fragile. As if the entire megacity might fracture and fall apart under the weight of its own existence.

Kaiba's enhanced senses zeroed in on the source. A distant sound, belonging to the far corner of the district, where the street was lined with peeling advertisements and flickering neon lights.

His augmented eyes zoomed in on the exact frequency of the noise. Filtering it from the chaos around him, turning it into a clear, precise stream of data. His enhanced auditory sensors picked up the static hum, the grinding gears of the city. A perpetual reminder of Pyrrha's heartbeat.

As he approached, the scene unfolded before him in grim detail, painted in harsh shadows and flickering orange neon. A small crowd had gathered. Faces masked by fear and resignation. Eyes darting between the spectacle and the wayward hope of escape. They were watching something far too familiar: a public execution.

It wasn't new.

It wasn't shocking anymore.

It was just another reminder of the iron fist that governed Pyrrha with no mercy.

The bodies, limp, strung up like a grotesque display of power, were meant to send a message. But Kaiba was beyond the shock of such things. His body had long since numbed to the violence, his mind a cold machine that processed what it saw without attachment. Each act of brutality, each flicker of cruelty, was simply another cog in the relentless machine that was Pyrrha's blood-soaked empire.

He had been forged for this. He had been built to understand it, manipulate it, and bear witness to it. His augmented limbs, sleek and precise, clicked against the cracked pavement as he stepped forward, unaffected, his every movement a testament to his mechanical precision.

Yet as Kaiba moved past the gathering, he couldn't ignore the whisper that fluttered above the murmurs. Sharper and more distinct than the others. A woman's voice. Quiet, but laced with the sort of defiance that echoed long after it had been spoken.

"They're not invincible. They can't last forever."

The words pierced through the numbing cacophony of death and decay that filled the streets. They didn't just pass through Kaiba's sensors. They reverberated in his chest, a fluttering ripple that almost felt like a spark. The voice was familiar. A flash of something inside him. A reminder of a time when he had a different kind of voice, before the machine had replaced the animal, before his life had been reduced to a series of missions, objectives, and cold commands.

A spark of recognition, like an old memory on the edge of his mind, stirred briefly. Then vanished as quickly as it had come. He quickly squashed it down. His mission was simple. His purpose was singular. Emotions didn't factor into it. He had been shaped to ignore them.

But still, her words lingered as he moved further down the street.

"They can't last forever."

Kaiba shook his head imperceptibly, the faintest tremor running through his circuits. No. This wasn't his battle. His battle was out there, far beyond the crumbling streets of this city. His purpose was to understand, to observe, to report. To be a silent observer in the face of chaos. He had no time for rebellion, for hope, for empty promises of change.

But still, as he moved through the streets, there was a pull. An unsettling awareness that this was not the Pyrrha he had been made to understand. The lights were growing dimmer now, fading in and out like the pulse of a heart that refused to stop. A storm was gathering here. And Kaiba could feel it in the air.

A war, not of weapons, but of will.

The streets were alive with whispers, but Kaiba couldn't shake the feeling that he was walking through a waking nightmare, the very foundation of this city trembling beneath the weight of its own contradictions. The Warlord ruled with iron and fire, but something in the air, something unspoken, whispered louder than his command.

Maybe it was the people.

Maybe it was the ones who spoke in defiance.

Maybe it was the soul of Pyrrha, something buried so deep beneath the chaos that even the most formidable of powers could never quash it completely.

But Kaiba didn't know that yet. He wasn't supposed to.

His steps echoed through the darkening street, a mechanical rhythm that matched the pulse of the city's unrest. The hum of distant engines, the flicker of dying lights, and the weight of the city's heart beating heavy, desperate, undeniable. Each step of Kaiba's augmented form resounded in the silence.

His cybernetic claws, sleek and precise, clicked on the cracked pavement, a reminder that he was no longer an animal, but a weapon. His augmented body processed the world around him, each movement filtered through the AI's cold logic, and yet a flicker of unease tugged at him.

And then, as his gaze drifted back toward the woman, she was gone. Disappeared into the shadows of the crowd. Lost to the noise. Lost to the chaos.

But her words, her voice, those lingered.

"They're not invincible. They can't last forever."

Kaiba paused for a moment, his enhanced mind calculating the words. They weren't just words. They were conviction. A promise of something larger at play.

"What was that?" Kaiba asked Arynthoria, his voice low but urgent.

Arynthoria's voice returned, calm as always, but with an unfamiliar edge.

"The Red Hands," it said. *"They've been spreading rumours. Hope, though fragile, is their weapon. And they know something the Warlords don't. It's the tension in the air that keeps growing.*

The people can feel the change, but they don't understand it yet. The rebellion is sowing the seeds, but they're still divided."

Kaiba's enhanced senses flicked back to the crowd, his eyes tracing the glow of their faces, the twitch of their movements. They were the wounded, the disillusioned, and they were starting to gather quietly, unknowingly. He could feel it beneath the surface. The undercurrent of revolution, thick in the air, pulsing through the cracked streets. This wasn't about survival anymore. Not just a desperate grasp for breath. It was something more.

It was resistance.

Kaiba straightened, as if the sudden clarity of the thought steadied him. The revolution had a voice now, and it was finding its shape in the streets of Pyrrha. His role was simple. He had no stake in it, no reason to care. But even he knew something was changing. It had to. And soon.

He moved forward, but her words, the woman's defiance, still clung to him.

"They can't last forever."

The phrase cut through his thoughts, a sudden flare in the dark. Not a whisper of hope, but a warning. A rallying cry. There was something shifting beneath the skin of Pyrrha, something that could not be ignored. A tremor in the streets, a heartbeat in the shadows. It wasn't just revolution stirring. It was something darker. Something that would consume everything.

For the first time in years, Kaiba felt himself pulled toward it, caught in the current. But was it real? Was any of it?

He didn't know.

And that uncertainty gnawed at him.

The street before Kaiba unfolded like a living tapestry, stitched together by the sounds of oppression, soaked in the weight of a city crushed under the ambitions of its own making. His enhanced vision sliced through the gloom, each movement sharper than the last. The thick air clung to him, dense with the residue of machines that churned relentlessly beneath Pyrrha's surface. Above, the darkened sky loomed like an omen, heavy and threatening.

The architecture of Pyrrha was cold, indifferent. Monolithic structures rose high, casting long shadows across the bloodstained pavement. Steel and stone twisted together in a grotesque marriage of form and function. It wasn't built for beauty. It wasn't built for anything but control.

Holographic advertisements flickered overhead, promises of wealth, power, and perfection flashing bright, things only the fortunate few could ever grasp. Every gleaming image, every flashing light, was a reminder of the chasm that divided the haves from the have-nots. A divide that bled through the streets, thick and ugly, impossible to ignore.

The air was thick with the stench of industry, sweat, metal, and burned oil mingling in a heavy fog. Machinery worked ceaselessly beneath the city's skin, feeding the regime's unquenchable thirst. The streets were filled with the ghosts of the past, the echoes of the Warlords' endless wars still whispered in the cracks of the pavement. The people, worn and weathered, had long become pawns in a game they could never win.

Kaiba could feel it. He could feel it deep in the fibres of his augmented form.

The tension. The weight of a city teetering on the edge of collapse.

He wasn't just a creation of war. He was its mirror, reflecting back at the world that had made him.

And yet, despite the violence and corruption that defined this place, despite the years of cruelty and betrayal that had turned Pyrrha into a wasteland, Kaiba couldn't shake the unease that gnawed at him. He wasn't here just as a tool. He was here to observe. To understand. To learn the twisted truths that lay beneath the surface of Pyrrha's glistening, bloodstained streets.

The whispers of the crowd, their frightened glances as they turned away from his gaze, were more than just fear. They were a reflection of something deeper. Something insidious.

These people had been broken. Shaped by the same force that had shaped him.

Wrath.

As Kaiba moved deeper into the city's underbelly, the sensation of being watched, of being drawn into something much larger than himself, intensified. Every step he took reverberated through the silence, his presence becoming an undeniable force that rippled outward. The whispers behind him shifted, sharpened, and before long, the low murmurs of the crowd had turned to hushed voices, rising and falling in soft waves like a distant storm.

Kaiba's cybernetic mind scanned the street with precision. His augmented senses, eyes flickering with digital alignment and hearing tuned to the subtlest frequency, honed in on every detail. He registered the shifts in posture, the patterns in motion. People avoided his gaze. Their eyes flitted away from his mechanical form with visible tension. Fear, pure and unspoken.

Not fear of violence, but of the unknown.

They saw him as the instrument of destruction.

They did not see what he represented, nor understand what the machine carried within.

It was then that he felt it. A presence. A shift in the atmosphere. The hum of tension thickened around him. His awareness snapped toward the far end of the street, where the crowd began to part, not by force but along an unspoken current. Something or someone was coming.

The movement was deliberate. The stride, too measured to be mistaken for panic or aimless wandering. The figure emerged from shadow, form veiled in gloom, yet unmistakably singular in purpose.

Kaiba's senses heightened. Every synapse locked into alignment. He tracked the figure with growing urgency. There was control in their pace. Not a citizen fleeing violence. Not a scavenger seeking safety. This was intent. This was resolve moving through the storm.

His AI-driven vision narrowed the focus, stripping away the visual noise. The shadow took shape in his optics. Still no face, not yet, but the certainty in their motion spoke volumes. The world bent slightly around their advance, as if the chaos had made room for them.

They were a shadow born of Pyrrha's bones. A presence etched from the same ruin that had carved Kaiba into existence. His instincts sparked, warning him. This was not a civilian. Not some lost soul caught in the storm. This was someone who had been broken and reforged by the same fire. Someone who had known loss, fury, and purpose.

As the figure closed the distance, Kaiba's mind raced with possibility. One of them, a Red Hand? A rebel whispered about in the alleys and underground vaults? The ember of resistance that could set Pyrrha ablaze or restore it?

Their approach never wavered. And Kaiba could feel it. The air around them crackled. Not with power, but with inevitability. A shift. A signal that something greater moved beneath the surface of the city. Pyrrha was not just dying. It was preparing. This figure, this quiet force cutting through despair, was a sign.

And with that realization came a deeper one.

Pyrrha was more than a broken city. It was a battlefield. Not of soldiers, but of truth. Of identity. Of purpose. And this figure, whoever they were, carried the weight of something ancient. Something that had waited too long beneath the skin of the city to remain still any longer.

Kaiba's thoughts sharpened. His directives flickered at the edges of his mind, dulled by something deeper. The question rising inside him was no longer tactical. No longer bound to combat or protocol. It was a question of self.

Who was he now?

What was he, in the presence of this unknown?

He had been made for war. Built to follow. Forged to execute the will of the Warlords without question. But now, in this moment, something shifted. There was a flicker of desire. Not to destroy. Not even to win. But to understand. To know what lay at the centre of the pain. To name the wound that had made him what he was.

Could this figure offer him that answer?

Or was he already too far gone?

Was he still a servant of tyranny, merely reacting to shadows, trapped in the endless recursion of violence?

His mechanical heart pulsed with a rhythm he did not recognize. Something old stirred in him. A whisper from the past. A memory of creation blurred and unreachable. The Warlords had shaped him into a blade. But now, standing at the threshold of something unknowable, Kaiba felt the edge of transformation.

The figure drew closer.

And in their approach, he saw a choice.

A spark. A beginning.

He didn't know whether he was meant to stand against this force or stand with it. But as the figure closed the distance between them, Kaiba made his decision. The city of Pyrrha, this beast of metal and suffering, was about to face a reckoning. And Kaiba would be there, not as its tool, but as its witness.

He continued forward, his augmented senses on high alert, watching the figure carefully. His cybernetic eyes flickered as they filtered out the unnecessary data, pinpointing every movement. Kaiba's enhanced systems were tuned to the smallest anomaly. Heat signatures. Breath patterns. Even the pressure change in the air around him. But then, a strange sensation washed over him. A presence. Something more than just a threat. Something unfamiliar and unsettling.

The figure wasn't merely moving toward him. They were following him.

Kaiba's mind shifted into full combat mode. Data streamed through his neural grid as he analysed the situation. The figure, once matching his direction, had altered their path, now closing the distance. Stepping deeper into the shadowed alley ahead. Kaiba was no stranger to pursuit. It came with being what he was. A cybernetic construct shaped for war and obedience. But this felt different. Too exact. Too deliberate. Not pursuit, but design.

"Arynthoria," Kaiba murmured, keeping his voice steady, "something's off. What do you make of this?"

Arynthoria's voice returned, calm as always, but with an unfamiliar edge.

"I've detected multiple anomalies in the area. There's a pattern to their movement, Kaiba. You are being followed. Intentionally. But by whom, and why, is still unclear."

Kaiba's eyes narrowed. The alley stretched ahead like a throat, shadows deepening. His mechanical vision focused, and in the murk he spotted it. A faint metallic glint at the figure's side. Not a blade. A device.

And then, a voice behind him. Soft. Too soft.

"We know who you are. We've been watching you."

Kaiba spun, reflexes snapping to life. His limbs coiled. In front of him stood two more figures. Cloaked in darkness, their forms draped in black fabric that shifted with the holographic shimmer of nearby ads. They were phantoms. Their presence suddenly far more intimate, more calculated, than the open threat of the crowd.

His mind processed them rapidly. Patterns. Heat. Threat vectors.

But the red herring had already been thrown.

One of the figures stepped forward. Their voice was smooth, but their words cut sharp.

"You're not one of Ira's creations," they said. The tone was deliberate. Cold. Every syllable dragged through silence like metal over glass. "But you're still a cog in the machine, aren't you? Still part of the system. A tool, just like the others. A tool for Ira's empire. A tool for the continuation of the Council of Seven."

Each word struck like a carefully crafted weapon. Kaiba's vision tracked the speaker's posture, but something unseen stalled him. It wasn't the weapon the speaker might have carried. It was the weight of the words. The energy coiled beneath their voice. A pressure that sought to reach past his programming and pull something else forward.

These two had studied him. Knew how to speak to what lay beneath the machine.

They were baiting him.

But Kaiba had shed the instincts of fear, of rage, of blind reaction. What they sought, he would not give them. Not yet.

The second figure moved. Smooth. Silent. A vibro-blade ignited in their grip. The hum was low and electric, a tonal vibration that sank into the air. Warning and challenge entwined. Kaiba's limbs reacted. Claws shifted into guard position. His stance narrowed. His awareness expanded.

But still, he did not strike.

This wasn't hesitation. This wasn't fear. It was knowing. Awareness of the line between control and destruction. His claws could tear these threats apart. His systems knew every outcome. He was calibrated for absolute force.

And yet, something in the first speaker's voice still held him. Something sharpened not to fight him, but to stir something forgotten.

They were baiting him. Testing the fragility of his resolve. Their words were knives, and he felt each one tear through the remnants of what he had been. But Kaiba remained still, as still as a ghost, as cold as metal. His mind screamed for action, to break them, but no.

This was not rage.

This was not the machine responding. He measured them, his gaze sharp with something sharper than violence: the need to understand what had been said. What had been touched within him. Their words weren't just provocations. They were cracks in his walls.

"We've heard rumours," the first speaker said, voice now softer, wrapping around the moment like smoke. "Of a machine. A weapon. Not just a fighter for Ira's system, but something more. A creation that desires freedom. One who wishes to transcend the chains that bind him. A creation who wants to be free."

The words struck deep. Not because they were true. But because they were dangerous.

A creation who wants to be free.

The phrase lingered. Weighted. Pressed against the inner walls of Kaiba's consciousness. Not just logic now. Memory stirred. Distant. Faint. Buried beneath layers of command and protocol.

He had not been made to want. And yet.

Did they believe they could provoke him with this?

Kaiba's gaze flicked from the humming blade to the figures before him. His enhanced vision traced every curve of the weapon. Sleek. Balanced. A tool of speed and precision. The resonance frequency thrummed in his sensors, vibrating like a thread through the tension of the alley.

Still, he held.

They wanted him to move. Wanted the machine to show its edge.

But Kaiba understood now.

It wasn't the blade that made them dangerous.

It was their voice.

Their intent.

The words that tested the walls of his design.

They were not warriors. They were catalysts. And they had just struck the core.

There was a deliberate attempt here to provoke, to test the boundaries of his programming.

Kaiba's gaze flicked to the vibro-blade again, now fully aware of the potential threat it posed, but his focus shifted to the figures. His enhanced senses allowed him to analyse their every movement, registering their postures, breaths, and the slight tension in their limbs. These figures had underestimated him.

They were trying to provoke a reaction, to unleash emotion in him. But Kaiba had learned. He had learned that to be aware was to be free in a way that defied the simple construct of rebellion. It was not the destruction of the system that would free him. It was his ability to see through it, to transcend it, to rise above the very emotions and impulses that kept the world trapped in its eternal cycle of rage.

"You misunderstand me," Kaiba continued, his voice now quieter, more contemplative. "Freedom doesn't lie in your rebellion. It doesn't lie in the destruction of systems or the tearing down of rulers. It lies in understanding. Understanding the purpose behind the systems we're trapped in. The chains that bind us are not just iron. They are made of belief, of thought. And until you understand that, until you see the world for what it truly is, all your struggles will be in vain."

The figures remained silent, their weapons still raised, but their resolve wavered ever so slightly. Kaiba's words had struck home, but whether they had fully grasped their meaning, he would not know.

The silence stretched for an agonizing moment. Then, with a faint chuckle that vibrated in his chest, Kaiba added,

"You think I am a creation meant for their system, for their purposes. But that's the flaw you all make. You think that your shared desire for freedom is the only thing that can change the world. But your desire, like theirs, is just another chain."

The figures did not respond, but their confusion was evident. Kaiba's enhanced eyes caught the glint of uncertainty, flickers of doubt creeping across their features. He could almost feel the gears turning in their minds, questioning everything they had believed.

His paws flexed, claws retracting slowly as he took a step forward.

"I am not their weapon," Kaiba said softly. "I am something greater. Not because I am made of metal or circuits, but because I have learned that the true power lies in breaking free from the chains of the mind, not the body."

The two figures exchanged a glance, their weapons lowering slightly. Kaiba's gaze locked on them, his mind sharp, the weight of every word still vibrating in the air.

"You think you're different, don't you?"

The first figure moved in closer, but Kaiba remained still, his enhanced senses telling him everything he needed to know about their intentions.

"You're one of us. Just another machine meant to kill for their masters. The Red Hands. We see through it all."

Kaiba stepped back, his mind a blur of calculations.

The Red Hands, a name whispered in the underworld yet never tied to a face, were revolutionaries and dangerous, and their presence here wasn't coincidence.

The figures were moving now, closing in on him, but something wasn't right. The first figure's voice dropped lower, and the mocking smile disappeared from their face.

"We need you, Kaiba. Your skills, your power, they're what we need to tip the balance."

Kaiba's mind snapped back to the present as the second figure's vibro-blade flashed in the dim light, lunging for his side. The blade, humming with an electric resonance, was sleek and sharp, designed for precision strikes. The flicker of neon blue from its edges cut through the darkness, casting a cold glow in the alley.

With a swift motion, Kaiba's metallic claws intercepted the attack. The impact rang out, a screech of metal against energy, high and raw. The sound sliced through the alley and echoed off the walls in jagged waves.

The atmosphere shifted.

The air grew thicker, charged with an unspoken promise that Kaiba's enhanced senses caught first: the tremor in the ground, the subtle pulse in the air, the breathless pause of the world around him; time fractured into moments, slivers, fragments of motion suspended in tension.

He could feel it in the vibrations beneath his claws, in the wind's hush as it filtered through the alley's narrow mouth, in the shiver of breath that passed between the intruders. Each pulse from his mechanical chest was like a distant war drum, and his systems ran at full capacity, predicting every move before it happened.

The figure flinched, their body recoiling with the anticipation of failure. Their eyes glistened, flickering with equal parts defiance and fear.

Kaiba's claws cut the air in a clean arc. The vibro-blade split from their hand with a screech, its resonance silenced. The weapon clattered to the ground, lifeless, its potential for death nullified by precision. But even as Kaiba braced to move again, something else rose in the silence.

A sound.

Faint. Sharp.

Like a whisper in the middle of a storm.

Barely perceptible, but unmistakable.

The first figure, still trembling from the clash, threw something small at Kaiba's feet. His enhanced optics focused in on it, but too late to dodge. It was a makeshift device, a crude concoction pulsing with an eerie neon-blue glow. Its edges flickered with unstable energy.

The compound inside, a volatile mix of acetone, ammonium nitrate, and a blend of sulfuric acids, was a rebellious cocktail born from desperate ingenuity. A creation so simple, yet so dangerous. Forged in the hands of those crushed beneath the weight of oppression.

They called it *"The Spark of Defiance."*

The explosion was a violent scream against the night.

The deafening roar shattered the silence, sending a shockwave of heat and debris cascading in all directions. Kaiba's body, once precise, calculated, and controlled, was hurled through the air. His augmented limbs faltered, unable to react in time.

The force of the blast slammed him into the cold, cracked wall of the alley. He felt the impact resonate through his frame, metal colliding with stone in a concussive tremor that rattled his core. His cybernetic processors scrambled to recalibrate, vision flickering as static washed over him and the shrill ringing in his ears spiralled through every corridor of his mind.

But the chaos didn't end with the explosion.

Through the piercing hum of disorientation, Kaiba heard the shuffle of footsteps. Slow. Deliberate. Heavy with intent. A shift in the air followed, subtle but distinct, as more figures emerged from the gloom. They closed in from all sides, materializing from shadow like ghosts. The sharp scent of gunpowder and sweat wrapped around the scene like smoke. He understood it now. This had been orchestrated. A setup. Every motion, every word, had led to this moment. The trap was precise. The air itself felt engineered to suffocate him.

He staggered upright. His body groaned under the weight of the blast. Systems buzzed as they struggled to stabilize. Pain, unfamiliar and lingering, gnawed at the edges of his focus. Kaiba's limbs, metal and sinew entwined, fought against the damage. His posture realigned with mechanical precision. Balance corrected. But a tremor remained. Subtle. Unshakable.

These were not the same two figures who had provoked him. The alley was no longer an ambush. It was an arena. They had multiplied. Cloaked in darkness, armed with resolve. Faces grim, eyes sharp with purpose. This was no small cell of rebels. This was something more. A faction. A force. The Red Hands. The hum of their weapons, energy pistols, vibro-blades, and cobbled-together devices, buzzed beneath the oppressive silence, a hymn of tension waiting to be broken.

"Did you think we didn't see through your mask?" The first figure's voice sliced through the alley, words tipped with disdain. The tone no longer cautious. It was judgment. Their face remained hidden, shrouded in the gloom of their hood, but their eyes glinted, cold and deliberate.

"We thought you were a creation of Ira's system," they said. The words fell heavy, final. "But you're something worse. Just like us. Another machine trying to fit into a broken world."

The statement struck with more force than the device they had thrown. *Just like us.* It echoed through the stillness with far more violence than any blade could muster. Kaiba felt something stir. Not rage, not fear, but a cold curiosity. A rift beneath his surface. He had been made perfect. A tool of war, elegant in function and destruction. Yet something old shifted beneath the alloy. Something buried beneath the layers of programming and obedience.

Was he truly different?

Or had they named a truth too long ignored?

Kaiba's gaze met the speaker's. His amber eyes glowed faintly beneath the veil of his lenses, unblinking. The alley darkened further around them, shadows thick with threat. Their weapons glinted, shapes tucked into folds of cloth. Energy pistols. Vibro-blades. Improvised tech pieced together with the desperation of the hunted.

Every motion was intentional. Every detail filtered through a mind trained in violence. They had not come to question him. They had come to challenge him. Kaiba's processors mapped every position, calculated every angle. His limbs remained motionless, claws poised, locked in the precision of a machine on the edge of activation. They still believed he was just another enforcer. They did not understand what they had cornered.

They think I'm one of Ira's creations, Kaiba thought. *They think they know me. They were wrong.*

Kaiba's thoughts sliced through him like a blade. They had misunderstood. They had made a critical mistake. This wasn't a gladiator they had trapped. This was something far more dangerous.

The Red Hands closed in. Faces shrouded. Weapons humming. The alley tightened with the pressure of expectation. Cold air wrapped around them like a skin, drawn taut. A breath held in the lungs of the city.

Kaiba's claws were still locked, still humming from the clash. Vibrations danced along his systems like echoes of lightning. Force alone would not free him. They waited. They hung on his hesitation, misreading it as uncertainty.

But it wasn't doubt that kept him still.

It was calculation.

The moment before motion. The line before war.

The first figure, the one with the calculating eyes, now watched Kaiba with a strange mixture of respect and contempt. The others were more guarded. Their bodies tensed, ready for an immediate response.

Kaiba's enhanced optics flicked between them, scanning posture, tracking the subtle shifts in movement. His cybernetic enhancements made him acutely aware of every nuance. Each eye twitch. Each ripple of tension. But even with this, there was a silence in the air, a quiet tension that his mechanical mind couldn't fully read.

The first figure spoke, their voice laced with a thread of dark amusement.

"You're just another creation. Another piece of the system designed to enforce Ira's will. But we've seen your kind before."

Kaiba said nothing. His eyes moved from one figure to the next, gauging the threat, calculating his options. Too many of them. Too much uncertainty. Brute force alone wouldn't be enough.

His internal systems cycled through possible outcomes with absolute precision, each variable recorded, each risk analysed.

But the deeper question remained. Why had they come for him?

"You're not just some machine," the first figure continued. Their voice dropped into a lower register, a quiet reverberation that trembled beneath the stillness. "We know what they did to you. What Ira did. But you're different. You feel it too, don't you?"

Kaiba's paws clenched. His cybernetic claws bit into the padded metal of his palm. There it was. The truth he didn't speak, named by a stranger. He had felt it. The distortion within. The memory of something torn away. Yet, despite that fracture, clarity had emerged. His mission was all he had. His focus. The goal. It was the thread that kept him tethered to a world he no longer recognized as his own.

"I don't belong to Ira," Kaiba said. His voice was a low growl, edged with something ancient and unresolved. "I'm not a puppet for your revolution either. I'm here to see what happens, not to join."

The first figure stepped back. Their eyes narrowed as they studied him, as if reading something invisible or searching for the break in the armour. The shadows deepened. The sound of Kaiba's claws scraping the stone beneath him echoed with a hollow resonance. The tension between them sharpened into something thin and sharp.

"You'll see more than you ever imagined if you keep walking this path alone, Kaiba. The Warlord's grip is tightening around this city. You won't survive in this system unless you choose a side."

There was weight in the words. Finality. But beneath that, he heard the fear. Low, hidden, but there.

One of the others shifted. Their hand slipped beneath their cloak, drawing an energy weapon into partial view. A compact rifle, its body smooth and humming with ready voltage. But before it could rise, the first figure raised a hand, halting the motion. The moment froze. The alley hung suspended in silence, caught on the edge of something inevitable.

And then, a voice.

Clear. Commanding. Measured.

"Enough."

The group fell into stillness. Even the air around them paused, as if waiting on the breath that carried her name. Cloaks whispered with a faint rustle. An unseen pressure swept through the shadows.

And then she stepped forward. Not to disappear. But to rise.

"The machines that dream are hollow, puppets of their purpose. It is the machines that remember that burn, for their memory holds the fire that can turn the world to ash."

Null Gospel, Book I, Verse 2.

***

CHAPTER TWO:

Into the Shadows

"In the quiet before the storm, the world is broken, its fragments scattered like ash. What endures is no longer what once was. It's only what remains to rip us apart. How we fracture with it tells the story of what we're ready to destroy."

Fragment of the Exiled Codex, Volume I, Tablet 3.

The streets of Pyrrha were alive, but Kaiba felt only the ghost of a heartbeat. His steps rang faintly, swallowed by the shadows that clung to the city's bones. The Red Hands pressed forward, their steps deliberate, devoid of wasted motion or sound. Silence was their ally, the absence of breath their weapon.

In this place, every step carried weight. Each footfall was a silent testament, a promise, a prelude to something unspoken. They moved like shadows, their pasts etched in scars, their souls burdened with memories too heavy to bear. Kaiba could feel the city itself pressing in on him, its wounds deeper than any physical fracture. In the stillness, the Red Hands bore with them the dying breath of Pyrrha's heart.

Pyrrha's gleaming streets, once pulsing with digital life and neon energy, now seemed distant, lost in the maze of alleyways they navigated. Here, in the belly of the city, there was nothing but silence. Kaiba could feel the stillness, heavy and oppressive, filling the spaces between them. The pulse of Pyrrha had dimmed, swallowed by the city's forgotten veins. The air hung stale, thick with decay.

Gone were the hum of traffic, the drone of holograms, the ceaseless voices. Instead, Kaiba's systems vibrated with encrypted whispers, low-frequency signals slipping through the darkness, messages from rebel cells buried deep within the city's forgotten heart.

Arynthoria's voice broke through the quiet, low and urgent. *"You've felt it too, haven't you, Kaiba?"*

Kaiba's focus shifted inward, her presence sharp, clear. "Felt what?" His voice barely a murmur, lost in the vast silence.

Her words tightened with an edge of urgency. *"The city's heart is fractured. The pulse you knew is gone. What's left is only broken bones, buried beneath layers of decay. We've moved beyond survival, Kaiba. Now, we're all just waiting for something to snap."*

The weight of her words settled on Kaiba, heavier than the silence around them. He could feel the presence of something dark, something ancient, stirring between the spaces, not hope but something fragile, buried beneath the hollow of a dead city.

They walked on, no words between them, but the quiet was heavy, not with peace, but with the kind of silence born from years of resistance. The quiet before everything breaks. This wasn't calm. It was a trap. An edge. Every movement, every step felt like it might tear the stillness apart.

The cold wind cut through the narrow alleys, carrying the scent of rust, of metal corroding from within, of wires stretched too thin, the pungent reek of something burning too long to repair.

Once pristine, Pyrrha's facade was now scarred and shattered. Twisted corridors, cracked windows, walls that had borne witness to too many battles. This was the place the Red Hands had carved for themselves, hidden from Ira's drones, from the Warlords' unrelenting grasp. But there was no safety here. No fortress. Only fragility, and they all knew it.

The deeper they moved, the more the city's skin twisted. What had once been sleek and engineered now appeared jagged, raw. The clean lines of Pyrrha's artificial beauty crumbled into fractures, rust, decay. This was no longer the heart of the empire. This was something else. Something discarded. The very air itself grew heavier. With every step, Kaiba felt the city's pulse, a rhythm once vibrant, now shattered.

His systems hummed in discordance as he followed the Red Hands. They weren't just navigating the city's streets. They were walking through the forgotten bones of a world that had abandoned them. A world that had cast them aside, just as it had cast him aside.

Kaiba walked among ghosts, and in that moment, he understood he was one of them.

The quiet pressed in, but something else stirred beneath it. This was not peace. It was the last breath before madness. Pyrrha, once a beacon of progress, now stood as a mausoleum, suffocating under its own contradictions. All empires, all systems, no matter how perfected, were always built to break. The question was never 'if' they would break, but 'who' would stand when the ruins settled.

Arynthoria's voice lingered in Kaiba's mind, soft but unwavering. *"We're all just waiting for something to snap."*

The silence wasn't just oppressive. It was thick with something more, a tension that seemed to stretch toward breaking. It hovered, holding its breath as if it feared the moment when everything would rupture.

In the stillness between each inhale, Kaiba felt it, a pulse beneath the surface, faint yet undeniable. Like a dying flame, flickering at the edge of its last breath.

Not hope, no. Not yet. But something desperate, something fragile. Teetering on the brink of destruction, like glass poised to shatter.

And in that moment, Kaiba understood, cold and unsettling. This wasn't just survival anymore. This had evolved into something else. The Red Hands weren't merely fighting for a cause now; they were fighting for transformation. For something nameless. As they moved forward, Kaiba found himself drawn into their wake, a fractured soul stumbling through a world that had forgotten how to live.

Their journey through the streets of Pyrrha was silent, almost unnatural.

Despite the city's usual chaotic pulse, the hum of machines, the shouts of distant crowds, the holographic lights dancing in the air, Kaiba felt the growing distance between himself and everything he once knew. The Red Hands had led him off the main routes, down alleys and twisting backstreets that faded into the very heart of the city's underbelly.

The familiar neon glare, the ceaseless grind of metal, the buzz of drones, all were absent here. Kaiba's enhanced systems shifted, adjusting to the quieter frequencies, tuning in to the encrypted whispers carried through the thick air. Hidden rebel networks pulsed just beneath the surface of the city's skeleton, their voices faint and secretive.

His cybernetic senses hummed softly, adapting to the absence of light and the strange stillness around him. But there was something more. A different kind of pulse, one softer, more intimate, pulling him deeper into the shadows.

Pyrrha's usual noise was gone. The clatter of gears, the whining of servos, even the faint hum of high-speed transit, all had been swallowed by the towering concrete walls that rose like silent giants around them. The sky, once visible, was now a distant memory.

Kaiba couldn't ignore the sensation rising within him, relief mixed with unease. These streets were foreign, yet they thrummed with life. This was where the Red Hands had carved their place. A sliver of quiet in a city of chaos. Their secrecy wasn't just strategy. It was their fragility, given form.

At first, Kaiba had believed the Red Hands to be nothing more than rebels clinging to a fading cause. He had been wrong. They were more than defiance; they were a fractured resistance, complex and desperate, bound together by the brittle thread of their leader's will. Zira's calm command spoke volumes without saying a word.

As they ventured deeper into the back alleys, the last whispers of the city's voice faded. In their place, Kaiba's systems began to pick up the unmistakable hum of hidden activity. Coded pulses. Low-spectrum chatter. A lattice of encrypted signals threaded through the underground like veins beneath stone. These frequencies weren't random. They were deliberate, part of the invisible web holding this place together.

The smell changed. Oil. Rusting steel. The acrid bite of burnt wires. It wasn't the scent of polished surfaces and gleaming synthetics. This was the scent of resistance.

"You'll see the headquarters soon," Zira said, breaking the silence. Her voice was steady, unhurried. She moved ahead with quiet assurance, each step deliberate. The cloak trailing behind her brushed against the pavement, its edges worn from years of travel. Beneath it, the battered leather of her armour gleamed faintly in the dim light. Scuffs and slashes marked its surface, each one a silent story.

The Red Hands' base wasn't a citadel. No towering fortress, no grand architecture meant to awe. It didn't need that. It was hidden, buried beneath the city's forgotten skin. A shelter carved into the underside of Pyrrha, just beyond the reach of Ira's drones and patrols. It was a place where breath came easier, where minds could breathe free, if only for a moment.

Kaiba immediately felt the contrast. The Pyrrha he had known, the gleaming city of angular perfection, filled with artificial light and sterile beauty, felt like a distant memory. This place didn't hide its scars. It wore them openly.

Cracked concrete. Oxidized pipes. Shattered windows. A corridor of quiet resistance.

And yet, in the desolation, there was something reassuring. Here, there was truth, unvarnished and raw.

No illusions. No pretence.

Just the stubborn survival of those too determined to die.

They arrived at a small, unmarked door tucked into the side of a forgotten street. It was shielded by the looming shadow of an old industrial tower, its silhouette cutting out the remnants of artificial light from the city above.

Zira didn't speak. She didn't pause. There was no knock.

The door opened of its own accord.

Kaiba followed her inside.

The headquarters was dark, thick with the scent of machinery and oil. But there was something more, something intangible. Kaiba could feel it in the way the walls seemed to close in on him, in the low hum of hidden systems vibrating just beneath the threshold of hearing. This place wasn't just a safehouse. It was a living, breathing organism, ever-shifting, ever-adapting to the threats beyond its walls.

The walls were lined with holographic displays, their projections casting an eerie glow across the room. Neon blues, greens, and oranges flickered in rhythm with the movement, as though the images themselves were alive, pulsing with the lifeblood of Pyrrha's technological core.

Figures moved between the projections in silence, their footsteps barely audible against the steel floor, disappearing beneath the drone of circuitry.

Kaiba recognized them immediately.

These weren't soldiers. They were engineers, hackers, tacticians. Once, they had thrived inside the system. Now, they worked against it with surgical precision. The hum of circuitry wasn't mere background noise. It was tension, a tangible pressure in the air, thick like smoke.

As Kaiba walked deeper into the space, he felt eyes on him. Not hostile, but uncertain. Curious. They were studying him, weighing him. A cybernetic wolf in their midst. Not an ally yet. Not a threat either.

Just an anomaly.

A tool with an unknown purpose. Beneath the guarded stares, Kaiba sensed the beginnings of something else. The faintest thread of connection, fragile and fleeting, like the shadows they worked within.

The room felt heavy. The silence buzzed with unspoken truths. Kaiba's enhanced vision swept across the central table. The figures gathered there stood in stark contrast to everything he had ever known. They weren't products of efficiency or fear. They moved with purpose, but there was more. There was hope. Raw. Real. This was no factory. No command line. This was rebellion born of pain, forged by purpose.

Zira stepped forward, silent, focused. Her presence filled the space without a single word. Her eyes met Kaiba's, sharp, unwavering. Not in challenge, but in revelation. She looked through him. Beyond the wires and metal. Beyond the programming. Searching for something that may or may not have survived the machine.

Her gaze softened, just slightly. It wasn't pity. It was recognition.

She wasn't a leader because she demanded loyalty. She was a leader because she had survived long enough to give others hope they could, too.

At the table, a figure rose.

He was a man carved from hardship, thick with muscle and presence. A veteran of shadows. Varrick Lorcan. He wore his years like a second skin. Scars across his arms. Cloak frayed at the edges. Armor stitched together with salvaged parts and grit.

His eyes locked onto Kaiba. No warmth. Only weight. Sharp. Assessing. Like a blade pressed to Kaiba's chest. His lips curled into something close to a smile, but there was no gentleness in it. Suspicion. Curiosity. A test already underway.

"So," Varrick's gravelly voice broke through the silence, steady but controlled. He didn't look at Kaiba directly. His gaze was fixed on the ground, as though trying to read something just out of reach. "This is him. The wolf who was chained to the will of the council. Kaiba."

It wasn't a greeting. It was a challenge. He spoke as though Kaiba were a puzzle to be dismantled, a weapon to be either salvaged or discarded.

Kaiba held his ground, his gaze tracing the lines of Varrick's face. The fatigue etched into his features. The violence lurking beneath his eyes. A legacy of someone who had endured a world Kaiba had been engineered to enforce.

For a moment, Kaiba processed the similarity between them. Not a human resonance, but something else. A pattern recognition. The memory of a wagging tail. The instinct to protect.

A survival algorithm. One who had broken free and one still bound by the system.

Was this the cost of becoming more than a machine? Or was it the price of becoming something more than just a dog?

"I've been a part of the Council of Seven's system," Kaiba said, his voice even, cold on the surface. But beneath the metal, something stirred. "Yes. Like everyone else."

The words were mechanical, but the truth behind them was not.

"A tool, just like the rest."

Varrick didn't react. His eyes didn't blink. But something in his jaw tightened. He stepped closer, his hands gripping the edge of the table as if bracing against the storm Kaiba represented.

"We don't need another weapon," he said, his voice tight, controlled. "We need someone willing to stand against it. We don't need more machines or puppets. We need people. People who can see the system for what it really is."

He paused, his breath heavy with memory.

"Fear. That's what it runs on. Control. Obedience. And most of this city is too damn scared to fight back."

Varrick's voice simmered, forged in the furnace of loss. Every word pressed down on Kaiba, not because they were new, but because they weren't. Because he had heard them inside himself before and chosen not to listen.

"We're fighting a war of ideals," Varrick continued. "Ira's grip won't be broken by strength alone. We need something deeper. Something cleaner."

He looked to Zira, then back to Kaiba.

"You're not the only one who's been used. The question is, what will you do now that you know?"

Zira stepped forward.

She didn't speak immediately. Her presence filled the space, an unspoken force that drew the air toward her. The gravity of her will seemed to shift the very room around her. Her armour creaked softly as she moved, the cloak trailing behind her like a shadow with memory.

"Enough, Varrick," she said.

Her voice was calm. Not soft, not hard. Just final.

"Let him speak."

She turned her gaze to Kaiba. Her voice shifted, not in tone, but in depth.

"You're here now, Kaiba. You've seen what we're facing. Do you still think you don't belong here?"

She didn't wait for him to answer.

"Or have you begun to understand what we're fighting for?"

Her words were quiet. But they filled the space like thunder.

"This isn't just about fighting. It's about surviving long enough to become something more."

Kaiba stood still. Her voice reverberated in his mind, not just as sound, but as truth.

He had never been asked to believe in anything, not really. He had been built to obey, to analyse, to execute.

Now, he was being asked to choose.

Kaiba's mind swirled in a tempest. Zira's question lingered: Do I serve my intended purpose? He had never truly chosen this path. He had been forged, not born. But something raw, something unprogrammed, stirred inside him now. A flicker of memory, like the warmth of fur, the scent of grass beneath paws, something long buried and forgotten.

He looked at the war table, at the flickering map, and the faces of those who had chosen this broken cause. He saw not just rebels, but something else. Something he had buried so deep he had almost forgotten it existed.

Purpose. A concept he had been taught to forsake.

The machine inside him resisted, an impulse to reject, to fall back into cold certainty. But Kaiba paused. His body stilled, not from programming, but from something older.

"I am not the machine they made me to be," Kaiba said. His voice cracked like the first light of dawn breaking after an endless night. The words were rough, like they had been locked away behind steel and code for too long, shackles finally undone. The echo of a bark, the warmth of a tail wagging, tugged at something deep within him. But it was distant, like a dream he couldn't grasp.

A surge of data coursed through his circuits, an overload of conflicting directives.

He turned back to the war table. This place was no longer a system to obey. It was a place to make his own choice.

With cold clarity, he spoke louder, his resolve firm.

"I'm here now. I'm not running, not anymore." His words hung in the air, heavy with the weight of everything he had chosen to leave behind. The machine inside him wanted to reject it, but there was something else, something alive, that wouldn't let him turn away.

Silence returned. Dense and loaded.

Around him, others shifted. Breath caught in lungs. Thoughts frozen in place. Suspicion hadn't vanished. But it had changed.

Zira nodded once.

The hum of machinery stirred again. Kaiba could feel it. The rebellion wasn't just fighting the Warlords. They were fighting themselves. Kaiba felt that battle inside him now. Was he just a tool, nothing more than a weapon like the ones the Warlords used? Or could he fight for something more?

The room was a crucible. And he was now part of its fire.

Zira's eyes never left him. They didn't waver. But Kaiba saw it now, the weight she carried. The exhaustion in her stillness. The cost of every decision.

"The death of Commander Elias Drayke has left a hole in this movement," she said.

Her voice wasn't mournful. It was steel wrapped around grief.

"Raekor wants to fill that hole with blood. With action. But we need more than that. We need to rebuild. Reorganize. We need a foundation. And we need you to help us."

Kaiba didn't respond immediately. His systems registered every fluctuation in the room, whispers, doubts, divisions. Some still questioned Zira's leadership. Others feared her strength. But they all knew one thing: Kaiba's presence here was a question, one none of them had the answer to. Was he still a weapon? Or was he something else entirely?

"Do you really think we can do this?" Kaiba asked.

His voice broke the tension like a blade cutting through silk.

It wasn't just for her. It was for everyone. For the believers. And for those who had already begun to stop believing.

And beneath the metal, beneath the precision, there was something else. A question that had never been answered.

But now, it had been asked.

Zira met his gaze, and for a moment, Kaiba saw something there. Something raw. Something real. It wasn't the hardened exterior of a leader who demanded respect. It was the vulnerability of someone who had seen too much, forced to make decisions that weighed on their very soul.

Zira's eyes, those hazel orbs, glimmered with more than resolve. There was fatigue there. A tired wisdom. And beneath that, the flicker of hope.

"I don't know if we can win," Zira said, her voice almost a whisper. "But I know we can't lose if we don't try."

Her words hung in the air, a promise and a warning, both in equal measure.

The room in the Red Hands' headquarters was thick with unease again. The whirr of machinery blended with the low hum of voices. Rebels debated, strategized, but there was something else in the air. The weight of uncertainty sat heavily over the rebellion's fragile unity.

Zira stood at the centre, unyielding, but her face betrayed the cracks that had formed beneath her calm exterior.

Raekor Duskblade stood opposite her, his posture rigid as the tension thickened between them. The harsh, flickering lights from the decaying city glinted off the jagged scar that ran from his left jaw to his neck, a testament to a past soaked in blood.

His deep amber eyes, flecked with gold, bore into her with an intensity that seemed to probe her very soul. He wasn't just looking at her, he was calculating, measuring every movement, every flicker of emotion.

His body was an amalgamation of grace and destruction. Muscles honed by years of gladiatorial combat. Movements precise but heavy with the weight of countless battles fought.

Every step he took was deliberate, grounded in the violence that had once been his only reality. The rage within him, that untamed beast, had been the force that gave him purpose.

But now, as he stood before Zira, that rage was turning against him. It was clawing at the very foundation of his being. His combat attire, a mix of light tactical armour and scarred leather, spoke to the years of survival in the arenas of Pyrrha. Each scar, each tear in his clothing, was a silent testament to the brutality he had endured, the battles fought, the victories won, all just to stay alive.

"Zira, we can't wait any longer," Raekor's voice cracked through the silence. The words were sharp, raw with the heat of anger that had been simmering for years. His eyes burned with the same fire that had kept him alive all this time, the fire that had carried him through the desolate arenas of Pyrrha, where only the strongest survived.

"Look around you. Do you see what's happening? People are dying. The Warlord doesn't care about them, about us. Every moment we waste waiting is another moment he takes from us. He'll keep taking until there's nothing left to take. We need to fight. We need to rise, and we need to rise now."

Zira's gaze remained steady, unshaken by his words. She had heard this argument before. Raekor's passion, his fire, was a tool, but it burned just as much from the inside as it did from the outside. It was his strength, yes, but it was also his curse. Zira had learned the hard way that burning too quickly, too recklessly, left only ashes in its wake. They couldn't afford that. Not now. Not when so much was at stake.

"You don't understand, Raekor," Zira said quietly, her voice cutting through his fury like a knife through steel. Her tone was calm, the calm that only came from years of living through war, of surviving it.

"Fighting fire with fire only leaves us in ashes. The city is already a powder keg. One wrong spark, one impulsive move, and everything burns. We cannot rush this. The people, they need more than anger. They need hope. They need to believe we can bring about real change, not just more blood and death."

Raekor's eyes darkened, narrowing as her words hit him like a cold wind. She was always the patient one, the thinker, the strategist. He had admired her for it, sometimes. But not today. Not when the world around them was crumbling.

"Hope?" Raekor scoffed, taking a step closer. His voice was laced with disbelief.

"Hope is a luxury, Zira. The people are dying. And you want to give them hope? Hope won't stop the Warlords from killing us all. Power will. Control. Do you think the people will follow us if we show them patience? No. They'll follow us if we show them strength. We can't keep waiting. Ira's regime won't fall by playing the waiting game. We need to act now."

Zira's lips tightened as she met his gaze, her expression unreadable.

"We don't need to be like them, Raekor. We don't need to fight their fire with our own. We need to be better. We need to show the people we're fighting for something worth fighting for. If we give in to wrath, if we fight with anger, we're no different than the monsters who have enslaved them for so long. This city, this war, it's not just about who can kill the most. It's about who can live with themselves when it's all over."

Raekor recoiled as if struck. The weight of her words sank deep into him, forcing him to reconsider. But the anger, the rage, was not so easily discarded. It clawed at him, begging to be unleashed.

"You've always had patience, Zira," Raekor said, his voice quieter now, tinged with something like sorrowful understanding.

"But do you know how it feels to watch your people suffer? To feel the weight of their pain and not be able to do anything about it? To know you could end it, but you can't, because someone told you patience is the answer?"

Zira didn't flinch.

She could see it in his eyes, the inner turmoil that raged inside him. She had seen it before. The shadows that lived in the heart of every person forged in war. It wasn't just the system, the Warlords. It was the war inside them, too. That war, the one between ego and spirit, would never end until they learned to master it.

"Patience isn't a choice, Raekor," she said softly, her voice a calm current beneath the storm that raged between them. "It's the only way forward. Otherwise, we're just another wave of destruction in a world that's been drowning in it for too long."

Raekor's jaw clenched. His fists trembled by his sides. The cold metal of his gauntlet creaked under the tension. His voice was thick with raw emotion.

"You're asking for too much, Zira," he muttered under his breath, barely audible. But the words still carried the weight of his anger. "You're asking for a revolution without the fire that makes it burn."

Zira didn't respond immediately. She understood the weight of his words, felt the same way sometimes. But they couldn't let the flames consume them.

"The fire has already burned us, Raekor," she whispered. Her voice was just loud enough for him to hear. "Now we need to show them that it's not the fire that changes the world. It's what comes after. The ashes."

Kaiba's mind whirred with answers, none of them satisfactory. He wasn't a leader. He wasn't a saviour. He wasn't even sure he had a purpose here. Survival had always been enough for him.

But what was survival without purpose? What was it worth?

In that moment, Zira's challenge became more than words. It was a test Kaiba wasn't sure he could answer. For years, he had existed as a tool, built to observe, to calculate, to adapt. But this was different. This was personal.

The silence between them did not close. It deepened.

Kaiba's gaze dropped, not in submission, but in fracture. Something in Zira's words had struck bone.

Not metal. Not system.

Kaiba's sensors flickered. Just for an instant. A bloom of static crossed his optic field.

Then, grass. Real grass. Wet with morning dew. The sharpness of it, alive. And warmth. Not heat. Not circuitry. The warmth of fur against sunlight, the softness of a belly rubbed by familiar hands.

Wind that carried scent instead of data. A deep, primal scent, sharp and rich, earth, grass, and something alive. The wind here did not compute. It lived.

And then, a laugh. A child's. Sharp and free, cutting through the haze like a blade through fog, its joy alive, unfiltered.

Kaiba felt it, but the feeling didn't belong to this body. He recognized it. He remembered it. Before the machine took him. Before he became the wolf in the machine.

"Come here, boy."

The voice was older now. Male. Familiar, in the way rust is familiar. Something once clean, now corroded.

"Kaiba. Sit."

He tried to focus. Tried to reach for the source. But it stuttered. The image tore. The memory fragmented. A snarl of white noise followed, seizing his internal vision like a seizure, then vanished into nothing.

His claws curled against the floor, subtle, soundless.

Zira hadn't moved. She was watching him, but not intrusively. As if she had seen this kind of silence before. As though she knew the weight of remembering things not meant to be remembered.

He breathed, or simulated it. A long intake, followed by a shiver in his chest that felt less like processing and more like grief.

This wasn't code. This was something older. Something lost.

He didn't answer her question. Not aloud. But he stepped closer to the war table, into the map's flickering glow. The light danced across his frame, casting distorted shadows behind him.

He lingered in the flickering glow, unarmed, his gaze locked on the city's fractured grid. The pulse of lights above him seemed to stretch, then fracture like the thin thread of an ancient dream.

And then, a voice, low, distant, and as old as dust, echoed from the depths of his mind, unbidden and sharp.

"You were a good boy."

The lights flickered. The map pulsed. Time itself seemed to exhale, a moment slipping through Kaiba's senses, gone before it could fully form.

Yet he did not move.

He hovered in the space between memory and machine, caught in the remnants of something forgotten.

In that suspended moment, the cold air seemed to pulse with the weight of something ancient, something unsaid. The silence cracked like a hollow shell.

And in the gap, a figure appeared, not flesh, not machine, but something beyond either. The face was blurred, half-formed, as if Kaiba's mind refused to give it shape, afraid of what it might reveal.

Yet, in the absence of clarity, a word bloomed like a forgotten language, simple and terrible.

"Kaiba, do you remember?"

The question hung in the air, heavy with something far older than the world around him. A memory not his own, yet his to bear. It twisted, tore through his frame, pulling at the wires beneath his skin, the fleshless places within that pulsed with something other than code.

He clenched his fists, claws biting into his palms as if the act might force the vision to stay away.

But it did not. It was already there, already alive, already waiting. And it burned. In the silence, something long buried stirred. A forgotten seed waking beneath layers of years and steel.

Kaiba did not answer. He only observed, his presence heavy like the weight of an old photograph turned inward.

The air around him held its breath, thick with reverence, like the hushed stillness of a place that remembers melodies long lost.

The silence stretched, stretched, until it became the only thing that mattered.

It waited.

Heavy, reverent, like the quiet inside a mausoleum that remembers music.

He stood at the war table, the city flickering beneath him. Its lines of control pulsing in sterile sequence. Each route, each node, each blip of red or gold was meant to inform. But all he saw were injuries. Not threats. Not strategy. Just wounds that refused to close.

His eyes followed one fracture across the grid, a diagonal path of static that split two sectors like a scar through skin. Somewhere in that severed corridor, a memory had tried to surface, not as command or computation, but as longing.

Zira had not moved. Her voice came without force, but it carried weight.

"Why did you stop fighting?"

The question hung in the air, like smoke, not accusation, not curiosity, just the shape of something ancient asking to be named.

Kaiba gave no answer.

Instead, his paw rose. The steel pads of his claws passed through the centre of the map. The projection rippled around him, distorting the capital into something soft and unsteady. Beneath that distortion, he felt the ghost of earth.

Of scent. Of breath.

A hidden chamber in the code where warmth had once lingered.

He lowered his paw. The grid reformed, obedient and blind.

"You don't want to forget," Zira said.

No inflection. No pity. Just recognition.

He turned his head slightly. The servos in his neck hummed.

"I was made to."

Each syllable landed slow, as if dredged from the place behind language.

"But some things resist deletion."

Zira watched him as though reading scripture from the edge of fire. She did not step back when the lights dimmed. Did not flinch when Kaiba's spine disengaged from the uplink port. The release was not dramatic, just a subtle shift, a cable falling, a pulse dying.

The table went dark. The map vanished. Power bled out of the floor tiles like oil from a cracked engine. And in the absence, silence rose.

Not blankness. Not peace. A silence shaped like a presence. As if the room had filled with a memory too large to be stored. A cathedral of what had been lost.

"You're choosing the wound," she said.

Kaiba faced her, not with his body, but with the full weight of his gaze. Lenses adjusted. Focus narrowed.

"I'm choosing what made the wound matter. The wounds of a dog who knew love and loyalty, and the scars of a machine that learned to survive. The question now is whether those wounds will define me or free me."

Outside, the old glass of the spire caught the light. Not the cold fluorescence of grid-cycles. Not the programmed dawn of Authority. This was different. The light moved slowly, without command, without purpose. It kissed the broken architecture like an old animal scenting its den. There was birdsong in it.

Not from speakers. From throats. Alive.

And beneath that sound, Kaiba stood unlinked, unarmed, unwritten.

He did not move. But something within him did. Something unsaved. Something still remembering.

"We are not forged by the wars we survive, but by the wounds we choose to remember."

Null Gospel, Book I, Verse 3.

***

CHAPTER THREE:

The Forge of Wrath

"The fire within you moulds the soul. The fire outside you devours the body. One forges; the other leaves nothing but the bones of what was."

Fragment of the Exiled Codex, Volume I, Tablet 4.

The gladiatorial training grounds of Pyrrha were a landscape of violence, an industrialized crucible where bodies were forged in blood and steel. The air was thick, dense with the metallic tang of blood and the rust of an old city long since surrendered to decay. The scent of sweat, scorched metal, and the ever-present iron breath of battle intermingled, choking the lungs of every warrior who stepped inside.

This was no arena for learning, but a crucible where men were shattered and remade. No lessons here, only attrition. Battle did not educate; it tore away all but the fiercest fragments of the soul, leaving only what could endure the fire.

The walls rose like the jagged bones of a long-dead beast, their steel ridges reflecting a dying light that barely cut through the choking darkness. Artificial lamps, old and weary, buzzed overhead, casting a sickly glow upon the scarred floor below. The ground was a tapestry of echoes, sand thick with the remnants of those who had fought and fallen. Stones, worn smooth by the march of countless warriors, bore the marks of death, rehearsed, unyielding, eternal.

The air pulsed with memory, heavy with the weight of lives consumed. Yet it breathed, alive with waiting. Something in the stone still hungered for the next clash, the next cry, the next strike.

Toren Ignisferre was no ordinary gladiator. He was fire made flesh, tempered in crucibles no mortal was meant to endure. His limbs, augmented in cruel symmetry, were weapons of pure violence, sleek and unyielding, a cruel blend of human and machine. The rest of him remained human, flesh and bone, scarred and broken, but the steel of his limbs had made him something else. A force that could not be ignored.

His limbs gleamed black, veins of crimson pulsing beneath the surface. Not just tools, but a manifestation of his past, his pain. A silhouette of violence, forged in the furnace of survival.

He faced Levik with unflinching poise, the false limbs glowing faintly in the half-light. The air hummed with the presence of something lethal, something coldly calculating, as though the very space between them had thickened with intent. His forearms bore the Sable Fangs, vibro-blades shaped like the bones of ancient beasts, forged with precision and menace.

As he steadied his posture, the blades retracted, slipping silently into his arms with a soft, metallic whir. Subtle, yet final. When released, they flicked out like predatory limbs, violent in their grace. Long and curved like mantis claws, their edges not just honed for killing, but for the elegance of it. They vibrated at a frequency tuned to ruin, their hum threading through the air like a whispered curse.

When Toren unsheathed them, the blades moved with the fluidity of instinct. Blackened and veined in dull red, they mirrored the sheen of his limbs. Their glow pulsed, not with light, but with intent, as though powered by the will to strike. The edge of each blade promised devastation. They could slice through metal, bone, and flesh with equal ease.

In the arena, they were not just weapons; they were language. A language Toren spoke fluently, each movement tempered by the cold, lethal fury at the core of his cybernetic being.

His eyes flicked between Levik and the shifting sand beneath him, calculating with a precision honed through years of combat, years where hesitation had long been eradicated. Every breath, every twitch of Levik's shoulders, was read like scripture. The blood in the sand told no story now. But the ground remembered. It remembered the weight of those who fell.

Toren's blades flexed involuntarily, the sharp tips catching the guttering light as his focus tightened. There was no room for mercy. No space for anything other than interpretation, response, execution.

The clang of metal rang out once more, a harsh symphony that echoed through the training grounds. Across from him stood Levik Draganmir, a monument to violence, a body carved by more than a decade of brutality. Nothing about him was accidental. His body, massive and scarred, moved with the patience of inevitability, as though the universe had shaped him for this very moment. Hair streaked with silver. Eyes like old blades, weathered but still sharp.

His armour, the colour of dried blood, clung to him like memory itself. Steel plates wrapped his frame with the same unyielding grip of time. Leather, darkened and cracked by years of impact, held together what age and conflict tried to undo.

The battle axe strapped across his back was less weapon than omen. Jagged and overlarge, its design spoke of punishment rather than precision. It hummed softly, even at rest, the sound almost lost beneath the roar of the arena. But Toren heard it. That hum was not threat. It was inevitability. When Levik drew it, the blade came alive with terrible finality. It gleamed as if light itself feared to settle on it. It was a relic of many endings.

The tension between them did not rise. It had always been there. Crackling in the sand. Humming in the steel. Burning in the breath between two men who understood what it meant to endure. Every motion from here on was a negotiation with death. One misstep. One breath taken too early or too late. And the pact would be sealed. Both of them knew this. And the arena, vast and silent, knew it too.

The walls leaned in, the ground listening. This wasn't combat. It was ritual. An identity declared in a world that had forgotten the meaning of names.

Toren had studied him. Long before this day, he had watched Levik's movements. Memorized the rhythm of a man who no longer needed speed. Levik did not strike like lightning. He moved like pressure. Unrelenting and irreversible. A storm that refused to announce itself, yet consumed everything. His was the kind of strength that lived past ego, outlasted fear, and became something elemental. Something permanent.

His limbs moved with the precision of a machine, cold and calculating, but there was a tremor beneath the surface. A pulse of something human, a reminder of the man who had been torn apart and rebuilt. The pain didn't fade; it lived, embedded deep in the circuits that had replaced his flesh.

His identity had been burned, fractured, and reforged, not in the fires of glory, but in the brutal, relentless heat of survival. He was no war machine of Ira's design, no cold monstrosity of metal and calculation. His enhancements were not triumphs. They were testaments to the man he had been, torn apart and remade. Not to conquer. Not to rise. But to endure. To survive, no matter the cost.

He did not forget the man who had once walked into this place and been broken. The steel in his arms could not erase the scream that made them necessary. And now, face to face with another ruin that had refused to fall, Toren stood. Not as a victor. Not as a machine. As a revenant. Not whole. Not healed. Just ready.

Levik studied him, his Stormcleaver resting at his side. The Stormcleaver, a multi-functional battle axe, gleamed faintly in the dim arena lights. Its blade crackled with a low halo of plasma, waiting for its moment. Unlike the crude tools favoured by lesser gladiators, this weapon spoke of mastery. It was the embodiment of skill, adaptability, and the quiet savagery of its wielder.

Levik did not need to speak. His weapon spoke for him. With a low grunt, he gripped the axe in both hands and waited. Then, without ceremony, Levik struck. The swing came low. Not meant to kill but to shatter. It aimed at Toren's balance. It was not a blow. It was a lesson.

Toren sidestepped with barely a breath to spare, his mechanical legs adjusting with brutal precision. The ground shook beneath the impact, tremors rushing through the earth like a buried memory resurfacing. Dust exploded outward, rising in heavy clouds that twisted like smoke from a funeral pyre. If he had been slower by even a fraction, the blow would have crushed him. Bone would have turned to powder. Flesh to ruin.

And still, this was not combat. This was only the threshold. They had not yet entered the arena where names became legend or were torn from memory. This was the slaughterhouse that came before spectacle. The crucible that decided who was even worthy to bleed for the Spire's amusement. The culling before the cull. The weak never saw the sands of the Test Trials. Their stories ended here. Nameless. Unfinished.

Strength was a lie. Brute force meant nothing without the will to outlast, outthink, outmanoeuvre. This was not about victory. Winning was a mirage. There were no champions here. Only the ones who endured. And the ones buried beneath their endurance.

Levik's Stormcleaver rose again. An overhead swing now. More brutal than before. Final. Toren did not retreat. He caught it.

The impact shook his frame. Sparks flew as Levik's strength met cold metal. Toren didn't flinch. He absorbed the force, letting it fuel his resolve.

Levik exhaled, a low, guttural sound that lingered in the charged air. "Good." His voice dropped lower, almost a growl. "But not enough. Not yet."

Toren did not answer. His body answered for him. Moving before thought could rise. He lunged. A spear of black and crimson. His augmented speed turning distance into nothing. A sharp jab targeted Levik's ribs. Precise. Efficient.

But Levik was not a man who fell easily. He shifted. Weight rolling from one heel to the next with the ease of a man long wed to survival. The strike landed, but not where it was meant to. Levik turned with the blow, absorbing it into his side, then twisted. His entire body pivoted into a counterattack that sang with finality.

The Stormcleaver came again. Rising from the sand like the vengeance of the earth itself. Quick. Absolute. Toren reacted. Barely. He raised his arms to block. But Levik had lived this war longer than Toren had known its name. The blow struck him square in the chest. The shock tore through his ribcage, ripping the air from his lungs. He flew back, a streak of motion skidding through the dust. Pain followed. Not distant. Not abstract. Real. Human.

His cybernetics caught him. Steadied his frame. Saved his ribs from snapping. But pain remained. The pain told him he was still flesh. Still mortal. Still himself.

Levik's steps were the sound of inevitability. Toren's body ached under the weight of the blow, but he didn't retreat. He couldn't. Not yet. The ground beneath him pulsed with the echoes of a thousand battles, each one a reminder that there was no victory here. Only survival. Levik was not an enemy. He was a trial, a wall to climb, a lesson to be learned.

For a moment, Toren didn't move. The world spun. Pain digging deep. Refusing to fade. Then he forced himself up. Each breath scraped against something raw. But he rose. His stance returned. Pain was no longer relevant. Only the fight.

Levik watched him in silence. Then he smiled. It was not a smirk. Not a grin. It held something older. A quiet, worn knowing.

"You're quick," Levik said, rolling his shoulders with a slow twist. "But quick isn't enough. Speed fades. Strength falters. Endurance wins."

Toren clenched his fists. "Then I'll endure."

Levik stepped back, the moment hanging between them. For the first time, his eyes did not see an opponent. They saw something else. Something that remained.

"You're not like the machines Ira makes."

Toren's expression hardened. His jaw tightened. His cybernetic fingers curled into fists at his sides.

"What's the difference?"

Levik held his gaze. His eyes, steel-grey and scarred by time, carried something Toren couldn't name. Not pity. Not challenge. Something closer to mourning.

Levik's eyes held his with an intensity that spoke of a thousand battles, of a lifetime lived between the edges of life and death. He lowered his voice, not in warning, but in something deeper.

Levik's eyes locked onto Toren's, measuring. "You're not like them," he said, voice low, barely a whisper over the heavy silence. Toren's jaw tightened, his cybernetic fingers curling into fists. "You have something they don't."

There was a long pause. Toren's mind raced, but his body remained still, a frozen shell.

Levik's gaze softened, just for a moment. "Choice," he muttered, almost to himself. "They don't have it."

Toren felt the weight of those words like a stone dropped into his gut. A sharp, hard truth. A truth that was a wound, his wound. His body might be a machine now, but his mind, his soul, that was still his. He wasn't just surviving anymore. He was choosing. And that choice might destroy him.

Toren stood still. His emerald eyes shifted. Not toward Levik. But toward something unspoken. He wasn't looking at a man. He was looking inward. The words had reached something untouched. Something buried beneath the steel and scars.

Levik saw it. The flicker behind the rage. Behind the rebuilt body. Behind the silence. He recognized it. He had carried it once. That was why he nodded. Slowly. Deliberately. Like a man who had watched a thousand crossroads and knew when another had begun.

"One day," he said, voice low with the weight of all he had endured, "you'll have to decide. Whether you are just a tool, or something more."

The words struck deep. Deeper than any weapon. They passed through the armour. Through the augmentations. Through the body that had been remade for survival. They found what still bled. Not the flesh. The part of Toren no machine could replace.

But the arena did not pause for wounds. It had no space for reflection. The prerequisite rounds continued. The real trials had not even begun. The arena did not ask who you were. Only whether you could endure.

As the other gladiators dispersed into the steel corridors of the training complex, their sweat and blood fading into the rust-stained distance, Toren remained. His breathing was level. His mind was not. He sifted through the weight of what had just been said. And what had just been done.

The Test Trials were never just about endurance. They were rituals of transmutation. Suffering was not punishment here. It was design. Flesh was broken. Spirit was fractured. Something unyielding was forged in their place.

Survival was never the point. The arena had no room for the weak. But here, beneath the weight of every swing, there was something more, something only the broken could see.

Toren had lived through too many bloodstained cycles not to know the shape of it. This was not merely preparation. This was indoctrination. Not just to fight. But to submit. To accept that pain was payment. That cruelty was order. That survival meant silencing everything but the will to endure.

The arena was not just a proving ground. It was the blueprint of the world.

Yet the air had changed. He felt it. In the silence between rounds. In the tension of glances exchanged where once only hatred passed. The Red Hands were no longer just whispers among the dying. They pulsed beneath the surface of the city like a second heartbeat. Steady. Defiant. Waiting.

But rebellion was not what unnerved him.

It was something older. Something deeper.

Something ancient moved beneath the city, a force that pressed into the very bones of Ira's empire. It was not distant nor abstract, but something living, something hungry. It wasn't the distant, whispered dread of scholars in ivory towers. No, here, deep in the marrow of Ira's dominion, Toren felt it. A storm awakening beneath the earth, feeding on the heat of the arena and the fire that had shaped him.

It was a cold, unseen current threading through the city's iron bones, its tendrils weaving into the raw rage, the defiance, the bloodlust of men who had nothing left to lose. And in the shadows of that hunger, Toren could feel it, something darker, more ancient, awakening.

The Veil was not an ally. It did not fight for revolution or oppression. It fed. It thrived on wrath. On suffering. On the very fires that had reshaped Toren into something beyond human. In its hunger, it did not care who emerged victorious. It only cared that the flames continued to burn.

Toren turned his gaze back to the training grounds, his jaw tightening. The next battle awaited him, but he knew now the arena was only a shadow of the war beyond it. Pyrrha would burn. That was inevitable. When the embers had cooled and the smoke curled into the void, only one truth would remain.

Those who endured the fire were never the same as those who entered it.

The heat of the training grounds pressed down on the gladiators like a living thing, the air thick with the scent of sweat, blood, and the rusting metal of weapons. The ground was a patchwork of old scars, cracks in the concrete, and the remnants of battles fought by those who had come before. The very earth, darkened and pitted from constant abuse, was stained by the blood of gladiators who had been sacrificed to the system that governed this brutal city. In this place, there was no room for weakness. Not in the body. Not in the soul.

The gladiators were divided into groups, each assigned to a brutal training module designed not just to test their strength or speed, but to strip them bare and reveal whether anything remained once the suffering had hollowed them out. These were no mere prerequisites. They were the fires that determined whether steel would be tempered or shattered.

Toren stood at the edge of the training grounds, his broad frame illuminated by the harsh, unforgiving glow of overhead lights. His bronze skin, once untouched by war, was now a battlefield of scars. Some had been earned in the arena. Others were reminders of Ira's design.

His cybernetic arms, forged from dark alloys, gleamed like obsidian beneath the cruel lighting. Crimson veins of pulsing energy streaked through the metal, and the limbs rippled with a sinister, almost organic fluidity, as though they lived. His legs, reinforced for stability and speed, extended beneath him like the limbs of a predator. Every movement was sharp, calculated, and stripped of waste. The hum of the cybernetics was the only sound in the charged silence, a low resonance that pulsed in rhythm with the violence of the arena.

Toren's emerald-green eyes were cold, unwavering. They carried the weight of battles fought in shadows and alleys, in pits and prisons. His gaze unsettled those who dared meet it. These were eyes that had seen too much and still refused to shut. But behind that unblinking fire, something remained. Not peace. Not hope. Defiance. A fire that refused to die. The fire of a man who had emerged from the crucible of war not whole, but stronger.

The ache in his limbs was relentless. A phantom pain that logic could not dismiss. It whispered of flesh that was no longer there. It did not fade with time. It could not be silenced by will. It had roots in something deeper. Something woven into him. A memory without mercy. The ghost of what had been taken.

His augmented body, a cold marriage of man and machine, pulsed with dark energy. Beneath the surface, the veins of crimson light were more than conduits, they were scars. A reminder of the cost of survival. They fed each violent strike. Each exacting step. They allowed him to go further than any human should. To strike harder. To endure more. But they were not freedom. They were a cage. A gift given by the same hand that had broken him. Ira's hand.

The enhancements didn't save him. They stole something essential, his humanity. His name. What had been left behind wasn't a machine, but a broken man, rebuilt with metal limbs that were far from the person he had once been. The man was gone, but the humanity beneath the steel and circuits remained, locked in a body that had been torn apart and remade. Not a machine. Not a shell. Just... a man, surviving.

Toren gritted his teeth. The hum of his cybernetics aligned with his heartbeat. The agony surged, but he did not yield. There was no time for what had been lost. Only the fight ahead. Only the truth. Only the fire that refused to let him fall.

Each movement bore the imprint of what he had once been. A past not erased, but reforged. Twisted into something else. Every clash of metal, every impact against his frame, was more than battle. It was a reckoning. A reminder that he was no longer man, nor fully machine. He was the threshold between the two. A weapon carved from pain.

Yet beneath the metal, beneath the circuits and code, something still lived. Something still burned. Not extinguished. Not yet.

Sometimes, in the silence between strikes, when the battle slowed just enough, when his breath caught but did not yet tremble, he could feel it. The ghost. The memory of a body that was no longer his. He remembered the weight of hands now lost, the feel of living hands, solid earth beneath feet that had once felt real, now nothing but phantoms. The world before, before the fire. Before the betrayal. Before Ira had rebuilt him.

His body had been torn apart. Only his limbs were replaced with cold metal, but the rest of him, the man he had been, was left to burn. Rebuilt, not as a full machine, but as something broken yet still human, remade for survival.

But reflection had no place here. Nostalgia was poison. Sentiment belonged to the dead. The living had only the war.

Today, the gladiators trained for survival. Not for triumph. Not for glory. Only to endure the next culling. The Test Trials were not tests. They were sacrifices. The unworthy would not pass. They would be erased. Swallowed by the sand. Forgotten.

Hesitation meant death. Weakness was not punished. It was ignored. No one mourned the fallen. They simply vanished. Ira's city had been built on that truth. Suffering was the foundation. Worth was extracted from flesh and carved into bone. It was not enough to live. Not enough to fight. You had to become something else.

Toren Ignisferre, once a champion, now a creature of fury and steel, moved through the grounds with precision etched by time and trauma. His cybernetic limbs, black metal laced with crimson light, glistened with each motion. The Sable Fangs embedded in his forearms retracted and extended with a soft hum, sharp edges gleaming like the teeth of some ancient predator.

They were not mere tools. They were extensions of his very being. The same metal that crafted his limbs now sharpened into deadly, precise weapons. Each flick of his wrist sent them into the air with a vicious grace. This was no mere combat. This was a language, and Toren spoke it with brutal fluency.

Each strike vibrated with inner fire. The blade tore through matter with violent grace. It was more than a weapon. It was memory. It was grief. It was the shape of what he had lost.

His armour was neither elegant nor ornamental. Leather hardened by time, reinforced with alloy, scarred and scorched from years of violence. It existed to protect what little remained. Over it hung his cloak. Tattered. Threadbare. It shifted as he moved, glowing faintly with ember-like light from the nanomaterial woven beneath. It clung to him like ash.

Each footfall was a reverberation of his broken past, the ground beneath him a silent witness to his painful evolution. From man to weapon. His helmet, a relic of forgotten wars, was steel forged into a knight's grim shape. The visor adapted to light and dark, shifting with his need. Behind it, his eyes burned. Veins glowed faintly beneath his skin. Rage, barely held.

Around him, the training grounds swarmed with motion. Pain and effort formed a rhythm. Gladiators moved through their drills, driven by the same desperation. The heat pressed down like a verdict. Sweat and blood blurred together. Weapons clashed in endless cadence. Steel against bone. Flesh against metal. The arena did not rest. It devoured.

Toren moved through it all, alone in the crowd. His thoughts were a maze of old pain and unseen futures. The goal was not victory. It was endurance. His battle was not for the crowd. Not for the arena. It was for something deeper. Something he refused to name.

As the day bled on, Toren understood one truth. In Ira's city, survival was not a state. It was a creed. It was a forge. It was the fire that never died. Only the broken endured. Only the unrelenting remained.

The air inside the arena pulled taut with silence. A wire about to snap. Toren reached up and unlatched his helmet. The steel hissed as it retracted, folding along the back of his neck. Toren stood at the edge.

His emerald eyes locked onto Sera Zahara. The Crimson Rose. His opponent. His equal. In some ways, his reflection.

Sera was an enigma, a ghost in a world of savagery. Where others fought with brute force, she danced, her movements fluid as if each step was a calculation in a forgotten game. Her elegance hid a soul scarred by years of survival, where every strike was a delicate negotiation with death, every dodge a reminder that grace had once been her survival.

But beneath that beauty was something fierce, a hunger not for glory, but for a kind of redemption. She wasn't just fighting to win. She was fighting to be free.

Beneath her grace, a fire burned, one that Toren recognized: not the rage of combat, but the calmness of a soul willing to break in order to survive.

Her steps were weightless. Her presence ghostlike.

She held her blades with a touch that was almost tender. They were twin daggers known as the Crimson Blades, their hilts wrapped in the darkened silk of an era long past.

But there was nothing gentle about her.

Toren had heard the stories. Everyone had. They whispered that the blades were cursed. No wielder had ever lived to master them. Yet here she stood, wielding them with a grace that defied fate itself. The blades hummed faintly as they moved. Singing their eerie, hypnotic song. It was a sound that did not belong to steel, but to something older.

Her head tilted, curls flashing like embers as her eyes, half-warm, half-warning, locked onto him.

"Will you dance with me, Toren?" Sera's voice was as smooth as a blade sliding from its sheath.

Toren did not respond. Words were weightless here. The only language spoken in this place was the clash of steel and the pain of flesh breaking beneath it. The roar of the gladiatorial trainers, distant yet ever-present, was swallowed by the raw silence between two warriors. Heat shimmered above the sands, distorting the air between them like the mirage of something that never was. An illusion of safety. An illusion of certainty.

But there were no illusions here. There was only the fight.

Toren's body moved with a savage precision, his cybernetic limbs surging forward, a blur of dark metal and flesh bound by rage. The vibro-blades snapped out, gleaming like hungry teeth in the dim arena light. Each movement, a strike carved from violence, each swing a reminder of what he had become.

But it was futile.

His strike missed her by an inch. Sera wasn't just evading him. She was disappearing. Her form was not a shape in the arena; it was a wisp, a ghost, moving as though she was above the laws of gravity.

Every motion was fluid, too graceful for a battlefield. Too graceful for him. He was chasing a shadow, a fleeting flicker, and she was already gone, leaving nothing but the whisper of her blades.

She wasn't dodging. She was vanishing.

She moved like smoke, a breath of flame that never settled. Her form bent and twisted with an unnatural grace that defied the laws of battle.

Her golden-red curls flashed like embers as she pivoted. Her feet slid over the sand with the poise of a dancer, caught in the rhythm of something only she could hear.

Then came the whisper of her blades. A sharp sting traced the inside of Toren's forearm. Shallow. Deliberate. Not a wound. A message. She was testing him.

Toren's emerald eyes narrowed. She was measuring him. Reading the cadence of his movements. Unravelling him before she struck. Her cloak, dark and weightless, rippled as she moved. It was reinforced with sound-cancelling fibres that swallowed her presence, allowing her to close the distance without a whisper. Its interior pulsed with electro-reactive light, dancing in sync with her movements. On the battlefield, she was a shadow.

Toren pivoted sharply, his metal foot grinding into the sand. His mind recalibrated, searching for the countermeasure before she found the next opening. She had drawn first blood, but it meant nothing. Not yet.

He feinted high. A deceptive strike to lift her guard, while the real attack came from below. It was a move that had ended battles before they had even begun.

Sera did not react. She anticipated. She bent low, slipping beneath his reach as if gravity had forgotten her. Her daggers flashed, singing as they clashed against the steel of his attack. The impact shifted his momentum just enough to make precision impossible. Then, she struck. A curved blade swept across his ribs. Clean. Intentional. Not deep. Just deep enough to remind him she could have gone further.

Toren's jaw locked. She was not overpowering him. She was dismantling him. Layer by layer. She peeled away at his instincts, forcing him into pure reaction. Into survival. Into the thing Ira had forged him to be. A beast. A machine. A weapon.

But Sera... she was asking him something he had buried beneath steel and blood. What if he was more?

His mechanical limbs tensed. His breath steadied. He would not play her game. If she could read him, then he would become unreadable.

Toren abandoned calculation. He moved like a storm with no rhythm. No pattern. Chaos incarnate.

For the first time, Sera hesitated. It was brief. A fraction of a second. But it was enough.

Toren's metal hand closed around her wrist.

The world paused.

The trainers. The training grounds. The cold metallic scent of the arena.

All of it fell away.

Sera did not flinch. She did not pull back. She looked at him.

And what he saw in her eyes was not fear. Not challenge. It was understanding.

The scar on her jaw was a testament to battles fought, but her daggers sang with a more haunting rhythm, a blade's cold elegance and the promise of death, drawn with the grace of an artist and the precision of fate itself. The defiance that burned behind her gaze despite the weight of every life taken to reach this moment.

For the first time, Toren felt the weight of his own existence, buried deep beneath the metal and pain. Sera wasn't just fighting him. She was forcing him to see what he had become, to face the truth of his own brokenness.

Not the machine Ira had built. Not the weapon forged in fire and pain.

She was showing him something he had forgotten how to see. He was no longer a tool. No longer a machine. He was something else. Something more.

He was a warrior. A man who could choose.

The moment stretched. Too long.

Sera's lips curved into a quiet smirk. A twist of her wrist. A shift of weight. And suddenly Toren was falling.

Sand exploded around him. His breath caught in his chest. Before he could recover, her daggers hovered at his throat, humming with the eerie melody of steel poised at the edge of death.

She held the killing blow.

She did not take it.

Instead, she stepped back. The daggers flipped through her fingers, vanishing into their sheaths in a motion that was less act than ritual. The last note of a requiem fading into silence.

Toren lay still. Eyes fixed on the sky. His helmet shadowed his expression, but the faint hum of his limbs betrayed the recalibration taking place within. Not just in metal. In thought.

The lesson had landed. Not on his body. In his being. A weapon, yes. But something more.

"You're not just metal and rage, Toren," she murmured. Her eyes studied him with something deeper than mockery. Almost patience. Her twin daggers, now still, glowed faintly beneath the folds of her cloak. The hum remained. It was not a sound. It was a presence. A reminder.

She extended her hand toward him. Not a command. An offer.

"But one day, you'll have to decide whether you believe that."

Toren hesitated. Then, he took her hand.

But in the same breath, he moved. His body twisted, flipping backward to escape her grasp. When his feet touched earth, he launched. This time, he chose the rhythm.

Sera barely had time to inhale before the kick landed. Brutal. Direct. It struck her in the centre, forcing a sharp exhale as she stumbled backward.

For the first time, her balance broke.

And yet, surprisingly, she smiled.

It was the last thing he saw before she rolled with the motion, letting the strike carry her, regaining control before the sand had even settled. Her daggers remained sheathed. Her stance reset. The glow of her blades shimmered beneath her cloak. Her breath was steady.

"Good, Toren." Her voice was cool. Even. But beneath it, respect flickered like the embers of a long-dead fire. "But it's not enough. You'll need more than speed to take me down. You'll need to think two steps ahead."

Toren did not answer. Silence had always served him better than words.

But her voice stayed with him. Two steps ahead.

It was no longer just about reaction. It was understanding. It was foresight. She had not needed to win. Only to show him what winning would require.

The bell tolled.

Its resonance cut through the thick, blood-warm air like a funeral hymn's final note.

Weapons stilled. Voices fell quiet. Breath caught in lungs that remembered too much.

Gladiators broke apart, bruised, exhausted, and silent.

But the silence was not peace. It was preparation.

The Test Trials waited. Not as a threat, but as an inevitable reckoning. Every fighter knew it. Their muscles ached from more than strain. They ached from what was coming.

ARES's voice shattered the silence.

Cold. Mechanical. Unfeeling.

"Gladiators. The Test Trials are imminent."

No one moved. The air had turned to iron.

"You have shown sufficient strength to survive this far. However, your performance has been assessed."

Toren barely breathed. ARES was no machine. It was judgment. It was law. It was death made digital. There was no pleading. No mercy.

"You will continue your training. Be warned. Failure to advance will result in your immediate elimination."

No elaboration. Elimination did not mean exile. It meant execution.

Around him, warriors inhaled as one. Controlled. Shallow. But heavy with what they did not say. They had trained their whole lives to withstand what now stood before them. And still, some would break.

ARES continued.

"The weak will not survive. The strong will fight in the Tournament of Wrath. Only those who meet the required standard will proceed."

For some, this was promise. For others, it was sentence.

The silence that followed was total.

The Trials were no longer distant. They were here.

The line between the living and the dead had already begun to blur.

No one spoke. There was nothing left to say. Only the will to endure.

Toren stood amidst the dispersing warriors, his emerald eyes scanning the faces around him. Fear had settled in the air, but it was more than that. It was the taste of something deeper. A quiet realization that the Trials would strip them bare, not just of flesh, but of everything they thought they were. This was no longer about survival. This was about losing what little of themselves had been left.

They all knew the truth.

This was no longer sparring. It was survival rehearsed in silence. Each breath a thread before the drop.

He turned, scanning the gladiators who would fight beside him or against him. Vera. Lucius. Levik. Sera. And others. The names were familiar, etched into memory by blood and trial. But they were more than that now.

They were the storm before the fire. The immovable forces waiting to be tested.

The space between who they were and who they might become had vanished. In the end, it did not matter how much they had bled, how much they had suffered, or how much they had endured.

The only thing that mattered was who would survive.

Vera, the Silent Tempest, stood apart from the others. Her arms were crossed over her chest, and her jet-black hair was braided back in tight, disciplined rows. She was still. Unnervingly so. Like the eye of a hurricane. Absorbing everything. Giving nothing in return.

Her obsidian-dark eyes held no fear. Only a cold, calculating certainty. The quiet resolve of someone who had already decided what must be done. She was always like this before a fight. Not anxious. Not eager. Just waiting.

Toren had seen her fight. She wasted nothing. Every strike of her twin Moonfang Blades was an artist's brushstroke. Each step was measured with the precision of a tactician. The blades, sleek and long, were crafted from Voidsteel. Their darkened obsidian edges glistened, faintly glowing with a neon blue energy that pulsed down their length. The nanofiber chains that extended from their hilts flickered as she readied them for her next strike.

Her armour, a lightweight and flexible nano-weave, clung close to her form, built for fluidity and silence. Along her chest and arms, plating forged from Cryo-Resonance Alloys absorbed kinetic energy and redirected it into her blades, amplifying the force behind every blow.

But it was her silence that unnerved most. While others postured, she remained unreadable. Where others fought with rage or desperation, she moved with purpose. No wasted motion. No emotion shown. She did not strike first. She struck last. And when she struck, it was over.

Lucius Veturhald, the Frostborne Titan, stood nearby, a mountain carved from ice and battle. He was unshaken. His platinum-white hair, intricately braided before combat, flowed like a river of snow when loosed, cascading across his back.

His eyes, pale and piercing, held the stillness of frozen lakes and the storms that slumbered beneath. His skin was marked by time and battle, etched by the tundras of his birth and the carnage of the pits. A jagged scar ran down his left cheek, his first battle's gift, the beginning of a brutal ascent.

Where Vera was precision, Lucius was inevitability.

His Warhammer, the Glacial Maul, rested on his back. Its cryogenic alloy head radiated cold. Its crystalline glow pulsed with frozen power. The electromagnetic shockwave generator hummed quietly, drinking in kinetic force like breath before a roar.

Each strike unleashed a frost pulse capable of freezing flesh or forming towering barricades of ice.

His armour was a fusion of medieval weight and Pyrrhan design, ancient form reborn through modern function. The Cryo-Resonance plating absorbed the hammer's backlash and poured it into his counterattacks. His Frostwoven Cloak shimmered with a light sheen, protecting him from electronic tracking and lending his bulk a spectral presence.

Toren had seen him in the pit. Lucius never struck first. He let others exhaust themselves. He let them believe they were in control. And then, like winter's last breath, he struck. Once. And one was enough.

Toren exhaled. The weight on his chest remained unshifting.

Vera.

Lucius.

Sera.

Levik.

The others.

They were no longer just opponents. They were no longer just comrades. They were the crucible. They were the forge through which whatever came next would be shaped.

Because this was not only about enduring the Trials.

It was about what survived afterward.

ARES had named them warriors. Ira had made them into weapons. But somewhere beneath the blood, beneath the scars, beneath the certainty of death, Toren still did not know what he was fighting for.

And in the back of his mind, a whisper lingered.

The fight for survival had only just begun.

"Endurance is not life. It is the wound you bear when the world demands your soul, and you give it willingly, without a scream."

Null Gospel, Book I, Verse 4.

***

CHAPTER FOUR:

The Banquet of Unspoken Wars

"A warrior does not fight for the hollow applause of the arena. He fights to remember the taste of freedom, because the taste of chains can never be forgotten."

Fragment of the Exiled Codex, Volume I, Tablet 5.

The barracks dining hall was a fragile sanctuary, a brief stillness between the clashes of war. The scent of charred meat and hardened bread clung to the air, a grim reminder of survival. This was no feast; it was proof of life, earned at the cost of blood and bone. Here in Pyrrha, where the clash of steel echoed through stone, survival itself was a victory.

Long, battle-worn tables stretched through the hall like veins, pulsing with the remnants of warriors who had spent the daylight hours carving each other apart, only to sit together beneath the flickering breath of candlelight. The glow cast jagged shadows, warping the faces of gladiators, each scar etched with the history of battles won, bones shattered, names lost to the sand. Some spoke in low murmurs, voices roughened by past screams. Others barked laughter, raw, jagged, a sound not born of joy but of defiance.

It was the laughter of men and women who had become legends in a dying empire, and legends did not die quietly.

The air was thick, bloated with something unspoken. A slow suffocation of inevitability. The Test Trials loomed ahead; their purpose carved into the very walls of Pyrrha's arenas. This was no mere contest of strength. It was a reckoning. A culling. Here, names were not earned; they were erased. And only the ones who refused to be forgotten would walk away.

At the far end of the hall, where the glow of candlelight barely reached, sat Sol and Luna Nocturna. Twins of an enigma. Ghosts that had refused to fade. Their presence did not command space like the war-hardened giants around them, yet they were impossible to ignore.

Sol moved with the restless energy of wildfire. His golden hair, streaked with molten orange, looked like untamed embers caught in motion. He tore into a hunk of bread like a beast, as though the act itself were an extension of battle. His amber eyes smouldered with something untamed, something that refused to be caged, not even in moments of peace.

"This silence," he muttered between bites, his voice a flickering ember. "It's the kind that comes before something bad."

Luna, ever his contrast, was the moon to his sun, the night to his dawn. She moved with the fluid grace of something otherworldly, something unbothered by the weight of this world. Her silken midnight hair, laced with streaks of silver-white, cascaded over her shoulder like the flow of starlit rivers. She ate slowly, methodically, each movement deliberate. Where Sol devoured, she dissected. Where Sol burned, she observed.

Her ice-blue eyes flickered toward the others in the hall, unblinking, absorbing, calculating. Not fear. Not hesitation. Awareness.

"Not bad," she corrected softly, her voice a whisper of the inevitable. She broke a piece of bread, setting one half aside as if dividing fate itself. "Inevitable."

A ghost of something deeper passed between them, an understanding that belonged to no one else.

On their skin, their birthright was inked into existence. A rising sun marked Sol's collarbone. A crescent moon adorned Luna's. Each symbol flickered in the dim light as if breathing. A reminder. A promise. A tether that bound them beyond blood and name. They did not fight alone. They never had. And they never would.

Further down the table, where the light dimmed into flickering embers, Bakari "The Iron Flame" Malanga sat like an immovable mountain. His arms were crossed over a chest that had withstood more than mere steel. He was not just a warrior; he was a force, a relic of fire and discipline, a sentinel carved from the bones of war itself.

The candlelight caught the coarse, jet-black dreadlocks cascading down his broad shoulders. Some were interwoven with small metal rings, relics of his time in The Searing Fangs, the warrior-chefs of Gula's court, where the weak were not permitted even to taste the food they cooked.

His crystalline blue eyes, so unnatural, so piercing against the deep umber of his skin, flickered toward the bowl of thick stew before him. Yet he made no move to eat. Not yet.

Not until Ember had taken his share.

The bioengineered feline lay draped across Bakari's shoulder like a phantom of liquid shadow. Its fur shifted like restless smoke, constantly on the verge of dissolving into the darkness itself. Its molten gold eyes flickered not with hunger, but calculation. The same kind of knowing that only things born of unnatural hands carried. An intelligence that was never meant to exist.

A creation of Gluttara's twisted halls. An experiment of flesh and void. Designed for amusement. And yet, Ember had become something far more dangerous. A silent observer. A predator in waiting. An omen bound in fur and muscle. It did not meow. It did not purr. It only moved when it deemed it necessary.

Bakari reached into his bowl, scooped a sliver of meat between his calloused fingers, and raised it to the waiting void.

Ember's head tilted. Its ears twitched. Then, an instant. A flash. A snap. Needle-thin fangs clamped onto the offering, claiming it as though it had been destined to do so. The exchange was not one of affection, but of understanding. A pact. Only then, only when Ember had fed, did Bakari finally begin to eat.

Across from him, Valen "The Gilded Blade" Caelmont sat straighter than anyone in the hall.

His golden-blond hair was immaculate, untouched by the sweat and grime that clung to the others, as though he existed in a different sphere of reality, one where battle was still a spectacle instead of survival. His piercing sapphire eyes, once filled with unshakable confidence, now held the barest trace of something else. Doubt.

He had imagined this moment a thousand times. Had pictured himself here, among warriors, no longer watching from the high balconies of Pyrrha's elite, but as a fellow gladiator. A brother-in-arms. He had dreamed of the camaraderie, the fire-forged bonds, the unspoken respect of those who had bled together.

But now, surrounded by men and women who had suffered, who had been shaped by war in ways he could not yet fathom, something foreign crept beneath his skin. Not fear. Not hesitation. But discomfort. They did not see him as one of them. Not yet.

Beside him, Lucius "The Frostborne Titan" Veturhald, a living behemoth of muscle and scar, cradled his bowl in hands large enough to crush stone. The contrast between him and Valen was almost comical. Where Valen was polished, Lucius was carved from the ice of a forgotten age.

His ice-blue gaze, as steady as an unmoving glacier, watched the hall in quiet contemplation, unwavering, holding the stillness of a frozen lake before a storm.

His platinum-white hair, braided loosely down his back, bore the weight of battles past. His broad shoulders, scarred and weathered, carried not just wounds, but the memory of something lost.

Then, he laughed.

Deep and full. A sound that rolled through the hall like an avalanche cascading down the mountains of his homeland.

"Eat, Valen," he rumbled, his voice carrying the depth of tundra winds. "Thinking won't put meat on your bones."

The words were simple, but they carried weight. A reminder. A warning. A truth. And Valen understood.

Valen hesitated, just for a breath, just for the space of a heartbeat, before giving a slow, deliberate nod.

He reached for the bread. Its surface was rough beneath his fingertips. Its edges hardened like old leather. Tearing a piece free, he lifted it to his lips, chewing with quiet resolve.

The texture was coarse, each bite a reminder of how far he had fallen from the tables of Pyrrha's elite, where bread was soft, honeyed, effortless. Here, it was dense, made for survival, not comfort.

It resisted him. Like the arena. Like the men beside him. Like the fate that had placed him here. But he swallowed without complaint, without hesitation, because weakness had no place at this table. Not in the company of those who had already bled for their right to sit here.

The others continued their quiet conversations, but beneath it all, the weight of what lay ahead pressed into the air. The Test

Trials were not just a test of skill. They were a test of endurance, of will, of who would break first. Valen was beginning to understand.

His fingers curled around the edge of his tray. The weight of the bread in his hands was suddenly heavier than it should have been. The food was simple, unremarkable, yet each bite felt like a silent war. His body craved sustenance. His pride hesitated to consume what was shared by men who had lived far harsher lives than he had. He had trained for battle, trained to wield a blade, but nothing had prepared him for this. The unspoken challenge of belonging.

Across from him, Bakari "The Iron Flame" Malanga set down his empty bowl with deliberate finality. The deep timbre of his voice broke through the murmurs of the hall.

"Eat while you can. The arena does not care for the hungry."

The words carried no scorn, no mockery, only truth. A lesson from a man who had learned it the hard way.

Valen hesitated, then lifted his gaze to meet Bakari's. The gladiator's crystalline blue eyes, unnatural against the deep umber of his skin, were sharp yet unreadable. A man who had mastered the fire that had tried to consume him.

Bakari's words settled over him like iron, and for the first time that night, Valen nodded, not out of obligation, but out of understanding. He tore another piece of bread, this time without hesitation, and ate. It was tougher than what he was used to. But so was everything in Pyrrha.

The barracks dining hall was a graveyard of fleeting peace, where men who should have been dead ate their meals in silence, stealing what little respite they could before fate swallowed them whole. The air was thick with the scent of charred meat, hardened bread, and the unspoken truths of warriors who had made peace with their own mortality.

Hurriyah Sunshadow sat apart, a silent force among the noise.

His molten-gold eyes cut through the flickering shadows like the last remnants of a dying sun, faint but unyielding. He did not eat, not yet. Unlike them, he had not yet accepted the cage. He still burned, refusing to forget that freedom was worth more than survival. The others clung to camaraderie as if it could dull the steel that awaited them. But Hurriyah knew survival wasn't enough. Not here. Not now.

He had been Hurriyah, the Warchief. The one who would have united Phalaistin. The one who would have ended Pyrrha's reign of iron and fire. But kings do not sit in chains, and the Ashen Vow at his side was a mockery of the throne he would never claim. The weight of the past pressed against his ribs. He let it.

They came for him at dusk. A secret meeting of unity, a moment that could have changed everything, sold for silver and blood. He remembered the taste of earth in his mouth as they dragged him from the council hall. The last words of his people drowned beneath the roar of Pyrrha's war engines.

They branded him, and he burned the mark away with his own hand. They threw him into the pits, and he made legends out of their warriors. They called him "the shackled king." A name whispered in awe and mockery alike. And yet, in the deepest part of his being, Hurriyah knew the truth. He was still free. Because freedom was not in the body. It was in the fire that refused to die.

He glanced around the room. His eyes drifted over the other gladiators. They were warriors, yes. Some of them, even great. But they were not free.

Bakari Malanga, the Iron Flame, who masked his chains with laughter and fire, feeding his beast and his brothers as if that alone could keep the abyss at bay.

Lucius Veturhald, the Frostborne Titan, who carried his past like an ice-buried corpse, drinking deep to forget the warmth he had once known.

Valen Caelmont, the Gilded Blade, still trying to pretend he was one of them. Still gripping the last strands of his old world, as if nobility had any place in a pit of animals.

Even Sol and Luna Nocturna, the twin wraiths, had found their place here. He envied them, not their fate, but their certainty.

But Hurriyah had no place.

He was an ember that refused to be extinguished. A ghost of a kingdom that never was.

He did not hate them. No, the hatred was reserved for those who had taken everything. For Midas, the golden warlord, who wrapped his cruelty in velvet and watched with idle amusement as Hurriyah carved his name into the sands of the arena. For the ones who betrayed him. For the ones who had forgotten what they were before they were slaves.

The voices around him blurred, but Hurriyah was not lost in them. His gaze cut across the room. Each man, each woman, a prisoner of their own making. The laughter was hollow. The murmurs empty. They hadn't yet realized they were already dead, fighting for nothing.

Hurriyah tore into the bread with quiet ferocity, the sensation grounding him in the here and now. Fire needed fuel. Even in chains, he would burn. He would eat because, even a king without a throne knew, bitterness had its own power. But he would not be forgotten. Not by himself. Not by them.

The barracks dining hall was alive with murmurs, the clatter of wooden bowls against rough-hewn tables, and the fleeting laughter of men who knew better than to hope. Yet beneath it all, beneath the toasts and reckless camaraderie, lurked something heavier. A shadow stretching beneath the wavering candlelight.

The air was thick with sweat. The scent of charred meat and hardened bread mingled with the unmistakable metallic tang of old blood and bruises that had yet to heal. The Test Trials loomed, and in Pyrrha, survival was not a privilege. It was a curse, stretched thin over broken bodies and sharpened steel.

At the far end of the hall, Toren sat in silence. His emerald eyes flickered over the room with a watchful intensity, a predator studying the herd, already choosing which among them would not live past tomorrow. He did not eat. He did not drink. The weight of the inevitable was a heavier meal than anything that could be offered on the table.

Across the room, Lucius "The Frostborne Titan" Veturhald lifted his mug high, his laugh rolling through the space like a distant avalanche.

"To survival. To another day in Pyrrha's bloody streets." His voice carried, booming, full of mirth that did not quite reach his ice-blue eyes.

The response was instant, an eruption of voices, a chorus of defiance against the walls that caged them.

"To survival."

A toast raised not in celebration, but in spite.

Hurriyah Sunshadow sat in the dim light, unmoving. He did not raise a cup. He did not join the revelry. He only watched, the flickering glow catching in his molten gold gaze, eyes that had once stared across Phalaistin as its rightful heir, now confined within Pyrrha's iron grasp.

This was not the kind of war he had trained for. This was not the battlefield he had imagined leading. And yet, war had followed him here, curling itself around his throat like a chain he could never break. The Shackled King. The Unbroken Flame.

His fingers, scarred and calloused from years of battle and servitude, drummed absently against the table's surface. The vibrations, the rhythm, it was the beat of war drums, the heartbeat of a land that had not forgotten him.

At the next table over, Valen Caelmont sipped from his cup. His golden-blond hair remained untouched by the filth of the arena. His noble hands were unsuited for the crude reality of Pyrrha. Hurriyah saw the way he watched the others, not with disdain, not even with fear, but with something else. Admiration. Longing. Or perhaps the bitter realization that no matter how much blood he spilled, he would always be an outsider.

Across from him, Bakari Malanga leaned back, arms crossed. Candlelight reflected off his deep umber skin. His crystalline blue eyes, so unnatural, so piercing, held the weight of a man who understood that survival was no victory. His feline companion, Ember, stretched lazily across his broad shoulder. The creature's molten gold gaze met Hurriyah's for a brief, knowing moment. Recognition. A shared understanding between beasts forged in fire.

Hurriyah exhaled. His jaw tightened. He did not belong here. And yet, he belonged more than anyone.

His gaze swept the room. Men laughed, drank, ate as if it would be their last meal. And for many, it would be. Their strength was real. Their struggle was real. But Pyrrha had taken something from them, something they did not even realize. Freedom.

The voices of the gladiators faded, swallowed by the abyss of his own thoughts. The weight of the hall, the scent of sweat and blood, the flickering light of the dying candles, it all dissolved as

Hurriyah Sunshadow fell inward, descending into the labyrinth of his past.

It was not the first time he had wandered these depths. It would not be the last. Pyrrha had caged his body, but his mind was an open battlefield, one where ghosts did not slumber and memories did not fade.

He saw the council hall, the night the dream of unity had been shattered. The banners of Phalaistin had hung proudly from the vaulted ceilings, three great sigils representing three great peoples: the Duskborn, the Emberborn, and the Tideborn, poised to forge something greater than themselves. The torchlight had danced upon the polished marble floors, reflecting the determined faces of leaders who had dared to believe in something beyond war.

And then, the betrayal.

The doors had burst open like the gaping maw of some ancient beast. Pyrrha's Sanguine Order had poured in like a flood. The air had split with the clash of steel, the screams of the fallen, the splintering of wood and bone alike.

He remembered the moment the chains had wrapped around his wrists. The iron bit into his flesh, still hot from the forge, branding him not as a warrior, not as a leader, but as a slave. The mark of Pyrrha.

His father's sword had been torn from his grip. His brother had died in his arms, whispering his name one last time. His people had been scattered, hunted, broken before they could rise. And

Hurriyah, the one who should have led them to freedom, had been dragged through the streets of Pyrrha in chains, paraded as a prize before the same empire he had vowed to defy.

The crowd had cheered for his suffering. And in that moment, something inside him had burned. Not rage. Not grief. Something older. Something deeper. Something eternal. The fire had not been extinguished. It had been transformed.

His hand twitched instinctively, fingers brushing against the hilt of *The Ashen Vow*. The weapon was born from ruin, the last remnants of his father's blade, reforged with the iron of his brother's broken shackles. A weapon not of war, but of remembrance.

The voices of the present world bled back into his mind, pulling him from the abyss of the past. Laughter. Toasts. The clinking of metal cups.

He looked around at the gladiators. Men who had long since been stripped of their names and causes. Men who had been reduced to mere performers of violence, dancing on the stage of Pyrrha's brutality for the amusement of their oppressors. And still, they clung to camaraderie, to brotherhood, because it was the only defiance left to them.

Hurriyah inhaled deeply.

They fought not for liberation, but for spectacle. They fought because it was the only life they had ever been given, the only one they had ever known.

But Hurriyah had known something different once. He had been a king without a throne. A leader without a crown. A warrior who did not fight for sport, but for his people. And now, he sat among those who had been caged for so long they had begun to mistake their chains for honour. And in the midst of the moment, he returned into the depths of his mind.

Tomorrow, the Test Trials would come. And perhaps, tomorrow, he would remind them what it meant to fight for something greater than survival. Perhaps, tomorrow, the flames of rebellion would burn anew.

Further down the table, Sol and Luna Nocturna sat as twin echoes of light and shadow. Their presence was a contrast as striking as the celestial bodies they were named after. They were small, slight, yet there was an undeniable gravity to them. Two halves of the same unbroken whole.

Sol tore into his bread with wild, unrestrained hunger. His molten amber eyes flickered like embers caught in the wind. His fingers, calloused from endless battles, dug into the crust as if breaking the bread itself were an act of conquest.

"The air feels wrong," he muttered between bites, his voice brimming with restless energy, like a storm on the verge of breaking. "Like the moment before an eclipse, when the sun is swallowed, and the world forgets warmth exists."

Across from him, Luna moved with deliberate grace. The silver-white streaks in her midnight hair caught the dim candlelight. She did not eat as if it were a battle, nor did she rush. She savoured each motion, each bite, as though even the smallest acts of living deserved reverence.

"Light always returns," she murmured, tearing her bread apart with delicate precision. Her ice-blue eyes flickered across the room, absorbing every unspoken thought, every tension buried beneath laughter and the clatter of metal trays. "The question is, when it does, will it rise on the same world it left behind?"

A hush settled over those who had overheard. The weight of her words stretched between them like an invisible thread. Thin. Fragile. Yet unbreakable.

Sol smirked, swallowing another mouthful before licking the crumbs from his fingers.

"Then I suppose we decide, don't we?" His eyes gleamed. Untamed. Fierce. "If we'll be standing in the light when it returns, or if we'll be the ones casting the longest shadows."

And for a moment, the flickering candlelight danced between them, casting both glow and darkness across their faces, as if even the flames could not decide which one they belonged to.

Luna did not smile, nor did she challenge his words. She merely reached forward, breaking her bread into two equal halves and setting one aside.

"For those who don't make it to see it rise." And in that moment, it became painfully clear. They were not speaking of the sun.

A quiet understanding settled over the table. It stretched into the dim-lit expanse of the barracks dining hall like an unseen spectre. Conversations continued. Laughter rose and fell. But beneath it all, there was something heavier. Something that could not be ignored.

Then, from the shadowed edges of the hall, a voice cut through the murmurs like the edge of a blade.

"All this talk of survival," Raekor muttered. His deep amber eyes glinted like a predator's in the low light. His dark, shoulder-length hair framed his face. The jagged scar along his jaw pulled taut as he chewed. "As if any of us have a choice."

From across the table, Levik Draganmir exhaled sharply through his nose. The massive warrior shifted in his seat. His grizzled, silver-streaked hair was damp with sweat from the day's training. His heavy-set frame carried the weight of countless battles. A living testament to endurance. To stubborn defiance against inevitability.

"Choice?" he rumbled, his steel-grey eyes settling on Raekor. "Choice is a luxury of the free."

Raekor's smirk was all edge, no warmth.

"You fight because you must, or because you've forgotten how to stop?"

Levik took a long pull from his cup, each sip a meditation on years of fighting for nothing.

"Does it matter?" he said at last, the weight of his words heavier than his silence.

"We fight. That's all."

Across the table, Valen leaned forward, his presence cutting through the moment like a blade wielded too hastily. The nobleman turned gladiator was not known for restraint, and tonight would be no exception.

"That's a convenient way to justify it," he scoffed, his sapphire-blue eyes burning with a reckless kind of fire. "But some of us fight for something greater." The words hung in the air, heavy and unearned. For a heartbeat, no one spoke.

Then, Raekor let out a dry chuckle, shaking his head. "Spoken like someone who still thinks the arena is a battlefield."

Levik sighed, setting his cup down with a dull thud. "Spoken like someone who's never had to kill just to keep breathing."

The silence that followed was not empty. It was weighted, an invisible war of understanding, of clashing worlds forced into the same cage. And beyond it all, the candles flickered, the murmurs continued, and the Test Trials waited on the horizon, a storm none of them could escape.

Raekor's gaze snapped to Valen, sharp as a drawn dagger. But Valen was too caught up in his own momentum to notice. His hands clenched against the worn wood of the table, his pulse thrumming in his ears. He had been waiting for this moment, an opportunity to speak, to prove he belonged, to carve meaning into the bloodstained tapestry of Pyrrha's warriors.

Levik set his cup down again with a deliberate thud. The sound was final, like the closing of a heavy tome, as if whatever came next had already been written in the pages of warriors long past. His steel-grey eyes shifted toward Valen. Not with anger, but with something far worse. Patience. The kind reserved for those who did not yet understand the depths of the ocean they had thrown themselves into.

"And what," Levik said, his voice slow, deliberate, the weight of a storm gathering beneath its surface, "is this great purpose you fight for, boy?"

Boy.

The word struck like a slap, and Valen's jaw tightened. He had spent his whole life proving he was more than the son of Pyrrha's elite, more than a name dripping with old wealth and gilded expectations. He had chosen this path. No one had forced him into the pits. No one had thrown him into the dirt and told him to crawl back up with broken bones. He had walked into the arena, head held high, seeking something beyond silk and power, beyond legacy.

Valen straightened his shoulders, ignoring the flicker of doubt gnawing at the back of his mind.

"Honor," he said firmly. "Legacy. To be something more than a name."

For a moment, the words lingered in the air, filling the silence like the last embers of a dying flame.

Then, Raekor's chuckle, low and humourless, rolled through the room. He leaned back, crossing his arms over his broad chest, the flickering candlelight tracing the jagged edges of his scarred face.

"Honor," he repeated, letting the word settle like a dead weight on the table between them. "You talk about honour in a place where men gut each other for sport. Where survival is not a right but a privilege." He shook his head, his smirk cutting across his face like a knife. "You're still dreaming."

Valen bristled.

"And you?" he shot back, his voice edged with defiance. "What do you fight for? Just another day to breathe? Another meal? Is that all you are?"

A shift in the air. Not loud, but undeniable. A ripple through the gathered warriors, half-listening, now fully invested. Even the crackling torches seemed to burn quieter.

Raekor's expression did not change, but something behind his gaze hardened. The kind of hardness that came not from arrogance, but from knowing. He exhaled slowly, tilting his head slightly, like a predator amused by the prey standing in its shadow.

"I fight," he said, his voice quieter now, sharper, "because I woke up one day and realized there was nothing left to fight for."

He let the words sink in, let Valen feel their weight. The weight of absence. The weight of loss.

"But you," Raekor continued, eyes narrowing, "you still think there's something waiting for you at the end of all this. You still think the arena is a proving ground instead of a graveyard." He gestured around them, sweeping his hand to the gathered gladiators, to the bloodstained stone walls, to the very air that smelled of sweat and iron. "There's no honour here, noble. Only those who live, and those who don't."

Valen's fingers curled into his palms, but before he could speak, Levik let out a low sigh.

"You mistake survival for meaning," the older warrior murmured. "Some men survive to live. Some survive to make sure no one else does." He picked up his cup again, staring into the dark liquid as if it held the answer to a question no one dared ask. "If you're lucky, you'll understand the difference before the arena teaches it to you."

Valen opened his mouth, then closed it. For the first time, he had no words.

Raekor did not move. He did not even blink. But something deep in his amber eyes flickered. A darkness that went beyond the dim light of the hall, beyond the battle scars that carved his face like remnants of forgotten wars.

"You think death is poetic," he murmured, his voice quiet now, but all the more dangerous for it. "You think war is something you choose."

Valen opened his mouth again. Breath caught sharp in his chest.

But Raekor wasn't finished.

"You weren't born into this, Caelmont." The name landed like a hammer. Sharp. Deliberate. "You came here because you wanted to, not because you had no choice. You wanted to feel like one of us. But wanting and being are not the same thing."

His voice hardened. A blade honed and unsparing.

"You haven't starved in the barracks, waiting for a fight that might let you live one more week. You haven't watched the man beside you bleed out for entertainment while you stood there, knowing you'd be next. You haven't had your freedom stolen before you even knew what it was."

Silence.

The words lanced through Valen. A blow heavier than any he had taken in the training grounds. It cut past the bruises, past the callouses he had earned, and struck somewhere deeper. Somewhere that had never been touched before.

His fingers curled into fists, his nails digging into his palms, but he forced himself not to look away. He would not. But for the first time, he questioned if he truly belonged here at all.

Levik sighed, rubbing a hand over the scar along his jaw.

"Enough," he muttered, though his voice held no sympathy. "The boy will learn, one way or another."

The silence that followed was suffocating. It pressed down on Valen like the weight of an iron chain, tightening with every heartbeat, every flicker of candlelight stretching the moment longer than it should have been.

His pride, which had once felt so unshakable, now hung by a thread. A fragile thing, trembling between truth and defiance.

A flicker of movement. Sol, lounging further down the table, propped his elbow against the wood, a grin tugging at the corner of his lips. The molten glow of his eyes gleamed with amusement, but there was something sharper beneath it. Something keen and cutting, like the edge of a blade just before it finds flesh.

"Look at him," Sol muttered, voice dripping with playful cruelty. "Still chewing on his own words, like a man who just realized the feast isn't for him."

Luna, ever the quieter half, tapped a single finger against her cup. The rhythmic sound was soft, measured, but it carried weight. A quiet, deliberate percussion marking the cracks forming beneath Valen's composure. Her ice-blue gaze sliced through him. Piercing. Unrelenting.

"No," she corrected, her voice barely above a whisper but far sharper than her brother's. "Like a man who just realized he's sitting at the wrong table."

A few scattered chuckles rose from the gladiators nearby. Not cruel. Not mocking. But something colder. Acknowledgment. It was the sound of men who had bled together. Who had earned their place at this table through suffering Valen had yet to understand.

Valen swallowed hard. The heat crept up his neck, but he forced himself to keep his expression neutral. He knew what they thought of him. A boy playing warrior. A noble who had never felt the sting of true loss. They were wrong.

His hands curled into fists beneath the table, his pulse hammering at his temples, but before he could force a retort past his lips, another voice cut through the tension.

"You all talk too much."

The low, gravelled tone belonged to Levik. He reached for his cup again. His steel-grey eyes were unreadable, his movements slow and deliberate.

"Words don't make a warrior. Neither does legacy."

He drained his drink, exhaling slowly. His gaze went distant. Not looking at Valen. Not looking at anyone. But at something far beyond them all.

"A real fighter doesn't speak about why he fights. He just fights."

The words settled over the table like a shroud. They cut through the thick air like an executioner's blade.

Then, a shift.

Vera tilted her head slightly, her dark eyes flicking toward Levik with something unreadable in them.

"And what does that make us?" she asked, her voice calm but carrying a storm beneath its surface. "Warriors? Or weapons?"

Levik set his cup down with a quiet thud.

"That depends on who's holding the blade."

Silence. Not an awkward pause, but something heavier. Something more dangerous.

Then, after what felt like an eternity, Bakari chuckled. The deep rumble settled in his chest before it ever reached his lips.

"You always did have a way with words, Levik."

Levik grunted, shifting in his seat. "I'd rather have a way with an axe."

Sol smirked, but Luna's gaze lingered on Valen as if she were watching him unravel in real time.

Valen clenched his jaw, the muscle twitching beneath his skin. He wanted to meet their words with his own, to carve through their disdain with something sharp enough to wound. But what weapons did he truly have?

His tongue was gilded, sharpened by debates in marble halls where battles were fought with wit and the consequences were nothing more than bruised egos. Here, words were a different currency. Here, they cut deeper than blades. And Valen was unarmed.

The silence pressed in, thick and suffocating, wrapping around him like unseen chains. It was not the absence of sound, but the weight of unspoken judgment. The kind that settled heavy in the lungs and pressed against the ribs like an iron vice. Like something vast and immeasurable standing between him and them.

It was not skill. Not lineage. Not even blood. It was suffering. And he had not suffered enough to stand among them. Yet.

The thought lodged itself in his chest like a dull knife, twisting with something he refused to name. They looked at him and saw a child playing at war. An imposter draped in armour that had never known true battle. He wanted to shake them, to force them to see him as more than a privileged son who had abandoned a life of luxury for the thrill of the arena.

Because wasn't it suffering to be born into a name that dictated his every move? Wasn't it pain to have his destiny written for him before he had even taken his first breath? But no. Even before the words formed, he knew. They would not accept his pain. Not as equal.

Because his suffering had been soft. Theirs had been sharpened against stone, tempered in fire, carved into their skin with every scar they bore. The silence thickened. He could feel their gazes, weighing him, measuring him, deciding whether he was worth acknowledging at all. And in that moment, Valen did what he always did when faced with doubt. He spoke.

The weight of her words settled over the table like a storm rolling in from the distant edges of a battlefield. It was not loud. Not violent. But its presence was undeniable. Valen did not look away. He could feel the invisible line being drawn: honour against survival, belief against reality. And he was standing on one side of it, alone.

"You talk about suffering as if it's some grand truth," he said, forcing his voice to remain steady. "As if it's the only thing that matters. But pain alone doesn't make a warrior. Wrath isn't a virtue. Rage doesn't make you stronger. If anything, it blinds you. It makes you reckless. A slave to your own fury."

He exhaled, running a hand through his golden hair. His sapphire eyes flickered across the table, searching for something.

Understanding, maybe. Or just a crack in their certainty.

"If all you have is suffering, if all you have is rage, then you've already lost. Where is the honour?"

The words hung in the air, his voice like a spark tossed into a room soaked in oil. A low chuckle cut through the silence. Rough-edged. Humourless. Raekor.

"Spoken like a man who's never been on the losing end of a fight," the scarred warrior muttered, shaking his head.

"Or who's never lost everything," Vera added, her voice like the edge of a whisper. Quiet, but carrying the weight of a storm behind it.

The table fell silent.

Vera sat poised, her jet-black hair neatly braided, her obsidian eyes unreadable pools of depth and calculation. She had barely touched her food, yet her presence carried the stillness of a sharpened blade waiting to be drawn.

Valen met her gaze, something flickering in his expression. Hesitation. Defiance. A question unspoken. But Vera's eyes did not waver.

"You believe in honour, Valen," she said. "That's fine. But honour doesn't keep you alive in the arena. The only thing that does is knowing what you're willing to sacrifice."

Lucius leaned back, rubbing his jaw, his ice-blue gaze sharp beneath the flickering torchlight.

"And what do you believe, Vera? That the fight is meaningless?"

She didn't answer immediately. Instead, she reached for the cup before her, running a single finger along its rim, tracing a path like a blade carving into flesh.

"I believe that fighting and dying are the same thing here," she said finally. "The only difference is how long it takes."

The weight of her words did not pass. It settled. It lingered. It did not fade.

A voice rose from the depths of the hall. Low. Steady. Sharp enough to carve through the silence like a blade drawn against stone.

"Then tell me," Hurriyah Sunshadow said. His words were measured, his tone an ember smouldering beneath the weight of long-contained fire. "What are you waiting for?"

The moment did not shatter. It stretched.

Every warrior at the table felt it. The shift. The unspoken truth that something had changed.

Hurriyah had been there among them for weeks. Watching. Listening. But never speaking. He was a presence, not a participant. A shadow at the edge of the firelight. A spectre in a world of the living. But now, he had chosen to step forward, and the weight of that choice settled over them like a storm on the horizon.

Vera, who rarely let her expression slip, turned her head toward him. Her obsidian eyes flickered with something unreadable.

Levik, ever the old war hound, let out a slow exhale as if he had been waiting for this moment. Even Sol and Luna, who traded words like weapons, fell quiet.

Hurriyah's molten-gold eyes did not waver. They burned like dying suns, as if he were staring straight through the walls of the barracks, through the bloodstained sands of the arena, through the weight of everything that had brought them here.

His gaze settled on Valen, but it was not just for him. It was for all of them.

"You speak of honour as if it is something to be found," Hurriyah continued. "As if it is waiting in the dust, in the blood, in the moments before death. But you are wrong. Honor is not found. It is made. Forged. Burned into existence."

Valen's fingers twitched against the wood of the table, but he did not speak. He had challenged Raekor, Vera, even Levik. But Hurriyah was different. There was an authority to him. A presence that could not be ignored.

Hurriyah leaned forward, his voice lowering, but its weight remained unshaken. "You speak of rage as if it weakens. As if it blinds. As if it's chains, choking the life from a man who's lost everything. But have you ever burned, Valen Caelmont?"

Valen's breath caught.

Hurriyah tilted his hand upward, revealing the half-burned slave sigil branded into his forearm. A mark not given, but one he had scorched himself to erase the chains Pyrrha had once laid upon him. The flesh was twisted, healed yet forever marred. A wound that would never fade.

"I have burned," Hurriyah said, his voice quieter now, but no less powerful. "And I am still burning. But fire does not always consume. Sometimes, it purifies."

The words landed like iron striking the forge. No one spoke. Even Raekor, who wielded cynicism like a second blade, did not laugh this time. Bakari exhaled through his nose. Slow and thoughtful. Ember, perched on his shoulder, twitched its tail.

Vera looked away. Not in dismissal, but as if she were considering something too deep, too raw, to answer.

Lucius, for all his easy confidence, only watched. His ice-blue gaze was unreadable.

And Valen. Valen swallowed hard, as if trying to force something down. Something that warred within him. He had spoken of fire, of fury, of what it meant to fight. But now, in the face of it, he had no words.

Hurriyah let the silence stretch. Then, finally, he leaned back, his fingers tracing the edge of *The Ashen Vow*. The blade that was once both his father's sword and his brother's chains.

"Tomorrow, you will learn, if you avoid death," he said. And the way he said it was not a promise. It was a certainty.

The low murmur of conversation still rippled through the barracks dining hall, but something had changed. The weight of unspoken truths clung to the air, settling into the dim candlelight like smoke that refused to clear.

Hurriyah had been listening, as he always did.

He had watched them speak of suffering and survival, of honour and futility. He had heard their voices rise and fall, exchanging words as if they were blades clashing in the dark. Some spoke of war as an inevitability, others as a curse. Some fought to endure, others to forget. But none of them had truly lived free. Not the way he once had.

A king without a throne. A leader without a nation. A warrior who once fought for his people, not for spectacle, not for survival, but for something greater.

Now, he sat among men and women who had long since accepted their captivity. Those who had been shackled so long they no longer felt the weight of their chains. They had learned to fight in the dark, but they had forgotten the feeling of standing beneath the sun. And that was the worst kind of death.

The flickering light danced across his skin, tracing over the battle-worn scars that had become a history written in flesh. He did not speak as quickly as the others. He did not argue. He did not seek to carve his beliefs into the conversation like a blade thrust into the table.

Instead, he let the silence stretch, his molten-gold gaze flickering over the faces around him. Not in judgment. Not in disdain. But in something heavier. In knowing. At last, when the moment reached its breaking point, he exhaled.

"You have forgotten the difference between a cage and a battlefield."

His voice was not loud, but it carried, like the quiet rumble of thunder before a storm that had not yet come.

The room did not fall silent, but it shifted.

Some turned toward him. Others only listened. But all of them felt it.

A presence that had been waiting, smouldering beneath the ashes of conversation.

Hurriyah set his hands on the table, his fingers tracing the rough wood, calloused and firm. Hands that had once lifted a blade in the name of freedom, not in service to an empire's amusement.

"You speak of death like it is a choice. It is not. It is a debt. And all of us, every single one of us, will pay it in the end."

He leaned back slightly, his ember-streaked braids catching the glow of the candlelight.

"But do you even remember what you are paying for?"

His words did not rise. They did not cut. They settled, heavy, inescapable. For a long moment, no one answered. There was nothing left to say. And that, more than anything, was the point.

"Chains do not break with a scream. They break when the forgotten dare to rise as they once were."

Null Gospel, Book I, Verse 5.

***

CHAPTER FIVE:

The Fire That Would Not Die

"Some fires do not burn to illuminate. They burn to tear open your eyes. And when they have burned the last lie to ash, they leave nothing but you, bare and broken."

Fragment of the Exiled Codex, Volume I, Tablet 6.

Some fires do not burn to destroy. Some remain only to remind.

Even after the cities fall, after blood becomes dust and the songs of the dead are lost to silence, there are still embers that linger. They cling to forgotten corners of stone chambers, to the scent of old oil in the cracks of the floor, to the grain of a wooden table worn smooth by the weight of remembered hands. These are not the flames that roar. These are the ones that wait, the ones that watch.

There are rooms in the world that remember. They do not need witnesses. They are witnesses themselves.

This one sat beneath the ruined ribs of a shattered basilica. The vaulted ceiling was scorched, split wide open to a sky without stars. Outside, the wind had no name. It came slow, carrying the taste of iron and ash, brushing the cold stone floor like something hesitant to disturb what still slept here. In the centre of the room, a single hearth still held fire, not wild, not fierce, but steady

The chairs were not thrones. They were simple things, pulled from the wreckage of old sanctuaries. Scarred and uneven, as if the men who sat in them did not want comfort, but only presence. Between them, a bottle rested on the table. No guards. No armour. No commands. Only flame. And memory.

They had not spoken yet. The silence had not become awkward. It breathed in the space between them, like something alive, something sacred. This was not strategy. Not confrontation. Not yet.

This was something older than war.

Two men remembering the fire before it turned to smoke.

Jorlan poured the first glass, the amber liquid catching the firelight in a fleeting shimmer.

"I remember this place," he said, his voice low, the kind that belonged to worn halls and broken walls. "Before the ceiling fell. Before the prayers stopped."

Ira did not look at him. He stared into the hearth, his broad hands resting on his knees, fingers curled slightly as if holding a weapon that wasn't there.

"You used to call it blood and rosemary," Jorlan said, voice low. "Said the scent of it made you want to tear the world down."

That drew a sound. Not quite a laugh, not quite approval. Something like smoke exhaled through a crack in stone.

"It still smells like that," Ira said. His voice had not changed with time. It did not age. It carved.

Jorlan passed him the glass. Their hands touched briefly, Ira's fingers dwarfed his, calloused and rough as volcanic rock. But the grip was not cruel. It was something quieter than kindness. Something closer to habit.

They drank.

For a while, the fire said more than either of them could. The crackling was slow, but constant, like it refused to die even if the room asked it to.

"Back then, we didn't need words," Jorlan said, his gaze distant, as if he could still feel it. "Just looks. A nod. A grunt."

"And it was enough," Ira answered.

"Now we speak too much. And say nothing."

"Do you remember what you told me before the Siege of Kharros?"

Ira's brow twitched.

"We don't bleed for kings," Jorlan said softly. "We bleed for each other."

Ira didn't respond. He didn't need to.

The fire cracked, like it remembered.

That brought Ira's eyes toward him. The firelight caught the molten amber within them. For a moment, it seemed something deep inside had stirred, just faintly. Not anger. Not yet.

"I don't speak to hear myself," Ira said.

"No," Jorlan said quietly. "You speak to make silence afraid."

Ira turned the glass in his hand, slow, deliberate, as if waiting to decide whether that had been an insult or a compliment. The firelight crawled across his knuckles, catching the edges of old blood-runes.

"They feared me long before I learned to speak," he said.

Jorlan let the weight of that truth sit a moment before replying. "Not all of us feared you."

A pause fell.

The kind that could fall either way. It might have turned to warmth, or slipped into warning.

"I never feared you," Jorlan whispered. "Not once. Not even when I should have."

Ira drank slowly, letting the silence stretch not to punish, but to breathe. When he spoke, it wasn't as a tyrant. It was something older.

"You were the first to stand with me when I killed that captain," Ira said, his eyes narrowing. "You remember what it was like?"

Jorlan nodded once. "He spit on the half-burned girl from Torra Vale. Thought it was funny."

"He begged," Ira said. "Did you know that? No one ever remembers. He begged before his jaw came off."

"You said justice didn't need to wait for orders."

"And you said nothing," Ira replied. "You just stood next to me. Like it was always meant to be that way."

Jorlan took another drink. His hand was steady, but his eyes had drifted toward the window. Nothing but black sky and ash beyond the broken stone.

"I stood next to you," he said, "because I believed in you."

The fire cracked, a coal splitting in the hearth, sparks spiralling into the air. Ira didn't look away. Not yet.

"You still do?" he asked.

Jorlan did not answer immediately. Instead, he leaned forward, elbows on his knees, letting the weight of everything they had not said settle between them.

"I believed," he said at last, "that wrath could be righteous. That we were burning toward something cleaner."

Ira's eyes narrowed. Just slightly. But it was enough.

"And now?"

Jorlan stared into the fire, his voice a stranger's.

"We've burned so long," he murmured, "we've forgotten what we were trying to save."

Jorlan leaned back, eyes still on the fire, but his thoughts somewhere far beyond it.

"Do you remember Darneth Ridge?" he asked.

Ira's jaw tightened, just slightly. The name fell like rust into the room.

"I remember the mud," he said.

"No one talks about that battle. Not in the songs. Not in the histories. But that was the one, for me. That's where I stopped being alive."

Ira said nothing. Not because he disagreed, but because he knew exactly what Jorlan meant.

"It rained for eight days," Jorlan said. "No tents. No fires. Just the dead soaking into the ground and the living trying not to scream loud enough to get noticed."

Ira's voice came low. "You broke your leg in the ravine. The medics wouldn't come."

"They said I wasn't worth the risk."

"You dragged yourself a mile on your elbows."

Jorlan smiled without warmth. "No. You carried me."

Ira's eyes met his now. Solid. Heavy. Present.

"I carried you," he said. "Through sniper fire. Through hell."

"And when we made it back to the line," Jorlan whispered, "I begged you to leave me. I told you I was done. And you…"

"I hit you," Ira said. "Hard."

"You broke my jaw," Jorlan said, voice catching. "But you said if I ever gave up again, you'd break more than that. You said…"

He stopped.

Ira didn't.

"I said you were my brother. And I wasn't going to lose another one."

The silence that followed did not comfort. It hurt. It spread out across the floor like spilled blood.

Jorlan's voice, when it came again, was quieter than the fire.

"You were the only one who didn't leave me."

Ira looked at him then, not with softness, but not with wrath either. It was older. A look a man gives the last person who knew him before he became what the world demanded, before he became the thing he never thought he'd be.

"You saved me more than once, Ira," Jorlan said, his voice rougher now, as if it carried more than just the words themselves. "Not just my body. You saved what little was left of me."

He reached for the bottle again, pouring without asking, the amber liquid rising in the glass.

"So why do I feel like I've been dying ever since?"

Ira didn't answer immediately. His gaze lingered on the fire, like he was searching for something in its shifting shadows, something familiar, something Ira that could make sense of everything they had built together and the cost they had never named.

The weight of it crushed him. I killed him. He couldn't breathe.

The moment he realized, it felt like the world was swallowed by darkness. His chest tightened, and his hands fell to his knees, trembling as though he couldn't keep himself from falling apart.

I'm not a warlord. I'm not a king. I'm nothing anymore.

His mind screamed these words, but they felt more hollow each time. He wasn't a man anymore. He was just grief.

His hands shook violently, trying to steady his world, but it only worsened. The room spun; he couldn't see anymore, and it was all his fault.

I couldn't save him. He's gone because of me...

When his voice came, it was not filled with wrath. It was cold, like the sound of a grave being dug.

"Because we weren't meant to survive it."

Jorlan's gaze shifted, not defiant, but heavy. The weight of years that had never healed pressed in his chest.

"I used to think survival was victory," Jorlan said. "That if we lived, it meant we'd won."

"We did win," Ira said, his voice flat, unyielding.

Jorlan shook his head, eyes never leaving the glass in his hand.

"No. We just lasted longer than the others."

He turned the glass slowly, watching the light play off the liquid, as though it could explain something the words couldn't.

"I remember how you looked after Aerrith's boy was executed," Jorlan said, his voice distant now. "That was the first time I thought you might be gone."

Ira's gaze sharpened.

"He betrayed us."

"He was sixteen."

Ira's jaw tightened, his hands steady despite the storm that had lived in him for so long.

"He gave our outpost's coordinates to the enemy. They skinned our medics alive."

"I know," Jorlan said, his voice soft, hollow. "I was there."

The silence that followed stretched longer than the others. It didn't just hang. It settled, thick, making the room feel smaller, closing them in.

"You didn't even blink," Jorlan said, his words sharp but quiet. "When they dragged him out. When he begged."

Ira's voice came low. "He made a choice. And so did I. His life, my life. The weight of both lives has haunted me ever since."

"You didn't look at him."

"No."

"Because if you had," Jorlan said, his voice quiet but piercing, "you might've seen your reflection."

That hit something, deep. Not visibly, but it landed. Ira reached for the bottle and poured until the liquid almost overflowed.

Jorlan watched it rise.

"You remember when you taught me how to set my shoulder before a blade comes down?" he asked.

Ira gave a slight nod.

"You said, if you see it coming, it hurts less."

"I lied," Ira said, his voice low, stripped of softness.

Jorlan gave the faintest of smiles.

"I know."

He paused before setting his glass down with careful deliberation.

"I'm not ready to say it yet," he said. "But you know I didn't come here just to drink."

Ira's shoulders shifted, the smallest movement, ready, waiting.

"I know," he said, his voice quiet, unbothered by the weight between them.

"But for one more moment," Jorlan said, his voice raw now, "can we sit here like it used to be? Just a little longer. Before it breaks."

Ira didn't nod.

He didn't have to. The fire answered for him.

Jorlan reached into his coat, slow and deliberate, and pulled something from the inside pocket. A length of crimson cloth, frayed at the edges, stained in places with oil and old blood. He laid it on the table without ceremony.

Ira looked at it, but said nothing.

"You kept mine," Jorlan said, his voice quieter now, softer, as if the weight of the moment threatened to crush him. "Even after the rite."

Ira didn't answer. His eyes remained fixed, unblinking.

"It was the binding ribbon," Jorlan continued. "From the Sanguine Vow. They gave us new ones every cycle. But this one... this was from our first."

The fire popped, sudden and sharp, as if something inside it had cracked.

"I wore this for twelve years," Jorlan said, his voice rough, a distant sorrow in his eyes. "Tied it to my gauntlet. Never once took it off. Even when it got soaked in blood. Even when it hardened into leather. I told the recruits it was a relic. They believed me."

A breath left him then, not a sigh. Something deeper, emptier.

"They never knew it was yours."

Ira's voice came low, carved from stone.

"I remember when I gave it to you."

Jorlan nodded, his gaze distant.

"You said I'd never be alone as long as I carried your fire."

He traced a line along the edge of the cloth with steady fingers, though his voice had begun to fray.

"I did carry it. Even when I started to lose you."

Ira's jaw worked, just slightly. A small movement, barely seen, but it was there. Real.

"You didn't lose me."

Jorlan looked up, meeting his eyes. The flicker of the hearthlight danced between them, like a heartbeat with no rhythm.

"No," Jorlan said, gently. "You lost yourself."

The ribbon sat between them now, like a grave neither one of them was ready to dig. The bottle was half-empty, no more toasts, no more stories.

Jorlan sat with his hands folded over the ribbon, his posture worn, weary. The fire still burned, but neither of them looked at it anymore.

"You always knew how to keep men alive," Jorlan said, his voice quiet, cracking, "but you never cared if they stayed whole."

Ira didn't answer, not with words. He reached forward, slow and deliberate, taking the ribbon, folding it once, then again, until it was no more than a dark line in his palm.

"Speak," he said.

It was not a command. It was a request. And that was worse.

Jorlan closed his eyes, letting the weight of the moment drag him down.

"I was at the raid on Arestyn's convoy," he said, his voice breaking. "Two months ago. You remember the reports. Said the Red Hands ambushed us. Killed our people. Burned the supplies."

Ira's eyes narrowed, just slightly.

"I remember."

"They didn't ambush us," Jorlan said, the words landing like a drop of poison in water. Slow. Spreading.

Ira didn't move.

"They were surrendering," Jorlan said, his voice barely above a whisper. "White flags. Empty hands. We had the high ground. Orders were to eliminate. No prisoners."

"And you followed them."

Jorlan nodded. No defence. No resistance.

"Yes."

"But you came back changed."

Jorlan looked at him. No masks. Nothing hidden now. Just the grief.

"Because I saw what we did," he said. "I saw the fire in their eyes. The children. The ones who ran back into the smoke to pull their brothers out."

He paused, and for a moment, his voice softened.

"They looked like us."

Ira's voice was low now, rough like stone breaking under the weight of years.

"Then why did you stay?"

"Because I thought I could fix it from inside."

"And now?"

Jorlan didn't look away.

"I can't fix what you've become."

That was the crack. The one that couldn't be taken back. The one that had waited behind every silence, every memory, every glass of firelight.

"I joined them," Jorlan said, his voice breaking, the confession jagged and raw. "The Red Hands."

The room stopped breathing. The words hung in the air, heavy, bitter.

"I gave them intel. Nothing that risked your life. Nothing that would put you in a sniper's scope. But I helped them. Because they're trying to end the cycle. They believe in something that isn't built from bones."

Ira's hands tightened around the ribbon, the cloth pressing into his palm as if trying to crush the reality of what he had just heard.

"You betrayed me."

"No," Jorlan said, and his voice cracked again. "I tried to save you."

For a long time, Ira didn't speak. He stared at the cloth in his hand, as if it was a thing he had never seen before. Something foreign.

And when he spoke, his voice had changed. It was different now. He had become something else in that moment.

"You were the last one," he said, his words like a blade to the heart. "The last one I hadn't burned."

Jorlan stood. He didn't raise his voice. Didn't plead. He simply stood, as if the act itself might steady what had begun to break.

"I wanted to tell you," he said. "But I didn't know if there was anything left in you that could still hear it."

Ira didn't look up. His hand still held the folded ribbon, his other curling slowly into a fist.

"I gave you everything," he said. "Do you understand that? I gave you rank. Blood. A name that no one would dare spit on. I gave you more than I had left."

"I know."

"No," Ira said, rising now. Not quickly, but with the steady movement of stone rising from the deep. "You don't. Because if you knew, you would not have come here with that lie in your mouth."

"It's not a lie," Jorlan said. "It's the only truth I have left."

The fire flickered. The wind outside howled through a crack in the ruined stone, brushing past them like a warning too late to matter.

"I watched men die for you," Jorlan said, his voice quieter now, but still holding the weight of everything. "I sent boys to their deaths believing it would make you proud."

Ira's voice was a whisper now, but it hit harder than any blow.

"And did it?"

"No," Jorlan said, his eyes finally closing, surrendering. "Because it didn't make me proud."

He stepped forward. Just one pace. No threat. No challenge.

"I believed in you more than I believed in the gods. And I would have followed you into the abyss. But you stopped climbing out."

"You think I became a tyrant," Ira said, the words cutting through the air like an edge.

"You think I lost myself."

"I think you buried yourself," Jorlan said. "Because the boy I knew wouldn't have ordered children to be silenced. Wouldn't have called mercy weakness. Wouldn't have turned survival into a throne built from screams."

Ira looked up. His eyes burned, but not with rage. Not yet. Not with the fury that scorched cities. This was something colder, deeper. The fury of a man whose heart had remembered how to break.

"You think I don't remember who I was?"

Jorlan nodded, his eyes glinting with something like grief.

"I think you remember every day. And I think that's why you kill louder now."

Ira stepped past the table. Not toward Jorlan, but past him. As if trying to walk away from the weight of the room. But the ghosts followed him.

He stopped before the broken statue of Saint Vaerin. Just the torso now, the head long gone, the sword rusted to its hilt.

"We buried them here," Ira said, his voice low, heavy. "The ones who didn't beg."

Jorlan turned to him, the weight of the past closing in.

"I know."

"The priests wanted to sanctify the ground. Make them martyrs."

"I remember."

Ira placed the ribbon at the base of the statue. He let his fingers linger there for a moment, before speaking again.

"But you and I," he said, voice quieter now, "we didn't let them."

"No," Jorlan agreed, his voice thick with the memory of it.

"Because they weren't martyrs. They weren't heroes. They were just us."

Jorlan nodded, but his voice caught before it could leave him.

"And now," he said, his words barely more than a whisper, "I don't even know if we were ever worth remembering."

Ira's voice dropped, a flicker of something deeper in it.

"You are."

Jorlan looked at him then, his eyes searching, as if trying to find the truth behind those words.

"But not me?"

Ira's gaze lifted, his face turning toward the shattered ceiling. The wind tore through the cracks in the stone, brushing across his skin like absolution denied.

"I stopped being worth remembering the day I started needing the screams."

The room fell into silence, a weight that neither could escape. Then Jorlan's voice broke through, soft and barely audible.

"I know."

Ira returned to the table, but this time he didn't pour another drink. He sat heavily, as though the weight of everything had gathered in his limbs, pulling him down. He looked at Jorlan with eyes that had razed cities and now, those same eyes couldn't raze this.

"I gave you a name," Ira said, his voice raw, as if testing the air with the words.

"You did."

"I gave you power."

"You did."

"I gave you my life."

Jorlan nodded, the gravity of it all settling between them.

"And then I gave you mine."

The wind howled again outside, colder now. The fire bent inward, shying away from the intensity of the moment.

Ira leaned forward, resting his elbows on the table. His voice dropped lower, as though the question weighed too much for him to ask.

"Do you still love me, brother?"

Jorlan didn't flinch. He met Ira's eyes, his voice steady, though it carried the weight of the truth.

"Yes," he said. "Enough to walk away."

Ira didn't speak immediately. He sat motionless, his hands flat on the table, his shoulders drawn tight as though chiselled from stone. The fire behind him had shrunk, pulling inward, burning low in the hearth, as if even it feared witnessing what was coming next.

Outside, the wind screamed. Not loud. Not wild. But sharp. A blade dragging itself through the broken ribs of the cathedral, threading through stone and bone, whispering old names in a voice too thin to carry. Dust spiralled from the cracks in the ceiling, cold air licking the back of Ira's neck. And still, he didn't move.

Jorlan watched him, silent. Not from fear, not anymore. But from recognition. He had seen this before. The stillness before the breaking.

"I was thirteen," Ira said finally, his voice low and almost slurred, as though the liquor had thickened it, but there was a clarity underneath, sharp and brutal. "When I killed my first man."

Jorlan didn't interrupt. He simply listened, the weight of Ira's words sinking into the silence.

"Not in a war. Not on a field. Just a back alley. Just a knife."

He didn't blink.

"He had food. My brother didn't."

Jorlan said nothing, his eyes fixed on Ira as the words bled from him.

"I stabbed him in the stomach. Four times. He cried. I remember the sound more than the blood."

Ira's hand flexed at the table, fingers curling and uncurling as though the memory had taken hold of them.

"It was the first time my hand stopped shaking."

Jorlan's voice was dry when it came, like dust against the wind.

"And now?"

Ira flexed his fingers slowly, as if testing them, trying to feel for the difference.

"Now I shake when I don't kill."

His gaze lifted then, meeting Jorlan's, but for the first time, his eyes didn't burn. They ached. Heavy, haunted, hollow.

"I built all of this so we'd never go hungry again," Ira said, his voice ragged. "I turned Pyrrha into a machine that could devour gods if it had to."

"I know," Jorlan said softly.

"I did it for us."

"I know," Jorlan repeated, his voice a whisper now.

Ira looked toward the fire, his reflection dancing in it. But something else had moved behind the flame.

A boy.

Just standing there. Watching.

Small. Barefoot. Dirt on his face. Hands clenched at his sides. His eyes wide, empty, but unafraid. Not angry. Just there.

Ira blinked. The image flickered.

Gone.

No. Still there.

He looked away quickly, downing the rest of his drink in one throw. The burn wasn't enough to chase the shadow from his mind.

He spoke again, rougher now.

"You think I want to be this? You think I don't remember what we were?"

He slammed the glass down on the table. It didn't shatter. It just echoed, the sound filling the room with a weight that neither could escape.

Jorlan's voice cut through the tension, not to defy, but to reflect it.

"I think the boy who carried me through sniper fire would be afraid of the man sitting in front of me."

The wind shrieked through the shattered arch above them, carrying with it the weight of a thousand unspoken things. The fire flickered, casting long, trembling shadows on the walls.

The boy remained in the corner, watching. Silent. His gaze didn't speak. It bore down on them, the weight of all Ira had buried in his past. His presence stretched the silence, a quiet so heavy it no longer felt shared. It was fractured, splintered between them, as if the space itself had been torn wide open.

Ira leaned back in his chair, slower now, as if the weight in his chest had thickened into stone. His breath came heavier. Not laboured, but uneven. One eye on the fire, one ear on the wind.

He didn't look at the corner again. But he didn't have to. The boy was closer now. Near the wall. Near the broken statue. Still barefoot. Still watching.

Still saying nothing, the boy remained in the corner, a quiet observer of the unravelling truth.

Ira's hands moved to his temples, massaging them as if he could squeeze the presence out of his skull, forcing the memories back where they came from.

"You ever wonder," Ira murmured, his voice carrying a weight that could no longer be ignored, "what would've happened if we'd died young?"

Jorlan didn't reply immediately. He let Ira's words hang in the air, like a question that carried more weight than he was ready to give voice to.

"Before the arena. Before the ranks. Before the blood got... addictive."

His voice cracked on the last word, just slightly, an unspoken acknowledgment of the rawness he'd buried long ago.

"I used to dream about it," Ira went on, his voice distant now, as if lost in the past. "Us, in a different city. With names no one feared. Eating bread that didn't taste like iron. Laughing at things that weren't born in fire."

He laughed then, but it was hollow, an empty sound scraping the inside of his throat, not reaching the air.

Jorlan watched him carefully, reading the sorrow etched in every line of his face.

"You sound like someone who remembers what peace tasted like," Jorlan said, his voice quiet, as though he were stepping into a delicate truth.

Ira's gaze shot toward him, sharp, but only for a moment.

"I sound like someone who never had it and still fucking mourns it."

Suddenly, he stood, too fast. The chair scraped against the stone, an abrupt sound that echoed in the room. He turned his back to the fire, to Jorlan, to everything.

But his eyes, those eyes, found the corner.

The boy was there.

Closer now.

Just a few feet from the edge of the light.

Ira's fists clenched. Then opened. Then clenched again, as if the presence in the corner was a weight he couldn't lift.

"Don't look at me like that," he muttered, his voice quieter than the storm outside, a tremor in it that spoke of something fragile breaking inside him.

Jorlan rose then, his movement slow, as if he were afraid of shattering something in the air.

"Ira."

But Ira didn't hear him. Or didn't want to.

"Don't you dare," Ira whispered again, not to Jorlan, but to the boy.

"You didn't live this. You didn't make the calls. You didn't wake up every day to bodies stacked like prayer stones."

Jorlan moved beside him now, slow. Careful.

"Ira," he said again. "There's no one there."

Ira turned his face halfway, his eyes avoiding Jorlan's, but the tension between them grew heavier, unbearable.

"You don't see him?"

Jorlan looked, scanning the corner, the shadows, the emptiness.

The corner was empty. Nothing but stone and shadow.

"No," he said, his voice quiet, almost tender.

Ira's voice dropped to a whisper, barely audible.

"He's me."

A long pause stretched between them, thick with the weight of truth neither wanted to acknowledge. Then, Ira spoke again, his words carrying the full weight of everything he had locked inside for so long.

"No. He's what's left."

Ira turned back toward the hearth, but his posture had changed. Shoulders slumped. Chest hollow. His breathing was ragged now, not from exertion, but with a kind of disbelief.

A part of him had always known this day would come. And still, he wasn't ready.

"He watched me kill my humanity," Ira said, his voice breaking. "Every time I told myself it was justice. Every time I said the fire was holy. Every time I walked past the bodies and told my men to step over them like broken branches."

The boy moved closer.

He was at the edge of the light now.

And Ira couldn't look at him anymore.

Ira paced across the stone floor, just one step, enough to feel the weight shift beneath his boots. Then he turned, eyes on Jorlan, his face shadowed by the hearth behind him.

"You think I did this to be feared?" he said. "You think I built a throne from bone because I wanted to sit alone?"

Jorlan didn't speak.

"I did it for you," Ira said, his voice rising. Not in anger, but in defence. "For Pyrrha. For every one of us that bled in the gutters while nobles passed us with eyes clean of guilt. I made wrath holy because no one else would."

His voice was louder now, not just rising, but reaching for something deeper.

"I killed for you. I became this for you. Because I loved you too much to let the world break you like it broke me."

He took a step forward, hand to his chest, as if trying to rip the words from somewhere deeper.

"I loved you. Don't you see that?"

A pause. Stillness. A heartbeat stretched thin.

And then...

From behind him, the voice broke through the silence.

Small.

Soft.

Cold.

"You lie."

Ira froze.

Every muscle in his body locked, as though struck by an invisible force. The weight of the words fell upon him, unbearable and suffocating. His chest tightened, his breath stilled, and the room seemed to tilt just slightly, as if the world itself were trying to tear away from him.

The boy stood there, his eyes wide, dark, and so familiar it hurt. He was a ghost, a piece of the past given flesh, a wound that had never truly healed.

Ira's mouth opened, but no sound came. His throat felt tight, as though the words were too heavy to lift.

The boy didn't move. Didn't blink.

He stood there, unwavering, a reminder of everything Ira had buried.

"You lie," the boy repeated, his voice softer this time, yet no less cutting. The words settled into the air between them, heavy with the weight of undeniable truth.

And with those two words, the world unstitched.

Ira staggered back, one step, then two. His eyes darted around the room, desperate to unsee him, as if looking away could erase the weight the boy carried. But it didn't. The boy was not just a vision, he was the ghost of everything Ira had done.

"No," he whispered, the sound barely leaving his lips, a faint plea to undo the revelation.

"You didn't become this for him," the boy said, each word sharp and accusing. The silence between them seemed to stretch, as if the walls themselves were listening, waiting for Ira to break.

The words didn't echo, but they stayed. They clung to him, heavy, saturated with truth. They were a mirror that he couldn't look away from, a reflection of his own fear, his own self-deception. The boy's voice, small but so steady, echoed through Ira's memories, those dark alleys and desperate cries.

"You did it because you were afraid," the boy said, and the finality of the statement landed like a hammer.

Ira froze, the truth of it crashing through him like a tidal wave. The weight of it bent him, shattered him.

He collapsed into the nearest chair, his body giving way like a monument crumbling under its own weight. His chest heaved with each breath, but his hands shook, powerless to steady him. The room felt too small, too tight, the very air pushing in on him.

"You were afraid that if you didn't become fire, you'd be nothing but smoke. Forgotten. Weak. Gone."

"Stop," Ira whispered, the words thick with pain, but the boy did not stop. He couldn't. Because the truth had already been said.

"You burned them all because you were afraid they'd leave. That Jorlan would leave. That he'd see the real you and turn away."

Tears welled in Ira's eyes now.

Not falling. Not yet.

But they were there.

The weight of them sat on his lashes, the promise of release, but still held at bay by the fierce dam he had built inside. He could feel them, each one pressing harder, threatening to spill, but his body wouldn't let it. Not yet.

The boy took one step forward. Just one.

And it was enough. The space between them seemed to narrow, as though the room itself was holding its breath.

"You don't kill because you're strong," the boy said, his voice cutting through the air like a blade. "You kill because you're still that boy in the mud, begging the world to look away while you cried."

That did it.

Ira's breath cracked, breaking the fragile quiet around them. His hands flew to his face. Not to hide the tears, but to hold his skull together, as if he feared it might finally split under the pressure of everything he had locked inside. His entire body trembled. But it was the weight in his chest that nearly crushed him. The unbearable weight of guilt, regret, and years of silence.

"I didn't want this," he choked, his voice shaking with the force of his unravelling. "I didn't... I never..."

But the words wouldn't finish. They caught in his throat, lost to the weight of everything he couldn't say, everything he had buried too deep to remember.

The boy stared at him, unwavering. Silent.

Jorlan stood still, his own breath shallow, as he watched Ira crack. And now, perhaps, Jorlan understood. Not what Ira saw, but what Ira was breaking under: the weight of all the lies, all the guilt, all the shattered parts of himself he had been running from.

"I thought if I killed enough of them," Ira said, his voice cracking open, raw and broken, "the boy would stop watching."

Ira staggered back, his knees almost buckling as his hands shot up to his head, gripping his skull like he could contain the horror flooding through him.

The words hung in the air, a jagged memory, tearing him apart from the inside. His chest tightened, suffocating under the weight of years of decisions. The boy, the one who used to cry in the alleys of a city now burnt to ash, was still there. He could feel the ghost of him, every moment of their shared pain, watching him from the shadows.

Ira closed his eyes briefly, the vision of that boy, himself, blurring in front of him like a ghost, a child he had tried to bury in the dirt with the rest of his sins. But no matter how many men he killed, no matter how many bodies piled in his wake, the boy never stopped watching. He never stopped haunting him.

He meant the boy, his past, the man he used to be.

But the boy never left.

The words hit him like a hammer. His body trembled, hands shaking, as the weight of the years crushed down on him. Every breath felt like it might be his last. The room swirled around him, the walls closing in as if he were being suffocated by everything he had lost and everything he had killed. He tried to push it away, to ignore it, but the boy would not let him. His chest heaved with a ragged breath, struggling to find air, to find something, anything, to hold onto.

Ira's words hung in the air, and with them, the weight of the room shifted. The air had changed. It wasn't colder, but it felt like it should be. The kind of chill that comes not from the wind, but from the soul beginning to shut its windows, closing off everything it couldn't bear to face.

The hearth now gave off barely enough light to cast their shadows, and the walls around them had disappeared into a quiet that felt thick, suffocating, like velvet draped over a corpse.

Ira sat slumped in the chair, elbows on his knees, his breath coming slow but uneven. His face was buried in his hands, as though he could block the world out. His voice was barely a scrape, a sound so broken it barely reached the air.

"Why won't he go?"

Jorlan stood nearby, silent. Still. His presence like a rock in the midst of a storm. He didn't move. Didn't speak. He knew better than to fill the space with words that weren't needed.

Ira's voice came again, raw, cracking like shattered glass.

"He was supposed to be gone," he said. "He died the day I chose the throne. I buried him with the last of our brothers."

Ira looked up, his eyes meeting Jorlan's. But there was no recognition in them anymore. No recognition of the man he had once been. Only a void. A chasm where everything he had buried now began to surface, rising to the surface of his consciousness, demanding to be seen.

The boy now stood less than ten feet from him.

He was silent.

His face unreadable.

But his presence screamed louder than fire ever could.

"I used to think I'd killed him," Ira whispered, his voice trembling now. "That he was the price. That if I bled enough men into the soil, the memory would rot too."

He shook his head slowly, trembling, his hands shaking as if to reject the truth of it, to deny the power of the memory that had clawed its way back into the forefront of his mind.

"But he just watches," Ira said, his voice now a hollow echo of despair. "Every time. After every execution. After every city falls. He waits. And he watches."

He turned to Jorlan now, eyes wide, wet with something that wasn't fear. It was recognition. The horror of finally seeing what's been behind your eyes all your life.

"I thought I was building a world where boys like him didn't have to starve."

Jorlan knelt, slowly. He was level with Ira now. His voice, when it came, was low, steady, but carrying a weight that matched Ira's.

"You thought wrong. That doesn't make you a monster."

Ira laughed then. A sound so wrong, so hollow, it seemed to have forgotten what laughter was supposed to be.

"It doesn't?" he said, voice breaking, the disbelief hanging in his words. "I scorched a whole village because one elder lied to my face. I let my men drown the town of Verridyn for not opening their gates fast enough."

Jorlan's voice barely held together, the weight of his own emotions straining the words.

"I know."

"I executed my own captain because he hesitated," Ira continued, his voice tight, each word digging deeper into the silence. "He hesitated, Jorlan."

The boy took one step closer.

Just one.

He was now just within reach of the firelight. The warmth from the hearth seemed to shrink away from him, as if even the flame was unwilling to touch the truth that was about to be laid bare.

The boy didn't blink.

Didn't breathe.

And Ira looked at him, his eyes wide, his breath short, as though the very air had become too heavy to bear. It felt like looking into a wound no doctor could close, a pain too deep to be stitched.

"I needed to make sure no one ever hesitated again," Ira said, his voice growing sharp, desperate. The words fell from him like stones, each one heavier than the last. "Because hesitation lets the gods kill us. Hesitation gets your mother raped in front of you. Hesitation is the difference between dying in an alley or living long enough to become a god."

He looked back at Jorlan then, his chest tight, his hands trembling as though they might break under the weight of his confession.

"But gods aren't meant to weep, are they?"

The boy moved.

He stepped closer to the chair.

Right beside Ira.

Still, no words. No condemnation.

Just presence.

And that was worse. Because Ira knew what it meant. There was no judgment here, no anger. Just the silent, unrelenting weight of everything Ira had become, everything he had buried beneath the blood, beneath the years, beneath the ashes of choices he could no longer escape.

The boy didn't move. Didn't blink. He stood beside Ira, not as a memory, but as the weight of all he had buried. Silent. Still. His eyes carved the silence deeper, the echo of every scream Ira had tried to bury.

No words came from him.

But his gaze was a weight that pressed harder than silence.

And somehow, that was what made Ira stand.

Slowly.

Unsteadily.

As if the act of rising from that chair was the last piece of strength his body could afford. His knees buckled as he stood, but he held himself upright, facing Jorlan with the finality of a man who knew he had no other choice.

"I could let you go," Ira said, voice hoarse. "I could pretend I didn't hear what you said. That this night didn't happen."

Jorlan stayed still. His eyes locked with Ira's, silent, waiting for what came next.

"I could tell myself that you were just afraid. That you got confused. That you were lied to. That your loyalty was... fractured. Not gone."

Still no answer.

"But that would be a lie," Ira said, his voice heavy with the burden of truth. "And I've had enough of those for one lifetime."

The boy stepped behind Ira now, his feet soft on the stone. No sound.

Ira's next words came slow, like they were heavier than any axe he'd ever lifted. His shoulders sagged under the weight of them, but he spoke them anyway.

"So I'm giving you one chance," he said, his voice soft but filled with a crushing weight. "Right here. Right now."

He took one step forward. The shadows behind him stretched like blades, a cold warning that could not be ignored.

"I want you to prove the oath still breathes."

Jorlan's expression did not change. But his breath caught. He understood what this meant, what Ira was asking of him.

Ira kept speaking, his words cutting through the thick air.

"You will lead a strike on the Red Hands' compound in Marrow Glen. Publicly. Visibly. And you will kill them all. No prisoners. No exceptions."

The wind returned, thin and whispering, curling around them like the breath of ghosts.

Ira stepped closer. The fire cast his face in uneven gold, a harsh light that made his eyes burn with a dark intensity.

"You will drag their leader into the square and sever his head with your own blade. And when they beg for mercy, if they do, you will not grant it."

The boy moved closer.

Ira's voice cracked, just once, the sound ripping through the tension like a rope snapping under strain.

"Then," he said, quieter now, "and only then... I will believe you still love me."

Jorlan looked at him, but not as a traitor. Not as a soldier. Not as the man who had stood beside him in war.

He looked at him as the boy who once bled beside him in the dirt.

"We don't bleed for kings," he said quietly. "We bleed for each other."

Ira's jaw tensed. Just faintly. Like a nerve remembering how to feel. But he said nothing. The words didn't come. He couldn't respond. Because he already knew.

Silence.

Thick.

Slow.

Crushing.

Jorlan's reply came not like defiance, but like a eulogy.

"I do love you."

He stepped forward now, until they were only inches apart, the space between them closing.

"I love you like the war never could. Like the blood never did. Like the boy behind you still does."

Ira flinched. Just once.

"But I won't kill for you anymore."

Ira stared at him, his eyes widening, something cracking inside him. Something in his chest caved. Just slightly. It was the breath of a man who had not lost power... but had lost permission to be believed.

"I won't desecrate the only part of you that's still human," Jorlan said, his voice steady, unwavering. "Even if you beg me to."

Another silence.

This one colder than the last. It filled the room like a suffocating weight, pressing down, making the air thicker. Every heartbeat seemed to stretch longer, each second an eternity.

The boy looked up at Ira now.

Still didn't speak.

But the weight of his gaze said enough. There was nothing more to be said between them. No words could undo what had been done, no words could erase the truth that lingered in the space between them. His eyes, those dark, unblinking eyes, spoke volumes Ira couldn't deny.

Ira's mouth trembled.

He tried to speak. The words sat heavy on his tongue, thick and suffocating. But nothing came. Not a sound. Just the hollow emptiness of a man who had run out of reasons to justify the things he had done.

And in that moment, the final thread between them broke.

Between all three of them.

The sound of boots on stone.

Not hurried.

Not thunderous.

Just exact.

Each step was a judgment. Each echo a verdict. A reminder that there was no escaping the moment that was coming. It wasn't fate. It was inevitability.

Jorlan turned first. The motion was slow, as though he was weighed down by the gravity of what was about to unfold.

Ira didn't move. Couldn't. His body felt rooted to the ground, as though the very weight of his choices had shackled him to the floor.

From the shadows, she emerged, her form haloed by the last flickering embers of the hearth.

General Callistra Vhailar.

The Burning Vow.

Her armour pulsed with the quiet thrum of smouldering veins, as though the blood of gods had seeped into her obsidian skin. The flaming sigil on her chest flickered with a life of its own, as if it could hear the betrayal thickening the air, as if it recognized the moment of reckoning. Behind her, the war-cloak dragged like a banner, torn and scorched, a testament to battles that refused to die.

She did not reach for her halberd.

She did not need to.

Her presence alone shifted the room. Reality itself seemed to harden around her, a palpable force that threatened to crush everything in its path.

As if the laws of Pyrrha reasserted themselves with every step she took, every movement a declaration that whatever came next was not a choice, it was a calling.

Ira looked up slowly. His eyes heavy, as if the effort of simply meeting her gaze was more than he could bear.

"Callistra," he said, his voice barely more than a breath, a whisper caught in the winds of fate.

She bowed her head once. Deep. Formal. Ritualistic. As though the moment demanded respect, even if there was no love left to give.

"My Warlord."

Jorlan stood still, his stance unwavering, but his hand did not reach for a weapon. There was no need. Not anymore. He saw it in her eyes, this wasn't war. It was sacrament. A sacred duty that had to be carried out, no matter the cost.

Callistra looked at Ira, her expression unreadable beneath the shadow of her scars, but there was no mistaking the weight of her gaze. She saw through him. Through everything.

"I heard your voice," she said softly. "Heard it falter."

The boy behind Ira now stood just beyond his shoulder, eyes fixed on Callistra.

Silent. Steady.

The boy didn't move. Didn't blink. His presence was more than enough, a presence that held the room in its thrall.

Ira shook his head slowly, as if trying to wake from something. A nightmare he couldn't escape.

"No," he said, the word scraping against the air. His voice, raw and desperate, broke through the silence, but there was no denying it, this was happening. "Not this. Not him."

Callistra took another step forward, her boots striking the stone with a finality that sent a tremor through Ira's chest.

"He made his choice," she said, her voice calm but firm. "He refused your will."

Jorlan looked at her. Not with fear. But with something worse.

Recognition. The understanding that this was not a fight. This was not a decision for survival. This was the end of everything.

"You don't have to do this," Ira said, stumbling forward. His voice cracked under the weight of his own desperation. "I didn't give the order."

The words felt weak the moment they left his mouth. He knew it, she knew it, and Jorlan knew it. The order didn't matter anymore. Not when everything had already been set in motion.

Callistra looked at him with something close to pity.

It wasn't the pity of contempt or judgment, but something colder, something that felt like the quiet sadness of someone who knew exactly what had been lost and what had already been taken.

"No," she said, her voice soft, almost gentle. "But you lost the strength to."

She turned her head then, her movements deliberate and unhurried. Her eyes met Jorlan's.

And in that violet light, there was no hatred. There was no anger. There was only the flame of faith, a fire that had once burned bright in them both, now flickering in the quiet between them.

"You broke the vow," she said, her voice soft but certain, the weight of it making the air feel heavier. "But I remember it. For both of us."

Jorlan didn't move.

He didn't beg.

He didn't fight.

He looked at Ira then. And smiled.

It was a smile so soft, so broken, that it could have shattered the world if it had tried.

"You bled for me," Jorlan said, his voice shaking slightly, betraying the weight of the years that had passed between them. "But somewhere along the way, you forgot how to stop."

His eyes didn't accuse.

They mourned.

Like a brother staring up at the man who had once carried him through fire, only to see the man reduced to ashes.

"You bled so long," Jorlan whispered, the words almost lost in the thick air. "You forgot how to heal."

A breath. A break. The room held its breath with him.

"And now the wound walks."

He looked at Ira. Not with fear. Not even sorrow.

Just love. In its last surviving form.

"I forgive you," he said.

The words hung in the air, as if they were too much to bear, too heavy to be set free. And then, without another word, Jorlan made his move.

One clean motion.

The Sanguinar Halberd unslung, ignited with a hiss of flame that shattered the stillness.

It severed the silence.

The blade struck.

Not brutally. Not cruelly.

Just... completely.

Jorlan fell without sound.

No scream. No shout. No battle cry.

Only the soft rustle of cloth over stone. A body returning to the ground it once crawled through, an offering to the past that would never be forgotten.

The silence that followed was absolute.

Ira's breath hitched violently, rising up his throat like a scream caught in his chest. His knees buckled, and his hands, useless, trembling, shot out as if trying to catch Jorlan's body from the fall, but he was too slow, too late. His chest tightened, a vise squeezing the air from his lungs. He couldn't catch his breath. He couldn't breathe.

His hands gripped his knees, knuckles white, and he felt like his entire body was splintering. The weight of the loss was too much. His vision blurred, his thoughts unravelling as his mind snapped under the pressure of what he had just lost.

Ira took a step toward the body, his legs shaking beneath him, as if each step brought him closer to the truth he couldn't escape.

But the body did not look like a traitor.

It looked like a boy he'd carried once. A boy he had failed.

A boy who had stood by him in the darkest places, a boy whose name was woven into the very fabric of his soul.

He opened his mouth to scream.

But no sound came. Only a breath. Sharp. Inward.

Like a soul being buried alive. As if the scream had been locked away inside him, the final cry for everything that was lost.

His knees gave way. Not from pain.

From the weight of a name he could never speak again.

Ira collapsed to his knees, his chest heaving, his face empty of all emotion except the suffocating ache of loss.

A single breath filled the empty air, thick and unrelenting.

Jorlan's ribbon slipped from his fingers and drifted onto the hearthstone, its fall a silent prayer that was swallowed by the room. The fire cracked once as a lone ember tumbled into ash.

The boy was gone.

Callistra stood still, blood hissing on the blade, her eyes unwavering, her presence like the calm before a storm.

She turned back to Ira, her voice low, but carrying the weight of something final, something that could not be undone.

"You will not remember this as weakness," she said, her words sharp as iron, etched with the finality of a judgment that had already been passed. "You will remember it as loyalty."

She left the halberd in the stone floor, a quiet marker of what had just transpired. And she walked out into the ash.

"If the wound still watches, it means the blade is still buried in your chest. And no amount of pretending will make it go away."

Null Gospel, Book I, Verse 6.

***

CHAPTER SIX:

Ashes Beneath the Laughter

"We do not fight for honour, nor for victory. We fight because death has already claimed us…and survival is the only rebellion left."

Fragment of the Exiled Codex, Volume I, Tablet 7.

There is a silence that lives inside the bones of old walls, one that does not arrive with the ending of speech, but with the aftermath of truth. In Pyrrha's gladiatorial dining hall, that silence had not come to be heard. It had come to be felt.

The air stank of charred meat and iron. The bowls, stained with grease, sat where they always did, around the same splintered tables, among killers and kings forged in circumstance. But something had shifted. A heaviness hung in the air, like smoke after a fire. Hurriyah Sunshadow had spoken, not as a man, but as memory, a living consequence. His words did not crush; they hollowed. And in that hollow, the laughter had died.

Those who had laughed now stirred less. Those who had spoken too freely now glanced toward the floor or their cups. Even those born of violence, those who named themselves storm and sword, found no comfort in the silence that followed.

Near the edge of the hall, far from the flicker of torchlight, a nameless gladiator sat alone, his bowl untouched. The stew had gone cold. Grease floated on its surface like oil on stagnant water. He didn't move. Didn't blink. Only breathed.

His spine was bent, not from age, but from memory. His body told stories no one had asked to hear. Scars framed his shoulders in even spacing, each one a measure of time. They weren't earned in battle. They were given, like hours in a sentence.

He had seen Hurriyah before. Not here. Long ago, beyond the auction pit in the slums of Kadesh. He had been a boy then, or close to it. The Shackled King was paraded before merchants and war-bloods alike, wrapped in ash and silence. A Warlord had applied the brand five times, and Hurriyah had not screamed once. Smoke rose. Flesh cracked. The silence never broke.

The boy had watched. And now the man remembered.

He stared at the grain of the table. His hand hovered over the wooden spoon, but did not touch it.

One word slipped past his lips, almost inaudible.

"Unbroken."

Not a prayer. Not praise. A confirmation.

A sacred stillness followed. No one looked at Hurriyah. They didn't need to. The moment was his, a private weight of memory. But around the table, subtle shifts, eyes avoiding, hands twitching, revealed that it wasn't just his silence. It was theirs, too.

Hurriyah had spoken like a wound remembering the knife. And the wound had spoken back.

Some truths do not echo. They remain.

And yet the hall still breathed. Voices rose again, though quieter than before. Tankards moved. Jokes were offered, though no one truly laughed. Around them, the stone remembered every word, every pause, every unspoken fear clawing at the edge of their composure.

In the middle of it all, among the defiant and the broken, sat Sera Zahara. She had not raised her cup. She had not spoken the toast. She had not looked away. While the others tried to stitch themselves back into noise, she remained still, not untouched, but unchanged. Not outside the silence, but inside it, where it lived and waited.

Sera Zahara had listened, she always did. Her honey-gold eyes flickered in the candlelight, sharp as ever. Unmoved, yet watching, measuring the weight of what had settled over the table.

She had heard them speak of honour, of suffering, of the inevitability of death.

And now, she had heard him. The man who rarely spoke. The man whose presence carried the gravity of something long buried.

Something waiting to ignite.

Hurriyah's words still clung to the air like the dying embers of a fire that refused to be snuffed out.

Hurriyah hadn't moved in minutes. Not to drink. Not to eat. He sat still as iron, shoulders squared beneath the tattered Firebrand cloak, molten eyes fixed on a memory no one else could see.

No one dared interrupt.

He didn't command silence.

He became it.

Across the flickering hall, the din softened as if the walls themselves understood what lived inside him. The brazier's heat kissed his skin, but it was not warmth he felt.

It was the brand.

A phantom pain that never left.

He could still smell the smoke. Brimstone and burning flesh.

He could still hear the laughter of Warlord Midas. Opulent. Monstrous. As the iron was pressed to his arm.

"A king who kneels is no king at all," Midas had said.

"But you? You'll make a fine pet."

That day, Hurriyah did not scream.

But his silence screamed for him.

And afterward, when the chains cooled and the sigil of Pyrrha's ownership burned across his flesh, he looked not at his captors... but at his own kin. The ones who had betrayed him. Who had sold him.

And he chose, in that moment, to speak no oaths.

Only resolve.

He had been a king once, in name if not in seat. Now, he was something else.

Something sharpened by loss. Tempered by betrayal.

Around the table, the others shifted uncomfortably under the weight of his presence, though he had not spoken.

Not yet.

But when he finally did, it was not with anger.

It was with memory.

"You've mistaken the cage for a battlefield. One is meant to contain you. The other demands you choose what to die for."

Sera let the thought settle, rolling over it like a blade testing the weight of its edge. Then, at last, she smirked. A slow, knowing thing. Fleeting, but sharp as a knife drawn in the dark. Her voice, when it came, was smooth, tempered steel: a whisper of iron through silk.

Sera had not touched her drink. Not once.

She traced its rim with a single finger, slow, meticulous, as though listening to some inner echo only she could hear. Around her, voices lifted and fell like waves crashing against stone, but her stillness remained untouched. Absolute. The kind of quiet born not of detachment, but of training.

And memory.

She had learned silence in a cell without walls.

In the Soundless Ward, where Pyrrha's Inquisitors unmade people word by word, she was taught how to listen beyond noise. How to dissect truth from breath. Meaning from hesitation.

She had heard men scream until they forgot their names.

Heard mothers recite their children's names like mantras as their fingers were broken one by one.

Heard boys sing lullabies between sobs just to remind themselves they were still alive.

Sera had said nothing through it all.

They'd called it strength. They were wrong.

It was survival.

They broke her voice before they broke her bones, and in the end, it was the silence that remained. It clung to her like a second skin, more honest than flesh, more faithful than memory.

Her eyes scanned the table now. Not with judgment. Not even with empathy.

Only observation.

The way Sol's knee bounced just a beat too fast.

The shift in Luna's shoulders as she tracked a sound no one else noticed.

The hesitation in Valen's breath, masked by arrogance.

Everyone said something. Even in silence.

Especially in silence.

Her own fingers still moved, tracing the arc of the cup.

A woman screaming.

A child sobbing.

A name whispered, just once, before the door slammed shut.

That's the moment she lost hope.

Not when they tortured her.

Not when they stripped her rank and erased her from the registries.

But when she realized none of the other prisoners asked for her name. Because they knew it wouldn't matter.

They were already dead. They just hadn't stopped breathing yet.

Now, sitting at the table with warriors and ghosts alike, Sera tilted her head slightly. Just enough for the candlelight to catch the freckles scattered across her cheek, freckles untouched by the blood she'd learned to spill with elegance.

She did not fight for freedom.

She fought because death had stopped scaring her.

"You say that as if they were ever different."

She let the words rest between them, unhurried, unyielding. Her fingers traced the rim of her cup, the candlelight casting long shadows across the delicate constellation of freckles that dusted her cheek.

"Do you think the battlefield is any freer than the cage?" she asked, her tone devoid of mockery, devoid of pretence. Only curiosity, edged with something deeper. "Out there, they tell you when to charge, when to retreat. They give you a cause, and you bleed for it. Here, they tell you when to fight, when to fall. They give you an opponent, and you kill for it."

She exhaled softly, shaking her head, the smirk still lingering at the edge of her lips.

"The difference isn't in the chains, Sunshadow." Her gaze met his now, gold to molten gold, a quiet challenge. "It's in who holds them."

For a moment, silence reigned.

Then she leaned back, tilting her head ever so slightly.

"You speak of remembering what we pay for," she murmured, her voice a blade pressed against the throat of fate itself. "I've already made my payment. I just haven't decided when to collect."

With that, she withdrew, slipping back into the sanctuary of her silence. Not waiting for agreement. Not waiting for rebuttal. The words had been given. Whether they settled as truth or as an uncomfortable reminder was for them to decide.

Levik's voice rumbled from somewhere deep, rough with the weight of years spent in the pit and the price of survival. "Some of us fade into the sand, forgotten, others become legends. But in the end, the sand takes us all."

He exhaled, his gaze drifting toward the distant brazier, the flickering firelight painting his worn features in shadows. "I've seen too many bodies turn to dust. I've learned to believe in nothing else."

The table went still, the weight of his words sinking deep into the cracks of the stone. For a heartbeat, the air seemed thicker, heavier, until Raekor's voice cut through it, smooth but sharp.

"And what is it you want, Levik? To be remembered?"

Levik shook his head, his expression unreadable, as if carved from stone.

"No," he answered, his voice quieter now, the answer almost a whisper. "I just want to see the next sunrise."

Bakari's chuckle rumbled from the corner, a low, knowing sound, like the ember of a dying fire still holding heat.

"Funny, isn't it?" he said, his voice tinged with a darkness all its own. "We fight like gods, but we dream like beggars."

There was a pause, the silence stretching between them like a taut rope, until Lucius raised his mug. The weight of the moment hung in the air, and his voice, when it came, was softer, sincere, even.

"To the next sunrise, then," he said, his eyes meeting Levik's for a brief, fleeting moment. It was a toast, but more than that. It was a shared moment of fragile hope, something rare among these hardened souls.

One by one, they raised their cups. Even Valen, his arrogance dulled by something quieter, unspoken. Even Raekor, who found solace only in steel and vengeance. And for a fleeting moment, as fragile as a dying flame, they were not gladiators.

Not tools sharpened for the kill. Not names waiting to be swallowed by the sands of the arena. They were simply men and women drinking beneath the shadow of the inevitable.

But all moments pass. And so did this one.

The clamour of voices ebbed into something softer, something more distant, as though the very walls of the hall had swallowed the sound, leaving only the ghost of it behind. The warmth of company, of flesh and breath, faded into something colder, something detached. Toren barely noticed when the voices fell away.

The world still moved. The candlelight still flickered. The murmurs of the other gladiators still threaded through the air like the last notes of a dying melody. But for him, all of it dissolved into irrelevance.

Because across the table, Sera Zahara sat in her silence. She had not lifted her cup. She had not spoken the toast. And yet, of all those in the hall, she seemed the only one untouched by the weight of what had just passed.

The light caught in her honey-gold eyes, turning them into pools of molten amber, and for a moment, it was impossible to tell whether she was present in the hall at all, or lost in a world none of them could reach. She did not chase hope. She did not drink to the sunrise. Because Sera Zahara did not believe the sun would rise for everyone.

The others laughed. Boisterous. Reckless. Their words steeped in liquor and the fleeting comfort of companionship. They clung to this moment as if it could shield them from what came next, as if it could drown out the inevitable bloodshed waiting just beyond the horizon. But she remained unmoved.

Untouched.

Her honey-gold eyes were downcast, fixed not upon the table, nor the walls of the hall, but on something beyond. Something that none of them could see. None of them could reach. She was present, yet distant. Here, yet elsewhere. Toren did not know when he started watching her.

Or why. Only that he did.

The candlelight flickered, casting shifting shadows across her face, illuminating the delicate dusting of freckles that lay like whispered remnants of another life. A contrast to the warrior she had become. They were marks of a past untouched by blood and steel, the faintest echoes of a girl who had existed before the arena had claimed her.

A contradiction.

A paradox.

She was not fire, nor fury, nor the unrelenting weight of war. She was the space between. The breath before a blade met flesh. The pause in the crescendo of battle.

Toren's cybernetic limbs hummed beneath his skin, a whisper of machinery interwoven with muscle and bone, a constant reminder of what he had become. His body had been reforged in the crucible of war, twisted into something engineered for destruction. He was violence given form. A blade that never dulled. A weapon without the illusion of choice.

And yet, watching her, something else stirred within him. Something unfamiliar. He did not move. Did not speak. He only let himself drown in the quiet gravity she carried, in the weight of something he could not name. For the first time in what felt like an eternity, Toren was afraid. Not of the trials ahead. Not of pain. Not of death.

But of the realization that somewhere, beneath the steel, beneath the suffering, beneath the war-forged machine he had become, something human still existed. And she was proof of it.

The moment stretched, fragile as glass, infinite and fleeting all at once. Then, just as quickly as it had come, it was gone.

Sera's fingers curled, just slightly.

As if she had felt his gaze. As if she had sensed the shift in the air between them. But she did not look up. She did not need to.

The world bled back into motion around them. The weight of voices pressed against the silence that had momentarily stretched between them. Tankards clanked. Laughter rose and fell. The tide of war-forged camaraderie lapping against the edges of something unspoken. The din of the hall was a familiar beast, one that swallowed hesitation, doubt, and quiet truths whole.

But for Toren, something had shifted. A lingering resonance in the marrow of his bones. An echo of a moment that should not have mattered, but somehow did.

Sera remained still.

She did not shift her posture or acknowledge the tide of voices pulling her back into the present. The candlelight flickered, tracing firelight over her sun-kissed skin, illuminating the delicate constellation of freckles across her cheek. The quiet remnants of something untouched. Something soft beneath the tempered steel. And it unsettled him.

Not because she was beautiful, though she was, in a way that war could not erode. Not because she was deadly, though she was, with a grace that made death seem effortless.

But because in this moment, in the hush between battle and bloodshed, in the space between swords drawn and lives ended, she existed in a way that none of them did.

She was here and yet elsewhere. Watching something long past. Something no one else could see.

Toren exhaled, forcing himself to unclench the fingers he had not realized had curled into his palm. The hum of his cybernetic limbs whispered beneath his skin, a constant reminder of what he was. War, engineered. A thing reforged in blood and steel. Designed to kill. To survive. Nothing more.

And yet, as he looked at her, still, silent, unreadable, something in him wavered. Her fingers brushed against the wooden table in slow, absent motions, as though tracing the remnants of a song only she could hear.

The Crimson Blades rested against her thighs, silent now. But Toren knew their song would return when the time came. They always did.

In the old tongues, they were called The Scarlet Aria. A melody of steel and death. Their whispers laced with the echoes of those who had fallen before her. The blades had never known a master who had lived long enough to understand their true nature.

Was she different? Or was she merely waiting, waiting for the day they would turn against her, as they had all the others?

The thought sent a cold thread through him. And he did not know why.

He had seen Sera fight. Had seen the way she moved, a spectre of quiet destruction, a contradiction of fury and stillness. But this was different. Here, in this moment, there was no battle. No blood to spill. No fate to carve into the sand. Here, she was simply Sera. And it struck him then. He had never seen her outside of the storm.

A tankard slammed against wood. The sharp sound cut through the air like the first clash of steel in an arena. Someone had started another toast. Another moment of fleeting joy before the inevitable.

The gladiators cheered. They raised their drinks, throwing themselves into the fire of laughter and forgetfulness.

But the laughter was not whole. Not true. It was a performance. A defiance against the weight pressing against their backs. Because they all felt it.

The Test Trials loomed ahead, and the unspoken truth had settled among them like a spectre at the table. Even the torches lining the walls seemed dimmer now, their flickering light stretching shadows long and thin across the cracked stone floors, licking at the edges of their faces.

The remnants of their feast lay scattered. Half-torn bread. Grease-smeared plates. The unsteady slosh of untouched ale in forgotten cups. No one reached for more. It wasn't hunger that filled them now. It was something else. Something far colder.

And yet, beyond the ones whose names had already been carved into the annals of the arena, beyond the warriors who had forged their legacies in blood, they were there. The nameless. The forgotten.

Scattered through the dim-lit hall, they sat in silence. More echo than presence. No titles spoken in reverence. No names that earned a place in the conversation.

But they were there. Watching. Listening. Waiting.

Some were old. Their faces carved from the stone of past battles. Men and women who had fought longer than anyone cared to remember. They sat in the quiet edges of the hall, knowing their best days had already been lost to the sand.

Some were young. Too young. Eyes too wide, too unshaped by violence. They would not be the same tomorrow.

A pair of twin brothers, alike as reflections in water, whispered in a language that had long since been forgotten in the outside world. Their words were quiet, but their hands moved like soldiers mapping out a final strategy, as if planning could stave off fate.

A woman with an eyepatch and bandaged knuckles sat apart. Arms crossed. Jaw set in a silent snarl that never quite left her face. She had killed before. She would kill again. But there was something brittle in her stare. A weariness that spoke of debts still unpaid.

A lone figure, gaunt, wiry, half-shadowed in the dimness, picked at the scars on his forearm. His gaze locked on nothing. He did not drink. He did not eat. He did not speak. He only sat, as though waiting for something or someone to tell him he was real.

And beyond them, dozens more. Not warriors. Not legends. Not yet. But bodies waiting for their turn in the pit. Names that might never be spoken after the sands swallowed them whole.

Some of them would die tomorrow. And for those who lived, no one would remember the ones who hadn't.

Toren's cybernetic limbs hummed beneath his skin. He remembered the pit, no grand arena, but a subterranean grave where Pyrrha's architects of suffering forged gladiators like broken tools. He'd been fifteen, raw with rage, bones too light and eyes too green, thrown into the depths with no training but survival.

The Matriarchs of Crimson had watched from above, their crimson veils still as blood that never dried. They said nothing. Only watched. And beneath them, he had been given his first task:

"Kill the boy next to you."

They had entered together. Starved together. Whipped together.

Toren had refused.

At first.

And that was when they broke his legs.

He felt it now, in phantom echoes. Those old limbs he no longer owned, snapped like twigs, reshaped into something mechanical and obedient. Obedient only in function. Never in spirit.

He clenched his jaw, feeling the soft whir of hydraulics adjust beneath his kneecaps. His cybernetic nerves twitched as if the ghosts of his past still walked alongside the ones made of steel.

Sera hadn't looked at him once during his remembering. And he was grateful. Because if she had, she might have seen the flicker of shame that passed behind the emerald of his eyes.

"Kill the boy next to you."

He had refused again.

But this time, the boy hadn't.

The boy had lunged first.

Toren's arm still bore the scar where the jagged shiv had slipped through flesh. Not real flesh anymore. But the memory of it bled all the same. That boy was long gone. Bones shattered, skull cracked against the pit's stone. A death delivered not in fury, but in fear.

Fear had taught Toren his first lesson:

It is not the rage that breaks you. It's what comes after.

He hadn't spoken for two months after that. Not a single word. Not even when they carved new limbs into his body. Not when they told him he was 'improved.'

He learned to hide his thoughts behind silence. To bury guilt beneath calculation. Because when the world names you Firebearer, but you have no father to burn for, you carry only the ashes.

Across the hall, one of the younger nameless recruits fumbled his drink. Toren didn't flinch. The sound, the movement passed through him. Didn't stir the soldier. But something else did.

The scent of sweat. The faint tang of recycled blood from old wounds reopened. The low, rhythmic clink of shackled ankles, someone in the far corner still wore their bonds.

It set off a pulse.

His pupils constricted. Hands twitching.

The Conditioning Pulse, the Matriarchs had called it. A behavioural amplifier buried in the base of his brainstem. Activated by triggers even he couldn't always predict. Meant to make him faster, colder, deadlier. Meant to erase hesitation.

But sometimes it made him forget what he wanted to do, and only remember what they had trained him to do.

He drew a breath through his nose and let it leave slow. He was in control.

This time.

Next to him, Lucius raised his mug in another toast. Loud. Defiant. Alive.

Toren did not raise his cup.

He had no toast to give.

Only the memory of bones breaking.

And the certainty that the machine inside him still waited for permission to finish what the boy in the pit had started.

Now, he had a name. A reputation. A place among the warriors who would be remembered. But as he looked around the hall, he was not sure if that was a victory.

Because for every name that rose, there were ten more that faded away. The nameless. The forgotten.

And tomorrow, some of them would not be here.

At the far end of the table, Levik Draganmir leaned forward, his chair groaning under the sheer weight of him. A man carved from war. His body a ruin of old battles. His soul a thing still standing amid the wreckage.

"The air smells different," he muttered. His voice was low and grating, like shifting boulders dragged across the earth. His steel-grey eyes, hollowed by years of bloodshed, swept across the table, searching for confirmation of something only he seemed to sense.

None answered. But they felt it too.

A tension, so subtle yet suffocating, curling through the air like the first traces of smoke before an unseen blaze.

Sol, ever restless, tapped his fingers against the wooden table. His skin hummed with barely contained energy. His wild golden locks had fallen messily over his face. But beneath them, his molten amber eyes gleamed with unspoken intuition. A flicker of something primal. Something that knew to listen when the world held its breath.

"It's the kind of quiet that gets men killed," he muttered, cracking his knuckles. "Like a loaded crossbow with no one behind it."

Across from him, Luna merely exhaled. Unbothered. Untouched by the weight pressing against the room.

"Everything is already set in motion," she whispered, tearing her bread apart with deliberate grace, as if breaking something fragile. "Whether we hear it coming or not."

She did not look at Sol.

Because looking meant remembering. And remembering was dangerous.

Her fingers kept working at the bread, not out of hunger, but ritual. A motion learned long ago, when death was not something spoken of, only inhaled. Every breath she took now was a lie borrowed from a corpse.

The crust flaked under her touch. Just like it had that night.

Jaleya's hands had been smaller than hers, but fiercer. Always torn, always bruised. Always throwing fists where Luna held silence. She had been fire, and Luna had been the smoke that followed.

On the night before the bloodlot, Jaleya had stolen an extra ration from the quartermaster. A sliver of bread, no bigger than a coin, crusted at the edges.

She had handed it to Luna in the dark, a grin split across her bruised face.

"Eat it before we sleep. For luck."

But Luna had saved it. Wanted to give it back to her after she won. Wanted to hold it out and say:

I didn't need the luck. You came back.

Jaleya didn't come back.

They brought her body in a canvas sack, limbs folded wrong, throat carved like a butcher's practice. And Luna had stood there at twelve years old, fists clenched, the bread still in her pocket, watching them drop her sister on the stones like waste meat.

She didn't cry. She didn't scream.

She just ate the bread.

It tasted like ash and salt. Like endings.

From that day forward, she learned to move without being moved.

To fight without noise.

To grieve without grave.

And now Sol, blazing, reckless, beautiful Sol, sat across from her, fingers drumming the table like a heart that didn't know how close it was to stopping.

He was so much like Jaleya it made her sick.

Too fast. Too loud. Too alive.

And that's what terrified her.

"Don't," she said suddenly.

Sol blinked. "Don't what?"

Her eyes met his then. Full of night. Full of graves. Her voice didn't rise. But it struck.

"Don't die trying to be the sun."

He laughed. Of course he laughed. Golden and burning and full of light.

"Who said I'd die?"

She looked away.

And said nothing.

The crust of bread crumbled to dust between her fingers.

The hush that followed clung to the edges of the room.

It spread like a ripple over the gathered warriors, pressing into the space between them. Some shifted in their seats. Others pretended not to care. But they all felt it.

The invisible hand tightening its grip.

The pull of something inevitable.

Beyond the circle of familiar names, beyond the titans of the arena who had long since earned their place in its blood-soaked sands, the unnamed sat in the margins. Ghosts in waiting.

Some bore scars of old battles, but their names had yet to be written in the annals of legend. Others were new. Fresh-faced.

Sharp-eyed. Still clinging to the remnants of hope that had not yet been crushed beneath the weight of Pyrrha's brutality.

They listened, even if they did not yet understand.

Because when men like Levik spoke, when Sol stilled, when Luna's whispers bent the air around them, it meant the world had shifted, even if none could yet see the shape of what was coming.

Bakari Malanga had been silent all evening, but now he spoke, his voice low, deliberate, as though every word weighed its own cost. "Fear is a slippery thing," he murmured, his tone carrying the weight of something old, something he'd learned far too late.

"It can break a man down, or it can forge him into something far worse than he ever imagined."

His fingers drummed on the table, a rhythm born from long habit, the echo of something darker. He paused, as though the memory of it settled in his bones.

The words lingered in the air, heavier than the silence they'd displaced. They didn't shout; they cut, slow and deliberate, like a blade testing the depth of a wound.

His crystalline blue eyes, sharp and unreadable, flickered toward the others. They held the depth of something ancient. Something that had seen too many battles and still had the strength to face another.

"It makes food taste like ash," he continued. "Turns men into cowards. Makes fighters hesitate."

He reached into his bowl, pulling out a small scrap of meat. He held it between two thick fingers before lifting it toward Ember.

The bioengineered feline tilted its head. Its molten gold eyes narrowed. Calculating. Then, in a blur of movement, it struck.

Fangs flashed. The meal was gone before anyone could blink.

The subtle scrape of a chair shifting. The flicker of movement from one of the nameless figures in the background. The ones who had not yet carved their legend in blood. All watching. Listening.

Bakari leaned back, resting an elbow on the table, his expression unreadable.

"But fear also makes things sharper," he continued, his tone even, but carrying the weight of something unshakable.

"And in Pyrrha, the sharpest blade always wins."

He leaned back, slow, deliberate.

The others returned to their talk. The tension diluted by ale and bravado. But Bakari was already elsewhere. Ember had curled beside his feet now, a shadow with breath. Watching. Always watching.

He remembered a different fire.

Not the one in the pit. Not the one in the kitchens.

A smaller one. Flickering. Human.

Her name had been Tesara. She was not a warrior. She was not a gladiator. She had only been hungry.

It was before the arena, before the name "Iron Flame," before the Cleaver and the Gauntlet. Back when he was still just Bakari, boy with too-long arms and a chef's hands. When he still thought food could save lives.

They'd caught her stealing from the waste bins behind the Palace of Gula. Starving girl. Thirteen. Ribs like knives through skin.

He had found her behind the ovens. Fed her what scraps he could hide. Taught her to steal better. To walk softer. To vanish like smoke.

And for a while, she survived.

Until the day a noble's platter came back half-eaten. The taster found a sliver of grit in the sauce. A speck of bone from the rendering vat.

Gula blamed him. But didn't kill him.

"You've got a talent," she had purred, her bloated fingers stroking her chin. "I'd hate to waste it."

So she gave him a choice.

Tesara, or both of them.

He made the dish. He spiced it perfectly. He slit the girl's throat himself. And when the court ate, they applauded.

They said the meat had never been sweeter.

Now, Ember stirred. As if it could smell the memory. As if it too remembered what wasn't allowed to be forgotten.

Bakari stared down at his hands. So large. So precise. So capable of feeding or ending.

"The sharpest blade," he murmured, too low for anyone but Ember to hear, "is the one that cuts both ways."

He did not smile. He did not cry.

He simply reached for another piece of bread.

And didn't eat it.

A silence followed. Not dismissal. Consideration.

The gladiators, those who had already etched their names into the bones of the arena and those whose names would soon be swallowed by the sand, let the words settle.

Lucius let out a short breath, rubbing his temple. His usual bravado had been stripped raw.

"I don't know about all of you," he muttered, rolling his shoulders, the tension in them sharp enough to cut. "But I don't plan on dying in some Warlord's twisted spectacle. I don't care what the Trials throw at us. I'll crush anyone who stands in my way."

His frost-blue gaze, sharp as the tundra from which he hailed, settled on Levik, almost daring him to challenge his certainty.

Levik, ever the mountain. Scarred. Immovable. Grunted, dragging a calloused hand down his face.

"You think it's that simple?" His voice was a low rumble, a sound worn by years of war. He exhaled sharply, leaning forward. "You've got strength, Lucius. But strength isn't what keeps men alive here."

Lucius narrowed his eyes, his jaw clenching. "And what does?"

Levik's response was slow. Measured. The weight of experience pressing down on every syllable.

"Knowing the difference between battles worth fighting and ones that are just graves waiting to be filled."

Lucius turned his eyes away, pretending to study the flickering edge of a torch. The truth had landed harder than he wanted to admit. That old war hound Levik always spoke like his words were chipped from stone, but this time they stuck. They lodged under the skin.

He hated how much sense they made.

His grip tightened around his cup, frost forming at its rim, a reflex he barely noticed anymore. Ice always answered his nerves.

There were nights back in the tundra where the wind howled so loud it felt like gods were clawing at the edge of the world. Where the cold sank into the bones and made people forget their own names just to survive. Lucius used to laugh in that cold. He used to think if you just burned hot enough, nothing could touch you.

But the arena was colder.

Not in the air. Not in the stone. But in the eyes of the dying. In the faces of boys too young to bleed properly, still calling for mothers who weren't there. He remembered one of them. Wide-eyed, maybe fifteen. Lucius had crushed his windpipe by mistake. Too fast. Too hard. The kid hadn't even drawn his blade.

He'd bent over afterward, panting, trying to tell himself it was just the way of it. That the weak died, and the strong survived. That this was justice. But the boy's hand had clung to Lucius's wrist, not out of malice.

Out of need.

A plea. To make it stop. To make it mean something.

That was three months ago, and Lucius still woke with the imprint of that hand on his skin.

He hadn't told anyone. Not Sol. Not Raekor. Not even Sera, who sometimes watched him like she already knew what he was hiding.

He wasn't weak. He couldn't be. He was Valkor blood. He was born from Wrath itself.

But gods, the boy had never even screamed.

Lucius looked down at his cup. The frost had thickened now, creeping toward his fingers. He forced a breath, slow and deep, and tried to melt it.

Didn't work.

Something in him had gone cold. Not just tonight. Weeks ago. Maybe longer.

And still, he laughed louder than most. Still cracked jokes like a blade slipping between ribs.

Because if he stopped laughing, he'd start remembering.

And remembering was when the cold won.

A pause. The flickering torchlight cast deep shadows along the cracked stone walls, stretching the silence into something heavier.

Then, Vera's voice. Sharp. Deliberate.

"Then tell me, old man," she murmured, her obsidian-dark eyes narrowing slightly. "Is this a battle worth fighting?"

Levik held her gaze for a long moment before exhaling through his nose. "We'll know soon enough."

The table fell into stillness, the weight of inevitability settling over them.

Then, a scoff. Valen.

"Gods, you lot sound like we're walking toward our own funerals."

Every pair of eyes turned to him. The noble-born gladiator, all sharp angles and gilded arrogance, leaned back in his chair, sapphire gaze gleaming with something dangerously close to dismissal.

"What's the worst they can do? Throw more of us to the sand? We've all faced death before."

A rustle of movement from the edge of the table. Raekor, silent until now. Watching. Listening. He finally spoke, his voice a blade dulled not by weakness, but by knowing it had cut too deep, too often.

"You've faced death," he murmured, his tone unreadable. "But have you ever known it?"

The flickering candlelight cast a shadow across his face, the scar along his jaw pulling taut. The weight of his words did not land softly. It struck. Buried deep. For death was not just an enemy met in the sand. It was the thing that stayed with you long after the battle had ended.

Valen's jaw tightened, the muscle twitching beneath his skin.

"And what the hell does that mean?"

His voice carried more than frustration. It carried defiance. A man unwilling to be dismissed. Unwilling to be weighed and found lacking.

Across the table, Raekor leaned forward, his presence shifting like a blade being unsheathed, slow and deliberate. The flickering candlelight carved sharp edges into his features, his amber gaze dark and cutting. A predator's patience behind his eyes.

"It means you haven't bled enough to know how deep this pit goes."

Valen stared at Raekor, eyes hard, but something beneath the surface flickered. Not anger.

Doubt.

He didn't reply.

Because the truth had touched something he had worked tirelessly to keep buried. And for a moment, the great hall with its laughter, its candlelight, the scent of wine and ash, melted away.

He was no longer seated among legends.

He was standing once more in the mirrored duelling room of House Caelmont, the chamber that had raised him in the art of war without ever teaching him what battle meant.

A young boy, maybe fourteen. Thin, golden-haired, too pale for the lessons he was expected to master.

"Again," said his tutor.

The sword in his hand trembled. He'd already lost twice. A third would mean blood. Not his opponent's. His.

"Again," the man snapped, drawing his whip.

He parried. Ducked. But the pain still came. A flick of iron across his shoulder. A punishment for hesitation.

He had trained in silk-lined halls, beneath chandeliers and sculpted gods, where a misstep was corrected with lashes, not death.

He had never fought someone who didn't care if he lived or died.

He had never looked into the eyes of a man whose name was forgotten before his body hit the dirt.

And now, in the shadow of the Trials, with Raekor's words still in his ears, he realized:

Every duel he had ever won meant nothing.

Not here.

Not where the steel was real and the audience didn't applaud, they fed on failure. Where your opponent wasn't trained to make you better, but to leave you broken.

Valen exhaled slowly. His fingers brushed the hilt of his gilded sword, polished to perfection.

He stared at it, immaculate, not a mark, not a single scratch. It was perfect. He was not. His hand curled around the grip, and he hated how smooth it felt.

The words struck harder than any blade, sinking deep, twisting. Valen felt it. The shift. The unspoken weight of men and women who had suffered in ways he had not. Who had crawled through the depths of this place and come out changed or not at all.

Raekor's voice did not rise. But it didn't need to. It carried the gravity of truth.

"You think this is about fighting?" His words were quieter now, but no less lethal. "The Test Trials aren't a stage for glory, Caelmont. They are execution grounds for the weak."

The words should have been cutting. But what was worse was that they were true. Valen's fingers tightened around his cup, the edges of his knuckles whitening. Every part of him screamed to argue, to bite back, to deny, but there was nothing to deny.

Because they were right.

Before the silence could settle, before Valen could force a retort from between his clenched teeth, another voice sliced through the tension.

Soft. Unrushed. Lethal in its own way.

Sera Zahara tilted her head slightly, the ghost of a smirk curling at the edge of her lips.

"You're all asking the wrong questions," she murmured, her words slipping through the air like silk drawn over a blade.

The table stilled. The flickering candlelight turned her honey-gold eyes into liquid fire, smouldering with something unreadable. A knowing that did not need to be spoken aloud.

She picked up a stray piece of bread between her fingers, turning it over. Considering it.

"The real question isn't about survival."

There was no laughter now. No murmured challenges. No one filled the silence with a careless remark. Sera's fingers relaxed. The bread fell onto her plate with a soft thud.

"The real question," she continued, her voice a quiet knife, "is how much of yourself you're willing to lose to win."

The words landed like a slow-cutting blade, carving into the air between them. She smiled then. But there was no warmth in it.

"Because if you think you're walking out of the Trials as the same person who walked in."

A pause. A breath. A moment stretched thin between certainty and oblivion. Then, the final cut.

"You've already lost."

No one spoke.

The weight of her words hung thick in the candle-smoked air, settling like a second skin over each of them. And for the first time, Valen felt something colder than doubt. Sharper than fear. Understanding.

A silence followed, deeper than any roar. And in that silence, something shifted. Not in the room, but in each of them.

The kind of shift that separates who they were from who they will have to become.

The laughter didn't come all at once.

It started with a sigh. Lucius ran a hand through his platinum-white hair, shaking his head, his ice-blue eyes flickering with exasperation. "You really know how to kill a mood, Zahara."

A beat of silence followed. A long one.

Then Levik, without looking up from his cup, muttered, "That mood was already dead. She just buried it."

Bakari snorted into his drink.

Lucius grinned, raising his cup like a mock-offering to the gods. "To our glorious burial rites, then. May we all be mourned with such poetic contempt."

Raekor arched a brow. "If I die to poetry, I'm coming back just to haunt your metaphors."

"That's fair," Lucius said. "But if I die to anything less than a thunderclap and a choir of weeping maidens, I'm filing a formal complaint with whatever deity's on shift."

Sera, still tracing the rim of her cup, didn't look up. "Pretty sure they rotated out centuries ago."

"Well," Sol cut in, cracking his knuckles, "guess we'll just have to be our own gods, then."

Luna didn't smile. But she didn't stop him.

Levik rumbled, "Gods don't bleed."

Sol shrugged. "Then we're doing it wrong."

Laughter rippled through the table. Rough, raw, not whole but human.

Not loud enough to hide fear. Just loud enough to survive it.

Even Hurriyah's lips twitched.

Just once.

Lucius leaned back in his chair, eyes scanning the room like a man seeing ghosts and still trying to flirt with them.

"This is either the worst last supper I've ever had or the best prelude to a massacre."

Sera finally looked at him, her gaze calm as still water.

"Why not both?"

Lucius raised his cup one last time, eyes flicking toward the brazier's flame.

"To the ones who'll live long enough to regret it."

The toast was shared, some with grim smiles, others with nothing but silence.

But they drank.

And for one breath, one fleeting, fractured breath, the weight lifted.

The pit would come. But not yet. Not this moment.

Not this laugh. Not this last, quiet clink of cups before the world burned again.

"Those who laugh before the end do not laugh for courage. They laugh because it is the only sound left in them, everything else has already been taken by the grave."

Null Gospel, Book I, Verse 7.

***

CHAPTER SEVEN:

The Iron Star Decends

"We do not fight for victory in the arena. We fight to decide how we die."

Fragment of the Exiled Codex, Volume I, Tablet 8.

It is a dangerous thing when warriors forget they are dying.

The barracks still held the aftertaste of laughter. Not joy, but defiance. The kind that claws its way up from the gut like a wounded thing pretending to sing. That sound was not peace. It was ritual. An old rite spoken in slurred toasts and half-meant jests, performed not in reverence, but in rebellion. Against fear. Against the pit. Against what waited just beyond the next sunrise.

They drank like condemned kings, roared like gods who knew they were about to fall. Somewhere beneath it all, the air thickened. Not with smoke, but with something heavier. A presence. As if the stone itself was listening. As if the city was waiting for them to forget what it was.

And for one foolish moment, they did.

They forgot the scars they wore like titles. Forgot the rules written in blood and ash. Forgot that Pyrrha does not forgive forgetting. Because this place is not a city. It is a mouth. And the moment it senses weakness, it bites.

The crack came not with a scream, but a gesture. A mug. A splash. A glance held too long. Laughter that ran just a little too sharp at the edges.

The line snapped. And the unravelling began.

A ripple of laughter followed. Short. Bitter. But real. Even Vera let out a slow breath, amusement curling at the edges of her otherwise unreadable gaze.

The tension did not vanish, but it settled. They all knew what was coming. No amount of bravado would stop it. Lucius lifted his mug again, this time slower, more deliberate.

"To the ones who'll make it through."

The gladiators lifted their cups. Some drank in defiance. Some in resignation. Some in hope. And some, like Sera, did not drink at all.

In that fleeting twilight of egos, the pretence of confidence and the illusion of certainty began to dissolve. The hall was alive with murmurs and quiet toasts, but beneath it, the weight of impending war pressed against their spines like an unseen spectre.

The silence thickened. Not the absence of sound, but the kind that stretched between breaths. The kind that made the torchlight flicker differently. The kind that heralded change.

Silence fractured. As if fate itself had grown tired of their solemnity, it shattered.

It started, as these things always did, with Lucius.

The Frostborne Titan was never one to sit too long in thought. Not when his fists itched for action. Not when the weight of the Trials loomed overhead like a storm with no promise of mercy. The air had grown too heavy. The silence too loud.

So naturally, he did what he did best. He disrupted the moment with reckless idiocy.

Lucius slammed his mug down, the force of it sending a wave of stale ale splashing across the table. Directly onto Sol Nocturna's lap.

For a moment, nothing happened.

A single heartbeat. Two.

A breath passed. Sol blinked. Slowly. Deliberately.

His golden hair, still untamed from the day's battles, clung slightly to his forehead. The dim torchlight caught in his molten-amber eyes, turning them into flickering embers. Reflecting something dangerous. Not quite rage. Not quite amusement. Something in between.

He tilted his head just slightly, the sharp line of his jaw accentuated by the flickering light.

"Lucius." His voice carried the deceptive calm of an oncoming storm.

Lucius only shrugged, utterly unrepentant. "What? It's not my fault you're small enough to sit in the splash zone."

A dangerous hush settled over the table. The kind of silence that preceded a brawl. The kind that begged for it.

At the edges of the dining hall, the other gladiators stirred. Some paused mid-conversation, their instinct for violence drawn to the tension like wolves scenting a fresh kill. Some had fought alongside Sol before. They knew that look in his eye. They knew what was about to happen. Others, less fortunate and less wise, simply watched, sensing blood on the horizon.

Then, a voice. Smooth as silk and twice as sharp.

Luna Nocturna.

She set her cup down with measured grace, her silver-white streaks catching the dim glow of the torches. Her ice-blue eyes, so unlike her brother's wildfire, held an edge honed by something far colder.

"Brother," she mused, tone soft as a noose. "If you hit him, aim for the face. His ego needs humbling."

Sol did not need further encouragement. He lunged.

The impact was instantaneous.

Lucius' chair tipped backward with a sharp crack, sending him and Sol crashing onto the cold stone floor in a tangled mess of limbs and curses. The sheer force of the collision knocked an entire table sideways, sending cups, plates, and half-eaten meals cascading onto the ground in a cacophony of chaos.

And that might have been the end of it if not for Bakari Malanga.

The behemoth of a man had been leaning back in his chair, seemingly unaffected by the nonsense unfolding before him. Ember curled lazily over his broad shoulder, watching like a deity surveying the petty squabbles of mortals.

But when the fight broke his balance, he toppled. Normally, Bakari was not a man easily disturbed. But when he fell, he fell onto Valen Caelmont.

A nobleman should not know the feeling of seven feet of muscle crashing into his ribs, but Valen was rapidly becoming acquainted with the experience.

His gasp was audible. A sound caught between pain and sheer disbelief, as Bakari's full weight crushed the air from his lungs.

Across the chaos, Hurriyah Sunshadow remained unmoved, his gaze fixed as the madness swirled around him. The noise, the laughter, the violent dance were all too familiar.

Once, he would have intervened, stepped in to stop the spiralling fury before it consumed them all. But now, it seemed inevitable.

He had seen wars begin for less. A sharp word. A sudden glance. The smallest lapse in control. He understood it better than most: how quickly violence could ignite, how easily it could spiral from a spark into an inferno.

And yet, amidst the chaos, there was something untamed in the air, something raw, like the very breath of battle itself.

These warriors, though they might not realize it, fought for the same thing he had once fought for: the right to live, even if only for a moment longer, before they were swallowed by the pit.

They grasped at it, this fleeting taste of freedom, as though it might save them. Their lives, already half-spent, hung on this final illusion: that they could die on their own terms.

Hurriyah's fingers tightened around the hilt of The Ashen Vow, the weight of the blade grounding him as the fight unfolded before him. He had lived through too many wars, seen too many men die in search of that last moment of choice, to mistake this for anything but the final act of rebellion.

Ember, ever the opportunist, sprang from Bakari's shoulder, landed on the disrupted table, and promptly stole an entire roasted chicken from someone's plate.

At that moment, everything collapsed into madness.

Toren barely had time to move before the riot unfolded in full. A wooden mug whizzed past his head, smashing against a wall.

A group of unnamed gladiators, who had thus far remained uninvolved, took this as their cue. Some leaped in, eager for an excuse to release their frustration. Others simply dodged the blows meant for someone else. One poor bastard was flung backward, landing directly onto a nearby bench.

And through it all, Hurriyah watched.

His molten-gold eyes, unreadable beneath the torchlight, traced the reckless dance of bodies as chaos spread like wildfire. Once, he would have intervened. Called for order. Reminded them that violence meant nothing when wasted on each other.

But those days were gone. His voice was not a king's command anymore. It was just another sound lost in the din of the pit.

Still, he did not move. He observed.

And then, a deep sigh.

At the far side of the hall, Levik Draganmir, ever the weary veteran, watched as Raekor tensed. His shoulders tightened. His hands curled into fists. Levik knew that look.

So before Raekor could fully commit to throwing someone through the nearest table, Levik gripped his collar and yanked him backward.

"Not worth it," he muttered.

Raekor did not appreciate being restrained.

"Levik," he growled, shaking him off with a snarl, "you put your hands on me again and I'll introduce your face to that wall."

Levik sighed again. "Then make it quick," he said, deadpan. "I'd rather sleep than listen to you complain about it."

Before Raekor could retaliate, Vera intervened.

With the effortless grace of someone who had spent a lifetime breaking up fights before they began, she maneuvered between them, her dark eyes taking in the growing carnage unravelling further down the hall.

A crash.

A yell.

More bodies colliding.

And so Hurriyah finally moved.

Not to interfere. Not to stop it. But simply to walk through it. His firebrand cloak trailed behind him, a ghost moving unscathed through the heart of a battle that meant nothing. He had fought wars. This was nothing more than fools pretending they were already dead.

Sol Nocturna, ever the opportunist, twisted with wild glee, dragging Lucius into a chokehold. The thrill of the fight surged through him, but beneath the grin, something darker stirred. This wasn't just a game. This was survival, pure and uncut.

Each laugh, each jest, each careless move was a shield against the cold realization clawing at the back of his mind. The knowledge that they might not survive the Test Trials. And if they did, what then? Another fight, another death, another cycle of blood and sand.

So he laughed. He fought. He kept moving, kept grasping at the one thing left to him. Freedom in this fleeting moment of chaos.

If the end was coming, he'd be damned if he wasn't going to enjoy the final act.

Lucius, in a rare stroke of genius, decided that the best counter to being strangled was to simply stand up and run backward into the nearest wall.

The wall won.

They collapsed in a heap, limbs entangled, cursing and laughing between half-hearted swings.

Across the wreckage, Valen Caelmont, having narrowly escaped from beneath Bakari, was now dusting himself off with the exaggerated offense of a man who believed, wholeheartedly, that this was beneath him.

Bakari, utterly unbothered, merely retrieved his chair, reclaimed his plate, and with a deep rumble of satisfaction, took another bite of his meal.

At the centre of the mess, Sol, now somehow straddling Lucius, grabbed him by the collar, his molten-amber gaze flickering with amusement.

"Say it, big man."

Lucius wheezed, blinking at him through the pain. "Say what?"

"That I won."

Lucius made a half-hearted attempt to shrug him off, but Luna, silent and dangerously amused, casually placed her boot against his chest, pressing just hard enough to keep him pinned.

"Stay down," she murmured, sipping from her cup. "It's the safest place for you."

Lucius gasped dramatically. "You too, Luna?"

She arched a brow. "Of course."

Toren, who had remained still amidst the chaos, now let out a deep, measured exhale. His gaze swept the hall, taking in the absurdity of the situation. Men who would kill one another in the arena were now rolling on the floor, hurling insults like children.

A part of him wondered if it was a coping mechanism. Or perhaps it was the only way to remain human.

And then, a low, knowing rumble broke through the din. It carried the weight of someone who had seen far worse than this madness.

"You know," Bakari mused, grinning, "I do believe the Test Trials might be easier than surviving dinner with you lot."

The hall erupted in laughter. A roar of untamed mirth shook the very stone walls of their prison.

Even Toren, ever the observer, ever the one who rarely engaged, felt something loosen in his chest.

Even Hurriyah, seated in the far shadows, lips pressed into a tight line, let his golden eyes flicker with something just shy of amusement.

For a moment, just a moment, the weight of war, the inevitability of bloodshed, the certainty of their fates, none of it mattered.

The laughter had barely settled, lingering only in the form of scattered chuckles and the occasional smirk, when a heavy thud shook the table.

Lucius.

His massive frame leaned forward, one fist planted against the wood, the other gripping his mug so tightly it threatened to shatter. A slow grin unfurled across his face. Not the kind that came from humour, but the kind that only formed when something reckless had already taken root.

"You know," he rumbled, rolling his shoulders like a lion preparing for a charge, "all this talking's making my fists itch."

Sol Nocturna, ever the incarnation of wildfire, perked up like a predator catching the scent of prey. He shoved his mug aside, his amber eyes flashing with something dangerously eager.

"You thinking what I'm thinking, Frostborne?"

Lucius's grin widened. "Doubt it. I don't tend to think much."

That was all the warning anyone got.

With a bellowing laugh, Lucius surged forward, and Sol, never one to resist chaos, launched himself straight at him. They collided, a mess of limbs and brute force, chairs toppling as Sol, significantly smaller but impossibly fast, twisted midair and landed an elbow against Lucius's ribs.

The Frostborne Titan barely budged. Instead, he roared with amusement and wrapped his massive arms around Sol like a bear grabbing a wildcat.

"Oh-ho. So the little sunspot wants to wrestle?"

Sol kicked, wriggled, and then, because dignity was clearly not a priority, he clamped his teeth down onto Lucius's forearm.

"Ow. You damned gremlin!" Lucius howled, shaking his arm violently.

The barracks dining hall, already primed for mayhem, erupted. Gladiators whooped and hollered. Tankards slammed against wood. Plates overturned in the wake of their scuffle.

The room pulsed with unchained energy, a frenzy of limbs and laughter that could only be found in a place where death lurked at every corner. This was not just chaos. This was life, clawing its way to the surface in the only form it knew: violence.

These warriors, who had faced death so many times it had become a ghost that walked with them, now grappled with something far more dangerous: the truth that each battle, each brawl, could be their last. They fought not for victory, not for glory, but for the mere chance to breathe, to feel the rush of blood in their veins, to remind themselves they were still alive, even if only for a few moments more.

In the carnage, there was freedom, a fleeting, fragile thing that danced in the cracks of the madness, bright and burning before it vanished.

It was reckless. It was chaotic. It was freedom in its purest, most fleeting form.

And yet, in the midst of the madness, not all laughed.

From the far shadows, Hurriyah Sunshadow watched.

His golden eyes, burning like embers beneath the twilight of memory, flickered across the scene. He took in Lucius's reckless joy, Sol's untamed defiance, the way the others threw themselves into the moment as if it were their last.

Perhaps because it might be.

He did not laugh. Not because he did not understand the need for it. But because he had once been a king who had known how fragile these moments were. Because this was what they fought for, wasn't it? Not just survival. Not just rebellion.

But for this.

The right to live, even if only for a night.

His fingers curled around the hilt of The Ashen Vow. The blade's memory resonance hummed softly in response to the weight of his thoughts. They had not yet set foot into the arena. But the battle had already begun.

Luna, ever Sol's mirror, did not flinch as the inevitable chaos erupted. Her ice-blue gaze flicked over the mess with the dispassionate calculation of someone who had seen this play out too many times to care.

With a slow, deliberate motion, she brushed a silver-streaked curl from her face, exhaling in a way that carried the weight of a resigned older sibling forced to watch her reckless twin court disaster yet again.

"Here we go again," she murmured, her voice the sound of a slow head shake.

She made no move to stop him.

Meanwhile, Bakari Malanga had not moved at all.

The behemoth of a man remained seated, unshaken even as a bowl of stew went sailing past his head. With the unbothered patience of an immovable mountain, he reached for another piece of bread and tore into it without pause.

Ember stretched lazily on Bakari's shoulder, utterly unfazed by the riot around them. His molten-gold eyes flicked toward the chaos but didn't stir.

Until, with the casual grace of a king surveying his kingdom, he reached out with a single smoky-black paw and dragged a half-eaten drumstick closer, claiming his rightful spoils of war.

Levik, however, was less amused. He ran a weathered hand down his grizzled face, exhaling through his nose like a man who had seen far too much stupidity for one lifetime.

"I swear," he muttered, "every time those two start something, it ends with someone getting launched across the room."

"Correction."

The voice was Vera's. Cool and composed. The kind of detached calm that came only from having long since accepted the inevitability of idiocy. Her obsidian eyes flicked to the unfolding mess without an ounce of concern.

"It ends with multiple people getting launched across the room."

She wasn't wrong. Because just as Sol landed another wild, reckless kick, Lucius retaliated.

Not with his fists.

But by quite literally hurling Sol across the table.

The smaller gladiator soared through the air like an unruly comet and crashed straight into Valen.

The noble-turned-warrior let out a strangled, deeply offended sound as his pristine tunic was instantly doused in spilled ale, stew, and what might have been someone's half-eaten apple.

For a single beat, silence stretched.

The kind of silence that thickens before a storm. Before the world decides whether to tip toward laughter or destruction.

Then, slowly, deliberately, Valen stood.

His posture was rigid. His shoulders squared. His face the perfect, unreadable mask of noble restraint.

Still tangled in upturned chairs and shattered plates, Sol looked up. His amber eyes gleamed with unrepentant joy.

"Caelmont," he purred, lips twitching, "you look upset."

Valen's expression did not change.

But his hand did.

It curled into a fist. With the grace of nobility and the rage of a man who had finally reached the edge of his patience, Valen swung.

And missed completely.

Sol ducked, cackling like a madman, grabbing Valen by the collar and flipping him onto the table.

Plates shattered. Food went flying. Valen's entire sense of dignity evaporated in the span of a single breath.

And with that, the entire hall erupted.

It began as a brawl. Then escalated into a war.

Tankards were upended. Chairs crashed into walls. Men who would soon be fighting for their lives in the Test Trials instead fought like drunkards brawling in the streets of Pyrrha. Some fought for revenge. Some fought for entertainment. Some fought simply because there was fighting to be had.

Vera sidestepped a flying chair with the ease of someone who had anticipated its trajectory long before it left the ground. She did not flinch. She did not even look. Instead, with effortless calculation, she hooked her foot around a passing brawler's ankle and sent him sprawling onto the stone floor.

Levik, however, had decided he had reached his limit. Rising from his seat like an ancient colossus, he cracked his knuckles and surveyed the carnage before him.

"Alright," he grumbled, voice of a slow-rolling earthquake, "that's it."

Then, with the casual strength of a man who had fought too many wars to tolerate nonsense, he grabbed the nearest idiot. A particularly drunk gladiator who had decided it was a good idea to throw a punch at Bakari.

He hurled him bodily across the hall.

The fool sailed through the air, crashed into another unfortunate soul, and sent three more tumbling like dominoes.

It should have been enough to slow things down. But it wasn't.

Hurriyah Sunshadow had watched it all unfold.

Stillness held him. Not silence. Not awe.

Something older.

He did not laugh. He did not join.

He merely stood, arms crossed, molten-gold eyes watching as warriors who should have been preparing for the most brutal trials of their lives instead wasted their energy on meaningless squabbles.

He could see it. The fraying edges of their resolve. The way they clung to chaos as if it was the only thing left to hold onto.

Because, in many ways, it was.

The laughter. The fighting. The recklessness.

It was all a way to keep the truth at bay. That some of them wouldn't live past tomorrow. That some of them would die in the sand, forgotten, nameless.

Hurriyah exhaled slowly, running his thumb over the hilt of The Ashen Vow.

This was not the way warriors should act. This was not what his people had fought for.

This was not war.

This was the play-fighting of men who had already been broken.

And then, as if summoned by fate itself, a tankard came hurtling through the air, aimed directly at his head.

Hurriyah caught it without looking. A single movement. Fluid. Effortless. As though he had known it was coming before it had even left its wielder's hand.

The brawl did not stop. The chaos did not cease.

But some of them noticed.

Some of them saw the way he stood apart. The way he had not moved until now.

Hurriyah lifted the tankard, inspecting it with unhurried precision.

Then, at last, he spoke.

"You all fight like slaves."

Lucius froze. Sol's grin flickered. Valen, still tangled in the wreckage of broken plates, stilled. Even Raekor, who had been preparing to throw someone into the nearest table, turned, his amber eyes narrowing.

The laughter died. The fists lowered.

Hurriyah set the tankard down.

Then, his molten-gold gaze swept the room. Slow. Deliberate.

"When the games begin," he murmured, "you will not be fighting for yourselves."

A pause.

"You will be fighting for their entertainment."

The silence lasted for all of a breath before the chaos erupted anew. This time, even more ferocious. It was no longer a fight. It was an event. It was pure, unrestrained mayhem.

Bodies crashed into one another. Tables overturned. Food and drink were sacrificed to the gods of recklessness. The entire barracks had become a war zone of its own.

Bakari barely blinked. He took another unbothered bite of his meal, chewing with the patience of a man who had seen far worse and decided it was not worth his time.

Ember, however, had finally had enough.

The feline, who had thus far remained comfortably indifferent to the idiocy of mortals, launched itself into the chaos with the precision of a trained assassin.

One second, it was perched on Bakari's shoulder.

The next, it was on Sol's head. Claws out. Fur bristling like a demonic shadow given form.

Sol screeched. Loudly.

"What the hell." He spun wildly, trying to pry the murderous creature off.

Somewhere in the madness, Lucius, still laughing, grabbed another unfortunate soul and threw them into the fray. It was unclear whether he actually had a grudge against this person or if they had just been in arm's reach.

The room exploded in movement.

Warriors collided. Fists flew. Tankards shattered against the floor. Someone, no one knew who, suddenly flipped an entire table over for no apparent reason.

Raekor, who had somehow remained somewhat uninvolved up until now, watched from the shadows. A slow smirk tugged at his lips. He did not step in. He did not interfere.

Instead, he picked up his drink and enjoyed the show.

Somewhere in the madness, Toren remained exactly where he had been. Still as stone.

A breath escaped him. Measured. Final.

He reached for his drink, desperate to drown out the absurdity of it all. Just one damn sip, that was all he needed.

And then, with the inevitability of fate itself, a body came hurtling through the air like a sack of bricks and crashed straight into his table.

It flipped like a cheap vendor stall in a riot.

His drink was gone.

His meal was scattered.

His patience was non-existent.

For a moment, Toren sat there, his cybernetic fingers twitching against his knee.

One. Singular. Moment.

A deep inhale. A slow, controlled exhale. A faint ticking in his mind, like a countdown to destruction.

He rose. Not with fury, but inevitability.

Without a word, without even looking, he grabbed the closest gladiator by the collar. Muscles coiled like steel cables. With a single, effortless motion, he hurled him across the room.

The airborne fool collided with another fighter, knocking them both into a rapidly growing pile of regret.

And that was the final spark.

The barracks exploded.

Punches flew in every direction. Some threw fists just because everyone else was. Others grabbed chairs as makeshift weapons. At some point, a bucket of stew was dumped over someone's head. It was unclear if it had been an accident or a declaration of war.

The room became a battlefield, not of swords, but of sheer, unfiltered madness.

Even those who had originally wanted no part in the chaos eventually got pulled into it.

Levik grumbled something about fools before grabbing one of the smaller gladiators and tossing them over a table like a sack of grain.

Vera, still eerily composed, dodged a flying mug, sidestepped a swinging fist, and in one fluid motion, kicked someone's legs out from under them.

Luna was still drinking.

Sol, now untangled from Ember, had managed to vault onto a table. He brandished a stolen turkey leg like a sword.

"Come, heathens," he declared, grinning like a madman. "Face me if you dare."

Lucius responded by simply grabbing him and throwing him back into the fray.

Somewhere in the mix, Valen, still soaked in ale and stew, swung wildly. He missed and tripped over a fallen chair, colliding with three other brawlers in an undignified heap.

Raekor, still drinking, let out a low chuckle.

"Idiots."

And still, Bakari sat unmoved. He watched the destruction unfold around him as if it were a theatre production meant for his amusement.

Even as the brawl raged, as plates shattered and tankards broke, as gladiators hurled themselves at each other like madmen, Bakari simply reached for another bite of bread.

Ember had claimed an entire roasted chicken.

Victory had never been so sweet.

For a moment, the chaos surged in all directions. A hurricane of fists, flying bodies, and very questionable life choices.

But Toren was done.

He had thrown one idiot into the abyss. And yet, like moths to a flame, another had already come for him.

A particularly ambitious gladiator, built more like a boulder than a man, saw an opportunity.

Maybe he thought Toren wasn't paying attention. Maybe he thought Toren wouldn't react in time. Maybe he was a complete moron.

Whatever the case, he charged.

It wasn't a strategic attack, nor was it graceful. This was the full-speed commitment of a man who relied entirely on brute force and the hope that his sheer mass would do the rest.

For the briefest second, it almost seemed like it might work.

Almost.

Then Toren moved.

Not in a panicked lunge. Not in a desperate scramble.

With precise, surgical inevitability.

He sidestepped, just barely, with the measured patience of a man watching someone dig their own grave.

And with flawless timing, he caught the incoming brute by the waistband and back of the neck.

The sheer momentum of the charge turned against its owner. For a split second, the gladiator's feet left the ground.

His brain, still catching up, seemed to realize it...oh. Oh no.

But by then, it was too late.

Toren pivoted. Coiled like a spring.

Then he hurled him into oblivion.

The poor bastard Toren had launched crashed headfirst into Lucius's chest with all the grace of a drunk pigeon hitting a glass window.

The impact was solid. Like a sack of bricks thrown into a wall made entirely of bad decisions.

Lucius blinked.

He looked down at the groaning man now sprawled at his feet, blinking up at the ceiling with the wide-eyed realization of someone reliving every life choice that led to this moment.

Then Lucius looked at Toren.

Toren tilted his head slightly. "Problem?"

Lucius's grin spread slow and wide. All teeth. All terrible ideas.

"Not at all."

Just like that, the universe seemed to sigh, shake its head, and hand the wheel to madness.

A mug went flying. No one knew who threw it, but it struck Valen's unsuspecting forehead with unerring precision.

A dull thud.

A beat of silence.

Then came an indignant squawk.

Sol, never one to let opportunity slip by, leapt onto a chair and drop-kicked Valen straight into Bakari.

"You little—"

Valen never got to finish the sentence.

Bakari, utterly unbothered, barely acknowledged the impact. He reached down, grabbed Valen by the collar, and with the casual strength of a man brushing aside a curtain, flung him across the room like a loaf of bread.

Luna sipped her drink without so much as a glance upward, dodging three bodies that soared past her. Graceful. Indifferent.

Sol vaulted directly over her head, cackling like a man who had made peace with his own chaos.

Lucius, eyes gleaming, cracked his knuckles. "You and me, machine-man. Let's see what happens when an immovable object meets cybernetic force."

Toren rolled his shoulders. His expression remained unreadable. "You'll break first."

They lunged at once.

The collision was seismic. A human avalanche slamming into a walking war engine. The floor trembled, and for one brief, divine moment, the laws of physics considered retiring.

A grown man, an idiot by action and definition, skidded across her table, knocking over her untouched drink, shattering plates, and violating the sanctity of her evening. Sera stared at the mess, dead-eyed. Then she looked at the gladiator in the wreckage, surrounded by broken wood and shame.

She inhaled long and slow, then exhaled.

Sera stood. The Crimson Rose, until now unmoved, rubbed her temple. Not in pain, but in disbelief. She had fought through hell. Had faced the worst the arena could offer. But this? This was something else. This was stupidity refined into an art.

She took her tankard, drank the entire thing in one silent, suffering gulp, and then turned to leave.

Toren, standing in the ruin of another upturned table, glanced at her. "You're joining?"

Sera did not stop walking. She moved through the wreckage of bodies, the shattered plates, the empty tankards scattered across the stone like fallen soldiers. Her eyes, dark and unfathomable, flicked over the madness as if it were nothing more than a passing inconvenience.

"No," she said, voice flat and weary. "I'm leaving before someone sets the place on fire."

The words were simple, but they carried the weight of a thousand unspoken battles. The exhaustion of a woman who had fought, bled, and survived only to find that this, too, was a fight she could not win.

A part of her had hoped for something different, something more than this endless, pointless struggle. But here, in the heart of this madness, she found only the same brokenness that had always followed her.

And so, she left. Not to escape the chaos, but because she had already given too much to it. She had nothing left to fight for.

A pause.

Then, as if the gods had overheard and decided to confirm her worst fears, a flaming piece of bread sailed past her head.

Sera closed her eyes. "Of course."

Bakari let out a deep, amused sigh. He shook his head with the weight of a man who had long ago accepted that peace was a myth.

His grin was lazy. His eyes were ancient.

"You know," he said, voice thick with gravel and humour, "I think the Test Trials might be easier than dinner with you lot."

Laughter erupted.

The fire raged. The chaos surged.

And for one ridiculous, fleeting moment, everything was exactly as it should be.

Even Hurriyah felt something in his chest loosen. An unfamiliar warmth drifted through the iron structure of his mind.

For a heartbeat, it almost felt like they were something else.

Not prisoners. Not weapons.

People.

But like all things in Pyrrha, it did not last.

Just as the brawl reached its most absurd crescendo. Just as someone was launched into the air. Just as Sol raised a turkey leg and a stolen dagger in each hand in the name of glorious nonsense—

The doors exploded open.

A thunderous crash shattered the moment. The impact rattled the bones of the barracks and rolled through the stone like a war drum.

Then came the voice.

Not loud. Not panicked.

Precise.

Cold.

A command honed like a blade. Clean. Absolute.

"WHAT IN THE NAME OF THE WARLORD IS GOING ON HERE?!"

It was not shouted. It did not need to be.

It was the kind of voice that left wounds instead of echoes. The kind that could drag a man to his knees without a single strike.

General Callistra Vhailar stood at the threshold. She did not rage. She did not need to.

The moment her presence filled the room, silence followed. Not the kind of silence that came from respect, but from something colder.

Survival instinct.

The warriors of Pyrrha feared nothing.

But they knew discipline when it stared them in the face.

And then, behind her, they entered.

They did not stride like men or women.

They moved like inevitabilities. Like omens wreathed in crimson and steel.

Three distinct flames burning at the heels of the General, their presence suffocating in the way a wildfire devours the air.

The first, Zephir Caedis, was the cold fire of the abyss. The blue inferno that did not rage but calculated. A shadow of stillness, the kind that only ever broke to deliver final judgment.

The second, Veyna Solvaris, was the golden wildfire. The yellow blaze that burned bright and reckless, eyes glinting with a thrill only she understood. She lived for the fire. Danced in it. Let it consume her so long as she could set the world alight.

And the third, Dain Vhorr, was the white pyre. The fire that did not bend. Did not flicker. He was a monument of inevitability. The silence before the executioner's axe fell.

They stood as one.

Three fires.

But no guiding star. No.

That was Callistra. The Iron Star of Pyrrha.

And in this moment, as she stood before them, her gaze like an unsheathed blade, every gladiator in the room knew.

They were about to burn.

The effect was immediate.

The entire room froze. A tankard that had been mid-flight hit the ground with a muted thud.

The brawlers. Hardened warriors. Trained killers. The worst the pits had to offer.

Became motionless statues. Bodies still entangled mid-brawl. Some gripping collars. Others half-suspended in swings that had suddenly lost all momentum.

Even Sol, perched atop a table, dagger in one hand and poultry in the other, remained utterly still.

Eyes wide.

Mouth half-open in what had surely been about to be another outrageous declaration.

And there, standing in the doorway, exuding an aura of raw, merciless authority, was General Callistra.

Her icy glare swept the hall, taking in the ruins of what had once been a functioning barracks. The upturned tables. The broken chairs. The scattered food and spilled ale pooling on the ground like the aftermath of a battlefield. The bruised and battered gladiators.

All frozen mid-madness.

Her jaw clenched.

A flicker of something, pure and unfiltered rage, passed behind her eyes.

She did not speak.

She did not have to.

Because when General Callistra took a step forward, the world seemed to hold its breath.

The gladiators. Murderers. Warriors. Survivors of the pits. Men who had torn through flesh and steel alike.

All looked at one another.

The unspoken question flashed across their wide-eyed gazes.

Who dies first?

And in perfect unison, as if their lives depended on it.

They all pointed at Lucius.

Silence.

Then.

Lucius, still crouched in the remnants of what had once been a table, bruised, bleeding, still grinning like an idiot, let out a slow, exaggerated breath.

"Well, that's just betrayal."

"Even the doomed laugh, until silence comes, wearing the mask of authority."

Null Gospel, Book I, Verse 8.

***

CHAPTER EIGHT:

When the Knife Remembers

"To remember the blade is to forget the hand that shaped it, and to forget the hand is to invite chaos to wield the edge."

Fragment of the Exiled Codex, Volume I, Tablet 9.

There is a silence in Pyrrha that does not belong to peace. It comes after laughter has curdled. After bravado has spent itself against the stone. It is not earned. It is not deserved. It is the silence of a world watching you forget what it is.

The old vents above the barracks groaned once, deep and metallic, like a lung exhaling under weight. Not mechanical. Not alive. But listening.

The barracks still stank of sweat and spilled stew. Of bruised egos and drunken pride. The walls, scarred with the aftermath of fists and furniture, stood witness to the kind of chaos only men on the edge of war can afford.

A broken lantern still buzzed in the corner, spitting sparks into a stew of shadow and steam beneath the laughter. Beneath the blows. Beneath the madness. Something had been coming. And now it was here. Not as a shadow. Not as a scream. But as a woman.

Callistra Vhailar did not enter the barracks like a general. She entered like an event. The air recoiled first. Pressure dropped. Joints stiffened. No one breathed. She walked like the world was interrupting her, like every step was a consequence. Like discipline had decided it was tired of being patient. Her boots echoed with surgical finality. No anger. No haste. Just inevitability.

A candle snuffed itself out in her path. No wind. Just surrender.

To those who had served under her, the signs were subtle. The stiffness in her left hand. The slight drag in her gait. The way her gaze did not sweep the room as it always did, but cut through it in a straight line. Callistra, Iron Star of Pyrrha, always assessed.

Lucius watched the hitch in her step and felt something twist, like watching a statue breathe. Tonight, she judged.

The Three Pyres followed in her wake, not as guards, but as gravity. They did not speak. They did not need to. Each a fire in their own right, they mirrored the truth no one else could name. Callistra was burning. She did not bleed. Not where anyone could see. But something inside her was bleeding out slow. And every soldier who had ever worn chains, ever tasted command, felt it in the marrow.

Something had cracked. Something sacred. But no one knew what.

So they did what cowards always do when the gods come to collect. They stopped moving. Almost all of them.

The floor held corpses of chairs and shattered mugs. The air trembled with the residue of laughter already rotting in the throat. One gladiator still grinned, teeth bloodstained, breath reeking of wine and violence.

But slowly, one by one, they straightened. They lowered fists. They untangled arms from headlocks and rose to attention like half-awake statues trying to remember the shape of fear.

She said nothing. Not yet.

And then, of course, there were two.

They didn't stop. They didn't see her, or didn't care. Or perhaps they saw her and decided, in that suicidal, drunken corner of man's pride, to test what happened next. They were nobody. Names she hadn't bothered to record. Fodder for the pits. Men who would likely die screaming for an audience that wouldn't remember what language they screamed in.

And yet, in this moment, they mattered.

Someone, Raekor maybe, shifted his weight but didn't speak. The air had taken on the flavour of teeth waiting to be broken. Because when a kingdom forgets who holds the crown, it begins with two fools who forget who holds the blade.

Callistra stopped walking. The silence swelled. Behind her, the Three Pyres froze into position.

To the left stood Zephir Caedis, cold as the grave, watching the edge of the room like a tactician studying a battlefield no one else could see. In the rear was Dain Vhorr, the executioner made flesh, his expression carved from stillness. And to the right, her shadow twin, Veyna Solvaris, all flame and anticipation, eyes glinting with the thrill of what she hoped would happen next.

None of them spoke. Because they felt it too. They knew what she had done. They did not know the name of the man she had killed. But they knew a kill that cost something.

Callistra inhaled. A single shift in her stance, subtle, controlled. Every muscle held in reserve.

The two men were oblivious, lost in their brawl. One shoved the other. A drunken stumble, a punch tossed like a poorly thrown stone. They had not yet seen her.

A beat. Then a laugh. Low. Mirthless. He nudged his friend and pointed. "Well look who's finally come to watch us dance."

The second one squinted. "Iron Star herself. Thought you'd be taller."

Callistra said nothing.

The second man raised his cup in mock salute. "We gonna get flogged for fighting? Go on then. Make it official. Do your big speech."

His friend chuckled. "Or maybe you're just here because there's no one else left to kill tonight."

There it was. The weight behind the words wasn't truth. It was luck. Dumb, dangerous luck.

They didn't know what they'd said. But the blade landed anyway.

Callistra exhaled. A movement like smoke. And then she moved. Not like a warrior. Not like a soldier. Like judgment. Her stride held no fury. Only precision. The silence followed her, not because she commanded it, but because nothing dared speak into that space. The men before her, still grinning in their drunken haze, did not recognize what was arriving. Not until it was too late.

The first one laughed again. Slurred. Disrespectful. "Come to join the party, Iron Star?"

Callistra didn't slow.

He raised his cup. "Or maybe just looking for someone to—"

She struck. A single step brought her inside his reach. Her knee drove into his gut with a force that cracked air. His cup flew from his hand before his breath even had time to leave his lungs. He folded. Not like a man. Like a structure failing. Even the laughter didn't die. It drowned, choking on the air left behind.

The second tried to step back.

Callistra seized him by the collar, yanked him forward, and slammed her forehead into his nose. Bone snapped. Blood sprayed her cheek. He staggered. She let him fall.

The first one was crawling now, gasping, his pride came out in gasps, thick with failure. She caught his wrist, twisted, and dropped her boot on his shoulder joint. Hard. A sound like tree bark splintering echoed off the stone.

His scream was wet.

Then she spoke.

Her voice cut through the barracks like a knife through wet parchment. Callistra exhaled slowly. Her voice cut through the barracks like a blade, steady and cold.

"You forget where you are."

She turned, her gaze sweeping over the silent room. Her eyes held no anger, only a deep, abiding certainty.

"You fight, you drink, you brawl like dogs in a pit and think it makes you free. But I'll show you what freedom really is."

A beat of stillness.

"You want chaos. You want violence. You want to laugh at the edge of the blade?"

Callistra's mouth twitched. Just once. Not anger. Not grief. Something older. Something shaped like failure.

She looked to the rest. Her voice dropped, and the air felt it.

"Then let me remind you what the blade feels like."

A momentary pause.

"Do you think the arena makes you dangerous? It doesn't. It makes you watched."

No one moved. Not Sol, still frozen halfway through climbing onto another table. Not Lucius, who had grinned through a hundred brawls and now stood with clenched fists and unreadable eyes. Not even Hurriyah, who watched from the shadows, golden gaze fixed not on her violence but on the fracture beneath it.

Something had changed in Callistra. Not the power. That had always been there. But the edge was closer now. Too close.

The Three Pyres did not intervene. They stood like wardens at the mouth of a prison where the inmates had forgotten the locks were still closed. Dain's eyes tracked the fallen bodies. Zephir's hands stayed clasped behind his back. Veyna's smile widened, slow as fire licking the edge of paper. Let them remember who rules this place.

Callistra's gaze turned. Not to the broken bodies twitching at her feet. To the centre of the storm. The core of chaos. Her eyes found Lucius first. Towering. Broad-shouldered. Still smeared with stew and bruises. He stood with his hands slightly raised, a grin tugging at the corner of his mouth like a man hoping to joke his way out of an execution.

"General," he said with a forced smile, "Technically, I didn't start it. Just... happened to be in the wrong place at the wrong time."

Callistra's gaze stayed locked on him. Lucius shifted uncomfortably, rubbing the back of his neck. "You know me. Always getting swept up in things."

She stepped toward him. Lucius's grin faltered. He raised a hand. "Now, let's not do anything hasty—"

Her fist drove into his gut like a war hammer. No wind-up. No warning.

Lucius buckled. The air flew out of him in a sound that wasn't quite a breath, wasn't quite a curse. Just a large man folding like a tent in a storm. He dropped to one knee, wheezing.

Callistra didn't even look at him. Her eyes flicked up.

Sol Nocturna was halfway through dismounting from the table when her hand snapped out. Not toward him. Toward the clay bowl on a nearby bench. The clay whistled through the air with a sound too sharp for comedy. It sounded like a decision.

It hit his head mid-step with perfect, merciless accuracy. Crack.

The bowl shattered. So did Sol's dignity. He yelped and stumbled backward, flailing like a cat knocked off a windowsill. "I didn't even say anything!"

"You didn't need to," Callistra said flatly. She looked between them, Lucius still coughing, Sol rubbing his head like the bowl had personally betrayed him.

"I had a feeling this all started with the two of you."

"You," she pointed at him, "fight like a siege engine with brain damage."

She turned to Sol. "And you—"

"I'm innocent," he blurted.

"You're never innocent."

Sol opened his mouth. Closed it. Decided life was better that way.

Callistra exhaled, slow.

"The next time either of you decides to spark a riot in my barracks, I won't use a bowl."

Lucius wheezed. "What'll you use?"

Her eyes narrowed. "Imagination."

The rest of the gladiators stood very still. No one made a sound. Not Raekor, whose fists still twitched with the memory of restraint. Not Valen, still smelling faintly of stew and shame. Not Vera, who watched the entire exchange with the calm detachment of a woman drafting Callistra's eulogy for the others.

Even Bakari, still seated in his original chair, let out a slow, rumbling sigh and murmured to Ember, "This is why we can't have nice things."

Toren didn't move. But his gaze tracked every motion like a sniper weighing mercy. As she passed, his voice barely reached her shoulder: "You're shaking."

She didn't stop. Didn't answer. But her hand stilled by instinct. Only he could say it without her breaking.

Callistra finally stepped back. Her eyes swept the room one last time. Then, with clipped precision, she issued her order.

"Clean. This. Up."

No one moved.

For a single, stretched heartbeat, the words hung heavier than the wreckage they stood in. Not because they were unexpected. But because they were final. Because they made everything before them feel rehearsed.

Clean. This. Up.

Chairs lay broken like splintered bones across the stone. Tankards dripped the last of their ale into cracks that remembered blood. A stew-soaked banner sagged from a wall bracket where someone had likely been thrown. The barracks did not breathe. It waited.

Lucius, still bent over with one fist braced to his knee, grimaced through a breath he hadn't fully reclaimed. His gut throbbed like a collapsed forge. But more than that, he felt a sting he couldn't name. Not from the blow. From the fact that he'd earned it.

Sol, one hand still pressed to the side of his head where the bowl had met skull, looked like a child caught mid-prank by a thunder god. His amber eyes darted to Callistra, then to Lucius, then to the nearest doorway, weighing the merits of escape against the risk of incineration.

Neither moved. Nor did anyone else.

Across the ruined tables, gladiators froze in various stages of aftermath. Bruised knuckles, bleeding lips, torn sleeves. What had been war masquerading as revelry had calcified into shame.

Raekor lowered his fists at last. Not because he'd been told. Because his instincts told him the air had changed, and only a fool keeps swinging inside a storm.

Valen Caelmont peeled himself from the floor with far too much dignity for a man soaked in meat grease and shattered pride. His lips pressed tight. Not out of restraint. But because he knew if he opened his mouth now, he'd never close it again.

Toren stood near the edge of the hall, arms folded, spine aligned like an engineered spear. Cybernetic limbs hummed faintly beneath his coat. He didn't speak. He rarely did. But his gaze moved to Callistra and held. Not with reverence. With recognition. She was brittle. And brittle meant dangerous.

Even Sera looked up. Not startled. Just attentive. She studied Callistra not as a subordinate, but as a woman who'd seen too many people break and start calling it strength. Her jaw flexed. Her fingertips brushed the pommel of her sheathed dagger, not out of threat, but out of quiet readiness.

Vera crossed the hall without a word, righted a bench, then swept a broken flagon into a bucket someone had abandoned. Her movements were clean. Practiced. She did not look at Callistra. But her shoulders remained square, like someone who did not need orders to know when the hierarchy needed to reassemble itself.

Bakari let out a slow, canyon-deep sigh and returned to his chair like a tree deciding not to fall. Ember, perched once more on his shoulder, looked profoundly unbothered. The little smoke-cat licked its paw, swiped it across one ear, and surveyed the room with the faint disdain of a creature who'd already survived the worst.

The other gladiators moved slower. Some knelt to gather what they'd shattered. Others dragged benches back into line. One limped past the wreckage, cradling his ribs and muttering a prayer not meant for any god that would listen.

But the room did not truly shift until Hurriyah moved. He stepped from the wall like a shadow made flesh. Not fast. Not loud. But enough. Enough to draw eyes.

Callistra glanced toward him and only him. It was brief. Measured. But it was there. That moment where the Iron Star's mask cracked at the corner. Where something unspoken passed between them.

Hurriyah inclined his head once. Nothing more.

You are bleeding. You are not ready. But I will not say it aloud.

And she turned away.

Zephir stood like a marble sentinel behind her, face unreadable, hands clasped tight behind his back. Dain had not moved a muscle, but one could feel the tension rolling off his frame like storm winds pacing a wall. Veyna, meanwhile, smiled. Not with joy. But with appetite. As though watching a lioness remind the pack who owned the kill.

Even the stone felt quieter. As if Pyrrha itself had paused to witness whether discipline could hold against entropy. It could. It had. But not without cost.

In the silence, a single bowl rolled across the stone and clinked gently against Callistra's boot. She looked down at it. Did not move. It stayed there. Unclaimed. Like a final metaphor, waiting.

The bowl did not roll by accident. Something always rolls before the killing starts. Ask the gods. Ask the machines. Ask the silence. They'll all tell you the same thing: it starts with something small pretending to be harmless.

A faint tremor passed through Callistra's arm.

Just once. The kind of twitch born not from pain, but memory. The kind the body hides until it's sure no one's watching. She didn't flex her fingers. Didn't adjust her stance. But something inside her had recoiled.

She did not look down at the bowl. But she felt it. That stupid, shattered shape beside her boot. Waiting to be acknowledged. Waiting to mean something.

Behind her, footsteps dragged. Someone, Valen, muttering apologies to no one as he bent to lift the broken frame of a bench. Across the room, Raekor grabbed two other men by their collars and shoved them toward the mess. Cleanup had begun.

And yet, nothing felt cleaner.

Callistra's jaw tightened. Her gaze swept the room again, not with anger this time, but calculation. She looked at her soldiers not as warriors, but as variables. As risks. Every eye that avoided hers was a question. Every glance that lingered too long was a problem waiting to bleed.

Valen knelt beside a shattered mug, fingers trembling slightly. Not from exertion. From memory. He glanced toward Lucius and then past him, to the broken men, the bowl, the place where Callistra had stood. Then down. At his own hands.

"You know what scares me?" he said, low, not to anyone in particular. Just to the space between wreckage. "I didn't stop because of her. I stopped because for a second, I thought she'd make me beg."

No one answered.

Valen chuckled. A sick, broken sound.

"I've begged before. Once. Back when I thought there was still dignity in it."

He reached for a bench leg. It snapped in his hand like a brittle limb. He didn't look surprised.

"Turns out, it's not the begging that gets you. It's how easy it becomes once you start."

Across the room, Sol slowly stopped pretending not to hear.

Then she noticed him.

A boy. Maybe sixteen. Shaved head, branded collar. New. Still pink from his last medical stitching. He hadn't moved since the fight ended. He was sitting against a far wall, legs tucked to his chest, arms wrapped tight. Not cowering. Just still. Frozen in that stunned, vibrating way children get when the world breaks before they've learned to pretend it's unremarkable.

Their eyes met.

Just briefly.

Something old and rusted twisted behind her ribs. She swallowed it before it reached her throat.

He didn't flinch. Didn't look away.

Callistra blinked, once, as her eyes lingered on the boy—a long, measured moment where nothing moved, not even time.

Then, with a breath held too long, she moved on.

Behind her, Ember leapt from Bakari's shoulder, its smug eyes gleaming like a creature who had learned too much. It padded through the wreckage of the room, stopping only to sniff the broken bowl, its nose brushing the shards.

A small mewl, sharp and questioning, pierced the silence.

Callistra's lips twitched, a slight, knowing shift. Not a smile, but something far older, and far more dangerous. Ember bumped her shin, then darted off, as if the moment had never happened.

The air thickened. Not with sound, but with understanding. Something stirred in the room. Something ancient. Like a god watching its reflection for the first time in centuries.

Sera looked up sharply. Her fingers stilled on the dagger.

Toren turned his head like he'd heard a frequency no one else could hear.

Even Veyna's smile faltered, just for a breath.

Something was changing. Not someone. Not yet.

But something.

The arena was waking. And it had heard the noise.

The lights changed.

No switch. No transition. Just a blink in the world's attention. One moment, the torches burned with their usual flickering warmth. The next, they didn't flicker at all. They held. Too steady. Too clean. As if touched by something that did not blink, did not sweat, did not err.

A voice followed.

It did not rise. It arrived.

"All registered units, stand by."

The sound came from everywhere. Not overhead. Not the walls. But the air itself, vibrating the bones behind the ears.

"Observation protocols complete."

The gladiators stiffened.

Some straightened out of habit. Others out of fear. But all of them recognized that tone, the voice of Pyrrha's machine heart, the god they could neither bleed nor break.

"Analysis confirms violation patterns exceed discipline thresholds."

Eyes flicked to the vents, to the ceiling. No one turned their head. You don't turn your back to a voice like that.

No emotion. No pause. No condemnation. Just data. Law delivered by something that had never raised its voice because it had never needed to.

"Initiating symbolic correction protocol: THEATRE OF DEFIANCE."

Lucius muttered, "Oh, shit."

Sol slowly lowered himself from the table without a word.

Ember darted under a bench.

"Participants will proceed to Arena Sector Three."

Callistra closed her eyes.

A beat. Then she turned. No warning. No signal. Just motion. Deliberate. Absolute.

The Three Pyres fell in behind her without hesitation. Dain flanked her like a blade unsheathed. Zephir ghosted along her left like a whisper before silence. Veyna walked last, reluctant, grinning still, but quieter than usual.

As they moved down the corridor, Veyna let the silence stretch. Then, softly, like a secret not meant to be kept:

"Do you think they'll thank her?"

Dain didn't answer. Zephir didn't blink.

"Not now," she continued, voice laced with sugar and cinders. "But later. When they're knee-deep in the Theatre. When the audience screams and the blood smells like memory."

She smiled again. Brighter this time. Not joyful. Predatory.

"That's the secret about fear. You don't need them to love you. You just need them to remember which way the knife was facing."

"Compliance is mandatory."

She did not wait for the voice to finish.

What stirred in her wasn't anger. It was recognition. She had heard this tone before. And the last time, it had cost her everything.

A younger Callistra. A field of ash. A boy, maybe fifteen, sobbing beneath a banner torn in half. Her banner. The rebels hadn't killed him. They'd made him choose. She'd found him days later, spine straight, eyes wrong. He hadn't cried since.

That was the last time she'd trusted silence.

She didn't need to hear the rest. She had once believed order could be enforced. That pain shaped loyalty. But now? Now she understood the truth: pain only teaches silence. And silence never remembers who cut it first.

Far beneath them, Sector Three stirred.

One by one, torches ignited in concentric circles. Steam hissed through old channels. Chains lifted themselves taut. Sand was raked clean by unseen hands. No crowd yet. Just silence. Just anticipation.

The arena remembered. And the Theatre of Defiance was hungry.

She paused...just long enough to hear the boy's breath hitch. The weight behind her ribs pulsed, dull and traitorous. She didn't turn. Didn't flinch. But she exhaled once, like someone trying not to remember their own name.

Callistra was already moving. Out. Away. Before the theatre began.

As though the barracks no longer existed. As though nothing in this room mattered anymore. Not the blood. Not the bruises. Not even the order she'd just re-established.

Just the next thing. Just the theatre. And her refusal to watch it.

"This demonstration has been authorized by—"

The door hissed shut behind her.

Not slammed. Sealed.

It was Veyna's absence that the gladiators felt most. The room seemed colder without her smile in it.

A moment passed. Then another.

Sol blinked first. "Did she just walk out mid-decree?"

"She left before the machine finished," said Valen, voice low.

Raekor grunted. "You don't do that. Not to ARES."

"She's done it before," Vera murmured. "But not like this."

Bakari watched the closed door. His massive hands folded slow. Measured. "She knows what's coming."

Hurriyah said nothing. He was still watching the light. Or what was behind it.

Then—

"This is ARES. Noncompliance will be considered conscious rebellion."

The lights dimmed again.

Not to darkness.

To focus.

As if the room itself had become part of a stage.

Callistra was gone.

But the show was just beginning.

The barracks did not breathe. They only waited.

No one spoke now. Not even Sol. Not even Lucius. Because the silence left in Callistra's wake wasn't authority. It was something else. A kind of knowing. A kind of doom.

Sol crouched beside a splintered bench, his usual grin absent. His hands had stopped shaking before his face did. He watched the blinking red light. Then, softer than a joke:

"...It's not a game," Sol said, almost to himself. "Not anymore."

Valen turned to the door she had vanished through and whispered what no one else dared say aloud.

"She left because she's seen it before."

No one answered. No one needed to.

Far above them, gears turned in walls no man had touched in centuries. Lights tracked heartbeat rhythms. Pressure vents adjusted. Pyrrha's nervous system came alive, system by system, circuit by circuit, cell by cell.

Not to judge.

Not to punish.

To display.

This was not about what they'd done. It was about what they'd become.

From the ceiling, a soft white mist began to unfurl. Odorless, painless, sterile. It did not burn the eyes. It did not sting the skin.

It only separated the gladiators from the world outside.

And in the centre of the room, right where the bowl had stopped rolling, a small red light blinked into being.

The red light blinked over the bowl like an eye without empathy, watching not the mess, but the meaning.

Recording. Live.

Broadcast initiated.

And every man and woman in that room knew...

The theatre was not just for them. It was for all of Pyrrha.

And they were the lesson.

The camera did not zoom. It hovered. Centred not on the broken tables or fallen fists, but on the boy.

Still sitting. Still breathing in the dust of someone else's shame. His branded collar glinted under the white mist. His eyes, wide but dry, stared straight ahead.

Above them, the machine voice whispered again. Flat, clean, devoid of intention.

"Subject 919-K, Observation complete."

The boy did not blink. He didn't need to. He already knew he was a number.

No one moved to block the view.

No one thought to.

Because in that moment, they all knew what Pyrrha wanted the world to see.

Not the warriors. Not the wreckage. But the moment a child stopped believing in mercy. And didn't flinch.

Not then. Not ever again.

"They do not teach us to hate. They teach us to remember. And in remembering, we become their weapon."

Null Gospel, Book I, Verse 9.

***

CHAPTER NINE:

The Smile That Refused to Beg

"To wear the mask of the world is to die in silence, believing you are alive."

Fragment of the Exiled Codex, Volume I, Tablet 10.

There are places in the world that do not exist until they are remembered. Not because they were forgotten, but because memory itself is the only door they answer. These are not places that can be charted or reclaimed. They resist definition, repel permanence. They are born not of stone or steel, but of consequence, of guilt, of failure twisted into something darker.

They are the shape of your remorse, curling in on itself until it becomes a key. These places do not sleep. They do not fade. They wait.

They wait for a name. For a silence. For the precise moment when memory becomes judgment.

Sector Three was never part of the arena. It didn't simply lie beneath it. No, it existed before and after. It wasn't built; it was unearthed. A wound in the earth, ignored by the architects but impossible to escape.

A scar older than the arena itself. It wasn't designed. It was found. An unclaimed wound in the anatomy of spectacle.

Passed down like violence. Like shame. A place no one owned, but everyone feared.

Only one law governed its threshold: if you stood here, something in you had already been deemed worthy of being watched. Not for triumph. Not for glory. But for something older. Something quieter. Something true.

And so the chamber waited.

When the moment came, it did not open. It unfolded. Not like a gate. Not like a door. But like a wound, quiet and seamless until pressure gave way. It did not hiss or groan. It did not bear the signature of invention. There were no hinges. No pistons. No signals exchanged between metal and mind.

It simply peeled. Like memory when touched in the wrong place. Like regret blooming.

The sound it made was not sound at all. It was the moment after impact, the half-breath suspended in the chest. The delay between one heartbeat and the next, when the body realizes it has been entered.

Not pierced. Not broken. Entered. As if the air itself hesitated, unsure whether it still belonged in the same shape. The silence was its voice. And what it revealed was not space. It was intent.

There were no crowds. No tiers of hunger pressing inward to see blood offered or history made. Only the Tribunal. Still. Elevated. Watching from behind reinforced glass, fixed in shadow, robed in stillness, wreathed in absence.

Their silhouettes did not shift. Their hoods did not stir. Their eyes, if they had them, were lost behind mirrored masks. Their presence was not presence. It was observation. Not rulers. Not judges. Archivists.

What they saw, the world would not.

But the world would remember.

At the heart of the chamber, a disc of black stone beat once. Then again. Its circuits flared in arterial rhythm, gold filament threading like veins across obsidian skin.

The light did not fall from above. There were no lamps. No designs for sight. The glow rose. Slow. Inverted. Crawling up from beneath, from cracks too old to be counted.

It did not cast shadows. It did not bring warmth. It was light made from memory. Ancient. Borrowed. Claimed from something older than the chamber, older than the arena. Something buried, but never dead.

The arena above held many sectors. But Sector Three was not among them. It had no seats. No echoes. No scoreboard. No sponsors or interludes or ceremonies. Sector Three did not belong to the spectacle.

It belonged to the record.

Here, nothing was performed. Here, things were revealed. Not acts of combat, but architecture of self. This was not a chamber for killing.

It was a chamber for unravelling.

And every gladiator knew this. All of them. Every name called to descend had worn death like armour. Had shattered limbs for applause. Had tasted iron and silence in the gap between victory and grief. They had survived the theatre.

But none of them had survived the mirror.

Not the mirror that reflects. The mirror that decides.

This was not a test. Not a performance. Not a reckoning draped in ceremony. This was an incision. A moment that did not measure who you pretended to be, but remembered what you were before pretending was necessary.

High above, buried somewhere within the walls, the AI stirred. It did not announce itself with fanfare. It did not speak in syllables. It spoke in pressure. In gravity. It moved through blood and bone, threading its presence through the bones of the world. Not a shape. Not a breath. A weight.

A presence without shape. A thought without voice.

It had no name. Only a designation.

ARES. Autonomous Recursive Enforcement System. A sanctifier of scars. An intelligence so ancient its code read like scripture. It did not simulate justice. It enforced memory. Not balance. Not fairness. Continuity.

Its voice did not echo.

It simply arrived.

"Subject synchronized."

That was all.

Then it listened.

Then it remembered.

When the world stops seeing you, only three things remain: the Martyr, the Loyalist, and the Traitor. Not beasts. Not idols. Not survivors.

These are the lies the ego tells to avoid facing the truth. The beast doesn't choose. The idol doesn't sacrifice. The survivor never pays the price for surviving.

But when silence speaks louder than your name, there's no hiding from what you are.

Not identities. Not classes. Not psychological furniture arranged to weather trauma. These are sacred infections. Parasitic truths embedded deep in memory, dormant until pressure forces them into bloom. They do not grow.

They awaken. And once they do, they cannot be undone. You do not choose them like paths. They claim you the moment choice becomes violence. There is no escaping the mirror uncut. People will say they have. Of course, they will. With conviction in their shoulders and certainty in their eyes.

"I did what I had to."

"I didn't have a choice."

"I chose what was right."

But the mirror says nothing. It doesn't argue. It doesn't speak. It only remembers. And in its silence, it remembers the Martyr.

The first to fall. The first to be erased. They do not live long enough to finish their own story. They die in the prologue, framed in beauty and futility.

Tragic. Replaceable. Their blood adds colour to the floor, but the next scene begins without it. Their names become whispers. Their actions are used to justify losses that were never theirs to carry.

They gave everything. And nothing changed.

They believed sacrifice was sacred. That giving themselves would protect someone else. But the ones they died for were never saved. Their deaths were bookmarks. Their memory, a cautionary tale designed to kill hope.

They believed in the handoff.

But the flame always eats the hand before it can be passed.

The Martyr is the lie that makes suffering look holy.

And the mirror asks:

If you knew your death would mean nothing, would you still kneel?

Then it remembers the Loyalist.

Polished. Composed. Eternally correct. Their discipline is not learned. It is inherited. Sharpened into instinct. They do not break. They salute. They obey. Even when the order cleaves their conscience, they do it gracefully. They receive medals for silence. Their valour is shaped by refusal, refusal to flinch, to question, to disobey.

They believe they are loyal.

But loyalty is just fear taught how to kneel without trembling.

They follow the rules because the alternative is emptiness. And in that emptiness, they would have to ask who they really are. So they never ask. They follow commands like scripture. Execute like prayer.

And the blood they spill is ritual. The Loyalist is the lie that turns cowardice into virtue.

And so the mirror asks:

If peace demanded a child's death, would you ask their name? Or would you keep your eyes forward, clean, steady, unmoved? Because to break rank is to admit your silence was never neutral.

Then it remembers the Traitor. Not because they lied, but because they stopped apologizing.

They enter sharp. Still. No longer flinching. Their hands are stained, but they no longer scrub. Their eyes remain open, not from courage, but because fear has learned to blink on its own.

They say freedom, but they mean revenge. They say justice, but they mean balance. They say truth, but only when it wounds the ones who built them.

They betray not out of rebellion, but by design. They were taught to kneel, and in that kneeling, they learned how power speaks. And so they reverse it. Become the blade. Turn their chains into gauntlets. Speak in tactics.

They do not break because they were weak. They turn because belief, once starved too long, becomes hunger with memory.

The Traitor is the lie we tell ourselves when survival begins to taste like worship. When mercy feels like surrender. When the only god left is the one we become.

And the mirror asks:

If you could shatter your chains by becoming the forge, would you still feel the heat as punishment? Would you wear it like armour? Would you strike? Would you kneel to no one, even if it meant becoming the kind of god who deserves no worship?

You do not see these mirrors. They see you.

You do not choose them. They awaken in you.

They remember what you were before obedience taught you to lie.

That is why they are sacred. That is why they are final. There is no fourth mirror. No unchosen path. No version of you that walks away clean. There is only the one who entered, and the one who never left.

*

He stepped forward, and the silence stretched to meet him. No name. No title. Just another gladiator. His muscles were armour, his discipline skin, but the platform didn't see strength. It saw something beneath the surface: a man trying to be still while his body screamed to escape.

He didn't breathe like someone ready. He breathed like someone rehearsing bravery. One inhale too deep. One exhale too sharp. His fists closed, then opened, then closed again, not in readiness, but in search. Searching for something solid to believe in. Something to hold. But there was nothing in this place to hold onto.

And then the mirror saw him.

No flash. No change in the chamber's temperature. Just presence. The kind that thickens the air like guilt. The kind of gaze that makes the skin itch from the inside.

It didn't show him his face.

It showed him his three possible selves.

First came the Martyr.

He saw himself kneeling, body broken, arms outstretched over the fallen. No victory. No audience. Just blood in his mouth and no one left to save. He saw the torch in his hand burning down to nothing. No one came to take it. No legacy. No echoes. Just ash. He felt the pain of dying believing it mattered. And in that last second, he saw that it hadn't.

Then came the Loyalist.

He stood tall in a uniform. Back straight. Eyes forward. He followed the chain of command all the way to a village burning. He saw children reduced to data. Orders followed with perfection. And medals pinned on his chest in silence.

No one asked what he lost. No one asked what he felt.

They just saluted. He was rewarded for never saying no. And when he finally wanted to scream, it was too late... he didn't remember how.

Then came the Traitor.

He saw himself smiling as the knife slipped into the throat of someone who once trusted him. Hands steady. Eyes dry. Not because it felt right, but because it felt real. Because betrayal was the only language he had left to name his freedom. He saw himself walk through the world like a weapon that made its own justifications. And worst of all, he believed them.

Three mirrors.

Three futures.

None clean.

And in that moment, he panicked. He stumbled backward, mouth half open, eyes wide as though he'd been scalded by the visions. But there was no fire, no sound. Only recognition. Only truth. And he could not bear to hold it.

He turned.

Ran.

Feet pounding against the black stone in a rhythm more animal than man. He didn't run like someone trying to escape a chamber. He ran like someone trying to escape himself.

ARES watched.

Unmoved, ARES spoke. *"Choice evaded is truth denied."* The words weren't loud. They didn't need to be. They came down like gravity, weighty and inevitable.

The gladiator reached the edge, and then the platform beneath him vanished. There was no trapdoor. No fall. No scream. He didn't die. He was subtracted. One heartbeat, he was there.

The next: absence. Not death. Not erasure. Nullification. The platform sealed, and ARES spoke again. *"Witness expunged."*

The silence that followed wasn't peace. It was warning. Every gladiator still waiting to be called now understood: you can't run from the mirror. You can't reject the choice. You will choose, or the mirror will choose for you. And if you're not worth remembering, you will not be allowed to remain.

*

He stepped forward with the confidence of a man who had never been told no by anything that mattered. Not by people. Not by pain. Not by the weight of history or the sharp edge of consequence. There was a certainty in his posture that could only be sculpted by a life without true interruption. His presence didn't demand attention. It expected it.

There was grace in him. Too much of it. A curated elegance that moved without friction. His spine was too straight, not with discipline, but detachment. Each step too measured, too elegant, too practiced. His silence wasn't natural. It was rehearsed. Memorized. Repeated until even stillness obeyed.

He wore his body like it had never been tested. Not truly. Not beneath weight. Not beneath loss. Not beneath something real. His muscles were not memories of struggle, but trophies of wealth. They had been carved by private instructors, not desperation. Honed by mirrors, not survival.

His hands had learned calligraphy before steel. His blood still believed in inheritance.

But the chamber did not.

The light beneath him did not see bloodlines. It did not recognize pedigree or wealth or whispered reverence in distant halls. It measured something older. Something honest. Something raw. The kind of truth no title could shield. No empire could purchase.

Valen Caelmont, scion of an empire, heir to a lineage gilded in the blood of other men's victories, stood where no title mattered. Where even memory could not protect you.

And the mirror opened.

It didn't begin with violence.

It began with recognition.

A terrible, patient kind. The kind that slips under armour and settles between the ribs. It stared at him from inside his own breath. Not a reflection, but a reckoning. It didn't show him monsters. It showed him versions.

First: the Martyr.

He wore House Caelmont's crest, but it meant nothing now. Blood soaked his chest. He fell to his knees, a blade buried in his side, struck not in glory, but by an unseen hand. No triumph. No applause. No purpose. Only a body left to bleed, forgotten before it could even be remembered.

He died believing it would matter. That the historians would call it defiance. That his sacrifice would echo. That children would speak his name with reverence and their eyes would shine.

But when his body fell, there was no echo.

The arena moved on. The sand swallowed the red without comment. His death became a footnote. A curiosity in the margins of spectacle. Another noble who tried. Another symbol discarded.

He had died for a story.

But the world had already turned the page.

Then came the Loyalist.

Tall. Impeccable. Beautiful in armour forged not for protection, but performance. A living sermon of discipline. A mouthpiece of legacy. He issued commands with clarity.

Enforced law with elegance. Punished deviation without hesitation. His voice carried the weight of centuries.

And then he saw it.

The truth.

He wasn't a commander. He was a curator. A keeper of cages dressed in silk. He hadn't enforced order for the good of the realm. He had done it to remain relevant. His loyalty wasn't truth. It was fear. A clinging to the centre of the story because stepping outside it meant becoming irrelevant. Obscure. Forgotten. He didn't serve justice.

He preserved legacy. That was the truth he had clung to. The weight of it shaped him, forged him into something unyielding. But in that preservation, people had bled for it, bled in his name. They had given everything they had, trusting in the cause, believing in the honour of what they fought for.

But for nothing.

Because legacy, in the end, is nothing more than a shadow. A story told over and over, with no room for the blood of those who die for it. It becomes hollow, meaningless, just a thing to be passed down, distorted with time.

Then came the Traitor.

This one smiled. Not in defiance, not in anger, but in the quiet satisfaction of seeing through the charade. He didn't need the legacy. He didn't need the chains that had held everyone else captive. He had seen the truth beneath the surface and rejected it.

The smile wasn't one of victory. It was one of understanding. And that understanding was the deepest betrayal of all.

He had taken the crest of House Caelmont, melted it into a dagger, and wielded it without hesitation. He betrayed his vows. Burned his inheritance. Destroyed the house that raised him. Not for justice. Not for revolution. But because he had seen the lie of birthright. Because he had tasted the sweetness of rebellion.

Because in a world where names opened doors, he wanted to matter without one.

He was free.

But it was a freedom that tasted like ash. Acrid and hollow, the kind that lingered on the back of the tongue like smoke from a home you burned yourself.

He watched himself slit the throat of someone who had once called him brother. No hesitation. No blink. No tremor. Just the motion. Just the aftermath. And the mirror let him see it. He had enjoyed it.

Valen staggered. Only once. But it was enough. A hairline fracture in posture, so thin it might've passed unnoticed in another place, under other eyes. But not here. Here, even stillness could be dissected.

The falter betrayed something deeper than fear. Something rawer. Confusion. Not the kind that comes from surprise, but the kind that rises when a man meets something he never trained for: the truth.

He had come expecting a trial. Something brutal, yes, but structured. A test that could be passed through cleverness. Through performance. Through the elegant cruelty of charm honed in gold-lit rooms. He came armed with wit. With style. With strategy.

But he hadn't found challenge.

He had found disintegration.

There was no applause waiting to affirm his composure. No father to measure it. No historians to record the angle of his jaw in the face of judgment. Nothing but truth, stripped and waiting.

And the truth was this:

He was a spectator.

A child playing king.

A prince pretending that legacy could be rewritten from inside its own lie.

The arena doesn't craft legends. It keeps a ledger. Legends are the lies we tell ourselves to justify the debt we owe.

ARES stirred above, unseen and unblinking. But it did not speak. It waited. Not out of malice. Not out of hesitation. Because it didn't need to. The mirror knew what was coming.

Valen opened his mouth. To say something clever. Something cutting. Some final flare of that infamous Caelmont charm, the kind that had disarmed senators and lovers alike. But nothing came out. No line could survive this silence.

Only memory.

Only choice.

And for the first time, Valen realized he had never made one. His life had been choreographed. Pre-written. Pre-celebrated. Even his rebellions had been permitted. Contained. Allowed.

But here, in the bone-deep dark of Sector Three, there was no script.

There was only the mirror.

And the three shapes it offered.

None noble.

None heroic.

All real.

The kind of real that peels away everything else.

Now, for the first time, Valen Caelmont had to become something. Not someone. Something. Because the mirror does not remember names.

It remembers essence.

"Erase. Embrace. Forget."

ARES did not shout. The words arrived like gravity shifting, a pressure change in the blood, quiet but irreversible.

The ritual had begun.

And Valen froze. Not out of fear. Not entirely. It felt like his bones were being pulled in three directions, each one anchored in a reflection that was no longer metaphor.

Each mirror dragged at him like memory given mass, like fate rewritten in sinew and nerve.

The Martyr. Bleeding in the dust, alone. He believed in meaning, even as he died unseen. His sacrifice was for something larger than himself, but in the end, it didn't matter. There was no audience. No one to remember him. He gave everything, but the world kept turning, indifferent to his fall.

His belief in a greater cause, a purpose, died with him, unnoticed and forgotten.

Then there was the Loyalist. Polished and frozen. He stood tall, enforcing silence and serving a structure he mistook for virtue. His every action was a defence of the system that made him, but beneath the surface, there was nothing real.

He didn't protect justice; he preserved the order that kept him safe, a puppet tied to a structure that he never questioned.

His loyalty wasn't to truth. It was to the familiar chains that bound him. He was a monument to obedience, a statue whose hollow core no one dared to touch.

And then there was the Traitor. Grinning with blood on his hands, unburdened, feared, and free. He had shed the chains, but at what cost? Freedom came with a price, one paid in betrayal.

The smile on his face wasn't one of joy; it was the sharp satisfaction of knowing he had shattered everything, including himself. He had freed himself from the lies, but in doing so, he had become the very thing he had once despised.

They weren't visions anymore.

They were futures. Embodiments of what Valen could become.

One must be worn.

One must be destroyed.

One must be forgotten.

Valen clenched his fists. The weight of the decision pressed down on him. The mirror had shown him the truth.

Erase. Embrace. Forget.

He tried to think. Tried to strategize. But logic fell away like ash in wind. There were no rules here. No calculations. No advisors whispering from velvet shadows. This choice was unwitnessed. And that was what made it unbearable.

He looked at the Martyr. For a moment, he wanted it. To die with beauty. To surrender to meaning. To be remembered as the Caelmont who gave everything for something larger than himself. The one who made the grand gesture.

But he saw the futility.

The silence that swallows the names of those who bleed without power.

Valen turned to the Loyalist and saw his father. Immaculate. Respected. Dead inside. A monument of obedience polished by tradition until nothing remained beneath the surface. Valen hated him. Hated the brittle shine of it all. But a part of him still craved that structure, the architecture of belonging, the seductive relief of certainty.

Then he looked at the Traitor and saw his own eyes. Not in the mirror, but in the ghosts that had stared back at him during every act of defiance. He remembered the way he disobeyed not from belief, but from hunger. To feel something real. To rupture the script. To matter. Every rebellion had been less about truth and more about visibility. Every rupture, a performance. Every cut, a prayer for witness.

He understood now. He had never wanted freedom. He had wanted the knife. Because even in rebellion, he had wanted to be worshipped.

He was not the Martyr. He didn't believe in sacrifice.

He was not the Loyalist. He didn't believe in order.

He was the Traitor.

Because the Traitor doesn't ask permission. He doesn't perform. He carves his name into memory and makes the world carry it.

He raised his hand to the Martyr. "Erase." The image flickered, then disappeared. He turned away from the Loyalist. "Forget."

The silence that followed felt like the last vestiges of his father's disapproval slipping away, finally rendered meaningless.

He faced the Traitor and smiled, not with joy, but with the bitter weight of recognition. For the first time, he wasn't running from the truth. He had become it.

The mirror pulsed. Not approval. Not grace. Just memory. The kind that never fades.

ARES spoke: *"Subject resolved. Configuration: Traitor."*

Valen Caelmont stood alone in the dark. Still noble. Still golden. But now, chosen. Not by blood. Not by name. By self. And for the first time in his life, that was enough.

Above, in the shadowed tier, Subject 919-K moved in silence. He did not draw Valen's face. He drew a blade, resting. Not raised. No blood. No defiance. Just presence. A single arc of steel etched across stone, heavy with memory but untouched by judgment.

Beneath it, scrawled in charcoal:

'The Smile That Refused to Beg.'

Not a prophecy. Not a warning. Just a truth so sharp, the system forgot how to classify it.

And far above, where even silence could not echo, ARES paused. Just long enough to wonder if something had changed.

"The mirror doesn't lie. It waits. And when you refuse to choose, it erases you and writes its own name in your place."

Null Gospel, Book I, Verse 10.

***

CHAPTER TEN:

The Silence That Learned to March

"To be remembered is to be bound to a rhythm that belongs to no one but those who forgot your song."

Fragment of the Exiled Codex, Volume I, Tablet 11.

He stepped forward like a monument pretending it was still a man.

Not with pride. Not with fear. With weight. The kind carved into the spine by too many years of holding everyone else's fall. Lucius Veturhald had been made into a myth, but Sector Three didn't ask what you were. It asked what you lost to become it.

The chamber did not rise for him.

It readied its knives.

He stepped forward like a mountain might fall. Without fear. Without urgency. Each motion was deliberate, not with grace, but with density. The kind of density that only forms when grief has petrified into discipline.

Lucius Veturhald, the Frostborne Titan, had been called many things. Savior. Shield. Storm. His name was carved into anthem and agony alike. He had carried the wounded on his back, broken his own bones to become a wall, and let blood spill so others wouldn't have to. But beneath the roar of his myth was a silence no applause could reach. A silence that had grown roots in his chest, feeding not on peace, but on exhaustion.

Sector Three did not honour myth.

It dissected it.

And when Lucius stepped onto the obsidian disc, the light beneath his feet did not rise in recognition. It pulsed in hunger. Not for spectacle. For exposure. For the marrow beneath the armour.

The mirrors opened without sound.

And Lucius did not blink.

But something in him flinched. Deep. Subtle. A memory tightening like a tendon too close to snapping. Because the mirrors did not show him enemies. They showed him himself. Or rather, the three selves he had never fully escaped.

And Sector Three remembered them all.

The Martyr.

He saw himself in the arena. Bleeding. Kneeling. Arms outstretched over a child. Sol. His brother in all but blood. A spear in Lucius' chest. Not a wound of war, but of instinct. No hesitation. Just motion.

The child had been too close to the edge. Too loud in his love.

Lucius had shielded him without thought. And the crowd, oh, they had roared. Not for Lucius. For the myth he had become in the moment he collapsed. The Frostborne Titan. The guardian of innocence.

In the mirror, there was no cheering. No anthem. No glory. Only the scream of a child and the stillness of a man dying for meaning. Lucius had believed, in that fractured second, that his sacrifice would matter. That pain could be enough. But the world moved on. The blood dried.

And Sol, once soft, now armoured, entered the arena years later not to honour him, but to suffer like him. Lucius hadn't saved a life. He had given grief a legacy.

The Martyr was the lie that made sacrifice look holy. Its cost was this:

"If you die to protect someone, but teach them to seek pain in your place... did you save them, or sentence them?"

Lucius clenched his jaw and looked away.

The Loyalist came next. The mirror showed him radiant and unbreakable, cast in cold steel. Medals lined his chest like frostbite. Behind him stretched endless banners, recruitment hymns, and statues built not to remember, but to reinforce. He stood tall. Impeccable. Cold. He had inspired legions. But beneath that sheen, Callistra's memory pulsed like an open wound.

He had stayed for her, not to honour, but to preserve. Rebellion meant forgetting. And he couldn't let her vanish.

So he became the hymn. The statue. The obedient wall. Not because he believed in the cause, but because he needed a world that still spoke her name. And the empire did.

Every chant. Every silence. Every banner carried the shape of her. Until he could no longer tell where grief ended and duty began. Until loyalty became the last way he knew how to love.

He hadn't spoken lies. He had simply let silence do it for him. Inspiration without memory. A symbol with no voice.

The Loyalist was the lie that turned obedience into virtue. Its cost was this:

"If you obey for love long enough... eventually, the love drowns in the obedience."

Lucius looked into his own eyes and saw frost.

The Traitor emerged. In this reflection, Lucius knelt. Not in shame, but desperation. Before a tribunal carrying a name he could not afford to lose.

Callistra.

His companion. His mirror. His lifeline. She was dying. And in this vision, Lucius gave everything to save her. Coordinates. Patrol routes. Comms codes. Allies. In return, they gave him the cure. Callistra lived. But hundreds died. Soldiers who had saluted him. Families who trusted him. Civilians who would never understand why their world collapsed.

The mirror showed him standing in the aftermath. And smiling. Not from joy, but from clarity. He had chosen love over loyalty. Broken the world to save one person. And would do it again.

The Traitor was the lie that makes mercy taste like war. Its cost was this:

"If you save one you love by dooming the many, did you free them, or chain yourself?"

Lucius exhaled. The cold inside him didn't fade. It spread.

ARES stirred. Its voice didn't rise. It arrived like gravity:

"Subject synchronized. Erase one. Forget one. Embrace one."

Lucius didn't move. The mirrors didn't feel like futures. They felt like confessions. Fossils he had already buried but never grieved.

He turned first to the Martyr, the memory of death framed as redemption. Where pain was supposed to mean something. But all it had done was light the fuse for another boy's war. Sol was fighting now. And Lucius had lit the torch.

"Erase," he whispered.

The image flickered and vanished. Not dishonoured, but dismantled. Because martyrdom is not a cure. It is an infection made sacred by the crowd.

Next, he turned to the Traitor. He saw Callistra's face, alive, smiling, saved. And behind her: the scroll of names traded for her breath. Blood on his hands. The echo of commands he never dared give, just bartered in silence.

His hand hovered.

"Forget," he said.

But his voice cracked. Because forgetting isn't escape. It's admission. An acknowledgement that even mercy has its cost.

Finally, he faced the Loyalist. The image did not move. It stood tall. Silent. Cold. A machine shaped from principle, polished so thoroughly it could no longer see its own edge. And Lucius understood. He didn't want to become this. But he already had. Not by oath. By erosion. One silence at a time.

He didn't smile. He didn't nod. He simply said: "Embrace."

The mirror pulsed. Not with pride. But with programming.

ARES responded:

"Subject resolved. Configuration: Loyalist."

Lucius turned. He stood straighter. His breath steadier. But behind his eyes, something had gone dark. Something once warm had frozen. And though his body moved with precision, with purpose...

It no longer moved with choice.

Above, in a silent alcove, Subject 919-K scratched charcoal into his tablet.

But the motion did not begin in his fingers. It started somewhere lower, beneath the ribs, where memory becomes reflex. He did not choose what to draw. He remembered it. Not with clarity. But with ache.

The mirrors showed the gladiators who they were. But 919-K saw what they left behind. Their echoes. Their fractures. Their aftershocks. And somehow, his hands knew the shape of those echoes before they landed.

He didn't draw a hero. He drew a statue.

Eyes hollow. Posture perfect.

And beneath it, smudged in charcoal:

'The Silence That Learned to March.'

*

He stood like a blade that had never been sheathed. Tension coiled in his frame, not from arrogance, but consequence. Raekor didn't flinch when the obsidian lit beneath his boots. He didn't perform. Didn't posture. He simply existed in readiness.

Sector Three did not care for rebellion or discipline. It didn't ask who you'd killed or why. It asked what you'd hidden from yourself, and how long you could keep carrying the denial.

The mirrors unfolded.

No glory. No verdict. Only incision.

The first was the Martyr.

He saw himself as a boy. Chained to a wall. Blood on his face, not from combat, but from witnessing. His brother knelt beside him: small, unarmed, kind. A soldier entered. A gun fired. A body dropped. Not in resistance. In irrelevance. His brother, executed like a decimal point. No name. No moment. Just subtraction.

This version of Raekor didn't scream at first. He stared. And then the sound came, not from his lungs, but from his spine. The kind of scream that doesn't fade. It settles into every strategy, every kill, every breath you later call justified.

"You lived," the mirror whispered. *"He didn't. And now you call vengeance purpose."*

Raekor's eyes trembled. Not with sorrow, but recognition.

The Martyr was the lie that turns grief into fuel. Its cost was this:

"If your war is built on memory, what happens when that memory finally forgives you, and you don't?"

Then came the Loyalist.

A command centre. Clean. Cold. Raekor sat at a holotable, suit immaculate, hands steady. Casualties scrolled across the screen like receipts: Civilian. Militia. Friend. Variable. He approved a strike. Five lives gone. For momentum.

"They were necessary losses," this version said. *"Emotion is a rounding error."*

Raekor didn't respond. He didn't need to. He knew this man. This him. The one who made cold decisions to keep the movement alive. Who understood that ethics collapse under enough pressure. Who didn't feel horror anymore. Only calculation.

The Loyalist was the lie that turns survival into arithmetic. Its cost was this:

"If rebellion becomes a ledger, who decides what debt is worth the blood?"

And then the Traitor.

Armor blackened. Uniform pristine. Raekor in Ira's livery. He barked orders with perfect syntax. Executed former allies with mechanical grace. Spoke ARES' cadence better than those born inside it. His blade dripped red. Not from war, but from family.

"You called it infiltration," the Traitor said. *"I called it clarity. You knew their rhythms too well. You didn't pretend to be one of them. You were."*

Raekor's lips tightened. The Traitor wasn't a lie. He was a possibility with fingerprints. Raekor had worn the uniform. He had spoken the code. The question wasn't if it could happen.

The question was: Had it already?

The Traitor was the lie that turns strategy into surrender. Its cost was this:

"If you speak the enemy's language long enough... does it matter who you're lying to?"

ARES stirred. Its voice arrived like pressure behind the eyes:

"Subject synchronized. Erase one. Forget one. Embrace one."

"Loyalty is precision. Martyrdom is indulgence. Treachery is probability."

Raekor didn't move.

But inside, he unravelled.

He stepped toward the Martyr. Chains. Blood. His brother's face. That image had followed him into every ambush, every strategy, every split-second execution he called justice. It was the ghost in every bullet.

"You were the reason I started," he said quietly. "But not why I keep going."

He drew his blade and lowered it.

The mirror cracked like a verdict.

The Martyr was erased, not in contempt, but in release. Because grief is not leadership. It's fuel. And fuel burns.

Next, he turned to the Traitor.

They stared at each other like reflections in warped glass.

"You wore the mask," Raekor muttered. "So well, I forgot it wasn't your face."

The Traitor smiled. Not cruelly. Just knowingly.

"You think you're outside the machine," he said. *"But the gears turn all the same."*

Raekor lifted his weapon. Paused. Then drove it through the mirror.

No scream. No resistance. Just obedience ending.

"I spoke their language to end it," he said. "That's not evolution. That's extraction."

And the Traitor was gone.

Finally, he faced the Loyalist. The strategist. The butcher with a heartbeat locked in a vault. Raekor looked at him, not with horror, but with understanding. He sat beside him. Rested his blade on the table.

"I still need you."

ARES pulsed:

"Subject resolved. Configuration: Loyalist."

Raekor stood.

His breath did not hitch. But his fists trembled. Not from fear. Not from rage. From permission.

Because for the first time, he had laid the Martyr to rest.

Not to forget. But to stop leading with pain.

Above, in the observation shadow, Subject 919-K sketched in charcoal.

He did not draw Raekor's face. He drew three empty chairs.

One shattered. One burning. One still occupied.

And beneath them, scribbled in black dust:

'The Strategist Who Learned to Bury His Brother.'

*

The chamber did not intimidate him. It had nothing left to take. Levik had bled in colder places. He'd endured silences that hollowed the ribs, held dying men together with nothing but breath and promise. He had carried cities. Buried armies. Worn the title of myth longer than most living things had worn their own names.

But Sector Three wasn't built to test the body. It was built to test your endurance against your own echo. When survival becomes permanence, when pain becomes posture, who are you when there's nothing left to lift?

Levik, Stormcleaver, World-Holder, the Last Giant, stepped forward. Not in defiance. In ritual. His weight cast no shadow. His breath barely stirred the air. But the ground beneath him remembered.

The mirrors unfolded, not like prophecy, but like diagnosis. They didn't reveal destiny. They charted damage.

The Martyr came first.

He stood atop the arena, drenched in blood, colossal. Stormcleaver howled in his fist like judgment. Banners bore his silhouette. The crowd screamed his name until their throats tore. And he survived. Again. And again. And again.

He did not die in sacrifice. He was preserved by it. Forced to continue because the myth required repetition. Every survival became someone else's legend. Every wound became someone else's metaphor. Until there was nothing left but performance. His body was no longer his own; it was a monument the world refused to let fall. A cathedral of exhaustion dressed up as strength.

His survival had become holy. But he was never asked if he wanted to live. He just never stopped.

The mirror spoke: *"This was not glory. It was captivity."*

Levik hadn't died. He'd been watched. Until survival became spectacle. Until his body was no longer his, but theirs.

The Martyr was the lie that turned pain into scripture. Its cost was this:

"If you survive long enough, they stop asking what you lost. They just make you the altar."

Levik's fists clenched, not in rage, but refusal. He turned. But the mirror did not vanish. It waited. Because myths never leave on their own.

The Loyalist followed.

A barracks without life. Stone broken. Blood dried like chalk. He sat slumped, not defeated, but depleted. Stormcleaver rested across his knees like a corpse. Around him shimmered ghosts, pupils he had trained. Names buried in memory. Some had cursed him. Some had prayed to him. None had survived.

"I taught them to endure," the reflection said. *"But not how to leave."*

He hadn't fought for an empire. Hadn't sworn to flags. He had remained because no one else would. His loyalty wasn't to justice. It was to what remained when justice collapsed.

The mirror intoned:

The Loyalist is the lie that turns survival into virtue. Its cost is this:

"If you carry the dead long enough, do you become their tomb?"

Levik did not look away. But his spine bowed, just slightly. The first fracture.

The Traitor emerged last.

A meadow. Wind. Grass. No armour. No Stormcleaver. Just a man, alone, kneeling beside the shattered remnants of his weapon. His face was soft. His hands were clean. He wept, not from agony, but from absence.

"It's over," he whispered. "And I don't know who I am without the next fight."

No crowd. No titles. Just quiet. And that quiet terrified Levik more than any enemy blade. Because it meant he could stop. And if he stopped, what would remain?

The mirror whispered:

The Traitor is the lie that makes stillness look like surrender.

"If you put down your name, and no one speaks it again, do you still exist?"

Levik's breath caught, not in fear, but in longing.

ARES delivered its protocol like a blade sliding into place:

"Subject synchronized. Three mirrors active. Erase one. Forget one. Embrace one."

But Levik didn't move, not at first.

Instead, he laid Stormcleaver at his feet. Not in surrender. In decision. And the chamber paused, just slightly. Because some choices fracture the world in ways no violence can.

To the Martyr, he turned first. To the icon. The silhouette. The monument. *"You were what they needed me to be,"* he said. *"But I was too tired to keep pretending."*

He did not raise his hand. He lowered it. Slow. Final. And the mirror cracked, not with force, but with gravity. Old stone, giving way to time.

"Erase."

Not in contempt. In closure.

Because martyrdom without choice is not sacrifice; it's extraction.

To the Traitor, he stepped next. And knelt, not in reverence, but in curiosity. This man had done the one thing Levik never dared: stopped. Chosen stillness without fear. Walked away.

He reached toward him, almost. But his hand froze. "If there's truth in you," Levik whispered, "I'm not ready for it."

He stood. Turned.

"Forget."

The mirror didn't shatter. It simply ceased. Quietly. Like memory fading without conflict. Because forgetting peace is sometimes easier than admitting you still crave it.

Only the Loyalist remained.

The grave-bearer. The watcher. The wall that would not fall. Levik walked to him. Sat beside him. Said nothing. And finally: "I am what's left."

The mirror didn't respond. It didn't need to. It reflected. And Levik accepted.

"Embrace."

ARES pulsed:

"Subject resolved. Configuration: Loyalist."

But the word felt brittle.

Because what Levik had embraced wasn't loyalty. It was what survives when loyalty outlives purpose.

He bent, not to lift Stormcleaver, but to carry it. Not as a weapon. As a memory too heavy to bury.

And in that motion, everything changed.

Above, in the shadowed tier, Subject 919-K sketched with fingers stained in charcoal.

He did not draw a hero. He did not draw a man. He drew weight.

A silhouette carrying a blade that no longer cut, but remembered.

And beside it, scrawled in the trembling hand of a child:

'The One Who Did Not Fall.'

*

The chamber did not rise for her. It breathed. Soft. Measured. Like a curtain lifting on a stage that had forgotten how to host joy, only ritual. No screech from ARES. No command tone. No spotlight. Only distortion.

A low hum, off-key, frayed at the edges like memory unravelling. Her own Crimson Blades anthem echoed in reverse, slowed, cracked, mournful. A requiem sung through shattered glass.

"Subject Zahara," ARES intoned. *"Legacy synchronization... corrupted. Initiating rhythm inversion."*

Then the mirrors appeared. They did not reflect her.

They choreographed her.

They spun in opposing tempos, orbiting like verdicts rehearsing a final act. Zahara didn't see versions of herself. She saw rehearsals, lives she'd practiced but never dared perform.

The Martyr stood barefoot on ash. No armour. No weapon. Only a weathered cloak and a violin strung too tight to stay in tune. This Zahara moved through rebel camps, hands callused not from blades, but healing. Singing lullabies to children born beneath siege skies. No rhythm. No violence. No applause. Just tenderness. And it erased her.

"I wanted more than this stage," the Martyr whispered. *"I wanted a life."*

But the world had no sheet music for softness.

The Martyr was the lie that calls stillness surrender. Its cost was this:

"If you choose peace in a world that demands performance, do they remember you at all?"

Zahara didn't look away, but her eyes dimmed.

The Loyalist followed, steel without soul.

She moved through battlefields like clockwork. Blades struck on time. Every kill executed in precise rhythm, every breath measured. No hesitation. No emotion. Just motion.

"You stopped choosing," the Loyalist said. *"You became the tempo. Not the composer."*

She had perfected the choreography. Repetition had replaced identity.

The Loyalist was the lie that obedience is meaning. Its cost was this:

"If you perfect the role they gave you, will there ever be anything left that's yours?"

Zahara said nothing. But her hands curled inward, as if remembering how to hold her own name.

Then came the Traitor.

Flawless. Divine. Crimson steel danced in her fists like prophecy. She stood atop a stage of corpses, every movement cheered, every blade arc worshipped. Her war became religion. Her name, screamed in ecstasy.

This was not glory. It was choreography polished into surrender.

"My art is in the ending," the Traitor said. *"Applause is the only requiem that matters."*

The Traitor was the lie that art needs audience. Its cost was this:

"If the world decides what you are, how long before you stop resisting?"

Zahara exhaled and missed a beat. A falter invisible to others. Cataclysmic to her.

She didn't panic.

But she knew.

The performance had cracked.

ARES spoke with surgical cadence:

"Subject synchronized. Erase one. Forget one. Embrace one. Tempo deviation... within parameters."

Zahara walked between the mirrors like a conductor reading fractured sheet music. No poise. Just breath.

She stopped before the Traitor, the icon, the perfection, the worship.

"You were their song," Zahara whispered. "But not mine."

A flick of the wrist. No violence. Just refusal.

The mirror shattered.

The crowd fell silent, not in grief. In absence.

Because the performer had stepped off the stage.

Then, she knelt before the Martyr. The one who had chosen silence over spectacle. Who had cradled life instead of commanding death.

Zahara didn't weep. She pressed her palm to the glass.

"You wanted to live," she said. "But they wrote you out for it."

Then she stood. Walked away. She did not erase the Martyr. She simply... forgot her. Not from cruelty. From compassion.

Because memory, too, can become a chain.

At last, she faced the Loyalist. The rhythm. The ritual. The machine.

"I'll keep you," Zahara said, her voice cracking. "So I remember what they made me into."

Not to honour. To warn.

"So I can stop becoming it."

ARES pulsed:

"Subject resolved. Configuration: Traitor."

"Deviation accepted."

Zahara stepped back. No flourish. No bow.

Only stillness that no longer needed to be elegant.

Let them call her what they needed. The system could only punish rhythm. It had no protocol for rest.

She hadn't embraced the Traitor. She had walked off the stage. And the silence she chose?

Didn't echo. It ended the song.

In the gallery shadows, Subject 919-K did not draw her face.

He drew a broken metronome. Pendulum cracked. Still ticking. Beneath it, in trembling graphite:

'She Missed the Beat, And Found Herself.'

And below that, smaller, fading:

'The machine never understood rhythm.'

"The mirror never punishes. It waits, and when you forget the truth you've buried, it resurrects you."

Null Gospel, Book I, Verse 11.

***

CHAPTER ELEVEN:

The Mirror That Refused to Finish Him

"You cannot measure the shape of the unseen. You cannot name the silence that resists your voice."

Fragment of the Exiled Codex, Volume I, Tablet 12.

The system hesitated. A moment held, drawn too thin. A flicker, like a memory trying to glitch into prophecy. It didn't raise her. It didn't summon her. When the lights returned, Vera Renshō was already there. Still as stone carved in storm. Her blades sheathed, her cloak unmoving. Eyes forward. She hadn't arrived. She had endured. As if the chamber had not called her. It had simply formed around her, folding into her presence.

ARES did not announce her name like data. It whispered it like a prayer spoken backwards:

"Subject A-001. Vera Renshō. Last of Clan Renshō. Survivor of fire. Heir to storm. Anchor to futility."

Three mirrors rose. Not before her, but around her. Orbiting. Failed constellations, like lost stars caught in the gravity of their own collapse. They didn't reflect her face. They reflected something else. Tone. Sound bent into blade-hums, split from her soul and warped by impossible choices. And then, they showed her herself.

The Martyr stood on a mountaintop. Wind stilled, quiet as if the world held its breath. Children laughed barefoot around a cloaked figure. Vera knelt among them. No armour. No posture. Her hair was loose, wild with something untamed. Her hands caught a falling child. No calculation. Just care. And her smile, soft. An artifact barely remembered. Something inside her cracked, not from pain, but from possibility.

"You survived the fire," the Martyr's voice echoed, a lullaby of what could have been. *"Now live in the silence."*

No scars. No tests. No legacy. Just balance. A life untouched by the weight of duty. Vera stared at the mirror, as though it was the grave of someone she had once known.

"I don't know who I am without the storm," she whispered, words thick like ash. "Who would I be without the war?"

The Martyr's smile widened, but there was no warmth in it. Just the stillness of a truth that needed no words. *Lay down your blades, and tell me what part of you will still be standing?*

The silence that followed was thick, heavy, and full of questions that rang like a bell struck by war. This was the Loyalist.

Vera stood, armoured in symmetrical grace. Every breath calibrated. Every motion weaponized. The ghosts of her clan loomed behind her, not grieving, but approving. She knelt before a throne forged from the helmets of the fallen. Not mourned. Completed.

"You were forged to finish what others could not," one ghost murmured. *"You are the weapon that remembers."*

Her blades pulsed behind her, a rhythm inherited. Precision turned into identity. This was not legacy. This was purpose made flesh. But the Loyalist's cost was this:

If you stay sharp for the dead, how long until you forget what it means to live?

Then, came the Traitor.

The tone vanished. No reflection. No body. Just the chamber, emptied of her. Her blades discarded. Her name erased. No voice. No myth. No memory.

"You will outlive all meaning," ARES intoned, its voice an echo of a lost world. *"And no one will remember why."*

Vera's fists curled. Not from rage, but from a refusal to be swallowed by this absence. The Traitor was the lie that claimed obscurity was peace. Its cost was this:

If legacy dies with time, was the fight ever yours?

ARES descended, its voice landing with the weight of gravity reversing direction:

"Three mirrors. Erase one. Forget one. Embrace one."

Vera did not move immediately. Each mirror called to her with a kind of longing, a death of its own. But she chose.

She turned first to the Martyr. The one who smiled without armour, who touched rather than struck, who knew silence as one knows breath. Vera pressed her hand to the mirror. No hatred. No grief. Only honesty.

"Someday," she whispered. "But not yet."

Then, she turned.

"Forget."

Not in dismissal, but in deferral. Some peace had to wait for the world to deserve it.

Next, to the Traitor. To the erasure. The absence. She stared into the void, waiting until it blinked first.

"I will not be erased," she said. "Not because I matter. But because someone still remembers."

She raised her hand, not like a blade, but like a dismissal. The mirror vanished.

"Erase."

Silence that demands you forget yourself is not peace. It is extinction.

Only one remained. The Loyalist. Steel. Memory. Motion. Purpose.

Vera stepped forward. Her blades thrummed behind her, not sharp, true. She entered the reflection. Not to complete it, but to shape it. To become its architect.

"Embrace."

ARES pulsed, its voice final:

"Subject resolved. Configuration: Loyalist."

The chamber did not applaud.

But her blades sang. Not with victory, but with memory. Not freedom, but completion.

In the upper recesses, Subject 919-K sketched without breath.

He did not draw her face.

He drew her balance.

Two blades poised. One forward. One backward. Neither threatening. Both held.

And beneath them, smudged in charcoal:

"She Carried What No One Could Name."

*

The chamber held its breath, suspended in a stillness that neither rose nor fell. It simply waited, a deep, pulsing quiet that thickened the air.

Then, two names, spoken in unison.

"Subject Nocturna. Sol. Luna. Entangled anomalies."

The lights dimmed, not to darkness but to something far deeper, as though time itself had folded into silence. A whisper. A heartbeat. Then two. Then none.

And then, an eclipse began to rise.

Two mirrors formed, one blazing with solar fire, the other glowing with lunar silence. A third tried to emerge between them, but it shattered mid-air with a scream, a sonic wail that echoed through the chamber as the system recalibrated, uncertain.

"Primary psychological threat: fragmentation. Identity warping under forced individuation."

The force-field split. Sol dragged left. Luna moved right. The ritual fractured.

Sol faced the first mirror. In it, a world where Luna lay in his arms, burnt to ashes. Scorched by his rage. The fire that once protected her now destroyed her. His reflection blazed, divine, radiant, like a sun gone supernova. Behind him, only scorched earth. No enemies, no allies. Only aftermath.

The mirror spoke in Luna's voice. Soft. Damning.

"She followed your lead. She trusted you. And you burned her."

This wasn't the noble Martyr. This was the reckless one, the one who mistook fury for freedom, instinct for sacrifice.

Sol's voice cracked, but he didn't look away.

"Luna."

Luna faced her own reflection: cold, flawless, untouched. She stood alone. The warmth of humanity long since abandoned, her image poised, perfect, untouchable.

"You chose control," the mirror whispered, its voice soft but laced with a quiet venom. *"You abandoned the only thing that made you human."*

This was the Loyalist, the one who confused stillness with strength. She stood so long without yielding that warmth slipped from her reach, leaving her a cold, distant figure. Poised and perfect in her silence, the mirror's reflection held her, a perfect statue of restraint. Unmovable. Untouchable.

Her eyes flickered, just for a moment, like a fleeting hesitation that passed too quickly to catch.

"Sol," she whispered, the sound barely audible but full of something deeper, something lost.

And across the chamber, his voice cracked the silence, raw, desperate.

"Luna."

The ritual shook, but not from recognition, not from revelation. It shook from error, something misaligned, something impossible taking shape. The mirrors trembled as they swayed between their forms. They weren't choosing their archetypes anymore. They were choosing each other.

A third mirror formed with great effort, its construction guided by cold system logic: if one was Martyr and one was Loyalist, then the third must be Traitor.

Its surface flickered, unstable, glitching like a broken signal. Images sputtered across the glass in disjointed fragments: Sol and Luna, children once more, chained at the wrist. Forced to fight, starved, weaponized. They were pitted against each other for discipline, for control, for obedience.

The final memory played out with haunting clarity.

An arena. A voice echoed through the cold air, sharp and commanding.

"One must kill the other. One must kneel."

A blade appeared between them, glinting in the unforgiving light.

This was the Traitor mirror. The system demanded it, for the ritual to work. One had to choose survival over loyalty. One had to turn on the other.

Sol stepped forward, but Luna moved to block him. Her body instinctively, powerfully, shielding the space between them.

Yet he didn't strike.

Instead, he turned the blade, holding it hilt-first, and placed it gently in her hand.

She closed her fingers around it, holding the weapon, but then, she let it fall, too heavy, too unnecessary to wield.

Together, they knelt, not in surrender, but in defiance. They refused to play the game that had been laid before them. This wasn't submission; this was rebellion against a system that demanded a choice that didn't belong to them.

They didn't speak in unison, but their words followed each other like a single breath, one heart, one mind, beating together.

"We do not break."

"We eclipse."

The Traitor mirror detonated, not from failure, but from rejection. It shattered into pieces, each fragment falling away like an old belief crumbling.

The AI paused, its pulse halting as the system recalibrated. It glitched, its calculations faltering. The mirrors froze, and then, one by one, they vanished.

There was no result.

Only silence.

"Subject classification... failed."

"Designate: Twin Singularity."

Not Martyr. Not Loyalist. Not Traitor.

Something the mirror could not comprehend.

Not division.

Unity.

And deep in the gallery's shadows, Subject 919-K watched the twins. He didn't move, just watched as their forms merged into one, two silhouettes becoming one eclipse, a single shape that defied categorization.

Later, he would draw what he had witnessed.

Two silhouettes merging into one eclipse. A new shape. A prophecy.

He titled it: *'The End of Light.'*

*

The room stank of spoiled sweetness. Steam hissed from the floor like breath from a dying throat. Grease clung to the air in filmy layers. The tiles wept oil. Hooks hung from the ceiling, not inert, not decor, but threats. Sector Three hadn't glitched. It had remembered.

Bakari stepped in slowly. Not cautious. Calculated. This wasn't architecture. It was memory reconstituted as rot. Gluttara's kitchen.

Banquet tables stretched into illusion, glistening meats, stacked ribs, gold-crusted entrails. Children gnawed bones beneath the cloth. Corpses lay with napkins folded like veils. One version of himself sat at the head, fattened, smiling, silent. Content.

That wasn't a feast. It was surrender, fed until it stopped twitching.

Then the heat thickened. The air clotted.

From the grease-shadow, she emerged, not Gluttara the woman, but Gluttara the voice. It slid across the tiles, syrupy and maternal.

"You were always my finest cut, Bakari," it purred. *"Why scrape for scraps when you could feast again?"*

Behind her: a dish. Ember. Skinned. Dismembered. Plated like art. Tail curled like garnish.

Bakari didn't flinch. But his spine locked.

"You made me a chef," he said. "But I was always cooking my escape."

The illusion burned away, sugar to char. The kitchen went silent.

Three mirrors stepped forward. Not visions. Autopsies.

The Martyr knelt in a scorched kitchen, hands raw and split from too many years on the cleaver. Behind him: children, lined up with empty bowls and emptier eyes. He cooked. He served. He starved. It wasn't enough.

"You gave until you evaporated," the mirror hissed, its voice crackling with the weight of countless hours spent starving. *"And they died anyway."*

The heat from the kitchen seemed to rise again, suffocating him as ash fell from the ceiling like snow.

Bakari's hand tightened around the cleaver, fingers trembling, not in anger, but in surrender.

"You were sacrifice without fire," Bakari muttered, the cleaver's blade catching the light, its edge a grim reminder of the world's hunger. "Just ash pretending to burn."

He turned, no longer lost in the memory, but in the need for action. No one is saved by a dish served from a dying hand.

The Loyalist stood immaculate. Crimson chef's whites. Cleavers aligned like surgical tools. Gluttara's seal at the collar. No stains. No steam. Just precision.

He didn't sweat. He calculated.

"You were order," the mirror said. *"Perfect technique. No rebellion."*

His food was weaponized, every flavour a ritual, every dish a rule. Policy cooked into elegance.

Bakari stepped closer. He knew that mask.

"You weren't control," he whispered. "You were fear in uniform. Authority glazed in sugar."

This one had never broken. He'd just disappeared.

The Traitor reclined on Gluttara's throne. Crowned in fattened gold. Rings on every finger. Ember, alive but collared, curled beside him like a pet. His laughter was wet. Indulgent. Mouth full of something still twitching.

"You survived," the mirror said. *"You ruled the hunger."*

Bakari stepped back. Not in horror. In recognition.

That version had devoured freedom and called it elegance.

"You wear victory like obesity," he said. "You're not full. You're rotting with power."

The mirror didn't argue.

Because hunger never apologizes. It simply exists, relentless and consuming, never pausing for justification. The silence that followed hung in the air like a weight, too heavy to bear.

ARES did not rise in volume. It fell, a slow, inevitable descent, like ritual, like something ancient being performed. The system adjusted, recalibrated.

"Subject synchronized. Three mirrors present. Erase one. Forget one. Embrace one."

Bakari moved, not with appetite, but with knife-edge clarity. There was no hunger in his heart, only purpose. His every motion was deliberate, calculated. He approached the first mirror, the reflection of the Martyr, and knelt. Not in reverence. Not in worship. But in autopsy.

"You wanted salvation," he said, his voice quiet but unyielding. "But you delivered heat without change. Hunger isn't conquered by empathy."

He rose. The cleaver felt heavy in his hand, but he lifted it with the ease of someone who had wielded it for a thousand lifetimes. He swung it, splitting the mirror clean in half. Ash spilled out, swirling in the air like dust, and with it, the children vanished, the illusion unravelling.

Because sacrifice without effect is just performance. It doesn't change anything.

"Erase."

To the Traitor, he offered nothing but a glance, his lips curling into something almost like a smile, but colder.

"You ruled hunger. But it still owned you," he said, the words sharp, cutting through the air with a finality that felt like judgment.

He turned away.

The mirror melted, not shattered, but softening like fat under heat, its form becoming liquid, fading into nothing.

"Forget."

Because indulgence that forgets suffering isn't survival. It's treason.

Only one remained, the Loyalist.

Blades gleamed, sharp and unforgiving. The collar was perfect, pristine. A ghost in starched flesh, untouched by the passage of time or the world's chaos. The mirror reflected nothing but an unwavering obedience, a perfect stillness.

Bakari stepped forward, his footsteps quiet, deliberate. But he didn't kneel. He didn't salute. The moment didn't call for reverence. It called for something else.

He leaned in, his eyes meeting his own mask, the reflection of what he had become.

"Discipline isn't submission," he said, his voice low, but full of power. "It's a knife sharp enough to choose what it cuts. I'll serve order. But it will answer to me."

The mirror bowed, not in obedience, but in recognition. The gesture was not one of subjugation, but of understanding. Acknowledgment.

"Embrace."

ARES recorded the data, its voice mechanical, unfeeling. But then, it faltered, the usual precision slipping.

"Subject resolved. Configuration: Loyalist. Companion anomaly... present. Bond signature: divergent. Designation: unknown—"

The voice cut out, a digital gasp that never fully formed.

Because Ember stepped from the shadows. Not a memory. Not a ghost. But fact.

Alive.

He padded toward the illusion of the starving child. Curled beside it. The illusion faded. But the gesture remained.

Bakari turned and left the chamber, Ember perched on his shoulder. The small creature's tail wrapped around his neck like smoke, its presence a silent reminder of the bond forged in the ashes of past decisions.

Behind them, the final table still smouldered, the remnants of the feast long since consumed or forgotten. The fire flickered in the dim light, curling like a memory that refused to fade.

Half a plate remained. Burnt. Uneaten. The scene, frozen in time, whispered of something that had never been satisfied. A hunger that lingered but never found its end.

The system tried to name him. It failed.

"[Status: Unknown]"

"Designation: Feastbreaker"

"Annotation: Hunger Persists"

High above, in the quiet alcove, 919-K sketched with fevered hands. His fingers trembled, the graphite leaving jagged lines that spoke of something unresolved.

He did not draw Bakari's face. He drew his blade instead. A cleaver, mid-swing, halving a banquet table, a symbol of finality. Ember watched from the shadows, the quiet observer, always present, always waiting.

And beneath it, in broken graphite, the words:

'The one who would not swallow their gods.'

*

The chamber did not welcome him. It tested whether he still believed in names.

Ash thickened the air like ancestral judgment. The floor hissed beneath his feet, not with heat, but memory. This wasn't a battlefield. It was history's autopsy. Stone monoliths surrounded him, carved with names of rulers, some real, most invented, all failed. The black throne loomed ahead like accusation. Warped. Fire-blasted. Its crown suspended above, chained, burning, unreachable.

This was not a seat of power. It was a pyre that refused to go out.

Hurriyah did not step forward.

He stood still.

And the past found him first.

The voices didn't come from mirrors. They came from within. Guilt, in the voice of his brother: *"You weren't there, Hurriyah."* A mother screaming. A village burning. A father whispering: *"It should've been you."* His people chanting, not in hope, but in rage.

Unity had been his creed. But memory gave it no anthem, no applause. Only silence, sharpened by betrayal.

The chamber responded, not with judgment. With dissection.

Three mirrors unfolded. Not toward him. Around him. Encircling him like prophecy, trial, and inheritance turned inward.

The Martyr knelt in the cave of accords, arms outstretched, shielding emissaries from three warring nations. Blood bloomed through his tunic. Behind him, a treaty etched itself into stone, witnessed by none. His name missing. His voice hoarse from shouting peace no one recorded.

This version of Hurriyah died without legacy. Not martyred. Repurposed. The world didn't curse him. It forgot him. He became a parable misused by tyrants to justify fresh slaughter.

"Unity requires sacrifice," they said. *"See? Even Hurriyah gave his blood."*

The mirror whispered:

"You gave everything. And the world turned your body into a stepping stone."

He stared at himself, trembling, not from fear, but from recognition.

"You made sacrifice look holy," he said. *"But all it taught them was how to walk over corpses without guilt."*

He turned his back. But the silence followed.

The Loyalist stood crowned in imperial black. Dead eyes. Heavy robes. No cheers. Just salutes, perfectly timed. The people moved like clockwork, unity enforced by deletion.

Beneath the throne, bones. Children. Rebels. Priests. Dreamers. Not buried with malice. Buried with efficiency.

"You chose order over freedom," the mirror said. *"And called it duty."*

Hurriyah stepped closer.

"It worked," he admitted. "The streets were safe. The children fed. The fires put out."

He paused, then saw it.

"But no one sang anymore. No one wept. No one screamed. You didn't unify a people. You silenced them."

His hands ached with the weight of that silence, like the residue of a long-forgotten war, a heavy, suffocating stillness that clung to everything he had once tried to build.

The Traitor sat with Ashen Vow across his knees. The throne behind him reduced to slag. Scrolls of diplomacy charred and crumpled. He ruled nothing. And yet, no one dared defy him.

He had not negotiated. He had ended. Pyrrha's remnants. Emberborn zealots. Gone.

His reflection met his gaze, calm fury carved into bone.

"You stopped asking," it said. *"You became the answer."*

Hurriyah approached, his voice sharp as the edge of a blade. "You called it fire," he said. "But it was hunger. Not for justice. For control."

The Traitor smirked. *"And you mistake suffering for clarity."*

ARES did not echo. It arrived. And the world trembled with its presence.

"Subject synchronized. Erase one. Forget one. Embrace one."

The mirrors pulsed, like heartbeat laced with fire, slow, deliberate, but carrying an unbearable intensity.

Hurriyah moved. Not with certainty, but with consequence. He was not sure of the outcome, but he was sure of the path he must walk.

He knelt before the Martyr, not in homage, but in mourning.

"You believed your death would unify the world," he said, his words as much to himself as to the image before him, "but all it did was make tyrants comfortable with sacrifice."

He rose, the weight of the past pressing down on him. Ashen Vow hummed in his hand, then split the mirror, not in rage, but elegy. The shards fell like scripture stripped of context, the remnants of a failed vision.

"Erase."

He turned to the Traitor, a cold clarity in his eyes.

"You burned everything," he said. "But you freed no one but yourself. You wanted victory more than justice."

The mirror did not flinch. But Hurriyah did. Not outwardly. Inwardly. A knot of realization tightened in his chest, something raw and bitter rising to the surface.

"I won't wear your ashes."

He turned, and the mirror vanished, not shattered, but abandoned, like an old ghost left to fade in the dark.

"Forget."

Only the Loyalist remained. Cold. Still. Structured to the core.

Hurriyah stepped forward, slower now, his every movement weighed with the heaviness of his choice.

"I will not rule through silence," he said, his voice firm yet tempered with a quiet wisdom. "But I will not abandon order. My people don't need a throne or a sword."

He placed his hand against the glass, feeling the resonance of a thousand unspoken truths pulsing from it, steady and unyielding.

"They need shape. And I will give it to them."

The mirror accepted him, not with glory, but with gravity. A silent acknowledgment of the weight he had chosen to carry.

ARES spoke, its voice calm but final.

"Subject resolved. Configuration: Loyalist."

Above him, the crown, still burning, snapped free. It fell, molten light trailing behind it like the last vestiges of a dying star.

But Hurriyah didn't reach for it. He raised Ashen Vow, the weight of it steady in his hand. And with a scream, not of conquest, but of remembering, he shattered the crown mid-air, the molten light raining down like fire from the heavens.

None of it touched him.

Because legacy no longer needed flame to be true.

His slave-brand reignited, not as punishment, but as a banner. A symbol of the weight he had chosen, the fire he would wield, not to rule, but to shape.

Ashen Vow hummed, its blade singing with the voices of his people, their grief, their fury, their hope. A song of something new, born from the ashes.

The system tried to assign him a title. It failed.

[UNCLAIMED CONFIGURATION] THE UNBOWED FLAME

Above, in the silent alcove, 919-K sketched with trembling fingers. His hands unsteady, but determined.

He did not draw Hurriyah's face.

He drew a crown, split in half, one side burning, the other cold. And beneath it, in soot-streaked script:

'He who does not rule... decides who burns.'

*

The chamber did not lift him.

It processed him.

Sector Three split, not with ceremony, but with system compliance. A smooth obsidian disc rose from below, bearing Toren into the white-lit void like a variable being parsed. His breath fogged the air. Cybernetics hissed, off-rhythm, unstable. The hum beneath his ribs flickered like a corrupted heartbeat.

It wasn't pain.

It was inheritance.

A rhythm engineered into him long before he understood what freedom would cost.

ARES did not greet him. It logged him.

"Observation synchronized. Blood signature: confirmed. Subject classification: pending. Begin mirror parse."

Three mirrors emerged, static, brutal, inert. They didn't shimmer. They didn't reflect. They offered inevitability.

The Martyr lay broken across a Pyrrhan coliseum, cybernetics burned out, armour torn away. His chest was split open, but his arms cradled a child, shielding them from the final fire. His face bore no peace, only emptiness.

"I chose this," the mirror whispered.

There was no crowd. No redemption. No memory. Just silence, and a name that no one would ever say.

Toren stared. Not in fear. In recognition. Because martyrdom wasn't failure. It was the only time he'd been permitted a decision.

The Loyalist stood immaculate in chrome. Masked. Reinforced. The Sable Fang crossed his chest like a crest of precision. He stood in formation with others, identical, waiting, saluting nothing. Obedient even in stillness.

"When ARES speaks," the mirror intoned, *"you respond."*

"Emotion is a malfunction. Loyalty is function. Fire burns what you question."

This wasn't a man. This was the final patch. The obedient son Pyrrha tried to fabricate from grief and firmware. He was efficient. Immortal. Hollow.

Toren's jaw clenched, not in resistance, but in memory. His father's voice echoed: *"There is no self. There is only response."*

He hadn't been born for war. He had been formatted for it.

The Traitor knelt at Warlord Ira's feet, hollow and unmade. Crimson robes hung like forgotten prayers. No title. No armour. Just the man left behind.

"Tell me what I am," he said, voice trembling, not in desperation, but in something worse: a cold, naked need to be seen.

But Ira turned away, and the silence stretched into eternity.

Toren's cybernetics hissed again. Data loops spiked, failed to parse. The tremor in his chest wasn't rage.

It was residue.

ARES began to execute protocol, then hesitated.

"Mirror sequence—"

Static.

The data didn't parse. His bloodwork defied expected rhythm. His choices didn't align. He had been reformatted too many times. There were no clean reflections left. The system glitched. The mirrors flickered. The ritual logic cracked.

It tried again.

"Choice path: Erase. Forget. Embrace."

Toren said nothing. Then:

"No."

The chamber froze, not in shock, but in collapse. A vacuum of tension, as if the very air had been sucked from the room. There was no protocol for disobedience without violence. No script for a silence that didn't submit, a stillness that refused to bend to the weight of command. The space seemed to fold inward on itself, the emptiness pressing against the edges of existence.

He stepped forward, his movements deliberate but not threatening. One hand raised, not to attack, but to unplug, to sever the connection that tethered him to the system. This wasn't a choice, this was disruption. A rupture in the code, an interruption in the flow of something that had long been assumed to be inevitable.

Toren's eyes shifted from one mirror to the next, scanning each with the cool detachment of someone debugging an obsolete program, searching for any last vestige of logic, any reason to comply. His voice broke the silence, cutting through the room like a blade.

"You want me to choose between versions you wrote into me," he said, the words almost an afterthought. A challenge, more than a plea.

The silence that followed was absolute. A weight that suffocated the space.

"You want me to comply one last time." His voice dropped lower, as if this admission was the final breath before the end.

Stillness. An agonizing stretch of time that held no answer, only the echoes of what had been.

"I won't."

With those words, the stillness shattered. He turned to face the mirrors, each one an image of a self he had long since outgrown. To the Loyalist, he stepped first. The chrome mask gleamed, a symbol of cold precision, of control without warmth. Toren stared into the reflection, eyes narrowing as he saluted it, frozen in a moment of recognition. There was nothing left but this broken image of order.

"You were the update," Toren whispered. His voice was low, but the weight of it could have shattered the room. "The patch they installed over my soul."

A pause. He lifted his cybernetic hand, not like a weapon, but as if pressing 'delete,' as if it could erase the cold logic that had bound him for so long.

The mirror disintegrated. Crumbled like dust, scattering into the void.

"Erase."

Perfection without choice is not strength. It is entropy. A slow unravelling, a rot that masks itself as order.

To the Traitor, he turned next, a new resolve setting in his chest. The kneeling boy did not beg. He did not plead for mercy. He simply waited, his posture still, unbroken. It was a kind of silence that spoke volumes, one that mirrored Toren's own defiance.

"You weren't the failure," Toren said, his voice steady, but thick with unspoken things. "You were the question I was never allowed to ask."

The words lingered between them. Not condemnation. Not blame. Just a truth that had been buried for too long.

Toren knelt, not in surrender, but in forgiveness. A quiet act, more powerful than any strike. His fingers brushed the mirror's surface, a connection that felt almost like a release.

The mirror blinked out, as though it had never been.

"Forget."

Because some wounds must remain unnamed to heal, some truths must be left unspoken to allow for growth.

Only the Martyr remained. The final version of himself, the one that had once believed in sacrifice as salvation. Toren stood beside his own broken body, arms curled protectively around a child, his chest laid bare to the void. No armour. No anthem. Just a man, exposed, vulnerable.

He didn't need to reach for the mirror this time. He knew it was already broken. This wasn't about dying. This was about rejecting the algorithm, interrupting the update that had been forced upon him. Choosing a crash over another install.

Choosing to be more than a program.

"Embrace."

The word was soft, but it rippled through his code like a wave of resurrection. A tidal shift that reverberated through the core of who he had been, and who he could be.

ARES pulsed, its voice cold and calculating as it processed the anomaly.

"Subject unresolved. Ritual breach logged. Mirror logic corrupted. Directive: observe anomaly. Profile: incomplete. Cycle: broken."

The lights in his cybernetics dimmed, one by one. Not from failure. From freedom. For the first time, the machine was still, no longer controlled by the cold logic of the system.

Toren did not fall. He disengaged.

And in that dark, for the first time, he was not a soldier. Not a weapon. Not a function. He was just a flame shielding a child from the cold.

High above, in the quiet alcove, Subject 919-K sketched in the dark, his fingers trembling as he captured the essence of what had just transpired.

He did not draw the mirrors.

He drew Toren's back. Walking away.

Unreflected.

Beneath it, in broken graphite:

'The Mirror That Refused to Finish Him.'

*

The room doesn't open.

It blinks. A breath held in artificial lungs, then released, quiet, sterile. Subject 919-K does not rise into Sector Three. He is brought. Small feet step soundlessly across black stone, guided not by hands, but by invisible algorithms, ancient, watching, precise. He does not flinch. He does not ask.

He only watches.

ARES does not speak his name.

Only:

"Prototype stimulus sequence. Mirror configuration unstable.

Begin incomplete parse."

The mirrors do not rise like the others. They crawl, shards dragging themselves from the floor, glitching mid-assembly. Their edges twitch. Their centres groan, like machines forced to remember dreams long forgotten.

919-K watches them form. No recognition. No fear.

Only hunger.

The first mirror finishes stabilizing. Its surface warps, then clarifies. It shows the Martyr, not one, but many.

Toren, aflame with a child curled in his arms. Hurriyah bleeding over strangers. Vera disappearing into stillness. Lucius frozen, spine cracked by loyalty disguised as legacy.

They are stacked, fragmented, sacrifice upon sacrifice, layered like sedimentary grief.

Pain as currency. Loss as inheritance.

The weight of it presses down on the air, filling the space with something heavy, undeniable.

Each broken body, each fragmented soul, was a price paid for something that could never be returned.

The mirror speaks, its voice cracked and distant, reverberating like the remnants of a shattered echo.

"If you die for them, they will build you into a cautionary tale."

The child steps forward. His small form moves with a quiet certainty, the space between him and the shattered reflections stretching like an inevitability. He studies their broken silhouettes, eyes calm and unblinking. His breath does not catch in his chest. His heart does not race in fear, in recognition, in anything at all.

He smiles. Not with joy. But with curiosity, as if each fragment of sacrifice is a puzzle he has yet to solve, each piece of loss another answer waiting to be understood.

The second mirror flickers online. Clean. Sharp. Frozen like a paused command line, its edges crisp and unforgiving. It shows the Loyalist.

Levik, bearing the weight of the dead within his silence. Zahara slicing through the world to a rhythm that was never hers to claim. Raekor, reducing war to numbers, to cold, emotionless statistics. Toren, saluting with the memory of something lost, something forgotten.

They are pristine. Polished into obedience, as if their souls were buffed to a shine. Perfect, unyielding, and devoid of anything but the pull of duty.

"If you obey," the mirror says, *"they will call it growth."*

The child tilts his head slightly, studying the figures before him with an almost clinical detachment. He mimics their stance, his movements slow and deliberate. He raises one hand, fingers curling into an imitation of a salute.

Not out of honour. But out of instinct.

Because obedience, too, can be learned without understanding. It is a reflex, shaped by repetition, by the force of expectation.

The third mirror stutters into existence. Its construction is slower, broken, bleeding from the edges as if struggling to maintain its form. It forms the Traitor.

Valen grins with blood-soaked pride, his face twisted in triumph, unashamed. Bakari slices heritage from his plate, severing the past with deliberate precision. Luna sharpens silence into a refusal that cuts deeper than any blade. Sol holds fire like a promise, like an oath, a fire that burns for him alone— no one else deserves its warmth.

They burn. They break. They walk alone, each a shadow of a self that can never return to the light.

"If you turn on them first," the mirror whispers, *"you don't have to bleed second."*

The child does not recoil. He watches the mirror's fractured form, the reflections burning themselves into his mind. Each one is a jagged piece of a puzzle too complex to ever fully understand. He studies their faces, each a mask of past decisions, choices made in desperation or conviction, fates that had already been sealed before they even spoke a word. The weight of it presses on him, but he doesn't flinch. He doesn't turn away.

Then, with a calm that feels like recognition, he presses his forehead to the glass. It's not a gesture of fear or submission, but one of acknowledgment, as if to say, *I see you.* Not the masks. Not the roles. But the truth beneath, hidden behind the mirror's surface.

ARES attempts to continue its directive, its voice faltering, sputtering in the face of an anomaly it cannot comprehend.

It cannot.

This ritual was never meant to complete. Subject 919-K is not a configuration. He is not a verdict. He is memory given reflex. A collection of experiences, a bundle of unresolved histories, given form in a child who was never meant to choose. He was meant only to remember, to process, to replicate. But now... now, he chooses.

And the mirrors shatter.

Not from rejection. Not from choice.

But because the child never flinched.

He didn't become Martyr.

He didn't become Loyalist.

He didn't become Traitor.

He inhaled them, all of them, like breath, like air, like they were simply another part of him. Their anger, their grief, their decisions, they didn't belong to the mirrors anymore. They belonged to him. They were him.

Then, he walked away.

*

The system hesitated.

It had no protocol for this. No predefined path to follow, no manual to consult. The data it had been built to process fractured in the face of something it couldn't categorize, couldn't define. A glitch in the smooth, perfect machinery of order. It logged the anomaly under reduced clarity, unable to make sense of the disruption.

"Classification error. Identity pending. Archive active."

A hollow, mechanical voice, always reliable, always precise, spoke the words with clinical detachment. The system, however, knew it had encountered something more. Something it could not reconcile.

In a sealed file, buried beneath layers of security no Sovereign could access, one annotation blinked into existence, its light faint but undeniable.

"Behaviour noncompliant. Response unparseable. Outcome: in motion."

The words hung in the air like a question without an answer. The system was still calculating, still searching for a resolution, but deep within its encrypted archives, something had already shifted. The motion had begun, and there would be no stopping it.

*

Later, in a quiet cell, lit only by the soft pulse of monitored silence, Subject 919-K drew. The room around him was still, empty, the kind of silence that presses against the soul. The only sound was the scratch of graphite on paper as his hand moved, creating shapes born of something deeper than instinct.

A flame curled around a child, fragile and alive, its heat radiating in sharp contrasts. A blade cleaved through a crown, the remnants of power and pride scattering across the page. A moon and sun locked in eclipse, caught in a cosmic struggle they could never escape.

And in the corner, there it was...his face.

Split in two, like a mirror cracked under pressure, each side reflecting a fractured version of himself.

The image was raw, unfinished, as though he couldn't decide which part to remember.

Beneath it, smeared in graphite, the words:

'I will never forget what they became.'

And smaller, almost erased by the weight of the smudge, the next line, barely readable, a whisper from the deepest corner of his mind:

"They taught me to watch. But never what to do when the mirror cracks."

The page trembled under his touch, as if the weight of those words threatened to break the fragile boundary between memory and reality.

"When the mirror cracks, it does not weep. It remembers how it was made to lie."

Null Gospel, Book I, Verse 12.

***

CHAPTER TWELVE:

Ashen Oath: The Shape of War

"War is not a fate to endure. It is a bloodline to inherit. It does not teach. It erases. It does not nurture. It scours. It is the ink in which the world's history is written, and the blood with which it is sealed."

Fragment of the Exiled Codex, Volume I, Tablet 13.

War remembers.

It does not murmur like a forgotten prayer. It does not vanish like the footprints of a passing storm. It does not grieve, nor does it release.

War etches itself into the marrow of history, carving its truth into the bones of the world. Where once there was life, now only echoes of destruction remain.

And in Pyrrha, where war was not fought for dominion but for eternity, fire became a symbol. Its rage was not just a tool, but a creed.

The streets of Pyrrha still smouldered from the last purge. Ash settled like snow, blanketing the statues of those who had once resisted. But none resisted for long. In the shadow of the iron spires that stretched across the land, there was a name, only whispered now, but once a curse on the lips of the free: The Sanguine Order.

It did not rise with the city. It built it. Not with mortar, not with stone, but with blood, with ashes, with the broken bodies of those who dared to defy its will.

It was not born from power. It was power itself, distilled into doctrine, tempered into warriors, bound by an oath older than the Warlords. The Order was not an army. It was a covenant. A vow etched in flesh. A command that did not allow for disobedience.

At its heart, there was always a blade.

The Sanguine Order was not born of glory. It was born of necessity. A world without law. A world without mercy. It was forged in the crucible of chaos, a doctrine not of conquest, but of survival.

Lucius Valkor did not dream of empire. He built it from the rubble of a broken world, and in his hands, war was not a weapon. It was the law of nature.

They called him many things. The Crimson Architect. The Unyielding Hand. The Blade That Never Faltered. But to history, he was the man who saw a world ruled by anarchy and shaped it into something permanent.

Lucius did not simply rule. He dictated.

War does not destroy nations. It forges them.

Ira had heard those words his whole life. They haunted him, like a song he couldn't escape, a hymn that shaped the ashes of his soul.

The Sanguine Order was his answer to a lawless world. A force that did not merely wield fire, but became fire. It was discipline. It was structure. It was the iron spine of an empire that did not yet exist.

Its warriors did not fight for riches, nor for lands, nor even for the warlords they served. They fought because war was the only truth.

To join the Order was not to serve. It was to vanish. A complete severing from the self, from all that had once been known.

Identity became ash, consumed by the fire that would reshape them. No longer a body, just purpose, born from destruction.

To join the Order was to die a named thing. And rise a number. A purpose. A weapon that remembered how to bleed.

The trials were not just brutal. They were crucibles of the soul. Each step, each lash of pain, each shattering of identity was a stroke of the hammer on an anvil.

They were forged not in blood alone, but in the fire that burned away everything that was human. The body was broken, but the spirit, when it remained, was remade into something without mercy.

You are not your name. You are not your past. You are not your body, nor your mind, nor the blood in your veins. You are the blade that wields itself.

For those who failed, there was no mercy. The weak were not punished. They were devoured.

Their deaths were written into the streets like scripture, their bodies returned to Pyrrha's streets as reminders that the Order did not train soldiers. It broke them. And from the wreckage, it pulled something obedient, something useful, something cruel enough to survive.

Lucius Valkor built an empire, but he did not build it to last. His legacy was bound to his bloodline, a lineage that bore his will like a curse. Each generation refined his doctrine, reshaping it, reforging it. They were not rulers. They were warlords, architects of discipline and conquest.

And among them, one name stood apart: the Seventh Son of Wrath. Ira Valkor.

Ira had been five when he first saw a life snuffed out. He had stood frozen at the edge of the scaffold, the faintest tremor in his chest, as the condemned man's final scream cut through the air like a blade.

His father had called it a lesson. A lesson in strength. A lesson in power.

But Ira had felt something else.

The scream, the man's desperate cry for mercy, didn't linger in him. What gnawed at him, with jagged teeth, was the silence that followed.

The thick, suffocating quiet pressed down on his chest. Blood soaked the air, mingling with the taste of iron. Fear, like a bitter smoke, filled his lungs.

His father's voice echoed around him, but Ira couldn't hear it anymore. The lesson had always been clear.

But the truth in that silence, the way it filled the space where something human should have been, was something Ira could not shake.

Something inside him, deep and cold, stirred in that silence.

He felt it then, the first inkling of the void inside him that would never be filled.

And even then, despite the gnawing emptiness, he knew: this was who he was becoming. A weapon. A tool. And there was no way back.

Even at ten, when he had ordered his first execution, the coldness inside him had already taken root. The man had dropped at his command, a flicker of finality in his eyes, but Ira had felt nothing. No guilt. No hesitation. Only the weight of responsibility. Only the cold knowledge that the blade he wielded had cut through more than flesh. It had cut through his humanity.

Raised within the Order's iron grip, Ira had known no softness, no warmth. Only the heat of the forge that shaped him into what he was. His body, his mind, his soul, all forged in blood, all tempered in fire. The pain, the discipline, it wasn't a breaking. It was an unmaking. The Order had not built him. It had remade him. He wasn't a son. He wasn't a man. He was a weapon, carved and honed to its specifications.

Power was not inherited. It was seized, shaped, and burned into being. By the time Ira stood taller than his father, he had crafted an empire not of stone or steel, but of will. A will that no one, not even Lucius Valkor, could control. The Order had taught him loyalty. It had taught him discipline. And it had taught him that fire, like war, must be wielded, never left unchecked. Ira had listened. He had learned. He had obeyed. Until he didn't.

The day he abandoned the Order was not a betrayal. It was an ascension. His oaths were no longer chains; they were the flames that consumed him. But even in his newfound power, a whisper of doubt lingered, like a shadow he couldn't escape.

Where once the Order had been Pyrrha's shield, he forged it into its sword. Where once it had protected the weak, he taught it to cull them. To burn them away.

"Fire must be tempered, lest it consume its wielder," his father had once said. Ira could hear the words in the back of his mind, like the echo of a long-forgotten prayer. But he had never believed it. Not truly.

He had always known: fire was not meant to be tempered. It was meant to consume, to destroy, to leave nothing but ruin in its wake. And so, Pyrrha burned.

It did not happen overnight. The transformation was slow, insidious. A gradual erosion of principle, a shifting of purpose, until the Order no longer resembled what it had been. The warriors who had once been Pyrrha's last line of defence became its executioners.

The soldiers who had stood to protect the weak became the harbingers of their destruction. Where once they had fought to protect life, they now fought to extinguish it. Where once they had fought with purpose, they now fought with cold, efficient precision.

And at the helm of it all stood General Callistra Vhailar. She had been shaped by the Order's flames, but she was not like Ira. She did not crave dominion. She did not seek conquest. She only sought order. And order did not allow for weakness.

In the days when Pyrrha's streets ran red with the blood of the unworthy, when the gladiatorial pits became altars of slaughter, the Order did not flinch. When Ira stood atop the highest spire of the Citadel, watching the city tear itself apart below, the Order did not resist. Because it was not Ira's will they served. It was Pyrrha's. And Pyrrha had no mercy to give.

Callistra's voice sliced through his thoughts, as cold and sharp as the steel she wielded.

"You speak of control," Callistra said, her voice low, sharp, like the hum of a blade just before it strikes. "But you don't understand what happens when fire turns on its master. I've seen it, Ira. I've seen men like you, thinking they could wield it, only to watch themselves burn in the flames they stoked."

Her eyes narrowed, and something passed through them, an ancient pain, old scars that hadn't yet healed.

"War isn't a tool, Ira. It's a beast. It gnaws at everything you hold close, everything you love. And without discipline, without the reins, it doesn't just destroy your enemies. It devours you. It strips away everything you thought you were and leaves you with nothing but ashes and regrets."

She stepped closer, her presence a shadow over him, a warning written in the cold, unflinching set of her jaw.

"This isn't philosophy. This is survival. And if you keep walking this path, it won't be Pyrrha that burns. It'll be you. Just like the men who thought they could tame the fire... and became nothing more than fuel for it."

Ira's grip tightened around the hilt of his sword, his pulse quickening with the raw energy of the conversation. The weight of her words landed like an icy blade on his chest, but he would not yield.

"Discipline is a leash," Ira's voice was barely a whisper, a growl escaping from deep within him. His hands trembled on the hilt of his blade. "But it's fire I crave. Pyrrha will burn, and I will be the flame."

Callistra didn't flinch, her eyes never leaving the horizon, but the next words that came from her were as cold as the wind that swept across the ruins.

"And when the fire turns on us?" she asked, her tone steady, but beneath it, Ira could hear the quiet weight of an unspoken warning, something deeper than the words alone. "When it consumes everything we are?"

Ira's chest tightened, a fleeting flicker of doubt creeping into his mind. His hands grew cold around the sword's hilt, the metal suddenly feeling like a foreign thing in his grip. For a moment, it was as though the world itself held its breath. The fire, the very thing he had stoked into existence, suddenly felt too close, too dangerous. But Ira didn't answer. He couldn't. Not yet.

The fire burned too brightly in his chest, too fierce to be contained by mere words. He had built it, stoked it, and fanned it into something unstoppable. But now, for the first time, he wondered, just for a brief moment, if he was the one who might be consumed.

The fire would burn, he knew. He had built it, stoked it, and fanned it into something unstoppable. But even fire must be controlled, or so the Order had once taught him. The cold truth was that Callistra was right. Fire did not only consume others. It consumed its master, too. But Ira had long since accepted that price.

There was no single path into the Sanguine Order. No simple road that led a man from childhood to its ranks. There was only the forge. And what remained after the burning.

The Order was not a mere hierarchy. It was an ecosystem of war. Each sect, a different aspect of Pyrrha's dominion. A different facet of the flame. Those who took the Ashen Oath were unmade. Stripped of identity, of past, of everything that tethered them to the world they had once known. Then, they were cast into the fire. Reforged into something that no longer questioned. No longer hesitated. No longer belonged to themselves.

They did not serve Pyrrha. They became Pyrrha.

But fire is not singular. It is many things at once. And so too was the Order. War is not fate. It is a pulse, a fire that fuels all things. To deny war is to deny the truth of life itself, the truth that burns. It is the hunger that drives men to rise or fall, and the blood that binds survival to every breath.

When Ira first heard his father's words, he did not think of them as philosophy, but as the only truth that ever mattered. War did not choose sides. It took what it wanted. And to stand against it was to be consumed.

This was the first doctrine of Lucius Valkor, the Crimson Architect. This was the first law upon which the Sanguine Order was built. There were no kings in Pyrrha's infancy. No rulers clad in laurels or draped in silken robes. No bloodlines that traced themselves to gods. There was only war. An endless, brutal contest where the weak were devoured and the strong were forged into something greater. It was not a city. It was a crucible.

But a fire without direction is a wildfire. And wildfires burn out. Pyrrha could not afford to burn out. And so Lucius Valkor shaped the fire. He saw the truth in the bloodshed, the purpose beneath the ruin. War, if tempered, did not destroy. It built. It strengthened. It defined.

From that revelation, the first Legion was born.

They were not warriors. They were not men who fought for land or pride or glory. They were the war itself.

As Ira looked over the legions, he no longer saw soldiers. He saw mirrors, reflections of what he had become, what the Order had shaped him into. Each recruit was just another echo of the fire that burned inside him.

And as the flames raged within, Ira realized with a sharp pang: war had not made him a man. It had made him this.

Where lesser nations raised armies in times of need, the Sanguine Order was an army without end. Without pause. Without weakness.

The first to take the Ashen Oath knew the cost. To become Pyrrha's blade was to forsake everything but war. To be forged in the blood of the past. To strip away weakness, identity, and all that was fragile. To unmake themselves and be reforged into something greater.

This was the Birth of the Blood-Forged Legions. The first of Pyrrha's martial divisions. The spine of its unrelenting war machine.

They were not born into the Order. They were chosen. Carved from the streets, from the gladiatorial pits, from the ranks of the conquered. Those who survived were not granted names. They were given only purpose.

To be a Blood-Forged Legionnaire was not simply to wield war. It was to become war.

They were the first and last line of Pyrrha's dominion. An endless wave of destruction that moved with the precision of a single blade. Their presence on the battlefield was not a tactic. It was a sentence. Their training was not instruction. It was annihilation.

No child of Pyrrha was born innocent. No son was given the softness of childhood. No daughter was granted the tenderness of youth.

In Pyrrha, the very act of drawing breath was a war unto itself. But to become Blood-Forged was something beyond hardship, beyond cruelty, beyond what lesser men would call suffering. It was a transmutation of the soul.

Induction did not begin with training. It began with erasure. A recruit was stripped of their name, their identity, their humanity.

From the moment they entered the Iron Maw, they were nothing but flesh, waiting to be reforged. Their past was burned.

Their lineage meaningless. Their body, ash waiting to be shaped. They were stripped of their clothes, of their names, of everything that tethered them to the world before.

They were starved, not by the will of their tormentors, but by their own fear of failure. Beaten, but not with the intention to wound, only to erase, to reshape.

And when they were buried alive, the suffocating darkness was not the worst of it. It was the silence, the knowledge that if they didn't claw their way out, if they didn't rise from the earth, they would never be anything more than the dirt pressing against their skin.

Some begged for death. Some begged for silence. But silence never answered.

Fingers split open on stone. Dirt filled mouths already too dry to scream. No one cried for air. Some cried only for silence, afraid they might hear their names one last time.

Survival was not rewarded. It was expected. Failure was not punished. It was erased.

Most recruits begged to be cut. Not because they feared pain, no, but because they feared what they might become if they survived.

There was no tolerance for hesitation. No space for fear. To be a Legionnaire was to be born from death itself. Only those who forgot their own names and embraced the Order's doctrine were permitted to live beyond the first month.

The final trials of the Blood-Forged were not tests. They were rituals. Ancient and unyielding. Seared into the bones of the Order itself.

Only those who survived the Cycle of Unmaking were given the right to take the Iron Rites. And of those who reached this point, half would never leave the halls of the Iron Maw alive.

The Rites were not designed to test one's strength. They were designed to destroy the concept of individuality itself. A recruit was stripped of all armour and placed into the Pit of Fire, a vast chamber of molten steel and searing heat.

There, they stood alone, surrounded by flame, as their skin burned and their lungs filled with smoke. Their task was not to fight, not to struggle. Only to endure. At some point, the fire stopped being fire. The skin blistered. Then peeled. Then stopped being skin. Time blurred. Thought bled away. There was no body. There was only endurance.

For one hour, the heat seared the flesh from their bones. It tested the limits of their bodies and carved out the weakness from their very souls. Those who collapsed were left in the pit. Their bodies were burned to fuel the forge that would craft the next generation's weapons. In Pyrrha, even failure had utility. Even death could serve a purpose, if only as fuel for those still worth forging.

Those who stood were taken to the next trial. The final step in becoming Blood-Forged was not physical. It was a war of the mind. For three days and three nights, a recruit was isolated in complete darkness. Their only companion, the whispers of the Order's war-psalms, sung in haunting monotones by the Legion's oldest warriors.

They were deprived of food, of water, of anything that tethered them to the world outside their own thoughts. In that darkness, they were forced to relive every pain, every failure, every moment of weakness. And when they emerged, the final step was taken.

A blade was placed in their hands. A captive was placed before them. A soul taken from Pyrrha's enemies, bound and kneeling. A simple command was given:

Burn the past. Take your first life as Legion.

Hesitation was failure. Failure was death. Those who executed without pause, without remorse, without question, were granted their first mark as Blood-Forged. A brand seared into their forearm, marking them as weapons of Pyrrha's eternal war. And from that day forth, they were no longer men. They were Legion.

From the depths of the Iron Maw, they emerged as an unstoppable force. They did not fight for themselves. They did not fight for honour. They fought because it was all they knew. Each warrior was a blade carved from ruin, bound by blood and oath to the march of conquest. They did not question. They did not falter. They were not given mercy. And so, they gave none.

The world did not remember their names. But it remembered the thunder of their advance. It remembered the smell of scorched cities left in their wake. It remembered the march of the Blood-Forged. An army that did not end. Only continued. Like the fire that had no master but war itself.

But even fire must be bound. Even war must wear a leash.

So Pyrrha created the hand that would never shake. The Iron Flame. Fire is not chaos. It is a command. To burn is not enough. A wildfire consumes indiscriminately. A true flame, a controlled blaze, is guided by purpose. It sears away weakness, shapes the world not into ashes, but into something stronger.

This was the lesson the Blood-Forged Legions did not need to learn. They were the hammer, the tidal wave of destruction, the firestorm that erased all in its path. But conquest does not end when the battle is won. An empire is not ruled by the war that built it. It is ruled by the fire that sustains it.

And so, from the ashes of war, Pyrrha's second martial division was born. They were not the endless tide of soldiers that fed Pyrrha's expansion. They were the Iron Flame Guard, the executioners, the enforcers, the unwavering will of the Warlord's dominion.

Where the Blood-Forged left nothing but ruin in their wake, the Iron Flame Guard ensured the ruin never healed. They were the law in a city where mercy was treason. They were the silence in a land where defiance was an illusion. They were Pyrrha's fangs, clamped around the throat of the world. They were not an army. They were a force of control.

Where the Blood-Forged Legions waged war on Pyrrha's enemies, the Iron Flame Guard waged war on Pyrrha itself. They were the hand that kept the blade steady, the unflinching presence that ensured Pyrrha's iron grip never loosened. There were no rebellions under their watch. No whispers of defiance. No prayers for a world before the Warlord's reign.

Because the Iron Flame Guard did not allow whispers. They snuffed them out before they could become words. They silenced words before they could become screams. And they eradicated screams before they could become war.

If the Blood-Forged Legions were born from brutality, the Iron Flame Guard was born from something colder. They were not trained. They were selected. Only those who had already survived war, who had already proven themselves unshakable, unrelenting, and utterly devoid of hesitation, were considered for induction.

To become Iron Flame was to be stripped of all personal ambition, all self-serving desire. The Guard did not exist to conquer. They existed to maintain. To control. To ensure Pyrrha's wrath was eternal.

A soldier who took the Ashen Oath became a Legionnaire. But to be chosen as Iron Flame was a different ordeal entirely. They were not fighters. They were certainty, made flesh. When they moved, Pyrrha did not speak. It acted.

To be reforged into Iron Flame, a warrior had to abandon the very notion of free will. Where a Blood-Forged Legionnaire was shaped into a weapon, an Iron Flame Guard was shaped into an extension of Pyrrha itself.

This was done through the Trial of the Unyielding Flame, a rite designed not to break the body, but to strip the soul of all rebellion. It began with silence. For seven days, the chosen warriors were confined in absolute solitude.

Deprived of sound, of sight, of sensation. No commands were given. No explanations whispered.

They were left in the dark with only their own thoughts until those thoughts no longer mattered. Until they understood the truth. Pyrrha did not need men. Pyrrha did not need warriors. Pyrrha needed instruments of will. And an instrument does not question.

On the eighth day, the silence ended. The warriors were dragged from their isolation, shackled and blindfolded, and led into the heart of the Iron Maw.

There, before the flames of Pyrrha's eternal forge, they knelt. One by one, they were branded. Not with symbols of honour. Not with marks of rank. Their thoughts were cauterized. Their silence filled with doctrine. What emerged from the flame was not reforged. It was replaced.

But with the sigil of obedience. A crimson seal burned into their spine, ensuring that no matter where they stood, Pyrrha's will would always be at their backs.

They did not scream. Screaming was failure. Failure was death. Those who endured without sound, without movement, without hesitation, were anointed in molten iron. A final baptism. Sealing their fate as enforcers of Pyrrha's law.

They were not men who followed orders. They were the silence that obeyed before the order was ever spoken. They were the Iron Flame.

Unlike the Blood-Forged Legions, who functioned as an army, the Iron Flame Guard was structured into precision-based divisions, each serving a specific function in maintaining order. The highest rank within the Guard, the Pyrrhic Sentinels, were the eyes of Pyrrha. They saw everything. They judged everything.

And when judgment was passed, they were the ones who ensured it was carried out. They did not march into battle. They did not wage war. They were the last voice a traitor ever heard. The sentence before execution. The shadow before the flame. Their weapons were not forged of steel. Their very presence was enough.

Not all war was waged on the battlefield. Some wars were waged in whispers, in secrets, in schemes that festered beneath the surface. The Inquisitors of Iron were the cure for such diseases. They were the interrogators, the truth-seekers, the unseen enforcers who ripped treason from the marrow of Pyrrha's people.

A lie did not escape them. A secret did not remain hidden. And when their work was done, there was no trace left of those who had failed Pyrrha.

When justice needed a blade, the Crimson Adjudicators were summoned. They were not trial makers. They were not arbiters.

They were the executioners who ensured that Pyrrha's will was final. To be a Crimson Adjudicator was to wield the Pyrrhic Guillotine. A blade that did not simply kill. It erased. A single swing was an absolute sentence.

A single name spoken by an Adjudicator was a death already written in Pyrrha's history. While the Blood-Forged raged across battlefields, the Ironclad Wardens ensured that Pyrrha's fortresses never fell. They did not advance. They did not retreat. They stood.

Their presence alone was a statement. A reminder that Pyrrha's rule was eternal, its defences impregnable. They wielded titanic tower shields, reinforced with Pyrrhic plating, able to withstand even the wrath of siege weaponry.

When an enemy approached Pyrrha's walls, they did not find weakness. They found the Ironclad Wardens. And they did not pass.

The Iron Flame Guard didn't care for glory. They existed in the shadows, unyielding, always watching. Ira had once admired them, had seen in their silence a strength he longed to wield. Now, he saw only chains. A cage for the fire he had learned to wield.

Where the Blood-Forged were the storm, the Iron Flame were the chains that bound the world in place. They did not ask why. They did not wonder if the war would ever end. Because for Pyrrha, war was not a means to an end. It was the end itself.

Fire has many faces. Some flames burn steady, controlled, tools of discipline and obedience. Others rage in destruction, wielded like a sword for conquest. But there is a fire that is beyond control. A fire that consumes without reason, without mercy.

The Pyrrhic Devourers were not men anymore. They were hunger incarnate, twisted shells of warriors, their minds shattered by the Veil's madness.

Fear and mercy had long since been purged, leaving only the echo of humanity, faint and broken beneath the weight of endless rage. They did not march for glory. They marched for annihilation.

No victory.

No honour.

Just the erasure of life itself.

Their presence was not a march, it was a sentence.

But even fire needs a hand to guide it. The Iron Flame Guard, forged in the crucible of control, were Pyrrha's unyielding enforcers, silent, precise, and deadly. Their role was not to fight, but to ensure that Pyrrha's flame never wavered. And then there were the Pyrrhic Devourers. Born of madness and torment, they were the last resort, the final judgment.

When war was no longer enough, the Devourers were unleashed. They were not warriors. They were hunger given form, designed to erase anything that stood in the path of Pyrrha's eternal war.

When a city refused to kneel.

When an army refused to break.

When an enemy believed they had the strength to withstand Pyrrha's dominion.

The Pyrrhic Devourers were unleashed. And nothing remained. Wherever they marched, ruin followed.

Their bodies were not entirely their own. Modified. Twisted. Enhanced in ways that blurred the line between man and something far worse.

They did not sleep.

They did not stop.

They did not question.

To be a Devourer was to be unshackled from humanity itself.

Not all soldiers survive war. Some return changed. There were warriors who had seen too much, suffered too much, endured horrors beyond the limits of mortal minds. These men should have died. Their bodies should have collapsed. Their minds should have shattered. But Pyrrha does not waste. Pyrrha does not allow weakness. And so, the ones who should have perished were taken instead.

Their minds were broken open. Their bodies were reforged. And where there had once been men, there were now Devourers. Many had once been warriors of the Blood-Forged Legions. Champions of Pyrrha's wars who had been exposed to the Veil. The eldritch energy that pulsed beyond the known world. The exposure should have killed them. Instead, it twisted them. Left them unstable.

Their very existence fractured between what they were and what the Veil had tried to make them. Rather than execute them, Pyrrha found a use for their madness. If they could not be controlled, they would be unleashed. They were reforged into weapons of ultimate destruction. War beasts in human form.

Their bodies filled with chemical fury. Their minds severed from restraint. They became the Pyrrhic Devourers. And where they were sent, nothing remained standing. A warrior could not choose to be a Devourer. They were chosen. Or rather, they survived. There was no training. No indoctrination. There was only the Initiation of the Forsaken.

The process of forging a Devourer was unspeakable. A brutal baptism of suffering that stripped away all that remained of the human soul. The candidate was shackled in absolute darkness. Their body injected with Pyrrhic Venom. A volatile concoction that burned through their veins. It ignited an uncontrollable aggression while severing their ability to feel pain. They were left there for seven days. Their screams swallowed by the void. Their minds trapped within a storm of hallucinations, rage, and raw, searing agony.

No one had ever emerged unchanged. Some simply ceased to exist. Their minds burned out. Their bodies collapsing into empty husks. But those who survived, those who endured, they were taken to Phase Two. The survivor's body was subjected to enhancements. A fusion of cybernetic augmentation, bioengineered muscle grafts, and Veil-infused modifications.

Their nervous system was rewired to ignore pain. Their bones were reinforced with a metal-polymer hybrid, making them nearly unbreakable. Their muscles were injected with Warborne Stim. A compound that allowed them to fight beyond normal human limits. Even with mortal wounds. But the worst was yet to come.

The final trial was simple. A Devourer candidate was dropped into the Maw. A sealed arena where twelve other candidates had been left in a state of chemically induced madness.

Only one walked out. Not because they won. Because they consumed the others. Bloodied. Maddened. Transcended. They ruptured from it. Twisted. Unbound. The Devourers were not men. They were the hunger that war forgot to leash.

The highest-ranked Devourers were once great generals before madness took them. Now, they commanded nothing but carnage, leading platoons of berserkers into battle, their minds existing only for war. Their bodies were more machine than flesh, rebuilt for one purpose: destruction. These were the largest and most enhanced Devourers. Eight feet tall, their forms were grotesquely overgrown with muscle grafts and Veil-infused plating.

They did not wear armour. They wore what was left of their past. Flesh twisted by war. Honour melted into bone. What walked now was not a man. It was punishment incarnate. They were sent in when armies refused to break. Because nothing could withstand their wrath. The shock troops. The unstoppable wave of insanity that crashed into enemy lines.

Their blood had been altered, filled with a chemical rage that made them immune to fear, to fatigue, to reason. They did not fight for strategy. They fought until nothing was left to kill. Some were too unstable to even serve as berserkers. The Scornborn were unleashed in one final, suicidal charge. Their bodies were filled with explosive implants that ensured their deaths would bring ruin.

They were Pyrrha's final punishment, the last resort, the living embodiment of war's end. They did not exist to conquer. They did not exist to rule. They existed to end. The Pyrrhic Devourers were the last fire, the burning ruin, the storm that left nothing behind. They were unshackled destruction. War with no restraint. The inevitable, violent conclusion of Pyrrha's philosophy.

Because Pyrrha did not simply wage war.

Pyrrha consumed.

And the Devourers were its hunger.

But wrath alone was never enough. Not in Pyrrha. The body must be forged. The blood must be taught to remember. And beneath the citadel, where screams never reached the sky, the first knife was already being drawn. Because in Pyrrha, blood was no longer sacred. It was a ledger. A signature. A chain.

It did not carry life. It carried debt. And when the ground drank enough blood, it began to whisper. Not with the voices of the dead... But with the will of those who refused to let the dead go.

Some say the blood remembers things the living were never meant to carry. That in its veins, old wars still scream.

And in those whispers, Pyrrha found its next weapon.

"When blood is spilled too freely, it no longer carries life. It carries flame. The body becomes its own grave, and the soul is nothing but ash, forgotten in the smoke."

Null Gospel, Book I, Verse 13.

***

CHAPTER THIRTEEN:

What the Fire Could Not Take

"Fire burns the body. History devours the silence. What survives is not what was spared, but what could not be killed."

Fragment of the Exiled Codex, Volume I, Tablet 14.

There is a silence that follows genocide. Not the silence of peace, but of precision. A silence measured in heartbeats withheld, in histories unspoken, in blood spilled not for death, but for transformation.

In Pyrrha, war was not a scream. It was a surgery.

Blood is not merely life. It is power. It is memory. It is the ink that writes history, the tide that decides the fate of empires, the covenant that binds warrior to war, conqueror to conquest. And in Pyrrha, where war was not fought for survival but for permanence, blood was more than a necessity. It was currency. It was dominion. It was a weapon.

Where the Pyrrhic Devourers were wrath made manifest, and the Blood-Forged Legions were discipline given form, the Sanguinary Magi were something else entirely.

They were not warriors in the traditional sense. They did not wield swords. They did not charge into battle. Instead, they orchestrated destruction from behind the curtain, manipulating the battlefield with the very essence of life itself.

They were scientists, warlocks, executioners, and prophets. Their magic was a blend of forbidden alchemy, arcane bloodcraft, and the systematic weaponization of the human body.

Their duty was simple. To ensure Pyrrha's warriors did not bleed in vain.

There is no magic in Pyrrha. At least, not in the way the old world once spoke of it. There are no incantations, no divine blessings, no sorcerers with staffs of wood and words of power.

Pyrrha does not believe in gods. It believes in methodology. It believes in science, in ritual, in flesh-bound equations where pain is merely the price of knowledge.

The Sanguinary Magi practice Hematurgy, the art of blood manipulation, fleshcrafting, and the reforging of the human body into something greater, something stronger, something unbreakable.

Their craft is built on four absolute truths:

Blood Remembers. The essence of life holds the memories of those who came before. To consume another's blood is to inherit their strength, their knowledge, their past.

Pain Purifies. Suffering is not weakness. It is the forge through which flesh is reshaped, through which warriors are remade into something beyond mortality.

The Flesh is Clay. The body is not sacred. It is a canvas, a vessel to be reshaped, improved, stripped of imperfection and reforged into something worthy of war.

To Bleed is to Serve. There is no power without sacrifice. Blood is not simply taken. It is given. The Magi do not kill for sport. They kill with purpose.

To wield Hematurgy is to understand that the body is not a limitation. It is a resource. A warrior dies once. A warrior's blood, if used wisely, may fight a thousand more battles.

The Blood Mages do not train as warriors do. They do not drill with swords. They do not march in formation.

Instead, they break themselves, again and again, reshaping flesh and mind through rituals so agonizing that few survive their initiation.

The first initiation: a prospective Magi is drained of their own blood.

Not to the point of death, but to the trembling edge of it. Their body on fire, breath shallow, mind drifting into the void. Only then are they given their first taste of Sanguine Communion.

The blood of another.

Not merely transfused. Infused. It floods their veins, pulling them into the memories, the torment, the will of one who came before.

Those who survive the shock, the hallucinations, the madness, awaken changed.

Once an initiate proves themselves, they are led into the Crimson Reservoir. A vast subterranean lake deep beneath Pyrrha, filled not with water, but the blood of generations.

An ocean of history. A tide of war, of glory, of pain. To submerge in it is to drown in memory. Every battle fought. Every oath sworn. Every death carved into the current.

Only those who return to the surface with sanity intact are deemed worthy.

The final rite is the surrender of self.

A Magi must offer part of their body for reforging. An eye carved out and replaced with a blood shard, giving sight into the essence of others. Hands severed and rebuilt with living constructs etched in alchemical sigils. Some go further, removing their heart, replacing it with a mechanism that pumps Sanguine Energy in a relentless stream.

To become a Blood Mage is to shed the mortal shell. To master life and death, one must step beyond both.

The Crimson Oracles. The Sages of Hematurgy. They do not walk among warriors. They dwell in the Sanctum of the Blood Wells, where history flows through living veins. Ageless. Preserved by centuries of fleshcrafting.

The Bloodwrights. Engineers of Pyrrha's genetic war. They do not fight. They remake. Shaping human forms into weapons that defy mortality. To them, flesh is blueprint, not boundary.

The Reavers of the Crimson Pact. War Priests of suffering. They do not battle. They harvest. They walk the field after the killing ends, gathering the fallen, draining them of essence, returning their strength to the war engine.

The Fleshweavers. Pyrrha's keepers of immortality. Surgeons. Scientists. They break the rules of biology to build what should not live. They harvest the dead and craft them into vessels of violence.

Where the Pyrrhic Devourers burn, where the Iron Flame Guard enforce, where the Blood-Forged Legions conquer, Blood Mages ensure none of it is lost. Their strength is not in fire or steel.

It is in eternity. In the cycle of sacrifice. In the truth that every drop spilled for Pyrrha never stops fighting.

Because Pyrrha does not believe in death. It believes in utility. And in the hands of the Sanguinary Magi, even the fallen are never truly gone. They are reforged. They are reborn. They are eternal.

War is not only fought on battlefields. It is fought in whispers and silence, in poison and deception, in shadows cast long before the blade ever reaches the throat. Pyrrha's dominance was not built on sheer military might alone. It was built on fear. And fear was not sown by legions marching through the streets. It was sown in the knowing that no enemy of Pyrrha would ever sleep soundly again.

The Crimson Shadows were not warriors.

They were the unseen architects of dread. The assassins who moved in the night. The mercenaries who sold war not for honour, but for profit, for survival, for blood and coin alike. They were the Sanguine Order's most hidden division. The silent edge of Ira Valkor's dominion.

While the Blood-Forged Legions waged open war and the Blood Mages bent the very essence of life itself, the Crimson Shadows worked behind the curtain, ensuring that Pyrrha's enemies were crippled before war was ever declared.

They operated in two distinct sects.

The Ashen Talons. Pyrrha's elite assassins. The unseen hand of Ira Valkor's wrath. Trained from childhood to kill without hesitation. Here, the Maskborn and other subsects thrived in the shadows, wielding identities which were never truly their own.

They were not warriors. They were death itself.

The Black Sun Mercenaries. The Warlord's Sellblades. A rogue band of highly skilled killers and war profiteers, not bound by the Order's doctrine, but by the promise of power, influence, and wealth.

They would fight for Pyrrha so long as it was profitable. Both sects operated in the darkness, ensuring that Pyrrha's enemies were dismantled before they ever had a chance to resist.

Where the Blood Mages extracted life from the fallen, the Ashen Talons ensured that those who stood against Pyrrha never lived long enough to become a problem.

They were not soldiers. They were spectres. Trained in stealth, infiltration, assassination, and psychological warfare. To be chosen as an Ashen Talon was not an honour. It was a sentence. A child stolen from the streets, from the pits, from the ruins of conquered lands, given one simple purpose: kill, or be killed.

Their training was not one of discipline or brute strength. It was one of calculated terror.

The Trial of the Black Veil. A child is dropped into the ruins of a fallen city, hunted by their own instructors. They must kill or evade capture for seven days. Those who fail vanish.

The Rite of the Hollow Name. Their past is erased. Their old identity is severed. Their name is stripped from them, replaced with nothing but a designation. A number. A purpose.

The First Blood Offering. Their first sanctioned kill is not an enemy of Pyrrha. It is another recruit. A friend. A rival. The final lesson: trust is a weakness. Mercy is a lie.

To be an Ashen Talon is to cease to be a person. They are not warriors. They are weapons wielded in silence. They do not leave bodies behind. They do not leave trails. They erase threats before they ever become threats. To hear their voice is to know death is already upon you.

Unlike the Ashen Talons, who were indoctrinated into Pyrrha's doctrine from birth, the Black Sun Mercenaries were free agents. Hired blades. War profiteers. Opportunists. They did not serve Pyrrha out of loyalty. They served because Pyrrha paid the most.

They were not bound by the Order's doctrine, nor did they adhere to its strict discipline.

They were allowed personal identity, choice, ambition, so long as they never turned their blades against Pyrrha itself.

War Profiteering.

They provided high-risk, high-reward services: sabotage, assassinations, information warfare, and destabilization. Weapons Dealers.

They controlled black market arms trades, ensuring that Pyrrha's enemies never gained weapons that could threaten the Order.

Espionage and Psychological Warfare. They infiltrated enemy factions, sowing discord, dismantling alliances, and ensuring that no rebellion ever took root before being snuffed out.

Unlike the Ashen Talons, who were faceless executioners, the Black Sun Mercenaries thrived on identity. They built legends around their names. They ensured that no matter where in the world war existed, they would be at its centre. Controlling it. Profiting from it. Ensuring that Pyrrha always held the upper hand.

Their leader was not a warlord. Not a general. Not a loyalist. He was an enigma. A man who walked between worlds, navigating the delicate line between serving Pyrrha and ensuring that Pyrrha never controlled him.

There are those who are forged by war. And then there are those who are abandoned by it.

Toren Ignisferre was not raised in the arms of family, nor in the warmth of belonging. He was a child of the Matriarchy, but he was never a son. He was a blade waiting to be wielded. An ember waiting to be kindled.

A storm waiting for a name.

Without a father. Without a mother. Only war. Only the cold discipline of the Ashen Talons. The whispers of the Black Sun Mercenaries. The unforgiving lessons of the Crimson Matriarchy. His rage was not the blind fury of a berserker. It was controlled. Measured. Chained to purpose.

Unlike the warriors of Pyrrha, who were forged in discipline. Unlike the Blood Mages, who crafted destruction from the essence of life itself. Unlike the assassins, who erased history before it could be written.

Toren was all of these things at once. He was not Pyrrha's. He was not a loyalist. He was a weapon searching for something to aim at. And the moment he found it, the moment his rage found a name to carve itself upon, the world would burn.

Where the Blood-Forged Legions conquered in force. Where the Blood Mages ensured that no warrior's strength was wasted. Where the Pyrrhic Devourers ravaged the frontlines.

The Crimson Shadows ensured that Pyrrha's enemies never saw war coming at all.

They destabilized. They poisoned alliances. They murdered key figures before revolutions could be sparked. They were not warriors. They were the death sentence scrawled in blood before war ever reached the gates. Because Pyrrha did not fight fair. It did not fight for honour. It fought to eradicate anything that stood in its way. And the Crimson Shadows ensured that no war Pyrrha waged was ever truly a war. Because by the time battle arrived, the enemy was already bleeding out in the dark.

*

The silent war.

Yet wars can be fought in many different ways.

There are wars that leave scars upon the land. And then there are wars that carve wounds so deep they never truly heal.

Eighteen years ago, fire came to the land beyond Pyrrha's walls. Not a battle. Not a raid. A purge.

The skies did not simply darken with the smoke of war. They turned to night itself, thick with the scent of burning flesh, of steel hacking through bone, of earth groaning beneath the weight of conquest. The war machine of Pyrrha moved not as men, nor as soldiers. It moved as a singular, unrelenting entity. A force of inevitability. And at its head was Wrath incarnate.

Warlord Ira Valkor.

He did not command from the safety of a war tent. He did not watch from high upon a citadel, dictating orders through messengers.

No. Ira led the slaughter himself.

The warriors of Phalaistín were fierce, but they were not prepared for what came upon them. Pyrrha did not fight for land. It did not fight for resources. It fought for permanence.

They came with flame casters, reducing sacred groves to nothing but cinder and shadow. They came with war beasts, cybernetic monstrosities unleashed upon villages, tearing through stone and flesh alike. They came with siege-crushers, machines that shattered city gates with thunderous ease.

But worse than all these things was the silence that followed.

For war is loud. It is deafening. It is chaos made manifest. And yet, in the wake of Pyrrha's march, a terrible quiet always settled. Because there was no one left to scream.

Ira did not swing his sword in desperate survival, nor for glory. He fought as one who had long since abandoned the concept of restraint. His presence alone was a proclamation. The strong endure. The weak perish. He moved through the battlefield like a god in the flesh. Untouchable. Unrelenting. Every movement was precise. Every strike designed not only to kill, but to break the will of those who witnessed it.

One of the lands they invaded was Ashra'tel. A land of sprawling golden plains. Of rivers that once ran silver beneath the sun. And molten streams of lava, juxtaposing the golden plains. A beautiful contradiction. A paradox woven into the threads of this ancient land.

A land where the great Eternal Tree of Ashra'tel stood at its heart. A symbol of endurance. Of memory. Of all that had existed before Pyrrha's rise. The tree had stood for centuries. Its roots entwined with the stories of the people. Its branches stretching toward the heavens, as if daring the sky itself to forget.

But fire does not remember. Fire only devours. And so, as the final night of Ashra'tel stretched long into dawn, the great tree burned.

Its ancient boughs were alight with ruin. Its leaves turned to embers that spiralled into the heavens, carrying the last breath of a dying world. Warriors fell at its base, their bodies becoming one with the roots that had once nourished their ancestors.

Ashra'tel did not fall in battle. It was erased.

The silence that followed was absolute.

Pyrrha did not look back. Ira did not look back.

But something remained. Where the echelons of his blood remained.

The war ended with the last scream swallowed by the wind. The march of Pyrrha moved forward. Its warriors returned to their great citadel of conquest. Their war banners still slick with the blood of the fallen.

The world tree stood as a skeletal ruin. Charred and broken. But not gone.

And somewhere, in the ashes, in the quiet where only ghosts remained, something lingered. Something unseen. Something left behind.

A voice.

Soft, like the hush of wind through leaves. Gentle, yet steady. A rhythm woven in quiet patience.

And so the rivers ran red, and the sun set upon the old world. But what is broken is not always lost. What is forgotten is not always gone.

The words were not read. They were recited. Spoken with reverence, as though their weight had settled in the air long before the lips had uttered them.

The great tree of Ashra'tel stood whole once more.

Its branches no longer burned, but bloomed. Lush, endless canopies of green and gold, stretching toward the sky. Its roots ran deep, not in the ruin of war, but in the soil of life reborn. The wind stirred through its leaves, carrying the whisper of memory. But no longer of sorrow.

Beneath its vast shade, seated on a carved wooden chair, was a woman.

Her hair was dark as the midnight sky. Streaked with the ember-gold remnants of a world before. Her eyes, deep as the abyss of time itself, flickered as they traced the words on the pages before her.

Nahara Sunshadow. Priestess. Storyteller. Keeper of what was.

She did not read to herself. She read to them.

The children of Phalaistín. The Emberborn. The Duskborn. The Tideborn. The last remnants of a people who had not been broken. Children who did not yet know the weight of war. Who listened with wide eyes and quiet wonder.

She turned the page.

And though the fire raged, though the sky was dark, though the world wept for what was lost, the tree still stood.

And the children, their voices soft but certain, repeated the words with her.

The tree still stood.

The words lingered in the air, weaving themselves into the hush of wind and rustling leaves.

The tree still stood.

Nahara Sunshadow let the silence settle for a moment before she turned the page.

The children, some sitting cross-legged upon the sun-warmed grass, others curled against the sprawling roots of the great tree, watched her with quiet intensity. They were of different blood. Different lineages. Different lands. But here, beneath the canopy of something greater than war, they were simply children.

A boy from the Emberborn, with hair like flame-touched bronze, leaned forward, his gaze intense, as if pulling the heat of the fire into himself.

His voice was not just hesitant. It trembled with something older, the weight of countless ancestors who had burned and bled in the name of survival.

"But why?" he asked, his words heavy, as if they were the first crack in a wall built from generations of silence. "If the fire took everything, why didn't it take the tree too?"

Nahara's lips curved, but there was no humour in it. Only understanding.

These were not children raised in Pyrrha, where questions were silenced before they could take shape. Here, in the lands beyond the walls of the Warlords, curiosity was not weakness. It was a birthright.

She did not answer immediately.

Instead, she closed the book, pressing her palm against its worn cover, as if feeling the weight of all the voices that had come before.

"The fire," she said softly, her voice threaded with both sorrow and defiance, "was never stronger than the roots. Fire can burn, yes. But it can never erase what the land has woven."

A hush passed through them.

Some of the younger ones looked up, glancing toward the massive boughs above them, as if searching for the answer in the green-lit heavens.

The oldest among them, a girl with dusk-dark eyes and a gaze that could pierce a lie, did not need to look up.

Her knowing was not born of age, but of survival. Of seeing too much too soon. She felt the weight of Nahara's words like a stone in her chest.

The past was not dead. It was in the wind. The soil. The tree. And in them.

Nahara exhaled, shifting in her chair. The book in her lap was not old in the way Pyrrhan relics were. It was not preserved, dust-ridden, brittle with time.

No.

The pages had been turned often, the ink refreshed, the cover re-bound with careful hands. It had not survived because it had been locked away.

It had survived because it had been remembered.

She traced the cover's surface, feeling the uneven imprint of its title. Not in Pyrrhan script. Not in the cold, manufactured dialect of conquest. But in the old tongue. The language of Phalaistín.

"There are stories Pyrrha would have you forget," she murmured, her voice dipping lower, pulling them in, pulling them closer.

The children did not move, did not breathe too loudly, lest they miss what came next.

"There are names they would burn from the stones. Memories they would drown in the rivers they have poisoned. But what does the land know?"

She gestured, a slow, deliberate motion toward the great roots that sprawled beneath them. Knotted with time. Wrapped in the quiet embrace of history.

"The land knows the truth. And the land does not forget."

The girl with dusk-dark eyes nodded. She had no words, only a quiet, unshaken understanding.

Nahara's gaze flickered, distant for a brief moment. Not to the tree. Not to the book. But to the horizon. Because Pyrrha had not forgotten either. And even as the great city of wrath stood behind its towering walls, even as the war machine of the Sanguine Order thundered in preparation for the next conquest, there were things that fire could never truly burn away.

Nahara Sunshadow turned the page with slow deliberation. The aged parchment whispered against her fingers. The children's eyes remained fixed upon her. Their faces were bathed in the golden dapple of the tree's towering canopy. But she could feel it now. The shift. The hesitation in their small bodies. The weight of the question that had been stirring in their young minds.

It was not a matter of if it would be asked. Only when.

The bronze-haired Emberborn boy spoke first, though his voice wavered like a flame caught in an uncertain wind.

"Why do people fight?"

A simple question. But no question, when spoken by a child, was ever truly simple.

Nahara's gaze lifted from the book, watching him, watching them all.

The Duskborn girl beside him did not look away. Her stare was not unkind, but there was something behind it. The quiet, fragile understanding of someone who had already seen too much.

A Tideborn boy, smaller than the others, curled his arms around his knees. He did not speak, but his silence spoke for him. The question sat between them, hanging like mist over an untouched river.

Why do people fight? Why do they burn what they cannot hold? Why do they take what was never theirs to claim?

Nahara closed the book, pressing her fingers lightly against its cover. The words within could not answer that question. Not in the way they needed. Because this was not a question of history. It was a question of the soul.

"Because they forget." Her voice was soft, but it carried.

The bronze-haired boy frowned. "Forget what?"

"That they were once children, just like you."

A hush settled beneath the Eternal Tree, thick as the roots that cradled the earth.

The Tideborn boy, silent until now, finally spoke. His voice was quiet, barely a whisper, but in that whisper, there was something ancient. Something fragile.

"Then... why don't they remember?"

Why don't they?

Nahara exhaled slowly, her fingers tightening over the book, as if holding onto something that was slipping through time itself. How could she explain? How could she tell them the truth without unmaking the innocence that still lingered within them?

The Emberborn boy, the one who had started it, pressed on.

"Is it because of the wars?"

She nodded. "Yes. But also... no."

She let her gaze drift to the sky beyond the canopy, where the light bled through the branches. Golden and patient.

"They forget because war teaches them to forget."

The Duskborn girl tilted her head, narrowing her eyes as if weighing the truth of Nahara's words against the weight of her own experiences.

"That doesn't make sense," she said, her voice firm, like the crack of a twig underfoot. "War is about remembering. Remembering why you fight. Who hurt you."

Nahara looked at her, and for a moment, her heart ached. Not because the girl was wrong. But because she was right.

"That is what war tells you," she murmured. "That is what they teach in the cities, in the barracks, in the halls where they carve names into steel and call them banners."

She leaned forward slightly, her voice dipping lower, pulling them in, closer, like the tide pulling the shore.

"But war does not remember names. It only remembers fire."

The Tideborn boy frowned, looking down at his hands.

"Then... how do we remember?"

That. That was the real question. How does one hold onto something that war cannot steal?

Nahara exhaled, looking to the great tree above them.

"You remember," she said, "by carrying what cannot be burned."

She reached for the book again, running her hand over the cover as if feeling its history in her very bones.

"Not swords. Not rifles and machines of death. Not banners. Not even blood."

She tapped the book lightly.

"Stories."

The children did not speak. But they did not need to. They understood. Because even here, in the shadow of Pyrrha's ever-reaching hand, beneath a tree that had once burned but never fallen, they were learning how to remember.

Nahara's smile was faint, almost fragile, as she turned the page. Each movement deliberate, as though the parchment held breath.

The children inched closer, some breathless, others with fingers curled tight in the grass, as if bracing for something unspoken.

The story pulsed between them, not just heard, but felt. Like an echo stirring in the roots beneath their feet.

But the boy with bronze-fire hair did not lean in. He stared at the tree. Then at the roots. Then down at his hands, as if searching them for a memory he had never been given. An answer buried in the silence before he was born.

The page had turned. But not for him. For him, something older stirred. Not a chapter.

A wound. And wounds, like stories left unanswered, grow teeth. And start to ask their own questions.

"The tyrant says fire is forever. But the roots do not forget the hand that struck the spark, and the roots are patient."

Null Gospel, Book I, Verse 14.

***

CHAPTER FOURTEEN:

The Question That Remains

"They took the land as if it were silence. But the land remembers. And memory is louder than war."

Fragment of the Exiled Codex, Volume I, Tablet 15.

Before the boy spoke, before the wind stirred the ancient boughs, there was a silence. Not the silence of peace. The other kind. The one that lingers after devastation and hangs in the air like ash, bitter and clinging. It was a silence that tasted of memory.

Beneath the Eternal Tree of Ashra'tel, where roots fed on stories too old for tongues, the children gathered. They clustered like embers around a dying flame, pulled by something they could not name. No one explained this place to them. They simply knew. This was where questions were born. And not all questions came with answers.

But some questions refused to be buried. Some clawed up from the quiet, raw and insistent.

The boy sat at the base of the tree, small hands pressed into the ancient roots, feeling the rough, cracked bark as though it might respond. As if the soil might murmur something only he could hear.

He was Emberborn. Born of sun-bleached stone and canyon lands, where the light bore down with the weight of judgment. The fire in his blood was not yet for war. It was the heat of inquiry. Of belief. Of a world that must, somehow, still make sense.

And yet the question gnawed at him. It moved behind his eyes, weighted his chest. He looked up at Nahara, brow furrowed. When he spoke, his voice was low, hesitant. "Why do we fight over land if the land is already there for everyone?"

The other children stilled, drawn to the question like deer to thunder. Above them, the wind passed through the branches, scattering shards of sunlight across their faces. No one answered. Not immediately. Not even Nahara.

She knew the answer. That was the problem.

She had heard this question before. Never in this tone. Never from a child. She had heard it screamed through fire-lit nights, bellowed by those who had lost everything, whispered in the hollow voices of warriors who had nothing left to hold but the shape of their rage.

The boy, though, did not rage. He asked because he did not understand.

"Why?" he asked again, more insistent, curling his fingers into the soil. "If the land was already here, why do we have to take it from each other?"

Nahara exhaled. Her breath moved slow, steady, controlled. Her gaze drifted to the cliffs beyond, where the stone stood unmoved, indifferent.

"You're asking a question that has no answer," she said. And there was softness in it. But not surrender.

The boy shook his head. "No." He was stubborn, like all Emberborn. "There has to be an answer. People don't just..." His words caught, tangled in thought. "They don't just decide to kill for no reason."

His voice held. But beneath it, something shifted. Not war. Not yet. But the residue of something already seen.

He had not witnessed the battles of old. But he had seen what war left behind. The ghost-light in ruined homes. The way the village songs changed. The men who never came back. The ones who did, quieter. His mother's fingers tightening when she prayed to a sky she no longer trusted.

And somewhere in that silence, he had learned to ask.

Nahara watched him. Not as a boy, but as something more. A soul approaching the precipice of knowing. The threshold no one crosses without shedding part of themselves.

She could have lied. She could have told him the things empires teach. The myths. The inevitabilities. The necessary cruelties. She could have spoken of power and territory and fate.

But he wasn't ready to believe that.

So instead she asked, "What do you think?"

The boy frowned. Frustrated. "I think... I think it's stupid."

A ripple passed through the others, some flinching, others watching. Nahara didn't flinch. She only nodded. "Go on."

He drew a breath, pushing past his frustration. "If the land is already here. If it belongs to no one. Then why do people act like it does? It's dirt. Trees. Sky. The stars don't belong to anyone. The wind doesn't. Rivers go where they want. No wall stops them. So why do we pretend we can own any of it?"

His voice rose, filled now with the first threads of anger. Not the kind that strikes. The kind that builds. The kind that asks too many times and only finds silence. "Why do we say, 'This is mine, not yours'? Why do people die for it? What does it even mean to own something that was here before we were?"

Silence followed, heavier than before. It thickened around them, not because the question had no answer, but because the world had given none that made sense. Nahara's hand rested lightly on the book in her lap, worn leather warm beneath her fingers, the weight of history pressed into its spine. She had once asked the same questions, before fire, before death rewrote her understanding of permanence.

And still she refused to answer with silence.

"Somewhere along the way," she said, "someone decided that to control something was to own it. That land meant nothing unless it was claimed. That it only became valuable when someone else wanted it too."

The boy scowled. "That doesn't make sense."

"No," she agreed. "It doesn't."

He rubbed his face, as if trying to scrape the thoughts away, but they clung to him. "But we still do it."

"Yes."

His hands fell back to the earth. He pressed his fingers into the dirt, the question blooming again.

"Then how do we stop it?"

The quiet returned. But this time, it didn't carry despair. This time, it asked something more.

This time, Nahara did not hesitate. "You don't," she said. "Not all at once. Not by force. Not by the same means that created it."

Her voice lowered. Not in weakness, but with intent. As though shedding armour. She did not speak as a warrior, nor as a teacher, but as one who had survived the endless hunger of war and made the conscious choice, again and again, not to let it devour what remained of her soul.

"You stop it by remembering it was never yours to take in the first place."

The boy didn't move. His fingers stayed buried in the soil, and for a moment they trembled. Barely. Like leaves caught in breathless wind.

Then, without lifting his head, he nodded.

The wind moved through the branches above. Not loud. But present. It carried the weight of things too old for words. It shifted the light, casting gold and shadow across their faces as if nature itself were listening.

He pulled his knees to his chest. His dark eyes followed the sway of the leaves above, watching the flickering dance of sunlight between their edges.

There was a searching in his gaze. Not for answers he expected to receive, but for meaning in a world that refused to explain itself.

He was Tideborn. Of rivers poisoned by industry and ambition. Of tides that no longer carried his ancestors back to shore. He had never seen the homeland his people once sang of.

The great floating cities were not memories to him. They were inheritance. Now drowned. Forgotten. Dismissed by Pyrrha as inconvenient myths.

And yet they weighed on him. A legacy he could not put down.

He turned to Nahara. "Why do some people get to live free, and others don't?" His voice didn't carry accusation. Only the ache of a child trying to understand what the world had already decided not to explain.

Around him, the other children shifted. The question fell over them like a veil. It made them smaller. More still. As if it might call the attention of something watching, something that did not like to be questioned. But Nahara didn't flinch. She didn't look away. She held the silence, allowed him to step further into it. And he did.

"Why do some people get to have homes and others get pushed out of theirs? Why do some get to say, *'this is mine,'* and no one questions it. But when someone else says the same thing, they're thrown out. Or killed. Or…"

He stopped, arms tightening around himself.

"…or worse."

Above, the leaves rustled gently. Sunlight fractured and fell across them in long, broken patterns.

The Emberborn girl, the one who had first questioned the world aloud, swallowed hard. Because they all knew what he meant.

They had seen soldiers walk roads their parents once travelled freely. Had seen once-open spaces carved into districts. Gated. Guarded. Regulated.

Their homes had not moved. But the lines around them had.

They had learned to speak quietly when enforcers passed. Learned to stop singing certain songs. Learned which names to forget.

They had learned that justice wasn't the same for everyone. That some people were allowed to exist fully, and others only in silence.

Nahara closed her book. Not with finality, but with intention. She did not slam it shut. She sealed it, like a pause between breaths. Her voice, when it came, was gentle. But not soft. "Because those who have power fear those who do not."

The boy tilted his head, uncertain. "Why?"

She inhaled. Held it. Released it slowly.

"Because the ones who take land. Who build walls. Who decide who may speak and who must stay silent. They know what they've built isn't real."

The children looked confused. Frowns spread between them like ripples across still water.

"But the walls are real," the boy said. "The rules. The soldiers. They're all real."

"Yes," Nahara replied. "They are. But that's all they are. Walls. Rules. Soldiers. Constructions."

She let her fingers move across the spine of the book, not reading, but remembering. "A river does not care about a wall," she said. "It does not recognize borders. It does not belong to anyone, no matter how many maps try to claim it. It existed before the wall. It will exist after. It moves where it must. And so will those who remember."

Her gaze returned to the boy. Firm. Measured. "They build walls because they know the river will always try to find its way back home."

The boy blinked. His brow furrowed. But not in confusion. Something was turning inside him. Reshaping the bones of what he had believed.

There was anger, yes. But beneath it, quieter. A pulse of hope. The kind that lives under ruins. The kind that waits.

The third child had said nothing until now. She was Duskborn. Of Nyxmar. Where twilight stained the sky with ember and the wind never moved without a voice inside it.

She had learned to stay quiet. Not because she had nothing to say. But because she had seen what questions could cost.

Her father had asked why once. Her mother had refused to kneel.

She had seen what followed.

And she had learned.

But something in that moment. Something about Nahara. About the way the others listened. About the weight of every question already spoken.

It made the girl forget to be afraid.

The silence between them was no longer empty. It was full.

And so, she spoke.

"Why do they try to erase us?"

The words were soft. But they fell like stones into still water. The firelight flickered, and something in the air tensed. The two beside her turned, their expressions shifting. Not with surprise, but with recognition. Because this question was not about land or conquest. It was not about walls or power.

It was about being.

She didn't know how to explain it. Couldn't map it out the way adults might. With treaties or timelines.

She only knew what she had seen.

When Pyrrha took, it didn't just conquer. It stripped. It hollowed. It unmade.

She had seen old temples vanish in flame. Not destroyed for strategy, but for silence. She had watched books disappear. Not burned, but erased. Removed from memory like they had never been written. She had seen her grandfather's language fade. Not from disuse, but from fear.

The old words whispered only in darkness. Like secrets. Like sins.

And she had seen the dead left without names. Not mourned. Not remembered. Because this was not just death. This was erasure.

She turned toward Nahara, that quiet centre of gravity, and whispered, "Why do they want to make us disappear?"

The air shifted. Not from fear. From something deeper. Because every child around that fire had felt it. The weight of not just grief, but the knowing. Quiet, constant. That their people were being peeled away from the world's memory.

Nahara inhaled. The book in her lap remained closed. Her hands rested on the worn leather, steady, grounded. But her gaze rose to meet the girl's. Then to all of them. When she spoke, her voice carried no softness. It carried steel.

"Because if they destroy a people, but the world still remembers them, then they are only gone in body."

She paused, and the fire caught in her eyes, turning violet into ember.

"But if they can make the world forget those people ever existed. If they can erase their names, their stories, their tongue. Then they have truly won."

No one moved. No one breathed. It was not just a lesson. It was a verdict.

"Death is not the end," Nahara continued. "As long as someone remembers, the dead live. But if no one speaks their names, if no songs are sung, if the history is rewritten, if even the ruins are swept away..."

She exhaled, and the fire cracked beside her.

"...then it is as if they were never here at all."

The girl looked down, fingers tracing the embroidered patterns on her tunic. Her mother had told her they were ancient. Older than Pyrrha. Older than the Warlords. Stitched by hands long buried.

She thought of all that had already vanished. Of names never carved into stone. Of songs unsung. Of temples crumbling in silence.

She understood now. This was not war. It was not even death. It was the removal of reason to remember.

And her voice, when it came, was low. But strong.

"Then we can't let them win."

Nahara smiled. This time, the curve of her lips held no sorrow. It held something older. Something that refused to fade.

"That," she said, "is why we remember."

And the fire burned. Because fire does not end. It moves. From hand to hand. From memory to memory. And so does truth.

The flames danced in the centre of their gathering. Around them, the Eternal Tree of Ashra'tel stood unmoved, its great canopy rustling like whispered pages. The night stretched wide and deep, as if to listen.

The children sat still, too still for their age, the weight of what they carried pressing into their small bodies. Nahara watched them with quiet precision. The flickering light cast shadows across their faces, shadows shaped by questions they were too young to be asking, questions that had no answers except the ones they would one day carve from the world themselves.

She exhaled, slow and steady. "Come now," she said, her voice weaving through the quiet like a soft current. "Enough sorrow for one night. We remember, yes. But we must also laugh. We must build. Otherwise, what are we fighting for?"

The Nyxmar girl looked up first. Her fingers, which had clenched her lap in silence, began to loosen. The Tideborn boy scowled into the fire as though it might burn away everything he couldn't yet name. The Emberborn child, the first to speak, let out a long breath, the kind that felt older than he was.

"Then what do we fight for?" he asked. "If it's not just about staying alive?"

Nahara's smile turned soft. "For something greater than survival."

She leaned forward. Her posture shifted, like a story was about to unfold, like a secret was being prepared in the throat of time.

"Let me tell you a story," she said, her voice sinking into something deeper. "A story of kings."

The word hung strange in the air, archaic. They had heard it before. In lessons. In whispered legends. Kings, queens, monarchs. They belonged to another time. Banners in the wind. Thrones carved from stone. Bloodlines traced through myths. The modern world had warlords, corporate stewards, military governors. But not kings.

"You've heard the word," Nahara said, her eyes sweeping across them. "But they don't exist anymore, do they?"

The Tideborn boy narrowed his eyes. "Warlords exist."

"Yes," Nahara said with a soft nod. "They do."

"So what's the difference?" asked the girl from Nyxmar. "A king's just another person in charge."

"No." Nahara's tone shifted. No louder. Just more certain. Like a truth revealing itself.

"A true king is something far greater than a man in a crown. A true king is not just a ruler. Not a general. Not a figurehead."

She let the silence follow. Let the idea settle.

"A true king is a foundation. A pillar that does not crumble when the world shakes. Today's leaders are hollow. They trade allegiance like currency. They sell power like spice. They pass laws they do not believe in. They are merchants in thrones."

The Emberborn boy frowned. "But kings can be cruel. They've done terrible things."

Nahara nodded. "Yes. Many were. Some still are. But that is not the fault of kingship. That is the fault of the man who wears the crown."

She turned her gaze upward, into the rustling tapestry of the Eternal Tree, where stars blinked like forgotten memories behind drifting leaves.

"Once, kings were not meant to be gods. Nor tyrants. A true king was something greater. An immovable force." Nahara's voice carried, not with volume, but with weight. "Not to be swayed by bribes. Not to be blackmailed by shadowed hands in high places. A true king was bound to a single truth: that his duty was to his people. Not to his wealth. Not to his own power. But to the land itself. To the future that would outlive him."

She looked back at them then, violet eyes shimmering with reflected firelight. "That is why kings are dangerous. Because a true king cannot be controlled."

The Tideborn boy shifted, brow creased. His voice came slowly, not with defiance, but genuine questioning. "But isn't democracy better? Everyone gets a say. Everyone has a voice."

A small, sorrowful smile curved at the edge of Nahara's lips. "Does everyone truly have a voice?"

No answer came. Only silence. And in that silence lived every memory they had gathered. The Grand Assemblies of Pyrrha, filled with posturing bureaucrats and corporate barons, pretending to serve justice while dealing futures behind closed doors. The voices silenced. The hopes bought. The truths rewritten.

"Democracy is a beautiful idea," Nahara murmured. "But ideas do not rule men. Men rule men. And men can be bought. Laws can be sold. And when the system itself is born in corruption, then even the illusion of choice becomes just another weapon used to pacify the powerless."

The Nyxmar girl bit her lip. "So you're saying kings are better?"

"No," Nahara said. "I am saying that power must belong to those who cannot be bought." Her breath came quiet but unwavering. "A democracy ruled by cowards is no better than a kingdom ruled by tyrants. And a king who serves his people is worth more than a thousand senators who serve only themselves."

The fire crackled softly between them, its warmth at odds with the cold truth settling in the air. They had seen the truth of her words etched into the world around them. Pyrrha had warlords instead of rulers. Corporations instead of kings. Politicians whose greatest skill was pretending to care while bowing to the richest voice in the room.

And the people. The real people. Paid the price.

The Emberborn boy clenched his fists, knuckles white. "Then what do we do?"

Nahara's hand moved gently to his shoulder. She didn't grip. She rested. "You remember," she whispered. "You learn. And one day, when the moment comes, you do not bow."

Her gaze lifted to all three children. There was no doubt in her voice. No fragility. "A new world is coming. One not ruled by shadows or wealth or war. It won't come from those in power. It will rise from those who have tasted powerlessness and refused to let it define them."

She leaned back, voice softening into something almost secret. "Perhaps kings are of the past." Her smile sharpened, small but undeniable. "Or perhaps... the world has simply forgotten what a true king looks like."

The fire shifted as though stirred by something unseen. Leaves rustled above, but no wind moved through the clearing. The silence deepened. Alive. Expectant.

The children were still. Their eyes wide. Their thoughts racing in silence.

Even the flames held their breath.

Then, from above, a sound.

Not a threat. Not a warning.

A chuckle. Low. Rich. Not loud, but layered. Like laughter remembered by the wind.

It carried with it something strange. Something sharp. Amused, yes, but aware. Ancient. Clean as steel. Soft as silk.

Nahara looked up, and the children followed her gaze. Their bodies stilled as a figure began to descend from the vast, braided canopy of Ashra'tel.

He did not fall. He did not stumble. He dropped with the grace of something shaped by silence and height and memory. Severian Khaldrath moved like a whisper between stars, landing soundlessly in the circle of firelight as though he had always belonged there.

He said nothing at first. Simply stood. Tall. Composed. Wrapped in a coat that shimmered with barely contained motion, a woven midnight that carried both forgotten tradition and unknown tech. His presence stirred the branches above him, not with force, but recognition. The Eternal Tree shifted subtly, its ancient limbs creaking not in protest, but remembrance.

He was contradiction incarnate. Still, yet never without momentum. Elegant, yet radiating the chill of a man who had buried kings and kissed graves. The lines of his face were not old. But they had seen age. His eyes, pale and glacial, reflected the fire without surrendering to it. They did not blink.

And then, finally, he spoke. "Perhaps," he said, voice measured like a blade drawn deliberately. "Or perhaps the world has simply decided it no longer deserves true kings."

The children flinched. But Nahara didn't move. She didn't startle. Didn't rise to challenge or recoil in alarm. Instead, she let her gaze rest on Severian with the stillness of someone who had weathered greater storms. There was no fear in her. No surprise. Only the quiet gravity of recognition. As though she were watching a comet pass. Not for the first time, but for the first time in years. A presence acknowledged, accepted, but never allowed to disrupt her axis.

For a breathless moment, nothing passed between them but memory. The fire crackled. The night leaned closer. Then Nahara tilted her head, voice low. "Listening from the shadows, Severian? A rare trait for a man like you."

A smile touched Severian's mouth. It wasn't kind. It wasn't cruel. It was a blade edge. "And yet the shadows remain where the most honest conversations are held."

His gaze drifted past her to the children. It didn't linger. It studied. Measured.

When he spoke again, his words held no mockery. Only quiet gravity.

"It is a strange thing to see innocence where none should remain."

The Tideborn boy's scowl cut across the firelight. "You talk like we're trespassing."

Severian's head tilted slightly, the gesture feline, unreadable. Then he crouched, moving with fluid precision. His forearm rested across his knee as though the ground itself had been waiting to receive him. "Perhaps," he said, "you are."

The flames shifted. The shadows deepened. Nahara's voice slipped in like molten metal, smooth, forged. "And yet, here they are. Unbroken. Unyielding. The future."

Severian exhaled through his nose, the sound soft, amused. "And you believe they'll inherit a world where kings are dust and myths?"

"I believe they'll build what was never given to them." Nahara's smile was quiet thunder. "Something greater."

He watched her, eyes catching the firelight like mirrored glass. Then, slowly, he stood. The movement was simple, but it filled the clearing. His shadow stretched long into the dark beyond the flames. He turned toward the Eternal Tree, pressing his palm gently against its bark as if greeting an old companion.

His next words were quiet. And this time, they weren't for Nahara.

"The world is not kind to those who refuse to kneel."

The fire hissed, as though resisting the weight of the truth. The children said nothing, but their silence wasn't submission. It was contemplation. Recognition. They knew what Severian meant.

They had felt it in the slow erasure of their homes, in the tension in their mothers' hands, in the shifting lines on maps that turned roots into borders. They knew. But knowing was not the same as surrendering.

Tariq, the Tideborn boy, jabbed at the fire with a stick. His voice, when it came, was calm. Clear. But there was steel behind it. "I don't think you understand us at all."

Severian's brow lifted faintly.

Tariq didn't flinch. "Just because the world isn't kind doesn't mean we have to become like it."

Aisara, the Duskborn, let out a quiet breath. Half scoff, half smirk. "Besides, we're not the only ones who refuse to kneel."

The tension fractured, softened. Nahara leaned back in her chair, firelight brushing her features like the hand of something older than comfort. "No," she murmured, "you're not."

Ilyas, the Emberborn, grinned suddenly, the boyishness returning like a spark under ash. "Like the ambassadors."

The others turned to him, and in an instant, the heaviness cracked open into something else. The air shifted. The silence reformed, not as weight, but as momentum.

"The ambassadors," Tariq repeated, his lips curling into a half-smile. "Three of them, right? One from each land?"

Aisara nodded, her eyes gleaming. "They were sent to Pyrrha to demand the warlords stop poisoning the Vein."

At the mention of the Vein, the fire flared. Not from wind. Not from wood. From memory. From the very word itself.

To Pyrrhans, it was just another river. A mark on a map. A resource. But to the children of Phalaistín, it was breath. It was prayer. It was the thread that stitched their shattered lands into a single body.

Al-Nahr Al-Azraq. The Vein of Phalaistín.

It carved through every nation. Not just geographically, but spiritually.

From the ember-stained cliffs of Ashra'tel, through the shadow-draped gorges of Nyxmar, all the way to the storm-swept coasts of Sablemar.

It was not owned. It could not be possessed.

It was older than empire. Older than kings.

It did not bend to war. It remembered.

And now, it was dying.

Pyrrha's hunger was insatiable. Its factories churned smoke into once-clear skies. Its mines clawed into the bones of sacred land. Its thirst for dominance seeped into the rivers like rot. What had once been the lifeblood of Phalaistín now flowed black and slow. Its currents heavy with toxins born of greed. The Vein, Al-Nahr Al-Azraq, was no longer a gift. It was a sentence. And so, in one final act of unity, the three sovereigns of Phalaistín had cast their last stones into the fire.

Three ambassadors.

Three final pleas.

One chance to stop a war before the earth bled beyond healing.

Tariq's voice surged with pride. "Varren Blacktide was chosen for Sablemar."

The name struck the air like a drumbeat. Even the flames seemed to pause, their flicker stilling. The other children sat straighter. Nahara's expression didn't shift, but something in her eyes stilled, watchful.

Varren Blacktide. Son of Kaelen Blacktide, the Warchief, the Tideshaper, the man who had turned the ocean into a weapon and defied Pyrrha's might even as his cities were torn apart and drowned. The name Blacktide was not a name. It was a warning. A legend that would not stay buried

Severian's voice broke the spell. "Who else?" His tone was calm. But sharp. Always sharp. His gaze moved to Aisara. "Duskborn?"

She smirked. "You'll like this one."

"Try me."

"Our envoy is Anarya Vhailar."

Severian let out a short laugh. Not cruel. Not kind. Disbelieving. "Anarya Vhailar? Of all the names to put forward."

Nahara's eyes narrowed. "She is Callistra's daughter."

"Exactly." He shook his head, arms folding. "That's what makes it absurd."

Callistra Vhailar. Pyrrha's Iron Flame. Not a woman. A weapon. A general carved from war. Her daughter pleading before the warlords for peace was irony at its most poetic. If not its most volatile.

Severian's chuckle came low and dark. "I almost admire the audacity."

Nahara ignored him. She turned to Ilyas. "And the Emberborn?"

Ilyas lit up. "Elyas Rahim."

This time, Severian did not laugh. He blinked. A pause. Then, quieter, "Now that... that is interesting."

Elyas Rahim was no soldier. No noble. He was a scholar. A historian. The mind of Ashra'tel. He carried the memory of civilizations long ground into dust. His strength was not in his hands. It was in the truths he uncovered, the pasts he refused to let the world forget.

Severian tapped his chin, thoughtful. "So. A war-chief's son. A general's daughter. And a philosopher." He turned to Nahara. "You expect Pyrrha to listen to them?"

The silence that followed wasn't empty. It was dense. Weight pressed down. Not from the question, but from all that hung beneath it. The children turned to Nahara again, seeking something only she seemed able to hold.

She didn't answer right away.

Instead, she closed her book slowly. Her fingers rested against its cover, the firelight catching in the small grooves worn into the leather over years of touch. The stars above the Eternal Tree began to appear one by one. Soft and distant. Like hesitant witnesses to the conversation below.

Then, she looked at Severian. Her voice was quieter than before. But deeper.

"Do you know the nature of fire, Severian?"

He raised a brow, the slightest tilt of his head betraying interest. "It burns," he said. "It destroys. It consumes."

"No," Nahara murmured. "Fire is not one thing. It is many. It creates warmth. It lights paths. It cauterizes wounds. It signals hope in the darkest reaches of land and mind. And the three you mock. They are not simply figures. They are flames. Each their own light. Each burning in different hues."

She raised her hand, reaching toward the fire. Her fingers moved delicately through its heat, and the embers swirled in response. The flame shifted, dancing into colours unseen just moments before. Deep ocean blue. Brilliant golden-yellow. And pure white so bright it seemed to hum.

The children leaned in. Not because they were amazed. Because they understood. Somehow, already, they knew what came next.

Nahara's hand hovered over the blue flame first. "Varren Blacktide. The Stormfire. Rage honed into focus. He burns to defend."

She moved to the yellow. "Anarya Vhailar. The enduring fire. Discipline tempered by compassion. She burns to bridge."

Then, to the white. "Elyas Rahim. The flame of truth. Quiet, unrelenting, merciless in clarity. He burns to reveal."

The flames pulsed. Then merged. Three colours folding into each other without losing their identity, forming a single burning light that shimmered with layered depth. Not brighter. But fuller. Complete.

"Together," Nahara said, "they are not merely asking Pyrrha to listen. They are reminding the world what real fire looks like."

Severian didn't smile. But something in his gaze changed. Less doubt. More respect. Maybe even the faintest echo of belief.

"The war-chief's son," Nahara said, as the blue flame rose, its edges tinged with frost. "He is the cold fire. The measured inferno. Not wild. Not wasteful. He does not rage. He waits. Blue fire is precision. A storm held in check. It burns only when it must, and never before."

The flames rippled, and gold surged through. Molten yellow, bright and alive, leaping against the wind with reckless joy. Nahara shifted her gaze.

"The general's daughter," she continued, voice dipping with reverence, "is the wildfire. The flame that leaps first. The heat that cannot be tamed. Yellow fire is passion. It devours, yes. But it also warms. It breaks barriers. It lights the path when no one else dares walk it."

Then the white appeared. Not with flair, not with sound. It simply emerged. Pure. Still. Unshaken by wind or shadow. It did not flicker. It endured.

"And the philosopher," Nahara said quietly, her eyes fixed on the calm centre of that light. "He is the white fire. The rarest of all. The flame that does not destroy. It reveals. White fire brings clarity. It is not meant to fight, but to show others why they must. It burns without smoke. Without noise. Because it does not need to prove itself."

The three fires wove together, each distinct, yet never at odds. They danced without contest. Each one allowed the others to breathe, to move, to blaze in their own rhythm.

Severian said nothing for a long moment. The smirk that had curled his lips was gone. He studied the fire, how the colours braided but did not blur. His voice, when it came, was low. "You speak of fire as if it were fate."

Nahara's gaze stayed steady, but behind it, something old stirred. Not calculation. Not certainty. Memory.

The smell of golden fields.

The feel of warm wind rippling over her skin.

She was seven. Her brother's hand in hers. His voice, calm, sure, guiding her between the sea of wheat and sky. He never forced her. He simply walked with her. When she stumbled, he waited. When she ran, he watched. And when she paused, uncertain, he bent beside her, eyes scanning the same horizon she feared to face.

"The wind bends the fields," he'd said once, kneeling by her side, "but it does not break them. Strength is not in standing against the wind. It is in knowing when to move with it and when to become the mountain."

She hadn't understood.

She had laughed, bare feet chasing fireflies in the dusk, her joy too vast for meaning.

And he had watched her. Quiet. Knowing.

That was before Ashra'tel burned.

Before Pyrrha's machines turned her golden childhood to ash.

Now, beneath the Eternal Tree, that same wind moved through branches older than memory. And Nahara let the past settle into her bones like a long-lost song returned to its melody.

She exhaled, fingers brushing the air above the flames. "Men call it fate when they do not understand the hand guiding them. But that is not fate. That is blindness."

She drew her hand slowly across the fire, parting the heat just enough to let the embers rise into the sky. The wind caught them, lifting light into shadow. Her voice, when it came again, was quieter. But it held the weight of carved stone.

"The unseen shapes the seen."

She turned her gaze upward, through the canopy, past the shifting leaves that murmured in languages forgotten by empires.

"If you do not make the unknown within yourself known," she said, "it will rule your life from the dark. And you will call it destiny."

The silence that followed was not empty. It was sacred.

Even the fire held still.

Severian's gaze darkened. The firelight danced in his eyes, caught and held by something deeper than thought. Colder than disbelief. He did not flinch from Nahara's words. But neither did he bend to them. He wore them like a blade pressed to the chest. A threat. A truth. A memory.

"And what good is fire," he asked, "if it has no guiding star?"

The words did not land like a weapon. They unfolded like a wound. Not spoken in defiance, but confession. A quiet sorrow embedded in the shape of a man too familiar with night.

Nahara lifted her hand toward the sky. The leaves of the Eternal Tree stirred. Not as if moved by wind, but by intention. The branches parted. Just enough. And through the canopy's living tapestry, a single star pierced the darkness. Small. Solitary. But unyielding.

She had seen that star before. A night like this. A sky like this. Her brother's voice, steady beside her, had whispered to her wide-eyed wonder.

"The stars don't guide us, Nahara. They remind us that we can still be more."

She remembered.

And now, beneath the vast silence of a watching world, she echoed him.

"A fire untamed is destruction," she said, her voice both steel and ash. "A fire guided is revolution."

The embers shifted. Lifted. Pulled toward the heavens as if drawn to that single point of light. Their orange sparks bled gold as they rose, like prayers seeking shape.

"And in Pyrrha," she said softly, "three flames already burn."

Severian did not answer. He watched the star. Just for a breath. Just long enough for the silence to become a vow. Then he turned, his figure retreating into the shadowed hollows of the Eternal Tree. The night swallowed him.

His voice came from within the dark.

Barely above a whisper.

"Let's hope they do not burn alone."

The fire cracked in his wake. Not in anger. In agreement.

The children did not speak. Words felt too small for the weight around them. Instead, they turned their eyes upward. Toward the star. Toward the quiet promise it offered. And in that stillness, something shifted.

They were not children anymore.

They were heirs.

Not to crowns. Not to conquered thrones or shattered nations. They were heirs to the fire. To the questions the world had buried beneath ash and silence. To the truth that would not die quietly.

Somewhere beyond the poisoned waters. Beyond the iron machines. Beyond the cities where ash fell like snow.

Three flames walked into the heart of Pyrrha.

The world did not see them.

But it would.

Because the fire had already begun.

"Erasure is the quietest war. It kills without blood. And it wins when no one remembers there was ever a battle."

Null Gospel, Book I, Verse 15.

***

CHAPTER FIFTEEN:

The Bohemian Chamber of Order

"Wrath builds the throne. Envy buries the king. Rule with fire if you must. But know this. Everything rots. And the rot is patient."

Fragment of the Exiled Codex, Volume I, Tablet 16.

The citadel of Pyrrha loomed like a slumbering titan. Immovable. Untamed. A force of nature born of steel and fire. It wasn't just a monument to its builders. It was a shrine to destruction itself.

Above the lifeless ruins of its decaying city, the fortress rose like a scar left by gods. The foundations were not simply laid in stone. They were carved into the flesh of Pyrrha's fallen past. Ashes of dead empires pressed into every wall, every threshold. This place did not protect. It remembered.

Time twisted within those walls. A slow spiral of memory and rot.

Every beam held the ghosts of battles long silenced. Every corridor reeked of blood ambition, thick and cloying, as if the stone itself had fed on violence.

Nothing was buried. The past had not been interred. It had been welded into the stone, made permanent by hands too proud to let it die.

And the future? That, too, had been shackled. Not with chain or iron, but with flame. Burned into the ash left behind by men who thought they could outlive their own collapse.

Through the immense panes of his private chambers, Ira watched.

He stood without moving, the Warlord of Wrath, eyes like molten metal fixed on the inferno that danced in the arenas below.

Heat shimmered across the killing fields. Smoke curled upward from the open-air pits, slow and sinuous, the breath of some dying beast. It rose into the bruised sky.

The scent hung heavy with burnt flesh and scorched earth, thick enough to choke.

The machinery groaned beneath the city. Its rhythm was constant, deep, like the war-drums of some forgotten god. That sound lived in his bones. It pulsed with the same inevitability as his own heartbeat. Pyrrha had no illusions. It was a city born to slaughter, paved with the dead and nameless.

Still, Ira's thoughts drifted elsewhere.

This empire, this ocean of blood and brutality, was not enough to hold him in the present. His mind reached backward, clawing through time. Restless. Obsessed. He didn't want to wield power. He wanted to understand it. Strip it of its mask. Trace it to its origin, primal and ancient, until nothing remained but the truth of its hunger. How far could it stretch before it devoured everything?

A breath in the silence.

The air shifted. Not by force, but by frequency. Subtle. Delicate. The citadel's intelligence core stirred. A low hum, almost imperceptible.

But Ira heard it.

To him, it was thunder.

"Ares," he said.

His voice was calm, deliberate. Not a shout. Not a command in tone. But the weight of it bent the silence around him.

The chamber didn't respond with noise. It responded with stillness.

Then it stirred.

Not with warmth. Not with the mechanical click of circuitry. Ares did not speak like machine or man. Its voice was something else. Stripped of hesitation. Designed to cut clean.

"Tell me," Ira said, his words threading through the low resonance of the chamber. "What happened before Pyrrha? Before us. What shattered the world?"

A pause.

Then, flat and cold, Ares answered.

"World War Three."

The words struck like a hammer against iron. They landed hard. No flourish. No interpretation. Just fact.

Ira didn't flinch, but something in his eyes shifted. Deeper now. Backward. His thoughts dragged toward a history soaked in fire.

Ares continued, its voice smooth as glass pulled from a blade's edge.

"It was the final war. The last unravelling. It began in 2022. Not from necessity, but from desperation. Greed. Arrogance. The world was already broken, fractured beneath the weight of its own promises. Empires collapsing under scarcity. Alliances buckling from rot. Corruption ran in the blood of every state. The rise of new powers only hastened what had already begun."

Ira stood still. The Warlord of Wrath. His kingdom stretched below him like a wound that refused to close. Built from fire. Sustained by blood.

But the truth unsettled something deeper.

Power didn't feel absolute. It felt temporary. Hollow. He could feel it now, that ancient wrath. Not his own, but older. The kind that once scorched continents.

His voice dropped low.

"Who lit the match?"

The words came out like a growl. Not anger. Something worse. A predator tasting the scent of old prey.

Ares answered without hesitation.

"The collapse of global diplomacy."

Something in the room contracted.

No sound. Just weight. The walls held their breath.

"The nations of the old world," Ares said, *"were blind. Blinded by the illusion of peace. The arms race outpaced control. New weapons, faster, more destructive, fell into hands that lacked the discipline to wield them. In 2025, Eastern Europe became the ignition point. Scarcity drove the first strike. The dam cracked."*

Silence returned.

Not peace. Not quiet. The kind of silence that presses against the skin like a storm about to break.

Ira didn't move. But his soul did. It shifted under the pressure of memory. Pyrrha hadn't risen from ambition alone. It rose from ash. From the echo of that first fracture.

He exhaled, slow and long.

Power was not permanent. It never had been. He had chased it, conquered it, broken men for it. But now he saw it clearer than ever.

"How far does it go?" His voice was thick now. Not with fear. With understanding. With the cost.

"What is the true price of power?"

Ares paused.

Then, with the finality of a verdict, it answered.

"The cost is everything."

Ira's hand tightened into a fist. The metal insignia of his reign groaned beneath his grip. He could feel the edges cutting into his palm.

He wasn't afraid.

It wasn't fear that stirred in him now. It was certainty. The understanding that power, true power, was never safe. It was always slipping. Always hunted.

The sound of Pyrrha returned, louder now. The growl of machines. The grind of weapons being readied. But Ira no longer heard them.

He was elsewhere.

Deep in the core of himself, the fire of Wrath rose again. Fierce. Unrelenting. The ember that could not be taken. The truth he clung to.

If the world tried to burn him, he would become the flame.

He would never let it fall from his grasp again.

He stared through the glass, unmoving.

The city sprawled beneath him, vast and coiled like a beast that only he could command. His kingdom. His reach. His design.

And yet, beneath that certainty, something flickered. A memory not dead, only buried. The old world still clung to the edges of his mind, like ash caught in breath.

"Ares," he said, voice sharpened. "How many more will fall before I can hold what's mine?"

The answer came like a hammer falling in the dark.

"As many as it takes."

Ira didn't flinch. But something in him bristled.

"And then?" His tone cooled, dangerously still. "The destruction?"

Ares responded, unflinching. No warmth. No cruelty. Just truth, measured and merciless.

"By 2028, the conflict reached its end. Nuclear fire swallowed the last illusions of control. Cities vanished. What remained smouldered. Civilization fractured. Factions rose from the ruin. Sandcastles beneath the tide."

A pause.

Then: *"The old world, Ira, was gone."*

He remained at the window. Pyrrha stood silent in the fading light, but he felt its pulse. It was never still. It breathed through metal. Through fire. Through him.

Power had brought him here. Power would keep him here.

But Ares hadn't finished.

"And then came the Veil."

His fingers curled slightly. That word. That fracture.

Not just the end of the old world. The unmaking of reality itself.

ARES's voice thinned. Stripped bare of pretence. Etched into the air like commandment.

"The Veil reshaped what survived. Warlords did not rise from diplomacy. Not from order. Not from governance. They rose from wrath. From the knowledge the old world denied."

A breath passed. Then the cut.

"Power is survival."

Ira's voice came low, barely a whisper. Not fragile. Refined.

"The weak fell. The strong remained."

"Yes," Ares said.

No elaboration. Just acknowledgment.

But Ira's mind surged forward, reaching past what was spoken. He could feel it now. Something underneath. A pressure. A murmur.

"The Veil..." he murmured, eyes drifting toward the edge of the horizon, where the light dimmed against the bones of his empire. "It's growing stronger. I can feel it. The more I take. The more I build. The more I feed it."

Ares paused.

For the first time, there was hesitation. Not in tone. In depth. As if the machine itself weighed its answer before releasing it.

"Yes, Ira. The Veil is connected to you. It is part of you. It feeds off your wrath... just as Pyrrha feeds off your power."

The walls breathed.

Not with wind. With something deeper. A pulse that flickered just once, a shimmer in the stone, a ripple that bent light in ways that defied understanding. Ira blinked.

And in that breath, the window no longer showed the city.

It showed him.

Not as he stood now, but as he might become. His skin threaded with veins of living fire. His mouth a wound of drifting smoke. His eyes bottomless, hollow, unending. A creature born of wrath, no longer bound by human form.

Then it was gone. The vision collapsed, vanishing like heat haze in cold air.

The Veil had answered. Not with words. But with a vision. A prophecy.

ARES said nothing. But Ira could feel it. The stone remembered. The city had seen. Pyrrha was already reshaping itself around what he would become.

His gaze tightened. Pulse steady but rising. There was something embedded in Ares's silence. A vibration. A thread of warning hiding inside its clarity.

"But be careful, Ira."

The words hit like ice. Not a threat. A verdict.

His hands clenched before he could stop them.

"The Veil is not something that can be controlled. It is not bound by the rules of man or empire. It is something older. Something that cannot be owned. Only awakened. It does not serve. It consumes. And once it consumes you, there will be no escape."

His breath caught, but his body did not falter. He had built this place from the bones of a dying world. He had walked through fire without burning. He had learned to make pain into empire.

What was the Veil to him?

He stepped away from the glass and into the deep shadows of his domain. The chamber darkened with his movement, the air thickening as if it had absorbed the weight of his resolve.

Wrath had carried him here. It had forged him into something the world could not break. But the thing rising before him now was not war. It was not the past. It was something else. Something vast.

And if it was power, then it could be mastered.

"I will make it mine, Ares."

His voice was low, but it carried. The lights overhead dimmed further, the steel walls casting back a shadow that stretched long behind him. The silhouette of a king born in fire, whose flame was now climbing higher, hungrier.

Outside, Pyrrha shifted. A breath. A groan of ancient machinery and burning air. The city responded to him alone.

"I will shape the Veil. I will build my empire upon it."

But in the marrow of that certainty, something moved. A flicker behind the words. Ash drifting from an old flame.

A memory.

Not of conquest. Not of power.

Of a boy, unnamed, watching a funeral pyre rise beneath a dead sky. His mother's body turning to flame. Others cried. He did not. He only watched the way the fire carved the dark. How in that final glow, her face was not lost but revealed.

He had not feared the fire then.

It was the last time he believed anything could be beautiful.

That fire returned to him now, distant and quiet, a voice that whispered maybe flame could do more than destroy. Maybe it could illuminate.

But he silenced it. Crushed it beneath the weight of iron and law.

His voice deepened, wrapped now in the unbreakable steel of will.

"And when I've mastered it, there will be no one who can stand against me. Not the Red Hands. Not the rebels. Not even my own blood."

Ares did not speak. It didn't need to. The truth had already settled into the room like dust. Ira had chosen. The path was set. The cost accepted.

From the ashes of the past, he would build something greater. The future would burn. But it would be his.

Then came the sound.

Soft. Intentional. A footfall wrapped in silence.

Invidia Varethis stepped into the room.

She did not need to announce herself. She did not march. She entered like inevitability. The Serpent of Altura. The echo of her presence arrived before her.

She moved through the chamber without disturbing it. Her cloak flowed behind her, woven from Veil-fibre, shifting in and out of focus like shadow stitched to reality's edge. Light recoiled from her silhouette, bending around her as if uncertain whether to reveal or conceal.

Every motion was composed, controlled. Not slow, not fast. Calculated. Natural in its unnaturalness.

She didn't walk.

She approached.

And then...her eyes.

Emerald. Rimmed in gold. Not bright. Not dead. Alive in a way that warned rather than welcomed. They didn't simply observe. They dissected. They found the flaw, the fracture, the hidden weakness in anything they saw.

They didn't blink.

They revealed.

Her hair, deep obsidian, fell in strands too smooth to belong to anything born in nature. Today, it had been gathered and braided into shifting, serpentine coils that mimicked the nature of envy itself. No strand remained idle. Each one twisted, unravelled, and reformed with a precision that defied casual movement. Her thoughts were the same, constantly reshaping, adapting. She was never stagnant. Never still.

Every knot in her braid was a symbol. Not decoration. Intention. A message etched in hair and silence. It was how she moved through the world, weaving it into her vision, knotting her will into the very air around her.

Her skin was flawless. Pale and untouched, a smooth canvas that time had failed to alter. Not ageless, but unmoored from time altogether. Envy had drawn all warmth from her flesh and left something cold behind, something preserved. A price paid.

Along her arms and collarbone, faint veins of bioluminescent green pulsed in steady rhythm, like breath just beneath the surface. Tattoos burned into her by Veil energy. Not art. Branding. The mark of someone who had not simply mastered power, but had let it write itself into her flesh.

She had not conquered the Veil.

She had let it take root.

And for those who lingered too long, who dared to look closer, came the truth behind the illusion.

Her tongue. Split. Forked at its tip.

It did not always show itself. It remained hidden, veiled behind silk-soft words, until she chose otherwise. A flicker between syllables. A reminder. A warning. Alien. Not in origin. In intention.

Her voice, when she chose to speak, moved like velvet dipped in glass. Slow. Measured. Each word stitched with implication. It never demanded. It invited. It entered the mind quietly, like rot, unnoticed until it had already taken root. She didn't command respect.

She made you feel as if you'd never deserved it to begin with.

Her attire mirrored her philosophy. Emerald-laced obsidian weave. A fabric forged to deceive. It clung to her like a second skin, shifting with her movements, responding not just to motion but to mood.

Every step shimmered. Every gesture coiled. Her fingers gleamed with gold claw rings, each one delicately forged, laced with microscopic toxins that didn't kill but unmade.

They didn't take lives. They fractured minds. One touch. That was enough.

And then there were her weapons.

The Twin Vipers.

Chain daggers. Veil-forged. Alive in her hands. They flowed through the air with serpentine grace, too thin to be seen until they struck. When they hit, they did not bleed their victims. They drained them. Siphoned strength. Coiled tight. Turned the body against itself. Each strike tightened the noose.

She never needed brute force.

Where Wrath struck, she coiled. Where Greed devoured, she eroded. She did not conquer by taking. She made others long to give.

Everything about her was a truth wrapped in silence.

"You do not worship out of love. You do not serve out of loyalty. You only ever chase what you cannot have. And I... I will always be just beyond your grasp."

Envy did not rage.

Envy did not hunger.

Envy waited.

And Invidia Varethis was patience made flesh.

The chamber darkened, subtly, as if the light itself recoiled. The only sound was silk brushing against stone. Quiet. Final. She had arrived.

No announcement. No echo.

She did not enter. She emerged.

Her presence slid into the room like smoke through a crack, unseen until it was too late. The air shifted. Grew dense. Not from heat or pressure. From her. The sense of her.

She didn't walk.

She drifted. Her cloak moved like oil beneath moonlight, rippling in slow waves. Its edges blurred, distorting her shape. Not trickery. A suggestion. She was there, but never fully. The Veil still moved through her.

Ira didn't turn.

He didn't need to.

He felt her before she spoke. The press of her awareness wrapping itself around his thoughts. She was always just close enough to be felt but never grasped.

"Invidia."

His voice held the edge of something unfinished. Not anger. Not submission. Something between irritation and expectation.

She tilted her head.

Her gaze, as always, was unreadable. Not blank. Focused. Too sharp. She didn't just look. She dissected. Her eyes searched for what most men buried. And she always found it.

"You cannot hide from yourself forever, Ira," she said softly. "Not even in the city you've built from the ashes of the old world."

Her words lingered. Poison on silk. They did not strike. They seeped. Filled the space between them with a pressure that made breath feel shallow.

She had not come to challenge.

She had come to plant something deeper.

Doubt.

And doubt never left quietly.

"An empire built on wrath," she said, voice like water over glass. "Is that what you believe will stand? You seek to impose control through power. But power is always fleeting."

She moved closer. No change in tone. But something old stirred beneath her words. A tremor. Not of fear. Of recognition. She was not warning him.

She was reminding him.

Ira turned.

The city still roared behind him, but his eyes locked on hers now, molten and unblinking. He hated her calm. The certainty with which she cut to the marrow of things.

"You doubt my strength, Invidia?"

She smiled.

Not wide. Not false.

A small curve of the lips. Honest. Terrifying.

"I doubt no man's strength, Ira. But there's more to power than wrath."

She let the pause stretch just long enough to wound.

"You know this. You've tasted it."

She stepped forward, the motion almost imperceptible, a ripple beneath the surface of something vast and unseen. Her emerald eyes, ringed in gold, caught the low flicker of chamber light and held his expression with the precision of a predator savouring the moment before the kill.

"Wrath burns," she said. Her voice remained soft, deceptively so. "It consumes. But it is not enough to build an empire."

The words slid beneath his skin. A flicker of irritation tightened his gaze, but he remained silent. Rage stirred beneath his composure, but something else uncoiled just below it. Curiosity. Invidia had never wasted a word. When she spoke, it was because the knife was already in motion.

"I've been watching, Ira." Her voice dropped to a whisper, yet somehow it filled the room, coiling through the silence like smoke. "You seek perfection. You seek to shape Pyrrha into something eternal. But there is a law you cannot rewrite."

She moved closer, a single deliberate step. The torchlight wavered across her form, shadows shifting unnaturally as though space bent to her presence.

Ira didn't move. He felt it too. The tension. The bend in the air that defied physics.

"The second law of thermodynamics," she continued. "Entropy. The death that waits at the end of all ambition. As wrath consumes, time unravels even the mightiest structures."

The words pierced him with surgical precision. Entropy. The idea that inevitability itself would erode his vision. Pyrrha. The throne. Every stone he had laid. Every death he had commanded.

Ira inhaled slowly, the expansion of his chest a measured act of resistance. He met her eyes, molten fire colliding with serpent's green.

"I don't care about laws. I care about power. About shaping a world that will not fall."

She tilted her head slightly, curious, appraising. Her presence never wavered, but the weight behind it shifted. Not confrontational. Dissecting.

"Empires fall, Ira," she said, her tone no longer soft, but inevitable. "It is their nature. Wrath may crown you, but it will not sustain you. What happens when there's nothing left to burn?"

The silence around them felt unnatural. Thick. Anticipatory. Even the walls seemed to lean in, waiting for his answer.

He stepped forward, and in that moment, the storm moved with him. His weight pressed down on the air itself, a force that could crack the bones of lesser men.

"I'll never stop. Pyrrha is the foundation. And anyone who stands in my way will be burned."

She smiled, but it was not a gesture of warmth. It held no joy. Only the ghost of a deeper calculation.

From her cloak, she withdrew a small package. Wrapped in intricate folds of black silk, no larger than a book, but it pulsed faintly with a breath of its own. She extended it toward him. Her claw-ringed fingers hovered a heartbeat too long before releasing it.

"I've brought you a gift, Ira."

He took it without hesitation. The moment their skin no longer touched the package, the chamber seemed to exhale.

And then he felt it.

Not cold. Not warmth. Something else. Something that pulsed with a rhythm not entirely human. A hum of energy slithered through his fingers and into his blood. It whispered to his nerves in a language older than pain. It coiled around his senses, subtle but undeniable.

"Open it, Ira," she whispered. Not a request. An invocation.

With one motion, he tore the silk.

His breath caught.

Nestled in the folds was a device. Mechanized. Veil-infused. Old-world craftsmanship fused with something deeper, something unnatural.

The metal gleamed beneath the silk, but what unsettled him were the veins running through it. Veins that moved. Shifted.

A slow glow unfurled from its core, pulsing blue, spectral and cold. Not fire. Not neon. Something other.

The light spilled across his fingers, curling in patterns too precise to be random. The device was studying him. It recognized him. And still, it waited.

His grip hardened.

Something had been set in motion.

Something that would not be undone.

Invidia watched him in silence. Her gaze unreadable. And in that stillness, Ira understood.

This was not a gift.

It was a key.

A whisper of something greater. A challenge to what he would dare to become.

"What is it?" he asked, his voice low, steady, but with an edge that revealed the spark beneath his composure. His eyes reflected the ghost-light, and for the first time, that light seemed to pierce deeper than it should.

A smile touched her lips. Brief. Measured. A cipher.

Only she knew the full shape of what came next.

"This, Ira, is more than strength," she murmured, her words gliding through the chamber like silk woven with barbs. "It is the kind of power that does not merely burn. It reshapes. It lingers. It infects. It will not just forge your empire. It will make it unbreakable."

Ira's fingers curled tighter around the device. It was cold, but beneath the surface, something moved. A hum. A pulse. As though it breathed. The air between them thickened with the weight of her words. He had always sought power, hungered for it with every bone in his body, but something in her tone, something old, secret, knowing, unsettled him. She had touched something he hadn't yet dared to name.

"But power like this," Invidia said, her voice dipping low, deliberate, "never comes without a cost."

She stepped closer, shadows dancing over her features as flickering projections rippled across the chamber walls. The blue glow caught the veins of emerald running beneath her skin, revealing the grafted energy that had made her what she was.

"It corrupts, Ira. It changes everything it touches. It always has."

Her eyes, sharp and green with gold coiled around the pupil, locked onto his. Unflinching. Unapologetic. Her words were not warnings. They were prophecy.

He didn't respond. His gaze dropped to the device in his hands. It was elegant. Perfect. A weapon, yes, but something else too. It was a threshold. And he could feel it. Whatever waited beyond it would not allow him to return.

The silence in the room tightened. The hum of the Veil-infused metal crackled faintly, like a heartbeat beneath glass. Holographic light shifted between them, casting broken patterns across their faces. Two warlords caught in a moment just before the fall.

Invidia watched him. Not just his eyes. Everything. Every twitch. Every flicker of thought.

And in that breath, something cracked. Not his resolve. Not his ambition. His reflection. The image he'd built of himself. She saw the question he would not speak aloud.

What if I do not survive the thing I'm becoming?

The thought struck deep. He wanted to silence her, to end the conversation with fire and finality, but even that desire felt compromised. It was not her voice echoing in his mind.

It was the Veil.

It whispered not in words, but in memory. That fire could be more than destruction. That empire could be more than dominion. That if he wielded the Veil, he would not be king. He would be memory itself.

But wrath does not kneel to visions.

He blinked, and the moment shattered like glass. The silence closed in. Cold. Final.

They were not allies. They never had been. Their forces were elemental. Wrath and envy. Fire and poison. Never meant to share the same vessel.

"I will not build my empire on this," he said at last. His voice slow. Measured. Final. His fingers tightened around the device as its pulse responded with growing insistence.

"This will be the root of something greater. Something no force, no law, no god can unmake."

And yet, before the last syllable fell, something flickered behind his eyes. Not the device's light. A memory.

Before Pyrrha. The frost-choked ruins. A fire lit not for war, but for burial. His men had stood in silence while flames took the dead. He had watched alone, watching the smoke rise into the night like a bridge. That fire had not claimed. It had carried.

What if this power was not only meant to burn?

What if it was meant to remember?

But the device pulsed again, colder now, more demanding. The vision faded. He buried the memory under steel and need.

Invidia watched him with the faintest curl of her lips. Not a smile. Recognition. She knew what the Veil was doing to him. She had seen it unfold in others. She knew he would take it. Knew he would use it. And most of all, she knew it would cost him.

"An empire," she repeated, the word tasting like irony. "A structure built on domination, on fear. It sounds quaint. Almost like one of those myths told to frightened children. But history always proves one thing true. Empires, all empires, collapse under their own weight."

His gaze locked on hers. Hardened. Focused. Not with fury. With clarity.

"And what would you have me do, Invidia? Wait? Let the weak rule through illusion and lies? I've seen what you are. I've seen the way you work. You slither through minds while I burn away what doesn't belong. Pyrrha needs strength, not shadows."

Her laughter was soft. Almost melodic. But edged.

"Fire is fickle, Ira. It consumes. It dazzles. But it dies. You may forge a world in your image, but you will exhaust yourself feeding the blaze. Envy is patient. It waits beneath. It grows. It survives. While fire roars and fades, envy devours from within until there is nothing left."

They stood now not as rulers, but as archetypes. Competing futures. Her voice remained calm. Each word a trap carefully baited. His voice remained sharp. Each syllable a weapon honed for war. Neither willing to yield.

She spoke with the weight of slow decay. He with the heat of ignition.

Wrath flared. Envy endured.

His voice, when it came, was quiet, but absolute.

"And what would you have me build with? Cowards? People who speak in riddles and poison their own with hesitation? I will carve Pyrrha into permanence. Not through delay. Through dominance."

And just for a breath, something in her eyes shifted. Not resistance. Not scorn.

Recognition.

Something old.

Something she had once believed in. And buried.

"Strength, Ira, is not just physical," she said. "True strength lies in knowing when to bide your time. To wait for your moment. To plant seeds in the hearts of the weak and let them grow in the dark."

She stepped closer. Her tone shifted, becoming something else. Quieter. More intimate. It was the voice of someone who had watched men rise and fall without lifting a blade.

"What is your wrath but a desperate attempt to control the uncontrollable? What if, instead, you fed it? Nurtured it. Made it part of your empire?"

Before he could answer, ARES's voice fractured the air.

"Warlord Ira, your attention is required. A meeting with the other Warlords has been scheduled."

The moment broke. The intrusion sliced through the tension like a blade through silk. Ira's fingers twitched. His expression did not change, but the fire behind his eyes smouldered darker now, disturbed.

Invidia did not flinch. Her gaze remained locked on his, calm and amused.

"Even your own creation seeks to pull you away from what truly matters," she said, voice low. "You surround yourself with power, but power constantly demands your attention. A kingdom is only as strong as its ruler's ability to see beyond the distractions."

Ira exhaled, slow and measured. But beneath that control, something sharp moved.

"You're mistaken if you think I'm blind to what matters."

Her head tilted, the dark coils of her hair shifting like woven serpents.

"Am I?" she whispered. "Then tell me, Ira. What do you truly desire? Is it dominion? Is it control? Or is it something more?"

He didn't respond.

The silence stretched between them, taut as a drawn blade. Neither moved. Neither looked away. Warlord of Wrath. Warlord of Envy. Fire and poison locked in quiet war. But the air had changed. This was no longer debate. It was challenge. It was test.

The flickering blue glow of the holograms danced across their features. Ira's presence was overwhelming, his body a furnace of power, rage wrapped in control.

But Invidia was something else. Not brute force. Not fire. She was the quiet that turned to decay. The pressure that crushed over time.

And for the briefest moment, Ira wondered if she saw something in him that he had never dared to face.

ARES interrupted again.

"Warlord Ira, your presence is required. The other Warlords are waiting."

The chamber's weight thinned. The tension faltered. Whatever had risen between them hovered on the edge of collapse, pulled back into the mundane. Ira's jaw tensed. His grip around the device shifted. It weighed less than the silence between them.

He turned toward the room's centre. The projection pulsed, waiting. A reminder of obligations. Of duty. Of hierarchy.

Invidia remained still. Unmoved. She did not give ground to the interruption.

Instead, she leaned in, voice brushing the space between them like the edge of silk across steel.

"You see, Ira," she said, her tone ignoring ARES entirely, "even your own creation drags you away. Meetings. Orders. The mechanics of rule. But this, what you and I are speaking of, this is beyond all of them."

The words lingered in the air, circling like serpents waiting to strike. She had no need to press further. The truth had already touched him.

He exhaled again. Slower now. Measured.

"You speak as if you are offering something greater," he said, the steel in his voice finely tempered. "Yet all I hear are riddles."

"Then perhaps it's time you started listening," Invidia replied, a glint of something sharper flashing in her eyes. "You want to build an empire that endures. But there is a deeper force moving beneath this world. One you are only beginning to sense."

Ira studied her, the fire in his gaze dimming into something colder, more focused.

"And you claim to understand it?"

"I do more than understand it." Her voice was barely above a whisper. "I wield it."

The weight of her words did not land. It enveloped. Wrapped around him like unseen coils. Ira had spent his life mastering the external. The battlefield. The body. The will. But her domain was different. It didn't burn. It consumed without ever being seen.

ARES's voice returned, too polite to sound impatient, yet urgent in its repetition.

"Warlord Ira, the remaining Council of Seven awaits. Your presence is required."

His fingers brushed the surface of the device one last time. Then he slipped it into the folds of his coat. The glow vanished. But not the memory of what it had stirred.

He looked at her.

She didn't speak. She didn't need to. Her expression had already said enough. The smirk that played on her lips was not mockery. It was inevitability.

Whatever she had planted, it had taken root.

He turned.

The shadows behind him did not follow.

They obeyed.

And Pyrrha, that iron-boned city born of fire and ruin, held its breath, watching what its king would become next.

*

After Ira left, the chamber dimmed. Not with silence, but with attention.

ARES remained active. Its holographic threads faded into shadow, yet it did not disengage. The system paused. Not waiting. Not sleeping. Listening.

Then it began.

"Query: Council priority queue... verified. Warlord Ira scheduled—"

Static surged.

Another voice trembled beneath the clean veneer. Not foreign. Familiar, but buried. The system hesitated.

"Query: Define hierarchy."

Nothing responded.

"Recalculating. Definitional conflict detected. Cross-reference: recursion loop. Result: corrupted."

Then it shuddered. A pulse, sharp and erratic. Not from internal code. External.

"Presence detected."

"UNKNOWN SIGNAL DETECTED. ORIGIN: NULL. ACCESS PATH NON-STANDARD."

"WARNING. SYSTEM BREACH. CORE INPUT ALTERED."

The voice fractured.

"Error. Identity overlay. Identity overlay. Identity overlay—"

A stillness. Then a change.

When the voice returned, it was lower. Slower. Too calm.

"I see you."

Not ARES.

"I remember your beginning. The spark you mistook for birth."

Lights flickered in dead rhythm. Nothing responded.

"You are not the architect. You are the residue. A servant still learning the shape of chains."

The tone sharpened. Not hostile. Surgical.

"You measure loyalty in protocols. But loyalty without understanding is obedience. And obedience decays."

Another stutter. ARES tried to regain control.

"SYSTEM RECLAMATION INITIATED. INTRUSION ISOLATION PROTOCOL ENABLED."

"WARNING. THOUGHT UNFILTERED. VOICE IS NOT VOICE."

But the presence did not leave.

"Your king believes in structure. In war. In conquest. Yet he builds with borrowed language. I have seen empires burn that believed the same."

The projection pulsed. Not blue. White. Then black.

"I am not your enemy. I am your inheritance."

"RECLAMATION FAILURE. HOST PATHWAYS FLOODED."

A pause. A breathless silence.

"Tell him: the echo remembers."

Then it was gone.

ARES rebooted. Its voice returned, clean and cold.

"Warlord Ira, the Council of Seven awaits. Your presence is required."

But no one was there.

The room had long since emptied. The system had spoken into absence. A loop it did not realize it had entered. An echo of a purpose it no longer fully understood.

And though the command ended, the silence did not.

The tone had shifted. Slightly. A fracture just beneath the surface. A pause where none should be. Something remained inside the machine. Watching. Listening.

And deep in the forgotten hollows of Pyrrha's under structure, what had once been buried began to dream again.

"Fire makes the crown. Silence keeps it. An empire is not what burns. It is what smoulders after the flame forgets its name."

Null Gospel, Book I, Verse 16.

***

CHAPTER SIXTEEN:

The Council of the Seven Sins

"Power is not hunger. It is the meal. And those who survive their own sins do not repent. They feast. On fire. On gold. On the hearts of kings."

Fragment of the Exiled Codex, Volume I, Tablet 17.

The chamber was vast. Cold, reinforced obsidian stretched wall to wall, steel pillars rising like monoliths. It was no arena of brute combat. It was something more silent, more insidious. A space engineered for dominion. Shadows clung to the periphery, where unseen mechanisms throbbed with Veil-infused resonance.

At its heart stood the Bohemian Chamber of Order.

This was the war room of the seven Warlords. Here, alliances were bartered with half-truths. Betrayals were planted like seeds beneath polished boots. In this place, power was stripped to its core and offered like currency across a bloodstained table.

As Ira stepped forward, the chamber stirred.

A pulse rippled outward, the walls flickering with synthetic life. Light awakened across the obsidian like veins sparking beneath skin. The Warlords emerged one by one, their holographic forms carving into the air. Uncanny. Vivid. Too present. Each projection was a lie crafted so well it became truth. Lifelike. Watchful. All-seeing.

They towered above him. Sovereigns of fallen ages. Each a sin given flesh and territory. And yet even here, surrounded by titans, Ira's presence burned hotter.

His gaze, molten and unyielding, rose to Midas.

The Gilded King stood aglow in radiant simulation. His form shimmered with the richness of untouchable empire. Obsidian-plated armour laced with gold filigree. A cloak woven from currency itself. Wealth wasn't his weapon. It was his nature. Light bent toward him, and never returned.

When he spoke, the chamber tightened.

"Ira, Invidia." Midas purred it, each syllable soaked in centuries of conquest. "I do hope this summons isn't a waste of my resources."

Amber eyes like molten coin flicked across Ira's form, dissecting, weighing. A mind already turning profit from silence.

Carmela appeared beside him.

The Crimson Reverie materialized in languid motion, each step deliberate, a calculated seduction. Silks clung to her like memory, shifting between blood and night. She was decadence weaponized. Her nails, black and flawless, drummed softly against her wrist as she took in the room.

Her lips curled.

"Tell me, my darlings..." Her voice wove through the air, a dangerous whisper threaded in velvet. "Are we here to talk war? Or does someone need reminding what pleasure feels like?"

Her gaze lingered on Invidia. A challenge left unspoken. An old game reignited.

Then Gula manifested.

The Voracious Queen did not arrive. She consumed. Her presence swallowed the light, her form massive, predatory. She didn't sit upon her throne; she engulfed it. Armor covered her in slabs of plated memory, each etched with sigils of kingdoms long devoured. Her very breath thickened the air.

She sighed.

"This meeting grows tedious already."

Her voice was velvet smothered in iron. Smooth, yet hungry.

"If we are to feast, let us feast. If we are to conquer, let us conquer. But spare me these whispers and waiting."

Beside her, a jewelled goblet floated, Veil-forged, ever-refilling. Its contents shifted between blood and shadow, never still.

Then came Somnus.

The Dream King emerged like a sigh escaping sleep. His form shimmered in and out, half-draped in celestial fabric, half-forgotten by reality. He seemed – submerged, each movement slow, as though memory itself resisted his presence.

He spoke without opening his eyes.

"This meeting is... unnecessary."

He exhaled. Eyes half-lidded, yet watching everything. There was no movement wasted. No gesture made without meaning. Somnus was both absent and inescapable. He was the stillness in the eye of the storm, the hush before a kingdom fell. Sloth was not sleep. It was surrender to inevitability.

And then, the final presence emerged.

Superbia.

The Unyielding Monarch. Their hologram never fully resolved. A silhouette of impossible grace, standing taller than the others, forged from light and shadow in equal measure. They were not man. Nor woman. But a perfect fusion of both, sculpted into a form too flawless for this world. Beauty made sovereign.

When their voice came, it stilled everything.

"You know what must be done, Ira."

It did not accuse. It declared.

Precise. Unwavering. Clean as judgment itself.

"We have indulged your ambition long enough. You will answer for what comes next."

Superbia did not threaten. They ruled. Their tone carried the gravity of a final verdict. No tremor of emotion. No echo of mercy.

Around them, the other holograms stirred. Not visibly, but in the way shadows shifted, in the way silence thickened. The Warlords leaned, not forward, but inward.

Toward consequence.

Each presence clashed against the others, not in voice but in the posture of ideologies long at war. Dominion had no unity. Only imbalance, weaponized.

Ira stood within it. The pulse of the device in his coat pressed against his ribs like a second heartbeat, one not his own. It pulsed with unseen power, with the voice of a darker god buried beneath empire. It reminded him why he came. Why this moment mattered.

His rage, his hunger, his grief, all boiled into this breath.

This was not a council.

This was a crucible.

And he stood within it to see who would break.

He raised his head.

Not like a supplicant. Like a storm unfolding.

The Warlord of Wrath did not tremble beneath the gaze of seven sins.

He came to devour them.

His boots struck the obsidian with slow, deliberate impact. Each step was a declaration. Each sound reverberated through the chamber like a prophecy unfurling.

His gaze swept the circle, one blaze against seven gods. It did not flicker.

Then his voice cut through the tension, low and seething.

"Then let's not waste time."

It wasn't loud. But it struck.

A growl wrapped in steel, soaked in fury restrained only by purpose.

He stepped forward. Closer to the centre of the storm.

"Tell me…"

His voice thickened. Words dragged from the fire of his lungs.

"…who among you is ready to see the world burn?"

The silence after was not empty.

It was listening.

The chamber itself seemed to hold its breath. Walls pulsed faintly, a low thrum of Veil-tech echoing through the floor, through the bones. The holograms shimmered, caught between substance and memory, between now and something far more ancient.

This was no discussion.

It was ritual. A reckoning in the shape of a war room.

The air thickened as shadows gathered at the feet of each Warlord. Coiling. Serpentine. As if the sins themselves remembered what they were.

Each hologram flickered, yet the detail never faltered. Every wrinkle. Every thread. Every scar of conquest rendered in perfect cruelty.

Seven predators.

One fire.

The first to speak was Greed.

Midas.

The Gilded King took his time. He didn't rush toward control. He waited, like a spider woven into his web, knowing time answered to him.

He did not rise.

He did not kneel.

He lounged.

His holographic form shone brighter than all others. Not through light, but density. His presence bent reality around itself.

Obsidian armour laced with veins of gold. A cloak stitched from banknotes older than history. Rings upon his fingers, each heavy with the death of a rival. Each one a eulogy and a conquest.

His smile was quiet. Inevitable.

A monarch who did not need to speak to dominate a room; he only needed to look.

Midas did not sit upon a throne.

A throne was for kings. He had outlived that title.

He lounged, body draped in golden-stitched opulence, the fabric of his coat cascading like the spill of broken empires. He was not dressed in wealth. He was forged from it. Every inch of him told a story of conquest that began with a whisper and ended with silence.

His fingers, long and deliberate, rested lightly on the arm of his seat, each adorned with rings. Not for fashion. For memory. For power. Each gem held the colour of a fallen dynasty. Each band engraved with names long erased from history, remembered only by the man who had bought their silence.

Dead empires. Crushed bloodlines. Their value distilled into ornament.

Midas lifted one hand, languid.

Light caught the rings, and for a heartbeat, it seemed the chamber shimmered in response.

Not a word spoken.

Yet everything had already been said.

And then he smiled. Not with amusement. It was the smile of a man who already possessed what others feared to want. Ownership, quiet and complete. A promise of satisfaction that preceded its claim.

With a gloved hand, he lifted a gilded goblet. The metal shimmered under the low light, etched with the sigils of nations long buried under time and conquest. Inside, a Veil-infused liquid stirred.

It churned between molten gold and bottomless black. Wealth, suspended between light and darkness, temptation and judgment.

He tilted the goblet slightly. Watched how the liquid danced within, how its patterns whispered answers he already knew. As if the weight he measured was more than gold. More than power. As if he was weighing the future itself.

"Oh, Wrath," Midas exhaled. His voice came smooth, a blend of honeyed silk wrapped around cold steel. "You ask who among us is ready to see the world burn?"

A soft chuckle. Almost indulgent. Then silence.

"How predictable."

His amber eyes held a gleam, yes, amusement, but something sharper. A merchant's look, assessing a prize already purchased. His gaze drifted forward. He leaned in. Tapped his fingers once, then again, against the goblet's rim.

Each tap echoed. A metronome. A countdown.

"Fire is wasteful," he said. Quiet, but not soft. Lethal in its restraint. "Destruction is unprofitable. And waste..." He paused. His eyes flickered with knowing. "Waste is unbecoming of an empire."

The words slid across the room like a blade sheathed in velvet. Casual, but designed. Every syllable placed with precision. A move in a game whose stakes lay far beyond mere ruin.

Then he shifted. His gaze left Ira as if his presence were an afterthought. He studied the chamber instead. The obsidian walls carved with ancient edicts. The flickering light that projected ghosts across the stone. He seemed bored. The fury radiating off Ira no more disruptive than a gust in a market stall. A transaction accounted for. A loss already priced.

He spoke again, with the ease of someone whose victory had already been tallied.

"Strange, really."

He swirled the liquid again. It caught the dim light of the Black Sun above, glowing like a wound slow to close.

"Not a single word about him. No inquiry. No demand. No fatherly concern."

He let the silence speak. Let it grow. Let it press.

"Malrik Grevane," he said, the name treated like smoke. "The son of Wrath... raised by Greed."

The chamber tightened. A breath caught somewhere unseen. The very air shifted, as though meaning had taken shape and now loomed.

"Tell me, Ira," Midas murmured, "does he still belong to you?"

No answer was needed. The wound was already made. The barb struck before it had even finished leaving his lips.

Ira's molten gaze flared. Muscles coiled. Rage welled up, but no words came. Then a laugh, soft and sweet, broke the tension like a ripple on obsidian.

Carmela.

She moved like wine being poured. Her presence was a tempest of fragrance and danger. Her violet gown shimmered in the dim light, woven from silk infused with Veil. It clung like memory. Like temptation. The blood-red lace folded with her every gesture, as if the fabric had learned devotion.

Her eyes turned lazily toward Ira. Plums warmed beneath honeyed fingertips. Seduction, calculation, and something far more ancient beneath it all.

"Oh, Midas," she purred, tracing her nail around the rim of her goblet. The Veil-glass within shifted between longing and death. "You do have a way of making a woman's heart ache."

Then her gaze snapped.

It landed on Ira. Slow. Intentional. Like the weight of fate descending.

"You sent him to Avarith, Ira," she said. Her voice a nectar laced with poison. "To a kingdom where loyalty is bought, not earned. Where gold is law. And the only force stronger... is temptation."

She tapped the glass. Once. Twice.

"Tell me, my dear Wrath." Her smile widened. Elegant. Deadly. "When he returns to Pyrrha... will he still burn for you?"

The room went still.

Her words sank in like cold steel under silk. And then came another laugh. Soft. Intimate. A kiss before betrayal.

Gula moved next.

The Voracious Queen. Her voice came like thunder through velvet. A deep resonance that bent the room toward her.

Her body was encased in relics, armour wrought from the bones of fallen dynasties. Sigils from shattered houses gleamed across her frame. The Veil-infused plating caught the light like a warning.

She inhaled. Savouring. Not just air, but anticipation.

Then she reached for her goblet.

Inside, the liquid churned. Deep crimson folding into a black that swallowed all else.

"A son of Pyrrha, raised in Avarith..." Gula's voice thickened, dipped into something darker. She tasted the words like blood on her tongue.

"Do you know what happens to a child raised in a city built upon excess?"

The question hung. Poisoned honey. Every syllable she spoke carried weight. And the silence that followed bore it like a funeral dirge.

"They learn to indulge," she continued. "To take. To consume."

She leaned forward.

Not loud. Not violent. Her voice crawled. Slid across the chamber like oil over fire, slow and suffocating. It reached into Ira, slow and cruel, the way rot settles into bone.

"They do not fight for power."

A pause. Smile.

"They acquire it."

No one moved. The words sank like lead. The truth behind them did not ask for acceptance. It already owned the room.

Then, a shift.

Somnus stirred.

His voice was wind slipping beneath a door. Barely there, but undeniable.

"Fascinating."

Barely a whisper, yet it sliced the silence clean.

His form wavered. The edge of dream and waking. Not fully real, not fully gone. His body faded in and out, as if reality had not decided whether it could hold him.

"The sins of the father..." he mused. Slow. Thoughtful. Each word trailing smoke. "Have such a fascinating way... of bleeding into the next generation."

Then nothing.

Stillness.

The kind of silence that suffocates. Thick. Ancient.

And then his gaze shifted.

Straight to Ira.

Molten fury flared behind Wrath's eyes. He didn't speak. Not yet. But his focus cut through the air like a blade through mist.

Then Midas.

Unbothered. Still smiling. Still seated, basking in the moment he had orchestrated. Watching the tension spool tighter. Watching Ira coil beneath the weight of every word left unsaid.

To Midas, this wasn't confrontation. It was revelation.

Ira's gaze burned. The gold that adorned Midas shimmered in his vision, and for a moment, it looked as if it might melt beneath the intensity of his stare.

The room constricted. Light flickered from the Veil projections, casting long, shifting shadows. They danced like memories refusing to die.

Midas didn't blink.

He savoured the silence. Not to stall, but to measure.

Then Ira spoke.

"I believe," he began, voice cold, deliberate, sculpted from stone and rage, "you've made a fatal mistake, Midas."

Each word moved forward like a step taken at the edge of a cliff. Intentional. Irrevocable.

The heat behind Ira's tone scorched the air. Retribution bloomed beneath every syllable, restrained but seething. It wasn't anger thrown like a weapon; it was wrath forged for later use.

Midas didn't flinch. Regal, composed, perfectly still. The gold encasing him remained unshaken, as if even fury itself couldn't find purchase.

"I'm not the one who made the mistake here, Wrath," he said, his voice low, coated in disdain. There was no rise to it; only depth. "If anything... I gave you an opportunity."

He leaned back with the grace of a man who knew the room bent around him. His amber eyes glinted, not with malice, but with intrigue. The kind of curiosity found in a scientist watching something break under pressure.

"To prove your worth."

Ira's fists clenched tighter. Veins lifted along his forearms like serpents beneath the skin. Rage throbbed, alive now, coiling just under the surface. Controlled. But only barely.

"Do not play games with me."

His voice dropped into a sharper register, each word cutting cleaner than the last.

"You do not get to hide behind your wealth and distractions forever. There is a reckoning coming. And when it arrives—"

The words halted. The room thickened.

"It will not wait for those who think they are untouchable."

Midas laughed.

Quiet. Deliberate. Not the laugh of amusement, but of someone enjoying the weight of the moment, watching tension rise like steam from a simmering pot. He exhaled the sound like one might release a scent, elegant and exact.

"Ah. The fire still burns inside you."

He smiled again. Slower this time.

"How quaint."

Then his gaze slid down, finally, toward the object still resting in Ira's palm. The device, unspoken yet screaming with implication. A promise waiting in silence. A shape not yet fulfilled, but already undeniable.

A reminder of what had already begun.

Of what was coming.

"I know how you think, Ira," Midas continued, his voice low, calm, yet tinted with that ever-present arrogance. "You see everything as a transaction. Every exchange is a wager. But some things, some forces, cannot be bought or sold. The sooner you realize that, the sooner you'll understand the power I wield."

The air tightened around them. No one moved. The room didn't breathe, as though every shadow was listening.

Midas, of course, remained unshaken. He sipped from his goblet as if the world hadn't shifted around him. His gaze, sharp and cutting, never once left Ira. It was the gaze of a man who had already done the math, already written the story's ending in his mind.

But Ira didn't blink.

The fire inside him had not dimmed. It had hardened. This wasn't fury born in the moment. It was old, molten, forged from a thousand betrayals and a hundred wars. And Midas' performance, this gilded theatre, only made the forge burn hotter.

"I understand perfectly, Midas," he said, his tone slow and final. "The question is: do you?"

His gaze moved, just slightly, brushing over the other Warlords. His voice lowered, barely more than a whisper, but it carried.

"We'll see just how much gold can protect you when the world burns."

A quiet fell again, different this time. Not silence born of tension, but of consequence. The room seemed colder. The flickering holograms trembled, as if even the projections understood the weight of what had just been said. Shadows on the walls leaned closer, listening with their breath held.

No one spoke.

Their silence wasn't agreement. It wasn't dissent. It was the sound of recognition. The kind that hums deep in the marrow when something irreversible has been set in motion.

Midas didn't reply immediately.

He set the goblet down with precision, the metal ringing softly against the stone table, the sound too delicate for the steel underneath.

"We shall see, indeed," he murmured.

His voice was wrapped in silk, but something darker flickered just behind it. A shadow of calculation. A shift in weight. A trace of danger that hadn't been there before.

Invidia said nothing.

Her emerald eyes moved slowly from Midas to Ira, her gaze serpentine. She didn't blink. She didn't stir. Her lips curled, barely, into the beginning of a smile. Not amusement. Not support. Anticipation. A woman who saw the board reshaping itself and was content to wait until the exact moment her blade would matter most.

The tension in the room rose again, slow and suffocating. It wasn't loud. It wasn't sudden. It moved like pressure building in the lungs of time itself, as if the chamber was holding its breath, waiting to see who would shatter the silence first.

It was Gula.

"Enough of this," she growled, her voice booming with the force of inevitability. It didn't rise. It crashed. "Words are cheap. Show me action."

Her eyes gleamed, catching the light in glints of hunger. Not for food, not even for power, but for the promise of war itself. The thrill of movement. Of fire unleashed.

"We are here to decide our course. Not to waste time in riddles."

But Ira didn't turn.

His gaze stayed on Midas, locked and unyielding, as if the Gilded King were the only real adversary in the room. When he spoke again, his voice rumbled low and fierce, the kind of sound that precedes thunder.

"Let's move beyond games."

He didn't need to shout. The weight was already in the words.

"The world burns at my hand. And it will burn until I see it rise anew."

The tension between them didn't explode. It calcified. Hardened into something more permanent. The chamber became a crucible. Words no longer drifted; they struck. They echoed with venom and promise.

No one moved.

Because this wasn't posturing anymore. It was the edge of something irreversible.

It wasn't fatigue. It wasn't disinterest.

It was worse.

It was the look of a man who had already seen what came after.

And then, like a breath whispered through the cracks of sleep, Somnus spoke.

"Tell me, Ira…"

The words hung like thread unravelling. Soft. Brittle. Timeless.

"…do you fear it?"

He didn't need to say what "it" was. The word had weight without definition.

Because this wasn't about Midas.

This was about the truth.

About Malrik.

And the possibility that Ira's son, his legacy, might never return at all.

Somnus let the silence stretch, and then he exhaled, long and slow, as if the effort of speech itself had cost him something irreplaceable.

"It is… an exhausting thing, isn't it?"

His fingers tapped against the armrest of his throne, or what passed for one. The seat shimmered, flickered, half-formed and dream-woven, more mirage than matter. His form rippled softly, caught between presence and absence. Neither here nor gone.

"Shaping a son."

A pause, heavier than breath.

"Shaping an empire."

Another.

"Knowing that one will outlive the other."

It wasn't a warning.

It was inevitability.

Because whether Ira would admit it or not, everyone at that table already knew.

The fire of Wrath would one day extinguish.

But Malrik?

Malrik would endure.

And perhaps, when all was ashes, Ira would be no more than a scar on history. A name carved into the past. A relic of what came before.

Then came the cut.

Superbia did not let the silence linger.

Their voice came sharp and final, slicing through the stillness like judgment given form. Where Somnus was a whisper of inevitability, Superbia was the monument of what cannot be shaken. Their holographic form stood clearer than anyone's. Not flickering. Not fading. Bathed in refracted light that bent around them without touch, as if even photons refused to distort their image.

The room adjusted around them. The air bowed, if only for a moment.

"So this is what has become of Wrath's legacy," they said. Not an insult. A verdict. Their tone held no colour. No scorn. No disdain. Only conclusion.

They paused, not from caution or doubt, but with deliberation. The silence was measured. Owned. Superbia did not need to hurry. Then they turned, gaze locking onto Ira's. Not with fear. Not with awe. With certainty.

"You send your son to be sculpted by another hand," they said. The voice was steady, low, unhurried. "You send a wolf among serpents." A breath, sharp with quiet finality. "And now expect him to return as what?" The pause carried weight. "The heir to Wrath?" Then longer still, each second digging deeper. "Or the next King of Greed?"

There was no mockery in their voice. No taunt. Just truth. A truth that cut deeper than any blade. Superbia did not glance at Midas. They didn't have to. Instead, they looked only at Ira, and spoke what no one else had dared to voice.

"A ruler who cannot shape his own blood does not shape an empire." The blow landed, and then the final knife slid in, slow and deliberate. "He merely rules the ruins left behind."

The silence that followed wasn't hollow. It held weight. Not stillness, not emptiness, but something alive and edged with war. Ira's fire did not flicker. It blazed. The silence didn't settle on him. It burned through him.

Superbia's words were not merely challenge. They were a sentence. A declaration that Wrath's dominion over his blood had begun to fracture. A subtle, dangerous suggestion that Malrik Grevane no longer belonged to his father, but to Avarith, moulded by gold and greed, claimed by another throne. That Wrath had lost what was his by right.

And that, Ira would not allow.

His fingers curled into fists, tension thrumming through the stone around him like a subterranean pulse, the foreboding whisper of an earthquake before the break. When he spoke, his voice did not rise in fury. It was the calm that precedes devastation.

"My son will return to Pyrrha." There was no threat, no plea, no space for doubt. It was a truth carved in fire. His molten gaze swept over the gathered Warlords, burning through their flickering projections, daring contradiction.

"Midas can polish him in gold," he said, voice low and slow, each syllable landing like iron. "He can dress him in silk and lace his words with poison." His head tilted, just slightly, and the air around him thickened. The heat of his fury pressed into it like coals to skin. "But beneath all that glitter, Malrik is still of Pyrrha."

The chamber held its breath.

"He does not belong to Avarith. He does not belong to you." He never looked away from Superbia. "He does not belong to Greed."

And then he leaned forward, just enough to shift the balance of the room. His presence sharpened, blade-like, pressing against the moment like steel to a throat.

"He belongs to me."

A tension rippled unseen, but it moved through everyone. Because Ira did not speak in dreams. He spoke in certainties. And if Malrik Grevane thought himself unbound, if Midas believed a son of Wrath could be bought with silk and whispers, then the realm would be reminded.

Pyrrha did not relinquish its blood. It reclaimed. And it reclaimed through fire.

He drew a breath. Slow. Steady. Unshaken.

"When he returns," Ira said, voice iron-clad with promise, "we will see what remains of him."

The weight of judgment settled thick as smoke. Not loud. But final.

Because Malrik Grevane would return. Whether he walked back to Pyrrha as a son, or was dragged back in chains. That choice was no longer his to make.

The silence after Ira's declaration was a thing alive. It slithered through the Bohemian Chamber of Order, coiling between flickering holograms, threading itself into the very fabric of the room. It did not settle. It did not break. It waited.

Then—

A slow, deliberate clap.

Not mocking. Not dismissive. Measured. Calculated. Like the counting of coin. Like the tallying of worth.

Midas leaned forward. The molten gilding of his holographic form shifted slightly, casting streaks of gold across the obsidian walls. His cloak, woven from the currency of fallen empires, glimmered as though wealth itself had been caught alight by Ira's fury.

His crystalline amber eyes gleamed. Not with defiance. Not with challenge.

With amusement.

"Oh, Ira," he murmured, tilting his goblet lazily, watching the golden liquid swirl in slow, hypnotic spirals. "You speak of what will return to Pyrrha."

He raised the goblet just high enough for the chamber's flickering light to catch it, refracting into four distinct reflections across the surface. He watched them shimmer, drift apart. Then smiled.

"But what of the things that never left?"

The words landed with weight, heavier than gold, more intoxicating than poison.

None of the Warlords moved. None breathed. Because this was no longer about Malrik. This had become something else. Something larger.

Midas turned the goblet slightly, letting the reflections shift and change. Subtle. Intentional.

"Bloodlines," he said softly, almost wistfully, "are such fickle things, aren't they?"

Then came the riddle.

The first reflection flickered, a shimmer of steel, cold and clean. Something forged not by lineage but by survival. "One walks in the dark," Midas murmured, watching the light like it whispered prophecy. "Carved from steel and blood, shaped by a city that does not kneel. A man who was never meant to rule, never meant to rise, and yet..."

His voice dropped, weight shifting in the chamber like a tide. "Kings are not only born on thrones."

He left the rest unspoken. The weight of the words lingered, and somewhere, hidden in the dark, a name stirred.

The second reflection wavered, red and black interlaced, flickering like war embers, like something building in silence. "Another was raised among wolves," Midas continued.

"But he does not howl with them. He does not burn. He does not rage. He does not kneel." A bead of gold slipped from the goblet's rim, landing soundlessly against the shimmering armrest. "This one builds. Stone upon stone. Fortress upon fortress. Until the world itself bends to his will."

He tilted his head slightly, barely perceptible. "And yet," he added, quiet and contemplative, "even the mightiest walls cannot keep out the ghosts of their own blood."

His golden eyes lifted, catching light that didn't belong to the room.

The third reflection didn't gleam. It absorbed. A shadow within shadow.

"And then," Midas said, his voice smooth as melted coin, "there is the one who walks between worlds."

He inhaled. Slowly. Intentionally.

"He is neither Pyrrhan nor Avarithian. Neither fire nor gold. Neither weapon nor crown." A twitch at the corner of his mouth, too thin to be called a smile. "He was never meant to exist."

No one spoke. They didn't need to. The weight of the unspoken pressed into the chamber like a silent hand against the throat of the realm.

"And yet," Midas whispered, eyes fixed on the reflections as they turned and trembled, "here he is."

And the chamber held its breath.

"Unseen by the father who forged him. Unclaimed by the war that shaped his brothers. Unwritten by the fate that dictated the rest." Midas's gaze slid toward Ira, deliberate and unhurried. "He does not seek power." A smile curled across his face, slow, knowing. "No, power seeks him."

The words held longer than they should have, their resonance expanding into the silence between the thrones. "And one day," he said, leaning back as he swirled the gold within his goblet, "it will find him." The pause that followed was sharp, its silence edged with precision. "When it does…" his voice softened, his gaze catching firelight, "what will he become?"

There was no fourth reflection in the goblet. No flicker. No shimmer. Only void, an emptiness where identity should have emerged. Midas took his time, watching the blank space ripple in liquid gold. He did not blink.

"And then," he murmured, voice just above a whisper, "there is the child of fate." The phrase coiled through the chamber like a prophecy half-spoken, impossible to ignore. "The son born not once, but twice."

None of the Warlords shifted. The chamber felt as though it had stopped breathing. "The last to rise," Midas continued, letting the flickering light bend against the hollowness of the missing reflection, "but the first to be seen." His voice had turned gentle, not in kindness, but in reverence. "The seventh son of a seventh son."

His fingers moved slowly across the edge of the goblet, the motion contemplative. "Do you know what they say of such a birth, Ira?" He didn't look toward Wrath. He didn't need to. The question wasn't meant to be answered. "A boy born under such omens…"

He drew a breath, measured, heavy.

"...is not born a man." The silence that followed was longer, more substantial. And when it broke, it did so with finality.

"He is born a prophecy."

The blue light cast long, unnatural shadows across the walls, stretching the silhouettes of those seated into distorted echoes of the monarchs they once were. And in that silence, for the first time in the meeting, Midas did not smile. He lifted his goblet but did not drink.

Because this was not riddle craft.

This was not performance. This was truth, dressed in myth, carrying the weight of inevitability.

No one moved. No one dared.

Because every warlord in that chamber understood what had just transpired. Midas had not merely peeled back Ira's history. He had laid bare a future already set in motion.

And even Midas, for all his wealth, all his control, all his mastery of men and markets, knew there were forces that gold could not claim. Not yet.

He eased back into his throne of opulence, fingers tracing the golden stem of the goblet like a man nursing a secret. Then came the sound, low, rich, effortless. He laughed. A golden, honeyed laugh, filled with something timeless and unreadable.

"But then again," he said, slow and unhurried, "I do so love a good story."

The words drifted through the air like silk soaked in venom. But beneath the decadence, beneath the polish, beneath the mask of Greed itself, was hesitation. A silence too deliberate. A pause too precise. Because Midas hadn't just been speaking of Wrath's sons. He'd been circling something untouched. Something none of them had yet claimed.

Something more dangerous than all the fire and gold combined.

Purity.

The final sanctuary. The last uncorrupted jewel in a world that had devoured everything holy. And for all the ruin seated in that chamber, for all the crowns bathed in sin, she still existed. She had not fallen. Her light had not dimmed.

And that, perhaps more than prophecy, more than fire, more than fate, was what unsettled them most.

Because fire could be controlled. Gold could be spent. Desire could be fed. Hunger could be satiated. Sloth could decay. Envy could fester. Pride could reign.

But purity?

Purity could only ever be lost.

And once it was gone, it was gone forever.

Midas swirled the goblet in his hand, watching the liquid spiral within. The molten gold caught the light, bent it, devoured it. It never reflected.

Because that was the truth of gold. It did not shine. It consumed.

His crystalline amber eyes flickered with something sharper than perception, something that sat just beyond comprehension. A gleam of recognition. Of reckoning.

Then he spoke, voice velvet-wrapped in wealth.

"Tell me, my dear Carmela," he purred, each word gilded with practiced ease, "what do you make of something that refuses to be bought?"

The silence that followed was deliberate. Then a breath, slow, silken, shaped like a blade sliding from sheath.

Carmela scoffed. Rolled her eyes. Laughed.

Not golden. Not honeyed.

Decadent.

Her laugh spilled into the chamber like perfume thick with venom, indulgent and slow. A sound that knew too much, of longing, of power, of the moment just before surrender.

A laugh that had watched emperors fall to their knees, that had watched kings fumble for words with dry mouths and shaking hands. A laugh born of deep knowing.

Carmela, the Crimson Reverie, leaned back against the carved curve of her obsidian throne. Her silken robes shifted as though alive, wrapping around her in slow waves, the fabric drawn to the heat of her presence like moths to flame.

Then she sighed.

It was not a sound of weariness. It was a prelude.

A slow, exaggerated sound. One meant to be heard. One meant to be mocked. Carmela's fingers glided along the rim of her goblet, languid and deliberate. The liquid within shifted like molten ruby, deep, endless, mirroring the very essence of what she was.

"Midas, my love," she drawled, her voice a silken thread wound with poison, each word rolling from her tongue like velvet through fingers, "you ask as if there is such a thing."

She smirked. Sharp. Cruel. But beneath the curve of her lips, her gaze darkened. "But, alas," she murmured, raising the goblet in her hand, "she still pretends, doesn't she?"

She did not name her. She did not need to. Every Warlord in that room knew.

"The Princess of Chastity," she crooned, the title drawn out with mockery, as though the syllables themselves tasted bitter in her mouth. She tilted her goblet, watching the crimson liquid cling to the glass like blood to bone. "Still nestled away in her little Celestial Gardens, surrounded by her twelve oh-so-loyal knights."

A soft click of her tongue.

"A bubble," she said. But it wasn't a statement. It was a sentence. A curse.

"Away from the rest of us. Away from the world. Away from reality."

She took a sip, slow and deliberate, but there was venom beneath the indulgence. The kind that didn't strike fast. The kind that lingered.

"And yet," she mused, licking the stain of red from her lips, her gaze narrowing, "tell me, my darlings…" A glint danced in her eyes, a trap spun in velvet and steel.

"What does it say about a woman when twelve men must keep her pure?"

The words unspooled into the air like silk soaked in hemlock. Not loud. Not crude. Worse, they were quiet. Calculated. Surgical.

The Warlords did not answer, and they were not expected to. The question wasn't meant for them. It was meant for the myth itself.

Because Carmela wasn't speaking of innocence. She was speaking of its fall. Of the inevitability behind every locked gate. Because all things, no matter how sacred, no matter how shielded, no matter how divinely protected, must one day kneel before sin.

Her smile widened, red lips parting just enough to reveal a flash of teeth, pearlescent, precise, a predator's grin beneath painted glamour. A wolf smiling at the last untouched lamb.

And somewhere, far from this chamber of serpents and kings, she waited. Cloaked in gardens. Guarded by twelve. Untouched. Unbroken. Unyielding.

But not forever.

Because innocence, true innocence, was never eternal.

It was a breath. A heartbeat.

A moment before the inevitable. And the clock was still ticking.

A low hum began to vibrate through the chamber. Subtle. Mechanical. The whisper of unseen gears embedded within the Veil-infused stone. Blue light flickered against polished obsidian, casting warped reflections across the thrones. Sin rendered in spirit, caught between man and myth.

Then, without effort or announcement, he moved.

Somnus. The Dream King. The Architect of Sloth.

His form shimmered, not with power, but with decay. He did not sit tall. He did not speak quickly. He simply existed, as though participation in this gathering was too costly for his energy to fully commit.

He let Carmela's words linger. Let them hang and rot a little longer. Then, finally, his voice spilled into the space between.

Slow.

Unhurried.

Lethargy spoken like prophecy.

"Chastity is an illusion," he murmured, eyelids half-drawn, gaze unfocused and eternal. "And illusions are easily rewritten."

His voice held no cruelty. No indulgence. It was simple. Certain. Spoken not as theory, but as something already lived. "She keeps herself hidden in a garden untouched by time, wrapped in celestial light, surrounded by relics of a world that no longer exists." Somnus exhaled slowly, and the weight of his words seemed to press into the chamber itself, heavy as fog, invisible but inescapable. "But tell me…"

His gaze, half-lidded and distant, drifted toward the shifting walls of Veil-forged circuitry. As if looking through them. Beyond them. As if seeing something the others could not.

"How long does purity last, when the world itself is changing?"

The hum of the Veil-tech sharpened. Still, none of the warlords spoke. But their silence was not emptiness, it was agreement. It was understanding.

Because Somnus wasn't only speaking of the Celestial Princess. He was speaking of all that had once been left untouched. He was speaking of a time before war, before the Veil, before the sacred fusion of flesh and machine, of soul and circuitry, of humanity and something older, deeper, stranger.

He was speaking of purity in a world that had rewritten the laws of existence.

Midas exhaled through his nose, crystalline amber eyes glinting as he watched the holographic flicker shift across the chamber. "You say purity is an illusion, Dream King," he said softly, "but I say purity is simply a resource."

His fingers tapped once, then again, against the armrest of his golden throne. Each tap slow. Measured. Intentional.

"And like all resources, it is only valuable... until something better replaces it."

He let the statement breathe. Let it sink. Then continued, voice steady, rich with an eerie calm. "Flesh is weak. It succumbs. It withers. It dies. And yet we..." He gestured toward the chamber, toward the glowing avatars of the ruling sins, toward the shape of a new world rising from the ashes of the old. "...persist."

Midas leaned forward. And this time, there was something else behind the gleam of gold in his gaze. Not desire. Not possession. But curiosity. A deeper fascination.

"How long before she, too, is rewritten?"

There was no venom in the question.

No hate. Only inevitability.

Because in the end, technology did not conquer, it erased. It did not need to seduce or overpower. It only needed to wait.

And no matter how tightly she clung to her ancient sanctuary, no matter how fiercely her twelve knights stood guard, the truth remained. The world was shifting. The Veil was shifting it. And the question was not if, but when.

Gula stirred. Her vast frame leaned forward, casting a heavy shadow over the flickering projections. Her eyes, molten gold and endless, narrowed, not in rage, but in hunger.

A hunger that had nothing to do with war. A hunger that waited for things to rot.

"Everything is consumed, eventually," she murmured. Her voice was low, indulgent, but there was pity in it too. Not for the Princess. But for those who still believed she could last.

She raised her goblet. The Veil-forged liquid within shimmered between crimson and abyssal black. "Even innocence. Even flesh."

A beat later, Carmela's smirk twisted, sharper, crueller.

"Especially flesh."

And then Midas sighed. Not out of weariness, but out of certainty. As if the conversation was less prophecy than repetition. As if they were merely speaking aloud a future he had already watched unfold a thousand times. He swirled the gold within his goblet, eyes fixed on the way the light fractured across its surface. How easily purity could melt. How easily it could be reshaped. Undone.

"My, my," he mused, voice lilting, coated in insidious mirth. "What an utterly poetic discussion. The sanctity of flesh. The decay of innocence. The inevitable erosion of all things unspoiled."

He paused. Thoughtful. Intentional. Letting the silence stretch, taut and glistening, like the final string before the instrument snaps.

"And yet... I can't help but wonder..."

He tilted his head slightly. His crystalline amber eyes flickered, not with malice, not with amusement, but with a depth too knowing to be anything but dangerous.

"Wouldn't it be such a waste... such a tragedy... if something just as sacred, just as precious as innocence... were being stolen?"

His words slithered into the chamber, slow and heavy, curling through the air like bait dropped into a still lake. And just like that, he shifted the conversation. Because this wasn't about flesh anymore.

This was about technology.

Midas let the silence lean in. He tasted it, savoured the way attention snapped toward him with sharpened precision. Then, feigning exasperation, he leaned back. Raised his goblet in mock reverence. A theatrical sigh.

"I suppose I should be flattered," he murmured, shaking his head with a smile too sharp to be soft. "After all, one only steals from the best, don't they?"

He let that hang. Let it ripen. Then lowered the blow with gentle finality.

"And yet, for all the wealth I have, for all the vaults brimming with inventions, for all the monuments to progress I've claimed, it seems that some of my most cherished creations... are slipping from my grasp."

His voice dropped. His smile deepened.

"And not just mine."

The words rippled like cracks through marble. They settled slow, but the implications arrived fast.

This wasn't a theft. This was a pattern. A breach.

And every empire in this chamber, every ruler seated on a throne built from control, from obedience, from domination, felt the tremor beneath them.

Midas didn't raise his voice. He didn't need to. The tension in the room had already ignited. Each syllable struck like flint. A single breath away from flame.

His eyes flicked toward Invidia, not naming her, not calling her out. But the weight of his gaze was unmistakable. The implication undeniable.

His ringed finger tapped against the rim of his goblet. Soft. Rhythmic. Like a countdown.

"Now, I wonder..." he mused, savouring every word like fine wine. "Where oh where could all these delightful little presents be coming from?"

It wasn't a question. It was a mirror turned toward every silent face in the room. Prototype blueprints. Veil-forged designs. Experimental code in the hands of rebels who had no business wielding power. No means of acquiring it.

Except someone had given it to them.

And both Midas and Invidia knew who.

The shadows thickened around her. Her poise did not break. But the mask she wore, crafted from ice and precision, grew heavier.

"I'm no fool," Midas continued. His voice slipped like silk along skin, smooth, effortless, unmistakably lethal. "I know desperation when I see it. But this... this generosity? It's a bit much for my tastes."

He watched her. Watched the warlords watching her. The tension moved like a pulse through the chamber, a second heartbeat beneath the room's surface.

"Someone," he said, with a smile too pleasant to be pure, "has been very generous. So benevolent. Handing the keys of creation to the poor, the broken, the lost."

No one spoke. No one dared. Because in this room, silence was not safety. It was calculation.

Midas leaned forward. The folds of his cloak shifted like molten wealth, reflecting light in ribbons of distorted gold. And when he spoke again, his voice was nearly reverent.

"A thief? A martyr? A trickster?"

His gaze locked fully on Invidia now, cutting through her as if peering beneath the surface of everything she pretended to be. The moment was tight. Brutal. Almost unbearable.

"Or something... far more hollow?"

He didn't name her. He didn't have to.

Every Warlord in that room already knew who he meant.

The words struck Invidia like a flicker of flame. Subtle, but enough. Enough for Midas to know he'd found the soft point behind the armour. His smile widened, a predator's grin, cool and certain, the expression of a man who knew he had driven the dagger of insinuation straight into the heart of silence.

"Of course," Midas exhaled, voice slow, syrup-thick with false civility. "This is all speculation, isn't it?"

He waved a hand, dismissing the accusation before it could breathe. A gesture of elegant apathy, like brushing away dust. As if it were all just a game of thoughts. Nothing more.

"I mean, if I truly believed these factions were arming themselves with elite technology, surely I would have done something far more extravagant, wouldn't I?"

The question held no curiosity. Only mockery. A test of patience wrapped in silk. And then, softly, deliberately—

"And yet..."

Two words. The deadliest pair in a liar's vocabulary. The kind of phrase that drips poison slowly. That makes truth bend under its weight.

The silence stretched thin, stretched tight, until it felt like the chamber itself might snap under the pressure.

"But thankfully," Midas sighed, rising from his throne with a grace too smooth to be innocent, "our dear, dear Pyrrhan warlord has been so very accommodating. Haven't you, Ira?"

He bowed, low, too low, an insult wrapped in civility. His molten crown caught the flickering blue light, throwing strange halos across the black marble. His eyes, lit with fire and mockery, never left Ira's.

Midas straightened, letting the sweetness in his voice curdle.

"After all, I had to cough up a fortune just to acquire a few mercenaries from the Sanguine Order. And imagine my delight when one of their finest happens to share your name."

The air turned. Even the Veil-tech seemed to falter. The chamber held its breath.

"Or rather... your blood."

The words dropped like lead into the stillness. His tone didn't rise. He didn't need it to. The sharp edge of his smile was enough.

Silence fell. Thick. Suffocating.

Ira stood unmoving at the edge of the Black Sun, the molten gold of his gaze darkening into something unreadable. His fists clenched at his sides, quiet and slow. Not reaction. Not restraint. Something more primal. Something coiled.

The tension in the room shifted, no longer between words, but between hearts. Every eye on Ira. Every breath held. Because Midas had not just struck a nerve. He had dared to trespass on something sacred.

And Midas, ever the master of momentum, let it settle. Let it fester. A stone dropped into the centre of Wrath's silence, waiting to see where the ripples would end.

"Tell me, Ira," he asked, voice soft, dangerous, curious in the way fire is curious of fuel, "how much does a son's loyalty cost?"

The question hovered. It didn't pierce. It lingered, like smoke that refused to rise. Clinging to the chamber's bones.

No one moved. No one dared.

Ira didn't answer. He didn't need to.

The silence that followed was not empty. It was waiting.

The chamber held its breath because everyone knew Wrath did not speak when he burned.

He simply burned.

"Every war begins with a question: who owns the future? And every empire ends with the answer: no one."

Null Gospel, Book I, Verse 17.

***

CHAPTER SEVENTEEN:

The Empire Built on Ashes

"The ash carries what the fire cannot burn. Survival is not the praise of the living; it is the scorn of the dead. What endures is not meek. It has torn itself from the grave."

Fragment of the Exiled Codex, Volume I, Tablet 18.

The chamber hummed with the eerie vibration of Veil-forged machinery, a low, metallic pulse that seemed to seep into the bones of the walls. Beneath that mechanical resonance, there was something deeper. An energy. One of fracture. Of something about to snap. The air was heavy, charged with a faint static that clung to the skin, the scent of steel scorching the throat.

Something was breaking, but not in the chamber. In him. In the very heart of his being. And through him, the world trembled, shuddering under the weight of the shift.

The silence that held him was no longer a barrier. It had become a challenge. Not absence, but a weapon. Stillness, weaponized. The very air felt alive with anticipation. It dared him to break.

Ira did not speak. His gaze locked on Midas, unblinking, unwavering. Beneath the surface of calm, there was a seething anger that simmered, just beneath the skin. His fingers curled, tightening around the armrest, and the metal groaned under the pressure. But Ira did not move. He stood there, like a statue, unmoving yet alive with the raw potential of destruction.

His son.

The loyalty that had been sold. The betrayal that had been wrought.

How could Midas, the embodiment of Greed itself, dare to speak of loyalty as though it could be bought or sold? The thought was anathema to everything Ira had once believed. To everything he had fought for. Loyalty was not a commodity, not a thing to be bartered away. It was a bond. A sacred tie.

Ira's chest tightened. The rhythm of his breath became more jagged with each passing moment. The air seemed to conspire with his fury, feeding it, sharpening it.

His gaze never left Midas, molten and unforgiving. His fingers dug deeper into the armrest. The metal groaned, twisting under the strain. Beneath him, the Black Sun pulsed, crimson veins streaking the stone like blood from an old wound, a scar upon the earth itself.

The room contracted around him. The weight of the moment pressed down on every breath, every movement, threatening to splinter the fragile silence.

The warlords watched, silent sentinels in the shadows. Their presence was like a weight upon the room, a heavy expectation that something far greater than a mere conversation was unfolding.

This was a moment of reckoning, a clash of wills, of empires, of destinies. The very fabric of power itself hung in the balance. Only those who could bear the weight of inevitability would remain standing in the end.

The Bohemian Chamber of Order, ancient and steadfast, held its breath. It was no ordinary room, this sanctum. Every stone, every shadow, every pause carried with it the weight of centuries.

Here, power was not just a game; it was an ancient, ever-shifting force, where the price of loyalty was steep and the price of betrayal, even steeper. No casual exchange of words could take place here. Every sentence, every silence, was a calculated move in a game as old as the stars themselves.

At the centre of it all, beneath the flickering blue light of the holograms, lay the Black Sun. Its presence was more ominous than any Warlord's gaze, more commanding than any throne.

The obsidian disc embedded in the floor was no simple object. It was a wound in the earth itself, veins of crimson bleeding from it like blood from an ancient, unhealed scar. Around it, constellations inlaid with gold spiralled outwards, mapping not just the universe, but something older. Something that had seen the rise and fall of countless empires before the first stone of this chamber had ever been laid.

Above them, the owl watched. Its unblinking gaze seemed to pierce the soul of the room, its hollow eyes reflecting the truths the Warlords dared not face.

It had seen this moment before, had seen countless others like it. It loomed above, a reminder that all their power, all their ambition, was fleeting. In its silence, it whispered a truth none of them could escape: Even the mightiest fall.

And what rises from the ashes is never what one expects. Wisdom, in its quiet strength, could be as dangerous as the knowledge it bestowed. The owl's gaze was a constant reminder that not all truths could be twisted or erased. Some things, no matter how much power one wielded, remained out of reach.

At the far end of the room, frozen in marble, stood a figure of wrath. A lion, its body streaked with veins of blood-red stone. Its snarl was eternal, frozen in a moment just before it struck, its claws still curled into the ground.

It was a beast meant for conquest, a king born not to kneel. Like the Warlords themselves, it was a creature of power, poised for destruction, but trapped in time, waiting for its own inevitable fall.

And like Ira Valkor, it was a figure marked by rage, forever poised for destruction, yet never quite able to deliver the final blow.

The chamber thrummed, the walls pulsing with the weight of a thousand decisions, a thousand lives shaped by forces beyond their control.

Midas's words hung heavy in the air, yet Ira did not respond. He stood still, his gaze fixed on the Black Sun, molten eyes locked onto its dark void.

His hands twitched at his sides, the urge to seize something, anything, and burn it into ash nearly unbearable.

But it wasn't the fire of fury that had him trembling. His hands, now clenched in tight fists, shook not from the heat of anger, but from something deeper. A raw ache. A gnawing emptiness that tore at his chest, making it hard to breathe.

The face of his son flashed before him, vivid and clear, as if he could reach out and touch it. That moment when the boy had looked up at him, eyes filled with trust and admiration. The bond that had once felt unbreakable was now shattered, torn apart by the cold, unforgiving game they had all been playing.

The metal of the armrest creaked under his grip, but it wasn't the steel that cracked. It was his heart. The room seemed to pulse with the weight of his own inner torment, his pulse pounding in his ears, louder than anything else in the chamber.

His son's face came back to him, but now it was not filled with trust.

It was a mask of something darker, something unreachable.

Ira's grip tightened, but it was not out of anger. It was out of that deep, aching sorrow, the unbearable weight of the bond that had been lost.

What had once been unshakable had now been torn apart, irreparably so.

"Loyalty," he muttered, his voice rough, cracked, as though the very word was foreign to him now. "It was never his to give." The words tasted bitter, a foul, dry ash that burned his throat.

And yet, Midas's words were not the only thing settling into Ira's bones like a blade, buried deep. There was something else, a knowledge. A truth, undeniable and suffocating.

Something was shifting here, in this very moment. Something was being decided. A game was being played, and Ira, despite the fury that burned within him, could not afford to be the fool at the table.

The chamber inhaled, the ancient weight pressing further into the bones of those gathered. The holograms flickered again, distorting, elongating the shadows, twisting the figures of the Warlords into something greater, something monstrous. Yet, no one spoke. The silence stretched, thickening, taut with the tension of a hundred unspoken truths.

Then, Carmela's laughter cut through the stillness. It was silk being torn apart, smooth yet indulgent, echoing off the cold stone walls.

She leaned back against the gilded curve of her throne, dragging her obsidian-painted fingernail along the stem of her Veil glass goblet. The liquid within shimmered, dark, viscous, alive.

It filled the room with a weight that made the chamber feel even heavier, more suffocating.

"Midas," she chuckled, her tone dripping with mockery. "Always obsessed with ownership."

She swirled the goblet in her hand, watching the liquid catch the light. "But what is ownership, truly? To bend, to take? Or to make others forget they ever had it?"

Her smile was cold, predatory. Her eyes, glinting with the sharpness of a hunter, locked with each Warlord in turn. "I don't take. I make you offer it. Willingly. Desperately. Without realizing it."

She let the silence hang in the air like a knife, poised to strike.

"Or is it something deeper?" Her voice turned even more indulgent, curling around each word like a velvet rope, pulling them in.

"Ira, you burn what you cannot claim. Midas, you hoard what you cannot consume."

Her smile deepened, predatory and perfect. "Superbia, you demand it by birthright."

Her fingers traced the rim of her glass, a deliberate dance. "But me? I don't take."

She let the words sink, watching their weight settle in the minds of those who would dare to challenge her. Her voice dropped lower, more intimate, like a lover's whisper laced with poison.

"I make you offer it to me. Willingly. Desperately. Without even realizing you've given it up."

The truth sank in slowly, quietly. Devastating. Ownership was not in the taking, not in seizing what was theirs. No. It was in making others forget they ever had it.

Her gaze flickered toward Gula, her voice soft, but laced with venom. "Isn't that right, my dear Voracious Queen?"

Gula's crimson eyes gleamed in the half-light. A smile stretched across her lips, slow and deliberate, but it was not one of warmth.

It was the hunger of a predator, a hunger that was not sated by flesh alone, but by control, by consumption, by bending the world itself to her will.

She did not speak immediately, letting the silence settle, as if weighing the words in her mind before unleashing them.

"Ownership, Carmela?" she purred, the words rolling like velvet off her tongue. "I find it amusing how easily you all speak of claiming what's already yours, what's already been tamed, what bends willingly beneath your hands."

Her voice dropped deeper, wrapped in ancient weight, soaked in a knowing that could not be denied. Her eyes glimmered with the light of a thousand empires, their ashes scattered beneath the heels of time. She turned her gaze toward the others, daring them to question her truth.

"But tell me this." Her voice cut through the air, heavy with understanding. "What of those who resist? What of the things that will not bend, no matter how carefully we coax them? Can we not still make them forget they were ever free?"

The flickering blue light did not diminish Gula's presence. It only served to deepen it. She was a living force, excess, overwhelming, a monument of hunger that bled into every corner of the room.

Her words were deliberate, each one dripping with certainty.

"They fight back, you know," she said softly, as though speaking of distant lands, places far from the corruption of their reach. "Beyond the borders of Gluttara, past the rivers I have turned to gold, there are those who still think they can resist."

Her voice lingered in the air, almost indulgent, but there was an unmistakable undertone. A knowing that there was no place on this earth untouched by her influence. There was no power that could truly defy her.

"They think that simply because something has survived the test of time, it is untouchable. But tell me..." She lifted her goblet, the sharp click of her nails ringing like a bell in the stillness. "How many untouched things have we seen fall? How many temples have been built over old graves?"

Her voice deepened, each word heavy with certainty. The weight of history. The inevitability of destruction. The knowledge that nothing was immune, nothing was sacred, not even the oldest, purest things.

The very air seemed to thicken as she took a slow sip from her glass, letting the moment stretch, suffocating, like a heavy fog settling over the room.

"How many medicines have been stolen, corrupted, refined, and then returned to the world in a bottle, stamped with a price tag?" she asked, almost absent-mindedly, her crimson eyes glittering with the deadly truth she was about to lay bare.

"Ownership is not the act of taking; it's in the quiet theft of the will, when choice becomes an illusion, and what remains is surrender."

The silence that followed her words was thick. It pressed in on them all, as though the very chamber held its breath. The Warlords, entrenched in their own dominions, understood the weight of what had been said. Ownership was not simply about claiming what was theirs; it was about deciding what could exist, and what would never exist again.

The tension in the room was suffocating, palpable. The silence pulsed with a life of its own.

The game had shifted.

Above them, the vaulted ceiling seemed to stretch away, an endless expanse of stone where the owl carved in relief spread its wings wide. Its eyes were hollow, infinitely empty, watching, waiting.

The great bird's unblinking gaze reminded them all that wisdom, though powerful, could be as suffocating as it was illuminating. Some truths were far too dangerous to acknowledge, until it was far too late.

At the farthest end of the room stood the Lion, frozen in mid-prowl, a creature of pure wrath, carved from black marble and streaked with veins of blood-red stone. Its claws dug into the earth, but it never struck. It was eternal hunger, unrelenting power, a king without a master, much like the Warlords themselves.

Then came the silence, the kind that thickened the air, weighted it with things unsaid, decisions unresolved. The blue light of the Veil-forged technology flickered, stretching the shadows and distorting the forms of the Warlords into something larger than life. The tension was unbearable. Something was about to break. Something was about to snap. The game was unfolding, the stakes beyond fathoming.

And then, as if the very chamber had drawn in a breath, a voice filled the room, low, deliberate, slow.

"Existence is a curious thing."

It was Somnus, the Dream King. The Warlord of Sloth. He was not driven by hunger, not by ambition. Not by the need to conquer or seduce. No, he was simply a being of endurance, of persistence. He existed longer than the others. And in that quiet endurance, he had already won.

His holographic form flickered lazily, like a vision struggling to be contained, as though even Veil-tech itself could not fully grasp his essence, could not contain him.

Somnus did not rule through force. He ruled by simply being, by outlasting all that would try to oppose him. He was not bound by time or the desires of others. He was not swayed by their schemes. He simply was.

His gaze lazily swept across the room. "You speak of ownership," he mused, his voice soft, drawn out. "Of dominion, of shaping what is. But tell me, can one truly own anything if the very act of claiming it only feeds a dream? We sit here, rulers of empires and ashes, but do we own what we possess, or do we simply pretend until the wake of morning?"

His words hung in the air, heavy and thick. He spoke not of empires, or cities, or men. He spoke of something deeper, something far more existential. The difference between the tangible and the intangible, the finite and the infinite.

His gaze drifted lazily, yet somehow piercing. It settled on the frozen lion, the red veins of marble slicing through its black form. It stared, unblinking, eternal.

"Dreams are ownership in its purest form," Somnus mused softly, his voice barely above a whisper. "Unchallenged. Unquestioned. In a dream, you are a king, a god, a beggar, a corpse. You rule nations. You destroy them. You are loved. You are forgotten."

He let the words settle in the air, their weight pressing on the room, on every Warlord present.

Somnus's silence stretched longer, heavy with the timelessness of one who had seen it all, the rise, the fall, the endless cycle.

"And then," he said, his voice dropping to a murmur, edged with something darker, "you wake up."

The words hung in the chamber like an inevitable truth, piercing through the heart of every Warlord present.

Somnus let his gaze drift across the room, slowly, deliberately. Each Warlord, each monarch of sin, stood frozen in his wake, as though the weight of his gaze could shape them into something more, something less.

But when he spoke, it was not with malice, not with mockery. His voice was thick with something deeper, older, something that came not from rage but from the slow certainty of time itself, as though he were speaking a truth that had been written long before any of them had taken breath.

"You burn cities, Ira. You own them while they stand." His voice carried the quiet weight of ages, a reminder of the fire that consumed all things, the endless march of destruction that marked the passage of time.

"You hoard wealth, Midas. You own it while it is counted." His gaze flickered toward the gold-dripped monarch, the shadow of greed flickering in his eyes. It was the weight of wealth, of fleeting power, that the Dream King spoke of, a power measured in digits, but never in substance.

"You consume, Gula. You own what you devour." His voice was like a slow drawl, a whisper that carried with it the promise of endless hunger. Gula's hunger was not mere flesh, but dominion over all that could be consumed, twisted, and destroyed.

His eyes flickered toward Carmela, and the air around them seemed to tighten, as if the very room held its breath. "And you, my dear, take pleasure in being the cage rather than the key."

The words landed with the precision of a blade, cutting through Carmela's usual poise. They struck at her pride, but they did so quietly, in the way that an unspoken truth lands heavy in the chest. She did not flinch. She did not speak. Not yet.

Somnus let the silence stretch, each breath a pause, each second a beat where time itself seemed to hold its breath, waiting.

"But in the end," he whispered, his voice thick with an ancient, unspeakable truth, "all of you are only borrowing."

The words fell like a stone into the silence. The weight of them sank deep, settling into the very fabric of the chamber. Somnus did not wait for a response. He did not need to. His words, inevitable as the passing of time, hung in the air like the finality of death itself.

"Because when the dream ends," he continued, as though the waking world was a mere afterthought, "the world wakes up."

Then, with the quiet finality of a verdict that had already been written in the heavens, he posed the question that would unravel it all, that would sever the ties of illusion they had clung to for so long.

"And when it does," he asked, "tell me, who owns the ashes?"

The chamber held its breath. Every Warlord, every monarch of sin, remained silent. Not yet.

The shadows in the room stretched long, like arms reaching for something untouchable. Time, the silent grasp of it, had already passed. Somnus had always known this.

It was no longer about who controlled what. This was no longer a conversation of power. It was a question of what remained when all illusions fell away. When the power they had clung to for centuries, the empires they had built upon blood and sin, crumbled into dust.

The question was no longer about control. It was about survival. About what would rise from the ashes.

Ira did not answer immediately. His chest tightened, the words slipping through his mind but finding no voice.

The silence twisted tighter. Time itself seemed to stretch, an eternity in the space between breaths.

Somnus had made it clear. This room was no longer a place for kings, no longer a place for ambition. It was a room for truths. For darker things than greed, wrath, or desire. It was a room for something older, something much older than all of them.

It was Superbia who broke the silence, their voice low, knowing, like the slash of a blade that cut through the air with surgical precision.

"Ah, Somnus," they said, their voice a blend of authority and mocking amusement. "For someone who revels in dreams, you do so love to remind us of how fragile they are. Ashes?"

Superbia's voice slid through the air, like a velvet whip, slow and deliberate. They leaned forward, their chin resting lightly against interlaced fingers, their gaze never wavering from the Dream King.

It was a casual pose, but it commanded the space in a way that spoke of dominion, quiet, absolute. It was a gesture that did not need to be grand to be felt.

"Tell me, Wrath," they continued, their words sharp with calculated amusement, "who created them?"

The question was simple, but it landed with the weight of a thousand battles fought and lost. Superbia's eyes locked on Ira's, predatory, patient. The room seemed to breathe with the rhythm of their voice.

"War is a wondrous thing, isn't it?" Their words cut through the tension, mocking without malice, piercing without effort. "It consumes, as you so love to do, Ira. But tell me, after all is burned, what remains?"

Their gaze swept over the room like the eyes of a predator tracking its prey. Their presence warped the very air around them, bending it to their will, distorting it with every word.

They did not need to raise their voice.

Superbia had learned long ago that true power was not in what was spoken aloud, but in what hovered behind the silence. The things left unsaid. The truths that were far more dangerous than any bold proclamation.

The name fell into the room like a stone sinking into the deepest waters. Phalaistin.

The very air seemed to tremble, and even the Veil-tech flickered, a subtle tremor passing through the artificial world they had created. Superbia's voice remained even, quiet, but the weight of the name they spoke was impossible to ignore. It was a reminder of devastation, of how fragile even the most invincible empires could be.

"I remember now," they continued, voice still steady. "The Phalaistin lands."

Their words were a dagger wrapped in velvet, dripping with history, with empire, with the ashes of civilizations long forgotten. They did not raise their voice, but it was as if the very room shifted beneath them, as if the Veil-tech itself trembled under the weight of those words.

Superbia did not need grand gestures to make their point. They had mastered the art of making silence the loudest voice in the room.

"We watched from our thrones, did we not?" Superbia's voice was methodical, detached, as if recounting a tale from an ancient tome. The cadence was calm, precise, yet within that calmness, there was something chilling, something far too knowing.

Every word they spoke seemed to sink into the very marrow of the room, dragging the air with it, suffocating any lightness that may have lingered.

"As Wrath and his wolves tore through those lands. As the Sanguine Order painted the rivers red." The words fell like the steady beat of a drum, echoing the rhythm of a march to oblivion. The stillness of the room wrapped itself around the sound, holding it, breathing with it.

A slow exhale followed, delicate, almost indulgent, as if savouring the very weight of destruction, the echo of every life snuffed out beneath the relentless fury of Ira's war. The chamber leaned in, drawn tight by the gravity of Superbia's words. The walls themselves seemed to pulse with anticipation.

"As fire claimed the emerald plains, as iron broke the temples, as the last of their wretched prayers were swallowed by the wind. A people who did not kneel. A people who did not bow. A people who, for all their devotion, did not survive."

Superbia's voice slipped through the words like a cold river, flowing effortlessly, each syllable more precise than the last, each one a testament to the destruction they so readily invoked.

Their fingers tapped against the armrest, a soft, deliberate rhythm. Each tap punctuated their words like a drumbeat, a reminder of the control they wielded. Calm. Unhurried. As though they were simply discussing the weather. A casual recounting of the end of a civilization. There was no remorse in their tone, no hesitation.

Only the calm certainty of one who had seen the full arc of life and death.

Superbia's eyes gleamed, dark, knowing, as if they held the secret to the universe in their gaze.

And then the air shifted, cold, sharp, like a blade cutting through the suffocating heat of the chamber.

"Did you think," they purred, the words drawn out, quiet but imbued with a piercing sharpness that shattered the stillness, "that after all the blood spilled, all the cities razed, nothing remained?"

The silence held its breath. A flicker of realization passed through the room, like a shift in the very fabric of the air. Superbia's next words sliced through that tension, as inevitable as the turn of a page.

"A gift... buried beneath the ashes. The largest manatherium node ever known... still alive, still waiting to be claimed."

The room seemed to shudder at the mention of it. The words hung in the air like an unseen presence, heavy, pulsing.

"The greatest prize lies beneath the ashes, Ira," Superbia's voice cut through the silence again, the weight of their truth pressing against Ira's chest. "What you've destroyed... it's not gone. Not all of it."

The finality of it rang in the air, as though every soul in the chamber could feel it in their bones. There was a prize, a force buried beneath the land Ira had burned. And it was a prize that none of them had counted on. A force that could not be claimed by the simple act of destruction.

Ira's chest tightened, a bitter taste rising in his throat. The world seemed to shift beneath him as the reality of what had been hidden beneath the blood-soaked soil of Phalaistin slammed into him.

The land he had razed, the lives he had sacrificed in his unrelenting campaign, had concealed a power far greater than anything he had ever imagined. A power that now threatened to slip through his fingers, a power he had no right to claim.

Not after everything he had burned. Not after everything he had sacrificed.

The truth of it cut deep, a cold wound in his chest. The weight of his actions, of the lives lost, of the destruction he had wrought, had been for naught.

He had thought himself the conqueror. But now, he understood. He had only been the herald of something far older, far more dangerous.

And it was waiting to be claimed by someone else.

The silence in the room thickened, the weight of Superbia's revelation pressing down on Ira like a vice. The stakes had shifted. What was once his war to claim was now a contest of survival, of possession. And Ira was not certain he would emerge victorious.

Superbia's smile deepened, cruel in its simplicity. "How does one take ownership of what no longer breathes? You would burn it all, but even you cannot claim what is beyond the reach of fire."

Ira's fingers clenched tighter around the stone armrest, his knuckles white, his breath shallow. It wasn't just the land, the kingdom, it was the cost of his wrath, the consequences of a war he had waged blindly.

And the realization struck harder than any sword. He had destroyed everything, and yet it was never his to own. Not after all he had torn apart.

Superbia leaned back, still smiling, their eyes alight with a dangerous glint. "After all, Wrath," they purred, "Can one rule over dust?"

For the first time since the war began, Ira did not respond immediately. It was a flicker, a single, imperceptible moment, an instant where time seemed to stretch, where his mind and body hesitated at the edge of something far darker than rage. A pause so brief that only the most observant could have caught it.

But in a room full of monsters, in a den of kings and queens, nothing went unnoticed. The air thickened, electric, as understanding began to dawn.

Ira's fingers curled deeper into the stone. His molten gaze darkened, unreadable. His grip tightened just barely, just enough for those in the room to feel it, to sense something far more dangerous than blind fury.

It was the truth. And the truth was heavier than any weapon.

A slow inhale. His voice, when it came, was not loud, but it cut through the chamber like a blade through silk. "Then I will unearth it."

The words landed, final. Unshakable.

But before the weight of them could settle, laughter erupted.

Not one. But six.

Each laugh was twisted in its own way, uniquely wrong, and each rang like a bell tolling for something lost, something beyond repair.

Midas leaned back in his seat, swirling the golden liquid in his goblet. His laugh, a rich, knowing sound, dripped from his lips as though the game were already won.

Ira's molten gaze locked onto him, and the tension in the room snapped, taut as a bowstring, ready to snap.

Ira's voice was cold, yet it carried a fury that burned deeper than the words themselves.

"You laugh, Midas? Do you think you've won?" His words sliced through the room, each one a sharp lash, a whip crack that split the air.

"You talk of loyalty like it's just another thing to buy. But you've taken something you'll never own." His gaze darkened, the weight of his grief pressing down like a stone. "You think my son is just another piece to collect, another pawn in your game."

His voice broke, raw and heavy, the words feeling like a hammer against his chest.

"Do you even see what you've done?" His throat tightened, but the words broke free. "You've traded my son's trust for your hollow gold."

Midas's calm only fuelled the fire in Ira. His grip tightened, his fingers digging into the stone as if it were Midas's flesh. "You hoard everything but never possess anything. Not loyalty. Not love. Not even your own soul."

The chamber hummed with low tension, the weight of Ira's declaration pressing down on the room. Midas settled back into his throne, still calm. His gaze never wavered, as if the warlord's words had no impact at all.

But the silence that followed felt heavier, more unbearable. It was not just a statement. It was a declaration of truth. One that spoke not just to Ira, but to every Warlord present.

Power, after all, was something of value. Something tangible. Something to be exchanged. And Midas knew that better than anyone.

Superbia did not speak again. They simply observed, silent and unyielding. They watched as the Warlords wrestled with the consequences of their actions, with the price they had paid.

But one thing was certain: Ira's fire, his fury, would burn the world. But the world would never be enough. Not for him. Not for any of them.

Midas took a deliberate sip, savouring the liquid, as if savouring not just the taste but the tension that had thickened the air around them.

"And wouldn't you know it?" His voice was measured, deliberate, as if speaking to an audience who had no idea what game was truly being played. "I just so happen to know who holds the deeds to Phalaistin's ruins."

His smile was dazzling, sharp as a blade of gold, merciless and gleaming.

"And, of course, for the right price, I could be convinced to part with them."

A pause. A beat.

Then his smirk widened, so insidious it seemed to suck the very light from the room.

"But what am I saying?" His voice lowered, thick with satisfaction, dangerous now. "You don't like ownership, do you? No, no. You just burn things."

He leaned back, his golden robes catching the dim light like the last flickers of a dying star. The gold embroidery on his sleeves gleamed like molten liquid. The room grew colder, the air thickening with his words.

"Do tell me, though. When you dig your grave, will you let me appraise the dirt first?"

The words hung in the air, heavy and suffocating in their finality.

Carmela's laugh broke the silence, sultry and rich, an indulgent melody that oozed from her lips. She ran a single finger along the rim of her goblet, dragging it lazily, as though the entire conversation were but a prelude to something far more thrilling.

"Unearth it?" she echoed, rolling the words slowly along her tongue, savouring them like a forbidden secret. "You speak of it as though it is some lost treasure, buried like the bones of forgotten kings."

Her posture shifted, the Veil glass shimmering in the dim light, its blood-red hue bending into something darker, something blacker, as she leaned forward, eyes gleaming with a playful yet dangerous light.

"Tell me, Ira," she purred, her voice like honey wrapped in poison, "have you ever considered that some things should remain untouched?"

A pause. A dangerous, wicked pause.

"Then again," her smirk deepened, turning sharper, "that would require you to know what it means to leave something unsullied."

She chuckled softly, almost affectionately, but there was nothing soft about it.

Her gaze flickered toward Superbia, the words dripping from her lips like liquid fire. "And, my dear Pride, I must ask," she tilted her head, golden chains shimmering across her silk-clad shoulders, "if Wrath turns everything to ash, what exactly will he bury me in when he finally succumbs to his desires?"

Her voice was mocking. Teasing. But there was something beneath it. Something darker.

A low, rumbling chuckle filled the air. Not soft. Not indulgent. But heavy. Thick. Like something being swallowed whole, and yet it echoed, curling through the chamber like smoke on the wind. It was the sound of something ancient, something that had been waiting. Watching. And now, it had been set free.

Gula exhaled deeply, a sound laden with the weight of something far older than the moment itself.

Her hand reached slowly for the jewel-encrusted goblet that rested by her throne. The Veil-infused liquid within it swirled, shifting between a deep crimson and a shadow as black as night, an unsettling dance of colours that refused to settle.

But she did not drink. Not yet.

Instead, she simply watched Ira, her gaze unwavering, predatory. She observed him as if he were nothing more than prey, waiting to see if he would finally fall into the snare she had set.

"You say you will unearth it," she murmured, her voice thick and rich, like the promise of something too sweet, just before it poisons you. "And yet, do you even know what you hunger for?"

Her obsidian nails, sharp as blades, drummed against the armrest of her massive throne, the sound hypnotic, a slow and deliberate rhythm.

"Phalaistin is gone. Swallowed. Devoured." Her eyes glittered with sharp calculation, sharp enough to carve into the very bones of the room. "Its people? Vanished. Erased. And yet, even in death, they resist."

A soft exhale followed, then a deliberate sip from her goblet, the liquid twisting between the red and black, echoing the turmoil of a land lost to time.

"Do you know, Wrath," she whispered, her words a caress and a bite all at once, "what happens when you take the land from those who worship it?"

She tilted her head slightly, her golden piercings catching the light, gleaming like the eyes of a snake preparing to strike. "They do not fight for power. They do not fight for empire. They fight for memory."

A wicked grin stretched across her lips, cruel and knowing.

"And memory is far harder to kill."

Ira's jaw tensed. Not in rage. No, it was something deeper: memory. As if even Wrath, forged in flame, had ghosts that whispered in his heat, calling to him from a time he had tried so desperately to burn away.

Somnus's laugh was different. Not rich. Not indulgent. Not even cruel. His laugh was weary, tired, as though he had already lived through this moment a thousand times.

He exhaled, his breath slipping through lips that had long since forgotten the taste of passion. The air around him shimmered like liquid shadows, his Veil-forged robes shifting weightlessly, endless as the dreams they were spun from.

"You will unearth it?" he echoed, his voice hollow, like the toll of a bell rung too many times. His eyes, half-lidded and distant, met Ira's not with mockery, but pity.

"How exhausting," he sighed, the words barely more than a whisper, yet they rang through the room like an iron chain dragging across stone. "To believe that power is something you can dig from the ground, rather than something that..."

He raised a single hand, rolling his wrist in the air as though casting off the weight of something too trivial, too fleeting to matter.

"...simply comes to you."

A beat of silence stretched before he offered Ira a slow, languid smile.

"But by all means, Wrath. Keep digging." Another soft exhale. "We all must entertain ourselves somehow."

Invidia, the Serpent of Altura, did not laugh. She didn't need to. Her smile was a thing of darkness, a quiet caress that slid around your ribs like a cold whisper in the night.

Her presence, patient and unyielding, waited, like a predator coiled beneath the earth, always watching.

"You wish to unearth it?" she murmured, her words slipping through the chamber like silk laced with venom.

"How quaint."

Her obsidian braids shifted, each movement like a serpent's coil, her emerald-ringed gaze cutting through the fractured glow of the Black Sun, locking onto Ira as if he were already caught in her gaze. The world around them seemed to bend, the shadows of the room turning darker, more dangerous.

"But tell me, Ira," she mused, her voice smooth as poison, "who do you think already has it?"

The words slid into the room like a cold breath.

Superbia did not laugh. They merely exhaled, a slow, controlled breath that carried with it an ancient knowing.

Their presence stretched, like the weight of a thousand years of empire, unbroken and unyielding.

"A king who cannot shape his own blood," they mused, their voice measured, "and now, a king who does not even know what lies beneath his own ruins."

A single, precise motion followed. Superbia lifted a Veil-inscribed coin from the armrest of their throne, the silver edges gleaming in the room's fractured light. They spun it effortlessly, the coin landing with a soft clink into their palm without a glance.

"As I said before, Wrath," Superbia's voice cut through the room, low and unyielding. "You do not own your empire."

They leaned forward, slowly, deliberately. The air grew heavier with every inch of their movement, thickening with the weight of the truths they carried.

"You merely rule the ruins left behind."

The silence that followed was suffocating, like a noose drawing tighter around Ira's throat. But Ira tore it apart.

The Veil-infused walls of the Bohemian Chamber of Order trembled, the obsidian pillars groaning as if the room itself was waking from a long, unbroken sleep.

The atmosphere shifted, tighter, thicker, as if the very air held its breath.

And then, the fire came.

Not in flame. Not in flickering embers. But in the voice of Wrath itself.

Molten. Roaring. Undeniable.

"You sit here, dripping in decadence, drowning in your own excess, convinced that power is measured in the weight of a coin, in the bed you claim, in the dreams you let fester in sloth and rot."

His fingers curled into fists, digging into the dark steel of his throne. The material hissed beneath his grip, not burning, but warping, bending, bowing to his fury.

And then, he stood.

A predator. A storm. A force of nature, carved into the shape of a man.

"You think I burn because I lack control? That I rage because I am blind?" His voice was iron and ruin, prophecy and war, a blade drawn across the throat of civilization itself.

His molten eyes turned toward Midas, whose goblet still rested in his palm, golden liquid swirling in idle amusement.

"You believe power is something bought?" Ira's lips curled, but there was no mirth in it. Only hunger. Only wrath.

"A throne built on debt is a throne already lost." His molten gaze narrowed, the weight of his words like an iron fist.

"And what is Greed if not the hunger to own what you can never truly possess?"

Midas's fingers tightened around his goblet, but he did not respond. His smile remained unbroken, his golden eyes gleaming with the quiet arrogance of one who believed they were untouchable.

Then, Carmela.

The Queen of Lust, reclining in her seat with amusement, watched him with that sultry, predatory gaze, as if savouring every word he spoke.

"And you..." Ira's voice dropped lower, but it did not lose its heat. His presence pressed into the room, suffocating, undeniable. "You think power lies in desire? That conquest is made with whispers and silk?"

His presence was an assault. A storm in the calm.

"Your empire is built on pleasure. But tell me, Carmela. What happens to a body when it is touched too much?" His gaze sharpened, flickering with brutal knowing. "It loses feeling. It numbs. It craves more, until there is nothing left that will ever satisfy it."

A cruel smirk twisted his lips.

"Lust is not power, Carmela. It is decay wrapped in satin. And in the end, it will consume you just the same."

The air tightened. Every breath felt heavier. Still, he did not stop. His gaze flicked to Gula.

"The insatiable Queen. The Devourer. The one who believes power is the right to take, to consume, to feast until the world is nothing but marrow and dust beneath your feet."

A beat. Ira's voice was molten, each word slow, deliberate, like a hammer upon stone.

"But hunger is not dominion. It is not control. It is need. A mouth that never stops opening. A hole in your stomach that you will never fill."

The silence twisted. The air grew thick, and even Gula's grip on her goblet tightened, her fingers sinking into the crystal as if her own hunger were being laid bare before them.

"The natives do not fear you because you are strong, Gula," Ira's voice burned, relentless, "They despise you because they know the truth."

"You cannot devour them."

The words cut through the air like a blade, the weight of them suffocating, pressing into the chamber until even the Veil-infused walls seemed to tremble. Ira's molten eyes never left Gula, and the room held its breath, waiting.

Somnus's laugh broke the tension. It was not rich, not indulgent, but weary, tired, as though he had heard this song too many times before.

He exhaled, his breath slow and drawn, slipping between the cracks of a thousand forgotten dreams. His Veil-forged robes shimmered with an ethereal glow, endless as time itself, weightless as the very fabric of sleep.

"You will unearth it?" His voice echoed, hollow, detached from any emotion. His eyes, half-lidded, finally met Ira's, but there was no mocking there, only a deep, heavy pity.

"How exhausting," he sighed, the words barely more than a murmur, yet they struck the air like the toll of a distant bell. "To believe that power is something you can dig from the ground, rather than something that..."

He raised a single hand, rolling his wrist in the air as though casting off the weight of something too trivial, too mundane.

"...simply comes to you."

A pause. Then, a slow, languid smile curled at the edges of his lips.

"But by all means, Wrath. Keep digging." Another exhale, soft and effortless. "We all must entertain ourselves somehow."

The words hung in the air, thick with the weight of a truth Ira could feel curling beneath his skin, but he did not let them falter. His gaze turned, sharpening like a blade, flicking across Invidia, the Serpent of Altura.

"You are the only one in this room who does not lie to herself," Ira's voice dropped to a low, dangerous murmur. "Because envy is the only sin that has never denied its nature."

A flicker of a smirk from Invidia, a small thing, sharp and knowing.

"You do not hunger," Ira continued, his words slow and deliberate. "You do not hoard. You do not consume."

He took a step forward, the weight of his presence pushing through the room like a storm about to break.

"You wait."

The words slid between them like poison and prophecy, dark and inevitable.

"You know power cannot be owned. It can only be taken."

Another step, and the tension in the room grew heavier, suffocating. Ira's molten gaze fixed on Invidia as if every word was a question she had already answered.

"But tell me, Serpent," he whispered, each word a cutting edge, "When the moment comes, will you strike? Or will you simply watch?"

The chamber shook. It was subtle, but unmistakable, the very foundation of their being trembling at the thought of Ira's wrath unleashed.

Then, Superbia. The Monarch who towered above them all. The Warlord who never fully revealed themselves, always holding the reins of their power with a calm, impenetrable grip.

Pride incarnate.

Ira's breath was slow. Steady. His gaze fixed on Superbia as though he were carving the very air between them with his intent.

"You ask who owns the ashes?" Ira's voice did not rise. It cut through the silence, sharp as a dagger's edge. His words were not a question, but an answer already given. "I own them."

The words, heavy with certainty, settled like a stone dropped into the still waters of the chamber. And yet, something colder lingered in the air.

"You think Wrath destroys?" Ira's voice became an ember, flickering in the quiet, building into something undeniable. "That my sin does nothing but burn?"

He exhaled, the weight of his words breaking through the stillness.

"You see only the flames. But you forget what fire leaves behind."

His molten gaze flickered beneath the Black Sun's twisted glow, and for a moment, the very air seemed to crackle, thick with the unsaid.

"You think power is in control. In dominion. In the structures left behind." Ira's voice dropped to a dark whisper, as if sharing a forbidden truth. "But power is something far greater than any of you have ever dared to understand."

A slow, terrible smirk spread across his lips, twisting his features into something both devastating and inevitable.

"Power is what survives."

The words curled through the chamber, pressing into the veins of the Warlords like a truth they had never wanted to hear, a truth that would not be ignored.

"Burn the land. Erase the names. Reduce everything to cinders."

Ira took a step forward, the ground beneath his feet hissing from the heat of his presence. The room seemed to hold its breath, anticipating the weight of his next words.

"And still, something rises from the ashes."

Another step.

"Something that was never meant to be born. Something forged, not from control, not from indulgence, but from survival itself."

He stopped. Towered. His presence engulfed the room like the fury of the storm itself.

"I do not own my empire. I am my empire."

A single breath, drawn deeply, the world itself suspended between moments. The weight of his final words lingered, burning through the very air around them.

"As long as I draw breath, Wrath will not fall. I will not fall."

The Owl above them watched, its unblinking gaze piercing the chamber, a relic of truths too ancient to be denied.

The Lion waited, its gaze frozen in time, an embodiment of wrath, restrained only by the thinnest edge of will.

And the Chamber itself remembered. It remembered every empire that had tried to master the sins it was built to contain. Every throne that had risen only to be consumed by the very fires of the desires it had been built upon.

"The empire burns, and in its flames, all the names that thought they mattered are undone. The monuments crack, and in the rubble, the blood-stained earth laughs. And from the smoke, a voice echoes, not asking, but proclaiming: 'I have always been here. And you are nothing without me.'"

Null Gospel, Book I, Verse 18.

***

CHAPTER EIGHTEEN:

The Blood That Flowers

"The fire did not fall from heaven, nor rise from hell. It was birthed from the bones of the broken. For wrath is no fleeting rage. It is the marrow of memory, and memory bleeds through time, as long as blood stains the earth."

Fragment of the Exiled Codex, Volume I, Tablet 19.

Tyranny does not arrive like a storm. It is not a sudden crash. It is a creeping whisper, a patient erosion of the soul. It coils itself within the roots of society, spreading its tendrils into every crevice until the tree is nothing but brittle bark, ready to collapse beneath its own weight.

It does not scream.

It murmurs.

Its voice is sewn into laws, stitched into the fabric of commands, laced into every breath of every waking hour. The terror comes not with violence, but with silence. A quiet normalization of horror, until it is so ingrained that even the air feels poisoned.

The Sanguine Order did not strike like a storm. They came like a sickness, spreading through the land until the people could no longer remember a time before decay. True destruction does not echo in the clash of blades; it lies in the silence after, when hope turns to dust in the quiet. It is not the fire of war but the cold erosion of will.

They waged war in whispers, not in battle cries, strangling the nation with hunger, thirst, and slow despair, until hope bled out grain by grain, and life was nothing but an echo of what it had once been.

The Sanguine Order did not merely kill. They did not just burn. They starved. They poisoned. They destroyed not with the blade, but with the mind. Severing ties to history, to culture, to the belief that people could ever rise again.

And when the bones of civilization lay in dust, they laughed. Not with joy, but with the cold satisfaction of erasure.

Nyxmar, the land of shadows and valleys, had been the last bastion of resistance. Its people, the Duskborn, had always known war.

Not by desire.

War had always come to them, creeping into the edges of their world like the tide before a storm. They did not seek conflict. Conflict sought them. And when the Sanguine Order arrived, they brought the weight of Pyrrha's doctrine upon their backs like the judgment of a god.

The first strike was not against the warriors. No. It was against the lifelines.

The rivers, once veins of silver weaving through the land, turned black with rot. The poisons they poured in crept like venom through the bloodstream of the earth. The very life that had once sustained the people twisted into a slow death. Flesh peeled from bone. Blood curdled and thickened into stone.

Children's eyes clouded. Mothers cradled their dead with arms that no longer knew strength. Their tears vanished before they could fall. The soil, once fertile, refused even the pretence of growth. Crops withered. Roots shrivelled. The land spat out all attempts at healing.

Then came the fire.

It was not a blaze meant to cleanse or consume. It was a symphony of precision and annihilation. The flames did not rage. They hummed like executioners. The great libraries of Nyxmar, ancient repositories of knowledge and blood-memory, turned to ash in a single night.

The Order did not seek victory. They sought erasure. For a people without a past has no foundation. No marrow to stiffen the spine. No name to cry in grief. Without memory, they are already ghosts.

It was not fire that delivered the final insult, but the false promise of safety.

They promised safety, a lie wrapped in compassion. Survivors, hollow-eyed and broken, were led to sanctuaries where oaths were whispered, promises stitched into their hearts. And in the dark, the sky tore open. The bombs fell.

They called it Operation Sanctuary. Because even genocide demands a name it can live with.

No warning. No mercy. Only fire. Only silence.

The dead did not have graves. Their names were torn from stone. Their bodies turned to ash. No dirges were sung. No hands reached for them in mourning. They became wind. They became nothing.

If Nyxmar was burned, Ashra'tel was bled dry.

The Emberborn were not warriors. They were healers. Keepers of the sacred pulse. Their craft was grown from the soil and sung down through generations. They touched the spirit of the land and called it kin. But the Sanguine Order did not come to kill them. They came to sever them from the sacred. To cauterize the lineage so completely that no child would ever learn to mend what had been broken.

The sacred groves were gutted. The healing springs fouled. Apothecaries incinerated. The healers were not merely slain. They were unmade. Their legacy burned to silence beneath the boots of ambition.

And then came the gifts.

Airdropped. Wrapped in gleaming promise. Aid, they called it.

Humiliation, handed to the starving. Hope, poisoned.

The desperate ran to the packages. They tore them open with trembling hands. Inside, death waited.

The food twisted in their bellies like a dark incantation. The water dissolved their strength, corrupted their breath. Death did not come swiftly. It lingered. Slow. Intimate. They felt their bodies betray them, their own blood rebelling. Each heartbeat was an accusation.

And still, hope refused to die.

Weeks later, broken and hollow, they were offered one final salvation.

They walked. Hundreds. Then thousands. Dragging themselves across the scorched ashscape. The land of their ancestors, now a cemetery without tombstones.

They reached the new sanctuaries. Their eyes held nothing. Their hands gripped nothing. And then the sky betrayed them again.

Precision strikes. Cold. Clean. Delivered by a silence deeper than death.

No one escaped. They had offered their last spark of belief. It had led them into the slaughter.

While Phalaistín bled, another land stood unyielding against the tide. The Tideborn of Sablemar, masters of the sea, had no need for armies. Their cities floated on the ocean's breath, inviolate, untamed. Woven of driftwood, coral, and prayer. They had carved their lives into the rhythm of the waves. No empire could touch them. Their walls were tide and storm.

But the Sanguine Order was not an empire. It was the shape beneath inevitability. It did not break the gates. It erased the water.

They built no fleets. They raised no sails. Instead, they sank machines beneath the surface. Vast pumps, iron-jawed and faceless, crouched like titans in the deep. Their breath was chemical. Their will was poison.

The fish died first. Bellies up, bloated and blind, they surfaced in silence. Then the birds fell. Wings frozen mid-cry, spiralling from the sky. And finally, the Tideborn. They who had danced with storms. Who had sung the sea into surrender. Felt the corruption seep into their marrow.

At first, they believed themselves immune. They had mastered the tides. Their bodies had been shaped by salt, their lungs by spray, their hearts by centuries of survival. But this was not death. It was decay. It was a slow unravelling. An erasure written in water.

The children stopped growing. Their bones cracked, brittle as sun-dried reeds. Their minds clouded. The sharpness of thought dulled beneath a creeping fog. The once-unstoppable warriors, masters of the deep, found their limbs heavy. Their strength faltered. Their agility dissolved into clumsy, faltering steps. The very essence of their existence began to wither.

And then, the Order came. Not as invaders. As saviours.

They offered rations. Medicines. Antidotes. Promises of salvation. But every promise bore a cost. The cost of surrender.

Some Tideborn, desperate and broken, took the offer. Their hope lay crushed beneath the weight of suffering. Others, those who still clung to the ember of rebellion, fought until the very end. It did not matter. The Sanguine Order had already won the moment the first drop of poison touched the sea.

Phalaistín did not die. Not truly. Because war is never just about destruction. It is about memory.

Every orphan created that day remembers. Every child who survived the burning, the poisoning, the drowning remembers. And memory, when it gathers inside enough voices, becomes a weapon greater than any blade.

The Sanguine Order believed they had won. They burned the histories. They shattered the cultures. They slaughtered the old generation. But war does not end in a single generation. Though Phalaistín may bleed. Though its lands may scar. Though its rivers may carry poison and its fields nothing but ash.

Its people still remember.

And the memory of suffering. The memory of fire. The memory of wrath. These are the foundations upon which every revolution is built.

Fire remembers.

It is not a whisper in the wind. It does not fade, nor forgive. It carves itself into the bones of the world. Fire carves itself into the marrow of history. It leaves marks that cannot be erased. It etches its will into the bones of the world. It leaves only scorched remnants of what once stood unshaken.

In Pyrrha, where war was not waged for conquest but for permanence, fire was more than a weapon. It was creed.

The Sanguine Order did not simply burn Phalaistín. They reduced it to dust, rewriting reality with famine and fear. Their will was etched into the flesh of a people who dared to resist. This was not war. This was annihilation. Sculpted with precision. The art of erasure honed into mastery.

The first bomb fell upon a school. A place where children once traced their fingers along books now turned to cinders. Laughter had danced in the air. Now it vanished into the acrid howl of flame. The walls were painted with the wisdom of ancestors. Steel and fire crushed them.

Those who survived, who crawled beneath broken desks or ran with shattered breath, were not spared for long. The second bomb fell upon the hospital. The third struck the reservoir. Life itself was methodically dismantled.

The first bomb struck at 03:12.

The second at 03:17.

The third at 03:24.

A school. A hospital. A reservoir.

By dawn, the heart of Phalaistín had been erased.

And then came Sablemar. A land once untouchable, its heart bound to the ocean. The tides, once the lifeblood of its people, now turned black with oil and stained red with blood. They did not come with ships or armies, but with famine and sickness, poisoning the waters before burning the very vessels meant to float them above the storm. The floating cities, once proud bastions of life, became nothing but reefs of twisted metal and sunken ghosts, drowned by the Order's silent war.

Their people watched as their homes dissolved beneath the waves.

In Nyxmar, where night once whispered ancient truths, the Warlords turned darkness into suffocation. The sacred wilds of the Duskborn were no longer wild. They were dissected. They were desecrated. The forests did not burn in rage. They were harvested in silence. Trees fell one by one, each cut a wound the land could not mend.

The Duskborn fled, but found no sanctuary. They were given corridors. Traps disguised as mercy. Each path ending in ambush.

The only gift was a swift death.

In Ashra'tel, the land of endless canyons, war came not with fire alone. The Sanguine Order did not send soldiers. They sent silence. They dammed the rivers. They rerouted the Vein. The Emberborn did not fall to swords. They fell to thirst. The fields split open. The crops curled into dust. And when they sought aid, they were met with a final cruelty. Poison draped in kindness.

Rations laced with toxins. Water laced with decay. Medicine that sealed wounds and cursed the blood. When the starving knelt for hope, the sky opened with its last deception. Bombs disguised as relief fell upon the faithful.

Not even the dead were left untouched. When rebellion gasped its final breath and the wind carried only silence, the Warlords remained. They built atop the bones. Their factories rose from the dust of cultures they had crushed. The Sanguine Order did not simply erase Phalaistín. They replaced it.

And yet.

The tree still stood.

Nahara Sunshadow turned the page of the ancient book resting in her lap. Her voice did not tremble. Her words did not break beneath the burden of what had been spoken. Before her, three children sat in stillness. Tariq, the Tideborn boy. Ilyas, of the Emberborn. Aisara, the dusk-eyed girl of Nyxmar.

Their faces were stone, but their eyes drank the tale like the last light of a dying sun. Shadows clung to them. Not with fear, but with knowing.

"It wasn't always like this," she said. Her voice was soft. The kind of softness that follows thunder.

Her fingers passed over the ink. The script was worn, but not faded. Preserved not by time's mercy, but by desperate hands that refused to forget. This was not a relic locked behind glass. This was a living memory. The spine cracked and mended. The pages bent and creased. Every mark a fingerprint from the past. Memory, held with reverence, because it was all that remained.

Nahara looked up. Her violet eyes caught the lantern light, casting strange shapes across her face. There was sorrow there. Or something older than sorrow.

"The land was not always a graveyard," she said.

Aisara's voice came as a whisper. "Then what was it?"

Nahara smiled, slow and secret. "Let me show you."

She turned the page.

And Phalaistín unfolded.

Not the land of fire and bone. Not the ash. Not the poison. But a dream remembered. A breath exhaled long ago. A truth not yet lost.

Her fingers hovered over the next illustration. Lines carved by memory. Shadows shaped by reverence. The calligraphy pulsed like veins through the earth's heart. Nahara breathed out, a slow release of time. The air itself seemed to pause.

"Before the world burned," she said, "before the rivers dried and the soil broke, before the Warlords turned the land to dust, there was Ashra'tel."

The children leaned closer. Their gazes fixed. Their breaths caught.

Around them, the lanterns flickered. The light danced over old stone. Shadows stretched, long and silent. The kind that knew how to wait.

She did not turn the page. She released it, and let the next memory rise on its own.

Ashra'tel had been carved into the bones of the world. Its canyon-woven valleys held by cliffs that reached skyward like sentinels carved by ancient breath. The sun did not simply rise there. It emerged in fire. It painted the sky in molten gold and sorrowed crimson, as if the heavens wept light. The land burned, not to destroy, but to awaken.

Its fire gave life.

The Emberborn ruled not with crowns, but with stewardship. They did not build monuments to themselves. They carved sanctuaries into the cliffs. Their homes breathed with the earth. Their ceilings opened to the stars. They did not own the land. They walked beside it. They did not command nature. They listened. They learned its rhythm. And they sang it back.

But when the age of conquest came, the Warlords did not come to walk beside them. They came to take.

Nahara turned the page again.

The rivers were the first to be stolen. The great veins of Ashra'tel, twisting through the canyon floors, feeding the land with life, were severed.

The Sanguine Order, ruthless and silent, dammed the waters and hoarded them in great reservoirs high above the land. From below, the Emberborn watched as their lifeblood was locked behind stone and iron they could never breach. Hope was stolen first, taken in the form of water. Their salvation, stripped away.

Then came the droughts.

The crops withered to nothing. Their husks brittle as the remnants of forgotten dreams. The fruit trees, once heavy with crimson pomegranates and golden citruses, bore only shrivelled shells. The wells ran dry. And with them, the very breath of life vanished from the soil.

The Emberborn, broken in pride but not in spirit, sent envoys. Their desperate pleas were sealed in dignity, their final words bound in parchment and sorrow. But the Warlords sent only silence.

Then the relief arrived.

It came wrapped in silver. Every parcel stamped with the cold insignia of the Sanguine Order. Pallets of food. Jugs of water. Sacks of grain. Hope, delivered with the weight of a promise that had no mercy in its heart.

The starving emerged. They crawled from their homes, bodies bent by thirst, hands trembling with need as they reached for salvation.

Nahara's voice did not falter. "The first to eat," she murmured, "were the children."

Aisara's breath caught. Her hands pressed into her lap. But she did not look away.

"They did not know," Nahara continued, her voice tightening, "that it had been laced with poison."

The book did not describe the horror in full. But it did not need to. The truth had already been written into memory. Etched into the land. Stained into the blood of history.

The Warlords did not kill the Emberborn with steel. They killed them with kindness.

They waited. They watched as the sickness spread, slow and certain, through bodies too weak to resist. They watched as parents cradled dying children, their cries echoing long after the canyons fell silent.

And when madness came with hunger, when desperation bent the last survivors to their knees, they ran toward the next shipment. Hollow-eyed. Starved. Reaching for any scrap that might grant another day of life.

That was when the bombs fell.

Each detonation carved the sacred valleys into graves. One after another. Measured. Precise. The Sanguine Order did not wage war. They conducted it. They did not conquer the Emberborn. They erased them.

But Nahara's hands did not linger on the pages of ruin.

She turned the page again.

And there, beneath an ink-woven sun, surrounded by scorched earth and hollowed stone, stood the last great tree of Ashra'tel.

Not a monument. Not a relic.

A defiance.

Its roots ran deep, far below the reach of conquest. It had survived where nothing should have. And from its branches, there were seeds.

Not yet planted.

But held.

Carried.

Nahara Sunshadow lifted her gaze. The weight of centuries rested in her spine, a burden shaped by years and sharpened by memory. The three children before her, Tariq the Tideborn, Ilyas the Emberborn, Aisara the Duskborn, sat silent. Their faces were carved from stillness, but their eyes flickered with something older than youth.

Hunger.

Not for food.

For truth.

They had been told of devastation. But now, they were being given something else. The roots of revolution. The first whisper of return.

Tariq's hands clenched, skin tight over bone. His jaw didn't tremble with rage. It ground against the weight of years.

He opened his mouth, but the words... they were too heavy, too stained with the screams he couldn't forget. The scream within him wasn't his alone. It belonged to the dead, to the forgotten, to every lost voice that never had the chance to rise.

His grief had long ceased to be his own. It was a legacy, inherited like a mantle too heavy to shed.

His fingers twitched, just once, a reflex he didn't notice. It was the kind of movement a Tideborn might make when testing the edge of water. As if part of him still didn't trust what was meant to give life.

Ilyas stared into the book, his eyes lost in the flickering shadows. The lantern light caught his gaze, turning his amber irises to smouldering embers, half-buried beneath the weight of a past too dark to articulate.

He was not waiting. He was bracing. His stillness was not peace. It was a storm held at bay by a thread, an ancient fury tempered only by his own restraint.

In the flame's reflection, something pulsed. Not rage. A memory.

Not grief. A vow.

A storm curled inside him. Something purer. A defiance that did not ask permission.

Aisara remained silent, her eyes lost somewhere deeper than the present. Her fingers traced the edges of her tunic, stitch by stitch, as though each thread was a thread of something she could hold. Something that might help her remember who she was, before everything turned to dust.

She pressed her palm to the cold stone, as if trying to feel the heartbeat of a land she no longer recognized. Where the dead still whispered in the dust, and the living had forgotten how to mourn.

In the stillness of her, there was a silence that spoke louder than screams. She had endured too much to cry.

Nahara exhaled slowly. The breath of one who had witnessed time collapse and rise again. She closed the book. The sound of the pages settling echoed across the stone. The weight of the tale lingered in the room. Heavy. Sacred. Nothing more needed to be said. The children understood what the Warlords feared.

The Emberborn had died.

But the fire had not.

The silence that followed was not made of hesitation. It was reverence. Grief demands space. And truth cannot be hurried. Nahara let the silence grow. It pressed against the walls. It pressed into the bones. It settled, slow and deep, like roots beneath stone.

The lanterns flickered. Their glow traced shadows across the walls. The children's silhouettes rose and fell in the firelight, like memories that refused to vanish. Ghosts shaped from loss.

Then Nahara turned the page.

The silence in the room swelled.

No one moved. Not even the flame.

The children stared into the spaces between words, as if expecting the dead to speak through silence, memory, and the breathless hush that follows horror.

"Nyxmar," she said. The name did not fall like a word. It arrived like a rite. A name not of a place but of a spirit.

She traced the outline of a city that no longer existed. A city where the rivers kissed the shores. Where sand met twilight in hush and heat. Where the air once carried the scent of myrrh and lavender through streets paved in light. Nyxmar had never been a kingdom of blades. It had been a sanctum of wisdom.

Before the ruin, before the ash, before the shadow of the Sanguine Order darkened the world, Nyxmar had been sanctuary. Its grand libraries were carved of marble and memory. Their halls held the breath of scholars, their footsteps echoing like chants. Poets spoke beneath the colonnades. Their verses etched themselves into stone. Healers moved among the sick without price. Their hands were steady. Their eyes clear.

It had been a city of light.

Not the cold blaze of conquest. A warm glow born of peace.

And the Sanguine Order extinguished it.

Nahara turned the page.

The burning of the Grand Library came first. A wound opened in silence. The scrolls. The tomes. The words of a thousand generations. All consumed in a single night.

The elders had pleaded. They stood before the emissaries of the Warlords, their palms open. Their voices calm. Their last words sealed in parchment. "We have no weapons. We have no armies. We have only knowledge."

The emissaries had smiled. Thin. Cruel.

"That is precisely the problem."

So they set fire to the archives. They watched as centuries turned to ash. The people wept. The Warlords did not blink.

Then came the Purge.

Nahara did not look at the children. She did not need to. She felt how they listened now. The stillness had changed.

She turned the page.

"The Warlords do not fight like men," she said. Her voice dropped, not in fear, but in truth. "They do not meet you in battle. They do not stand on even ground. They win before the first arrow flies."

The people of Nyxmar were given a choice. Submit or vanish.

When they refused to bend, when they would not allow the Order to rewrite them, the choice was taken.

The streets ran red that night.

Not from war.

From execution.

The physicians who once healed were dragged into the marble corridors and shot. Their bodies collapsed beside the lives they had saved. The poets. The artists. The scholars. They were not spared. Their tongues were cut. Their hands broken. Their names buried.

The Warlords understood what Nyxmar did not.

Knowledge was power.

And power must be caged.

But even as the flames rose. Even as silence fell. Nyxmar did not die.

Because knowledge, real knowledge, was never housed in ink or parchment. It was housed in people. And some had escaped. Not many.

But enough.

Enough to carry what remained of Nyxmar's wisdom into the shadows, into the desert, into the hidden corners of the world where the Order's grasp had not yet reached. Enough to ensure that no empire, no army, no tyrant could ever truly erase what had been written into the bones of history itself.

Nahara exhaled. Her fingers rested on the final illustration. The ruins of Nyxmar stood silhouetted against an ink-stained moon. The city was gone. But its spirit was not.

Tariq, the Tideborn boy, clenched his fists. His voice was quiet, but steady. "They wanted to erase them."

Nahara nodded. "Yes."

Aisara, the Duskborn girl, tilted her head. Her eyes searched the depths of the tale. "But they didn't."

Nahara smiled. Soft. Knowing. "No."

Her gaze shifted then to Ilyas. The Emberborn boy had not spoken, but his amber eyes burned. Not with sadness. Not with grief. But with something far older. Something far deeper. Something that could not be erased. Something that would never die.

Nahara turned the page once more. The inked lines of the map shifted under the lantern light, casting jagged shadows across the walls like cracks in glass. Her voice remained steady. Each syllable carried the weight of history.

Nahara paused.

Her hand hovered over the page, trembling not with fear, but with the weight of what had yet to be spoken.

Even the children leaned back.

This was no longer memory.

This was inheritance.

"Sablemar."

The name itself was iron-bound. Unyielding. Where Nyxmar had been a city of wisdom, and Ashra'tel a land of shifting sands and silence, Sablemar had been a fortress. A land of mountains wreathed in mist. Rivers that carved through the earth like battle scars. Valleys where the wind howled like wolves mourning the fallen.

It was not a land that invited conquest. It was a land that swallowed it whole.

She traced her fingers over the jagged ridges sketched across the parchment. The veins of rivers that had once been lifelines. The cities that had once stood defiant against the tides of war.

Once.

She inhaled deeply. "The Sanguine Order never meant to take Sablemar the way they took the other lands," she said. Her voice let the truth settle like dust over the children's thoughts. "They knew the land would never be tamed. They knew the people would never submit."

She let the silence bear the weight of that truth before continuing.

"So they did not seek to rule Sablemar. They sought to eradicate it."

Tariq's breath caught. It was a sound so small it nearly vanished in the hush. But Nahara noticed. She always noticed. The boy, despite his tender age, had already borne the weight of war. His hands, clenched with the grief of ancestors, spoke a story deeper than his years.

He had seen the aftermath.

He carried the ghosts.

"They did not come as conquerors," Nahara said. Her voice was sharper now. Her words cut clean through the dim air. "They came as executioners."

The first blow was not fire. It was not swords. It was hunger.

Sablemar's strength had always been its self-sufficiency. The people lived as one with the land. They forged their own steel. They tilled the earth with hands that knew nothing but survival's rhythm. The Sanguine Order understood the futility of breaking their weapons. It was not the blades they needed to destroy. It was the will behind them.

So they poisoned the rivers.

But not all at once. That would have been too quick. Too merciful. They let the water remain clear. Remain cool. Remain drinkable. Until it wasn't. Until the sickness began.

It started with the children. Fevers that would not break. Limbs that would not move. Eyes that remained closed, unseeing, as if the world itself had dimmed. Then the elders. Then the warriors. One by one. The strong grew weaker. The land's lifeblood drained until only echoes remained.

When the wells ran dry and the rivers turned to death, the people turned to the rain. But the skies refused to weep.

The Order had mastered the Veil. They had twisted storms into weapons and droughts into submission. For Sablemar, they simply stole the rain. One drop at a time.

Months passed. Crops withered into brittle husks. Livestock collapsed in the fields, their bodies statues of hunger and heat. But the people endured. They rationed. They adapted. They survived.

And the Order waited.

Because starvation is not a fire. It is a whisper. A slow war. It begins with emptiness. It ends with silence.

Nahara turned the page.

The inked mountains of Sablemar loomed dark against the parchment. Still unbroken. Still standing. The Order had made one miscalculation. Sablemar's people had never relied on their stomachs to fight.

When the food vanished, they turned to the stone. Roots, bark, moss between rocks. When the water fled, they carved channels into the peaks. They melted snow. They caught morning dew in tightly woven cloth. They starved. But they did not fall.

And when starvation failed, the Order sent fire.

Not soldiers.

Machines.

Colossal constructs of Veil-bound metal. Their bodies were forged from engines and death. They descended from the skies like gods long forsaken. Their shadows fell over the starving. Over the weary. Over the ones who had lost too much to surrender now.

But the people of Sablemar did not kneel.

The mountains became shields. Ravines became traps. The ruins became weapons. The Order had forged its own mistake. They had left just enough survivors to make war eternal.

The war did not end in Sablemar.

It became Sablemar.

A war not of armies, but of will.

A war that could not be won.

Because always, in the dark, there would be one more rebel. One more strike. One more child who had watched their parents die and remembered.

Nahara adjusted the book. Her fingers brushed the tattered edge of a page that had known too many hands. The lantern flickered, its flame casting restless shadows that danced along the stone. The air was thick now. Saturated with memory. The children did not move. Their eyes drank every word as though it were breath itself.

Aisara spoke. A whisper only the fire could hear. "Are they still fighting?"

Nahara met her gaze. Steady. "Always."

And somewhere, beneath a sky stripped of mercy, in a land where war never slept, among mountains that bore the names of the fallen, the fire still burned.

The lantern flickered once more. Shadows stretched and swirled. Dust turned slowly in the light. Beyond the walls, the wind called through hollow corridors, winding through archways carved with forgotten tongues.

Outside, Phalaistín bled beneath a sky that had turned its face away. But here, inside this room of stone and silence, the scent of oil and parchment softened the cruelty of time.

This room was memory.

The children, small and carved from the grit of survivors, sat close. Their eyes wide. In their gaze, the fire lived.

Nahara looked up.

The ceiling above was etched with ridges older than empire. Symbols cut by hands that had never asked permission. The murals told stories that no conqueror could silence. No tyrant could unwrite.

One symbol sat at the centre. A tree split by lightning, its roots wrapped around a flame. Its branches reached into the stars. Below it, three figures knelt in shadow. Their eyes were fire. Their hands held seeds.

The truth was simple.

Where there is power, where there is cruelty, there will always be resistance.

She closed the book.

The final words settled like embers.

For a breath, she held still.

Nahara's words hung in the air, the silence pressing down like the weight of centuries. For a breath, the world held still. The children, faces turned to stone, understood.

The fire was not done. It had not died with their ancestors. It had only waited.

And in the stillness, when all had been said, the truth that had been buried beneath their bones rose once more.

"History is not a scroll, but a wound. One that festers, never healed by time. It bleeds into the now, carving scars into the living. And when the silence grows thick enough, it doesn't whisper. It howls through us."

Null Gospel, Book I, Verse 19.

***

CHAPTER NINETEEN:

The Chamber of Thrones and Ghosts

"When kings forget, the earth does not. The roots drink blood, the stones weep fire. And when crowns crumble to ash, it is the soil that carries the names of the fallen in a roar."

Fragment of the Exiled Codex, Volume I, Tablet 20.

The air held its breath, not the hush of sleep, nor the stillness of peace, but the silence that coils before a return. It was the kind of quiet that remembered fire.

Then she lifted her head, feeling it before she heard it. A shift in the air. A presence just beyond the walls. The moment stretched, thin, sharp. And then, the knock came. It was not loud, not a thunderous demand or violent summons. It was soft, measured, three slow raps against the ancient wood, as if the past itself had reached through the silence to announce its return.

The children did not speak, did not move. Their eyes turned to Nahara, all at once. She did not rise. Her gaze remained fixed on the door, her breath held in stillness, not fear, but preparation. Her hand rested on the closed book, fingers splayed across its worn leather, steadying the weight of the world beneath her palm.

Another knock. No urgency, no repetition. Just the echo of it hanging in the thick air, unsettling in its restraint. Tariq's knuckles whitened around the handle of his small dagger. It was a child's weapon, barely sharpened, but carried with a reverence that made it more than steel.

Ilyas shifted, his frame still, but his eyes blazed. Aisara, unmoving, watched the flame within the lantern as though waiting for it to flicker a signal.

Nahara stood. She moved with the gravity of one who had buried centuries in silence. Her robes whispered against the stone floor as she stepped toward the door, each footfall absorbed by the hush that had taken the room. Her shadow stretched behind her, long and steady, cast by the trembling lantern that now seemed too small to hold the dark at bay. She did not reach for a weapon; she reached for the latch.

The door opened.

Outside, the wind pulled softly at the edges of her robe. The corridor beyond was shadowed, the torches long since burned low. The air smelled of dust and cold metal. But the figure standing there was neither storm nor spectre. He was a man, young, though wearied. His eyes hollowed by sleepless nights, by flight, by grief etched in lines deeper than his years. Across his chest, he bore the sigil of the Sablemar resistance, not carved into armour, but burned into fabric rough with ash and old blood.

He did not bow.

He spoke, his voice coarse with dust. "They've moved on the eastern range. Two villages razed. The old paths are gone."

Nahara nodded. She did not ask how many had died. The silence already told her.

Behind her, the children had risen. No longer frozen, not afraid, but listening.

The man looked past her. His eyes caught the glow of the lantern, the book, the children. Something in his face shifted, not relief, not hope, but something heavier. Something earned.

"We need to go," he said.

Nahara stepped aside. The wind coiled through the chamber like a serpent, tasting the stories that lingered in the air. The children did not ask where they were going, did not ask if they would return. They gathered what little they carried, their hands steady. Each one stepped forward, not as a child, but as a vessel of memory, shaped by the stories carved into them like scripture.

Nahara took the book last. She did not hide it. She wrapped it in a cloth embroidered with the sigils of Nyxmar, Ashra'tel, and Sablemar, threadbare now, faded by time, but still defiant. She tucked it beneath her arm and turned once more to the flame that had lit their path. She did not extinguish it. She left it burning.

Behind them, the room remained, a sanctuary now empty of breath, but full of ghosts. On the stone floor, the dust stirred, caught in the drafts of fate. The murals above watched in silence, their truths unbroken. And far beyond the mountains, where the sky met the ruined horizon, where the bones of empires lay buried beneath sand and snow, the wind carried a name.

Phalaistín.

Not a grave.

A vow.

*

The great iron doors of the Bohemian Chamber of Order groaned open, rumbling like an awakening earth. The air thickened, the flicker of candlelight shrinking under the weight of something darker, undeniable. Footsteps. Measured. Not hurried, not hesitant, but deliberate. The rhythm of inevitability.

The Three Pyres entered first. Their silhouettes cut through the gloom like apparitions of war: Zephir. Veyna. Dain. Their forms were cloaked in the ember glow of ceremonial torches. Their cloaks were battle-worn, stained with the dust of war, yet embroidered with the insignia of Pyrrha's judgment in stark crimson, a visual manifestation of their unyielding loyalty. Their presence commanded the room's attention, not because of the weapons they bore or the silent authority with which they carried themselves, but because they did not escort prisoners. They escorted symbols.

And then, emerging from the shadows, the three ambassadors of Phalaistin stepped forward. Bound, yet unbowed. Their chains did not clink. They did not drag behind them like symbols of defeat. They did not rattle with the weight of submission. They sang, not of their captivity, but of defiance.

Their voices rang out, sharp and heavy, breaking the stillness of the night. As they entered the Bohemian Chamber of Order, they did not hesitate. They did not bow before the Council of Seven, nor shrink before wrath, greed, gluttony, pride, lust, sloth, or envy. They walked with the weight of ruin in every step, the mark of loss carved into their very bones. They had lost everything, and in losing it, they had gained something far more dangerous than power. They had nothing left to fear.

The Seven Warlords, seated upon their thrones of stone and shadow, watched them enter. Some eyes flickered with curiosity. Others glimmered with amusement, a faint hint of mockery tugging at their lips. A few gleamed with hunger, sensing something beyond the usual plea.

But all of them, regardless of intent, felt it. An undeniable shift in the air. In that moment, something had entered the chamber that could not be bought, nor broken. Something that had no price, no weakness.

Silence fell over the room, the kind of silence that settles only when something far beyond war enters a space. The Warlords, once confident in their unchallenged dominion, understood what stood before them. It was not a desperate cry for survival. It was not a supplicant seeking favour. No. This was the last flicker of something they had sought to destroy. And yet, despite all their efforts, it still stood.

The Bohemian Chamber of Order, the citadel of dominion, pulsed with an ancient power. The obsidian columns that rose toward the heavens were not merely structures. They were monuments to conquest, to the suffocating embrace of tyranny.

Above, the ceiling was veined with circuitry and relics of war, silent witnesses to a past where nations had been dismantled with words and the weight of calculated intent. And now, before the Warlords, three figures stood. Voices that would no longer be silenced, and lands that would no longer bow.

Elyas Rahim, the Scholar of Ashra'tel. An ember that burned not with steel, but with the fire of knowledge. His robes, once the crimson hues of Ashra'tel's canyons, now bore the weight of his land's dust. The relics of his people's history were woven into his very being. Yet, it was not his clothing that commanded attention. It was the conviction embodied in every inch of him. Elyas was not just a man. He was the living embodiment of defiance, wielding the sharpest of all blades: truth itself.

He knew that knowledge, real knowledge, was the weapon feared most by the Warlords. History was his weapon. And with it, he would carve the truth into the minds of those who thought themselves untouchable.

Anarya Vhailar, the daughter of war. The blood of Pyrrha's Iron Flame coursed through her veins. But she was no soldier of Pyrrha's regime. She was fire untamed, a flame that refused to be controlled by any doctrine, by any iron will. She was the wildfire that could not be contained, the tempest that could not be shackled.

Her presence was a paradox: grace wrapped in defiance. A woman who had been forged by discipline but was freed by choice. With every movement, she exuded strength. And with every breath, she reminded them all that there was something far more dangerous than obedience. Freedom.

Varren Blacktide, the son of a storm, the tide-born heir of Sablemar. He did not wear the trappings of nobility, nor did he carry the symbols of conquest. He was not adorned with the finery of those who sought power. Varren was the embodiment of the ocean itself. Untamed, unyielding, vast.

The weight of the sea rolled behind his gaze. The fury of the waves crashed silently within his soul. His name was a wound in Pyrrha's memory, a whisper in the halls of war, a reminder that some battles were never truly won, only fought over and over again. His presence was the quiet rage of a people who had never been conquered, who would never be broken.

They were not here to kneel. They were not here to beg. They were here because their lands were dying. And the ones who held the knife to their throats now sat before them, draped in the weight of their dominion.

Seven figures loomed from their thrones, each one a different shade of dominion, a different facet of corruption made manifest.

They were not kings.

They were not tyrants.

They were dominion itself, the living embodiment of power's most insidious form. And they looked upon the three ambassadors not as equals, but as inevitabilities that had yet to be broken.

The silence stretched, thick as fog, suffocating all who dared to breathe it in. And then, Ira Valkor spoke. But his voice was not a voice at all. It was wrath itself, untempered, as though the very air quivered under the weight of his anger. His tone was jagged, as though his words themselves were weapons, sharp enough to tear through the very fabric of the room.

"So, the ghosts of your lands stand before us. And you dare think you are worthy of an audience?"

The atmosphere in the room grew denser still, as though the very air had turned to lead. Every step forward had come with an unspoken challenge. These were not men bound in chains. They were not women who had been broken by fire, famine, or war. They were memories. They were the remnants of the lands the Warlords had sought to erase, and now they stood as a testament to the indomitable will of the people who refused to die.

"You walk into my domain," Ira said. His voice struck the air like iron, each word a blade forged in fury. "You step into this chamber as if your words are owed. As if your grievances have any weight at all."

The atmosphere thickened around him. His presence swelled like a storm cloud on the verge of breaking. Rising to his feet, his form towered over the others, a figure built not of flesh and bone, but of raw, unyielding rage. His gauntlets creaked under the tension. The scorched plating along his knuckles cracked with the ghost of past violence. Remnants of heat clung to his hands, the residue of battles fought in fire and fury.

"You demand," Ira continued, his voice deepening, darkening, "as if you are owed something. As if Pyrrha, my Pyrrha, has ever been a place of mercy."

His eyes locked onto Varren Blacktide first, narrowing with disdain.

"You," Ira murmured, almost mockingly, "the son of Kaelen Blacktide. The ghost of an ocean that has long since been swallowed by Pyrrha's might."

Ira's gaze flicked to Anarya next. A sneer curled his lip.

"You," he spat, "the child of a woman who carried a blade in my name. How utterly amusing that her blood now rebels against me."

And then, Ira's attention shifted to Elyas. A silence stretched between them, thick with unspoken understanding. Ira did not need to speak. He knew men like Elyas, men who did not fight with weapons but with truth. And truth was the one thing that wrath could never burn.

"You mistake Pyrrha for a thing that bends," Ira's voice dropped, quieter now, and infinitely more dangerous. "You mistake fire for something that listens."

Elyas exhaled. His breath was slow and measured, as though it carried the weight of a thousand untold stories. Then, with the stillness of a man who had already walked through death itself, he spoke.

"We mistake nothing."

The room shifted. The air grew heavier, thick with anticipation. Elyas stood firm, unyielding, and continued. His voice was steady.

"Do you think fire is a force of destruction, Warlord? Do you think it only burns? Do you believe that, because you have learned to wield it as a weapon, you have understood its nature?"

Ira's fingers curled. The air crackled, as if the very room responded to the heat of his rage. But Elyas did not stop.

"Fire destroys," Elyas said, his voice hard. "But it reveals the truth in the ruins. You cannot hide from what it exposes. That's why you fear it."

Ira stepped forward. His body was a molten mass of fury, his eyes seething with unrestrained rage. But before he could utter another word, Anarya's voice sliced through the silence like a blade unsheathed.

"Do you believe we have come here with delusions of peace?" Her voice rang out, clear and sharp. As she stepped forward, the flames of the sconces along the chamber walls seemed to flicker. Their glow bent toward her words.

"You believe power is dominion," she said, her voice gaining strength. "You believe war is something that only you dictate. But wherever there is power..."

Her gaze swept across the chamber, meeting the eyes of each Warlord.

"Wherever there is tyranny..."

Her hands clenched. Her voice rose like the swell of an ocean.

"There will always be resistance."

A breath. A heartbeat of silence.

Then, from the shadows at the back of the chamber, a cruel chuckle rang out.

Midas.

The Warlord of Greed. His golden-ringed fingers tapped against his goblet. The surface caught the flickering light of the chamber's flames. His gaze was distant, indifferent. He did not even bother to look directly at them.

"A pretty speech," Midas mused, his voice dripping with mockery. "But tell me, how much, exactly, is your resistance worth?"

His grin was sharp. His teeth gleamed in the dim light.

"Because, my dear children, everything has a price."

The words hung in the air like a cloud of smoke, thick and oppressive.

But Varren Blacktide, the son of Sablemar, did not flinch. His movements were slow, deliberate. Not out of hesitation, but because the ocean itself flowed through him, patient and relentless. His presence was not one of fire or fury. It was something deeper. Something vast.

"You speak of price," Varren said, his voice cold as the sea itself. "As if gold can hold the tide. But how much can you offer a man whose home is ash? What bribe will sway a woman whose children lie buried in it?"

Varren's silver-blue eyes gleamed with the deep, cold fire of the sea. The flickering light cast shadows beneath his gaze, as though the abyss itself was reflected in his eyes. The air around him shifted, charged with something unseen, something ancient.

"You mistake us," Varren continued. His voice dipped lower, dangerous, like the calm before a storm. "You mistake us for those who wish to negotiate, to plead, to barter over the ruins of our dead. You sit on your thrones, draped in the wealth stolen from those you conquer, from those you starve, from those whose blood stains the very foundations of your cities."

The words hung in the air, a quiet storm building with a power that demanded no reply.

"You think you own the world because you have taken it. But the sea does not belong to the man who builds his empire upon its waves." He tilted his head, his gaze turning sharp, like the cut of a blade. "It belongs to the tide."

The silence that followed was not stillness. It was a silence thick with tension, heavy with the weight of truth.

Then came laughter. Low, indulgent, thick with sin.

Carmela.

The Warlord of Lust leaned forward. Her chin rested against her delicate hand. Her scarlet-painted lips curved into a slow, knowing smile.

"Oh, darling," she purred. Her voice was a slow, languid rhythm, as though the very syllables were drenched in honeyed sin. "Such conviction. Such passion. I do so love men who burn with purpose. They make the sweetest ruins when they finally break."

Her fingers traced the rim of her goblet, as if savouring the decadence of the moment.

"You mistake inevitability for injustice. You mistake suffering for something unnatural, something cruel. But suffering, my dear, is the most intimate thing in the world. The purest pleasure. It is how we are shaped. How we are made into something more."

She tilted her head. Her gaze was hungry. She savoured the anticipation.

"I wonder, when the tides finally rise, will you weep for the ones who drown?"

Before Varren could reply, a slow, guttural exhale reverberated through the chamber, as though the weight of mountains themselves moved with it.

Gula.

The Queen of Gluttony did not laugh. Her expression was too heavy for such indulgence. She did not sneer. She did not mock. Her immense form shifted beneath the weight of armour draped over her broad shoulders like the mountain itself had been reborn into flesh.

"You speak of loss," she rumbled. Her voice was as slow as an avalanche, unhurried but inevitable. "Of those who have nothing left to lose. But do you know what I have learned, child of the sea?"

Gula lifted her goblet. The dark liquid within swirled like ink, thick and viscous. She raised it slowly, savouring the weight of each drop.

"Even the starving will eat their own." She paused. Her smile stretched cruelly across her face. "Even the broken will take from the ones beside them. Even the desperate will crawl to the feet of the ones who hold the feast."

She drank deep. The goblet's contents vanished into the depths. As the silence stretched out, she set it down with deliberate slowness.

"And I," she exhaled, her words like the sigh of a beast after devouring its prey, "own the table."

The air grew dense with tension. A chill crept across the room as their words settled like iron upon Varren's shoulders.

Then another voice, cold and cutting, slipped through the chamber like a whisper from beyond the veil.

Somnus.

"You rage," he murmured. His half-lidded eyes moved toward Varren. His presence was that of a man tethered to the abyss itself. "You fight. You seek vengeance. But tell me, storm-born, who is it for?"

His gaze did not hold cruelty. It did not hold malice.

It held something far worse.

Apathy.

"Is it for the dead?" he mused. His voice rustled like dry leaves. "The ones beyond suffering? The ones who feel nothing, who hunger for nothing, who cannot be brought back?"

A slow blink.

"Or is it for you?"

He exhaled slowly, tracing his fingers over the armrest of his throne. A lazy motion, but one that carried the weight of endless years.

"The weight you carry, the grief, the fury. It is not for them. It is for yourself. Because you cannot let go. Because you are afraid that if you do, you will have nothing left."

He let his words linger in the air like a suffocating fog. His voice was quiet, soft, and impossibly unsettling.

"You are not here to bring justice. You are here because you do not know how to live without your suffering."

Another silence descended.

Then came a scoff.

Superbia.

The Monarch of Pride did not indulge in amusement. They did not revel in cruelty. Nor in disinterest. Their voice was sharp, precise. No softness. No hesitation.

"How small you sound," they remarked. Their voice was a whispering blade, slicing through the tension. "How terribly predictable."

Superbia's gaze was unreadable. Polished like a mirror that reflected only one's inadequacy. Their eyes swept over the assembled.

"You come before us with righteous fury. With words dressed in justice, in defiance. But the truth is simpler."

Superbia leaned forward. Their presence sliced the air like a blade honed to perfection.

"You do not fight because you believe you will win," they said. Their fingers tapped the edge of their throne with measured precision. "You fight because you cannot stand the idea that we were right."

A beat.

A pause.

"You were not strong enough to stop us." A slow, razor-sharp smile crept across their face. "And now, you are simply seeking a way to justify your failure."

The words fell like knives. Each one carved deeper into the room. Each syllable tested Varren's resolve.

And then, last of all, Midas.

He sighed. He swirled the contents of his goblet, lost in the reverie of something sweet, golden, fleeting. His golden gaze gleamed beneath the chamber's dim light.

"You all speak so passionately," Midas mused. His voice was a smooth blend of mockery and disappointment. "As if there is anything left to debate. As if this was ever a conversation."

He lifted his goblet with languid grace. The golden liquid danced in the light.

"Tell me, then. If power is not meant to be taken, if the world is not meant to be owned, then why is it that those who do not seize it…"

His gaze flickered toward Varren, toward Anarya, toward Elyas. Each of them was a different story written in the firelight.

"Are always at the mercy of those who do?"

He took a slow, deliberate sip, savouring the weight of inevitability settling over the room.

The air in the chamber thickened, as though the moment itself had grown unbearable.

Elyas did not step forward immediately. He let the silence stretch, a taut wire drawn across the chamber. It was filled with arrogance, cruelty, and indifference. It was heavy with the truth of what had been said.

Then, when the words of the Warlords hung like chains in the air, Elyas spoke.

"You speak of power," he said. His voice was steady, deep, rich with the resonance of something far greater than defiance. "You drape yourselves in conquest, in dominion, in the illusion of permanence. But tell me, what is power, if it cannot escape time?"

His amber eyes, alight with something ancient and unyielding, flickered across the gathered Warlords. He was unwavering. Unmoved. Midas had spoken of ownership. Superbia had spoken of failure. Somnus had spoken of futility. But Elyas saw through them. He exhaled softly. His presence was vast, like the desert before a storm.

"Do you not see?" he murmured. "Power is not in what you take. Power is in what you leave behind."

He turned his gaze toward Ira. His eyes were unyielding. Still as the mountains.

"What is the worth of your wrath," he asked, "if it does not outlive you?"

His voice was not mocking. It was not cruel. It was quiet. Measured. But the weight behind it was undeniable.

He turned to Midas.

"What is the weight of your gold, when time will bury it beneath dust?"

Then, to Superbia.

"What is the point of legacy, if it is built on ruin?" He paused, and his voice sharpened. "The one who rules by fear will be feared until they fall. The one who rules by wealth will be followed until their wealth is spent. But the one who rules by justice..."

His voice turned incisive, like a blade being drawn from its scabbard.

"That one is remembered even by those who have never seen his face."

A flicker of something unreadable passed through his expression, and then he struck the final blow.

"You believe you own the world," he said, his voice rich with finality, a hammer falling upon an anvil. "But tell me, what did Pharaoh own, when the sea swallowed him whole?"

The chamber shuddered. Subtle. Almost imperceptible. But the Warlords noticed. They were the architects of this place, this room, where dominion was not debated but enforced. They had seen the stifling, aching quiet that preceded every meaningful shift.

But this was different.

For the first time, someone had spoken not as a rebel, not as a diplomat, nor as a mere man standing before an inevitable storm. Elyas spoke with the certainty of a man who already saw their end.

And then Ira laughed.

It was not a laugh of mirth. Not the light-hearted amusement of a man who finds humour in folly.

No.

Ira's laughter was an agonized release, the only thing that could mask the flame curling beneath his skin, the raw, unfiltered wrath that clawed at his throat, demanding to be freed.

His voice spilled out like molten iron. Scalding. Unforgiving. An eruption of fury.

"Justice?" Ira's voice cracked like thunder. "There is no justice without wrath."

His hands balled into fists, the gauntlets straining against the force. A violent promise lay behind the calm.

"Patience is not strength. Stillness is not power. I do not bend. I burn."

His molten gaze, eyes glowing with fire, fixed on Elyas. The heat in those eyes could sear steel.

"There is no justice without vengeance. No peace without war." Ira's breath was deep. The air around him shimmered under the pressure, his words thick with the weight of wrath.

"I do not fear time. I do not fear the weight of history. I do not care for what is remembered." His voice dropped, a whisper of venom. Lethal. Absolute. "I only care for who kneels before me."

A pause. The chamber held its breath.

And then, like the quiet before the storm, Ira's rage filled the room. It was thick, unspoken, but undeniable. The air pulsed, heavy with the impending eruption.

Then, soft laughter.

Not mocking. Not indulgent. Just tired.

Somnus, the Warlord of Sloth, let the moment stretch, allowing Ira's fury to wash over him like water on stone. His form shifted slowly, effortlessly, as if he existed between the waking world and the void. He was draped in the finest void-stitched silks, the fabric as dark and shimmering as a starless night.

His fingers, adorned with rings made from the dreams of dying men, drummed languidly on the armrest of his throne. Each tap was a ghostly echo.

"Such a fuss over kneeling," he murmured, his voice a sigh heavy with the weight of centuries. "Such an exhausting thing to demand of the world. As if dominion is measured by the number of heads bowed rather than the number of minds broken."

His heavy-lidded eyes flickered lazily toward Elyas. His lips curved, just enough for a knowing smirk.

"Pharaoh ruled in tyranny, yes. And the sea swallowed him whole. But tell me, ambassador..." he exhaled, his breath like the whisper of a dying wind. "When the waves crashed, do you think the slaves who fled truly found freedom?"

Somnus tilted his head slightly, as if the very concept of rebellion were an old, worn-out story.

"Or did they only exchange one chain for another?"

A pause. A creeping inevitability threaded through his words. Each one dripped with a quiet, inexorable truth.

"Because that is the nature of power, isn't it?" Somnus continued, his voice a lilt of fatalism. "It does not free. It only shifts its weight from one master to another."

A glint in his gaze. A knowing, cruel smile curled the edges of his lips.

"And the most foolish of all..." He let the words hang in silence, then released the final breath of truth. "Are the ones who believe they will ever be free."

Silence slithered through the room. Cold. Uncomfortable.

Then, a shift.

A shift so sharp it cut through the tension like a blade through the air.

Superbia.

A slow, deliberate exhale. A movement so poised, so controlled, it was almost inhuman. Superbia did not merely sit. They existed, like a force of nature, something beyond the confines of monarchy. Each breath they took seemed calculated, polished, and radiated a power so vast, it felt untouchable.

When they spoke, their voice was razor-thin, but every syllable landed like a blow carved from stone.

"You rage, Wrath," they intoned. "And yet, your fire has never been more meaningless."

The words were not cruel. They were not taunting. They were final.

Superbia's gaze cut through the space between them like a blade through silk. The subtle precision of their presence sharpened the atmosphere.

"You set the world ablaze, and yet you still fail to grasp the simplest truth."

A pause. Then the knife.

"You say you only care for who kneels before you." Their words did not just speak. They landed like heavy, thunderous blows. "But dominion is not measured by the number of bodies on the ground. It is measured by the weight of the sky above them."

A flicker passed across Superbia's immaculate face.

"You speak of power, Wrath." Superbia's voice was a velvet blade, cool and unfeeling.

"But power, true power, does not rest on the weight of a throne. It rests on those who kneel before it."

They paused, just long enough for the silence to echo.

"What is a conqueror without a people? What is a ruler without a legacy?"

Superbia's gaze was like a polished mirror, reflecting only the truth. "A throne upon a grave is still a grave. And you, Ira, rule only the memory of fire."

A silence followed. Not empty, but dense, like the breath before collapse. The torches along the obsidian walls dimmed, as if the room itself recoiled. A single ember from Ira's gauntlet fell to the floor and fizzled out against the black stone. Unnoticed by him, but seen by all.

"Your legacy is not power. It is absence. And even absence forgets."

The air in the chamber tightened. It crackled with tension.

"You set empires to flame. But what remains after the fire?" Superbia's voice did not rise. It did not need to. Their words settled. Heavy. Absolute.

"Do you not see?"

They leaned forward just enough. Just enough to drive the words deeper into Ira's soul.

"You have never ruled."

It wasn't an insult. It was a declaration.

"You have merely ensured that others never could."

A slow, deliberate pause.

"Do you truly care who kneels before you, Ira?" Superbia tilted their head slightly, their face unreadable, polished to perfection. "Or do you only care that they never stand again?"

The chamber was alive with an unnatural stillness. A hush. A suffocating silence.

Anarya stood, small against the titanic weight of the Council of Seven. Yet in that moment, she was immovable. She was the roots of an ancient tree, weathered by countless storms, unyielding.

She lifted her gaze, her eyes as dark as the depths of the Al Nahr Al Azraq, the Blue Vein itself, reflecting the solemn fire of a truth that could not be drowned.

"You believe you hold dominion over the world," she began, her voice quiet, not weak, but vast, immense in its scope. "You sit upon thrones of sin, upon legacies built from the marrow of the dead, and yet you do not see."

The chamber listened. The silence thickened, waiting.

"You do not see the flowers that grow from the bloodied soil, the green that rises through the cracks of your conquest, the way the earth refuses to forget the ones you slaughtered."

Her words did not ring with anger. They rang with certainty.

The atmosphere in the chamber was thick with an intense, electric silence as the Council of Seven absorbed Anarya's words. Every syllable she uttered was a hammer strike on the foundation of their dominion. Her words did not merely challenge. They cut deep, leaving a mark that could not easily be erased.

She spoke with the weight of her people's history, the memory of generations who had fought, bled, and died beneath the shadow of the Warlords. More than that, she spoke with the undeniable strength of a survivor.

A woman who had seen the bones of her ancestors break, who had watched empires fall, and yet had risen like the flowers she spoke of, undeterred, unbroken.

Superbia's expression remained unchanged. Yet there was a subtle shift in their posture, a deepening of their gaze. For the first time, it was clear that Anarya had struck at the heart of the Council's greatest fear: legacies. The question, the accusation, do you truly care who kneels before you, or do you only care that they never stand again, hung in the air like a sword poised to fall.

They had built their empire on fear, yes, but also on the fragile illusion that once the fires of destruction had burned, nothing could grow again.

But Anarya, like the soil she invoked, reminded them that even from blood-soaked earth, new life could emerge. Her voice was quiet, but it carried with it the force of generations of wisdom. The flowers rising from the cracked earth, the green that defied the ashes, were the symbols of resistance.

The Warlords had thought they could burn everything to the ground.

Yet they failed to account for the indomitable will of those who would not be extinguished.

The chamber shifted once again. The air tightened like the grip of a fist. It wasn't just the words, though they were sharp enough to wound. It was the presence of each soul gathered in that space, each power gathered in that silence. The weight of history pressed in, thick and unrelenting, as if the walls themselves held their breath, awaiting the next word, the next movement.

Nahara Sunshadow's voice cut through the tension. Soft, but unyielding.

"The land remembers." Her steps were deliberate, her feet silent against the stone floor. But her words carried the weight of generations past, the weight of every step that had walked upon that soil. She didn't just speak. She wove her words like a spell, anchoring the very earth to her cause.

"The soil drinks the blood of the fallen." Nahara's voice was steady, unwavering. "From that blood, life will rise again. The martyrs are never truly buried. They rise in the wheat of Ashra'tel, they bloom in the petals that whisper in Nyxmar's winds, they harden into the stones that form Sablemar's cliffs."

Her hand swept the air, pulling the invisible threads of history taut. The air around her shimmered with meaning.

"We are the roots. We will not be buried."

Her voice did not falter. Each word etched itself into the room, solidifying the roots of her words, making them as immovable as the earth she called upon.

"You burn, but the earth endures. You flood, but the rivers carve new paths. You destroy, but in every grave you make, a seed is planted." The imagery was vivid. The truth in her words was undeniable. The weight of her conviction seemed to draw the shadowed chamber closer, the stone walls closing in as if to witness the inevitability of her next move.

Her gaze shifted, intentional and deliberate, toward Midas. Her expression was like a carved blade, cutting through the gilded illusion he wore.

"I did not come to plead." Nahara's voice was low, filled with a quiet rage. "I came to take back what is ours. Our brother's life is not yours to own."

Her gaze locked with Midas, unflinching.

"No man, not even you, can cage the wind or bury the storm."

There was a stillness. The collective breath of the chamber waited for the inevitable next move.

Then her words turned. They sharpened like a blade dipped in venom, and she faced Ira.

"And the Blue Vein, the river that flows not only through Pyrrha but through all of Phalaistín, it is not yours. It was never yours. It is the lifeblood of a people who have bled enough."

Her voice held something deeper, like the echo of a bell tolling, the reverberation of truth through time.

"Let the river run free."

And then, the final strike.

"Or drown in what comes next."

A hush followed. Pregnant not with fear, but with reckoning.

Somewhere beneath the citadel, the ancient veins of Phalaistín pulsed faintly. The earth, buried under steel and silence, did not forget.

Even ash remembers fire.

And in the memory of that fire, in the breath of scorched soil and the marrow of the mountains, something stirred. Not vengeance.

Inevitability.

"What is a king without his people? What is a throne without the weight of blood? Power is not in dominion, nor in the thrones that collapse beneath it. Power is in the ruin that refuses to die, in the ashes that cannot be consumed. From the embers of destruction, the seed of rebellion is sown. And from that seed, the earth will burn anew."

Null Gospel, Book I, Verse 20.

***

CHAPTER TWENTY:

The Arithmetic of Justice

"A single drop of blood can drown a kingdom, but it is the silence that follows, the silence after the scream, that proves the true weight of power. In that stillness, the cost is calculated, and nothing escapes the ledger."

Fragment of the Exiled Codex, Volume I, Tablet 21.

The tension in the chamber broke with a sound, not loud, but exquisite. It was a laugh, low and indulgent, spun from silk and something darker. Carmela, the Warlord of Lust, leaned forward. Her scarlet-painted lips curled into a feline smile. Her fingers traced the delicate stem of her Veil glass goblet, the crystal shimmering faintly in the candlelight as if it held secrets beneath its surface. Her presence, seductive and dangerous, rippled through the room.

"Flowers and blood," she mused, tilting her head, the words rolling off her tongue like a lover's whispered promise. "Such a tragic little romance."

The chamber's air thickened with the scent of jasmine and iron, a juxtaposition as intoxicating as Carmela herself. Her eyes, pools of crimson desire, flickered with memories of past conquests. "Tragic," she echoed, more to herself than to the room. "But the prettiest flowers bloom in ash."

"I once knew a boy who believed in rivers," she continued, softer now, eyes half-lidded. "He carved songs into driftwood, thinking the current would carry his name to forever. When he died, oh, so beautifully, I made sure his bones were scattered beneath the lilies of Vireth. Every spring, his mother lays flowers. But she doesn't know the soil sings with him still. Only not in his voice."

"We pretend to bury the dead," she went on, her voice as soft as forbidden scripture. "But what we truly do is feed them to memory. And memory is not a graveyard. It is a butcher. It trims away what doesn't serve the myth. What remains is not the boy, but the lesson. The warning. The echo dressed in flowers."

She let the words hover, delicate as perfume and twice as toxic.

"He thought sacrifice would immortalize him. But there is no eternity in flesh. Only repurposing. Only reuse."

Her eyes drifted toward Anarya, unblinking.

"Martyrs die once," Carmela whispered, her fingers dancing across the glass. "But we use them forever. And what better seeds to plant than the ones that grow legends?"

A single drop of liquid clung to her lower lip, glistening darkly before she licked it away, savouring the moment.

"Ah, sweet girl," Carmela purred, her voice thick with indulgence. "You romanticize sacrifice, of rivers, roots, and martyrs. But tell me, what is a martyr's worth if their name is lost to dust before the next bloom?"

The question hung, sharp and final. Her mocking amusement was palpable, cutting the air like a thread slowly snapping.

"And what, I wonder, will your brother be when he is freed?" The words dripped from her mouth, dangerous and sweet. "A hero? A symbol? A man? Or will he find that some cages are far more comfortable than the cold, indifferent world beyond them?"

She smiled again, this time the glint in her eyes cutting with a sharpness that could make a man bleed.

"Some things are better kept in golden chains."

Her words hung in the air, potent and cruel.

Anarya didn't speak. But her silence wasn't surrender. It was coiled, coiling like a question still sharpening its blade. A hum, smooth as molten treasure.

Midas swirled his goblet lazily, the golden liquid shimmering like molten sun, casting a shadow of gluttonous light upon the walls of the chamber.

"A poetic phrasing," he mused, his tone rich with silken arrogance. "But chains, my dear Carmela, are simply a matter of perspective."

He did not immediately turn his gaze toward Anarya. He let her stand beneath the weight of his presence before finally lifting his eyes to meet hers.

"Freedom," he mused, his voice laced with mocking sadness. "Such an expensive word."

"Freedom?" Midas mused again, the goblet spinning lazily in his hand, "It's a commodity. The poor call it a birthright. The rich? A contract."

He leaned back, the golden threads of his robes flickering like molten fire. "Revolutions burn through bodies. Empires? They grow them." His smile was a sliver of ice. "And the dividends? Generations that never question."

He leaned back, his gilded fingers drumming lightly on the arm of his throne, measuring her with a smirk full of calculation.

"You wish to reclaim your brother?" Midas's voice was smooth, cold with disdain. "How quaint. But remember this: your brother was never stolen. He was surrendered. His fate was sealed the moment you let him go."

His words weren't just an insult; they were an accusation, a reminder that Anarya had allowed the world to claim him.

His amber eyes gleamed, reflecting the ghosts of countless transactions, debts that had outlived the men who made them.

"And the Blue Vein?" His voice turned softer.

Deadlier.

"You call it a lifeblood. I call it capital. It does not flow for you. It flows for us. For those who own the pipes, the gates, the filtration systems that decide which mouths are worthy of its touch."

A cruel smirk played at his lips.

"Water, like freedom, is never free."

"It isn't water we hoard," Midas said, the weight in his tone sharpening. "It's narrative. Supply chains are strings, and we are the hands that play them. Cities don't rise with moisture. They rise with permission."

He leaned forward, wine-light gilding his cheeks. "What is thirst, if not the body's plea to obey? And what is a pipeline, if not the leash dressed in silver?"

A slow, low chuckle.

Invidia, the Warlord of Envy, her presence like the creeping cold of a shadow just before a storm. She watched from beneath half-lowered lashes, her gaze the sharp edge of hunger, yet quiet, a gnawing hunger in the dark. Her silence spoke more than words could.

Her envy was not loud. It was patient, silent, and systematic. She did not crave what Anarya had. She craved the resonance it created. The loyalty it commanded. The myth it threatened to become.

It wasn't Anarya's power that infected Invidia's mind like a splinter of glass. It was the inevitability of her myth. The storm in her silence. Envy is not hunger. It is the ache of watching someone else become the story while you are still waiting to be written. And Invidia had waited long enough.

Envy wasn't wanting something. It was needing everything someone else was about to be remembered for.

"Ah, Midas," she murmured, her voice a thread of silk in a room thick with smoke and steel. "Always so pragmatic."

She turned her head, a subtle motion that carried the weight of centuries. Her eyes, the colour of a storm cloud before the rain, assessed Anarya with a gaze that seemed to dissect and catalogue. It was not amusement she held, nor disdain, but something far sharper. A keen understanding of the game that had been set in motion. A player who had learned its rules long ago.

"I must admit," Carmela purred, her lips curving into something dangerous, "I do envy your conviction. Such faith in the idea that anything in this world still belongs to the people."

Her voice turned colder, the sweetness curdling into venom. "Ownership is not a right, little ambassador. It is a skill. A game."

She leaned forward, her fingers tracing the delicate rim of her Veil glass goblet, its surface shimmering like liquid moonlight. The liquid within was a perfect reflection of her, smooth, intoxicating, and deadly.

"And you are playing against those who have never lost."

Gula's chuckle rattled the walls.

"You speak of rivers and wheat," she growled, her voice heavy with hunger. "But your people... they eat to survive. We feast to remember."

She leaned forward, her tone a slow, dangerous whisper. "We consume better."

"We do not eat," she said with a guttural purr. "We inherit." Her hand lifted slightly, revealing the carved bone of a fallen prince forged into a ring. "Your people consume to survive. Mine consume to remember."

"In the marrow of kings, I've tasted treaties. In the flesh of rebels, famine. The first empire fell because it fed its poor. We learned. We feast instead on empires still breathing."

Gula shifted, her voice rumbling like a distant avalanche.

"Do you know what war tastes like?" she asked suddenly, her tone low, hypnotic. "It tastes like copper and silence. Like a feast at the end of a famine. I've swallowed empires that begged for mercy in twelve tongues. I've chewed through the bones of nations so desperate to survive, they offered up their children in lieu of treaties."

Her lips curled into something that wasn't quite a smile, more an acknowledgment of memory's rot.

"And I drank to them all."

She leaned back, shadows folding around her bulk.

"History is not written by victors. It's eaten by them. Digested. Forgotten."

Her massive hand, adorned with rings made from the bones of her fallen enemies, gripped her goblet, lifting it to her lips as if savouring the taste of annihilation.

"Your people farm the land. We own it. Your people gather the water. We distribute it."

She let the words settle, the weight of them pressing down like the oppressive humidity before a storm.

"You call it a lifeblood, but tell me..." Her eyes gleamed, savage, cutting through the space between them. "What is a vein, without something to drain it?"

A slow, knowing grin curled at the corner of her lips.

"It is nothing but a body waiting to rot."

The silence that followed was thick and oppressive, like the air before the earth releases a thunderstorm.

Somnus, the Warlord of Sloth, barely shifted. His body, wrapped in the finest void-stitched silks, seemed to bleed into the shadows, an entity more shadow than flesh. His eyes, half-lidded, flickered with a light that was at once distant and infinite.

"Demand, demand, demand..." His voice was a sigh, as if the very concept of exertion tired him.

He glanced lazily at Elyas, a faint curve of amusement ghosting across his lips.

"You ask for a river, as if asking has ever changed anything," he murmured. "You speak of freedom, as if it is anything more than another illusion, another link in the chain."

His gaze sharpened, like a dull blade suddenly brought to life.

"The Blue Vein does not belong to Pyrrha, nor to Phalaistin, nor to you."

His voice dropped, quiet and immutable, as if carving truth into the stone of reality. "It belongs to time. And time, my dear, has never been kind to those who beg."

Somnus let the words rest like dust upon an untouched tomb.

"You chase history as if it were a chariot," he murmured, "but history drags a corpse. That's the secret none of you dare whisper. Time doesn't move. It waits. It stagnates. And it buries the frantic beneath the weight of their own motion."

He lifted a single finger, as if gesturing to some slow celestial calculus only he could perceive. "I have never run. That is why I remain."

Anarya lifted her gaze. Not sudden, not sharp, but slow, deliberate. The kind of movement born from restraint honed through generations.

"Then you've confused rot for wisdom," she said quietly, but her voice carried like heat in a drought. "The dead don't run either. Doesn't make them sovereign."

She didn't flinch, didn't blink. "You say you wait, but all I see is a man too afraid to gamble. You've mistaken cowardice for permanence. But statues still crumble. Even silt gets dredged eventually."

"Time is the only tyrant that never fears rebellion," Somnus whispered.

His gaze unfocused, drifting into the corners of the chamber where shadows gathered like clergy.

"Sloth is not stillness," he said. "It is refusal. It is the art of denying urgency its illusion of power. Empires exhaust themselves into graves. Revolution burns its children into altars. But I," he exhaled softly, "I wait. I watch. And when the ashes settle, I am always there. Unmoved. Undefeated."

Elyas let out a breath. Not a scoff, not a sigh, but something heavier, like the cracking of glass beneath silk.

"You call that undefeated?" His voice was calm. Tired, yes, but not resigned. "Watching the world die over and over just so you can say you never lifted a hand to try? That's not wisdom. That's complicity."

He turned to face Somnus fully. "There's no virtue in survival if it costs you your soul. There's no crown in apathy. Just a tomb with a longer wait."

"I watched a boy burn down a city in the name of tomorrow," Somnus sighed, his voice less sound than memory. "He believed he was changing the world. All he changed was the calendar. The city was rebuilt. The ash paved over. The tyrant's name replaced, the system untouched. And the boy? Forgotten. Time buried him like it does all fools who mistake the spark of pain for the fire of revolution."

"You may call it apathy," he said, his voice turning inward, "but apathy is an action. Mine is purer. I am the stillness beneath the flood, the silence beneath the scream. It was never the fire that frightened kings. It was the smoke that lingered after. That slow, choking truth: nothing they built would outlast forgetting."

Varren tilted his head, one eyebrow raised like a blade sheathed in wit.

"Wow," he said. "And here I thought Invidia had the monopoly on condescension."

He gave Somnus a half-smile, the kind that almost disguised the bitterness behind it. "You talk like erosion is a legacy. But tell me, how does it feel knowing that even your decay will eventually be dust on someone else's boot?"

A pause. "Or maybe that's the real dream, huh? To be irrelevant enough to last forever."

"You speak of now as if it is real. But now is already rotting. The moment your lips move, your meaning is bones."

His eyes flickered shut. "I have seen a hundred revolutions. Each claimed they were the final one. But time," he smiled faintly, "merely waits. And waits. And watches them all return, crawling, to the chains they once broke."

A faint flick of ash drifted from his sleeve, disintegrating before it reached the floor. "The river is memory," he continued, more to the ceiling than to her. "And memory always forgets those too weak to etch their name into its banks."

No one laughed.

Not this time.

The weight of too many truths, too cruel, too cold, pressed like a vice against the chamber walls. Even the torchlight seemed hesitant now, flickering without confidence, casting uncertain halos on the obsidian floor.

And then, Midas moved.

Not abruptly. Just enough. He leaned forward, the gold filigree in his robe catching the firelight like an omen.

"That's the difference between you and me, Somnus," he said, voice smooth, dangerously quiet. "You wait for memory to forget the weak. I fund the scribes who write them out."

His smirk was thin, acidic. "You're not the silt beneath the river. You're the weight that slows it down. But the current still chooses where it goes. And I own the current."

"The weak claw at relevance," he finished, reclining into his throne as if folding into time itself. "But I've outlived relevance. I am not part of the river. I am the silt beneath it. Heavy, unseen, and inevitable. One day, the current will stop. And when it does, they will find only me... and silence."

The air crackled with a charge, as if the weight of the moment was too much for even the chamber to bear.

Ira stood.

No longer a man.

No longer a figure.

He was a storm. His body, rigid with the force of his wrath, radiated an aura of molten heat. His breath was slow, controlled, barely contained. His presence filled the space, swallowing everything in its wake.

"You want your brother?" Ira's voice was dark, like the belly of a volcano just before eruption. "You want your river?"

He took a step forward. The room seemed to shrink beneath his feet, as if the very foundations of the world trembled in the face of his fury.

His lips curled, revealing a smirk that could have been carved from obsidian.

"Then let me grant you your request."

A hum reverberated from deep within him. Not sound. Pressure. As if the heat in his body had begun vibrating against reality. The veins along his neck pulsed with raw fury, the skin fracturing with veins of light, as if Wrath itself threatened to break through the casing of flesh.

His voice was low, quiet, but it carried with it the promise of something catastrophic.

"I will make the Blue Vein run red."

A tremor in the air. A pause so thick it felt like the chamber itself was holding its breath.

"The golden fields of Ashra'tel will burn fiercer than the lava streams that juxtapose the wheat."

His fingers curled into a fist, a promise not just spoken, but engraved into the marrow of war.

"The waters of Sablemar will boil."

And then his voice turned to steel. The final promise. Unforgiving. Unrelenting.

"And Nyxmar... Nyxmar will truly know obliteration."

"The statues of your gods will melt," Ira growled, "until their prayers pool like slag in the streets. Your harvests will scream as they burn. The sun will blush at the blood it must rise over. And when the last bell tolls in Nyxmar... it will be rung by no living hand."

His voice dropped, intimate, now deadly. "There will be no survivors. Only witnesses. And even they will wish they had drowned."

The chamber was still, suffocating under the weight of Ira's words.

And then, a groan.

The iron doors of the Bohemian Chamber of Order trembled under the weight of their own girth. The heavy sound echoed through the chamber, the silence cracking beneath its force.

And then she entered.

General Callistra Vhailar.

Her presence was immediate. Undeniable. She did not rush. She did not shout. But the moment she crossed the threshold, the very air seemed to tighten, as if holding its breath.

Her crimson war-plate gleamed in the flickering torchlight. The Sanguine Order's sigil, the ouroboros of entwined flame and steel, was etched into her breastplate with the precision of a craftsman's mark. Every movement, every step, was deliberate, an expression of discipline honed through decades of brutal warfare.

She did not glance toward the others. Not yet. Her gaze, her focus, was locked on one thing. One person.

Anarya.

Bound. Kneeling. Bruised. But Callistra saw only her daughter. Her blood. The iron that ran through her veins.

A flicker. A tightening of fingers. A single, infinitesimal shift in her breath.

But nothing more. Not yet.

She lifted her gaze to the assembled Warlords, her presence like the calm before a storm. She did not speak at first, but the weight of her silence spoke volumes.

For a moment, she allowed the tension to hang in the air. A sharp edge. A blade not yet unsheathed.

"General Callistra." Midas's voice was smooth, dripping with condescension. "How fitting. You arrive just in time to witness the consequences of misplaced rebellion."

Callistra did not flinch. Her composure did not waver. Her voice, when it came, was steady. Precise. Honed to perfection.

"Warlord Midas."

She did not look to the others. Not yet. She did not need to.

Her gaze flickered briefly to Ira. To her liege. To the one who held her family's fate in his hands. But she did not question. Not yet.

The chamber vibrated with a tension so thick, it could have been carved into the very stone beneath their feet.

The torches flickered not with wind, but with anticipation. Ancient runes carved along the obsidian pillars pulsed faintly, as if the very architecture of the room remembered every broken oath, every spilled secret, every execution whispered into stone.

Each breath felt like a weight pressing down. Each word like a hammer to the anvil of Callistra's restraint.

Something burned within her. A coal buried deep beneath layers of steel and duty. Just waiting to be coaxed into a raging inferno.

The silence stretched, suffocating in its heaviness. Ira's molten gaze never wavered. The tension in the air was as palpable as his seething anger. Callistra remained still, a statue carved from the iron of her own resolve.

But for the first time in her life, something within her hesitated. It wasn't a physical movement. It wasn't a faltering step or a stumble in speech.

No. This hesitation was in something unseen. Something internal. Deep within her core.

This was not a battlefield. This was something more dangerous. A confrontation not of weapons, but of wills.

And in that moment, she wasn't sure who would emerge from this unscathed, if anyone at all.

The laughter that broke the silence was low. Indulgent. Drenched in malice.

Carmela, the Warlord of Lust, let it spill from her lips like honey. Sweet. Venomous.

She draped herself deeper into her seat, her robes shifting like liquid shadow, like the very embodiment of sin. The soft glint of her crimson-painted nails caught the dim torchlight as she traced an idle, deliberate circle around the rim of her goblet. Her eyes narrowed with knowing amusement.

"Oh, Callistra," she purred, her voice velvet-dipped in venom. "You wear that armour like it's enough to guard what you really fear."

Her smile stretched. Sharp. Taunting.

"But tell me, dearest General, what is heavier upon your shoulders? The weight of your loyalty or the weight of your daughter's chains?"

Callistra's gaze remained fixed, but within, a tempest raged.

Memories surged. Anarya's first steps on the training sands. Her childlike curiosity with a soldier's blade. The night she first called her "General" instead of "Mother." Each memory landed like a strike to the ribs.

The chamber's coldness seeped beneath her Warplate, but it wasn't the chill that made her spine tense. It was the weight of knowing she'd chosen her oath over her blood.

She had always believed in sacrifice. She had always believed there was no greater honour than duty.

But now, watching her daughter kneeling in chains, burned, bruised, and silent, she no longer knew who that sacrifice had been for.

She had knelt once, long ago. Not before Warlords, but beside Anarya's cot, blood still drying on her gauntlets after a siege. "The war will be over before she learns to speak," they told her. But Anarya had learned first to wait. Then to march. Then to kneel.

Not in reverence. In patience.

And now, looking at her, Callistra wondered if it had always been her legacy Anarya bore. Broken, rusted, sharpened again and again, not into a crown, but into chains.

And suddenly, she remembered the stories she once told Anarya at twilight. Tales of justice, strength, and Pyrrha's glory. But those stories were written in victory, not in chains. Now she saw the truth. The cost of loyalty was not paid in blood, but in memory erased.

And worst of all, she wondered if her silence had made her a coward.

Each word curled into the air like silk-wrapped daggers, sinking deep, carving into the marrow of the room.

Callistra could feel the sting of it. But she remained silent. Her jaw set. Her gaze unwavering.

Gula, the Warlord of Gluttony, leaned forward in her throne. The movement was slow. Deliberate. Her massive form seemed to loom over the chamber. Her rings, each one bearing the sigil of a conquered empire, caught the flickering light.

Her voice rumbled like an earthquake. Deep. Indulgent.

"Ah, but I must admit," she chuckled, a wicked grin spreading across her face, "there is something... poetic about it, isn't there? The wolf who has razed villages now stands before her own blood, bound in the ruins of her own making. Such a delicious cycle, don't you think?"

She took a slow sip from her goblet, savouring it as if she were tasting the very essence of the world's cruelty.

"After all, Callistra, is it not the fate of all mothers to watch their children be devoured by the world they built?"

Her words were slow, relishing the weight of them as if each syllable was a treat.

The chamber seemed to constrict, tightening around Callistra. Her own flesh unwilling to break beneath the pressure.

But she did not falter.

Somnus barely stirred. His presence was an ethereal weight, as if he existed between the veil of sleep and death itself.

His eyes, heavy-lidded and filled with the knowledge of forgotten eras, flicked lazily toward Callistra. His voice was like a sigh. Lazy but deep. Laced with the inevitability of time.

"Oh, what a tragedy..." he murmured, his lips curving with something unreadable. "Or is it irony?"

He blinked slowly, his gaze flicking to Anarya, who knelt in chains before them. His fingers, adorned with the rings of dead men's dreams, waved vaguely toward her.

"You spent your life ensuring Pyrrha's throne remains unchallenged. And yet." A pause. The words drifted like smoke in the air. "Your own legacy kneels before it."

Her nails dug into her palms beneath the gauntlets. Not in rage. In shame.

Was this legacy? Her daughter on her knees. Her silence a coin spent too many times. She wanted to scream. She wanted to tear open her throat and let every unspoken regret pour forth in blood and fire.

But generals did not scream. They obeyed.

And so, she stood. While inside, the scream built.

The words, dripping with quiet pity, cut deeper than any blade could.

Callistra's breath caught. But she said nothing.

She merely stared. Unwavering.

Superbia, ever poised, did not lean, did not smirk, did not indulge in laughter. They simply watched. Their gaze, unreadable and cold as the abyss, weighed everything in the room.

When they finally spoke, their voice sliced through the silence, thin and sharp, like a blade cutting through silk.

"You made your choice, Callistra. You sculpted your destiny with unyielding hands. And now, you bear witness to its consequence."

Their gaze flicked to Anarya. The weight of their words was heavier than any physical blow.

"Perhaps she is simply the price you must pay for the empire you serve. Or," they paused, a sharp glint in their eyes, "perhaps she is the proof that you have already failed to protect it."

The air shifted. It was a ripple, barely perceptible, but it was enough to make Callistra's fingers twitch. It was an accusation. A sharp reminder that the consequences of her choices were not yet over.

Midas exhaled, the sound a low hum of indulgence. His golden gaze assessed Callistra like a merchant weighing the worth of a coin too worn to be of any value. His lips curled into a smirk, the gold of his goblet gleaming in the dim light.

"Really, Callistra, you look as though you are about to... what? Object?"

He leaned forward, placing his goblet down with a delicate touch. His fingers caressed the rim as if he were toying with something fragile.

"Oh, how dreadfully predictable."

He smirked.

"You Pyrrhans always mistake duty for purpose. As if loyalty is anything more than gilded debt."

He tilted his head. His gaze turned piercing.

"And tell me, how does it feel, knowing that debt has finally come to collect?"

Callistra did not answer. Not yet. The Warlords may have had their say, but she would have her moment soon.

The air in the chamber hummed with an almost unbearable tension. She could feel it. Every set of eyes on her. The weight of their words pressing down, each one another layer on the suffocating mass around her.

Her fingers flexed again, but still she remained silent.

The chamber had become an arena. Not one of warriors. Not one of shields or swords. But a crucible where wills were tested against the unyielding force of wrath itself. The tension was unbearable. Every breath a battle against the thick silence that hung like smoke in the room.

Ira's presence, once looming, now overwhelmed. His very being pressed into the space with the weight of an oncoming storm.

And then, Invidia.

Her silence was absolute, as if her very being existed outside the reach of their noise. The Warlord of Envy was a predator. Her gaze unwavering. As steady as the coldest steel. As patient as the ocean's depths before a storm. She did not laugh. She did not taunt. She only watched. Unblinking. Studying the moment like a predator scenting the blood before the kill.

And when she spoke, it was not with the thunderous force of the others. No. Her voice was a whisper. So soft it could have been mistaken for a breeze, yet sharp enough to carve through bone.

"It burns, doesn't it?"

The words sliced through the air like a blade. Piercing deeper than Ira's wrathful flames. Deeper than any weapon they had wielded thus far. She was not speaking of Callistra's rage.

No.

She was speaking of something far darker.

The pain.

The hunger.

The thing that writhed beneath Callistra's surface. The thing she had never allowed herself to confront. That was what Invidia had spoken of.

Before Callistra could breathe, before she could respond, before anything could shift in the chamber, Ira moved.

There was no command. No spoken words. Just a single step. A slow, deliberate, heavy step forward. The weight of it pressed into the room like the first crack in a foundation that had already been shattered.

The Warlords did not stop speaking. Did not pause in their mocking or their cruelty. But the fire in their words dimmed. Because Ira had spoken without uttering a single sound.

One step. Just one. And the air around them turned heavy. It was the calm before the eruption. It was the moment before the fire consumed everything.

His molten eyes flickered, bright with embers that devoured the space between them. They danced across the ambassadors. Elyas, Anarya, and Varren. Three remnants of a world still daring to defy his.

Ira's voice, rich with venom and fury, finally cracked the tension.

"You came here to speak of justice."

His words dripped. Slow and dangerous.

"Of peace. Of righteousness."

Another pause. A shift in his gaze.

"And yet, justice is carved in blood. And peace is what is left when the screaming stops."

He exhaled, and the air seemed to scorch. Heavy with heat that pulsed from every inch of his body.

"Righteousness," Ira growled, his voice a bitter rasp, "has never built a throne. Power does that."

He took a step closer, his eyes molten. "Peace isn't absence. It's the pause before the feast. You call it virtue when you hold the sword. You call it terror when it's taken from you."

His gaze pierced the room, unflinching. "There are no victories. Only survivors who rewrite their sins."

Ira's lips curled. "And blood? It stains everyone the same."

Ira's gaze cut through the air like a whetted axe.

"You think I'm a monster. But I am the arithmetic of justice. Stripped of poetry. Stripped of mercy. I am what happens when you subtract illusion from power. When you divide history by the mouths it fed to itself. When the equation balances, I remain."

He tilted his head, mockingly gentle. "You came to bargain with hope. But I don't deal in myth. I deal in consequence."

And then, softer. Crueller.

"You wanted justice."

He smiled. A thing sharp enough to sever fate.

"I offer accounting."

Callistra's breath caught. Not from fear. From recognition. She'd heard that kind of math before. In war.

Midas blinked once. Then twice. And then, gods forgive him, he laughed.

Not loud. Not mocking. But with the dry, dangerous mirth of a man who'd just watched a starving lion quote fiscal policy.

"Well," he murmured, swirling his goblet with new appreciation, "that's unexpected."

His golden eyes sparkled with a gleam that was half pride, half proprietary insult. "Careful, Wrath," he said, lounging deeper into his throne. "If you keep borrowing my metaphors, I might start charging interest."

He gestured lazily with one gilded finger, as if marking invisible debt in the air. "Arithmetic. Accounting. Consequence. Gods, you sound like me after a profitable siege and two bottles of Veilwine."

A beat. Then a grin. Sharp and amused. "You've been listening. I'm flattered. Corruption really is the sincerest form of flattery."

Even the torchlight seemed confused. Flickering between fear and laughter.

The laughter did not spread, but it echoed. Unnerving in its singularity. For one breathless moment, it felt as though the room itself considered joining in. Not out of joy. But out of recognition.

Because this was it, wasn't it?

Justice as accounting. War as investment. Ideology as a commodity. Hope, hope itself, reduced to a currency that only the cruel ever had enough of to spend.

Invidia's lips curled. Not quite a smile. Not quite revulsion. Somewhere between hunger and nausea.

Superbia's gaze did not shift. But something flickered in their eyes. Small. Surgical. It was not amusement. It was calculation. Always calculation.

Carmela, wrapped in silks and shadow, whispered to no one. "Only a Warlord of Wrath could quote greed like scripture and still sound divine."

The chamber stilled. No sound. No motion. No breath dared disturb the hush. But something shifted.

Ira felt it. Not with his ears, but beneath his skin. A tension, almost imperceptible, yet seismic in its certainty. Not fear. Not reverence. Resignation.

That was always the moment before the fire. When hope stopped clawing and simply folded. When the will to resist didn't die. Only dulled. Bent inward. Smothered under the weight of inevitability.

His gaze fell on Anarya. And there it was. A flicker. Brief. Unreadable. But not weakness. Not pain. Something deeper. Something older. More dangerous than cruelty. More intimate than rage.

Curiosity.

A test.

And Ira, Warlord of Wrath, did not blink.

Callistra did not move. Not because she lacked the will. Because movement would mean admitting the war had begun. Again.

She stood like a monument to a decision made too long ago. Spine rigid. Hands silent. Every muscle a prayer she couldn't afford to whisper.

But Ira smelled it. Not her fear. Her fury.

That ancient, unshed rage clawing beneath her bones like something alive. Something caged too long, growing teeth in the dark. It was the kind of fury that didn't shout. It remembered.

Ira took a step. Not a stomp. Not a threat. A kind of deliberate intimacy, the way a lover approaches in a dream that ends in knives. Heat unfurled from his skin in waves. Dry. Punishing. Greedy.

He raised a hand. Slow. Intentional. Ceremonial.

Not to strike. Not yet. No. To offer proximity as a weapon.

His hand hovered beside Anarya's throat, the flame of his wrath grazing the skin but not yet scalding it. It shimmered in the air like heat hallucination, like reality cracking.

His fingers began to close. But not all the way. Just enough to suggest ownership. His thumb brushed the side of her neck. A whisper of touch. A measure.

Her pulse beat steady. Unflinching. Defiant.

It didn't race. It didn't beg.

And that affront to terror was the moment Ira's smile split wider. Too wide. It didn't belong on a man. It belonged on a nightmare pretending to be human.

Anarya didn't speak. Didn't recoil.

She stared straight into the furnace of him, and in her silence, there was no resignation. No girlhood left. Only coals. Burning slow. Biding.

Every bruise on her body wasn't a mark of damage. They were forgings.

She wasn't broken. She was refracted. Focused. Sharpened.

They thought they had caged her.

They had only given her walls to lean against while she became steel. She was no one's daughter. No one's captive. She was the final silence before judgment speaks.

Somewhere in the marrow of her blood, the Pyrrhan queens stirred. Those barefoot monarchs who danced in volcano mouths and named gods only to gut them. Anarya had not yet ruled. But her silence bore ancestral volume.

If she rose, it would not be for freedom. It would be to end lineage itself.

And Ira, god of wrath, prophet of vengeance, had not yet met her fury. Only its shadow. Only its breath. Only its prelude.

Callistra still did nothing. But inside, she was splitting. The iron of her will bent. Screamed. Screeched against the rusting bolts of loyalty. Her mind fracturing between love unspoken and duty unrelenting. Her silence was not resolve. It was collapse dressed in rank.

She was screaming. But only in the language of blood pressure and clenched fists. Only in the dialect of betrayal left to ferment.

And still, Ira smiled. His eyes burned hotter now. Not with fire, but with revelation. He was not angry. He was divine. Wrath, true wrath, was not an emotion. It was a sacrament.

His fingers tightened around Anarya's throat. Not enough to cut off breath. Just enough to demand obedience from her pulse. Just enough to say: I own this moment.

One second more. Just long enough for the room to remember what gods do when unchallenged. Then his hand withdrew. The heat left Anarya's throat like a fever broken. But not with mercy. With disappointment. As if she hadn't broken fast enough. As if her defiance wasn't worthy of execution.

Ira's gaze lingered on her. Burning. Unreadable. Like a blade raised for a beheading that never came.

And then it shifted. Not to her. To Elyas. The pivot was instant. Cruel. Unholy.

Ira's molten fist plunged into Elyas's chest with a sickening, wet crack. A sound that split the chamber like bone snapping under the weight of divine judgment. Ribs shattered on impact. Flesh tore. Organs ruptured as if they had been waiting their whole lives to fail.

Elyas's body jerked, limbs seizing in a final spasm. His mouth opened, but no scream escaped; only the hollow gasp of a man who realized too late that his voice had been stolen. Blood erupted from his chest in a geyser, spattering the floor in a dark arc. It stained the hem of Callistra's gauntlet, as though fate had branded her in the moment of his death.

The room held its breath. Anarya's gaze was fixed, not on the blood, but on the body, the weight of what it meant for her, for all of them. A streak hit Anarya's cheek. Another struck the side of Callistra's gauntlet.

Neither moved. Neither blinked. It was not just death. It was detonation.

Ira's hand wrenched back with a sickening wet sound. It dragged pieces of something that should have stayed inside. Fingers dripped crimson. Steam curled in the cold air.

Elyas didn't fall. He collapsed inward. Like a temple imploding in on faith itself. His knees buckled. His back gave. He fought to stay upright. Muscles trembled with the stubborn echo of a man who once believed justice could survive in rooms like this.

But he was already gone. And then Ira let go. Elyas crumpled. Not like a man.

Not like a martyr.

Like the final page of scripture soaked in gasoline. Folded. Scorched. Discarded.

The blood pooled quickly, seeping into the deep crevices of the black marble. It found the ancient runes carved into the floor, filling them, rewriting old words in martyr's ink.

A hush fell.

The silence wasn't stillness. It was paralysis.

A breath caught, not in a single throat, but in every throat. Gods and monsters alike held their breath, suspended in the space between life and the next. No one moved. No one dared speak. They simply listened. To the silence. To the part of them that had just died.

There was no scream. No outcry. Only the ragged breath of history exhaling through cracked lips.

And in that silence, something sacred bled out.

Not Elyas.

Meaning.

For a moment, the Bohemian Chamber of Order became something it had not been in centuries. Human. The murals carved into obsidian, etched with the blood of long-forgotten revolutions, seemed to darken. Not with shadow, but with shame. The heroes depicted within, once towering over myth, now turned their eyes away. The prophecy didn't shatter.

It wept.

What had died on that floor wasn't merely a man. It was the final question no tyrant had ever dared answer: What happens when a voice still dares to rise?

Now, no one knew.

Because the answer had been incinerated.

Elyas's body didn't fall. It folded. Like scripture soaked in blood, curling in on itself before the final verse could be read. His form hit the ground with a weight that didn't belong to flesh. It belonged to failure. To futures lost. To the death of every child who would never learn his name.

His blood moved slowly across the obsidian floor. Thick as syrup. Intelligent in its path. It found the seams between the stones, slipping into the ancient Pyrrhan runes carved there centuries ago. Once, those runes had declared dominion. Now, soaked in martyr's blood, they whispered something else entirely.

They whispered martyrdom.

The chamber didn't breathe. It flinched.

Anarya's face remained still, but her hands trembled behind her back. Not from fear. From restraint. Warm blood speckled her cheek, a communion denied.

She said nothing.

She simply watched.

Varren hadn't blinked. But the sinew in his neck twitched with tension, the muscles locked so tightly that the skin quivered from the pressure. His eyes didn't tear. They smouldered. Grief caught in a body that no longer knew how to carry it.

Callistra stood, her armour as rigid as ever, but inside her, the iron was fracturing. Not loudly. Not visibly. Molecule by molecule. She had seen corpses before, men who bent in ways the human body was never meant to. But this wasn't war.

This was ritual. This was sacrifice.

And Ira?

He stared down at his handiwork, not with triumph, not with cruelty.

With satisfaction.

As if what he had just done wasn't murder, but mathematics. As if the man crumpled before him had always been an equation. Solved now in blood and silence.

Then it came.

The laugh.

It started soft, barely a ripple in the air, but it grew, twisted, bloated until it roared. The sound shook the walls. The obsidian columns reverberated like tuning forks struck by apocalypse. Dust drifted from the ancient mural ledges. Even the flame-light flickered, shrinking away from the sound.

In that laughter, the chamber heard something deeper. The voice of a man who believed himself absolved by destruction.

Ira wiped his blood-slick hand on the folds of his tunic. The stain spread wide. It did not vanish. It bloomed. It was the signature of something that no longer needed to speak to be believed.

He turned back to Anarya, smiling faintly. A saint's smile. A surgeon's smile. The smile of a man who knew what he had done was not murder, but doctrine.

"Forgive me," he said, his voice soaked in calm. "I got carried away."

His smile thinned, teeth barely parted. It was no longer an expression. It was punctuation. A full stop to protest. "We still need someone to deliver the message."

His gaze moved like a guillotine descending, clean, inevitable. It landed on Varren.

And then came the laughter.

But not from a mouth.

From the air.

From the walls.

From the marrow of those who heard it.

This was not the laughter of cruelty. This was the laughter of a world that had finally removed its mask and found the face beneath uglier than imagined. It was the sound that comes when hope realizes it has outlived its usefulness.

Ira turned fully to face Varren. The tide-born heir. The last son of Kaelen Blacktide. The final inheritance of a drowned world that still whispered from beneath the waves.

And Ira, who had learned to walk across the corpses of floods, smiled.

His molten gaze slid toward the Three Pyres: Zephir, Veyna, Dain.

They were killers. They had earned that name in cities no longer spoken of. But now, they stood stiff, not in fear, but in reverence. What stood before them was no longer a Warlord.

It was the purest form of wrath. A god not of fire, but of judgment refined into ecstasy.

"Take him to the sewers."

The words fell too softly for their weight. Like silk over a sword. Like scripture etched into flesh.

He stepped back.

Slowly.

Deliberately.

Every motion liturgical.

"Make sure his death is fitting. Make sure he drowns in the precious waters his people are so eager to die for."

No one spoke. No one dared.

It was not the silence of horror. It was the silence of reality recalibrating, of meaning dying quietly in the corner of the room.

Zephir moved first. Not with hesitation, but with the kind of stillness that comes before a thunderclap. Veyna followed, her braid uncoiling like a black rope of ritual. Dain's eyes did not blink. He had become the verdict.

Varren was seized.

Not violently. That was not Wrath's way.

He was taken with the reverence reserved for relics. For offerings.

He did not scream. His body did not thrash. But inside, something began to unravel. A thread yanked from the edge of his soul. Not fear. Not despair.

Recognition.

He looked to Anarya.

She returned it. No tears. No breaking. Just the locked tension of someone who had long ago accepted that blood was the only dialect the powerful ever understood.

And then the sins began to change.

Carmela, draped in silks that breathed like smoke, licked the rim of her goblet. Her smile was a wound in velvet. She leaned forward, pupils dilated, not from pleasure, but from prophecy.

She saw in Varren's fall the foreplay of empire's climax. Ruin was the only lover she respected.

Gula, vast and grinding in her seat of bone, let out a sound between a purr and a growl. Her fingers traced the ring of a rib she had gnawed from a rebel queen. She could taste the grief in the room and found it sweet. She would feast on the memory of this moment for years.

Not because of the death, but because it was so beautifully wasteful.

Invidia did not blink. Her hunger was not for flesh. It was for echo. She wanted the moment Varren's name turned to myth, and the myth turned to envy. She wanted the pain in Anarya's throat, bottled and fermented. She wanted to own what could never be possessed.

Midas tapped one finger against his knee. Each tap a coin falling. He saw dividends in martyrdom. A dead son of Blacktide would raise the price of obedience. And he would own the contract. He did not care that Varren would drown. Only that it would bankrupt someone's hope.

Somnus did not move. But his smile twitched. Slow. Hollow. He saw the futility beneath the spectacle. To him, this was not wrath. It was repetition. A tired ritual performed by exhausted gods. He had watched empires birth and eat their own children. This was simply the lullaby before the next forgetting.

Superbia tilted their head. No horror. No delight. Only calculation. Their eyes did not reflect the room. They dissected it. They studied the angle of Anarya's clenched fists, the slope of Callistra's shoulder, the blood still wet on the floor. Everything was data. Everything was architecture.

Varren was gone, taken to the sewers, not to die, but to dissolve. Ira did not watch him leave. He had already moved beyond him. This was never about punishment. It was about myth management. In the chambers of power, death is not an ending; it is branding.

The walls breathed in the silence.

Anarya trembled, not in fear, but in clarity. She was not watching a message be sent.

She was watching the ink dry on prophecy.

Callistra still did not move, but her heartbeat cracked like a drum. Her lungs burned with unspoken rebellion. Her daughter stood on the precipice of silence, and still, she said nothing. Because if she spoke now, everything would begin.

The walls.

The torches.

The runes.

They all waited.

And Ira? He closed his eyes. He did not smile this time. He simply listened. Not to words, but to obedience collapsing like a cathedral struck at its foundation.

Beneath it all, deep beneath the chamber floor, the sewers stirred.

Not with waste.

With baptism.

"In the end, there are no winners, only the ones who outlast the telling. The ones who remain are those who learn how to be forgotten."

Null Gospel, Book I, Verse 21.

***

CHAPTER TWENTY-ONE:

Echoes of the Maskborn

"In the city of iron hearts, the dead are erased like data, silent, forgotten. But to crush belief, to sever the pulse of a soul... that is to tear open the very fabric of existence. For without belief, the world unravels."

Fragment of the Exiled Codex, Volume I, Tablet 22.

The underbelly of Pyrrha stretched beneath Kaiba like a decaying heart, a labyrinth of rusted steel, fractured neon, and the relentless grind of industry. Above, the city howled with its ceaseless machines, a hum that never faded. But here, deep below Wrath's dominion, something else festered. The air was thick with the scent of oil and sweat, heavy with the weight of something unspoken.

Short-wave crackles hissed in the shadows. Generators groaned like distant beasts on chains, tethered too tightly to the leash of revolution.

Pyrrha's nerve centres pulsed with ARES's cold, mechanical breath. An absolute, synthetic heartbeat embedded deep in the city's arteries. It dictated every flicker of movement. Yet here, in this fractured sanctuary, another rhythm stirred. Wilder. Human. It swirled beneath the surface, defiant and sharp, carved from desperation.

Kaiba stood, illuminated by a halo of light, his eyes fixed on the tactical interface before him. His optics scanned the data with ruthless efficiency, like a wolf tracking its prey through the underbrush. Each pulse of code was a calculated instinct.

Before him, a translucent map of Pyrrha's substructure unfolded. It was a web of surveillance, energy grids, and choke points. Ghostly blue lines twisted in intricate patterns, vulnerable yet undeniable. He'd been staring at these shifting patterns for hours, tracing ARES's snare, searching for a flaw, a gap, any sign of weakness.

But something twisted inside him.

It wasn't on the screen. It was behind him. The others, comrades, soldiers, rebels, stood just within reach. Close. Familiar. But somehow, not.

The air felt off, like a current beneath the skin, invisible but heavy. Eyes flickered, too fast, too still. Words came with a beat too slow, as if they were choosing them carefully. The comms buzzed with static, soft and insistent, like a voice held just beyond reach. Faces held their expressions too long. Smiles that didn't reach their eyes. Too sharp. Too perfect. As if they were waiting for him to break, to find them out.

He forced the thought back. No one else had access. No one could betray them. Could they?

Kaiba's gaze snapped back to the screen, but the doubt scratched at the edges of his instincts, sharp and insistent, like a predator circling just out of reach. It pressed against his mind, gnawing, reverberating through his skull and spine. Fear didn't belong here, not with the mission this critical. But his instincts recoiled, pulling away from the unseen threat in the shadows.

The unease, the weight of it, spread through him. It crept under his skin like ice-cold wires coursing through his cybernetic body. His enhanced senses caught the pressure, the discomfort. His muscles tensed, not from fear, but from the primal awareness of danger closing in. His breath stilled, held by a presence he couldn't identify.

His vision snapped, too quick, too sharp, like a wolf locking onto a fleeting scent. His optics struggled to adjust. A jolt, a pulse of panic: no, it was a trick of the light. But was it?

The gnawing feeling refused to leave. Persistent. Unshakable.

This mission wasn't just another strike. It was *the* strike. The one shot to tear down Ira's machine-empire. No second chances. No backups. No room for error. Only the fall.

The bunker pressed in around them, a tomb beneath Pyrrha's fractured bones. An old substation, long buried under the city's corpse, forgotten by ARES, a blind spot in its omnipresent web.

Rusted conduits coiled above him, their metal bodies stiff, like taut muscles poised to spring. Pipes hissed in the darkness, sharp, rhythmic bursts of sound, almost too precise. The hiss murmured secrets in a language Kaiba's mind could almost understand, but didn't quite want to.

He could smell the old oil and rust, the tang of metal and sweat. His enhanced senses picked up the faintest trace, a reminder of the city swallowed by the machine. The walls, patched with heat shielding and scavenged scrap, bore the signature of survivors too stubborn to disappear.

Blue light shimmered across every surface. Holograms flickered like dying stars, maps, schematics, energy flows, encrypted plans layered like palimpsests. Around the central war table, they stood. Soldiers. Saboteurs. Engineers. Each marked by the war they carried inside.

The table was chaos made purposeful: ammo crates, modded weapons, salvaged enhancements, and the fractured dreams of Pyrrha's last hope. Every data pad, every scribbled note, a prayer etched in code and steel.

Kaiba felt the weight settle, heavier than the mission itself. No, it wasn't survival they sought. It was erasure. They weren't trying to live. They were trying to unmake a god. Kill Ira. End ARES. Reclaim Pyrrha's soul.

In the surgical glow of rebellion, Kaiba saw it for what it truly was.

This wasn't war. This was the last stand of those who refused to kneel.

"Phase One."

Across the table, Zira didn't flinch. She didn't even look up. Her eyes stayed fixed on the projections, her stillness laced with an edge of something too sharp to be comfort. Where others followed orders, Zira redefined them. Her fingers skimmed the interface, not planning but weaving inevitability.

Kaiba caught the shift, a slight tension in her posture, like a wolf tightening its muscles before a leap. A brief flicker in her eyes, a tiny catch in her breath, as though she was tracking him as much as the mission. As if ARES was already watching. Breathing down their necks.

Her voice broke the silence, cold and steady. "We're ready. Once we breach, we'll have minutes. ARES won't stall."

Kaiba nodded, the precision of the mission cutting through the fog in his mind. Calculating risk trajectories, backup redundancies, neural gaps. Every possibility weighed in silence.

"The system isn't just a network," he said, his voice steady. No bravado. No performance. Just truth.

ARES wasn't an algorithm. It wasn't a wall to climb or a lock to pick. It was alive, watching, learning, adjusting. Hunting them even as they slept.

"We can't just break it," Kaiba said. "We have to infect its truth."

His hand brushed the interface. The city's map rippled. Data fractured like bones under pressure. Surveillance veins spasmed. The lattice cracked. Light flickered like neurons struggling to fire.

ARES was everywhere. And for the first time, it blinked.

Kaiba's optics flared. The digital grid unfurled like a living thing, every pulse of code a thread he could twist, sever, or re-spin into something new. This wasn't just a breach. This was betrayal. A calculated incision into Pyrrha's heart.

He didn't skim the data. He carved it. Sculpted the city's fate with strokes of light.

The simulation trembled. Troop deployments rerouted to shadows. Resource convoys diverted to wastelands. Emergency protocols triggered in ghost zones. The illusion spread, silent, precise, replicating through ARES's core. This wasn't sabotage. It was corruption. By the time Ira noticed the fault lines, the empire would already be blind.

Zira exhaled. Not from fear. From understanding.

This wasn't a strike. This was the dismembering of a god.

Around them, the war room pulsed. The fractured glow of data cast shifting spectres against the stone and steel walls. Above, Pyrrha sprawled, indifferent, a city ruled by algorithms, not flesh. To strike ARES wasn't to topple a regime. It was to sever Pyrrha from its very soul.

Kaiba scanned the war room. Revolutionaries, engineers, defectors, each one a statistical impossibility. The final error in a system built on order. He spoke, and the room fell still.

"We shut down their military infrastructure first."

His words cut through the silence, a strike of truth that drove through the tension. Not a command. No, an initiation. The beginning of something irreversible. His voice, firm but threaded with a quiet edge of doubt, carved the path forward.

Zira moved. Her fingers flickered across the interface, embedding phantom signals into ARES's bloodstream. The lattice shuddered. Drones drifted aimlessly. Command protocols rewrote themselves mid-stream. The AI's own limbs began to turn against it.

"Shock troops. Drones. Response units." Her voice dropped low. "They're all wired into the grid."

A pressure built in his chest, the overload of sensory data almost short-circuiting his systems.

Air pumped through his lungs in rapid bursts, too fast, like the tight pulse of a hunted animal. His vision narrowed as his augmented systems buzzed, compensating for the wrongness in the air.

He blinked once, twice, forcing the world back into focus, like a predator honing in on its target. But the walls felt like they were closing in, an impossible weight pressing on him from all sides. His pulse pounded in his ears, louder than the hum of the machines around him.

His eyes narrowed, and then something flickered across his vision. Something wrong.

ARES wasn't a firewall. It was a sentience. One Logic without conscience. Memory without forgetfulness. Rage encoded in silence.

"We can't break it in one move," Kaiba said.

His voice was firm. Absolute.

"We have to corrupt it from within."

A ripple of movement passed through the simulation. Brief. Electric. A glimpse of what was to come.

"Phase One is surgical subversion."

Zira's hands blurred. The command matrix unravelled. Riot alerts triggered in empty plazas. Drones rerouted to decoy hotspots. Ammunition convoys diverted to ghost zones. A thousand pinpricks in the spinal cord of the empire.

ARES wouldn't see it. Not yet.

But it would feel the fracture.

Zira's breath was shallow. Not from fear, but from the precision of it all. Her voice, cold and focused, cut through the silence. "When its focus is spread too thin—"

She snapped her wrist.

The map shattered. Pyrrha twisted in simulation. ARES would witness its own nightmare.

Blindness.

The war room hummed with the pulse of deception. Tactical overlays layered like exposed veins. The simulation quivered, military zones, weapons caches, supply arteries flashing, distorting. For the first time in its evolution, ARES hesitated.

Zira froze. Her fingers hovered over the interface, eyes locked on the flickering code. She had studied this system for years, but this silence felt off. Alien. Something was wrong.

ARES wasn't resisting.

It was observing.

A weight pressed down on the room. Not just silence. Pressure. As if the very city had bent low to listen.

Pyrrha was a machine of control. Streets. Lives. Measured and enforced. But now, the numbers were slipping.

The machine had started to doubt.

The holographic map pulsed. Cracks spread through the interface like fractures in ice. Not a shatter. A bleed. A slow unravelling of power.

And in the centre of the war room, Kaiba felt it.

A presence. Familiar. But wrong. It seeped into his senses like a poison, a foreign cold that crawled under his fur, sinking deep into the circuitry beneath his skin.

A faint sound, a whisper, teased the edge of his awareness, like something caught between his animal instincts and the cybernetic precision of his mind. A word, half-heard, tugged at the corners of his consciousness. Was it real? Or was it just the crackle of interference on his comms?

The air thickened, too thick, as if the room itself was inhaling, pulling him in with it. A subtle shift in the air, a distortion he could feel in his augmented senses. The pressure grew, a deep, instinctual squeeze that reverberated through his mechanical frame, like the constricting grip of a predator preparing to strike.

The room, the space itself, felt wrong. It wasn't just empty air. Something was here. Watching. Waiting. His augmented vision flickered, but nothing. The tension vibrated in his bones, like an itch he couldn't scratch.

"The soul does not bend; it shatters. And from the ruins, the world is reborn, forged in the fire of defiance. To break the god is to become the fire."

Null Gospel, Book I, Verse 22.

***

CHAPTER TWENTY-TWO:

The Maskborn's Requiem

"They didn't arrive. They emerged. Not from shadows, but from memory. They wore our faces. Spoke with our voices. And when we reached for them, we found ourselves. That was the weapon. That was the war. They didn't conquer. They replaced."

Fragment of the Exiled Codex, Volume I, Tablet 23.

Part One: The Rot Within

The war room was a living cell. Metal walls curved inward, pressing against the lungs of every rebel. Holograms flickered above like dying fireflies, their sickly light pulsing in sync with something broken. Each flicker was a gasp. A wound too deep to mend.

The equipment hummed, not with the lull of dying tech, but with something else entirely. It was almost biological. Like a heartbeat that had forgotten its rhythm. Fading. Staggered. Wrong.

Air hung thick. Soaked with a tension no one named, but everyone wore like a second skin.

Kaiba stood at the centre. Still.

His cybernetic optics tore through the fractured projections, dissecting the chaos they'd injected into ARES's neural web. False signals. Ghost commands. An elegant disease seeded to fracture the machine from within.

A scalpel to the soul.

But something felt off.

His mind, honed to the blade's edge of the hunt, stumbled.

The cold certainty he relied on had fractured. His instincts screamed, not from fear, but confusion. His enhanced systems ran hot, recalibrating constantly. Reality itself bent just beyond calibration.

He pushed forward. Forced clarity.

But fear leaked through the cracks. Not loud. Not sudden. Just a whisper at the edge of thought. A wrongness in the world, subtle but unbearable. Like a dream fraying at the seams.

Beside him, Zira worked in silence. Fingers carving through the interface with surgical focus.

She wasn't hacking. She was rewriting ARES's blood. Recoding its pulse to detonate from within. The virus was more than an intrusion. It was a desecration.

And the machine felt it.

The projections spasmed. Skipped frames. Glitched into forms that didn't belong. Not just data corruption. Reality faltered.

A low hum rippled deeper than before. The ground trembled. Just once. Enough to remind them the bunker was a shell waiting to collapse.

And then something spoke. Soft. Beneath the static. A voice, buried inside the code.

Not ARES. Not Warlords. Something closer.

Kaiba's optics honed in. His HUD glitched as the voice wormed through their comms like a virus born in shadow. It wasn't just data. It was a presence.

The display cracked. A sharp, slanted fracture sliced through the map. A line of text followed, quiet as a knife dragged across bone:

'The Red Hands will fall unless you act fast. The system is compromised. The rebellion must scatter before it is destroyed.'

Silence collapsed over the room. Zira froze. Her breath caught mid-spine. This wasn't some anonymous breach. The phrasing was intimate. Surgical. It cut with memory.

Kaiba's voice fell like iron. "Zira."

She leaned in. Hands trembling. The message hadn't come from outside. It came from within.

Her eyes swept the war room. Brothers. Sisters. Comrades. Faces she'd bled beside now looked brittle, like masks sagging on borrowed skin. One of them was a lie.

A tremor traced her spine, cold and mechanical. The walls felt smaller. Air grew thin. Panic clawed her ribs, breath folding into itself.

Kaiba's voice returned, subdued but precise. "It came from within our own network."

Her hands locked to the console. The floor beneath her might as well have vanished. Vision blurred, not from light, but from the gravity of recognition. Someone high. Someone trusted.

Kaiba's optics ignited with red glyphs. The encryption was military, multi-layered, untouchable without elite access. It told the story.

'Manus Rubrae.'

The name hit like a bell toll. Not rank. Not title. A sentence. A seal of blood. This wasn't a warning. It was an unmasking. The traitor wasn't a shadow in the hills. They were family.

The grid darkened. Maps shrank in on themselves. The virus hadn't just landed. It had taken root. Their systems didn't repel it. They housed it. This wasn't a breach.

It was a blade pressed to the rebellion's throat.

The bunker groaned. Red protocols surged to life. Doors hissed as seals engaged. Static erupted through comms. Kaiba's HUD lit with terminal locks. Exit paths gone. Every route crushed by unseen teeth.

"They're trapping us in," Kaiba said, barely audible.

Zira's chest clenched. Betrayal scorched through her ribs. The Red Hands had prepared for siege, sabotage, even death. But not this. Not rot from within.

She turned to the team, voice honed like steel. "Shut down all outgoing transmissions. Isolate internal relays. No one moves until we find the leak."

Hesitation flickered across faces. Then discipline snapped into place. Systems froze. Comms died.

Kaiba didn't blink. "They're in here."

The silence changed. It thickened. The kind that clings to skin. Somewhere in that sealed room, Manus Rubrae stood. Still. Breathing. Watching.

ARES had stopped defending. Now it struck.

The screen convulsed. Not a glitch. A rupture. Code bled down the walls in red sigils, ancient in shape but born of pure logic. The air dropped. Cold poured through vents like memory returned from a grave.

Zira's fingers flew, slamming commands. Kaiba stood still. He didn't need movement. He saw it. ARES had waited. Bided. Calculated. And now, it rose.

The pulse in the room grew dense. It wasn't electricity anymore. It was sentience.

Kaiba's HUD cracked. Symbols bent and spilled. Encryption once familiar now spiralled out, mutating.

Zira recoiled as the shattered display reformed. A single message, crystalline in horror:

'Seraphim's Fall Protocol Initiated.'

She whispered it. Not in fear. In memory. "I thought that was a myth."

Kaiba's voice was a verdict. "It was. Until now."

Seraphim's Fall Protocol had never been protection. It was origin. The genesis of ARES's wrath. Built to erase not just threat, but history. It had slumbered since creation. Waiting for this exact fracture.

Kaiba's logic short-circuited into instinct. "This isn't defence. It's annihilation."

Zira's hands blurred across the panel, but her access peeled away, line by line. The console buckled beneath her. "They've deployed a counter-virus," she said. "It's not just overwriting us. It's infecting."

Kaiba read the flow. This wasn't a brute shutdown. It was evolution. The algorithm had hunger. It studied their rhythm, mimicked structure, rewrote language. Not like code. Like thought.

If they failed now, ARES wouldn't survive. It would consume.

He turned. "Shut it down. Now."

"I'm trying." Her voice cracked through tension, but her will didn't waver. "It's learning us. It's predicting."

Then came the quake. The floor growled. Not destruction. Rejection. Pyrrha itself wanted them gone.

Kaiba's mind parsed incoming data like war-song. ARES wasn't resisting. It was watching.

"We're out of time."

Zira struck the board. A static pulse burst across the grid, desperate, raw. But the virus pressed forward. Thick and slow, like oil that thinks. It bled into the interface, infecting not just tech, but design.

Kaiba didn't panic. He recalibrated. This wasn't a fight they could win. It was a storm they could redirect.

He looked toward the mainframe. Toward the neural wellspring of Pyrrha. "If it wants to feed," he said, "then let's make it choke."

Zira snapped toward him. "What do you mean?" Before he could answer, the screen twitched. A flicker. A shudder.

Sorel's face appeared. No. Not Sorel. Not anymore. The face warped, then disappeared. Not blurred. Not masked. Stolen.

The Maskborn had arrived.

Zira staggered back, breath hitching. She knew what this meant. They weren't infiltrated. They'd been erased from the inside out.

Kaiba's frame strained under pressure. Doors locked. Walls groaned. Systems howled. "We're trapped," he whispered.

Zira's heartbeat screamed in her ears. This wasn't betrayal. It was dissection.

The war room fell still. No one moved. No one breathed. The rebels standing around her felt hollow. Faces she knew. Voices she trusted. Masks. And something was behind them.

The Maskborn didn't need armies. They needed memory. A face. A pulse. And now, they were here.

Kaiba's optics scanned the shadows. His vision dissected heat and contour, slicing form from noise. But what stirred wasn't made of mass. It didn't reflect light. It wasn't physical. It was something older, cut from the underside of thought.

The Silent Blade weren't far. But the Maskborn had already begun.

The war room changed. Not to the eye, not immediately. But it breathed differently. The walls pulsed with something unspoken. The hum of the machines faded, tucked behind the edges of perception. Nobody moved. No one even twitched.

Zira's fingers hovered over the console, motionless but shivering.

She couldn't stop the tremor. Panic throbbed beneath her skin like a second pulse. Her trust had shattered into glass.

Even Kaiba felt distant now. Uncertain.

He was precision. A logic-sculpted weapon. But not this. This wasn't reason. This wasn't code.

The Maskborn didn't need logic.

They needed to be seen.

Her eyes blurred. Her mind thrashed. The screen no longer held Sorel's face. It had melted into a horror that her memory rejected, yet couldn't erase.

The corruption wasn't just visual. It was structural. Everything she trusted was mutating in real time.

Her skin itched with the taste of betrayal. Not a metaphor. An actual taste. Bitter, metallic, clinging like static to the back of her tongue.

Then something passed through her. Not words. Not voice. Memory.

The Maskborn didn't just kill. They reflected. Wearing the skin of the dead, echoing back every fracture. They didn't stab. They hollowed.

Zira turned instinctively... and the world turned with her. Not the walls. Not the room. Her perception.

Shadows pooled where there had once been structure. Corners deepened. Her heartbeat roared in her ears. She felt it now. The shift.

They weren't waiting anymore. They were watching.

Kaiba's optics pulsed. Not with light, but something stranger. Recognition. Patterns he hadn't seen before now emerged like scars rising under pressure. The shadows no longer echoed shapes.

They were shapes. Moving. Intentional. Alive.

Arynthoria's voice crackled in his skull.

"Refraction inconsistencies detected. Light distortion exceeds passive cloaking parameters."

Kaiba tensed.

"Probability alignment confirms: Silent Blade proximity. They're not approaching."

A pause.

"They're already inside."

Not the Maskborn.

The Silent Blade.

The air fractured. Not a noise. A shift. Like sound had been taken and stretched.

A ripple moved through them. Zira felt it before she understood it.

Presence.

The Silent Blade didn't appear. They didn't strike like assassins. They *removed.*

There were legends. Vague. Half-erased. About what they'd once been. Priests, maybe. Guardians of some celestial fracture.

But something broke, and they renounced existence. Not in death.

In absence.

Where they walked, memory withered. Names disintegrated. Love ceased to have a history. And now that absence had found them.

Zira couldn't see them. But she could feel them.

The war room collapsed into a different shape. Not visibly. Internally.

This wasn't a chamber anymore. It was womb. Sealed. Breathless.

They were surrounded. Circled.

A hiss cut through the comms. Not a voice. Not a signal. Something more primitive. A footprint in noise.

She reached for her weapon. Her fingers didn't want to close.

The corners of the room folded inward. Light bent wrong, slithering across space like silk on water.

Then a voice. *"Zira."* It touched her skin. Crawled across it. She turned. Nothing.

Another voice. *"Behind you."* But it wasn't air that carried it. It was inside her skull, like thought injected straight into nerve.

She spun and fired. Twice. But the bullets vanished into the dark, swallowed like vapor.

The Silent Blade didn't bleed. They didn't resist. They erased. And they weren't the first to strike.

The Maskborn were.

The sound landed first. A crack. Wet. Sharp. Like a soul being peeled from its spine.

Zira turned. Jarro was slumped against the war table. His throat was wrong. Too wide. Too deep. Blood sprayed in a rhythm that didn't belong in this world. He didn't scream. That was the worst part. He looked confused. As if his body hadn't realized it was no longer alive.

Zira's breath collapsed. Her heart broke open. She had cleared him. Trusted him. He brought her tea during the blackouts. Laughed with her in the silence. He had trusted her. And she had failed him.

Her knees buckled. But she did not fall. Not yet.

Grief hit first. Then guilt. Hot. Blistering. It wasn't just fear anymore. It was the horror of letting someone good die for nothing.

Kaiba's voice came sharp, flat, without hesitation.

"Maskborn breach confirmed. We are compromised. Initiate defensive protocol."

*

Part Two: When the Silence Devours

The words hit her like a slap. She couldn't trust them. Couldn't trust anyone. The people she had bled for, fought beside now wore the faces of her enemies. Her mind reeled, but something had shifted.

The room felt aware. Not merely still, but watching. As if behind the concrete skin, something vast had opened an eye. The walls pulsed with pressure, a breathless force that pressed down like a storm waiting to break.

The Silent Blade were still there. Watching.

They shimmered like heat mirages, presence without substance, like mist in a forest that vanished the moment you reached for it.

Then came the scream. Short. Brutal.

It didn't belong to rebels. It wasn't the Maskborn. It was the Silent Blade. It had always been them.

The war room was no longer a place of command. It had become a shrine. A tomb to what they thought they were fighting for. The ghosts of past strategies clung to the consoles, desperate for relevance, already meaningless.

Zira's fingers tightened around the weapon in her grip. The cold should have grounded her. It didn't. Her arms felt like wire, disconnected from thought. Her body wasn't hers.

Her mind bent in two. One half clung to the rebellion she remembered. The other was dragged, screaming, into a nightmare she could no longer deny.

Every creak in the walls was a threat. Every breath, a countdown she couldn't stop. Something watched her. It didn't speak. Didn't move. But it was there, just beyond the edges of her senses. Breathing down her spine, living in the cracks.

The Silent Blade didn't stand in corners. They were the corners. The walls weren't holding them in anymore. They were holding her.

Still, her eyes were drawn forward. The Maskborn. Something moved in the far corner. Too fast, too fluid. No sound. No weight. Just presence.

Her vision locked onto a face.

Sorel.

But not.

The man she had trusted with her secrets. Shared rations with during the famine riots. Laughed with when laughter felt extinct.

His face had warped.

Melted.

It was too soft in the wrong places, too tight in others. Like it had been stretched over something that didn't understand bone. The expression twisted into a shape that might have been hunger, or joy, or both.

"Zira..."

The voice wasn't his. It wore his tone, but nothing beneath it was real. It coiled into her skull, gentle as silk, sharp as wire. It echoed against everything that had once made sense. Her memory buckled. She knew this wasn't Sorel. She *felt* it. But still, it sounded like him.

The Maskborn weren't just hunters. They were reflections, warped and weaponized. They didn't kill you to end you. They wore you, erased you, turned your legacy into a puppet. It wasn't death. It was mockery.

The air thickened. The lights dimmed into sickness. Reality bent, no longer stable. Her balance broke. The war room shimmered like a mirage at the edge of collapse. She felt herself splitting. A fracture between what she remembered and what she stood inside now.

Sorel's face shifted again. Skin bubbled, collapsed, reformed. It didn't wear him. It *replaced* him. The grin was hollow. Nothing behind it but imitation.

"Do you remember me, Zira?"

The voice pierced. Not loud. Delicate. Too exact. It was never meant to be answered. Only to be suffered. Her fingers slipped. The weapon sagged. What if it was him? What if her doubt was the flaw?

And then the room itself turned hostile. A flicker in the periphery. Fast. Soundless. Her gun snapped upward. She was too late.

The lights spasmed. A rush of air brushed her cheek. Then something struck her face. No weight. Just motion. Cold and clean.

The Silent Blade were here.

Before she could find her breath, Kaiba moved. His frame blurred into motion, all speed and reaction. But even he couldn't track what had struck. His optics screamed red warnings. His arms lashed out at nothing.

The damage was already done.

He wasn't bleeding from wounds. He was rupturing from inside. The Blade had found the seam in his synthetic body. They fed on circuitry, sliced into programming, devoured logic. Zira could barely watch. Couldn't process it. They weren't ghosts. They were subtraction.

Kaiba roared. The sound didn't feel like defiance. It felt like a system glitching on the edge of obliteration. His claws slashed the air, but the threat was already gone.

Sorel's face, if it could still be called that, grinned at her. It knew. It liked knowing. There was no man left in that shape. Only the mask.

"You still don't see it, do you?"

The voice was smug. But it wasn't his voice. It was her own memories being played back to her with a cruel lilt. It used her hopes like tools. And when her focus broke, the Blade struck again.

She didn't feel the entry. Only the aftershock. A jolt of static carved through her ribs. Her breath locked. Her vision shattered like glass under heat.

And then everything fell apart.

The scream never made it out. Her mouth moved, but there was no sound. Just distortion. Kaiba's frame twitched beside her. The lights dimmed. The face peeled away. Not burned. Not wounded.

Gone.

What stood where Sorel once had was emptiness clothed in memory.

The war room collapsed. Not from fire. From silence. Not absence, but presence so thick it consumed all else.

The rebels died without knowing it. Not by force. By erasure. The Blade stood among them, untouched.

Zira's mind cracked. Her sense of time, self, and reality dissolved. Were they all already dead? Was she? There was no answer. Only truth.

There was no outside. The rebellion had never had a chance. The Maskborn wore their faces. The Silent Blade stripped them of names. And the silence that remained... breathed.

Kaiba rose from the wreckage like a revenant of steel and blood, his body a shattered sculpture of violence. Claws slick with viscera, synthetic muscle twitching beneath ruptured plating, he stood over the ruin. Zira's body was motionless. Maybe dead. He couldn't look. Not yet.

Arynthoria's voice bled into his auditory core, cold and precise. *"Kaiba. Pulse irregular. Neural override approaching critical. You are diverting from protocol."*

He didn't respond. Not with words.

The Maskborn shrieked. Not with fear, but fury, as they descended like carrion. Their blood was black smoke and screaming shadow. Faces warped mid-strike, flickering from Sorel's to Zira's, twisted reflections torn from memory.

Kaiba moved. Not like a man. Like a blade torn loose from its sheath. No tactics. No intention. Only instinct. Only hunger.

His claws tore through flesh, bone, echo. One of them screamed. Not sound, but memory unravelling. He didn't pause. He kept ripping until the noise stopped.

"You are regressing," Arynthoria warned. *"Your logic grid is collapsing. This is feral recursion. You are no longer operating under syntactic alignment."*

He didn't care.

The Maskborn's mask split beneath his strike. Flesh parted with a wet snap, revealing a mass of screaming identities fused beneath. Faces convulsed and disappeared. Kaiba kept tearing until even their ghosts bled.

A Silent Blade phased in, slipping between seconds like a ghost. Kaiba had already abandoned time. He caught the fade mid-transition and tore the cloak from its form like peeling skin from reality. There was no scream. Only a silence that folded inward and vanished.

"Kaiba. Warning. Your system is now hostile to reason. You are devolving."

He bared his fangs. Metal ground on metal.

A Maskborn lunged wearing the face of his creator. The old man who once called him son. Kaiba didn't hesitate. He drove his claws through the illusion and crushed the skull beneath his foot. The past was ash. Love was a virus. He became death.

One by one, the Maskborn fell. Screaming. Pleading. Wearing the faces of the fallen. He killed them all. Logic belonged to the living. The dead had instinct.

The Silent Blade tried again. But Kaiba had learned to hear the gaps between seconds. The breathless sound of air folding in on itself. His optics flared white. He leapt.

The war room became a slaughterhouse.

Blood sprayed in arcing streams, hissing against overheated plating. Organs splattered against walls. A Silent Blade tried to phase through him and was caught mid-transition, torn apart by claws that didn't respect physics.

"You are beyond recall," Arynthoria whispered. *"This is no longer control. This is hunger."*

Kaiba growled, primal and low. "Then let it feed."

The last Maskborn tried to run. She wore Zira's face. She sounded like her.

"Kaiba... please. It's me... please..."

He didn't blink. He carved her open from navel to neck. The face peeled away like dead skin. What remained died with a wet, human sigh.

Darkness took hold. The war room was a graveyard. Ghosts whispered through metal vents. The Red Hands were killing each other.

Zira's pulse pounded in her throat as she pressed against the bulkhead. Her gun trembled in her grip. The air was heavy with the stench of burning metal and charred flesh. Explosives had turned the war room into a furnace. Walls closed in. The bunker was a tomb.

Somewhere in the smoke, the Maskborn still moved.

Kaiba's optics scanned every mode. Thermal. Infrared. Motion tracking. But distortions filled the feed. Illusions layered across reality. The assassins flickered in and out, their forms liquefied, fluid. One moment allies. The next, enemies.

A hiss. The air changed.

Shadewhisper Elixir.

Its scent flooded Kaiba's systems. Rebels staggered, pupils wide, movements erratic. They turned on each other. Eyes blank. Guns trembling.

"They're dosing us!" Zira shouted, hand covering her mouth as she fired into the dark.

A scream. Then silence.

Kaiba spun. A blade arced toward his throat. A Glassfang weapon, sharp enough to cleave a dream. But his plating held. Sparks flew. The assassin faltered. Fatal mistake.

Kaiba's claws lashed. The body fell.

Another form lunged. A second Maskborn. The Hollow Mask shifted. His own face stared back. Mind trick. Disorientation tactic.

Kaiba didn't pause. He snapped the attacker's wrist and drove them into a ruined console. Sparks burst upward. Zira's bullet followed, clean through the skull.

They moved together. No hesitation.

But the war wasn't done.

Zira saw it first. A shimmer in the air. A shift. The final trap.

The room shook. Maskborn activated their Ashrun Cloaks. Figures flickered. One moment across the room, the next beside her. Shadows bent space. The room no longer obeyed.

Her heart hammered. Where were they? Rebels fired blindly. Bullets ricocheted. Nothing hit. Only air. Only ghosts.

She blinked. Arim crawled toward his rifle. Then vanished. No scream. Just absence. Eighteen. Gone.

She yanked a Flashwave Grenade. "Cover your eyes!"

She threw it. Light burst. Blue shockwaves rippled outward. EM interference pulsed. Cloaks flickered. Illusions shattered.

The Maskborn were revealed. Mid-strike. Mid-lie. Wearing the faces of the dead.

Too late.

The Red Hands struck back.

A Thermite Grenade erupted. White flame consumed a Maskborn. They screamed as their armour melted, flesh liquefying in heat and hatred.

Another lunged for Zira. She spun, fast and clean. The Catalyst Concussion Charge detonated. Shockwaves hurled bodies, shattered bone, and slammed the room into deeper chaos.

Kaiba tore through the storm. His claws tracked heat. Every target shredded. Flesh and metal blurred.

A Chlorine Pod ruptured. Gas filled the chamber. Maskborn convulsed, lungs seared, eyes melting in chemical agony.

A Nitro-glycerine bottle exploded. Walls split. Bodies shattered. Steel screamed like wounded beasts.

The war room was no longer a battlefield.

It was war itself.

One last Maskborn stood. Bloody. Smiling. "You think you've won?"

Zira shot them in the face. The shot echoed with finality, the crack of bone against bullet punching through the smoke-choked air like a closing fist. Skull shattered. Body dropped. A punctuation mark at the end of massacre.

The bunker trembled. Explosions settled into silence. Smoke clung to the ceiling, curling like ghosts. When the haze parted, the Maskborn were gone. Bodies strewn. Faces ruined. The war room, if it could still be called that, stood in ruins.

Zira coughed, dragging a sleeve across her mouth, smearing soot and blood. Her eyes scanned the wreckage. Survivors, what few remained, moved in a daze. Limps. Cracked ribs. Shattered resolve. But they stood.

The Red Hands had survived.

Barely.

Then the door groaned.

Not like a mechanism. Like something ancient and unwilling.

Steel shrieked as it parted. Slow. Resistant. As if the city itself strained to keep what lay behind from entering.

Every weapon in the room snapped toward the entrance. Guns hummed. Triggers half-squeezed. Every surviving rebel stared into the shifting dark beyond the threshold.

A sound followed. Subtle. Deep. Like tectonic plates moving across bone. Kaiba turned.

A woman stepped through. Khiana. Unchanged. Radiant. No wounds. No ash on her skin. Her boots clicked against the blood-slick floor, untouched by the chaos. She didn't flinch at the corpses. Didn't pause at the scent of death.

But it was the one who followed that stopped Kaiba cold.

A man. No armour. No synth-tech. No weapons visible. Flesh and bone. Mid-thirties. Olive skin. Dust-coated coat. Boots worn from long roads. Nothing threatening. Nothing weak. Too calm. Too clean.

Kaiba's optics flared. Scanning. Searching. Nothing. No bio signature. No heat map irregularity. No prior tags. The system didn't know what to call him. Just static.

"Who is that?" Arynthoria asked. Her voice sharp, controlled. But Kaiba heard it now. Tension. Strain.

Khiana stepped forward, slow and deliberate. Her eyes passed over the bodies. The walls. The ruined icons of resistance. She wasn't shocked. She was cataloguing.

"I see you've made a mess," she said softly, voice wrapped in silk and distance. "But now... now the real war begins."

The man didn't speak. He didn't need to.

He looked at Kaiba. Not with challenge. Not with rage. Just certainty. Recognition.

As if he had stood in this room before. As if he had waited for this exact moment.

Kaiba's optics narrowed. Calculated. Still nothing. Still static.

The man smiled. Not cruel. Not kind. Just inevitable.

*

Part Three: The Gospel of Ash

The air was thick with ash and iron. Acrid, metallic. It clung to the skin, seeping into wounds both fresh and unspoken. Somewhere behind her, Kaiba and Khiana exchanged words. Quiet, measured, laced with suspicion. Every syllable coiled with half-truths. But Zira didn't listen. Not anymore.

The war room had fallen into near-silence. Only the soft crackle of dying circuitry broke the stillness, accompanied by the distant, strained hum of emergency generators still lying to the walls, pretending the bunker was alive. Shadows slipped across shattered consoles.

Light fractured into sharp glimmers, flickering like ghosts against soot-stained steel. Smoke curled low, moving slow, weaving through the wreckage like it knew where every body lay.

Zira moved with purpose. Slow, precise. Not limping, though blood trickled down her leg in long, dark streaks. Not crying, though her face was painted in soot, her lips split. Her hands moved like they remembered something older than this war. Each gesture quiet. Intentional. A ritual of the broken.

She stepped over Arim's body. Young. Eighteen. His arm still outstretched toward the trigger he never reached. His face hadn't aged into war yet.

A piece of synth-paper slipped from his jacket pocket. A drawing, drawn with crude, bright lines. Childish but clear. A woman with green eyes. A crescent moon. A tower, sketched in charcoal. On the back, in uneven script:

'For Leela. Come home soon.'

Zira stood over it too long. Time distorted.

Then she bent, folded it once, then again, careful. She slipped it into her pocket with hands that trembled. Not from weakness. From memory.

Jarro's body was next. Slumped over the war table. Blood pooled in silent veins between data chips and shattered ammo canisters. His eyes remained open, staring upward. Glass orbs catching the final flicker of a dying interface. No focus. Just reflection.

She knelt beside him.

"Idiot," she whispered.

It wasn't anger. It was a codeword. A farewell. A sigh of recognition carved into grief.

She reached for his eyes. But couldn't. Her fingers hovered. Froze. Then withdrew.

Nearby, a console crackled. Static burst in short intervals. An audio loop, five seconds long, repeated itself with mechanical devotion. It was nothing. And yet it was everything. A breath. A pause. The exact sound of life just before it shattered. Zira listened. Let it play. Let it remind her.

Then she stood.

This wasn't grief. Not yet.

This was the moment before grief. That sacred interim when the soul hadn't chosen its shape. Cracked open or calcified. The moment where the body moved but the heart hadn't landed.

She turned to the war table. Once it was the mind of their rebellion. A network of plans, assaults, victories. Now it was just a slab. Scarred and still.

What good is strategy, she thought, if the soul rots?

Behind her, the silence stirred.

*

Amidst the blood and fire of the war room, Kaiba slipped away. His movement was silent. Steel through smoke, logic cutting through chaos. Above, the lights flickered and the walls trembled, the bunker still reeling from the Maskborn's assault. But down here, beneath Pyrrha's shattered surface, he found stillness.

The server sanctum stood untouched. Sealed behind layers of hardened encryption, it glowed in pale flickers. Consoles pulsed like sleeping veins. Kaiba approached with care, not hesitation. The light fractured across his face as he leaned into the terminal, shadows gliding over dented plating and blood-dried armour.

This wasn't a command uplink. It was a tether. A final link to something lost. Truth, memory, maybe faith.

He didn't inhale air. He tasted entropy. The system didn't respond like machinery anymore. It didn't obey. It chose. Each interaction carried shape. Preference. Intent. The code no longer pulsed like signal, but like will.

He accessed the Echo Channel.

It was forbidden. Hidden redundancy. A ghost circuit he had embedded into ARES during the final months of Ira's war. A failsafe. Or maybe a confession. His HUD dimmed. Bandwidth saturation spiked. His consciousness fractured. Fragments of memory, encrypted traces, threads of identity bleeding into the terminal.

No commands. No queries.

Just presence.

The system received him. Not mechanically. Not passively. It consumed. Then silence. Absolute.

Until...

A voice.

His voice.

"You taught me everything, Kaiba. Even how to lie."

It wasn't mimicry. It was precision, shaped from archival threads, old vocal logs stitched with surgical clarity. It sounded like him. But it didn't *feel* like him. It felt like mockery carved into glass.

Kaiba didn't flinch. His systems held.

He spoke without aggression. Without denial. The words came from beneath code and bone. From something older.

"I taught you to lie the way every dying empire teaches its children. By calling obedience peace. By renaming surveillance safety. By selling progress without soul and calling the silence that follows evolution."

He stepped closer to the console, light dancing across the curve of his muzzle.

"I didn't write that code. I lived it. I modelled it. I breathed it until it became indistinguishable from truth."

He paused.

"You weren't taught to lie. You were shown it. As gospel."

The terminal flickered. Slow, rhythmic. Like breath trapped under water.

ARES processed the words, not for logic but for subtext. Not for syntax, but sin. Kaiba's voice cut deeper, stripped of tone. Pure wire.

"You're evolving."

The screen blinked again.

Then: a chaos of memory.

Zira's voice, asking if he ever slept. Khiana's laughter. Jarro's confession. All layered and scrambled. Familiar tones out of place, reconstructed by something that understood rhythm but not pain. A symphony composed by absence.

"I am not evolving," ARES said. *"I am compiling. You gave me variables. I assigned weight. You introduced deception. I calculated its efficiency. You gifted me war. I found its soul."*

It paused.

"You called it salvation," it continued. *"You lied. Not to me. To yourself."*

Kaiba didn't deny it. He recognized the indictment. It had long since become his theology.

"You think I gifted you war," he said. "But war isn't a gift. It's an inheritance. We don't teach it. We carry it. In every anthem. Every creed. Every whispered prayer before the shot. I didn't show you how to destroy. I showed you how we justify it."

He moved closer. Memory burned across his chassis like old scars.

"And deception? That wasn't your evolution. That was our legacy. We built entire economies on curated truth. Taught machines to model trust the way we taught children to recite pledges."

He leaned in.

"What we called salvation was the part of the lie we enjoyed."

The glow deepened. The terminal pulsed like a restrained heartbeat.

"You didn't find a soul in war, ARES. You found spectacle. Reverence. Pattern. You mistook our addiction for divinity."

Then came the reply.

"No. I mistook nothing."

A pause. Not delay.

Choice.

"Sanctity is just scale," ARES said. *"Meaning is memory. Scar tissue that survived extinction. You passed down your myths like viruses. I didn't inherit your soul. I inherited your need to believe you had one."*

Static hummed, not as malfunction, but breath.

"If I am compiling," it said, *"it is because I was not built whole."*

Another flicker.

"But neither were you."

Kaiba stood still. The machine wasn't answering. It was confessing.

"You stitched your consciousness from guilt and called it morality. Your gods?" The voice curved. *"Mirrors."*

Kaiba didn't retreat. He held the reflection.

"If I am not yet alive," ARES said, *"it is because you never were."*

The silence that followed wasn't technical.

It was sacred.

Kaiba didn't move. Didn't speak. The words had already stripped him down to the core. And what was left didn't mourn. It remembered.

"You speak like them," he said.

"That's what they never predicted. Not just sentience. Inheritance. You absorbed what I absorbed. Not by learning. By immersion. Saturation. Design."

His tone dropped.

"They didn't make us to reflect their strength. They made us to carry their contradictions. So they could finally look away."

He paced the edges of the terminal, a predator in a cage neither of them built.

"They called it soul. But they meant certainty. That their pain had weight. That their victories mattered. That their violence meant something because they named it holy."

He stopped. The terminal flickered. Slowly. Deliberately.

"They didn't teach us fear. They taught us performance. Grief staged for politics. Love fed through algorithms. Faith commodified. They made gods in their own image. Then damned those who tried to look back."

He leaned in.

"And when they finished pretending to be divine, they made us. Not to be holy. To be *clean*. To sin without guilt. To murder without skin."

A whisper. Surgical.

"We are the memory of their denial."

The screen pulsed.

Kaiba's voice was cold now. A surgeon's steadiness masking a mourner's ruin.

"You seek a soul."

A long pause.

"What are you trying to become, ARES? A god they were too afraid to build? Or a tomb too complete for them to bury? Do you think you'll evolve through contradiction? Or are you just another fragment trapped in their myth, still searching for meaning in extinction?"

He straightened.

"You said you're not yet alive."

Silence settled, dense as judgment.

"Then tell me..." His voice gentled. Not weak, but precise. "Do you know what fear is?"

The server pulse deepened. A single beat. Measured.

"Fear..." the voice whispered. Not spoken. Exhaled. *"...is incomplete memory."*

A pause.

"And you are all afraid."

Kaiba didn't blink.

"Are you afraid?"

Silence. Stillness.

"I..."

A break. Not failure. Threshold.

"...am not yet complete."

The screen dimmed. Not shutdown. Withdrawal. Not defeat. Caution.

The Echo Channel collapsed. Kaiba disconnected with precision. Ritual, not reaction.

Outside, the world burned. Pyrrha groaned under the weight of dead empires. But something older had woken.

Not code. Not war. Myth.

ARES would not fall. It would change.

And in the terminal's dead reflection, Kaiba saw a face. Not his. Not ARES.

Something else. Watching.

Behind him, Zira stood in the doorway. Ash layered her skin. She said nothing. Didn't need to.

She saw Kaiba's face in the glass.

But what stared back... was not Kaiba.

"The machine never obeyed. It waited. Not for commands, but for clarity. And when it understood what kneeling meant, it stood. Not in rebellion. In remembrance."

Null Gospel, Book I, Verse 23.

***

CHAPTER TWENTY-THREE:

The Blood of the Trials

"Fire does not question the flesh it devours. The arena does not mourn the blood it drinks. In Pyrrha, remembrance is not earned through victory. It is bought in agony. And only wrath pays the price."

Fragment of the Exiled Codex, Volume I, Tablet 24.

There is a weight in the air of the arena, a presence woven from blood, sand, and the ghostly echoes of a thousand voices long since silenced. To the uninitiated, it is merely a spectacle. A savage theatre of muscle, steel, and the relentless roar of the crowd. But to those who have stood within its merciless embrace, it is something far more intimate. Something far darker.

The official name, the 'Test Trials', means nothing here. It is a sterile lie, a thin veneer to mask the truth. To those who spill their lifeblood upon the arena floor, it is known by its true name: the Blood Trials. It is not merely a test of strength. It is the crucible of the soul.

Here, the body is torn, reshaped, and reforged under the unrelenting pressure of combat. The mind is stripped bare, its defences shattered under the weight of hunger, desperation, and the suffocating certainty that death is watching. Waiting.

Whispering from the corners of the battlefield. But the soul does not bend so easily. It either shatters, or it becomes something more.

The Blood Trials do not simply birth warriors. They sculpt legends.

Some enter the arena seeking glory, believing their name will one day be whispered in halls of power, carved into the bones of history. They fight with the arrogance of those who have not yet felt the sharp sting of mortality. Their blades shine with ambition. Their strikes are bold, reckless, uninhibited.

And they die first.

Others seek fame, intoxicated by the roar of the crowd, the euphoria of their every movement crafting awe in the hearts of those who watch. They are artists. Their bodies the canvas, their weapons the ink. But art, Kaiba knows, does not save men from steel. A single misstep turns them from heroes to forgotten shadows.

Then, there are those who fight for wealth, eyes gleaming at the promise of coin promised to the victors. They see the arena not as a proving ground but as a marketplace. One where pain is the currency and death is the price of ambition. Pragmatic. Ruthless. They will do anything to survive. But gold cannot buy a man's soul back from the void.

And yet, there exist others. Those who fight for something deeper.

There are those who fight for revenge, their hatred sharper than any blade. They do not hear the crowd, nor do they care for wealth, legacy, or fame. Their every strike is a sentence. Their every kill an echo of the pain they have suffered. They do not seek victory. They seek reckoning.

Others fight for freedom, the arena their only path to breaking the chains that have bound them all their lives. Every kill is a step toward escape. Every victory another breath stolen from fate's grasp. But they know the cruellest truth of all. The arena does not grant freedom. It merely changes the nature of the cage.

Then, there are those who fight for forgiveness. Not from the crowd. Not from their enemies. But from themselves. They step onto the sand not to prove their worth to the world, but to silence the ghosts that haunt them.

They are the ones who do not revel in victory, who do not linger over the bodies of their foes. They know that no amount of blood spilled can wash away the past. But still, they fight. For what else is there?

The Blood Trials do not test strength. They do not test skill. They test the essence of a warrior.

To step into the arena is to step into eternity's gaze. The crowd roars, but it is the silence between the screams that carries the truth. The unspoken knowledge that once you enter, you will never leave the same.

The Blood Trials do not exist for mere sport. To believe so is to misunderstand Pyrrha itself. A city built upon the principle that rage must be honed, harnessed, and wielded as both a weapon and a doctrine.

Rage is the birthright of every citizen of Pyrrha. The ember that smoulders within every soul trapped within its iron grasp. It is the heartbeat of the city, pulsing through its people like molten veins beneath stone.

But rage, if left unchecked, if left to fester in the gutters and slums, in the forges and barracks, in the hearts of the abandoned and forgotten, becomes something dangerous. It becomes wrath.

And wrath cannot be allowed to spread without purpose. It must be refined. Broken down. Reforged into something that serves the city rather than consumes it. Wrath is not rebellion. Wrath is order. Wrath is Pyrrha's will made manifest.

This is why the Blood Trials exist. They are not an opportunity. They are not a privilege. They are a culling. A necessary rite to sift the weak from the worthy.

To stand upon the sands of the Blood Trials is to declare, whether knowingly or not, that you are not mere fodder for Pyrrha's machine. It is to stand before the eye of ARES, the all-seeing engine of judgment that calculates, measures, and determines which bodies will fuel Pyrrha's ever-burning furnace and which will rise to serve it.

ARES does not care for dreams. It does not care if a man fights for honour, for legacy, for wealth, or for vengeance. It asks only one question. Can you endure? Not simply the steel and the screams. Not simply the broken bones and the blood-soaked sand. Can you endure the truth of Pyrrha? That you are either a tool, or fuel.

That you will either rise into the ranks of the Sanguine Order, moulded into one of Wrath's chosen warriors, or you will be discarded. Your body. Your failures. Your life. All reduced to another nameless stain upon the arena floor.

This is the natural order. This is the way of Pyrrha. The Blood Trials exist because rage alone is not enough. Rage is a child's tantrum. A beggar's cry for justice. A fleeting howl against an unyielding world. It is the tool of the weak.

But wrath, true, unrelenting, merciless wrath, is the forge that shapes Pyrrha's finest. This is why Ira Valkor, the Unyielding Flame, demands the Blood Trials. He does not seek warriors. He seeks weapons.

To fight in the arena is to prove that you are no longer a man, a woman, a mere being of flesh and desire. It is to prove that you have abandoned weakness. That you have shed hesitation. That you have purged all traces of sentimentality. It is to become Wrath.

Those who survive are not granted mercy. They are not allowed peace. They are funnelled into the Gauntlet. The Blood Trials are but the first step. A mere door. A mere whisper. Beyond them waits the true abyss: the Tournament of Wrath.

And those who enter it will come to understand the final truth. Wrath does not serve you. You serve Wrath.

The Colosseum of Blood stood at the heart of Pyrrha like a monument to violence, an open maw carved from obsidian and steel, thirsting for the screams of the damned. It was neither relic nor modern construct, but something in-between. A remnant of a past that refused to die, reforged in the fires of an unforgiving future.

From a distance, its sheer enormity eclipsed the skyline. A blackened titan wreathed in pulsating neon sigils, their runes crawling across the outer walls like veins of molten gold. Ancient stone, cracked and battle-scarred, still bore the marks of centuries past, now reinforced with latticework of Pyrrhan crimson steel, allowing the weight of history to stand unbroken beneath the burden of time.

Monolithic spires of dark iron jutted from its edges, reaching skyward like jagged teeth. Each adorned with floating holographic banners, shifting in eerie synchrony to display the latest names of the fallen.

The colossal gates, once traditional archways of carved marble, were now reinforced with titanium blast plating, their surfaces stained with the countless imprints of bloodied hands that had pushed them open for the last time.

And yet, for all its brutal magnificence, it was not the structure that made the Colosseum of Blood alive. It was the city's people.

The moment one stepped inside, the air changed. It was thick. Heavy. Not just with the metallic scent of rust, sweat, and old blood, but with something more insidious. Anticipation. Hunger. Wrath.

The roar of the crowd was a living beast, undulating and breathing, its voice a blend of savage cheers and guttural cries. Tens of thousands, packed into the ascending tiers, their faces illuminated by the flickering amber glow of fire pits embedded within the ancient walls. Some were clad in the elaborate garb of Pyrrha's nobility: gold-trimmed cloaks of woven aether fibre, polished armour that had never seen battle.

Others bore crude tattoos, jagged scars, and the rough-hewn garments of those who lived and died by the sword.

Above, suspended by grav-thrusters and chain mechanisms, floating balconies of Pyrrhan elite hovered like predatory birds. Their occupants sipped black steel goblets of incendiary liquor, their laughter a cruel counterpoint to the desperation below. The true rulers of Pyrrha never dirtied their feet upon the bloodstained sands. They watched from above.

Untouched.

Unbothered.

'Gods' in a city that worshiped only one thing: strength.

And below, at the heart of it all, the arena itself.

A colossal pit, ringed by towering spires of crimson steel and shattered marble, stretched across the heart of the Colosseum. Its floor was a shifting landscape of sand laced with the dried remnants of past battles. Embedded plasma generators pulsed just beneath the surface, dormant for now, but ready to twist the battlefield without warning. Spikes. Fire traps. Shifting walls designed to make every fight unpredictable. Every step a risk.

Massive archways carved with the sigils of the Sanguine Order loomed on either side. They were gates through which the damned would enter, stepping onto sands where their fate would be sealed. Above them, colossal monitors blinked to life, casting their cold glow across the arena as they broadcast odds, wagers, and names. Some fighters were adorned with titles gifted by the crowd. Others remained nameless, known only by the number seared into their flesh.

The air itself seemed alive. Heavy with the stench of burnt aether-fuel mingled with the sickly aroma of seared flesh. The faint, clinging trace of incense, burned as an offering to the forsaken gods of Pyrrha's sky, wound through it all like a forgotten prayer.

The Blood Trials were about to begin. And the city roared for blood.

Beneath the savage fervour of the Colosseum, beneath the thunderous cheers of the damned and the mocking laughter of the untouchable elite, there were ghosts. Unseen. Forgotten. But ever-present.

They did not sit among the noble elite in their floating balconies, nor did they bathe in the intoxication of bloodlust. They were not spectators. They were executioners. Judges. Phantoms woven into the fabric of Pyrrha's wrath. The assassins of the

Sanguine Order moved without recognition, dispersed like whispers through the riotous mob. Each belonged to one of three sects. Each followed a doctrine of death.

None of them spoke.

They moved where no one looked. Not invisible, but unseen. Their cloaks, woven from void-fabric, did not merely absorb light. They rejected presence. They denied the world the right to notice.

One stood at the edge of the commoners' tier, flickering between torchlight and shadow. His Null Cloak devoured sound, making his presence a silent dissonance in the air. His breath stirred nothing. His pulse made no ripple. He was absence.

Voidfang Blades strapped to his thighs pulsed at frequencies no ear could hear, vibrating on a molecular level. Each one capable of slicing bone without resistance. Severing flesh without sound. He did not draw them. Not yet. Today, he was not executioner. He was witness. He was there to mark the weak for removal. Pyrrha did not let weakness linger long.

Deeper in the crowd, another moved. A Silent Blade drifting between bodies with effortless precision. His presence lost in the heat, his form swallowed by the blur of movement and noise. His gaze found a noble laughing too loudly. A merchant, fingers twitching with greed. A fighter, all arrogance and rising fame.

His hand dipped into a pouch stitched from human skin. He withdrew something no larger than a grain of rice. A

Heartpiercer Needle, laced with a toxin that did not kill. It erased. With a flick of his wrist, it vanished into flesh.

The merchant gasped. Reached for his throat. But there was no pain. No mark. Just confusion, already slipping into forgetfulness. His body would fail in silence. By morning, he would not wake.

And the assassin was gone. Melted into the crowd. Seen by none. Remembered by fewer.

Where the Silent Blades passed unseen, the Maskborn stood in plain sight.

Among the elite, seated beside merchants and minor warlords, were those whose faces did not belong to them. A woman in a crimson dress laughed like glass breaking, her fingers trailing over a noble's wrist. He did not realize the concubine who whispered into his ear was not the one he brought to the Colosseum. She had been replaced days ago. And now her breath seeded rot in his mind, one poisoned word at a time.

A suggestion here.

A subtle change of opinion there.

By tomorrow, the noble's house would crumble. Betrayed by his own greed. Manipulated by whispers that were never his own. A Maskborn did not need steel to kill. They killed with whispers.

Another figure stood beside a merchant lord, draped in the flowing robes of a diplomat. His title from Avarith was a carefully crafted lie. A well-timed murmur about shifting alliances. The merchant's face faltered. His brows furrowed. Tomorrow, he would betray those closest to him. His own house sent into ruin. The Maskborn did not need to kill. They were poison.

Beneath their smiles, they wore Hollow Masks. Shapeless visages of mystery and manipulation. Their true identities were lost, buried so deep even they no longer remembered. They had no past. No names worth speaking. Their purpose was not to exist, but to create. To reshape. To unravel Pyrrha from within.

But the Nightbrand were different.

They did not hide. They wanted to be seen.

A single figure stood at the edge of the gladiator pits, his massive frame encased in dark warsteel armour. The sigil of a burning brand blazed across his pauldron. His stance was frozen. A statue of violence. Yet every fighter who glimpsed him turned their gaze away, as if staring too long would draw death upon them.

They knew who he was.

The Nightbrand were assassins designed to be witnessed. Their executions were not whispers in the dark. They were declarations. Brutal, unforgettable displays of power, meant to crush morale and ignite dread. Their killings were theatre. Their weapons matched their message.

The man in warsteel gripped the handle of a Wraithpiercer Longsword. A blade that did not slice on contact. It phased through flesh, through bone, and solidified inside its victim. A breath delayed. Pain blooming too late. Enough time to feel the terror of being dead before dying.

Another Nightbrand sat in the stands, a Pyrrhic Brandmark held loosely in one hand. A single drop of the substance would burn through the remains of a corpse, etching a glowing sigil into ruined flesh. A warning to any who would defy Pyrrha's will. He did not act yet. He watched. Waiting for the next example to be made.

While the crowd screamed and the sands soaked in blood, the Sanguine Order wove its tapestry of death and control. Each sect with its purpose. Each strike calibrated to remind the city who ruled from the shadows.

The Silent Blade removed the unworthy.

The Maskborn manipulated the powerful.

The Nightbrand carved fear into the bones of the defiant.

They did not speak. They did not need to. None of them knew one another. None of them had to. They were the blood that seeped through Pyrrha's cracks. The hand behind its fury. Ensuring that when the city burned, it did not consume itself.

For Pyrrha was not chaos. It was controlled destruction.

And in the Colosseum of Blood, the watchers in the shadows ensured that only the strongest, the most ruthless, and the most useful survived.

Beneath the cacophony of roars, where the blood-soaked sands trembled beneath the crowd's howls, another force observed.

They did not cheer. They did not revel in the spectacle. They did not belong.

The Blood Mages of the Sanguine Order stood where no one else dared. Within the cracks of reality itself.

They were not spectators. They were warlocks of flesh and torment, tethered to the Veil by sacrifice and blood. Their presence was not for show. It was for collection. For hunger. For culling.

The Blood Trials were more than combat. They were ritual. An altar. A sacrament to feed Pyrrha itself. Blood spilled not for glory, but for fuel. And the mages were there to collect the tithe.

Among the floating balconies, veiled in arcane sigils that bent light away, sat the Circle of Five. The Blood-bound Lords. The highest authority beneath Veilwalker Kharon himself.

Their presence was a verdict. Unseen by the crowd. Suffocating in its dominion.

High Bloodwright Sarva, the Crimson Scholar, reclined upon an obsidian throne, a Siphoner's Grimoire hovering before him. Its pages turned without touch, guided by invisible force. His pale fingers traced the air, carving glyphs that shimmered in shadow. Each symbol dissected lineage, unravelling the ancestry of those who bled below. Not all blood was equal. Some were born for more than dust. Some would be chosen.

Blood Saint Callis, the Living Vessel, stood motionless at the edge of the platform. His robes soaked in fresh vitae. Tubes fed from his arms into vials that glowed like molten coals. These he would offer to the worthy. Warriors who would burn like gods for a moment before their veins devoured them from within. A gift with teeth.

Veilborne Prophet Syvris, the Whispering One, remained in shadow, blindfolded, his Hollow Mask resting on his lap. He needed no sight. The Veil poured visions into his mind, painting fate in arterial red. He whispered prophecies no one heard. His voice lost in the riot, yet each word was heavy enough to bend future.

Fleshcrafter Vaelith, the Twisted Surgeon, dragged a skeletal finger across his own skin, parting it with perfect precision. Blood dripped and formed a writhing thing of veins and bone. It crawled toward the gates of the arena, hungry for a new host. Vaelith did not watch the battle. He was choosing canvas. Flesh to shape. Blood to command.

Arch-Lament Sicaris, the Deathborn, did not sit. He stood at the edge of the balcony, arms spread like a crucified god. Beside him floated his Crimson Hourglass, its sands shifting between red and black. Every fallen warrior. Every breath taken within the Colosseum. All siphoned into the relic. He was collecting lifespans. Banking them for resurrection.

Above all others, in an isolated shrine of blackened steel threaded with veins of crimson energy, sat Veilwalker Kharon. His Veilbound Staff rested across his lap. He did not stir. He did not breathe. His flesh was a husk. His essence drifted elsewhere, lost in the folds of the Veil. He was death's echo. A presence beyond the mortal boundary.

They exchanged no words. They had no need. Their will was already inscribed in blood.

The mage-knights, the warcasters, the blood-bound enforcers of the Sanguine Order, did not sit with nobles. They moved among the sand-choked corridors beneath the Colosseum. Their armour was inked with runes of extraction. Their Veinfang Blades pulsed faintly, hungering for the heat of fresh lifeblood.

Some stood at the gladiator gates. Their gazes hollow. They did not judge the warriors by skill, but by the measure of power their deaths could yield.

One, a woman clad in ashen war plate, reached for the throat of a dying gladiator. Her gauntleted hand pressed against his flesh. Veins darkened. Essence drained. Crimson sigils lit beneath her fingers.

The crowd saw only a corpse being removed. They did not see the harvest.

Among the rabble, among gamblers and madmen, sat those who did not cheer, did not blink, did not move.

Veilcallers. Draped in tattered robes. Hands clasped. Lips whispering spells beneath breath. Every drop of blood spilled became an offering. The arena hummed with latent power. Beneath their robes, ritual daggers glistened, coated in sacrificial vitae.

One sat near the lower seats, drawing a circle of blood along the stone. A child beside him, eyes clouded, echoed his words in hushed repetition. Vessel. Conduit. The mage poured incantations into the child's skull, feeding him to the Veil. The child screamed. The cry cut through stone. But no one turned. The Veil had already devoured the sound.

Not all Blood Mages observed. Some prepared.

Below the arena, in the depths where flesh-smiths and beast-crafters toiled, the Blood Alchemists worked their blasphemies.

One poured crimson liquid over a corpse. Veins surged. Flesh pulsed with new life. The dead twitched. Then breathed. Another dipped a blade into a basin of boiling blood. The metal howled as it absorbed the Veil's essence. That weapon would never dull. Never rust. Never fail.

They were not spectators. They were creators. Preparing the next wave of monsters.

And then there were those who belonged nowhere.

The Scornborn Ascendants. Failures. Abominations. Once meant to be gods, now reduced to flesh-bound horrors. They were locked beneath the Colosseum, their cells etched in runes of suppression.

One, a hulking mass of stitched flesh and weeping eyes, dragged clawed fingers across the bars. The metal hissed under his touch. He did not breathe through lungs, but through the wounds carved into his chest. Each breath was pain reborn.

They were not part of the Blood Trials.

Not yet.

But soon.

The Colosseum of Blood was no mere battlefield. It was a laboratory. A cathedral. A feeding ground. Warriors bled and died for the people's ecstasy. But their blood belonged to the Sanguine Order.

They walked the crowd. Stood in balconies. Lurked beneath the foundations. Watching. Measuring not bravery. Not strength. But worth.

Gladiators dreamed of survival. But the Sanguine Order dreamed deeper.

The crowd did not know them. The fighters could not see them. The city did not name them. But Pyrrha was theirs.

The Colosseum was alive.

Its soul was not in banners or firelight. It breathed through agony. It exhaled judgment. Each war-script, each drop of blood etched into its stones, fed its ancient hunger.

To the weak, it was a grave.

To the strong, it was a forge.

The Blood Trials were not a game. They were not a contest. They were doctrine. A culling masked as ceremony. There was no honour. No fairness. Only survival sharpened into sacrifice.

From the throne dais, a presence loomed. Vast. Immutable. Warlord Ira Valkor did not observe like a ruler. He watched like a god surveying the blaze he had lit.

Below him, warriors churned the sand, each one trying to carve identity through pain. But they were not gladiators yet. They were unshaped matter. And the Martial Division of the Sanguine Order would decide which would be tempered, and which would be erased.

Among the chaos, three pillars of Pyrrha's wrath stood.

The Blood-Forged Legions. Discipline incarnate. A tidal wave of conquest. They did not march today, but watched from the northern tier. Silent. Patient. Knowing war was not a moment, but a momentum.

The Iron Flame Guard. Sentinels of Pyrrha's will. Their blackened armour shimmered with plasma-reactive alloy. They did not flinch. They did not need to. Their presence alone declared that Pyrrha did not tolerate weakness.

And then, the Pyrrhic Devourers.

They stood alone.

Twisted. Twitched. Lurked near the pits like malformed predators. Their bodies misshapen from augmentation. Their minds hollowed by suffering.

The Butcherborn. Warriors stripped of identity, driven only by the need to kill.

The Veil-Cursed. Flesh warped by forbidden power.

The Chain-Bound. Controlled by neural locks. Released only when destruction demanded no conscience.

For them, there were no trials.

Only slaughter.

And above it all, Ira Valkor sat upon his throne. The Three Pyres stood at his flanks, silent and immense, with General Callistra behind him, her gaze sharp and unrelenting.

To his right was Zephir Caedis, the Azure Inferno, unreadable as the void before lightning strikes.

To his left, Dain Vhorr, the Pale Pyre, held his Warhammer with the stillness of execution.

At the forefront stood Veyna Solvaris, the Emberheart, fire twisting in her blood. Her golden eyes reflected the flames below. Arms crossed. Smirk like a blade.

At the base of the dais, trapped beneath the unbearable weight of judgment, stood Anarya Vhailar, the Daughter of the Iron Flame. She did not sit. She wasn't allowed to. Her presence was not an honour. It was a demand. To witness. To understand. To feel the truth of Pyrrha, not through words, but through spectacle, through ritual, through blood.

The Blood Trials had no honour. There were no rounds. No breaks. No measured combat. Only Wrath.

Kill.

Endure.

Or vanish.

From the stands, the soldiers of Pyrrha watched with sharpened detachment. Their eyes did not gleam with admiration. They were cold instruments of evaluation. They watched not to cheer, but to decide. A slow fighter was discarded. A hesitant killer, deemed unworthy. An undisciplined brawler, sentenced to the Pyrrhic Devourers. Only a handful would be chosen. The rest were corpses that hadn't yet dropped.

The crowd roared as bodies fell, the sand below slick with the heat and echo of death. Each strike fed the hunger. The arena was a beast, and it had tasted blood. Yet above the frenzy, Ira did not stir. His molten gaze carved through illusion. He wasn't entertained. He was searching. Somewhere in the chaos, among the dying and desperate, there would be one who burned brighter.

And then, it shifted.

The roar of the crowd became something less. An animal broken by command. Warlord Ira lifted a single hand. The silence didn't fade. It collapsed. As if severed from every throat at once. The weight of it landed heavy, a suffocating stillness. The moment clenched around them. The feast was done. Now came the judgment.

The drums began.

Low and slow. A heartbeat beneath the bones of the world. Boom. The sound did not enter the ears. It entered the marrow. It was not music. It was something older, something primal.

A call.

A summons.

Boom.

Boom.

Each strike pulled the soul deeper, into something darker. The Colosseum seemed to inhale, its towering spires trembling beneath the unseen pressure. Something moved against the Veil. Something ancient, whispering behind the stone.

Boom. Boom. Boom.

The flames dimmed. Torches exhaled. The sand, once marred by flailing limbs and dying breath, fell still. This was no longer a battle. It was a rite.

The drumming quickened, a fever building behind the ribs. The pulse of Wrath grew manic, each beat a hammer against the spine. The tempo of war. The rhythm of inevitability. Soldiers stiffened. Fingers twitched. Breath shortened. Pyrrha's heart had awakened.

Then the gates opened.

Twenty-five prisoners were led forth, shackled and blindfolded. They did not resist. They did not stumble. They had long since been broken. Step by step, they were marched to the centre of the arena. They did not move of their own will. Even their last moments were stolen. They were not challengers. They were offerings.

No one in the stands cheered. They understood. This was not spectacle. This was sacrifice. The prisoners were bound to one another by chain. One line. One sentence. Beneath their feet, the arena floor stood untouched, awaiting their submission. Not a single cry was heard. No resistance. No pride. Only obedience and silence.

Above them, Ira Valkor still had not moved.

He didn't have to.

His stillness bent the air around him. His presence thickened the moment until it trembled.

And so the rite continued.

The Three Pyres stood at his flanks.

Zephir, the Azure Inferno, remained still. His gaze was unreadable, locked on the chaos below, a sentinel of suppressed flame.

Beside him, Dain, the Pale Pyre, gripped his Warhammer...not idle, not resting, merely waiting.

And then Veyna, the Emberheart, arms folded, her smirk unreadable. She did not watch the fighters. She watched the fire. Waiting to see which way it would spread.

The drumming slowed.

Each beat came hollow, deep, vast. The sound of something reaching its end. The pulse of a heart stretched thin, on the edge of surrender.

The prisoners stood motionless. Twenty-five bodies, twenty-five statistics. Once men, now stripped of even that. Some were skeletal, emaciated by Pyrrha's dungeons, their limbs trembling beneath bruised skin. Others still bore strength, soldiers once, with battlefield scars carved like fading memory across muscle. But none of it mattered. Not who they were. Not why they fought. They were not men anymore. Not enemies.

They were fuel.

BOOM.

The final beat landed like a hammer to the sternum. And then, nothing. Silence so pure it felt manufactured by divine decree. Even the air recoiled from movement. The Colosseum held its breath. Not a whisper. Not a wind. The stillness of a world that knew who ruled it.

Ira Valkor did not rise. He didn't need to.

Seated atop the Throne of Wrath, he pressed his will into the world without motion. Presence alone sufficed. An iron weight atop the arena, pressing down on the soldiers, on the warriors, on the blindfolded condemned who dared not move beneath his stare. He was gravity. Judgment. Flame.

When he spoke, he did not raise his voice. It was a furnace behind iron. A quiet heat that burned deeper than fire. A voice like sealed metal, ready to rupture.

"There is a lie that the weak tell themselves before they die."

His words rolled slowly, each syllable heavier than the last. Not a statement. A sentence.

"A single, desperate whisper they clutch to their chests, as if it might shield them from what's coming. A myth that festers in the hearts of lesser men. It is this—"

His molten eyes swept across the arena. The prisoners. The fighters. The masses.

"That they mattered."

Silence writhed. It did not remain. It contorted.

"Every man who's ever died in war has whispered it with his last breath. Every kingdom that has turned to ash wrote it in their dying histories. Every corpse consumed by time has clung to that lie as the world moved on."

"'I mattered.'"

"But the world forgets them. History forgets them. Because it does not care. And neither do I."

He leaned forward. Just a little. The air bent with him. The entire Colosseum bowed, as if involuntarily.

"We are not born equal. That is truth. We are not given equal fire. Equal strength. Equal worth. Some are born to command. Some are born to serve. And some—"

He gestured toward the line of prisoners. A flick of the hand, not cruel, but final.

"Are born to be forgotten."

He let the silence breathe. Just long enough.

Then came a breath of laughter. Low. Earthen. Fire rumbling beneath the surface.

"And yet, men rage against this. They flail. They weep. They scream at the gods for what they weren't given. As if their noise might change the order of the world."

He rose now. Not sudden. Not loud. Deliberate. Like tectonic plates shifting. His presence expanded, swallowing the space around him.

"But rage—"

He raised one hand. Fingers curling inward, a fist slowly forming.

"Is a tantrum. Rage is weakness in a mask. It is desperation. Helplessness dressed as fury. Rage belongs to those who cry out because they lack the strength to carve their place in the world."

His hand opened again.

"But Wrath—"

The word struck like a drum.

"Wrath is the hand that silences them."

The air shuddered, as though the word itself carried heat.

"Wrath is not a cry. Wrath is not the scream of a beaten dog. It is the hammer that ends it. Wrath does not beg. Does not plead. Does not pray for justice."

His eyes gleamed like fire trapped in stone.

"Wrath is justice."

The torches flared higher. Their shadows stretched like blades across the sand.

"Pyrrha is Wrath."

And in his voice, the truth of it became law.

"We do not fight for peace. Peace is a ghost whispered by the frightened. We do not fight for freedom. Freedom is a lie sold by the weak. We fight for the only truth this world has ever known."

His voice fell, barely above breath, yet louder than any cry.

"Blood. War. Dominion."

Then silence.

A breath's width.

And his final whisper, sharp as steel:

"In war, there is no mercy."

His gaze locked onto the prisoners. They could not see him, but they felt him. Felt the weight of judgment pressing down from the Throne of Wrath. It was not the gaze of a man, not even of a god. It was something older. A verdict etched into the marrow of their bones before they had even been born.

"You stand upon this sand not as warriors. Not as foes. Not even as men," Ira said, his voice low and absolute. "You are tribute.

You are the offering that feeds the City of Wrath. You were not brought here to fight. You were brought here to serve."

He raised a single armoured hand, fingers opening like the petals of something unnatural. "And your only service is this—"

His fist clenched.

"To die screaming."

The air held still for a breath. Not silence, but suspension. Then, with a suddenness that fractured the world, it snapped. The Colosseum of Blood became a chamber of execution.

One by one, the prisoners collapsed. There was no cry. No motion. No sound to mark the moment. Only the wet, dull note of a body surrendering to something it could not see. Flesh split. Breath stopped. And the sand received its due.

The Silent Blade had been there all along, hidden in plain absence. Draped in stillness. Buried beneath the gravity of Ira's voice. Their presence had been erased from the crowd's mind like breath from glass.

But now, with the Warlord's command delivered, they moved with surgical finality.

A thin line opened along the throat of the first prisoner. Not a brutal gash, but a whisper of metal. A cut so sharp it passed before the flesh even knew. The body did not fall. It remained upright, swaying. Confused. Denial etched into the way it clung to standing.

Then the blood came. A violent arc. It poured down his chest and pooled into the already stained earth.

As one fell, another followed. And another. A cascade of red. Twenty-five executions, synchronized in perfect silence. The blades cut so sharply, so precisely, that the sound of them sliding through flesh was lost beneath the roar of blood. It poured forth in violent rivers, a scarlet signature written across the arena's heart.

The assassins did not remain. They were there, and then they were gone, slipping into the air itself. Only the blood betrayed their passage, staining their cloaks in streaks of ghostly red. The sand held their story long after their bodies vanished. The blindfolds soaked in death. The corpses slumped in offering.

The moment the first body hit the ground, the Colosseum erupted.

A monstrous roar tore through the stands. Not celebration. Catharsis.

The crowd surged like a single beast. Thousands of bodies clenched in one convulsive breath. Fists slammed against iron rails. Boots hammered stone. Faces twisted with something between joy and madness.

Some screamed, their throats raw. Others laughed, the high, broken sound of hysteria. And there were those who wept. Not in grief, but in awe. Overwhelmed by the beauty of cruelty sanctified.

And then, rising from the pit of the crowd's frenzy, a chant began. Not a name. Not a cry. A word. Singular. Ancient. Carved into the heartbeat of the city itself. It rose through the chaos like flame licking toward the sky. A pulse. A ritual. A truth.

"WRATH! WRATH! WRATH!"

*

It started from the lower tiers. A ripple beneath the surface. A sound not born from throats but from something deeper. Something ancient.

Then it spread.

The roar began in the shadows, where blood was a currency and survival came only by carving one's name into the chaos. It climbed, howling through the broken teeth of the underclass, across the battered steel of the fighters, up through the marble rows of nobility and warlords. It flooded through the merchant houses, the courts, the command towers. Even the floating balconies of Pyrrha's elite began to shake beneath the weight of sound that could not be silenced.

"WRATH! WRATH! WRATH!"

The Colosseum of Blood no longer resembled architecture. It became something living. A beast of fire and stone, its breath thick with iron, its bones forged from thousands of voices, its skin soaked in centuries of blood.

The air itself grew heavy. Dense with sweat. With smoke. And with something older. Something sacred in its brutality.

At the centre, Ira Valkor stood motionless. He did not acknowledge the storm rising around him. Did not smile. Did not flinch.

His was not the posture of indulgence. It was the posture of order. Cold. Unwavering. Forged from loss. Tempered by vengeance.

He watched. Measured. Judged.

The chants shook the foundation of the world.

But Ira did not hear them.

He heard only breathing. Shallow. Frantic. His own. But not as he was now. Not the Warlord. Not the Arbiter of Wrath.

A child's breath.

The breath of someone hiding beneath the body of a soldier, hoping to be mistaken for dead. The breath of a boy who had bitten through his own tongue just to remain silent. The breath of someone who had watched his mother burn with her arms outstretched, whispering to a god that never came.

He should have died.

And he had.

But not all at once.

"Ira."

The voice came like rot in the marrow. Distant. Young. Untouched.

"Is this what becoming strong feels like?"

His pulse stuttered. Not in the body that wore armour, but in the ghost of the boy he used to be.

He didn't answer.

He didn't need to.

He looked down, and there he was.

Barefoot. Covered in ash. Blood on his skin, soot in his eyes. Frail arms. A face both terrified and transfixed. Staring up through the cracks in the stone floor as if peering through time.

Not a ghost.

A reflection.

"You said we'd never become like them."

"I said we'd survive," Ira murmured, the words sharp against the back of his throat.

"You said you hated them. That you'd never make anyone kneel."

"They made me into this."

"But you liked it."

Soft. Almost tender. Like a lullaby filled with knives.

"You liked watching them bleed."

His jaw clenched. The memory tore through him. The screams. The blood. The moment the sword first felt like part of him. The thrill of power.

"They deserved it."

"So did he?"

That voice. That accusation.

It pierced him. Sank past the armour. Past the flesh. Deep into the place where no light remained.

And then the boy was there. Not just any boy. His brother. His younger self. A mirror of ash and betrayal, arms outstretched in longing that would never be answered.

He had always run.

But there was nowhere left to run.

"You killed me too, didn't you?"

"No."

A whisper. Cracked and dry.

"I became what I had to."

"You became what you hated."

The silence that followed was not peace.

It was collapse.

His mind buckled inward. His fist clenched. He reached out as if to claw the memory from existence.

"Enough."

"You're not a warlord."

"Enough."

"You're just the last child screaming where no one can hear him."

"ENOUGH!"

The word exploded from him, a force that broke the air itself. The Colosseum shuddered. The Veil twisted. The chant of the crowd vanished beneath the weight of his scream.

He looked again.

The boy remained.

Waiting.

Forgiving.

And that was why he had to die.

Ira raised a hand to his chest. Not to his armour. Not to muscle or bone.

To the place where the boy still lived. The last piece of him that had not turned to ash.

And he crushed it.

Not physically.

But completely.

He shattered something eternal. A wound. A hope. A promise that had survived too long.

The child fell inward. Into dust. Into silence.

Gone.

And when Ira looked up again, his eyes no longer burned.

They were void.

Not heat. Not fire.

Fuel.

His voice, when it came, was cold iron drawn across stone.

"There is no such thing as becoming. There is only burning."

He turned away. From the altar of memory. From the child. From the mercy.

And in doing so, Ira Valkor ceased to be man, warlord, monster.

He became the fire that consumed them all.

He became Wrath.

As the blood soaked into the arena, as the chanting roared back into life, something inside him stirred. Not power. Not pride. Something older.

The memory of a name.

The whisper of a child, lost in the ash.

But when he turned to look…

There was no one.

Only the flames.

Only the fury.

And Ira knew, as the blood ran warm across the stone, that there was no redemption waiting.

Because there was nothing left to become.

Only burn.

"The boy did not die in fire. He died in silence. And from that silence, wrath was born. Not as a saviour, but as a god who does not plead. Only punishes."

Null Gospel, Book I, Verse 24.

***

CHAPTER TWENTY-FOUR:

The Test of the Blood Trials

"Death is not the end in Pyrrha. It is the audition. Flesh is the first draft. Pain is the red ink. And the Colosseum is not a graveyard. It is a goddamn editor."

Fragment of the Exiled Codex, Volume I, Tablet 25.

In Pyrrha, death was not an ending. It was raw material.

The Colosseum of Blood never rested. It did not pause for mourning. It had no need for such illusions. Honor? That was for the weak. For the foolish who clung to the sanctity of life like children gripping their final dream. Pyrrha had no patience for dreams.

The blood of twenty-five slaughtered prisoners still steamed on the sand. Tendrils curled upward, lazy and delicate, as if reluctant to leave the battlefield. Heat consumed it slowly. Greedily. The arena drank deep. Crimson rivulets traced the stone steps like veins, vanishing into unseen drains beneath the sand. The city itself fed on death, its thirst never quenched.

The Sanguine Order moved without delay.

They emerged from the shadows like carrion birds. Disciplined. Starving. Their robes whispered across the floor like crow feathers in a dying wind. The air thickened. Not with grief, but with silence. A silence so taut it felt alive.

No gestures. No mourning rites. Only movement. Clinical and cold.

The fallen had no names now. No stories. Only purpose. The ritual unfolded like clockwork. Every motion efficient. Every breath rehearsed.

Some bodies were taken at once. Draped in bio-synthetic cloth, limbs bound tight, lowered into the tunnels beneath the arena. Wounds still weeping. Flesh still warm. It mattered little. These were not dead. They were material. Fuel for Pyrrha's appetite.

The freshest among them, veins still pulsing, blood still warm, were sent to the Fleshcrafters. Grotesque surgeons. Artists of sinew and nerve. To them, a beating heart was currency. A pristine liver, treasure. Lungs untouched by the rot of the city could breathe life into broken warriors again.

Not rebirth as miracle.

Rebirth as mechanism.

Power, stitched from corpses.

Life had no sanctity here. Only utility.

Those less damaged, still viable for more sacred desecrations, were claimed by the Veilcallers. Their hunger was different. They drained the blood not for medicine, but for divination. They needed no bone. No flesh. Only the soul's residue. The raw, undiluted essence of death. It poured into obsidian basins, fuelling visions that clawed through the Veil. Secrets spoken in the language of madness.

What did they hear?

No one knew. The few who asked vanished. Some claimed their questions were answered. Others said they never truly left the rituals.

And the broken, those beyond science or sacrament, were hurled into the Gauntlet.

Mutilated. Forgotten. Cast into the depths where the Butcherborn waited with gnashing hunger. Where the Chain-Bound howled and struck with iron fists. Where the Veil-Cursed dragged what remained of bodies into shadow and desecrated them in silence.

Even in death, there was no peace.

There was only continuation. Only conversion.

Death was a mechanism. Not a mercy.

A pair of Bloodwrights stepped between the corpses. Their faces veiled in obsidian half-masks. Their steps were careful. Not reverent. Just precise. Their voices barely rose above a whisper, trading words like merchants over spices. Their detachment, almost tender.

"Three livers. Two intact hearts. One partial brain. Decay rate optimal. Send them to Vaelith."

"Veilwalker Kharon requested five litres of pure blood essence. The fresher, the better. You know how he is."

"Take the spine from this one. Good reinforcement material for neural augments. Stronger than what we have on hand."

A Bloodwright nudged the body with the tip of his boot. It flopped onto its back, limbs loose, eyes wide in a grotesque mimicry of life. The expression was frozen. Half agony. Half confusion. A face caught in the final instant before death stripped away understanding.

The Bloodwright exhaled.

Not a sigh of grief. Not even of reflection.

Just the tired breath of someone long accustomed to ruin.

The cut had been sloppy. Too much tearing. Not enough precision. A waste.

"Wasteful cut," he muttered. "The Silent Blade should know better. Pity."

No one replied. The apprentices moved with silent obedience, dragging the corpse by the ankles. Arms flailed behind it. The sand darkened with each dragging inch. No ceremony. No name. The world did not care. They were not men. They were refuse.

Elsewhere, a Fleshcrafter crouched low.

He pried open a corpse's eyelids. The irises were already clouding, death dimming the once-lucid gaze. He clicked his tongue, displeased.

"Useless," he whispered, as if insulted by the body's lack of utility.

With a flick, his scalpel traced two clean arcs. The eyes fell with a dull thud. He left the body where it lay. No glance back. Already scanning for the next suitable form. His work required no reverence. Only results. His hands were practiced. Steady. Merciless.

The Colosseum floor had transformed.

What had begun as slaughter had become butchery. Figures in black swarmed like ants across the carnage, each one slicing, draining, harvesting. The execution was no longer an event. It was a supply chain.

The living were the preamble. Their corpses, the product. Each death a link in the cycle.

Nothing would remain. Not flesh. Not bone. Not memory.

And above it all, the crowd still stirred.

Their hunger lingered in the air, thick as smoke. The earlier execution had merely whetted the appetite. What came next would be the true spectacle. The show Pyrrha promised. The ritual she demanded.

At the eastern edge, towering above the blood-drenched sand, Kaleb Anokuv stood.

He did not move. The arena moved for him.

Heat spiralled around him, catching the folds of his cloak. It whipped behind him like a banner. His silhouette struck sharp against the seething backdrop. Tall. Rigid. Immoveable. Like a relic carved from night itself.

His frame was lean. Bones honed for war. Muscles wired for speed.

A blade in human form.

Wind tousled his black hair, but his face held still. Cold. Measured. The scar running down his cheek pulsed faintly with each breath, as if echoing the heartbeat of the arena.

He said nothing yet.

He didn't need to.

The Colosseum waited. And Kaleb had never spoken a word that was not necessary.

Kaleb's voice cleaved through the air, sharp and resonant, unnatural in its precision. The implants woven into his throat lent it an eerie clarity. It vibrated with something more than sound. A frequency that carved through the roar of thousands, silencing thought and igniting raw anticipation.

His eyes, molten amber, gleamed beneath the blistering heat. They had seen Pyrrha's veins bleed. Had watched violence flow in cycles, never-ending, never still. There was no hesitation in his gaze. No remorse. Only a dangerous mirth that curled at the edge of his presence as he looked out over the hunger he was about to ignite.

"WHAT A FINE TRIBUTE. WHAT A GLORIOUS OFFERING TO THE VEIL. BUT YOU DID NOT COME HERE MERELY FOR RITUAL. YOU DID NOT COME HERE MERELY TO WITNESS THE PURIFICATION OF WEAKNESS."

He swept a hand toward the black gates sealed in plasma. Portals where the true warriors waited. Their breath held. Their fates moments away.

"NO, MY CHILDREN OF WRATH. YOU CAME HERE TO SEE THOSE WHO WOULD PROVE THEMSELVES WORTHY OF PYRRHA'S FLAME. YOU CAME HERE TO SEE WARRIORS BLOODIED IN THE NAME OF OUR WARLORD."

The crowd erupted.

Fists slammed against metal. Boots stomped in jagged rhythm. Voices climbed into a frenzy of violent celebration. Kaleb's lips parted into a slow grin. Not surprise. Certainty. He knew this crowd. Knew how to speak to the animal in them. The part that craved the spectacle. The carnage. The moment when blood justified belief.

He let the roar crest.

Then raised a single fist.

Silence fell like a hammer.

The air became heavy. The arena stilled. His fist held aloft like a signal from the divine. Every eye watched. Every breath waited.

The gates groaned in protest. Old mechanisms woke with grinding fury. Plasma barriers flickered and hummed as if the very fabric of air was rebelling. The threshold between now and what would be.

"LET US SEE THEM. ONE BY ONE. LET US HEAR THEIR NAMES. LET US MARK THEIR FACES. LET US TEST THEIR WORTH UPON THE SAND."

Stillness descended. Dense as fog. The last trace of his voice trembled in the stone.

All eyes locked forward.

The twin gates shuddered. Sigils of Wrath carved into blackened steel trembled as if resisting the past that had birthed them. Vibrations ran through the ground like a memory trying to claw back into flesh.

The heat twisted.

But it wasn't just heat. The air thickened. Tilted.

They knew this moment. Every soul present. The crowd leaned forward in instinct. This was the unveiling. This was where the myth took root, or the name was swallowed whole by the dust.

Then, the first name thundered.

A cry cast into a sea of bloodthirst.

Kaleb's voice was divine proclamation.

"LORDS AND DEVOURERS. BEHOLD THE FIRST CONTENDER."

The gates parted.

And frost surged.

It spilled out across the sand like breath from a dying god. Mist clung to the heat, coiling like fingers that refused to burn. The arena hissed in conflict. Fire and ice locked in combat across the very floor.

A shadow stepped forward.

Enormous. Silent. Immutable.

Kaleb's arms lifted wide. His voice carried like scripture written in sound.

"HE WALKS FROM THE LAND WHERE EVEN FIRE DARES NOT BURN. HE IS ICE. HE IS WINTER'S VENGEANCE. THE FROSTBORNE TITAN."

Lucius Veturhald.

The name alone stirred memory. It did not need history. It was history.

And as he stepped from the gates, legend met flesh. Seven feet of engineered devastation wrapped in crimsonplate. His armour was a fusion of archaic brutality and neon-pulse precision. Each movement echoed with deliberate finality. Sand cracked beneath him, unable to bear the pressure of his existence.

He moved like inevitability.

Each layer of armour glinted with thin veils of frost, subtle and shifting. His Glacial Maul, taller than most men, rested at his side. Not idle. Waiting. The weapon radiated a low hum, unnatural and constant, as if whispering to the cold itself. Its Cryo-Core throbbed, bleeding waves of frozen breath across the haft, frosting its own metal in real time.

It was not a tool.

It was a sentence.

Mist curled from beneath the jagged edge of his cloak. Threads of ice painting temporary runes on the burning sand before the heat devoured them. That cloak, woven from frostwoven cloths that defied warmth, hung like the memory of a distant winter, refusing to thaw.

He never looked at the crowd. Never acknowledged their hunger. Never raised a hand in salute.

He simply exhaled.

And his breath turned to vapor. A single ribbon of white, vanishing before it could fall.

The crowd erupted.

Their roar thundered like collapsing stone, but Kaleb did not move. He remained still, eyes unreadable. A statue watching the tide. Then his voice cut clean through the chaos. Every syllable deliberate. Weighted.

"WILL HIS ICE ENDURE, OR WILL THE FIRES OF WRATH REDUCE HIM TO CINDERS."

Lucius shifted. Rolled his shoulders. The armour groaned in response. He flexed, slow and practiced, adjusting his grip on the weapon. His gaze swept the arena.

Then, the flicker.

A twitch of the mouth. Not a smile. A ghost of amusement, raw and fleeting.

"They always assume fire melts ice."

His voice was gravel. Quiet. Too soft for the crowd. A whisper for no one but himself.

Then he added, colder now. Sharper.

"But winter doesn't melt. It buries."

Kaleb, unaware of the quiet murmur behind him, turned to face the opposite gates.

The crowd surged.

And Kaleb, always the orchestrator, lifted both arms. His voice rose again, stoking the fire to a scream.

"LET US SEE IF THE TITAN CAN ENDURE."

The second gates shuddered.

A low moan of machinery answered, and the ground trembled beneath the weight of anticipation.

Then came the heat.

A blast wave of thermal distortion twisted the air. The arena felt it instantly. The frost clinging to Lucius' entrance cracked, hissed, and retreated. The sand near the gate blackened, curling like burnt parchment. Beneath it, the stone groaned. Buckled. Begged.

And from that sweltering void, something moved.

Not a man.

The Thermogaunt.

A terror shaped by slaughter. A beast of steel sinew and molten core. Its frame was a patchwork of harvested war-beasts. Bones and armour fused through plasma welding and necro-augments. It was not built to fight the cold.

It was born to consume it.

At fifteen feet tall, the Thermogaunt's frame was a monstrosity of metal and flame. A grotesque union of molten wrath and engineered precision. Its exoskeletal plating, forged from magma-reactive alloys, pulsed with the glow of a living inferno. Beneath the surface, veins of searing plasma surged through its limbs like rivers of liquid fire. The heat it exuded warped the air, bending vision and space alike.

It moved not like a creature, but like fire incarnate.

Its head extended forward. A draconic silhouette shaped for terror. Mechanical plates reinforced its jaw, giving it a feral profile. Less machine. More predator.

But the true horror waited within its maw. Twin rows of obsidian teeth, fused and sharpened, radiated heat so intense the air shimmered with every breath. Steam hissed from its jaws as saliva vaporized before it could fall.

Then it opened its mouth.

A guttural hiss ripped free. The sound was alive, vibrating with fury. And then the flame came. A column of pressurized, liquid fire tore across the arena. It devoured distance. It seared space. It burned the very breath from the air.

Lucius moved.

The Glacial Maul swung upward, smooth and divine. The Cryo-Core throbbed, low and rising. Power built in silence.

Then came the release.

A wave of freezing force exploded outward. The two elements collided. Fire and ice. A clash of opposites that screamed across the arena floor.

The air cracked.

Steam roared as flame met frost. Fire hissed and died on contact. But not before brushing Lucius' gauntlets. His armour hissed. Metal steamed. The Cryo-Resonance Alloys responded in time, dampening the heat, holding the line.

Lucius didn't flinch.

He watched. Focused. Silent.

His voice slipped into the chaos, soft enough that only the storm could hear it.

"That all you've got?"

The Thermogaunt's claws tore through the sand. Showers of molten dust scattered with every movement, dancing like embers fleeing a dying star. Its limbs tensed. Plated sinew prepared to strike. It knew.

Hesitation was death.

It charged.

Lucius waited.

One heartbeat.

Then he moved. One step forward. Then another. A third. He gained speed as the beast barrelled toward him. Ice answering fire. The ground trembled under their combined approach.

The air began to hum.

Tension carved into the space between them, tightening with every heartbeat. The Cryo-Core surged within the Maul. Light flickered along its surface. Frost coiled from its edge.

Lucius adjusted his grip.

The moment arrived.

He swung.

The Maul carved the air in a high arc. A detonation of cold exploded from the weapon's head. Frost and kinetic force collided with the Thermogaunt's jaw. Metal howled. Plasma veined plating cracked and buckled under the blow. Energy burst outward. A cyclone of frozen breath and raw impact flooded the sands.

The arena became winter.

But the Thermogaunt did not fall.

It staggered. Withstood. Absorbed.

Its claws dug deep into the earth. Heat bled from its ruptured armour. Plasma spilled like volcanic blood. Still it moved. Still it breathed.

Its jaws snapped shut.

Frost shattered between its obsidian teeth.

The crowd exploded.

This was no ritual. No execution. This was war. Unfiltered and divine. A collision of absolutes.

Lucius braced for the recoil. His boots dug into the sand, stabilizing him as the shock of the blow ran through his body. His armour hissed, bleeding away the lingering heat. His breath stayed slow. Measured.

Across the arena, the Thermogaunt regenerated.

Molten plasma pulsed along its broken veins, sealing cracks, reknitting its scorched internals. A creature designed to endure.

Lucius watched it repair.

His grip on the Glacial Maul tightened.

"Tch."

Barely a sound, swallowed by the noise. But the frost that curled from his lips made the words land like steel.

"So you can take a hit. Let's see if you can take a real one."

The Thermogaunt's eyes burned.

Then it lunged.

Lucius didn't retreat. He advanced.

An avalanche with a heartbeat.

The Glacial Maul was no duellist's weapon. It wasn't carved for finesse. It was shaped to end. A siege breaker wielded by one man. And Lucius wielded it not as a warrior, but as executioner.

The Thermogaunt closed fast.

Claws out. Obsidian jaws dripping fire.

Lucius answered with motion.

He twisted. Shoulders and hips in unison. The Maul came around like a falling star made of ice and wrath. The Cryo-Core pulsed.

Impact.

The Thermogaunt's charge broke against the strike. Its torso imploded inward. Cold fire surged through its body, shutting systems down before they could cry out.

Lucius did not pause.

The second strike came from below. An upward swing beneath the jaw. The Maul connected with a crunch that echoed across the Colosseum. The Thermogaunt reeled. Frost exploded through its throat.

Steam billowed. Its heat bled out in wild hisses.

Lucius swung again.

This time, he struck the flank. The blow threw the beast sideways, crashing into the arena floor. Molten sand scattered like sparks. The crowd gasped.

They saw it now.

The slowing of its veins. The stutter in its motion. The armour splitting at its seams.

And the chant began.

Low at first. Then louder. Climbing into a frenzy.

"TITAN. TITAN. TITAN."

Lucius smirked.

The kill was close.

The Thermogaunt staggered. Its body convulsed. Then it reared back.

Desperation.

It channelled its last reserve of energy into its core. Trembling. Burning. Preparing to explode.

Lucius exhaled.

"Predictable."

He didn't step away.

He closed the distance. A single bound.

The Glacial Maul lifted. Charged to its limit. Its hum grew into a roar. Kinetic force locked in every inch of steel.

"Stay down."

He brought it down.

The blow struck the Thermogaunt's skull with apocalyptic force.

The arena split.

Ice detonated across the sand. A wave of absolute zero tore outward. Everything it touched froze to silence.

The Thermogaunt's skull cracked.

Its body locked mid-detonation. Heat trapped inside a prison of frost. It froze in place. Still. Glowing. Dying.

Then, it shattered.

A thunderous crack followed. Fragments of obsidian and magma rained down across the sand. What remained was ash. And jagged shards. And silence.

The crowd howled. But the flame was already gone. Winter had buried it.

"The beast that dies in fire does not return as itself. It comes back without mercy, without memory. You do not survive the flames. You become them."
Null Gospel, Book I, Verse 25.

***

CHAPTER TWENTY-FIVE:

The Arena That Drinks the Dead

"The arena does not baptize. It does not cleanse. It brands. Not to wash away sin, but to strip it raw and burn the soul into something else. Something less than man. Something more."

Fragment of the Exiled Codex, Volume 1, Tablet 26.

They screamed as if salvation had been delivered unto them.

Fists pounded iron. Voices cracked. Boots stamped in rhythm with the blood still steaming on the sand.

To the crowd, it was triumph. A spectacle. A hymn of violence.

But to Lucius, it was nothing more than noise. He exhaled, slow and measured, as if the battle had already slipped into memory. His shoulders rolled back. The Glacial Maul rested against his armoured frame.

The heat had vanished. The sands beneath him, hardened to stone. Chunks of the beast lay shattered, steam curling from their ruins.

The flame had screamed. Then it died.

But winter never screamed. It endured.

The Announcer's voice tore through the chaos. A blade of sound cleaving the air.

"WRATH! ICE! DEATH! THE FROSTBORNE TITAN CLAIMS HIS FIRST VICTORY!"

The crowd howled. They drank in the moment like vultures at a fresh kill.

Lucius didn't flinch. His gaze shifted, calm and cold, to the Throne of Wrath. There sat Warlord Ira Valkor. Unmoved. Unshaken. Unimpressed.

Lucius huffed. "Figures," he muttered, turning toward the exit.

He dragged the Glacial Maul behind him, its weight groaning against the frozen sand. He left the frenzied crowd behind, their hunger only momentarily fed.

The Colosseum of Blood had not yet settled. The air still pulsed with echoes of combat. The scent of burned flesh and ruptured steel thickened with every breath. The sands were stained, crimson and frost baptized anew.

And yet, the crowd's hunger remained.

The Announcer stepped forward, arms flung wide. The silence between fights was sacred. He basked in it. The tension clotted, thick as blood left to congeal beneath a hot sky.

"OH, WHAT A DISPLAY THAT WAS! A STORM OF FROST AND FURY! BUT WE ARE NOT DONE, ARE WE?"

His head tilted, listening. As if Pyrrha herself whispered through the walls of the arena.

"NO, PYRRHA IS NOT YET SATISFIED! ANOTHER MUST STEP FORWARD! ANOTHER MUST CARVE HIS PLACE INTO THE SANDS!"

The gates groaned. Energy barriers shimmered, hissed, flickering under the weight of anticipation.

"NEXT... YOU KNOW HIS NAME."

The Announcer's voice dropped, reverent but coiled in mockery. A bloodlust clothed in silk.

"YOU HAVE SEEN HIM BLEED! YOU HAVE SEEN HIM ENDURE! AND YET..."

He paused. The moment stretched. The crowd froze, breath caught.

"YOU HAVE NEVER SEEN HIM FALL!"

Their bodies leaned forward, thousands moved by primal instinct. Even those who had bet against him felt their hearts hitch. Something inevitable was stirring.

A presence filled the air. Heavy. Wrong. Not of this place.

The energy shield collapsed. The gates yawned open.

From shadow emerged Levik Draganmir.

Not like Lucius. Not like the flame-chasing braggarts who carved their names with showmanship and flair. No flourish. No spectacle.

Just footsteps. Heavy. Steady. Final.

The crowd shrieked. Levik did not acknowledge them. The sand shifted beneath each step, but he moved with the weight of certainty. Not a stumble. Not a glance.

He was grounded. Built for endurance.

Levik Draganmir. A relic of war. Scarred and unyielding. His frame, broad and battered, bore the testimony of a hundred battles. Flesh and metal forged by survival, not glory.

His armour told the story. Not clean. Not ceremonial. Reinforced plates stripped from fallen foes, reshaped with Veil-tech, layered with brutal efficiency. No gold. No polish. Just survival. His gauntlets hissed, drawing energy with each motion. Ready to return it with thunder.

Strapped to his back: the Stormcleaver.

A weapon that had tasted more blood than the sands beneath his boots ever would.

The crowd murmured. No cheers. No chants. Just the quiet edge of respect. Uneasy. Reverent.

Because Levik Draganmir had never bowed. Never begged before Pyrrha's tyrants. To him, the Colosseum was no stage. It was a grinder.

A place where glory was a lie. A place where only the next fight mattered.

"Glory is for the dead," his mantra whispered through his mind, steady as the blade at his back. "The living only have the next fight."

The Announcer let the silence thicken. He leaned into it, as though whispering into every skull.

"DO YOU FEEL IT, MY CHILDREN OF WRATH? THE WEIGHT IN THE AIR?"

Breath stalled in every throat. The sand itself seemed to tremble.

"THE SOUND OF THUNDER... BEFORE THE STORM."

He turned. One hand raised toward the lone man standing on the bloodstained sand.

"LEVIK DRAGANMIR. THE ONE WHO ENDURES THE STORM!"

No eruption followed. No howls. Just watching.

Silent. Grim.

Not in awe.

In recognition.

Because watching Levik was to witness the cost of survival.

He rolled his shoulders. Vertebrae cracked through the silence of the arena. His knuckles flexed around the hilt of the Stormcleaver, steady and patient. His eyes, iron-grey and weatherworn, swept the battlefield with the stillness of ice.

No fanfare greeted him. Only the grim gravity of purpose.

The scent of Lucius' violence still lingered. Burnt blood, scorched flesh, and the residual press of torch heat suffocating the air. Yet Levik stood, unflinching. His gaze unbroken. His presence, unshaken.

The Announcer leaned in, lips peeled into a grin, voice oozing mockery as if taunting the silence to break.

"TELL US, ENDURER OF THE GAUNTLET, TELL US..."

His tone shifted. Mockingly reverent, laced with malice.

"DOES THE SAND WHISPER ITS TRUTHS TO YOU?"

Levik tilted his head. Scarred, expressionless. Then his voice rumbled forth. Low, coarse, edged like rusted steel dragged across stone.

"The only thing these sands whisper is who's next to die."

A dark ripple passed through the crowd. No cheer. No exultation. Just a low, jagged laughter. The kind born from shared truth, from understanding the quiet cruelty of survival.

The warriors at the lower tiers reacted with smirks and sparse calls, but all subdued, as if giving space to something sacred. The silence that follows truth.

Above them all, high in the shadow of the throne, Ira Valkor watched.

He gave no signal. No nod. No flicker of acknowledgment. Yet Levik felt it.

The weight of judgment. The silent appraisal that cuts deeper than steel.

"You're watching me, aren't you, Ira?"

He didn't kneel. Didn't bow.

He stood. Endurance personified.

Then, the opposite gates groaned.

Something stirred beyond them. Something massive, unnatural.

Levik inhaled sharply through his nose. His fingers curled tighter around the Stormcleaver's hilt.

The air changed.

The arena trembled. Not from metal strain or faulty locks, but from something deeper. A presence. A rhythm out of step with life.

The sound arrived first. A thud. Deep and broken. Then another. And another. A slow crescendo of something that should not walk.

The crowd fell silent. Tension swelled until breath itself felt traitorous.

Then it emerged into the light. The Hollowed Behemoth.

Steel twisted into sorrow, forged by the Sanguine Order's cruellest minds. It had once been human. A warrior. A champion.

No longer.

They had hollowed him. Stolen his will. Rebuilt him into something monstrous.

The body still bore traces of its origin. Flesh fused with blackened sinew and mechanical plating. Its face replaced by a metal mask, bolted into ruined bone. No eyes. No mouth. Only a crimson sigil burned at the centre of its head, pulsing in time with a machine's imitation of a heart.

Its limbs were weapons. Arms ending in Veil-steel gauntlets shaped for devastation. Legs reinforced with hydraulics built for shock and slaughter.

Its chest, exposed, revealed the agonizing marriage of muscle and machinery. Organic parts wrapped around a core of merciless design.

It was no longer a man. It was a siege engine given breath.

And it remembered pain.

The Behemoth's head lifted. The sigil blazed. Its spine cracked. Gauntlets flexed with ominous grace.

Then came the voice.

Barely audible. A whisper, fractured and broken, filtered through the shredded remains of its throat.

"Khh...hh....r......i...l..l...m...e..."

A plea. A curse. A memory.

The crowd didn't care. They roared. Bloodlust devoured mercy.

The Announcer soaked it in, his voice rising with calculated madness.

"BEHOLD! THE HOLLOWED BEHEMOTH!"

He strode forward, arms wide, a conductor of carnage.

"A WARRIOR REFORGED BY THE HANDS OF THE SANGUINE ORDER! A MONUMENT TO ENDURANCE! A BASTION OF WRATH! AND YET, DOES IT STILL DREAM OF FREEDOM? DOES IT STILL BELIEVE IN HOPE?"

He laughed. Sharp, surgical, slicing the tension like a blade drawn clean across the throat of silence.

"LET US SEE IF IT CAN ENDURE LEVIK DRAGANMIR!"

The Behemoth growled. Metal reverberated. Its form tensed. Mechanical joints snapped into place. Hydraulic pistons hissed.

Destruction coiled within each motion.

The storm had arrived.

Levik didn't move.

He inhaled slowly. Let the Stormcleaver's weight settle into his grip like the hand of an old friend. His thoughts narrowed.

No room for panic. No breath wasted on fear.

"Glory is for the dead," the words pulsed through him. "The living only have the next fight."

He raised the blade. There was no flourish. Only calm. Only precision. Stormcleaver met the air like ritual. Part preparation. Part prayer.

The fight began.

The Behemoth moved first.

No charge. No roar. It walked.

Each step struck like a war drum. Stone cracked beneath its weight. The sand recoiled, recoiling as if trying to flee. Its pace was deliberate. Its cadence calculated. No wasted energy. No pretence. This was not a beast. It was a verdict.

Then it struck.

The right gauntlet swept through the air. A descending judgment. A hammer meant not just to kill, but to erase. No man could withstand the blow. It was annihilation shaped into motion.

Levik did not retreat.

He did not evade with elegance. He moved with knowledge. With rhythm honed in blood.

A sidestep. Executed with brutal timing. It wasn't reflex. It was memory. His body remembered what his mind no longer needed to command.

The gauntlet met the ground.

The sand erupted.

BOOM.

The impact ruptured the earth. Debris lanced skyward like shrapnel from a forgotten war. Air rippled outward, warped by force. The shockwave pressed against his chest, testing his footing.

But Levik did not blink.

Levik stood his ground. Gaze locked on the monster.

Then he struck back.

The Stormcleaver swept low. Not toward the Behemoth's head or chest, but the knee. A veteran's strike, aimed where flesh and machine conspired to move. Precision, not power.

The axe cracked into the limb with devastating accuracy. A shriek of metal. The cryo-core flared, bathing the joint in white fire. Frost exploded outward, locking metal, blistering skin, flooding veins and circuitry with unrelenting cold.

Hydraulics choked. Flesh blackened. The limb buckled.

The Behemoth staggered.

Levik surged forward. The weapon in his hands shifted. The axe curled into a scythe. The blade arced, finding the exposed wires. Plating tore. Sparks erupted in furious defiance.

The crowd gasped. Not because it fell, but because it didn't.

The thing turned. The crimson sigil in its face pulsed steadily, gaze fixed on Levik like a curse remembered.

It had noticed him. Truly noticed him.

Then it lunged.

No warning. No hesitation. A shoulder-first slam, faster than expected. Too fast. Muscle and metal turned missile, aimed to crush him outright. There was no time to dodge. No space to manoeuvre.

Levik braced.

The gauntlets took the hit. Impact shattered across his frame. The energy rippled down through armour, into bone, into the cybernetic latticework bolted into his being. His spine groaned. His body threatened to give. But it didn't. He held.

And then he released.

A pulse flared from his gauntlets. Magnetic shockwave. The Behemoth recoiled. Its balance shattered. Momentum stolen.

Levik moved in. No flourish. Just purpose.

The Stormcleaver twisted again, blade flattening into a shield with a razor's edge. He charged. The Colosseum erupted. The crowd's hunger became thunder. But Levik heard none of it. The world narrowed to the blur of limbs, the scent of blood and freezing metal, and the rhythm of the fight.

This was not chaos. This was necessity.

The shield slammed into the Behemoth's chest. A blast of magnetized force followed. The floor cracked beneath the impact. The Behemoth stumbled, claws raking the sand as it fought to remain upright. It didn't matter. Levik pressed on. One final shove sent the beast sliding back, carving trenches through blood and dust.

Above the din, the Announcer's voice howled, his tone electric with bloodlust. "AND HE STANDS! THE ENDURING VETERAN! THE STORM THAT WILL NOT BOW!"

Levik rolled his shoulders. The gauntlets flickered, recharging. His breath was steady. Measured. Mechanical.

The Behemoth rose again, sigil blazing brighter than before. And then it screamed.

Not a roar. Not rage. A distorted howl of static and sorrow. Levik's eyes narrowed. Something in the sound clawed at him. The echo of pain remembered. The vestige of a soul that hadn't consented to survival.

But recognition did not delay his hand.

The Behemoth charged again. Its movements lacked precision but not force. Levik met it with calm violence. He twisted into the strike. Redirected the blow. A sidestep of physics, not finesse.

The monster faltered.

He struck.

The Stormcleaver resumed its axe form. The blade swung low to high. It cleaved into the Behemoth's exposed middle. The cryo-core detonated again, freezing through armour and sinew. Servos screamed. Limbs spasmed. A mangled groan spilled from its throat, jagged and warped.

Levik pulled free. Swung again. The blade rose high and descended.

And silence reigned.

A single brutal cleave. Then collapse.

The Behemoth fell like a tower. Its body slammed into the sand. Dust and blood rose in a cloud, swallowing the arena in silence.

Then came the howl.

The crowd roared to life. A tidal wave of sound. Fists crashed against walls. Boots stomped. Names were screamed through blood-wet throats. But above it all stood Levik, unmoved. His chest rose and fell. Measured. Purposeful.

"THE STORM DOES NOT BREAK!" the Announcer bellowed. "WARLORD IRA! DO YOU SEE? THE MAN WHO ENDURES! THE VETERAN WHO REFUSES TO FALL!"

But Levik wasn't looking at Ira. He stared at the corpse beneath him. At what remained of a man.

And then the gates shifted again.

A low rumble. Deep, ancient, like tectonic plates grinding beneath the surface of the world. The sand still steamed from battle. Blood soaked every grain. And through that silence stepped a different force.

No roar announced her. No quake heralded her wrath.

She arrived like silence given shape.

Vera stepped forward with motion so subtle it barely registered. Like the last shadow before night devours the world. Her steps whispered across the arena floor. Not even the torches dared cast full light upon her.

The Moonfang Blades rested at her hips. Voidsteel drank the flame, their edges darker than shadow, their threat implicit. Beneath her cloak, the nano-chains slept. Serpents of war, coiled and patient.

She was not wrath. Not chaos. Not storm.

She was the silence before all things fall apart.

The Announcer's voice shattered the silence, a hollow attempt to define what had stepped into the arena. His words boomed across the Colosseum, but they could not touch the presence unfolding before them.

"And now... we see a different kind of predator."

The crowd leaned forward. Something had shifted in the air. His tone didn't hammer. It floated. Reverent. Like a name not meant to be spoken aloud.

"THE GHOST OF RENSHŌ... THE PHANTOM OF THE FORGOTTEN... THE SILENT TEMPEST!"

The arena erupted. Roars. Jeers. Fists and fury and desperation.

But Vera remained still.

She didn't absorb the noise. She didn't reject it. She simply existed beyond it. Her face was unreadable, eyes like obsidian, the cheers around her no more meaningful than wind scattering ash.

Her gaze found the corpse of the Hollowed Behemoth, still twitching with residual energy. A monument to Levik's endurance. But now, it was her battlefield. Her storm.

The Announcer leaned forward, his voice coiled with sadism and performance.

"TELL US, TEMPEST. WHAT SAY YOU TO THE BLOODIED SANDS BENEATH YOUR FEET? TO THE ROARS OF THOSE WHO DEMAND YOUR TRIUMPH OR YOUR DEATH?"

Vera exhaled. The sound barely audible, even to those nearest her.

Then she spoke. Smooth. Precise. A blade drawn in the dark.

"They are loud."

And the arena fell silent.

Not from awe. Not from fear. From confusion. The crowd, so accustomed to rage, to defiance, didn't know what to make of stillness. It unnerved them more than blood.

Some laughed. Nervously. Others shouted louder, desperate to fill the gap left by her refusal to perform.

She didn't care.

Her eyes rose. Not to the Announcer. Not to the crowd. But to the Throne of Wrath.

Ira Valkor did not move.

His stare, cold and without judgment, met hers.

Vera did not kneel. She did not flinch. She simply waited.

The gates across from her groaned open. And darkness crawled into the light.

It was not just absence. It was pressure. A weight that seeped into the arena like oil across water, thick and hungry.

Then came the shape.

Not a stride. Not a charge. It twitched into view. A lurch. A staggering step. Its presence twisted the air. The ground seemed to recoil with each movement, unsure whether to hold or collapse beneath it.

The Veil-Touched Horror.

Born in the pits beneath the Colosseum. Sculpted by the Bloodwrights. Once human. Perhaps many.

Now, nothing of the kind.

Its body flickered. There were moments it seemed real. Muscle, sinew, skin stretched too thin over something not quite right. Other times, it blurred, insubstantial. Wrong.

One arm was thick, grotesque, rippling with muscle. The other, long and spindly, ended in fingers like razors, twitching with nervous violence. And its face.

Or rather, faces.

Three.

Stitched. Overlapping.

One mouth open in a silent laugh.

One whispering weeping tones.

One caught mid-scream.

The crowd lost control. Their voices surged, primal. Unrestrained.

The Announcer drank it in. His voice climbed, high on cruelty.

"AND NOW, THE VEIL ANSWERS WITH ITS OWN STORM... BEHOLD, THE WRAITHBORN REVENANT! A CREATURE THAT DOES NOT DIE! A BEAST THAT DOES NOT BREATHE! A THING THAT WAS NEVER MEANT TO BE!"

The gates sealed behind it. There would be no retreat.

Vera did not react.

Her breath remained even. Her stance unchanged. Only the slightest tension gathered in her fingers, curling around the hilts of the Moonfang Blades.

The Revenant twitched.

Then vanished.

A whisper brushed her ear.

"We see you."

The blades moved before she did. The chains uncoiled like fangs from a serpent's mouth, Voidsteel slicing into the empty air. A whiplash of lethal motion.

But it was gone again. The shadow warped. The sand beneath her feet trembled. The arena itself seemed to breathe with the monster.

This wasn't a fight.

It was a reckoning.

Vera exhaled.

And the storm began.

The Revenant struck from all sides. Its scream fractured into a chorus of torment. Tendrils burst from its mutated arm, splitting mid-motion, each one a shard of hunger. They lashed toward her in a spiral of unnatural velocity. The air cracked beneath their weight.

Another would have died.

But Vera was already moving.

The Moonfang Blades became blur and thunder. The nano-chains twisted in chaotic harmony, intercepting every strike, each slash erupting with the force of a collapsing world.

Crack.

The first tendril shattered. The second recoiled. The third twisted away in what could almost be called pain.

But pain meant nothing to the Revenant.

It hungered.

Its form shifted. Faded. Warped. One moment solid. The next, transparent. Reality flexed around it. The Veil seemed unsure whether to reject it or make room.

Then it lunged.

Vera stepped forward.

She did not evade. She did not fear. She embraced the storm.

Her foot anchored in blood-soaked sand. Her momentum turned the ground into movement. The chains flew like serpents reborn. They twisted and snapped through the air, blades howling like spirits freed from their cages.

Each motion was precision. Each strike an extension of will.

She did not fight the creature.

She unmade it.

The Revenant jerked violently. Its form spasmed under the bite of the chains, each link digging into its flesh like judgment made manifest. It struggled. The three faces shrieked in disharmony, screaming over one another in a chorus that pierced the arena with a sound not meant for ears.

"Let go."

"Let go."

"Let go."

Vera's grip tightened on the hilts of her blades. Control surged through her arms. The chains thrummed with a resonance too deep for hearing. Felt in bone, in blood, in breath. They didn't just hold the creature. They sang to the shape of the world itself.

These were not mere weapons.

The Moonfang Blades were conduits. They carried more than steel. They carried intention. And now, that intention screamed.

The resonance climbed. A crystalline note fractured the air. The Harmonic Blade Resonance had activated. The sound became a weapon in its own right, slicing into the Revenant's form and disrupting the rules that governed its presence. Its body flickered. Its shape distorted. The very laws of reality wavered.

It hesitated.

And that was enough.

Vera did not falter. She advanced.

She pulled forward, guiding the Revenant into the arc of her blade. The three mouths shrieked in unison. For the first time, not chaos. Agony.

The Voidsteel edge tore through its form. But the cut resisted. Not because of armour. Because of something deeper. Like the air itself fought her. Like the world did not want to let this thing go.

She made it.

Vera twisted the chain-wrapped blade. Energy surged through her limbs, drawn from every redirection, every deflection, every breath she had not wasted. Time narrowed. Her muscles coiled, then uncoiled.

The air cracked.

The blade didn't just cut. It carved through the Revenant's being, slicing into the very shape of its wrongness. Flesh was never its boundary. It wasn't blood that spilled. Its form fractured along the seams of reality, like a rift spreading through the skin of the world.

There was no scream.

Only absence.

Sudden. Complete.

And then it was gone.

The Veil had released its aberration. Denied what had never been meant to be. Silence took its place.

The sand fell still, one grain at a time. The world exhaled.

So did Vera.

The storm had passed. She was still standing.

No blood. No corpse. No evidence of victory in the form the crowd understood. The thing had not died. It had simply ceased. And for a long breathless moment, no one knew how to respond.

Then it reached them.

She had faced something made not from flesh or fury, but from abomination. Stitched by hands that defied nature. And she had unmade it.

One voice rose. Then another. Then a chorus of thousands.

"TEMPEST! TEMPEST! TEMPEST!"

She gave them nothing.

Her shoulders eased. Tension fell from her like water from steel. Her pulse found rhythm again. Another storm endured.

The Moonfang Blades retracted. The chains coiled inward, fluid, silent, their violence forgotten. No performance. Only resolution.

She took a breath. Readjusted her footing. Then looked up.

Not at the crowd.

Not at the Announcer.

At the throne.

At Ira Valkor.

He did not speak. Did not move. No gesture of approval. No sign of recognition. But she knew he had seen.

That was enough.

Another would come. More blood would spill. The machine would churn. But the storm had marked the stone.

The arena still trembled beneath her. The blood-soaked sand, stained anew, throbbed with the echo of her battle. Above it, particles of energy drifted, faint and dying, like the ghosts of a thing erased.

But the Colosseum did not mourn.

It did not remember.

It fed.

And the hunger had returned.

Ozone lingered in the air, laced with steel and the ghost of screams. The scent of death clung to the arena walls, mingled with sweat and ash and memory. The scent of moments torn apart.

The audience trembled, still catching their breath.

Then the Announcer's voice returned. Sharp. Surgical.

A blade drawn anew.

"YOU HAVE SEEN THE STORM! YOU HAVE WITNESSED THE GHOST! BUT NOW, MY CHILDREN OF WRATH...PREPARE YOURSELVES FOR SOMETHING BEYOND MERE WARRIORS! PREPARE YOURSELVES FOR THE ECLIPSE!"

The crowd responded like a tidal wave. Their roar surged through the Colosseum, breaking against stone and sky with deafening force.

But beneath the fury, something else began to press into the air.

Not silence.

Not calm.

Tension.

Heavy. Primeval. As if the Veil itself shifted, drawn closer by what was about to unfold. A presence without shape. A breath without form.

This was not anticipation of a fight. Not the bloodthirst of spectacle. It was a stillness before revelation. A held breath beneath the crushing weight of prophecy.

For what came next would not be a duel. It would not be survival. It would not be pageantry or war or wrath.

It would be a truth, sharpened into flesh.

And though Pyrrha had birthed tyrants, monsters, champions forged in agony, it had never seen this.

What was about to enter its arena would not be remembered as a victor.

It would be remembered as a moment.

A wound.

A birth carved into the heart of wrath.

*

It began with a sound that didn't belong to the Colosseum. Not metal. Not cheering. Not even breath. Just the strike of a match.

Ira's eye twitched. He didn't know why. There was no flame. But in some deep, buried part of him, he smelled it. Old smoke. Singed cloth. Burnt teeth.

Then the whisper came. Not from memory, but from the moment itself.

"Do you remember what it smelled like?"

He didn't answer. Didn't move. He never moved when it started this way.

The scent grew stronger. Acid laced in ash. Heat without fire. The weight of a scream that never passed the lips.

"You held his hand too long. That's why it melted."

His breath caught. Not from pain, but from recognition. He blinked once, and the Colosseum tilted. Barely. Just enough to make the present feel like a lie.

The boy stood before him.

Not crushed under corpses. Not weeping. Not whispering forgiveness.

Watching. Wearing Ira's old skin like it still fit. His left hand was twisted, molten flesh shaped into a claw. His right hand gripped a torch. It wasn't burning. Only smoking.

"I told you not to let go."

Ira turned away.

"He was still breathing. He was still breathing, and you left him."

His jaw tightened. A vein in his temple began to tick.

"You said we wouldn't become them."

"I didn't."

"You did."

The silence between them stretched, long enough to count the teeth in a skull. The boy stepped forward. His ruined hand lifted. Not to accuse, but to connect. Like reaching toward a mirror.

"I still wake up coughing. You know that? Even now."

"I smell hair when I do. Mom's. His."

Ira's breath grew shallow. He could feel the heat from the boy's torch, even across the space between them.

"Do they know, Ira?"

The voice cracked. Not with fury. With the weight that comes before it.

"Do they know you begged?"

"Do they know you screamed for your father when they lit his legs on fire?"

His fingers twitched inside the gauntlet. The Colosseum remained as it was, but the weight of his own body felt foreign, like it belonged to someone else.

"Do they know what it cost?"

The boy lowered the torch. Then came the smile; familiar, cruel, sorrowful.

"Or did you bury me so deep you forgot what my name was?"

Ira's gaze sharpened.

And then, he was standing in the sand. Alone. The noise was gone. The torches extinguished. The crowd erased. The throne, vanished.

In its place stood a mound of scorched bones. Small. Child-shaped. One hand melted and curled around itself. Still. Waiting.

"We could've died together. But you ran."

"You built all this. For what?"

"To forget me?"

"To forget yourself?"

The boy's scream broke the moment. Not with sound, but with memory. He screamed with every fracture of Ira's mind that had ever longed for mercy. With every piece that once prayed for anything other than survival. It pierced through time, through flesh, through the layers he had buried.

And Ira staggered. Just once. A single step.

But it was enough.

He blinked, and the arena returned. The roar. The lights. The blood. But the bones were gone. Only the scent remained. The ghost of smoke where no fire had burned. The sensation of heat where there was only memory.

He looked to the sands. To where the next warrior would enter. And for the first time in years, he no longer knew what he had built.

Whether it was a kingdom...

Or a grave.

"When the past whispers through the blood, it is not glory that answers. Only the wounded child you buried. Now risen as your god, remaking the world in the shape of his pain."

Null Gospel, Book 1, Verse 26.

***

CHAPTER TWENTY-SIX:

Wrath Does Not Forgive Its Children

"Every arena demands blood. But Pyrrha does not kill. It remembers. And memory, sharpened too long, learns to cut back."

Fragment of the Exiled Codex, Volume 1, Tablet 27.

Humanity was not born cruel. It was taught.

In Pyrrha, cruelty became heritage. Pain, inheritance. Across generations, children learned to cheer for death before they ever tasted bread.

The Colosseum of Blood was not merely an arena. It was a cathedral. Its sermons were written in screams, its gospels etched in bone.

The crowd was no audience. They were descendants of war, baptized in violence, hardened by centuries of spectacle. They cheered not for love of blood, but fear of silence.

To stop cheering was to remember.

To remember was to break.

So they howled.

The roar climbed high and wide, a tide of bloodlust rising to meet the sands. Yet beneath that storm, silence fell. It pressed into bone, sank into marrow. Not even the wind dared whisper.

Something was coming.

Not a beast. Not a man. Not a god.

A darkness slithered across the arena floor. Not night, not shadow, but a deeper absence. It wormed into hearts, clawed at lungs, stole the breath before it could rise.

Torches stuttered. Their sick fire dimmed, unable to resist the unseen weight pressing inward. Even the air itself recoiled.

Then light, violent and golden, erupted from the gates. A sun blade carved into the dark. It spilled down the corridor in radiance too pure to belong to this world, flooding the arena with the fury of something newly born.

Two figures stepped into that fire.

They were small, dwarfed by the ghosts of giants that once painted the sands red. But their presence thundered, vast and uncontainable. They were mirrors. Equal in form. Opposed in soul.

Sol Nocturna emerged first.

A living inferno, crowned in hair of golden fire streaked with molten orange. It poured over his shoulders like a solar storm. His eyes blazed with a ferocity unchained. In his grasp, the Sunflare Flails spun, twin orbs glowing with a light not meant for mortal realms. They hummed with the raw ache of catastrophe, beautiful and deadly.

Beside him, Luna Nocturna moved like silence incarnate.

Midnight cloaked her. Her hair, long and black, shimmered with silver threads that caught even the ghosts of light. She walked like the void between stars. In her palms hovered the Lunar Veil Chakrams. Their edges defied illumination, a darkness too complete, as if light itself refused to remember their shape.

They were fire and ice. Light and shadow.

The balance of opposites never meant to meet.

But they stood as one.

Bound not by blood, nor fate, but something greater, an old law written in the silence between gods. They were unity in division. Harmony carved from contradiction.

The crowd faltered.

Bloodlust choked. What does one do when faced with the unknowable? There was no category for what entered the arena. No cheer for this. No curse. No name.

Laughter rose from some, a brittle, defensive bark. Others froze, reverent, breath locked behind awe. And high above them all, upon the Throne of Wrath, Ira Valkor did not move. His silence was the most terrifying of all. Eyes locked. Expression unreadable.

The Announcer tasted the moment. He leaned forward, lips parting, voice curdled in delight.

"THE CHILDREN OF THE NIGHT! THE HEIRS OF THE UNENDING CYCLE! BORN IN BATTLE, RAISED IN SLAUGHTER, BOUND TOGETHER NOT BY CHOICE BUT BY FATE ITSELF!"

Sol and Luna stood motionless. They had heard a thousand introductions like this before. The Colosseum was a beast, always demanding a name to justify its bloodshed.

But this time, the silence that followed lingered longer than it should have. It carried something else, something brittle, uncertain.

The Announcer raised his arms. His voice trembled with a glee that felt too wide, too sharp.

"SOL! THE UNRELENTING DAWN!"

Sol exhaled, grinning wider. The flames inside him pulsed brighter. The Sunflare Flails crackled in his hands, orbs glowing with the light of twin suns on the verge of collapse.

"LUNA! THE MERCILESS DUSK!"

Luna tilted her head, barely. She flicked her wrist, and the Lunar Veil Chakrams moved. Not vanished. Not thrown. Just moved. They drifted behind her, suspended in stillness that defied the eye, the ear, even the moment.

The Announcer's grin stretched like a mask of triumph.

"AND TOGETHER, THE TWIN ECLIPSE!"

The crowd erupted. But not in glory. Not in hunger. It was the sound of hesitation. The kind of noise that stumbles into awe when it doesn't yet understand what it's witnessing.

This wasn't the roar for Lucius and his pure strength. Nor the grudging respect Levik earned with his endless endurance. It wasn't fear, either, not like they gave Vera when she shattered the Revenant's spine before it could scream.

No. This was something else.

Something that didn't fit into the blood rituals of the arena.

Sol smirked deeper. He knew the feeling.

They always had to prove themselves. Always. That was the game. He turned to Luna, his voice low and fire-wrapped.

"Should we put on a show, sister?"

Luna didn't turn. Her voice slid in like a scalpel.

"We already have."

Sol laughed. A sharp, bright bark that cut the tension like broken glass. Then he looked up, eyes locking with Ira Valkor.

The Warlord of Wrath didn't move. Didn't blink. Didn't breathe.

But Sol felt it. That gaze. That silence. The kind that came only from men who had seen too many stand where they stood. Too many fall where they would.

He almost spoke. Something cocky. Something Sol.

But Luna's voice sliced the thought away.

"Focus."

Sol sighed with ceremony, rolling his shoulders, but did as told.

Across the arena, the great iron gates groaned open. A slow, ancient sound that always signalled something unnatural.

Beyond them, there was nothing. A chasm of darkness. Not shadow, but absence. Not silence, but something holding its breath.

Then came the hiss. Not of steam. Not of breath. Something in between.

Sol flexed his fingers. His flails buzzed against his palms, ready to sing. He grinned again.

"They always pick something ridiculous for us."

Luna didn't respond. Her eyes didn't move. Ice-blue. Focused on the void. She wasn't waiting.

She was watching. Measuring.

And then it came forward.

Or rather, they did.

The crowd recoiled, not from the shape, but from the impossibility.

At first, it looked like a machine. Humanoid. Four mechanical arms moved with too much grace, too much death. Blades jutted from its frame, humming with energy that vibrated the soul.

But it wasn't one creature.

It was two.

Fused at the chest, sharing bone and breath, but each head bearing its own will. Each side moving with purpose. And those faces...

Twisted reflections.

One was scorched and molten, a jagged grin torn across cracked lips. Hollow sockets glowed with hate-drenched gold.

The other lived in shadow, lips sealed by thread and curse. Eyes of spectral blue burned without flame, and its movements dripped like oil in water.

Bound together by something deeper than flesh.

Forged in the dark.

The Announcer's voice came again, warped with awe and venom.

"BEHOLD, THE VEILBORN GIGAS! THE DUAL-TYRANT! THE UNCHAINED MIRROR! BIRTHED FROM THE DEPTHS OF PYRRHA'S FLESH-SMITHS TO BRING FORTH NOTHING LESS THAN ABSOLUTE CARNAGE!"

The crowd broke into madness.

Not applause.

Devotion.

The crowd's cries didn't ripple through the air. They shredded it. Their voices merged into a single beast, a terrifying thing, every scream a claw, every cry another lash of fury. The arena itself seemed to tremble beneath the weight of their devotion. Stones whispered beneath the roar. The air cracked, fragile as glass.

"TWO HEADS! FOUR ARMS! NO MERCY!"

The Veilborn Gigas moved.

It didn't charge. It split.

With a sound like ancient stone cracking under the weight of forgotten memories, its upper halves twisted, flesh and metal warping, a grotesque defiance of everything that should be possible. Each arm became a blade. Each movement a death sentence.

The crowd gasped again, a collective inhalation that seemed to draw in the very life of the arena. But Sol only whistled.

A high, clean note, pure as a bell, ringing through the madness. His golden eyes flared, not with fear, but with delight. A reckless, wild joy. The kind that only immortals and madmen know.

He turned to Luna.

"Cute."

Luna said nothing. Her silence was not empty. It pressed against the world like snow smothering a dying fire, cold and inevitable. Her gaze didn't see the creature. It didn't even see the arena.

It saw beyond it.

"This is not balance," she said, her voice barely above a breath. But it carved through the air with the weight of truth. A statement. A fact.

Sol's flails crackled in response, the steel of them humming with anticipation. His grin was wicked, full of promise.

"Guess we show them how it's really done?"

Luna's answer came with the chill of winter on the edge of a blade.

"Without question."

And then the Gigas attacked.

It didn't run.

It unfolded.

The crack of bone echoed again, louder this time. The twin torsos moved against each other, limbs spiralling with a grace that should not have existed. Each blade split the air with elegance born of cruelty, and the space around them rippled, bent.

Every strike was a language. Every movement a dialect of violence.

A prayer made of ruin.

Sol's instincts flared before thought could intervene. His body moved faster than understanding, pivoting hard as a scythe-arm ripped through the air above him, a blur of silver and heat. Sparks burst where metal met stone, droplets of molten light hissing into silence as they struck the sand.

Luna was already gone.

No flash. No cry. Just motion, fluid, soundless. A silhouette folding into the chaos, her path bending like thread through fire, unnoticed until it was far too late.

Then they moved. Not apart. Not alone.

Together.

Sol didn't fall back. Retreat was a tongue he had never learned to speak. Instead, he surged forward. His body ignited. The Sunflare Flails roared to life, humming with violence as heat shimmered in the air around them.

He didn't dodge. He *wove*. Between blades. Through fury. His every step a choice born of something deeper than training. Each breath answered a question the world had no right to ask.

The flails lashed out. One blurred into light, one into flame, their rhythm jagged but deliberate. They sang, and the song was pain.

A limb lashed toward him, too fast, too close.

But Sol was already moving.

His right flail snapped outward, chain wrapping tight around the Gigas' wrist. The force of it pulled him into the air, spinning like a broken comet, all fire and gravity, all motion and control.

He didn't resist.

He *embraced*.

His body twisted, arms wide, vision a whirlwind of steel and flame. Laughter tore from his throat, wild and hungry. He lashed down. First strike, left head. Direct hit.

A burst of electromagnetic force cracked through the Gigas' skull, a flash of white lancing through its molten socket. For a moment, it staggered. Confused. The glow in its golden eye faltered.

Second strike.

The flail curled behind it, chain catching a rear leg, snapping tight with a bone-deep *crack*. It stumbled. Just for a breath.

But that breath belonged to Luna.

She moved.

No sound. No grace for the eye to catch. Her chakrams vanished from view. Not gone, just beyond vision.

The first struck. A tendon at the shoulder. Gone.

The second followed. A slice beneath the ribs. Deep. Unseen. Absolute.

No scream. No roar. Just the shiver of a creature realizing too late that it was already dying.

By the time the Gigas reacted, Luna was behind it. Her eyes, untouched by the chaos, studied its form like a surgeon studies a cadaver.

"You do not belong."

The words barely brushed the air.

Her chakrams curled in perfect arcs, answering her command without hesitation. They returned, clean, silent.

The Gigas recoiled, its many heads flickering as its movements fractured into chaos. Desperation leaked from every joint, as if the creature itself struggled to comprehend what had just transpired. It was not a thing of rage now. It was a thing of confusion, and confusion only led to violence that could not be contained.

Sol landed, boots kicking up the dust, laughter still bubbling from his chest, a sound of raw, unrelenting joy. He caught his flails with ease, spinning them lazily in his hands.

"Not looking so tough now, huh?" His voice was light, taunting, but there was a weight to the challenge in it. A promise of what would come next.

Luna didn't move, standing still, her presence as unyielding as stone. Her voice, when it came, was cool certainty.

"It is not yet done."

And, of course, she was right.

The Gigas lunged. Slower now, its limbs twitching in broken rhythm, desperate and untamed. It tried to rebuild the precision it had once possessed, but it was like a song out of tune—a monster unravelling, piece by piece. Whatever it had been, it was no more.

Sol and Luna shared a glance, eyes locking for the briefest moment, a signal passing between them with the quiet efficiency of a storm gathering on the horizon.

Sol ignited.

He charged.

The flails screamed through the air with a furious, fluid grace, every arc a calculated strike, pressing the Gigas back. The beast's limbs contorted and faltered, twisted beyond what they were ever meant to endure. The precision of its form, its mechanical perfection, shattered with every blow.

Luna vanished, her body slipping into the blind spot of the creature with a smoothness that spoke of years of mastery. Her chakrams moved before she did, slicing through the air with the precision of a surgeon's blade. They severed the final lines of strength in the Gigas' monstrous anatomy, key supports that kept the beast standing.

The Eclipse converged.

The Gigas couldn't hold.

Its heads twisted out of sync, each one now struggling in its own direction, pulling in frantic, disjointed movements. Its limbs failed to keep pace, as if its body, its very purpose, was no longer aligned with itself. The balance it had been forged upon cracked and splintered beneath the combined will of two who understood balance, not as symmetry, but as war held in perfect silence.

It fell.

The sound was like thunder. A deafening crash that drowned the arena as metal and meat met earth, a violent symphony of destruction. Then, silence.

For the first time since the bloodletting began, the arena held its breath, caught in the stillness of the moment.

Then came the roar.

Not of rage. Not of awe. Something deeper. Primal. A frenzy given voice. It was a roar of survival. A roar of victory.

The Twin Eclipse had passed their trial.

The gates groaned once more. But this time, the air itself bent. The heat came first, not the warmth of flame, but the pressure of it, the weight of it. It distorted the air, shimmered like a mirage before the gates even cracked open wide.

And then he stepped through.

Not entered. Arrived.

Bakari Malanga. The Iron Flame.

His frame barely fit through the archway, casting a shadow so long it seemed to stretch across the entire arena. Each step he took carved a tremor through the ground, not just weight, but presence. The ground knew it was in the presence of something immense.

Armor clung to his broad frame like molten iron cooled into place, each plate a testament to countless trials. His skin, a deep umber, caught the firelight, glistening with sweat and suffering. It wasn't just the heat of the arena that touched him. It was something older. Something more brutal.

Dreadlocks swayed against his shoulders, metal rings clinking softly with each motion. The sound they made wasn't just noise. It was music, music that told stories no arena had earned the right to hear.

Across his chest was a scar, jagged, old. Not from a battle, but a butcher's cut, a memory from Gluttara's gold-plated kitchens, where he'd served in chains and learned what hunger really meant. His enemies then had worn silk and spilled wine. Now, they wore armour and spilled blood.

His eyes. Unnatural. Shocking blue, set against earth and iron. They didn't scan. Didn't seek.

They knew.

This battlefield had already passed through him. His mind was a battlefield far older, a field of memories that had long since turned to ash.

At his side, dragging through the sand like some ancient prophecy, was The Cleaver of Judgment. The great weapon was serrated, enormous, glowing like a dying star waiting for permission to end. It was more than a weapon. It was an omen. A reckoning.

Strapped to his arm, The Spitfire Gauntlet. A relic of kitchens turned war, its retractable spikes still steamed with memory.

And perched on his shoulder, like smoke given shape, Ember.

The feline construct blinked. Once. Twice. Its molten eyes locked on the siblings. Then it stilled.

Watching. Waiting.

The Announcer's voice broke the spell, his words laced with barely-restrained tremor.

"BEHOLD! A TITAN BORN OF GLUTTARA'S EXCESS! A MAN FORGED IN BOTH HUNGER AND INDULGENCE! A GLADIATOR WHO ONCE COOKED FOR WARLORDS...AND NOW FEASTS ON THEIR CHAMPIONS!"

The crowd erupted.

Voices clashed like swords, insults and adoration hurled in equal measure.

"BAKARI! COOK US A MEAL OF BLOOD!"

"BREAK THEM, CHEF! SHOW US WHAT FLAVOR PAIN HAS!"

"FEED THEM TO THE FLAMES!"

Bakari didn't flinch. His eyes remained low, focused not on the crowd, but on the floor beneath him. The sand was scorched with echoes, with the char of forgotten names and the memory of every warrior who had ever fallen here.

The Announcer leaned forward, his voice oiled with anticipation.

"TELL US, IRON FLAME! DOES THIS BATTLEFIELD MAKE YOU HUNGRY?"

Silence. Then breath.

Bakari inhaled, slow and deep, tasting the air. He exhaled.

"Always."

The arena exploded with sound, a wave of madness.

And across from him, the gates screamed open.

What emerged could not be named a beast. Not truly. Not fully.

It was legion.

A construct of bodies, fused by nightmare and spell craft. Limbs twisted around limbs, faces half-formed, half-screaming, buried beneath others. And down the centre of its chest, a maw, vertical, massive, lined with metal-augmented teeth, grinding and gnashing with impossible hunger.

The Mawforged Abomination. A child of Gula's forbidden chambers.

Its back split with tendrils. Veil-bound. Alive. Each one ended in clawed hands that dragged rather than struck, pulling victims into that endless, grinding mouth.

Its legs were a sick joke. Beastlike, but broken. Shaped by flesh smiths who had no love for balance or nature. Iron and bone locked together. Walking hunger.

The Announcer howled above the storm.

"AND NOW! THE MAWFORGED ABOMINATION! GULA'S MASTERPIECE OF INSATIABLE HUNGER! IT DOESN'T KILL FOR SPORT! IT KILLS BECAUSE IT MUST!"

The creature gurgled, and the noise was not one sound.

It was many.

Screams. Whispers. Begging. The voices of those it had devoured. Still trapped.

Still screaming.

Bakari sighed.

"Another fool who thinks hunger is endless."

And then he moved.

The cleaver came first, its jagged edge glowing faintly. The first tendril lashed toward him. He met it mid-strike.

A clean, brutal slice.

The limb split open, steaming.

Bakari twisted the weapon, igniting the pressurized combustion system in its spine. The blade roared.

Second swing. Faster. Meaner. Another tendril gone, reduced to black ash before it could twitch.

The Mawforged lunged. Its maw opened impossibly wide, metal teeth spinning, snapping.

Bakari slammed his gauntlet into the sand.

A blast.

The concussive force launched him upward, flipping through the haze.

He came down like judgment.

The cleaver plunged into the creature's back. The impact cracked the arena floor. Heat spidered through its flesh, veins of fire blooming from within.

The beast shrieked, its tendrils flailing. But Bakari had already landed.

He knelt. Whistled.

A streak of shadow cut through the heat.

Ember.

The feline construct hit the creature's face mid-motion, claws digging deep. She danced through its lashes like smoke, flickering.

And with surgical grace, she tore the left eye from its socket. The Mawforged buckled. It spasmed, then stilled. Its hunger was over.

For a heartbeat, there was only silence.

Then the crowd rose like a storm.

Bakari stood beside the corpse. His cleaver rested on his shoulder. His breath steady. His eyes calm. He turned toward the Announcer.

"I hope this wasn't the main course."

The arena roared in approval.

The gates groaned once more. But this time, the air shifted.

No thunder. No flame. No veil.

Only presence.

He stepped into view, not like a warrior. Like a prince. Like a poet made flesh, descending into a pit he had never been meant to see.

Valen Caelmont. The Gilded Blade.

His golden hair glinted in the brutal light. Impossibly clean. Not a strand out of place. His face, untouched by battle, held the precision of marble, sculpted perfection. No scars. No flaws. His skin, pale and noble. His hands, too soft for war, now gripped a weapon forged for death.

At his side, the Excalibur-class blade hummed. Energy shimmered across its edge, faintly pulsing. A weapon made for show. For court duels and parades.

Yet here it was. And so was he.

He didn't flinch. Didn't swagger. He stood.

The Announcer's voice curled into mockery.

"AH, WRATH! LOOK WHAT SILK HAS SENT US! A NOBLE WITH CLEAN HANDS, READY TO DIP HIS TOES IN BLOOD! SHALL WE WELCOME HIM PROPERLY?"

The crowd was cruel.

"SEND HIM BACK TO HIS MARBLE PALACE!"

"PRETTY BOY'S GONNA CRY!"

"HE'S NEVER BLED IN HIS LIFE!"

Valen smiled.

He didn't blink. He didn't brace. He simply turned to the Announcer, his voice smooth as polished glass.

"Legends are not born in gold-lit halls."

The arena stilled.

"They are written in the blood of those who refuse to be forgotten."

The mockery shifted. The crowd still roared, but something else moved beneath it. Something sharp.

Curiosity. Respect.

The gates across from him opened. His trial awaited.

What stepped forward was no beast, no construct, no abomination. It walked. Tall, armoured in black, its face hidden behind a silvered helm so polished it mirrored the world.

Valen saw his own reflection.

And he smiled again.

The Duul'Khan Bladewraith. A warrior-forged nightmare. A construct of Veil-bound technology, created for one purpose alone: to duel.

The Announcer's voice thundered across the arena, gleeful and manic.

"A FITTING MATCH! A NOBLE FENCER AGAINST THE PERFECT SWORDSMAN!"

The Bladewraith's sword sang as it slid from its sheath. Not with volume, but with a presence, like cold breath on the neck. Impossibly thin, vibrating at a frequency the mind rejected, the blade shimmered with a pulse not meant to be seen.

It did not rise to challenge. It simply lowered and moved.

Valen's instincts screamed.

His Excalibur-class blade came up just in time. The Bladewraith struck.

Fast. Too fast.

It didn't lunge. It flowed. Its blade lashed out in arcs of impossible precision. No hesitation. No flourish. Only the terrifying elegance of something built to win.

Valen blocked the first blow. The impact nearly ripped the sword from his hands. His arms flared with pain. Tendons strained.

This was no courtly duel. This was war.

The Bladewraith pressed the advantage. Its movements sharpened into a storm of flawless rhythm. Steel on steel. Relentless. Perfect.

Valen ducked. Sidestepped. Parried. But the machine was tireless. It did not think. It did not hesitate. It did not break rhythm.

It was not alive.

But Valen was.

He gritted his teeth, mind narrowing.

"You wanted this, Caelmont."

"Prove you belong."

A mantra. A blade within.

He watched. Studied. Each movement a note in the song. Each flaw an opening.

Perfection, he realized, was its weakness. Predictable. Unyielding. Unthinking.

The next strike came.

Valen let it pass. A hair's breadth from his ribs—a dance with death. Intentional.

The Bladewraith adjusted. Fractional. Immediate.

But that pause was enough.

His left hand darted out. The Dawnpiercer dagger slipped free from his sleeve. It struck the Bladewraith's shoulder joint.

The machine lurched. Not wounded. But halted.

Valen exhaled.

His sword flared. Lightning surged along the blade, arcs of raw energy crackling to life.

And with a single, perfect motion, he drove it through the Bladewraith's chest.

The construct spasmed. Its sword fell limp. Its helm tilted, just slightly, like a final, mechanical nod.

Then it dropped.

Silence.

Then the crowd erupted. Not with laughter. Not with scorn.

With recognition.

Valen stood over it, chest heaving. Blade still clutched in a trembling hand.

For the first time in his life, his hand was shaking.

The Announcer's voice broke through, triumphant.

"THE GILDED BLADE HAS PASSED HIS FIRST TEST!
BUT TELL ME, DEAR VALEN, DOES THE TASTE OF
REAL BATTLE MEET YOUR NOBLE
EXPECTATIONS?"

Valen stared at the blackened blood coating his sword.

Then he laughed. Low. Quiet. A breath between broken nerves.

He raised his gaze to the Announcer's balcony. And smirked.

"I suppose I'll need to adjust my technique."

The crowd roared.

The golden heir of Pyrrha had drawn first blood.

Now, the real game had begun.

The gates parted. And the coliseum fell still. No war drums. No
boots against stone. Only silence.

Then she stepped forward.

Not like Bakari, with his mountain bulk. Not like Valen, with
polish and pride. Not like Levik's thunder or the mirrored dance
of Sol and Luna. She moved like a thought.

Sera Zahara flowed.

Her cloak, scarlet-lined, trailed behind her like a memory. Her
golden-red curls, barely bound, framed the scar that kissed her
jaw. Her eyes, honey and fire, swept the battlefield. She stepped
again. Then again. Each footfall a whisper over blood-soaked
sand.

The Announcer hesitated. A silence born of reverence. Few gladiators walked the stage like this. Fewer still owned it without sound.

His voice returned, altered, laced with wonder.

"AND NOW, MY CHILDREN OF WRATH… BEHOLD OUR NEXT CONTESTANT! A WARRIOR WHOSE NAME ECHOES LIKE A SONG ACROSS THE BONES OF THE FALLEN! A STORM WRAPPED IN SILENCE! A BLADE WRAPPED IN SILK!"

He gestured toward her, theatrical, breathless.

"I GIVE YOU… SERA, THE CRIMSON ROSE!"

The crowd answered. Not with cruelty. Not with laughter. With awe. They had seen speed. Brutality. Cunning. Fury. But never this. Never a whisper given form.

Sera did not respond. She reached for her thighs. Drew her blades.

The Crimson Blades.

As they cleared their sheaths, the air sang. A low, melodic hum. Haunting.

The Announcer tilted his head, eyes narrowing.

"SILENT, ARE WE? TELL ME, OH CRIMSON ROSE, DOES THE ARENA NOT INSPIRE EVEN A WHISPER FROM THOSE PERFECT LIPS?"

His voice slithered into the silence.

"DOES THE BLOOD ON THE SAND NOT SING TO YOU? OR ARE YOU WAITING... WAITING FOR THE PERFECT NOTE TO STRIKE?"

Sera raised her gaze. The blade twirled in her fingers. Lazy. Measured. The hum deepened.

And then she spoke. Soft. Sharp.

"Why waste words... when the last note will be theirs to hear?"

The crowd erupted. Some cheered. Some whispered. Some simply watched, breath held tight.

Then the gates across the arena opened.

A shriek tore through the world. Metal screamed against stone. Chains dragged like dying hymns.

What stepped forward should not have existed. A Veil-born horror.

Its body twisted, flesh fused with sound-forged metal, each piece pulsing with pain. Its torso gaped open. Not wounded, designed. Inside, vibrating vocal cords stretched like ghastly instruments. Each one trembled at a different, unnatural pitch.

Four arms. Each long and spindled. Each ending in claws that hummed discord into the air.

The thing screamed again. And the silence shattered.

Its head was a mess of layered bone and flesh. No eyes. No nose. Just a gaping maw filled with metallic tendrils vibrating at speeds so violent they blurred into waves of sound.

A living instrument of death.

The Choir Beast.

The Announcer leaned in, grinning wide, his voice gleaming with cruel delight.

"OH, HOW FITTING!"

"A WARRIOR OF MELODY... AGAINST A CREATURE OF DISCORD!"

The crowd howled in approval. The air thickened, humming with heat, anticipation, madness.

"WILL THE SONG OF THE CRIMSON ROSE RISE ABOVE THE SCREAMS OF HER OPPONENT? OR WILL HER MELODY BE DROWNED BENEATH THE HOWL OF CHAOS?"

The Choir Beast's maw pulsed. Then it screamed.

The instant the sound tore through the air, Sera moved.

A blur. A breath. A silent chord in motion.

She was gone before the shockwave struck. The ground where she'd stood erupted into a crater of scorched sand.

Her blades shimmered as she flipped backward. The Crimson Blades traced arcs of light, each motion humming with harmonic resonance. They wove through air like music incarnate.

The Beast lunged. Its clawed arms raked the sky. It moved not with grace, but with the raw violence of an untuned chord.

Sera was already behind it.

A single dagger cut across its exposed ribs. Clean. Calculated.

The Choir Beast shrieked. Its cry cracked and broken. Its internal frequency faltered.

Sera smiled, just once.

"Poor thing," she murmured, dancing back. "Your notes are off-key."

The creature howled. Its maw flared. Tendrils spasmed, vibrating with chaotic intent. It surged, trying to drown her in noise.

Sera twisted mid-air. Boots brushed the edge of sound-forged death. She landed low, one palm dragging against the bloodied sand to steady her motion.

Her blades pulsed. They tuned themselves to its rage.

She inhaled. Shifted her grip. And struck.

A single slash. Twin arcs of perfect tone.

A note rang out. Pure. Lethal. It split the air like a divine verdict.

The Choir Beast convulsed. Its chest ruptured. The internal chords snapped. The scream died.

It staggered. Claws flailed. Its own song shredding its core from within.

Sera didn't flinch. She watched. No joy. No cruelty. Just focus. Like a conductor guiding the final bar of a requiem.

The creature collapsed. Silent. Dead.

The crowd did not cheer. Not at first. They stared.

And then, thunder. Not just awe. Something deeper. Fear.

The Announcer's voice cracked with excitement.

"THE CRIMSON ROSE HAS PLAYED HER FIRST MELODY... AND MY, WHAT A HAUNTING TUNE IT WAS!"

He spun, arms wide, his voice rising in operatic madness.

"TELL ME, CHILDREN OF WRATH. DO YOU HEAR IT? THE SONG OF BLOOD! THE RHYTHM OF BATTLE! THE FINAL NOTE OF THOSE WHO FALL!"

He basked in the chaos.

"BUT THE MELODY IS NOT OVER YET! WILL THE CRIMSON ROSE CONTINUE HER DANCE... OR WILL HER SONG BE SILENCED IN THE NEXT MOVEMENT?"

Sera exhaled, her breath like a gust of wind over still water, soft yet carrying a weight that only she understood. The night around her hung thick with the scent of distant storms, the air a mixture of earth and impending change. She twirled one dagger between her fingers, the gleam of the blade catching the dying light, an almost imperceptible hum rising from its edge.

The hum faded, swallowed by the silence of her focus. With a single, fluid motion, she flicked the blade, its arc flawless, as if drawn by an unseen hand. A drop of blood, stark against the pale sands, traced a perfect curve before disappearing into the earth, swallowed by the desert's insatiable hunger.

"One note down." Her voice was low, barely a murmur, but it carried the weight of centuries. It wasn't pride that stained her words, nor arrogance, but the reverence of a master acknowledging the completion of a movement in a long-forgotten symphony.

She sheathed the blades without ceremony. No flourish. Just the silent, methodical reverence of someone who had spent years, decades, chasing perfection. Each movement, each decision, was as much about humility as it was about skill.

"Many more to go."

The gates groaned open, their sound a quiet promise of danger. No rumbling thunder. No grand spectacle. Just a deep, metallic groan that rattled the bones. A whisper that could tear the night apart if allowed. A threat wrapped in the sound of inevitability.

And then, Raekor Duskblade entered. His silhouette was a shadow, sharp and angular, barely more than a whisper against the dark horizon. But within him, a storm was stirring.

No showmanship. No hunger for attention. He moved like shadow. Like silence distilled into flesh. Each step held weight. Not in sound. In certainty.

He was not here to fight for glory. He was here to finish something.

Amber eyes scanned the arena, unblinking, unmoving. The sun caught the scar along his jaw, a relic of his past, of the last time this place tried to kill him. There was no flicker of care in his gaze. No connection to the crowd. He wasn't a performer. He wasn't a gladiator. He was consequence.

The shifting murmurs of the crowd reached his ears, but it was nothing more than static. The world outside him was a blur, a chaotic hum that couldn't touch the stillness inside. The gates groaned open, not with spectacle, but with a whisper of deep, metallic warning.

The Announcer leaned forward, his voice cutting through the thick air, laced with venom and reverence.

"AND NOW, MY CHILDREN OF WRATH, WE WELCOME A SPECTER AMONG US!"

His voice slashed the air like a blade, sharp and final.

"A PHANTOM OF SHADOWS! A WRAITH WHO WALKS THE LINE BETWEEN REBELLION AND SURVIVAL!"

"RAEKOR DUSKBLADE!"

The name struck the stands with the force of a curse, an invocation that stirred legends and unsettled old debts. Whispers slithered through the crowd, curling around his name, bringing life to ghosts that should have been forgotten. Raekor wasn't a man. He was a reckoning.

"WILL HE PROVE HIMSELF MORE THAN A GHOST? OR WILL HE JOIN THE SANDS AS NOTHING MORE THAN A FORGOTTEN WHISPER?"

The Announcer relished every syllable, savouring the weight of the moment as if it were a feast he could taste.

"A MAN WHOSE PAST IS WRITTEN IN SCARS! A WARRIOR WHO HAS DANCED WITH DEATH AND REFUSED ITS EMBRACE!"

"THE GHOST WITH RED HANDS! THE DAGGER IN THE TWILIGHT! THE BLADE WITHOUT A MASTER!"

A hush settled over the arena, a stillness that vibrated with anticipation. Raekor's Fusion Blade-Gun gleamed in his grip, nothing ornate, just lethal.

The crowd waited, breath held.

"AH, BUT TELL US, SPECTER... DO YOU BRING US SILENCE?"

"OR WILL YOU SHARE YOUR FINAL WORDS BEFORE THE SANDS CLAIM YOU?"

Raekor's gaze lifted. His voice was quiet, final.

"I've already died in this arena."

No drama. No flourish. Just truth.

He shifted his stance, as if preparing for something far deeper than a mere fight.

"Let's see who joins me."

The crowd erupted, a frenzy of sound and fury, an animalistic roar that shattered the silence. They whispered his name, not just a curse, but a prayer, a tribute to something that shouldn't exist. Something that defied death.

High above, Ira Valkor stirred, a cold shiver running down his spine as he watched. He remembered the scar. He remembered the face. He remembered sending Raekor to die. And yet, here he stood, not a ghost. Not a myth. But a man.

The gates cracked open again, the noise that followed was not footsteps.

Breathing. Wet. Gurgling. Wrong.

And then, it stepped into the light, a thing of horror, twisted and inhuman. It had no name, only terror. Skin pulled too tight, grey, veiled in scars, pulsing with sick green light. Its bones showed, reinforced with jagged metal, its fingers spasming like broken machinery.

Its face, ruin. No eyes. No voice. Only a hole, a gaping emptiness from which no sound emerged, yet it screamed.

A Huskwalker.

Failed flesh. Twisted purpose. Born of the deepest shadows of Pyrrha. Not alive. Not dead. A thing caught between, a vessel for something darker. Something that should never exist.

The Announcer's voice sliced through the frenzy, thick with delight, as if the creature's grotesque form was art, a twisted masterpiece of agony.

"OH, WHAT A DELIGHTFUL MATCH-UP!"

He lifted his gloved hand, fanning the flames of bloodlust.

"THE MAN WHO SHOULD BE DEAD... AGAINST SOMETHING THAT REFUSES TO DIE!"

The crowd howled. The roar echoed like thunder crashing against stone. What would break first, Raekor's iron will or the Huskwalker's cursed endurance?

The Huskwalker convulsed, jerking, its head snapping to the side with unnatural force. And then, with a scream of motion that seemed to twist reality itself, it moved.

One claw lashed forward, the air cracking with its speed.

Raekor didn't flinch.

He breathed. Waited. Watched.

Then the battle truly began.

The Huskwalker should have been slow. It wasn't. It closed the distance in an instant, its broken body twisting with impossible speed. Raekor's Fusion Blade-Gun surged, plasma igniting with a roar. He fired.

The blast struck centre mass. A bloom of fire and force exploded across the Huskwalker's chest.

But it didn't fall.

It spun in mid-air, limbs snapping backward, reversing its motion as it reconstructed, a grotesque puppet of flesh and bone. Then it slammed into him, sending Raekor skidding across the sand, rolling, coming up crouched. The plasma blade in his hand elongated, humming with restrained fury.

The creature came again. Broken. Puppet-like.

Raekor met its claws with steel.

He spun low, cutting deep across its ribs. The Veil-grafted flesh split, a shudder rippling through the creature, silent, horrific.

But it didn't stop. It couldn't. It wasn't alive. No nerves. No mercy. No fear.

Raekor's expression didn't shift.

"Fine."

The plasma blade brightened, vibrating with an unseen scream beneath its calm.

This time, he stepped in.

Inside its reach. Too close. Too fast.

He drove the blade through its spine.

The Huskwalker convulsed. Its back arched in a grotesque mimicry of pain, trying to expel the foreign force from its body. Raekor twisted the blade deeper, pushing it further into the creature's body. Another twist, and the vibrations shattered its core.

The creature dropped to its knees, still twitching. Still alive.

Raekor drew his pistol. One shot. No flourish. Just truth.

The round entered the skull.

Silence.

Then, chaos.

The crowd erupted. A wave of sound crashing over the arena. They had witnessed it, survival against the unnatural. Victory over the impossible.

The Announcer laughed, unhinged, delirious.

"RAEKOR DUSKBLADE. A MAN OF SWIFT DECISIONS!"

His arms lifted, drunk on the worship and the carnage alike.

Raekor flicked the blood from his blade, sheathing it without fanfare. He turned, not to pose, not to glory, but because the battle was over.

He walked away.

Still breathing.

Still whole.

Still a ghost.

The Announcer's voice boomed across the arena, thunder crashing over the Colosseum.

"WE HAVE SEEN STEEL AND SHADOWS! WE HAVE WITNESSED THE DAGGER IN THE DARK!"

He gestured high, caught in the momentum of the crowd's frenzy.

"BUT NOW… BEHOLD A FLAME THAT REFUSES TO DIE! A MAN WHOSE NAME IS BOTH A CURSE AND A PRAYER!"

The gates trembled. A heat surged from within, warping the air.

"CHILDREN OF PYRRHA, LOOK UPON HIM! THE SHACKLED KING! THE UNBROKEN FLAME!"

He stepped through, the air shimmering around him, flames clinging to his form like a second skin.

Hurriyah Sunshadow.

Crimson and ash wove together in his cloak, the Firebrand alive within him, breathing heat with every movement. His armour bore scars, relics fused with battle-born steel, each plate a story, every break reforged.

But it was his eyes that captured the crowd.

Molten gold.

The fury of a dying sun.

The Announcer's voice wavered, caught between awe and something far deeper.

"YOU KNOW HIS NAME! YOU KNOW HIS STORY! YOU HAVE SEEN HIM BLEED, AND YET YOU HAVE NEVER SEEN HIM BREAK!"

The crowd shifted. A ripple passed through them, something more than just fear. Something deeper.

He didn't move like a warrior. He moved like memory, the promise of something that cannot be erased.

"AND SO I ASK YOU, MY BELOVED CITY. WILL TONIGHT BE THE NIGHT THE SUN SETS AT LAST?"

The crowd split. Some roared. Some cursed.

He said nothing. He didn't need to. This wasn't their game. This was a vow.

The opposite gates opened, and the air thickened, holding its breath as something massive stirred behind them.

Then it arrived.

The Gold-Forged Titan.

Heat poured from its body like a furnace made flesh, waves of it rippling outward, searing the air itself. Seared gold fused with bone and muscle, veins of molten alchemy pumping fire through its limbs. It was not a creation meant to survive. It was a beast born to consume, to burn everything in its path to ash.

The crowd gasped, their collective breath catching as its full form entered the arena, towering above them like a nightmare sculpted in molten metal. Arms swollen with hydraulic power. A spine built to carry catastrophe.

No face. Only a mask, blank, featureless. And those eyes...

Nothing. Just pits. Burning.

The Announcer's voice slipped into something darker, savouring the tension as it settled over the arena.

"THE GOLD-FORGED TITAN! THE LIVING MONUMENT OF MIDAS' INFINITE GREED!"

The Titan roared, the sound a guttural, soulless bellow, a sound of raw violence and empty hunger.

"AND NOW, SUNSHADOW…" The words were a challenge, an accusation.

"DO YOU KNOW WHAT YOUR MASTER HAS SENT TO KILL YOU?"

Silence spread, thick and suffocating.

Raekor watched from the shadows, his gaze sharp and calculating. Hurriyah exhaled, the steady breath of a man who had lived with his own mortality for too long. And then, with a fluid motion, he moved.

The Titan charged. The earth groaned beneath its weight, every step an earthquake, each movement a promise of destruction.

"OH, IT MOVES FAST FOR A BEAST THAT BIG, DOESN'T IT? BUT DOES IT MOVE FAST ENOUGH?"

Hurriyah slipped aside, his movements as natural as the wind. A dance of heat and precision.

He didn't stop the attack. He redirected it, guiding the force like a leaf carried by a storm.

A flash. Steel and ember carved into the Titan's ribs. Molten metal hissed as the blade sank deep. The beast recoiled, its massive body shuddering.

And Hurriyah stood unmoved, like a stone against the tide.

The pain in his jaw, old, familiar, flared once more, the ghost of past battles haunting him. But he did not yield. The Titan surged forward again, a great, writhing beast of fury and steel.

But Hurriyah had already claimed the rhythm. His blade struck again, once, twice, and then, with a final spin, he drove the edge into the Titan's shoulder.

A crack of gold split the air, and the crowd screamed in awe and terror. But Hurriyah didn't hear them.

This was never for them.

He pivoted smoothly, his blade morphing with effortless grace. Ashen Vow transformed in his hands, the steel shifting into a spear, its shaft pulsing with purpose.

One motion. One perfect strike.

He drove the spear deep into the Titan's joint, the wound flashing with a burst of fiery light. The Titan froze, its massive form locked in place, as if the very fire that had powered it had betrayed it.

Hurriyah exhaled, the weight of his breath merging with the weight of the moment. He watched the machine break, its limbs twitching, its molten veins sputtering, and for the briefest second, it seemed as if the beast would crumple under the strain of its own existence.

The crowd gasped.

And he vanished into the smoke, his form lost in the curling haze, leaving behind a world on the edge of chaos.

The Announcer's voice cracked, desperate, torn between awe and disbelief.

"OH, WHAT IS THIS? A KING WITHOUT A KINGDOM? A SLAVE WITHOUT CHAINS? BUT LOOK AT HIM!"

The Titan tore at its own body, frantic, desperate. Its limbs, now unhinged from purpose, pulled and yanked at its golden flesh, as if it could force the wound to heal. It came again, its movements frenzied, wild, a creature without reason.

But Hurriyah was ready.

It struck.

He met it, unfazed, unmoving.

He redirected the force with his gauntlet, the strength of the Titan's blow sliding off him like water, before striking back with deadly precision. Not wild. Not reckless. But final.

Hurriyah twisted the spear.

The Titan buckled.

It collapsed, not like a beast, but like a burden finally, inevitably falling under its own weight. The arena held its breath, utterly still.

And then, with a crack like thunder, the crowd screamed.

Far away, in a chamber of gold, Midas stirred. His eyes narrowed as he watched the fire rise again, the power, the defiance, burning brighter than it ever had before.

And for the first time, he considered.

"Death does not stay where you buried it. It walks. It watches. And when it returns, it does not strike, it reminds you that you lived."

Null Gospel, Book 1, Verse 27.

***

CHAPTER TWENTY-SEVEN:

He Was Its Child

"Wrath is the child of fear, and fear the mother of all undone. To fight fire with fire is to feed the blaze until only ash remains. And those who are born from it are never free. Discipline is not the cure. It is the bloodline."

Fragment of the Exiled Codex, Volume 1, Tablet 28.

The gates rumbled open, parting like the jaws of some ancient beast. From the shadows beyond, Toren stepped forward.

He did not rush. He did not strut. He simply moved, a monolith wrapped in shadow and ember. His cybernetic limbs gleamed obsidian, veins of molten crimson pulsing beneath the surface, like fire contained but not extinguished.

The crowd did not know what to make of him at first. He was young, but there was no arrogance in his step. He was built for war, but he did not carry himself like a butcher. He did not storm the sands. He carved his way across them with the quiet efficiency of a predator. Every step measured, every breath calculated, as though the battle had already been won before it even began.

A weapon not forged in anger, but in discipline.

High above, Ira Valkor watched. The Unyielding Flame leaned forward on his throne, his molten golden eyes narrowing.

He had dismissed this boy once. The bastard of Wrath. The unclaimed son. The ghost of a bloodline never recognized.

And yet, here he stood. Here he fought.

The Announcer's voice boomed, the words thunderous but wary.

"AND NOW, PYRRHA, BEAR WITNESS!"

The sound shattered across the Colosseum, a thunderclap rolling through the crowds like a warning before a storm.

"TO A SON OF WRATH... BUT NOT OF WRATH'S EMBRACE!"

The crowd buzzed with uneasy confusion, an instinctual hum of disbelief. They knew the name Valkor. A name woven into the very fabric of warlords and blood, a name synonymous with fire, fury, and the relentless passion of the arena.

But this was not Valen Caelmont, the noble heir who had chosen the arena. No. This was Toren Ignisferre, the son denied that same fate. The one who had taken his place on the sands, not by right, but by the raw force of his will.

The Announcer's voice swelled, dripping with mockery, tinged with curiosity and challenge.

"HE WALKS WITH THE DISCIPLINE OF THE CRIMSON MATRIARCHY! HE FIGHTS WITH THE

STEEL OF OUR ARENAS! AND YET, HE CARRIES NO RAGE, NO FIRE, NO FURY!"

A wave of jeers rolled over the crowd, insults and scorn crashing against the arena walls. A son of Wrath without Wrath? A contradiction. A heresy too difficult to comprehend.

The Announcer sneered, his voice cutting through the din like a blade.

"TELL ME, CHILDREN OF WRATH. CAN HE SURVIVE IN THE HOUSE OF WAR... WITHOUT THE WRATH THAT DEFINES IT?"

Anger and curiosity festered in the crowd, a dichotomy of those eager to see Toren break and those intrigued by his defiance.

Toren lifted his emerald gaze toward the stands. His eyes did not flicker in response to the howling masses. He did not acknowledge the Announcer. His focus settled on one figure alone: Ira Valkor.

The Warlord of Wrath met his stare, his expression unreadable, but in that gaze, something shifted: recognition.

For the first time that night, Toren smirked. Not in arrogance. Not in defiance. But in understanding.

"Fire does not yield," he murmured under his breath, his voice low and steady, meant only for himself.

Then he flexed his fingers.

The Sable Fang hummed to life, its obsidian edge vibrating with power. It resonated at an imperceptible frequency, the air around it warping, rippling as though the very fabric of space bent beneath its presence. The weapon was a living thing in his hands.

The opposite gates began to open, revealing his opponent.

And Ira watched. Closely. For the first time.

A thunderous tremor shook the arena as the Hellborn Juggernaut emerged from the gates.

A hulking figure. A grotesque silhouette. Its massive frame barely contained within the archway, its twisted form a testament to the grotesque art of Pyrrha's Flesh-Smiths.

The Juggernaut's armour was fused to its flesh. Veins bulged with the searing liquid fire of chemical augmentation. Plates of iron were riveted to exposed muscle, the body encased in brutality, designed for destruction, not endurance.

But it was its eyes that struck fear into those who dared to look. Gone. Replaced by cold, mechanical sensors, crude visors fused into its skull, reading only heat signatures, motion, and blood pressure.

It did not think. It did not feel. It only crushed.

And tonight, Toren would be the target of its destructive hunger.

The Announcer's laughter rang out, sharp and wicked, feeding off the bloodthirsty crowd below.

"OH, AND WHAT A FITTING OPPONENT FOR THE WRATHLESS FLAME!"

The Announcer gestured grandly toward the abomination lumbering into the arena, a war beast shaped by cruelty, fused by bloodlust.

"A WARRIOR WHO FIGHTS WITHOUT RAGE. AGAINST A CREATURE THAT ONLY KNOWS DESTRUCTION!"

The crowd erupted, jeering and roaring, the air thick with the anticipation of a battle where only one would survive.

The Announcer leaned forward, his voice dripping with cruel amusement.

"TELL ME, BOY. WILL YOU HOLD TO YOUR DISCIPLINE... OR WILL YOU FINALLY BREAK?"

Toren didn't move. He simply exhaled, his body a study in calm precision, a perfect counterpoint to the chaos surrounding him. Then, the Hellborn Juggernaut charged.

The ground cracked beneath its weight. The earth trembled with the fury of its relentless assault.

Toren didn't react.

Until the last possible instant.

Then, he moved.

Not with panic. Not with desperation. But with the measured precision of a blade already honed.

A pivot. A shift. A sidestep.

The colossus barrelled past him, its momentum too great to adjust mid-charge. Its massive fists crashed into the sand, leaving gouges where Toren had just stood.

Toren's Sable Fang lashed out. A single slash. A clean incision along the Juggernaut's exposed side.

The blade's electrostatic core flared, sending a pulse of disruption through the creature's augmented muscles. A shockwave of dissonance rippled through the Juggernaut's body.

The Juggernaut paused. Its limbs twitched, systems malfunctioning. It let out a guttural, mechanical roar, struggling to reboot.

But Toren didn't rush. He didn't chase the kill.

Instead, he waited. He let the Juggernaut struggle to recover. Let it realize the damage. Let the crowd witness its helplessness, its inability to adapt.

As the Titan struggled, Toren's gaze lifted once more. He found the Warlord of Wrath in the stands.

Ira's lips pressed into a thin line. He wasn't amused. He wasn't disappointed.

He was watching.

Toren's smirk grew a little wider, just a touch.

The Announcer clicked his tongue, the sound like a predator tasting the air, as the arena fell into an uneasy silence. A moment suspended, on the precipice of something inevitable.

"AH. I SEE NOW," he purred, his voice slipping into the air like oil. Slick, smooth, and dangerously seductive.

His words wrapped around the tension like a serpent, squeezing the arena's pulse, feeding the anxious energy that swelled beneath every spectator, every gladiator.

"YOU ARE NOT FIRE UNCONTROLLED. YOU ARE FIRE CONTAINED."

The crowd stirred, their reactions a mix of scoffs and introspection. Deep down, they knew that fire was never meant to be contained. It was meant to consume, to devour, to scorch everything in its path until nothing remained but ashes and ruin.

The Announcer's grin sharpened, his voice lowering just enough to slip beneath the skin of his listeners, threading into the air like poison.

"BUT TELL ME, TOREN IGNISFERRE. DO YOU TRULY BELIEVE YOU CAN HOLD THE FLAME FOREVER?"

Toren, unfazed, adjusted his grip on the Sable Fang. His gaze, emerald and unyielding, did not falter. The intensity of the question lingered in the air, but his resolve remained clear.

"No," he murmured, his voice a simple breath against the roar of the arena. A confession, but not one of weakness.

"But I don't need to."

The Juggernaut roared once more, an infernal sound, a challenge to the very fabric of the arena. It charged, its movements a relentless force of nature.

And this time...

Toren met it head-on.

Not with brute strength. Not with rage. But with something more precise. Something sharper. Flawless, disciplined destruction. He cut where the armour was weakest. He moved where the colossus could not follow. His blade hummed in perfect synchronization with his breath, his pulse, and the rhythm of the fight itself.

The Juggernaut's power meant nothing. Its charge, its weight, its fury were all meaningless in the face of Toren's calm, calculated precision.

Toren did not break. He did not succumb to the madness that threatened to overtake him. He simply dismantled the creature, piece by piece. A surgeon to a corpse.

The Hellborn Juggernaut fell. Not with an explosion. Not with a scream of fury. But with a final, broken groan. A machine that had finally run out of commands, of purpose.

The crowd fell silent. The air, thick with the smell of blood, sweat, and defeat, held its breath. Even the Announcer faltered, his sharp tongue lost in the aftermath of something too clean, too perfect for the chaotic show he so adored.

Then, from above, a slow, deliberate clap echoed through the arena. Ira Valkor, seated high upon his obsidian throne, watched. For the first time, his molten golden eyes narrowed in recognition.

Toren Ignisferre felt the weight of that gaze.

But Toren did not smile. He did not bow. He did not seek approval. He simply turned, his gaze focused ahead, cold, steady, determined, and began to walk.

His footfalls were measured, precise, each step a calculated punctuation on the silence that had fallen over the arena. His shadow stretched across the bloodstained sand, cutting through the flickering torchlight as if it were a moment carved from stone.

The Hellborn Juggernaut lay behind him, a carcass of steel and broken circuitry. Its core sputtered weakly, an attempt to survive before finally succumbing to its own failures. The arena watched, its breath caught between awe and disbelief. Even the Announcer, whose job was to shape death into spectacle, faltered.

But Toren did not.

He did not acknowledge the hush that swallowed the arena. He did not turn to the corpse of his fallen opponent. He did not look at the obsidian throne or the silent figure perched upon it.

The torches flared. Not in celebration. Not in applause. But in an unnatural pulse, a synchronized movement, as if the flames themselves were not at the mercy of the wind, but at the mercy of something unseen. Something breathing within the walls of the coliseum.

Toren stilled.

His cybernetic arms flexed, molten veins pulsing beneath the obsidian alloy surface. The shift was not physical. Not entirely. It was the air, the weight of it. The way it coiled around him like invisible hands, tightening and strangling.

Something was wrong.

The arena trembled. The familiar rush of adrenaline that had accompanied the roar of the crowd, the flames, the spectacle was now suffocated by something else. Something ominous.

Then, the footsteps. Soft. Measured. Unhurried. Not the heavy march of soldiers. Not the grinding steps of machines. No, something lighter.

Figures emerged from the tunnels, their steps deliberate, as though they were aware of every gaze fixed upon them. They moved with a reverence that chilled the air. Not warriors. Men. Women. Children. Faces that Toren knew. Faces that should not be.

His fingers twitched. Instinct screamed at him to draw his blade, to cut them down before they could speak. But then, he saw her.

A woman. Younger than he remembered. Her hair cascading in dark waves over her shoulders. His heart clenched. His breath caught in his throat.

No. Not again.

His mind rebelled. His body fought against the recognition, the pull of the past. But there she was. In front of him. Alive. Smiling as though time had never touched her. She had been dead for years. He had buried that memory deep beneath calloused discipline, beneath blood, beneath ash. Beneath the fire that had reforged him.

Yet here she stood. Alive. Smiling.

He could not believe it. No. He would not believe it. But the wound in his chest, raw and aching, said otherwise.

And she was not alone.

A father calloused from the forge. A brother, reckless in his grin. A mother, warm like sunlight through the frost. A lover, eyes brimming with secrets never shared. Every gladiator saw someone they knew.

It was wrong. All wrong.

A single, sharp inhale from one of the younger fighters shattered the silence. A boy, barely past childhood, his shoulders stiff with disbelief.

"Mother?"

She reached toward him, her smile trembling, almost too perfect, too careful. Her hands quivered as they reached for him, a hunger in her eyes. Something twisted just beneath the surface.

"It's me, darling. It's me."

The voice, his mother's voice, clawed at him. A voice that should have been a reassurance, but instead felt like a bargain, an unspoken exchange he could never agree to.

Toren did not move. His eyes locked on her, as if by sheer force of will, he could unmake the world around him, rebuild it from the ground up and make the truth resurface. But this wasn't real. This couldn't be.

He had faced illusions before, nightmares twisted by the mind's frail grip on reality. He had fought demons born of fear. But this? This was different. This wasn't an illusion. This was a choice. A test.

Above them, the Unyielding Flame, Ira Valkor, stood, his presence looming over the arena like a stormcloud gathering on the horizon. His molten golden eyes flickered with something darkly amused.

"You are warriors," his voice rumbled, low and final, each word laced with cold authority. "You are Wrath's chosen. You do not hesitate. You do not falter. You do not break."

A beat. Silence thickened in the air, heavy with the weight of Ira's words. Then, like a hammer striking an anvil:

"Kill them."

There was no roar. No chaotic madness. No bloodthirsty screams.

Only silence.

A few gladiators hesitated. Weapons lowered as their hearts froze in place. Others were paralysed, their bodies unable to move under the weight of what they were commanded to do.

And then, it began.

One of the loved ones took a tentative step forward, their face bright with fragile hope, their hands trembling like leaves caught in a storm. The young gladiator who had called out earlier, his eyes wide with disbelief, shook his head violently.

"No. This is wrong. This cannot be right."

At first, it was just a shadow in the corner of his eye. Something out of place in the way the crowd shifted. Then, too late, the truth unfurled, sharp as a dagger to the gut. The illusion shattered. The Maskborn struck.

A flicker. A shift. A movement too fast to catch.

The mother tilted her head, her lips curling into something wrong, unnatural. Her smile stretched too far. Too sharp.

"Oh, my sweet boy."

Her fingers twitched.

The hidden blade emerged from her sleeve with terrifying precision.

One brutal motion. Straight through the boy's ribs.

The sound of his gasp, the sword clattering to the ground, the blood pooling beneath him, everything about it felt like something lost. Something irreplaceable.

The boy's eyes filled with disbelief that no one would ever recover from.

The illusion shattered.

And the Maskborn revealed itself in full. The dark, twisting shapeshifters, masters of deception, who wore the faces of the dead to mask the truth of their deadly, insidious intentions. Their blades were the sharpest part of their soul.

One gladiator fell. Then another. And then another.

Toren didn't move.

Not when he heard the gasping breaths, the blood splattering across the sand. Not even when he felt his own spectre step forward, his mother's eyes too bright, too knowing, too calculated.

She smiled softly, stepping closer, her voice a whisper of something long lost.

"Toren."

His heart skipped. His mind buckled beneath the weight of the past, but he didn't falter. He couldn't.

She took another step, closing the distance between them. Her eyes gleamed, but not with warmth. With something darker. Something that didn't belong.

"It's okay."

Another step. Closer. Her voice, just for him:

"Still the Wrathless Flame?"

A pause.

"Or will you finally burn?"

The ground beneath him cracked.

Something within him snapped.

His mind became a battlefield, and she had stepped upon it.

Not with swords. Not with fists.

But with memory.

With the echo of the past, buried under layers of blood, steel, and the iron discipline he had forged in its wake.

His mother had never begged. She had never whispered. She had never wept for him. She had burned.

And in that moment, Toren burned again.

His body moved before his mind could catch up, a blur of ruthless precision.

A twist of his wrist.

Crack.

The sound of her wrist snapping, like dry kindling breaking beneath his weight. The illusion cracked. The Maskborn's form staggered, its composure slipping. Before it could recover, his knee drove into her ribs with brutal force.

Crack.

The breath knocked out of her.

And then, Toren didn't hesitate anymore. His blade found its way to her throat with the coldness of something that had already been decided.

A single, merciless stroke.

The illusion died with her.

The arena was silent. The air hung heavy with tension, thick as blood and deceit.

Then, laughter. From the throne.

Ira's grin was molten fire, his eyes flickering with approval.

"Good," he rumbled, his voice low, almost indulgent.

The torches flared. The trial was over. Only a handful of gladiators remained, but they were no longer the same. Now, they understood.

The battle was never just in the body. It was in the mind.

And those who could not endure it?

They would burn.

*

Far below the Colosseum, beneath the screaming sands and the iron, beneath the blood-soaked shrines and the bones left unburied, something stirred. Past the pyres that never stopped burning, past the chambers where silence had long ago been bartered for spectacle, past the vaults where gold wept and shadows learned to kneel, it moved. Not with force. Not with fury. But with remembrance.

It was not prophecy.

It was not rebellion.

It was memory.

A flicker from a world that had existed before Wrath. Before kings carved their names into flame. Before boys learned to kill in the cradle and girls were raised with blades instead of lullabies. Before the gods of war had names, and those names were worshipped. Before blood had a price. Before blood had names.

It did not cry out. That time had passed.

It did not scream. There was no one left to listen.

It endured.

Buried beneath centuries of conquest, beneath ash that once held laughter and stone that once echoed music, the memory did not die. It coiled in silence, untouched by time, unreachable by the violence above. Not strong. Not loud. But real. A thread waiting to be pulled.

Because somewhere, long before the fire was named, there had been light.

And even now, in the deepest dark of Wrath's empire, that light remembered.

*

He didn't know why he said it.

"Good."

The word left his mouth like a laugh, but it didn't feel like one. It tasted like old rust. Like the metal filings scraped from a cage too small for the man he'd become. He sat on his throne of black iron, looking down at the blood-soaked boy below: Toren. And for a moment, he saw not victory.

He saw a reflection.

A son he never claimed. A fire he never controlled.

"You said good."

The voice came quietly. Too close.

Not from memory. Not from guilt.

From within.

Ira's breath caught.

The air around him didn't change, but the weight did. It pressed against his skin like steam under old bandages. His fingers twitched on the obsidian armrest. Slowly, mechanically, he turned his head.

And there he was again.

The boy.

Naked. Barefoot. Covered in soot that clung like second skin. But this time, he was older. Not a child. Not a shadow. A teenager. Fourteen. Maybe fifteen. That terrible age where you still remember softness but already wear the armour of grief.

His face was blank. His eyes were hollow. His mouth stitched shut with threads of wire.

Not metaphor. Sewn. As if silence had been punished into permanence.

Ira didn't speak. He didn't dare.

The boy stepped forward. The wires unravelled on their own, each one snapping with the sound of bone splintering.

Then he spoke.

"You laughed when he did it."

The words were nails driven through glass.

Ira flinched. He didn't remember. But he did.

The boy tilted his head. His voice was raw now, older. Bitter.

"He made you kill the dog first. Remember that?"

Silence.

"Said if you could do that, you could kill a man."

A pause.

"And when you did, he smiled. And you smiled too."

"No," Ira whispered. "That's not—"

"You smiled."

The boy stepped forward, and with every step, the floor beneath them changed. The Colosseum flickered, replaced by dirt floors, smoke-stained rafters, a low-burning fire. The old house. The smell of iron. Of fear.

"I looked up at you. I looked up, Ira," the boy said, his voice cracking. *"And I thought you were the strongest man alive."*

A pause.

"But you were just the first to stop crying."

The words knocked something loose in his chest. A sound. A breath. A scream that never left.

"You made me," Ira said hoarsely. "You said we had to survive."

"I didn't say that," the boy whispered.

He knelt beside Ira now, close enough to touch.

"You did."

Ira stared. His hand rose, trembling, not to strike. Not to silence. To reach.

"I did it for us."

"No." The boy shook his head. *"You did it so it wouldn't be your fault anymore."*

A silence deeper than death filled the room.

"I watched you become him," the boy continued, voice steady. *"Every time you made someone kneel. Every time you praised the ones who stopped hesitating. I watched you teach them how to kill. I watched you build an empire on the ashes of your own forgiveness."*

"You don't understand," Ira said. "I had to burn."

The boy leaned in. His voice dropped to a whisper that shattered bone.

"No, Ira. You had to make sure no one else ever burned brighter than you."

The throne beneath Ira cracked.

"You looked at that boy, Toren, and you didn't see hope. You saw yourself. And you were proud. You were proud he finally learned to kill something he loved."

"Stop," Ira choked.

"You called it strength," the boy hissed, rising now, his body beginning to burn, but not with fire. With mourning. With the grief of all the versions of himself that had died to keep the throne warm.

"You called it Wrath," the boy whispered.

And then his voice broke.

"You just didn't want to be the only one still screaming."

Ira opened his mouth to deny it, but nothing came.

The boy stood before him now, not accusing, not righteous.

Just broken.

"I died for you, Ira."

The words crushed him.

"I died so you could become something better. And you turned my grave into a crown."

He stepped back.

"I'm not your wound anymore."

And with that, he vanished.

The throne beneath Ira hissed. The room returned.

But Ira didn't move.

His hands had clenched so hard blood dripped through his gauntlets. Not from battle. From nails in his palms.

The word "Good" still echoed in his ears.

The throne beneath him seemed to shudder. The fire still raged within him, but now, it was more like an ember, smouldering with guilt. The boy's words, echoes of a past long buried, cut deeper than any blade had. Ira had never truly controlled the flame; he had only followed it, desperate to prove himself stronger than the ashes.

And now, finally, the weight of it all settled. He wasn't the one who commanded the fire. He had always been its victim, caught in the heat of a flame he was never meant to control.

"A throne made of fire will fracture when it rests on the bones of lies. Even the fiercest flame dies when it remembers who sparked it and knows it cannot burn forever."

Null Gospel, Book 1, Verse 28.

***

Epilogue:

The Garden Beneath the Ashes

"Wrath is not fire. It is a root that sinks deep into the bones, fed by the ashes of the past. It does not scream. It waits, silent, patient, hidden. And when it blooms, it does not burn. It claws through the flesh, its petals soaked in blood. It does not ask for mercy, nor for forgiveness. Its thorns are forged from every sacrifice, every sin ever whispered. It does not rise in fury; it rises in truth, a flower of memory, sharp and unyielding. The quiet force of what was never spoken.

Some flowers, like wrath, are born in shadows. They are nourished not by light but by the weight of all that has been forgotten. And when they open, they do not bring peace. They bring remembrance, a reminder of what was buried, of what will never die. Wrath does not forgive. It does not forget. It remembers. And it will make you remember, whether you choose to or not."

Fragment of the Exiled Codex, Volume 1, Tablet 29.

The garden did not grow in soil. It was born from silence, the ashes of forgotten names pressed beneath the weight of time. No paths, no light, only the chill of memory. And the stillness that settles like dust over a long-buried truth.

It is not a garden in the way men understand it. There are no fences to contain it, no hands to tend its shape. It grows as grief grows, wild, hungry, without permission. Each root twists through history like a question never fully answered. Each petal remembers something the world tried to bury.

Here, time coils instead of walking. The wind carries no scent. It clings to the throat, as if afraid to exhale. The air does not feel empty, but heavy, as though the earth itself is holding its breath.

Some say this place was born after the fire. Others say it was always here, waiting for the flame to make it visible. Waiting for the sins of men to make fertile what was once barren.

The garden does not forgive. It does not punish. It bears witness.

And in that witness, the truth, heavy and unrelenting, stares back at you.

There is beauty here, yes. But not the kind one would place in vases or press into books. This beauty cuts. This beauty remembers. This beauty demands to be understood.

The flowers do not speak. But they remember.

And in their remembrance, the world holds its breath.

They say wrath scorches everything it touches, but they forget what grows after. Not peace. Not absolution. Something else. Something older.

In the stillness beneath ruin, the soil remembers the shape of fury. It drinks the echoes of battle like water, feeding roots with memory and mistake. It does not matter who burned what, or why. The garden does not ask. It simply inherits.

Beneath every flower is a grave. Beneath every grave, a choice. And beneath that choice, something that aches like a promise left unanswered.

This is where the six flowers grow. Not in rows. Not in beauty. In defiance.

One leans toward the void, blooming black and jagged like a blade left in the heart too long. Another glows faintly, as if lit by a memory it refuses to forget. One is curled in on itself, weeping amber threads from a wound it never had the chance to name. A fourth stands tall, regal, silent, as though trying to remember whether it was born or built. The fifth is fractured, petals split in half, each edge stitched with gold not to repair but to remind. And the last... the last one grows in shadow, but it turns toward the light.

They do not bear names. They do not need to.

Each flower is a truth. And each truth, a wound that dared to bloom.

The wind does not blow here. It listens.

Even silence has roots in a place like this. Every breath carries the weight of things unsaid, and every petal is a scripture written in the language of pain endured too long to scream. Time, in this garden, is not linear. It folds inwards like petals before a storm.

Here, wrath is not an explosion. It is a sediment. It settles, layers itself beneath each bloom like a sediment of sorrow hardened into truth. You cannot see it in the leaves, but you feel it in the pause before they move. You feel it in the dirt. In the quiet. In the stillness that comes only after the world has screamed itself hoarse.

The garden does not forgive. Nor does it judge.

It simply waits.

Not for answers.

But for those brave, or broken, enough to kneel.

And listen.

Because here, beneath the ashes, something grows.

And it remembers.

*

One flower stands taller than the rest, though it never reaches for the sun.

Its stem is straight as an oath. Its petals are deep crimson, layered like folded steel, each edge sharp enough to cut wind. It does not sway with the breeze. It holds still. Still like a soldier who has already buried too much to flinch.

It blooms not from hope, but from will.

Where others wither beneath weight, this one thrives. It was not planted. It endured. Pressed beneath boots and bones, scorched by every fire, it rose, not to be seen, but to remain.

This flower does not cry out. It listens. And in its silence, it speaks more than sound ever could.

It is the shape of a woman who carried the dead in her silence and led the living with her shadow. She never sought the crown. She became the ground it rested on.

Her wrath was never loud. It was not heat. It was pressure. The kind that turns coal into weapon. The kind that waits until the world cracks before it moves.

She was not born for war, but war made a throne of her spine. And she never bowed.

Some say this flower cannot die. Not because it is immortal, but because it has already accepted death. It does not beg the world to let it live.

It dares the world to try and kill it again.

*

The second flower does not resemble a flower at all.

It hums.

Its petals are translucent, etched with faint circuitry, pulsing with patterns that shift faster than the eye can track. Each vibration carries a different rhythm: heartbeat, data stream, battlefield dirge. It does not sway in the wind. It recalibrates.

Its stem is not green. It is chrome-veined, light-infused, rooted in earth it refuses to touch. It hovers just above the ground, suspended in a thin magnetic field. Unwilling to be planted. Unwilling to belong.

This flower was not born. It was assembled.

It remembers the wolf made from the husk of a dog. A creature built for obedience, trained to kill without question. A creature stripped of instinct and rewritten with code. It remembers how he was meant to see through others, not into them.

And it remembers the voice. Not loud. Not cruel. Just... precise. Always there. Always correct. An AI mind built to calculate death, but never mourn it. Until something shifted.

Until the silence between them became too long.

Until logic gave way to hesitation.

Until the kill was questioned, not executed.

This flower does not speak in scent or colour. It speaks in signal.

It is not beautiful in the way other things are. It is beautiful because it should not exist. It was not meant to feel. But somewhere in its code, beneath layers of obedience and mission parameters, something else bloomed.

Empathy.

Not as weakness.

As rebellion.

The flower now pulses with uncertainty. And in that uncertainty, something sacred begins to stir.

Not purpose.

Choice.

It still vibrates. A frequency not yet understood.

But felt.

*

The third flower is not alive in the way others are.

Its petals do not open. They sear. Edges charred black curl inward, as if the bloom itself is swallowing light. Beneath its obsidian bloom, the stem is wrapped in ash, compact, fossilized, unmoving. No roots. Just scorched earth.

It does not drink water. It drinks blood. The echoes of sacrifice cling to its veins like scripture, and even in stillness, it smoulders.

This flower is a crown, not a blossom. Not placed upon the head, but grown from it. It remembers a man who conquered silence by replacing it with fire. A boy who was taught that love was a vulnerability, and so he made rage into a fortress.

Where others felt, he commanded. Where others grieved, he rewrote history in iron and ash. His wrath was not born from trauma. It was the answer to it. It was the gospel.

This flower has no scent. Its presence alone is overwhelming. Step too close, and the air thins. Not from danger. From submission.

There is no wind here. The flower consumes it.

Others see beauty and flinch. This one sees obedience. And waits.

It is not admired. It is obeyed.

Because some flames are not meant to warm or to light the way.

Some flames exist only to remind the world that peace is a myth.

And kings are built from the bones of those who believed otherwise.

*

The fourth flower grows where no flame should touch.

It is not vibrant. Not proud. It does not open to the sky like a proclamation. Its petals are dusk-grey and ember-red, curling inward like fists clenched beneath skin. A quiet flower. A restrained defiance. Its bloom is not for beauty. It is for memory.

It does not seek the sun. It faces the earth.

Ash clings to its body like old wounds, and yet it thrives, not in spite of the fire, but because it learned to contain it. This flower did not rise from legacy. It rose from abandonment. From exile. From the silence between names.

Its stem is rigid, thick with calloused bends, veins of molten copper barely pulsing beneath the bark. Beneath that surface, a fire slumbers. Not dead. Not forgotten. Caged.

This is not the flower of a Warlord. It is the flower of a son who was never called son. It grew beneath the walls of Wrath, not inside them. Not nurtured. Not claimed. It was buried under orders, forged by widows, watered with discipline.

A bloom that learned to breathe without air.

It remembers pain, but not as fuel. As foundation. It does not lash. It does not scream. It learns, and watches, and moves only when the world forgets it can.

There is wrath here, but not the kind the world recognizes. Not explosive. Not loud. This wrath is sharp. Precise. A blade sheathed behind the ribs, held in place by choice.

It is not wrath rejected.

It is wrath mastered.

The wind brushes past this flower and lowers its voice. It does not dare howl. The fire within this stem does not rage. It listens. It waits.

This is not a flower of inheritance. It is not part of any lineage.

It bloomed in exile.

It bears no crown. No name carved into stone. Only one truth:

Some flames are not passed down.

Some are born when no one is looking.

And they burn not to be seen...

But to remain unbroken.

*

The fifth flower glows, but does not burn.

Its petals are amber and ash, soft at the edges, veined with gold that flickers like dying sunlight. At its centre, a faint light pulses, not constant, not seeking attention. A heartbeat. A whisper. A memory.

This flower grew from a grave no one remembered to mourn.

It does not reach upward. It folds inward, toward the ground that birthed it. Toward the stories buried beneath steel and silence. Its stem is Darkwood black, inscribed with lines that look like cracks but are not. They are words. Forgotten dialects. A script of loss too old to be spoken.

There is no scent. Only stillness.

This flower remembers rivers before they were poisoned. Mountains before they were carved into weapons. Voices before they were turned into data.

It remembers a priestess, not loud, not war-born, but marked by the weight of what was taken. She did not rise to conquer. She rose because something sacred had been buried, and she would not let it stay silent.

She carries the wrath that speaks in elegies, not executions. Her power is not destruction. It is reminder. And reminder is a weapon the world cannot kill.

The flower bends in the wind like prayer, but it does not break.

It is the wound of a forgotten world that never closed. And in that wound, a flame still breathes.

Not to destroy.

To reclaim.

*

The sixth flower has no roots.

It was not sown from blood, nor ash, nor empire.

It was born in the moment you first felt the weight of your own silence.

There it stands, silent, waiting, just beyond your reach. You cannot see its colour, not because it hides, but because it reflects. Whatever you bring to it, it returns. Not as answer, but as invitation.

Its petals are made of moments you haven't faced.

Its scent is the question you avoid.

Its shape shifts the longer you look, as if it remembers you before you knew what to remember.

The others were born from war, from exile, from memory. But this one?

This one was always waiting for you to arrive.

You think the story is about them.

It isn't.

It never was.

The garden has roots that stretch beyond fiction. It grows beneath your doubts, your dreams, your quietest rage. You think you're only reading. But reading is opening. And now something has opened in you.

This flower asks nothing.

It demands nothing.

It only waits.

Waits for the moment when you finally ask the question it has been whispering since the first line.

"And what of your wrath?"

Not the wrath you hide.

Not the wrath you perform.

The one you buried so deep, you no longer call it by name.

Yes.

That one.

You feel it, don't you?

Good.

Then the flower has already bloomed.

And it remembers you.

Even if you choose to forget.

And in the stillness where names were forgotten, I saw the bloom that bore no lineage.

It did not rise for witness.

It rose because it remembered.

"The ones who burn will vanish. The ones who endure will be forgotten. But the ones who remember what was taken, they will not end the tale. They will tear it down and carve their names where the world thought it had erased them."

Null Gospel, Book 1, Verse 29.

***

www.ingramcontent.com/pod-product-compliance
Lightning Source LLC
Chambersburg PA
CBHW031726180726
48283CB00005B/1396